THE SCORPION'S STING

STEPHEN FRANCIS MONTAGNA

PROLOGUE

June 5th, 1999. WASHINGTON D.C., 3:30 A.M. EST.

In a meeting being held between three young Iraqi terrorist in a small room they were renting from the Roland's Motel, a rather heated discussion was taking place. The three terrorists were sent to the shores of the United States to carry out an attack on a target they were ordered to select. The mission was devised to create mass fear, confusion, and concern in the United States. In an attempt to force an end to the stifling sanction imposed on Iraq at the conclusion of the Operation Desert Storm War.

Iraqi President Saddam Hussein gave specific orders to the members and officers of his military, and to all his special operations units of his country. They were armed with orders to create a terrible situation within the borders of the United States, to bring Iraq out of the eye of the world, and into the crosshairs of the present American leadership. He wanted and demanded to eliminate the two no fly zones installed over his country by the United States and England, and to have the sanctions lifted against his country. So the powerful Iraqi President could then get on with reconstructing his military might, and assume control over his entire country again, and his conquest of the Middle East to begin anew.

As long as the sanctions and United Nation's inspection teams walking the sands of his vast deserts, constantly looking over his country for any hidden weapons of mass destruction. Was forcing the angry Iraqi President to stop any further development on the weapons he desperately needed, to continue his thoughts of taking over the troubled Arab nations of the Middle East. This was his sole driving force, to control the Middle East, and become a military might equal to, if not more powerful than the United States.

As the three terrorist sat in the room of the dilapidated and filthy hotel used mostly by the local drug addicts and prostitutes who support them, to carry out their illegal activities in the streets of Washington D.C. Each of the terrorists offered targets they had selected to the leader of the small terrorist cell operating in the United States. Colonel Farseeha al-Mana, a member of the Secret Police and military of Iraq, leveled her eyes on the American President. She knew if they were successful in assassinating the American Leader, it would place the United States in complete turmoil, and it could be suggested the sanctions be lifted against Iraq in all the mayhem that would surely followed such an attack against the American leadership.

Iraqi Captain Jebril Brighteeth, the commander of the terrorist unit, believed that the American Leader was too well protected at all times to make a successful hit on, so he wanted to go after a much easier target to hit, a Saudi Arabian target within the borders of the United States. He was of the belief if a Saudi target was destroyed in their attack in the United States, it would cause hard feelings to fester between the United States and Saudi Arabia. Thus successfully destroying the Coalition Forces, and what they were trying to accomplish in Iraq. The leader of the terrorist cell voted down Colonel Farseeha's suggested target.

Seeing the upsetting confrontation taking place between the two fellow Arab terrorists, the youngest member of the cell offered his target to the radical leader. He cleared his throat, and when Captain Brieghteeth glared at him. The young man lowered his head, now he was afraid to speak. This infuriated Brieghteeth to no ends, and he snarled at the young man. "Fool, it seems that you have something to add to this cursed conversation, so now you have interrupted me. I'll wait for you to speak what you have on your worthless mind, young fool born in the sands of the desert. If it's anything you have on that useless mind of yours that is, young fool."

The angry commander of the terrorist cell waited not so patently for Mamdoul al-Qassan to find his water and speak. Al-Qassan drew in his breath in a sigh, and then offered cautiously to the commander. "Captain Brieghteeth, over the past weeks I been following a Senator John Hopkins, the leader of the Senate Oversight committee, who gives money to the American military, so they can carry on with their foul no fly zones in Iraq. I feel if we kill this one man, the funds to the American military would be cut off or interrupted, thus stopping the no fly zones order and bombing of our military equipment and soldiers and civilians in Iraq."

Captain Brieghteeth thought for a moment and then ordered the younger member to go on with what he was offering. The now interested Captain felt they might be on to something after all.

Mamdouh al-Qassan again drew in his breath and then offered his commander there was little security surrounding the old Senator, and he could easily be killed during one of his daily excursions in the gardens of the American Capitol Building. Over Farseeha's objections, the two male terrorists agreed with observing this elderly Senator for the day, to see if he was as easy a target as al-Qassan offered them.

While Captain Brieghteeth and the young al-Qassan went out to observe the senator, Farseeha decided to speak with the Libyan Captain, Badawl Badawlhmed Nabih Kamis. The Iraqi terrorist cell came to the United States with no weapons to complete their assigned mission, and when they finally selected a target. The leader of the terrorist cell had orders to approach this Libyan Operative and secure the weapons the cell would need to carry out their attack on the American interests in their country.

Farseeha al-Mana went to the Libyan Embassy, where she spoke to Captain Kamis, and convinced him to give her the weapon the cell would employ on the attack against the American President. The Libyan wormed the target the cell leveled their eyes on, by Farseeha admitting they have aimed their eyes on the American President. Upon hearing the radical cell was going to try and assassinate the American Leader, he was all for their attack and offered Farseeha the weapons the terrorist cell would need to carry out their hit against the American leadership.

But the ever cautious and wise Libyan began to go over the list of weapons he had available, and the special weapons Farseeha had requested from him. He became concerned and wanted to know how many terrorists were involved in this cell. Farseeha was forced to lie by suggesting there were four terrorist operating in their small cell. The Libyan was angry, but nevertheless he offered the weapons he had on hand, along with the orders she was to return to the Embassy later that night, so he could transfer the weapons to her car using the cover of night.

The moment the young and very pretty female terrorist was out of his office, the Libyan immediately placed a call to Iraq. He wanted to speak directly to General Hassan al-Zahar who he understood to be in command of all terrorist cells operating in the United States. His call was transferred to the General's private office, and when the Libyan was finally able to speak to the Iraqi General. General Hassan al-Zahar started to complain that Iraq was going through another attack on one of his SAM missile sites, from the American and United Kingdom aircraft constantly flying the skies over Iraq day and night. The fuming Iraqi General complained the fool operator stupidly lit up the American warplane with his attack radar from the missile site, and four F-18 Hornets immediately zeroed in and were currently attacking his missile installation.

General al-Zahar went so far as to rudely dismiss what he believed to be a nosy and rather troublesome Libyan Officer, by trying to give him the bum's rush off the phone while he attended to the defense of his country. So the General could get back to looking after his prized missile sites, and see if there was any other way he could hit the attacking American warplanes in the process of destroying another one of his SAM missile sites.

The Libyan Captain Badawlhmed was not to be dismissed so easily by the Iraqi General. Even over General al-Zahar's objections, the Libyan spoke as if he had the right to do so. He heard the Iraqi Officer let his breath out in a hiss, as he settled down and listened to the Libyan's words. The Libyan started to speak, and when he went over what Farseeha offered him, when she requested the needed weapons from his supply for their mission in the United States.

The Iraqi General became interested in the Libyan's words. The Libyan had the audacity to offer that he felt the terrorist cell was operating undermanned for such an important mission as the one they were on. He wanted more terrorists added to the attack cell to bolster this weak radical cell operating in the United States. The Iraqi Commander knew he was going to add more terrorists to this small cell for the same exact reason this Libyan was suggesting he do.

General Hassan al-Zahar was patient with the Libyan because he was aware he was their only source for weapons for his terrorists working in America. He could ill afford to create friction between his operatives and this Libyan. The Iraqi resided himself to allow the Libyan to babble on until he grew weary of his words. The General had to absorb suggestions on how his cell should be operating and manned. The Iraqi Officer glanced at the Heavens as he continued to listen to the Libyan's words, as the American bombs continued to fall about him and his missiles.

The Libyan Agent was well aware of the power he held over the feared Iraqi general over this knowledge. The brazing Libyan was making the best of it. Even daring to overstep his bounds with the powerful Iraqi Officer, by suggesting how many terrorists should be added to the general's cell operating in the borders of the United States.

The Libyan Captain smiled as he made the suggestions bordering on demands to the Iraqi General. One thing every terrorist control understood was they had absolute control over all terrorists operating in the United States. Because Iraq's Embassy was ordered closed by the then seated American President, since the first invasion of Iraq took place against the country, by the troops of the Coalition Forces during the short lived Operation Desert Storm War.

Iraq was forced to go through the Libyan Embassy, to operate and supply any terrorist cells working in the United States. This knowledge made the Iraqi Officer angrier, because he was forced to deal with the Libyan from the United Nations in the United States. The Iraqi was further angered because he felt he no longer was in control of his cell. Because he was forced to rely on the Libyan for arms his terrorists needed to carry out their orders in the United States.

This need to rely on the Libyan Captain and his weapons, took away a lot of the Iraq General's power over his cells in the West. Any terrorist control understood this was disturbing for the Iraqi General and his leadership, and it usurped his power over his cell. It caused other confusion and a lack of respect for his control over the cell. This confusion could very well spell complete disaster to the operation his terrorists were assigned to carry out in the United States.

CHAPTER ONE

Iraqi General Hassan al-Zahar was forced to listen to the Libyan, and he even allowed him to make suggestions for his terrorist cell. The General finally agreed with the Libyan Operative, knowing he was forced to agree because he was their only source of weapons to supply his cell. The Libyan waited until General al-Zahar offered he was sending his best, the most feared terrorist operative under his command to the United States in order to take control of the cell he was convinced, was coming apart at the seams. When General al-Zahar offered to send Colonel Abdulaziz Majd al-

Adwani to America to takeover this terrorist cell, this satisfied the Libyan.

The night came, and the Libyan Officer gave Farseeha the weapons she had requested from him. After forcing her to have oral sex with him, and then Farseeha left the Libyan Embassy with the weapons and a new hatred and vowed her revenge against the Libyan Captain.

While the pretty female Colonel Farseeha, from the special police of the Iraqi military picked up the weapons they needed for their mission's success. Captain Jebril Brieghteeth and the young Mamdouh al-Qassan returned to their one room apartment at the dilapidated and filthy Roland's motel. The Iraqi Captain was fuming with al-Qassan, because when they observed his intended target. They quickly discovered that the old Senator was suddenly surrounded by armed security guards, instantly removing him from their target list.

Captain Brieghteeth was further angered because now, he had to inform Farseeha the target they were interested in was now off limits to their attack, and they were going to settle on her suggested target after all. She returned to the motel room, and there she discovered the men quite upset. She was informed they no longer considered Senator Hopkins a target and they now were willing to aim their sights on the American President as she suggested.

Farseeha was pleased with the change. She admitted she discovered the best place to attack and kill the American President while he was boarding his aircraft they knew as Eagle Wings. She told the other terrorists of the no longer in use water tower she discovered which she located just off Joint Andrews Air Force Base where the special aircraft was parked, and they could easily kill the American

President from this location. She informed the terrorist commander that she had the weapons they would need to carry out their mission to its successful conclusion.

The terrorists left the filthy motel room for the night, and tomorrow they were to linkup and then stake out Joint Andrews Air Force Base, and wait for the American President so they could kill him. When Farseeha returned to her apartment, she took a quick shower and while she was showering, there was a knock on her apartment door which startled her. She wrapped a towel around her body then took her pistol and answered the door cautiously. Fearing it might be the hated Washington police authorities there to arrest her for her actions.

When she discovered Colonel Abdulaziz Majd al-Adwani her lover back in Iraq standing at the door, she flung the door open and pulled him in the room. She made love to him with her mouth as the Iraqi Colonel explained he was now the lead control over their small terrorist cell. The next day the Colonel informed Brieghteeth he was taking command of the cell, and he ordered the terrorists to setup in the water tower, once they read the American Leader was planning to visit New York City, and he was going to use Eagle Wings printed in the newspaper.

The wise and always cautious Colonel Al-Adwani watched from a safe place over a quarter of a mile away from the abandoned water tower on the outskirts of the American Airbase. His terrorists waited to kill the American Leader as he arrived on the airbase to take his aircraft up to New York City. The Iraqi Colonel watched as the first of four black stretch limousines slowly pulled up to the aircraft surrounded by a dozen special agents. The President along with a number of friends and new reporters, climbed out of the vehicles and the American Leader slowly climbed the stairs leading to the aircraft. The Colonel placed a disgusted look on as he saw a number of people head up the steps right behind the President, and he feared they would mess up Farseeha's shot, knowing she was the shooter on this mission. But then he smiled when the American Leader turned and he waved to other people who just arrived by the plane.

"Now! Take your cursed shot now, foolish woman." The Colonel roared as he waited for Farseeha to finally take her kill shot at the American President. Just as he heard the report from her weapon, a second man suddenly jumped up on the top step with the President, and his head instantly exploded from the heavy round hitting him. A woman standing with the President, who the Iraqi did not realize was the Vice President, also went down from the same shot. The Iraqi Colonel was fuming, because he saw the American Leader being pulled safely into the aircraft by his security agents, and it was obvious that he was unhurt by their attack.

Almost as soon as Farseeha fired at the President boarding his plane, return fire from security people, two attack helicopters, and a flood of military machines with a gaggle of soldiers in them charged the old water tower. All assets began pounding away with weapon fire at the terrorists hiding in the tower. The Iraqi control knew his attackers were killed in this onslaught. So he destroyed his small handheld radio and then left the area without bringing attention to himself.

Unknown to Colonel al-Adwani, a small slip of paper with his name printed on it Farseeha carried on her person, was discovered at the site once the police and agents started to check the bodies of the dead terrorists lay scattered on the walkway of the tower. The American

Command now knew there was a fourth member of this terrorist cell who had successfully escaped them. Instantly a massive manhunt was ordered, with special agents, CIA Agents, police and military personnel hunting him. Colonel Al-Adwani made it to a safe house, and with the help of a female agent from Iraq, ordered to assist al-Adwani. He hid until the female was able to make the needed preparations for him to escape the United States, and make his way back to Iraq.

The President ordered the special operations soldiers known as the Multi Nation Rapid Response Force, to be called in for special training, and if needed, send the troops to Iraq to bring back the missing terrorist. So he could stand trial before the American public and then be put to death for his attempt to assassinate him, and killing the national security director, and severely wounding his Vice President. The training went well for the elite troops, and when Colonel al-Adwani, who escaped the United States through Canada, surfaced in Iraq. A pair of CIA sleeper Operatives under the control of CIA Director John Raincloud took pictures of the terrorist while he was in Iraq. The American Leader ordered the troops to invade Iraq, and take the missing Iraqi Colonel prisoner and then bring him back to the United States to stand trial.

The troops set up operations in the Iraqi village of Dawral, and given twenty four hours to carry out their mission and at the end of the twenty four hours if the troops were unable to take the Iraqi terrorist prisoner. The elite troops were to change orders and kill the terrorist, and film it so the President could see the terrorist was dead. Then the troops were to get out of Iraq. During the time of setup and capture of Colonel al-Adwani, it was discovered his main control was an Iraqi General Hassan al-Zahar. So the

President cut orders informing the special operations soldiers he would not be upset if General al-Zahar happened to get in the way of a drive by bullet, and ended up dead during their mission into Iraq to capture the missing terrorist.

The special operations soldiers under the command of General John White, the Chairman of the Joint Chiefs of Staff training at Camp Lejeune by Colonel Bruce Leadbetter, set up outside the Iraqi General's headquarters in Iraq. Where they waited for Colonel al-Adwani to make an appearance, so they could snatch him in a snatch and scoot operation and then get out of Iraq with their prisoner. The elite group of soldiers was operating under orders to keep the killing of other Iraqis, whether military or civilian, down to the absolute minimum.

The President did not want his troops to create a blood bath in Iraq, mainly because they were upset this Iraqi terrorist tried to kill him. The concerned President was angry as hell, but he did not want to start a shooting war with Iraq just yet, not until he had hard evidence that proved beyond a shadow of a doubt that Iraqi President Hussein was the man behind the strings who controlled and then sent the terrorists to the United States to kill him.

When Colonel al-Adwani safely arrived back at General al-Zahar's main headquarters in Iraqi, he was greeted by a not so friendly Colonel Hamoodi al-Qaysi, who despised the Colonel and all he stood for in his terrorist ways and actions. Colonel Al-Qaysi was what he believed was a true soldier, and he did not like to be forced to deal with any spies, or and especially any terrorists, or actions and death they were responsible for during their evil actions. The two Iraqis Officers got into a slight altercation, and it was instantly stopped by General al-Zahar, when he came out of his office to meet with the terrorist, Colonel al-Adwani.

The Iraqi General realized his Colonel was angry with Colonel al-Adwani for the obvious reason. So he sent Colonel al-Qaysi out on a patrol to get him away from the Iraqi terrorist, before he ended up killing Colonel al-Adwani on him. The Army Colonel took off on his patrol with three vehicles, and thirty soldiers. He was out of the way, and the General and his terrorist spoke on a friendlier basis. During this conversation, al-Adwani went over why his mission failed to kill the American Leader. He suggested the General do an overthrow of Saddam and takeover control of Iraq and deal with the Americans on a more favorable term for peace.

General al-Zahar jumped all over the idea of deposing the weaken President of Iraq because of the one sided Desert Storm War, and he came up with an idea of releasing a false news press. Where he would announce to the world the Iraqi military shot down an American warplane involved in the constant no fly zone patrols over his country. This news conference infuriated Saddam, and at first he ordered his troops to arrest General al-Zahar then bring him to Baghdad.

The American troops who infiltrated Iraq, set up to snatch the wanted terrorist, but they discovered they were going to be forced to make an attack on the Iraqi headquarters if they intended to take Colonel al-Adwani prisoner, before they ran out of time on the mission. The elite soldiers hit the Iraqi building before midnight. The troops got involved with a heavy firefight with the Iraqi soldiers trapped inside the General's headquarters, and after a hard fought battle. The Americans were able to kill the enemy troops, including General al-Zahar, and they took al-

Adwani prisoner. The American forces lost one man to the battle in the brick building.

A battle hardened young Lieutenant Robert Walker, known to his fellow soldiers by the tag name Road Kill, was in command of the special troops as they assaulted the Iraqi headquarters. The Lieutenant ordered some of his troops to plant a number of explosives inside the building. He wanted the armory along with the building itself, destroyed as they left the small Iraqi village. Walker and his Special Forces was operating under pressure, because he was certain Saddam sooner or later, was going to send a mess of reinforcement troops once he discovered American troops were operating in his country. Walker was pushing his troops beyond their endurance, because the last thing he needed was to be attacked by a bunch of well trained Iraqi troops, and be forced to engage them in a firefight under these trying conditions.

From the reports Walker was receiving from his troops stationed just outside the building, informed him there was still no sign of any enemy reinforcement troops coming from Baghdad. Walker was at a lost as to why the Iraqi President refused to send support troops for his General. He had no way of knowing the Iraqi madman was angry at his General, and stopped his military forces from moving out, and offering any support to the under siege General and his troops.

Lieutenant Walker got the Iraqi prisoner out of the building and shoved him inside the lead machine, and then he ordered the commandeered vehicles to leave the Iraqi village A-SAP. As the troops were leaving, the trailing vehicle picked up a number of Iraqi war machines heading for the village at speed. The Ghost, (Sergeant Walter Casper) reported to Walker about the enemy vehicles entering the village behind them. The Lieutenant believed the vehicles were the reinforcements he was certain the Iraqi General requested from Baghdad. The Lieutenant ordered the Ghost to pop off the enemy armory as his vehicles started out of the Iraqi town.

Buckethead, (Sergeant Vincent Lombardo) named because of the size of his helmet. Along with Mother Flanagan, (Sergeant Richard Flanagan) was his tag named because he was always stuck training the new soldiers who joined their group. Opened fire on the arriving enemy Iraqi troops with M-60 machine guns, their fire disabled the lead vehicle of the small enemy convoy, and forced the other Iraqi war machines to bunch up behind the damaged and stalled vehicle. Mother Flanagan picked up a number of soldiers pouring out of the three Iraqi machines just as the armory inside the building exploded with a thunderous eruption of boiling flames and tumbling building debris and bellowing black smoke.

The two excited American soldiers watched as most of the Iraqi troops ran for cover when their headquarters exploded on them. The two American soldiers slapped sticks (forearms) together as Mother kept an eye on what the remaining Iraqi troops were doing in the village. Mother Flanagan wanted to make certain the undamaged enemy machines, did not come around the damaged one, and then they pursued them. Mother stared at the village forcing Buckethead to stop laughing and look at what Mother was staring so intensely at and causing him some alarm.

In Buckethead's eyes, he saw one lone Iraqi soldier standing directly in the middle of the road as the two story building exploded all around him. It seemed like this one soldier was not upset, or not very concerned with the exploding building. He looked like he was staring the American soldiers down from where he stood in the middle of the road. Buckethead stared at the same soldier as Mother, wondering who this crazy dude was.

"I wonder who the fuck that stinking guy is Homes?" Buckethead mumbled to Mother and then he added to his words to the second soldier with him. "He looks like he might be someone important back there man. He also looks really pissed off at us man."

"Beats the fuck outta my stinking ass Homes, but for some friggin reason I really don't think we have seen the last of this one lousy little scumbag, man. Look at the stupid motherfucker back there, Bucket. He's standing there and allowing himself to be pelted by the stinking debris from the exploding armory. There's something wrong about this sorry sonofa fucking bitch that has the short hairs on the back of my neck standing on end, and you know me. I'm not afraid of any man, woman or fucking beast, buddy. I think if anyone from Iraq is gonna give us any more grief from this shit filled mission, this is the friggin little prick who's gonna do it to us, man."

Mother Flanagan complained at his partner as he continued to stare back at the Iraqi soldier still standing tall in the middle of the village, like he was cursing them from where he stood standing in the road. Mother did the only thing he could think of doing in his attempt to threaten the Iraqi soldier staring at him so intensely, he shot him the bird.

Buckethead lifted his M-60 machine gun to his shoulder, and then aimed it at the Iraqi soldier as he announced. "Hey Mother, this mission has been seven shares of shit in a one shit suitcase. If you're that fucking worried about the sand swimming shitbird back there, I can pop a cap in his ass from here and end any trouble that might come from the motherfucker in the future, man."

"Naw, you know our standing orders big man, we're not to kill anyone on this damn mission unnecessarily, and just because this lousy little prick's mad dogging our asses like he's doing back there. It doesn't mean we hafta pop him just for the damn stare down, man." Mother Flanagan replied, but he was unable to rip his eyes away from this unknown Iraqi soldier, and the concern he was causing him. Try as he might, Mother just could not shake the ill feeling that he was getting from this one lone guy. He never feared any Iraqi soldier, until now.

"You betta let Walker know about this scumbag back there Mother, you know how he is. If he finds out we mighta left a possible threat still alive, he's gonna take it out on our asses but good, buddy." Buckethead warned Mother as he continued to stare at the enemy soldier also.

"Yeah, you got that right Bucket; I'll get on that right away man. Walker's getting to be a real motherfucker lately, ever since he got those damn gold bars pinned on his stinking ass." Mother complained as he hit the radio crystal in his robe then barked. "Walker, I need to talk to ya man. I got me something that's bugging the shit outta my ass, sir. Come in Lieutenant Walker. Over."

Walker immediately recognized Flanagan's voice and he fired right back in his helmet radio. "Yeah go, Walker here, whatdaya got going down Mother? What's bugging ya ass man?"

"Road Kill, can you look back at the Iraqi village and tell me what you fucking see?" Mother Flanagan asked Lieutenant Walker, he wanted the Lieutenant to see what he was looking at.

Lieutenant Walker did not reply as he merely glanced back over his shoulder, and he saw nothing but the exploding building, and three parked Iraqi war machines sitting in the middle of the road, with one of them smoking from the steaming radiator. He shook his head as he growled in is radio mike. "Yeah Mother, I see a rat filled building going up like an overinflated balloon, and some parked A-rab vehicles getting covered with the crap from that destroyed building, buddy. Is that what you wanted me to look at back there Homes? It's no big deal as far as I see Mother. I saw many a fucking building leave the face of the earth before, stupid."

"No Walker!" Flanagan snapped back at the Lieutenant, getting pissed off at Walker for calling him stupid over the radio as he offered him. "Walker, I want you to look at the left side of the third fucking machine, and then tell me what you see back there man, and thanks a shitload for the stinking slug you just fired at my ass, pal. Fuck you and the horse you rode in on man."

Walker smiled when he realized Mother was angry for the shot he just took at him, and he grumbled at the usual calm soldier. "Mother, you got a real fricking way with the big words I see, sucka. I'm looking at where you told me to look, and all I see is some stinking asshole standing out in the open, and he's allowing his sagging ass to eat a shitload of crap from the stinking building. What's up man? I still don't see what has your cockles in a fricking uproar, Homes."

"You got what I want you to look at man. I don't like the shit filled looks coming from that slimy motherfucker back there, Walker. From the looks of the lousy little bastard, I think he's gonna get back in our life in the future like the stinking cockroach he is, man. I know trouble when I see it standing before my ass, and this turd is gonna be a shitload of trouble in the future." Mother complained as he kept his eyes locked on the Iraqi mad dogging them from the village.

"C'mon for Christ sake Mother, what the hell do you want me to fucking believe about this one dumb shit back there man? That one lone sand scummer has you fricking worried about his rotten little ass?" Walker smirked back at Mother as he held the Iraqi soldier in his angry glare, as the machine he was in, passed the last building of the small Iraqi village, and it was now out on the open road and moving as fast as the machine could travel.

"I don't know what's with the fricking little dude and his stinking look that's upsetting my friggin ass like this, man. But something about the lousy scumbag has me sweating between my fucking balls, Walker. I think we might be leaving a little bit of trouble behind us, and I don't like leaving any fricking trouble alive, to come back and bite me on my ass later on, Homes." Mother Flanagan complained at the Lieutenant while allowing anger to enter his tone.

"Okay Mother, you have aroused my stinking interest, whatdaya wanna do about the little motherfucker, man?" Walker bitched at the Mother, trying to find out what had him so upset.

"I don't fucking know, Walker. I only know of the order to keep the killing down to nothing on this shit filled stinking mission into sand land, man. But this one back there is fucking trouble; I can see it written in his stinking eyes man. I can feel it in my guts as well Walker." Mother replied as he continued to stare at the Iraqi soldier behind his moving machine.

"Whatdaya wanna fucking do about it then Mother?" Walker snapped at the soldier.

"Again man, I don't really know what the fuck I wanna do about the lousy little prick, Walker. All I know is Buckethead must feel the same way I do. Because he has the dopey little bastard locked up in his sights, and he wants permission to take the little asshole out before we leave this stinking land of sand and scorpions, Lieutenant." Mother bitched at his commanding officer as he continued to stare at the Iraqi soldier who did not react when he shot the bird at the dude a few seconds ago. All the Iraqi soldier did was continued to stare angrily at both Mother and Buckethead, and he seemed to be cursing them as they left the village. Sergeant Flanagan shook his head again over this Iraqi soldier, and the concern he was causing him.

"Look Mother, I needed another fucking problem on this friggin mission on my ass, like I needed my balls beaten flat with a stinking wooden hammer, man. If you have a stinking hardon on for this lousy little puke back there then you're free to place a cap in his ass. I'm leaving the decision entirely in your hands, Mother. So take care of the problem anyway you wanna handle the damn thing, man. If you feel he might be a threat to us in the future, toe tag (kill him) the dopey bastard's ass. But make sure of your feelings first. You know our orders about taking one of these Iraqi bastards out, because we have a finger up our backside for the bastards. If you want him out then do him double quick and clear the radio. I gotta make contact with whatispuss, and let the stinking Colonel know we got the Iraqi dude he sent us out here to get, man."

Mother Flanagan let out his breath in a rush as he continued to stare at the Iraqi soldier, and the tumbling debris landing all around the man. He wished a chunk of the building would hit the Iraqi in the head, and take him out before he had to make a decision on the Iraqi's future fate.

Walker heard the deep sigh and asked Flanagan over the mike. "Well Mother, what the fuck's it gonna be man? Your machine's about to pass the last stinking building of the rat filled shit town. Then you're gonna lose your shot at the stinking bird back there man. Mother, if you decide to take the damn shot at him I don't want you to give the dude a fat shot. (Wound) If you take the shot, I want it to be a death shot or nothing, man. I don't need the fuck griping that we shot at the prick just for the hell of it my friend. If you do him then do him right Homes."

"God dammit Walker! Give me a fucking chance to think for a second will ya man. I know I wanna do the sonofa fucking bitch in nice and neat. But I don't wanna kill the lousy prick just for the hell of it, Lieutenant. Look Walker, if you hear some pop going off back here, just ignore it buddy. It'll be us doing the guy in, because he's still bugging the stinking shit outta my damn ass. Don't gripe in your radio, if and when you hear us fire at the slimy Iraqi bastard."

"You got it Mother, just make up your mind, I'm gonna make contact with the Colonel."

"You got it Walker." Mother replied as he looked at Buckethead for a second.

Walker glanced over his shoulder a second time and he found he could no longer see the Iraqi soldier who was bugging Mother's ass, or even the building burning in the village now. Because of the angle he was on as his machines left the small Iraqi town. All he could see left was parts of the building still tumbling in the air and crashing to the ground. He shook his head slowly, knowing full well he wanted Mother to take out the Iraqi soldier. He knew Mother long enough, and if he had a wild hair up his ass over this one enemy soldier. It was a justified worry, and he wanted it ended for the elite soldiers but quick by Mother.

Lieutenant Walker understood he was not going to be the one to tell Mother to take out an enemy soldier, especially because when he last saw the enemy trooper. He was unarmed and was not making any threatening moves against them as they left the village, except for maybe cursing at them. He knew he would be cursing up a storm if some Iraqi soldiers made a hit on his people back in the United States. He turned back and looked ahead as he keyed his mike and then made the call to Colonel Bruce Leadbetter, the Field Commander of the entire operation.

Buckethead knew what Mother Flanagan wanted, and he grumbled in a sharp tone at him. "Yeah Mother, I still got a clear shot at the dumb Iraqi asshole, man. Do you want his lousy hide for a fricking trophy for your stinking wall or what, buddy? You gotta make up your mind real quick like man. I don't know how much longer I'll still have the shot at the little prick. We're moving outta this dump real fast now man. I still have a good shot at the lousy little dude, but with each yard we travel, the shot's gonna be harder to take, buddy."

Buckethead's words about wanting the Iraqi soldier's hide for a trophy, made Mother rethink his thoughts about this enemy soldier. Now, he found himself questioning if that was why he wanted the enemy soldier dead in the first place, just because he was standing out in the open showing absolutely no fear of him, and the rest of his special operations troops who just attacked their main headquarters. Sergeant Richard Flanagan found himself still staring at the enemy soldier standing by the side of his disabled Russian built war machine. He could tell the Iraqi was getting pelted by junk falling out of the sky from the exploded building. He shook his head as then he glanced at Buckethead, and then grumbled at the huge soldier. "God dammit big guy, I don't know what the fuck to do with the dumb shit back there man."

"What's all the stinking sweat about anyway man? If you really want the lousy sonofabitch taken out, just say the stinking word and I'll drop the dopey little bastard right where he's fricking standing back there, Mother." Buckethead griped while still urging his fellow soldier to make up his mind about the Iraqi soldier one way or the other, before he lost his shot on the soldier and then they will have to forget about killing the enemy soldier.

"Dammit to hell and back again Bucket, now I don't know why I really wanna drop the lousy motherfucker. At first I thought he might be some kind of a possible future threat against us. Now I'm not so sure any longer man. Could it be I just want the little prick dead because he's standing there showing no stinking fear of us, man? And a soldier showing no fear of us, will somehow come back and end up biting us on the ass one way or the other, man. Dammit, shit, I just don't know any longer man, fuck it let me think about it for a second."

"Look Mother, I hate like hell to try and rush you any man, but no matter what the friggin reasons you want his ass dead, you gotta make up your mind on the double quick man. The shot's not so easy now, and the longer you wait, the harder the shot's gonna be for me to make. C'mon Mother, you gotta do something, even if it's fucking wrong you gotta do it buddy. Do you want the lousy fuck taken out or what man? You gotta make up your stinking mind now Homes." Buckethead glared at Mother.

"Crap, I don't know any fucking longer Buckethead. I still have a stinking hardon for the dopey little fuck, but is it for the right stinking reason I want him dead or what though, dammit. Is he really a serious threat in the future against us, or do I want him done in, just because he acting so fricking arrogant back there buddy? I never did another soldier in just because I hated the fuck like I do this fucking guy."

"Look man in another second or two your decision is gonna be academic man. Because the lousy dude's gonna be outta friggin range, and I ain't gonna shoot the fuck unless I know I can do him in right, Mother."

Mother shook his head, as he again looked at the Iraqi soldier still standing out in the open like nothing was happening around him, and then he mumbled at the Iraqi soldier as if he was able to hear any of his words he was aiming at him. "You're one lucky mutherfucker scumbag, because I'm gonna let you to live for a little while longer man."

CHAPTER TWO

AUGUST 7th, 1999.
THE LITTLE TOWN OF DAWRAL

Iraqi Colonel Hamoodi al-Qaysi was fuming as he watched the two American soldiers as their small convoy of vehicles quickly left the small Iraqi village of Dawral, with their prisoner Colonel Abdulaziz Majd al-Adwani in custody. Colonel al-Adwani was the terrorist who had masterminded the attempted assassination of President Albert Cole in the United States. In the attempt, the National Security Director, Norman Griffin was killed, and the Vice President

Mary Hirshfield was seriously wounded in the throat and right shoulder by the sneak attack.

The Iraqi prisoner was placed in the first of the commandeered Iraqi military vehicles taking the American soldiers back out to the deep desert. Where the specialized troops were scheduled to link back up with the reserve support soldiers and vehicles waiting by an ancient wadi or dried river bed. So the entire elite force could escape Iraq with their prisoner in tow. The Iraqi terrorist had no idea what was happening about him, because he was heavily sedated by the special operation soldiers, and he was also blindfolded and tightly handcuffed.

While Colonel Hamoodi al-Qaysi stood in the middle of the road of the town of Dawral and the explosion of his once headquarters did not make him flinch, as he stood glaring at the rapidly retreating American soldiers. Suddenly the Iraqi Colonel moved over to the first of his war machines gunned down and disabled by the invading American troops. Its radiator split opened by the heavy rounds fired at it. The angry Colonel was sent out on a patrol by General Hassan al-Zahar, who was the commander of the terrorist Colonel al-Adwani, when he returned to Iraq from his failed attempted assassination on the American President's life.

The fuming Iraqi Colonel al-Qaysi angrily cursed the backs of the American soldiers, and when he saw one of them do that disgusting hand signal at him, his anger grew more than before. He wanted nothing more than to be able to kill the hated American soldiers who had just dared to invade his country, and killed his General and the other Iraqi soldiers who were with his commanding officer. The angry Colonel had no doubt in his mind the General, along with the rest of the soldiers once in the headquarters were dead, now the building exploded and he did not see any soldiers outside, because the building was nothing more than a pile of rubble. The Iraqi Officer watched as the last war machine carried the enemy troops out of town.

The Iraqi Military Officer glanced over at the destroyed building once his headquarters, as the raging fire completely engulfed what was not destroyed by the explosives the American troops left as they fled his small village. All the upset Colonel could do was growl at the terrible carnage the American soldiers had created to their building and village.

The Iraqi Colonel's second in command, Major Serena al-Shaya came up to the officer's side, and offered him with concern in her voice. "Colonel al-Qaysi, what are we going to do now sir?"

The Colonel turned to his Major and then barked angrily at her. "What the devil do you mean by what are we going to do now, Major al-Shaya?"

"Colonel al-Qaysi, I asked you this question, because I'm in search of orders, sir."

"Foul woman of the hot desert sands, you offer me you're in search of orders? I'm in search of General al-Zahar and our headquarters in this foul village, woman. That is what I'm in search of, Major." Colonel Al-Qaysi growled at the female Major as he glared savagely at her.

"Colonel al-Qaysi Sir, I believe we have to think of our future, sir. We cannot possibly go back to Baghdad and think we'll be allowed to live peacefully there, sir."

"Why can we not go back to Baghdad, woman who speaks to me like I need her direction and guidance?" The angry Iraqi Colonel snarled at the staring Major.

The female Iraqi Officer let out her breath in a rush, and then she replied to her commanding officer.

"Colonel al-Qaysi Sir! After the press conference General al-Zahar gave about shooting down an American warplane, and trying to draw our civilians to his side. So he could overthrow our worthless President and understanding when we were attack. President Hussein had failed to send any reinforcing troops out to assist General al-Zahar when they came under attack by the hated American invaders. We heard all his pleas for reinforcement troops over our radios, and that was why we cut our patrol short and we rushed back to the town of Dawral. So we could help General al-Zahar with our few troops under your command, Colonel al-Qaysi Sir.

"We have to believe that we have fallen out of favor with our worthless President, and he was willing to allow what happened to the General and his troops, to take place uncontested. Colonel al-Qaysi Sir, we have to understand we're now a hunted group of Iraqi soldiers not only in our own country, sir. But I'm quite certain the cursed American soldiers will return to Iraq to finish us off some time in the future, sir. After seeing what they have done to our country and fellow soldiers makes me believe this is true, and soon to happen sir." Major al-Shaya grumbled at the Colonel who she was not certain was paying very much attention to her words and concerns.

Colonel Al-Qaysi did not reply to the Major's words which forced her to stare at him.

Suddenly, Colonel al-Qaysi shook his head slowly as if he was trying to clear the cobwebs clouding over his mind. Then he looked in the eyes of the worried looking Major, and snapped hotly at her. "Major al-Shaya, I know we and by we, I mean all the faithful soldiers with us. Are now hunted soldiers in our own country, woman. I assure you Major if our worthless President Hussein, who should've done what he was supposed to do as our leader of Iraq. We wouldn't have had to resort to that minor deception about destroying the American warplane, and our foolish President wouldn't be in fear of us either, woman. If he was our true leader, and he acted like he was supposed to, and he would've dealt with the hated American fools and their foul allies, and the worthless members of the United Nations, we'd be at peace with the world.

"But no, the great fool has to play his endless games of chess with the world, further infuriating the hateful American Forces, and their worthless allies. If the President confessed he sent all his weapons of mass destruction out of our country, and placed them safely in Syria. Then Saddam ordered the weapons moved to the Bakaa Valley in Lebanon for safe keeping until we were able to get the eyes of the rest of the world from our moves, foolish woman."

"Colonel al-Qaysi Sir, I'm well aware of all the cursed problems our foolish President has cost our faithful soldiers of Iraq, sir. I see no reason whatsoever to rehash these endless problems once again, sir. All I'd like to know from you is, what are we going to do now Colonel? We have to have a plan in mind, or we'll be hunted down like the loathsome jackals of the vast desert, and we'll be destroyed by our own soldiers loyal to our President, Colonel." The female Major allowed a trace of irritation to show in her tone of voice she was addressing the Colonel with.

Colonel al-Qaysi's eyes narrowed to angry slits as he glared at the female Major al-Shaya, and then he snarled at her. "You better take better care in your tone of voice that you dare to address me with, cursed witch of the desert sand. Although you might believe I lost power over our soldiers. I assure you woman, I'm far from a scorpion without a sting. I'll tell you this much though woman, beware of the Sting of This Scorpion. For you'll not live through my anger if you're foolish enough to push me until I lose my temper with you, my dear Major al-Shaya."

Major al-Shaya saw the look in the glaring eyes of the Colonel, and backed down. Then she cast her eyes to the sand and rubble covered street to avoid the harsh look from the Colonel.

"That's much better and wise of you Major al-Shaya. Woman, I'll explain to you even though I don't believe I owe you anything, least of all an explanation as to what I have planned for our future. Allow me to tell you Major, even though I deeply despise working with a lowly spy, or a hated terrorist such as Colonel Abdulaziz Majd al-Adwani is, and make no mistake about it Major al-Shaya. He's nothing more than a cursed terrorist for our country, woman. He has given Iraq and our cause something to dream about, be proud about, woman. We can dream about the removal of the cursed President Saddam from his foul office, and the control of Iraq.

"As much as I hate this worthless fool of a spy and terrorist, I swear this to you foolish woman. If it's the last thing I do in life. I shall kill the hated American Judge who'll dare try our worthless Colonel in their evil courts, along with as many of the hated American soldiers who had dared to invade Iraq to take Colonel al-Adwani their prisoner. Or I'll forgo the thought of spending eternity in Paradise. I will find the evil soldier's foul names and I'll destroy the lot of them."

"I agree with all you have just offered to me Colonel al-Qaysi Sir. But how are we going to seek our revenge against the loathsome American troops, when we'll have every soldier in Iraq looking for us, once our foolish President decides what he's going to do with us, sir. I believe if we leave this area and escape to the deep desert, maybe President Saddam Hussein will think that everyone who was with General al-Zahar, had perished in the battle in the village of Dawral against the hated American invaders, sir. Then we'll have more time to figure out what we should do, sir. Maybe we should also contemplate leaving Iraq all together, Colonel al-Qaysi."

"What the devil is this foolishness you now offer me Major al-Shaya, are you're suggesting that we flee Iraq like a bunch of lowly criminals, who are guilty and running from a crime we didn't committed? We are not criminals, if anyone is an evil doer in all of Iraq. It's our worthless leader who hides himself in Baghdad and surrounds himself with a small Army of security soldiers. If it was not for his foolish actions dealing with the rest of the world, Iraq would be at peace and we'd be dealing with the Americans, and their foul sanctions would be lifted from our hearts and minds, woman. I believe that the worthless Saddam cannot live with himself, unless he's sending the young males of Iraq on another war, another one he has started for the want of greed and foolishness. Bah, this talk is unnecessary for us to waste our breath on. I have an idea of revenge locked in my mind Major." The Colonel turned to the Major and smiled at her.

Major Serena al-Shaya let out her breath in a deep sigh, and her shoulders noticeably sagged as she asked her Colonel with concern in her voice. "Sir, I knew you had to have something on your mind, Colonel. Do you mind telling me what it might be sir?"

Still smiling, Colonel al-Qaysi added to his words. "Major al-Shaya! If I'm going to go over my plans then I want all our faithful soldiers to be in on the conversation. So in that way I won't have to repeat myself to anyone of our soldiers. But first Major, I need to know the soldiers will follow me in my plans to get back at the hated American soldiers, and their loathsome government, and that of our own government and foolish President at the same time. If I have these faithful soldiers swear their allegiance and they are with me. Then I'll know Allah will allow my ideas to bear fruit, and succeed for my wishes. I bid you to call all our surviving soldiers together so I can hear the words spoken from their faithful lips to me, woman.

"That they'll swear to me their faithful allegiance and follow me to the very gates of Paradise, and watch me bang on the door and order Muhammad to allow us to dwell with Him for all eternity. Go Major and bring the soldiers back to me and then we'll talk of my plans, and fulfill our dreams of revenge on all those who have dared to cross us." The Iraqi Colonel had to give Major al-Shaya a quick head movement in order to get her moving on his orders. He smiled as he watched the female Major scream at his troops, ordering them to muster by the last vehicle.

Their destroyed headquarters was the backdrop for the Iraqi Colonel's speech.

THE AMERICAN TROOPS HEADING INTO THE IRAQ DESERT

Lieutenant Robert Walker's machine was the lead vehicle of the column of commandeered Russian made Iraqi machines, and he smiled when he noticed Captain Wilson, who was ordered to remain with the Dinkies in the protective wade or dried up ancient riverbed coming at him. The fast moving sand buggies the American troops used to first invade the Iraqi desert a mere twenty six hours before. Three F-18 Hornets were flying over their heads, offering the elite troops cover from a possible attack by any reinforcement Iraqi soldiers.

Captain Wilson's buggy pulled up to Walker's lead machine, and the worried Captain spoke to the young Lieutenant without either of them leaving the vehicles. The concern Captain looked in Walker's vehicle and spotted the terrorist and barked. "I see you got the lousy little turd in one piece there, Lieutenant. Why don't you get out of those Iraqi pieces of shit and get in our own equipment, sir. So then we can get the hell out of this damn desert."

The young and pleased Lieutenant replied with a smirk. "The stinking prisoner's shaking like a French fucking soldier, Captain. But all in all, he's doing as well as can be expected, sir." Then he snarled in his radio. "Okay you sand rats, get the fuck outta them pieces of shit and get in our own damn machines. Just Bob, you and the two soldiers with you, take care of Sun Tan's body."

"Dammit! I guess we lost one of our guys in this action, Lieutenant Walker Sir?" The Captain mumbled in anger to his new military officer.

"Yeah, the motherfucking General that Colonel Leadbetter told us to make certain was hit by a drive by bullet, got Sun Tan before we got his slimy ass, sir." Walker bitched at the Captain.

"At least you got the scumbag back for Sun Tan, Lieutenant. You better get your troops moving before Leadbetter comes out here and takes chunks out of our asses for delaying, sir."

"You got that right Captain." Walker replied as he glanced behind him and snapped in his radio. "C'mon you slack asses we gotta get a stinking move on it. There's cold ass beer waiting for us in Arabia. I got word Leadbetter's shipping in a shitload of the crap for a job well done."

One soldier barked back at Walker in his helmet radio. "Hey Homes, why the fuck didn't you tell us that shit in the first place, man? We woulda been moving a helluva lot quicker if we knew that." The complaining soldier jumped down from the duce and a half they stole from the Iraqi's.

A female soldier bitched at Walker over the radio next. "Yeah Walker, and you're getting as bad as Leadbetter, mister. Ever since you got those set of railroad tracks tacked on your collar."

"Was that you Baby Tee?" Walker snarled in his helmet radio.

Baby Tee, (Sergeant Teri Dorland) who got her tag name because of the small size of her breasts, replied to Walker's bitch at her. "I'm afraid that I'm guilty as charged Walker dear, and what the devil are you going to do about it mister? We can settle this anyway you want to settle it, Lieutenant." Baby Tee sounded like she was actually angry at the Lieutenant.

"I'll tell you what I'm going to do about it little tits. When we get back to the real world, I'm gonna lick your body all over for that comment, baby girl." Walker warned her over the radio.

"Ooooooo, now I have something to look forward to when we get back to the real world." Baby Tee fired back at Walker then shot him a smile that would have melted butter on the table.

The Mutt, (Lieutenant Frank Hall) who got his tag name because he had a white mother, and black father, and helping Walker move their prisoner to one of their machines, groused. "Hey Road Kill, (Walker's tag name because of his body odor) what the hell gives here man? I thought I was the only lap dog around here man. Now you're gonna give Baby Tee a tongue bath. You betta find your own thing to make the chicks moan for ya, buddy."

As the soldiers moved Colonel al-Adwani over to the other vehicle, the Iraqi Colonel suddenly stiffened up and he then tried to stop the American soldiers from roughly shoving him around so much. This caused Walker to warn him in a harsh tone. "Look scumbag, you're one cunt hair away from finding fucking Paradise, man! So don't push it on me stupid."

Instantly, the Iraqi Colonel went in the direction he was being shoved towards.

Ice, (Sergeant Diane Morrison) who got her tag because she was as cold as ice whenever she was out on a mission, and was one of the soldiers who was wounded on this mission. She was hit in the shoulder and it was a bad wound, but not bad enough to stop her from continuing on with the mission. She heard the Mutt's gripe and immediately got right on his ass over it. "C'mon Walker, you know the Mutt would try and lick himself all over his filthy body if he could bend his neck against the laws of gravity, sir. I saw that lap dog's tongue in action a few times in my life sir, and it gave me the heebie geebies to watch him work it, Walker baby."

"Hey Ice, when it comes to the Mutt in the world of perversion, he wears the badge of honor, baby." Baby Tee offered with a slight twinkle in her beautiful blue eyes.

"Let me call you sweet heart cause I'm in love with you. I can't see your face dear, but your legs will do." No Neck began singing in the radio to Ice. Everyone started to laugh over the Neck's attempt at singing, but it caused the girls of the outfit to get on him as well now.

"Hey Neck, have you ever made love to a perfect ten in your ugly life, mista?" Blind Date, (Sergeant Regina Raphael) on loan to the American troops from the French, asked the big man.

"Naw, I never fucked a ten, but one night I fucked five two's, and I think that should count."

"You're as nuts as you look big man." The pretty French woman fighter taunted back at Neck.

"You better stay away from that big one if you know what's good for you Blind Date. I wouldn't let him stick that log he calls a dick between my legs for love or money, baby girl. I saw the damn thing a few times, and it scared the hell out of me girl." Ice added, trying to keep the attacks on the male members of the elite group of warriors going for a while longer.

"I understand a girl has to draw the line someplace." Neck fired right back at Ice, and then he asked her. "Hey girl, how are you doing anyway sister? How is the shoulder doing honey?"

"It's okay as long as I don't think about it." Ice replied as Blood Clot moved up to her, and checked the wound again. Blood Clot, (Sergeant Richard Brumback) was the unit's medic.

Walker shook his head and then he shoved their prisoner into the machine. Then he asked the Mutt. "Hey pal, are you doing okay man?"

"I don't know I'm usually kinda fucked up in general man, so it's kinda hard to gauge Walker. Why do you ask that man? You noticed something I didn't pick up?"

"Just asking, you look beat up from the feet up, that's all buddy." Walker replied as he and the Mutt climbed into the American made war machine.

"All I know Walker is I want a beer so bad I'll eat the fricking end off the damn bottle."

"What didja say Mutt?" Walker asked, because he was not paying attention to him.

"I don't know. What did you hear man?" the Mutt retorted with a grin at Walker.

"You know Mutt, at NASA they have fucking monkeys doing your fricking job, man." Walker fired back at the Mutt with a smirk on his lips.

"Funny, real funny Walker, now you're trying out for comedian of the year I see. You know Walker, has it ever occurred to you I might accidentally know what I'm doing around here?"

When the soldiers abandoned the Old Russian made Iraqi war machines, and were in their own vehicles again. Walker gave the order to start up and then head out. Before they moved, he made sure Sun Tan's (Sergeant Clifford Saldinger) body was tied down properly, and ready for the fast trip out of the Iraqi deep desert. He was the only soldier killed in the hard hitting action.

COLONEL HAMOODI AL-QAYSI BACK AT THE IRAQI TOWN OF DAWRAL

Colonel al-Qaysi leaned against his half track machine as he watched his second in command, Major Serena al-Shaya scream at his soldiers, ordering them to assemble by his machine. By the time his troops assembled, the colonel was taking a drink of water and glaring at the troops.

Major al-Shaya actually had to place her hands on the backs of some of the slow moving soldiers and push them in an effort to make them move a lot quicker than they were moving for the angry Colonel. The slower the soldiers moved, the angrier the female Major got at them. Finally she had the soldiers assembled before the Colonel, and he put his hand in the air and the soldiers stopped their conversations. The fires still consuming their headquarters were starting to burn themselves out, and the slowly brightening sky made the fires seem not so threatening.

Suddenly, the Major bellowed out at the troops. "Attention in the ranks!"

The Iraqi soldiers snapped to attention and then waited to hear what the Colonel had to say.

Colonel Al-Qaysi did not start to speak right off, instead he started to count the soldiers he had left in his command. There were nineteen soldiers in all not counting him or Major al-Shaya. He did some quick thinking and felt certain he had enough soldiers left in his ranks for his future needs. Next, he counted the women warriors he had seven women, including his second in command, Major Serena al-Shaya. He did not mind the women soldiers in the least because they seemed to follow orders better and much quicker than the male soldiers always did.

When the angry Iraqi Colonel was satisfied with the formation of his soldiers, he growled at the troopers. "My loyal brothers and sisters, we're now soldiers with no nation to owe allegiance to, except for our sacred allegiance to the Almighty Allah, and His quest to rid the world of the lowly infidels and non-believers to His faithful words. Like the evil ones who left our village in ruins, and killed General Hassan al-Zahar and the other troops to our cause, the reason why I say we have no nation to love and honor and seek comfort from, is because as surely as I stand before you. Saddam is giving orders to the Republican Guards to hunt us down and kill each of us out of his hatred against us as we speak. The reason I ordered you to formation my faithful brothers and sisters, is because I have a plan in mind that'll open the gates of Paradise for all of us. And, we shall sit by the right hand of Muhammad and then we'll enjoy watching Him rule over the

Kingdom of the Muslims. Once we have accomplished what I have in mind that is."

Lieutenant Malika Nabeel Elmasry took a step forward, informing Colonel al-Qaysi he had something to say. He was waiting for the Colonel to acknowledge his request to speak to him.

Colonel Al-Qaysi gave him the look and then he let out his breath in a disgusted sigh, and he snapped at the young Iraqi soldier. "Well my desert fool, you have my full attention. What do you have on that foul mind of yours, other than sin and lust soldier?"

The soldier stiffened as he drew in his breath and then said, "Colonel al-Qaysi Sir, what do you mean every soldier in Iraq will hunt us down and kill us, sir? We have committed no crime against our foolish President, sir. Why would our President want to slaughter us, Colonel?"

"It's enough you still breathe that makes President Hussein want you dead, fool. But I'll explain to you and the other fools who stand behind you. Since Saddam did not send any support soldiers to help General al-Zahar when he came under attack by the hated American invaders, you can believe he wants us all dead. Why you might ask me young fool? I'll tell you why, it's because we wanted to change what's happening in Iraq. We used Colonel Abdulaziz Majd al-Adwani as the weapon to bring about these changes we seek in Iraq. Since the worthless Colonel failed his task, gives us the situation we find ourselves trapped in. One we have to do everything in our power to crawl out from under. I can assure each of you I have such a plan in mind that'll get us out of the hateful eye of President Hussein, and in the light of the Iraqi civilians.

"Once we have accomplished what we set out on then every civilian in Iraq will flock to our side and back us as they have backed this great fool running our country for so many years past. But for me to explain my plan to you fools, first I have to know all of you will back me faithfully, as you have backed General al-Zahar in the past times. I'll make a roll call, and if any soldier wants to leave our ranks, and live his life running like the lowly jackals of the vast desert, he'll be free to do so at his pleasure. I'll not speak of my plan until I know all who stand before me are faithfully on my side. Once I know this, I'll tell you of my idea. Since you stepped forward first, I'll start with you, fool. Are you a loyal soldier to my command, Lieutenant Elmasry Sir?

"I'll assure each of you soldiers who stood before me on this foul day that I'm not anything like President Hussein is. If you don't want to back me then you'll be more than free to leave, and you'll live the rest of your worthless life as you may chose. I'm waiting for your reply to the question I have just asked of you Lieutenant, but I shall not wait very long I warn you, Lieutenant. Speak now! Are you going to back me and my future plans, young fool?"

"Lieutenant Elmasry stared at the Colonel for a brief moment before he replied. "Yes Colonel al-Qaysi Sir, I'll swear my allegiance to you, as I have offered to General al-Zahar, sir."

"Very good Lieutenant Elmasry Sir, but to be perfectly truthful with you, you didn't have very much choice left open to you in this matter my faithful Arab brother. To swear allegiance to me, will allow you to live. If you would have left our unit, President Hussein's henchmen would have surely hunted you down and killed you. Now, I want to hear from the rest of you fools starting from left and going right. I'll start with Lieutenant Abdel al-Atrash first now."

"Lieutenant al-Atrash replied he was with the Iraqi Colonel and the other soldiers.

Next, Sergeant Mustafa Adbullah said he was with the small group of soldiers. Then Sergeant Mohammed Mushtaha said he was in with the Colonel. Lieutenant Bashar al-Maluk offered himself to the Colonel's services. Captain Mohammed Oveidat readily agreed to stay with the Colonel and the rest of the soldiers swearing their oath to him. Sergeant Salama Nazzel, the first woman to speak up, and Private Mahmud Abdel Rezig both agreed to stay with the rest of the soldiers. They were followed by Sergeant Sufian al-Sharaa, Sergeant Aicha Said Damerdji, Corporal Bashir al-Beidh, and the remaining male Privates, Amr Onallah, Ahmad Abu Madani, and Abdel Harith Jama, they replied they would be honored to stay with the Colonel's unit.

Colonel Al-Qaysi could not hide the proud smile that suddenly crossed his lips, because he was that please his troops all put in with his plan. Next, he turned to the six young women fighters from his group who were all standing together, except for the seventh women soldier who mixed in with the male soldiers. He looked right at Major al-Shaya and then he snapped at her almost angrily. "And, the rest of the women of our Unit, are they with us woman?"

"Colonel al-Qaysi Sir, you know I'm with you in your plans sir, and I'm certain the rest of my soldiers are, sir." Al-Shaya turned to the first woman, and growled. "Lieutenant Miranda al-Mutta, I ask, are you with the Unit until we accomplished what we have set out to do?"

"Yes Major Serena al-Shaya, I'll follow the Colonel to the gates of Paradise, Ma'am."

Without waiting to be asked, Lieutenant Bahaa Handoni, Sergeant Hanan al-Wazir, Sergeant Yussa Shahid, and Sergeant Shurug Khalaifa, all agreed to remain with the small Unit, and Colonel al-Qaysi. All five women replied to the Major.

Colonel al-Qaysi was proud as the woman was now he knew he had support of the troops. He drew in his breath and then announced to his soldiers standing before him. "I thank my faithful Arab brothers and sisters for their loyal support. I'll explain what I have in mind. Once I explain my plan, you'll be forever bound to my Unit, because there'll be no backing out once you know of my plans. I'll kill anyone who wants out, or dare tries to desert me once you know what I have in mind for the future of our nation. So again, I'll give you a last chance to get out while you can. I don't want to be like our worthless President, who kills his loyal soldiers. But when I tell you of my plans, I'll do the same to maintain the secrecy of my idea, until we carried out my plan.

"Then we shall see where the wings of fate and Allah's great will leave us in the amphitheater of world manners. I have no fear whatsoever of my future plan succeeding, because I know well of everything that General al-Zahar was doing, and I also know of all his contacts both in Iraq and also in the hated land of Satan, the United States. This is why I'm extremely certain of our complete success with my plans, and now your mission for Iraq and her faithful people. So I say to all who are gathered before me today, if you're not absolutely positive you'll follow me, get out while I give you this last chance to do so. If you cannot keep up then don't step up, or you'll die right here. I need the positive, no second guessing later on. Now speak fools!"

The soldier's who made up the Iraqi Colonel's small patrol, everyone one to the last man and woman of the group, said they were part of his mission.

"Very good, I didn't expect anything less from my faithful soldiers under my command. I'll explain my plan to you my brothers and sisters. As you all understand, Colonel al-Adwani was sent to the land of Satan to kill the great devil himself, the President of the United States. His mission was to hit a high priority target, in an effort to stop the cursed no fly zones being enforced over our country, and the constant bombing of our soldiers at the pleasure of the American and hated United Kingdom planes of war, along with the stifling sanctions leveled against us from the worthless United Nations slowly killing the innocent civilians of Iraq.

"His mission failed miserably as I'm certain you all know this as fact by now. Nevertheless, he was successful with opening the door to show the American fools they weren't as safe in their loathsome country as they once believed. We my Arab brother and sisters will show the hated American jackals that they're less protected than they believed before in their worthless lives in their worthless country. The hated American invaders who left our village, and removed Colonel al-Adwani as their prisoner I'm certain will place him on trial. But this I promise you all standing before me today, he'll never stand trial in the foul United States. Since I'm aware of all General al-Zahar and Colonel al-Adwani's contacts in the great land of sin, I plan to leave Iraq with all of you. That is because we're no longer safe within our own country any longer.

"We understand we live our lives under the constant sentence of death in our own country as well as from abroad. So this is why it's absolutely imperative that we leave our land of Iraq as s0oon as possible. I plan to get us all safely into the hated United States, and once there, we'll begin my plan to set Iraq free of all those who wish her harm..." The Colonel stopped speaking at this point, because another soldier suddenly took a step forward that showed him this one had something he wanted to ask of him. He let out his breath in a hiss and then he allowed this soldier to speak up, but first he added to his words for all standing before him.

"Unlike our foolish and worthless President, I'll allow any of you to interrupt me at any time you believe it's necessary, if my words cause you any confusion or concern. I don't want my soldiers not to fully understand what I intend to do and what the outcome will have in Iraq, or in the land of sin." The Colonel stopped addressing the soldiers and then he placed the Lieutenant in his harsh gaze, and said. "Lieutenant al-Atrash Sir, you have just stepped forward to speak to me. Evidently, my words must have caused you some concern. Explain this worry and I'll lay them to rest for you, my brother of the endless sand. Speak for I'm better than Saddam Hussein is, sir."

The Lieutenant began the moment his commander stopped speaking at him. "Colonel al-Qaysi Sir, you have mentioned that you'll get us all into the United States to carry out your plan of attack against the lowly infidels of that country. Please Colonel, explain how you'll get us into the United States, sir. With all the cane the American public is raising of late because of the problems with their border between the United States and Mexico, and the public demanding their government do something about the flood of illegal aliens sneaking over the border into their foul country, how will you ever be able to get us into the United States safely, sir?"

"Ahhhhh... That is a very good question to ask of me Lieutenant al-Atrash Sir. I'm very pleased you're paying attention to all my words, sir. I shall explain to all of you how I'll get you into the hated United States safely. You see Lieutenant, we'll not try to get into the United States through Mexico, nor will we infiltrate the United States through the nation of Canada. Because I too feel the Americans will tighten the border security between these three nations. That is why I have decided to make our entry into the foul land of sin, through the Bahamas Island chain. I'm aware there's a small Island where many Cubans who fled Cuba, are taken out to this Island which is associated with the Biminis Island chain. The worthless fools are dropped off on this Island that is no more than a rock than an Island.

"Then the foul fools are smuggled out of Cuba by their relatives already living in the United States. These foolish Cuban relatives pay people in Cuba to ferry their loved ones out to this small Island, there they are left until their foolish relatives can find some American fool to go out and pick them up, and then smuggle them into the United States. Once they're on this Island, the fools wait for a paid American Captain to come out to them in one of their small pleasure fishing crafts. Once this Captain is paid two thousand American dollars apiece for each of the Cuban fools they pick up on this rock of an Island, he'll smuggle those foolish Cubans who he takes up to six at a time in his foul boat, into the United States through the Florida Key Island chain.

"These Cuban fools are then brought to such Florida Keys as Marathon, Big Pine Key, Key West, or Key Largo. Here, the smuggled Cubans are released on these small Key Islands, and are hidden by their fellow Cuban fools allowed to live in the United States when they fled their worthless country of Cuba, and the strong arm rule of President Fidel Castro. They're cared for until they're later on smuggled up to the city of Miami, and then they're free to move about the United States until they're given political asylum, or the worthless fools are arrested for some crime they might have committed, and then the fools are deported back to Cuba.

"I intend to make contact with one of these American Captain's, who'll sell out their own country by this illegal trade in human life and misery, for two thousand dollars a head. The American fools have no idea once they bring us in their foul land of sin and lust, we'll be the cause of many worthless American soldiers to lose their foul lives, for their last attack against our country. Yes my Arab brothers and sisters, there'll be many American jackals who'll call us terrorists, but if they're to brand us terrorists, they'll have to admit the American soldiers who took Colonel al-Adwani prisoner in our country. Are as likewise terrorists, something the American military minds will never do. And that my Arab brother and sisters, makes me certain that is why we, if we're taken prisoners in the United States, will never be branded terrorists.

"We'll be considered the same as their foul soldiers, taking revenge against another nation who made an attack on one's own country. Colonel al-Adwani tried to kill the American President in the United States, and the loathsome American Leader sent his troops on a just cause, to take the attacker back to their miserable country by a military insert of her troops into our country. So we'll basically do the same and we'll attack the cursed American soldiers and their judges for the same foul insult. If they brand us terrorists then they'll have to admit in court that their soldiers are as guilty of the same charge they'll be trying to bring against our soldiers.

"Getting back to our infiltration of the United States, I'll have this American Captain I'll hire, make contact with other American Captains and their pleasure boats to help him. Then the fools will smuggle us at the same time and day to the United States, so we can begin our plans to destroy the United States from within their own country of sin. I'll make my way to the United States, after we're on this foul Island. I know of one of these American Captains who'll meet me there, and once I'm in America, I'll have the fool setup more Captains to come and get the rest of you. I'll return to the Island with this deceived Captain, to make certain all of you are picked up safely, and then transported to the United States to begin our just cause against America.

"Once we're safely in the United States, we'll organize and begin our mission to not only free the worthless Colonel al-Adwani from the hated American's hands. But we'll also kill the loathsome Judge who was going to place our Colonel in jail, or worse, order him put to death. But our mission will not end there my faithful brother and sisters, we'll remain operating in the United States until we have successfully locate all the worthless soldiers who on this foul day, have invaded our great country of Iraq. I'll never rest peacefully until I have killed all the lowly dog eating fools, especially the one who have lead these fools into our country. I shall also want the head of the soldier who done that nasty hand signal at me as they left our small village.

"Once our revenge on these god cursed lowly infidels has been accomplished and if Allah is willing. He'll allow us to return to the safety Iraq where we can start our overthrow of the great fool still running our country. Once we rid Iraq of this great fool then we can get about our business of bringing Iraq back into the fold of the other nations. But under the conditions that we'll set for Iraq to rejoin the other nations of the world, not under the circumstances they continue to try and impose upon the heads of the people of Iraq. It's time the rest of the world realizes that Iraq is its own nation, and is not a nation other nations want Iraq to be.

"Bah, I grow weary of this most boring conversation. I'll tell you my faithful Arab brothers and sisters that I believe it's time we leave this small town of Dawral. I order each of you to search the ruins of our once headquarters. I want you to find any weapons still in working order. Find any ammunition, food, water, or anything else that'd be useful to us while we cross the vast desert of our ancestors to a safe place I know of, and where I can begin our preparations for getting us out of Iraq alive. Sergeant Mushtaha, take Corporal Oveidat and get what vehicles you can, running for our use. Any of the foul machines you're unable to get started you shall drain the remaining fuel and place it in the foul machines that are running for us.

"Any leftover fuel you'll place in holding cans, so we can carry it into the vastness of our great desert. Our trek will be a long and unbearable trip, and anything we have to make it any easier to endure, I want it with us when we leave this foul place. That's all I have to say to my trusted Arab brothers and sisters. Go now and carry out my orders as you have received them. Err... Major al-Shaya, you'll remain by my side while the others carry out my orders. If you cannot find any food and water remaining in the debris, you're to invade any homes in this worthless village and take from the foul civilians all you can carry in your arms. Check out the village good, if any of you discover vehicles that might be useful to our need. Commandeer the foul things and if the civilians give you any trouble over the matter, shoot them for their foolish trouble.

"We have to be supplied; Allah knows when we might come across any other much needed supplies and weapons as we flee across the vast desert towards the

Kingdom of Kuwait. You have your orders, so carry them out before the fool of our country sends his foul soldiers out to destroy what the hated American fools have failed to murder." Colonel al-Qaysi had to glare at the soldiers, before they broke ranks and the troops ran off to carry out their orders.

Major Serena al-Shaya smiled at the Colonel as she walked up to him, and then she joined him as they both watched the other soldiers running off in all directions to search for supplies.

The Colonel glanced at his Major and noticed her smiling at him, and he snapped at her. "Well my daughter of the Oceans of sand, I fail to see anything humorous in the situation that we find ourselves mired in, Major. Perhaps, you can tell me what you have found funny about this situation, foolish woman. We're wanted people in our own country, and the foul Americans hate us even more than our own people do, Major. We're going to try and invade the United States with a military force that I hope we can carry out my plan with successfully. Bah, all the foul cards are stacked against us, and yet here you stand before me, smiling like a jackal who has found the carcass of a prized camel to sink its cursed teeth into, woman."

"Please forgive me for my good mood Colonel al-Qaysi Sir. But it always brings a smile to my parched lips, whenever I see our faithful soldiers moving with a real purpose in their hearts. I, just as you, am a true and loyal soldier and as such, I live for that next mission, for the next battle, for the next war. Because as long as we're alive and fighting, we're carrying out Allah's great will and cause. I'm greatly pleased that we were out of the village when the cursed American soldiers attacked our headquarters, sir. Although I don't know of the size of the force the hated

Americans attacked General al-Zahar and his troops with. But judging by what I see spread out before my sorry eyes, they must have hit him with a sizable force of well trained enemy soldiers, sir. One I'm quite certain they would've been able to kill us, as well as they did with the other soldiers we left to protect General al-Zahar with, sir." Major al-Shaya mumbled as she watched a number of Iraqi soldiers enter their destroyed headquarters where the fires had died off, and began their search for useful weapons and food supplies.

"Yes Major al-Shaya, I believe you speak the words of truth to my worthless ears, young woman. If we were in the village when the hated American soldiers had arrived in our country to take Colonel al-Adwani as their worthless prisoner, I believe we would've all been killed in the same heavy enemy action, Major. I get some solace with the belief that if we were foolish enough to be in the foul village when the lowly infidels came out of the vast desert to attack us. There would have been a few American soldiers who would not be going home after the fight we would've given the foul fools for invading our country.

CHAPTER THREE

"What's the old saying we believe in, yes, ahhh... yes follow the Vulture and he'll surely lead you to death. Arrr... Allah and His divine ways are hard to understand at times my faithful sister of the vast desert. We, the true and faithful children of Allah, are being turned against by all nations of the infidel world of lowly jackals. If Allah wanted us to remain in His glorious eye then you'd think he would've given us small victories over his hated devils of the cursed lands that threaten us, my sister. Bah, I don't know what to believe any longer I fear, Major al-Shaya."

"Colonel al-Qaysi Sir, your words chill me to my very soul I fear, sir. If Allah does not love you then how could you have possibly accomplished all you have done in your life span, sir? Don't lead me to believe that you're considering turning your back on Allah and the sacred words of Muhammad, and the words printed in the Holy Qur'an. Because if you are then I'll have to reconsider my loyalty offered to you and your just cause that you speak of, sir." The suddenly concerned female Major said with much concern lacing her tone.

Colonel al-Qaysi glared angrily at his female Major while quickly collecting his thoughts for a brief moment. When he knew what he wanted to reply, he growled back at her. You strike me with words as hard as steel! Foolish sharmonta (bitch) of the desert, I'd no more turn my back on Allah and His great words of guidance, than I would turn my back on my own troops, Major. Do you think me a son of a low sand flea feeding upon camel dung to dare think of such a sin?

"Not at all Major al-Shaya, I just questioned His favor that's all, foolish woman. Don't dare speak to me again in this foul a manner, or I'll have your face tied to a bag of hot ashes. I wish for once in our many battles against those who don't heed the sacred words of the great Prophet Muhammad himself, to feel the awesome power controlled in one hand of the Almighty Allah.

"Always, when the hated American soldiers attack any Arab nation or our interest, the evil doers seem to come out on the top of the worthless pack. And, the foul things grind the bodies of the faithful into the soft sands of the great desert of our ancestors under the tracks of their massive machines of war. Bah, if the foolish nations of the Arab World were ever able to place their hatred of each other out of their hearts and minds for a time and joined forces together and aimed that once anger at the right evil of the world. Then even the feared great war machines of the powerful Americans could no longer defeat any Arab nation in the Middle East, woman.

"Major al-Shaya, it's the true stain against all Muslim lands that is Saudi Arabia. They speak and deal with the hated American fools, as if they're the true brothers to we Arabs. But then, in the background, the nation of Saudi Arabia supplies these same rebel Arabs with great sums of cash and military support, to make these hired rebels strong enough to attack any American or Israeli targets throughout the entire Middle East. If only Arabia informed the Americans how they truly felt about the great fools, and they joined our just cause against the lowly infidels of the world. The rest of the Arab nations would surely follow suite, and they'll join together with us. To defeat all the hated American interests in the Middle East region, and remove all the lowly infidels constantly invading Arab lands against us, Major al-Shaya." The angry Iraqi Colonel grumbled at his female officer as he turned his attention to what the other soldiers were doing.

Colonel al-Qaysi was pleased with himself as he noticed the undamaged weapons and the large amount of ammunition some of his soldiers successfully located within their heavily destroyed building. The Iraqi soldiers stacked fifteen operational AK-47s on the ground before his feet, along with fifty boxes of ammunition for the weapons. The soldiers also had thirty five extra clips for the weapons, and some had the ammunition stored in the clips. His smile grew broader when he noticed two other soldiers carrying four boxes of hand grenades out of the rubble of the destroyed building once their headquarters, one box was slightly burned, but the grenades were unharmed by the fire in the box. There were also a number of side arms added to the growing stack of salvaged weapons and military equipment. There were also a number of survival knives and a further wealth of other small arms weapons pulled out of the rubble by his soldiers.

The Colonel's attention was drawn to the other side of the destroyed building. Three of his war machines were started up, and slowly moving towards the front of what was left of their building. Colonel Al-Qaysi was relieved when he noticed one of the Russian made fighting machines rumbling out from behind the destroyed building. That made five operating machines for the protection of his troops, more than enough to transport the soldiers to the Kuwaiti, Iraqi border.

One of his soldier reported he found a number of other small arms and machine guns stored inside one of the parked machines from behind the building, along with the bodies of two of their fellow soldiers. The Iraqi soldiers were obviously killed by the American troops, and the bodies were then dumped inside the machines to keep them from discovery, until the American invaders carried out their attack on the General's headquarters. The longer the time passed, the more in the way of other weapons and military equipment, was being added to the Colonel's small Army. The Iraqi troops also found a number of undamaged military uniforms, and plenty of canned food stuffs and bottle water, and even a small cooking pot and portable stove.

Major al-Shaya rested her hand lightly on the Colonel's shoulder, as she again smiled and announced in a pleasant tone of voice to her commander. "Colonel al-Qaysi Sir, with all the weapons our soldiers are finding undamaged and still operational, we'll be more than able to hold off many small patrols I'm certain our foul President will send out to destroy us, sir."

"Yes Major we're finding more weapons than I dared hoped for recovering in useable condition. Seeing this renews my faith in Allah, and Mohammad's faithful words. The God of our fathers calls us to glory. Perhaps, the both of them will keep a shadow of protection over our shoulders, and bring us success on my plans at long last." The Colonel grumbled at his Major.

Their attention was brought back to the other soldiers, as another unburned uniform was brought out from the rubble of the destroyed building, and it was laid out on the ground before the Colonel's feet. It was General al-Zahar's extra uniform. Both Colonel al-Qaysi and Major al-Shaya stared at the undamaged uniform for several long moments, both soldiers with different thoughts in their hearts and minds. Colonel al-Qaysi was thinking of the murder of General al-Zahar, while the Major was thinking and then she offered to her commander. "Colonel al-Qaysi Sir, it wouldn't hurt my feelings in the least if you were to give yourself a rate increase, sir. That's if you so desired to do so sir. You have surely earned the right and the honor to wear a General's uniform for your many years of faithful service to Iraq and her people, sir."

The Colonel smiled for a moment and then he grumbled at her. "No Major al-Shaya, although it would be an honor to wear the General's uniform, and if I did, it'd only serve to be to honor his fine memory. I'm not in this plan for any self-enrichments. I'm a Colonel in the Army of Allah and Iraq, and that's what I'll remain until I'm called before the last Court of Muhammad for finally judgment, for the actions I have carried out while living on this earth, woman. I thank you for your thoughts, Major al-Shaya. Perhaps in the near future I'll take to wearing a General's uniform as my just reward for my work in the Iraqi military, Major." Colonel al-Qaysi turned and then he bellowed at his troops who had taken to gather around the officers as they spoke together.

"What the devil are you foul fools looking at for the love of Allah? I say enough of this foolish talk and worthless offerings for the true Iraqi soldiers. We found more than I had ever dared hoped for buried in the rubble of our once headquarters. We have enough equipment until we discover more supplies and weapons from elsewhere, on our unending journey we're about to begin for Allah's sake. I'll not allow my soldiers to become desert scavengers in order to survive in the harsh desert while we carry out a mission for our country, and for Allah's cause. We have to pack up all we have found and leave this cursed village immediately. Before we're attacked by our own troops, and killed before we can even begin our sacred quest for Allah and country.

"Load up all of what you have found in this debris of our destroyed headquarters and let us leave this area of the dead as soon as possible. Move rapidly my Arab sister and command these fools of ours. I want to be on our way within the next ten minutes at the latest. Major Serena al-Shaya, attend to your worthy troops and get them moving for us, I want to leave woman. We have other places that we must find, if we hope to be successful on our attack against the lowly infidels dwelling in the land of Satan." Colonel al-Qaysi ordered his second in command.

One of the filthy covered soldiers crawled out from the rubble of the building and showed the Colonel he found a slightly burned Book of the Qur'an, and handed it to his commanding officer. The proud colonel took the sacred book as if it was made of the finest glass, and he held it high aloft for his troops to see. Then Colonel al-Qaysi announced for the soldiers to hear his words.

"Look at me my faithful Arab brother and sisters and soldiers of Allah, I'll take command of this Holy Book, and when I have finally killed the one loathsome American soldier who is responsible for all this destruction committed against our soldiers and General al-Zahar in this small village. I'll lay the Holy Book upon the worthless body of the non-believer and lowly criminal. It'll prove to the world of hated infidels whenever anyone dares to encroach upon the sacred province of the Almighty Allah, that all lowly infidels will face His mighty wrath.

"It's time my faithful brothers and sisters, Paradise awaits its heroes. Allah has sent you to me so that we can spread His holy word for all non-believers to hear and then obey. We'll be the instrument Allah will employ to turn all the worthless non-believers of the world into believers of the one true Religion and that one Religion is Islam. Come my faithful brothers and sisters, we have to leave this foul area as soon as humanly possible I say and order."

THE AMERICAN TROOPS JUST CROSSING
THE IRAQI BORDER
BACK INTO SAUDI ARABIA

The newly appointed Captain Robert Walker's machine charged across the border and slid back into Saudi Arabia territory. The Captain wasn't made aware of the fact, but Colonel Bruce Leadbetter in command of the snatch and scoot operation completed in Iraq by his elite troops, boarded an aircraft, and he and Sergeant Dorothy Ramirez, Walker's future wife. Who was unable to accompany the other elite troops on the last mission because she was pregnant, came along with the Colonel. Colonel Leadbetter wanted to be there when Walker and his group of specialized soldiers returned to the unused Saudi Arabian military base of Camp Courage, first established in the old Operation Desert Storm war, inside the border in Saudi Arabia and Iraq.

The excited Marine Colonel wanted to be there to greet the returning soldiers, and to officially give Walker his latest rate increase being bumped up to the rank of Captain, himself. Besides, he was dying to see the face of the wanted terrorist of the cell that tried to assassinate the President of the United States a few months ago in his own country. To look him square in the eyes, and tell him what was in store for him when they finally dragged the Iraqi Colonel back to the United States, to stand trial for his crimes committed against the American President and his country. The American Colonel had steaks and cold beer on board his aircraft for his returning and obviously exhausted and battered soldiers. He wanted them to have a real meal for a change, and help them celebrate a successful operation with the soldiers involved in the operation.

Captain Walker's machine came to a sliding stop before the main area of the old base Camp Courage. He jumped out of the machine first followed by the Mutt. The two officers waited for the rest of the machines to join them, and the other soldiers still out on the mission. They climbed out of the machines and the soldiers linked up with the Captain as he stood on the sand.

As Walker started to speak with the rest of his soldiers, Colonel Bruce Leadbetter and Sergeant Dorothy Ramirez walked up behind him from inside the old camp. The Mutt picked up the two soldiers coming at them, but he did not warn Walker about them right off as they headed for the once young Lieutenant. Sergeant Ramirez walked out before the proud Colonel, and she went right up to Walker and grabbed his backside with both hands.

"Who the hell's fucking round with my god damn ass now, dammit? When the hell are any of you fricking people ever gonna grow the fuck up and start acting like real soldiers for once in your lives for Christ sake, shit?" Walker growled before he saw it was his lover greeting him.

"Hey baby, how did the mission go out there? I listened to most of the mission over the radio, Bobby." Ramirez asked Walker with a huge grin.

Walker turned, and Sergeant Ramirez immediately fell in his strong arms. He kissed her as he glanced over her shoulder at the Colonel. Colonel Leadbetter nodded kindly at the new Captain, and then he barked angrily at him. "Why the hell don't you two shitbirds go and find a damn room to carry out your sexual exploits in so the rest of us people don't have to watch you two asses pawing at each other's bodies for Pete's sake?"

"Colonel Leadbetter." Walker replied as he released Ramirez, and snapped off a half hearted salute at the commanding officer, and gave him a quick smile.

"What is it you're always telling me Walker? Never salute a fucking Officer out in the damn field, mister. It'll draw enemy fired at my ass, asshole. How did it go out there soldier?"

"It was a fucked up mission from the get go on us sir. I really hate any stinking mission where we're time poor on the damn things even before we begin the damn operation, sir." Walker growled at the Colonel, as Sergeant Ramirez took his hand and she leaned against him, trying to assure herself that her lover and soldier was standing safely by her side again.

"I understand and I assure you Captain, the next fucking mission you troops are sent out on, will be far different than this one was Walker. Causalities?"

"I have one dead, and three fucking wounded, Colonel Leadbetter Sir." Walker reported.

"Oh God in Heaven, one dead, one of our people was killed on the mission, who was it Walker?" Ramirez asked her lover in a concerned voice. She was scared to death at who might have died on the mission. She was pleased it was not Walker, or the Mutt, Lieutenant Frank Hall.

"Sun Tan, Sergeant Clifford Saldinger brought the fucking long dirt nap on this one, Raz. Ice is wounded the worst of the three; she's hit on the right shoulder. Of course, the Neck had to stop a round as he usually does on any mission we go out on, baby. The dumb ass still doesn't know enough to get the hell outta the way of a stinking bullet. Snatch got nicked by a round but his wound is barely worth talking bout, it just makes the grade of a fat shot, that's all baby." Walker grumbled as he let out an exhausted sigh and leaned heavily on his girlfriend.

"Oh Walker, how bad is Ice hurt? Where is she, I want to check on her condition, Bobby?" She cried at her lover and soldier as she started to look for Ice in the group.

"Bad enuf I guess, but she's a stinking soldier and she wouldn't pull back for a fucking moment to look after her wound. She toughed out the entire fucking mission with us like the trooper she is. She's in the third buggie of the group." Walker gave her a reassuring smile.

"I'm going to check on her condition Bobby. Maybe I can be of some help for her, baby. She is one of my favorite soldiers." She offered as she took off for the wounded soldier.

"Why don't you do that and let me know how she's doing while you're at it, Raz. That way I can speak to Walker without you hanging all over his damn ass and monopolizing all his time on me, Sergeant." Colonel Leadbetter snapped at the excited female soldier.

Ramirez shot a nasty look at the Colonel and then she was off like a shot heading for the third sand buggie and the wounded female soldier. She saw Ice was being helped out of the machine by Blood Clot, and the Ghost, (Sergeant Walker Casper). She could tell Ice was in a lot of pain just by the way she was moving with the other soldier's helping her.

Walker looked at the Colonel for a moment and then he began speaking to the new Captain. "Lieutenant Walker err... or should I call you Captain? You did real well on this one as always mister. Only losing one soldier to the damn action is just outstanding sir."

"Colonel Leadbetter Sir, that one soldier was one too many soldiers to lose on any fucking operation for my liking sir." Walker hissed at the Colonel as he took a deep breath for himself.

"Yeah, whatever you say mister. Where the hell's this fucking little prick of a fricking prisoner of yours that you brought in with your fellow troops, sir?"

Walker shot a look at Neck, (Sergeant Robert Abbot), who received his tag name because of the thickness of his neck, and McNip, (Sergeant David Nirajima) who got his tag name because he had an Irish father, and a Japanese mother, and he was on loan to the Special Forces Unit from Japan. Both soldiers were standing on each side of an obvious middle aged Arab man who was blindfolded, and he seemed like he was still out of it while swaying slightly on his feet, because each soldier was helping to support him in his stand before the Colonel. The Iraqi soldier was still suffering the effects of the drugs the soldiers injected into his body, to control him easier.

"That's the lousy little motherfucker over there, huh Captain? C'mon, I want to speak to the fucking prick one on one for a few minutes if he survives my talk if at all possible, soldier." Colonel Leadbetter snorted as he started walking towards the obviously drugged man.

Walker went to leave with the Colonel, but before he could move off he cast a quick eye to Ramirez to see how she was doing with the wounded female soldier.

She rushed over to Ice's side and then she helped Blood Clot with her. Once she was out of the machine, she dropped down to one knee, and Blood Clot forced Ice to lie down on the sand, and then he pulled at the bandages covering her wound. He did not like her color, and her eyes were slightly glazed over and she seemed to have not recognized Sergeant Ramirez's presence.

Sergeant Ramirez rested Sergeant Diane Morrison's head on her knees as Blood Clot quickly worked on her wound. She brushed some of her matted and filthy hair away from her face and then she ran her fingers lightly over her face, to let Ice know that she was there and helping to care for her. Three Martines, (Sergeant Cheryl Grantham), moved over and she watched the Marine medic quickly work on the downed woman fighter. She stared as Blood Clot removed the pressure bandages he had applied to the wound out in the field, and then he ripped half her shirt out of his way. The medic exposed her right breast, but no one seemed to notice, as some of the concerned specialized soldiers quickly gathered around Ice in order to check on her medical condition and to see if they could be of any help for her and the medic.

"I need a fucking stretcher over here double quick, god dammit!" Blood Clot suddenly roared out at the concerned soldiers gathering around them, and then he began to clean the wound again.

"How is she doing Richard?" Ramirez asked the medic with much concern lacing her voice.

"She's fucking dying on my damn ass, that's how she's fucking doing, Raz! Where the fuck's that damn stretcher at for fuck sake! I gotta get her someplace where I can work on her much betta, or she's gonna clock out on my sagging ass and I won't be able to stop it, dammit."

Ramirez looked around and she noticed both Buckethead and Mother Flanagan hustling over to them while carrying a stretcher. When they were by Ice's side, Blood Clot moved out of the way, and the two men picked Ice up like she did not weight a thing, and they dumped her out on the stretcher real careful like. Sergeant Ramirez could easily see the worry look etched in the two men's eyes, as they looked down at Ice with alarm.

"Take it fucking easy with her you two assholes. She's going bad on me fucking fast, dammit! Do we have any medical facilities operating on this fucking lousy base? If I don't start to work on her she's gonna die on me for the love of God. I told Walker she was turning bad on me when we were leaving that damn small Iraqi town for crap sake." Blood Clot growled at the two soldiers.

"Yeah Blood Clot I saw a fucking medical tent on base that seems to be still operational. I also noticed two medical personnel hanging round in the tent doing squat. So I think you'll have some kinda stinking help with the Ice lady when we get her over there, dammit. What's going wrong with her so fast man? I saw her out in the field, even though she was wounded, if you didn't know any better you could never tell she was hit, man. How the hell did she get so bad so quickly on us, buddy?" Mother Flanagan asked the Unit's medic with much concern on his voice.

"She lost too much fucking blood, she's going into shock and I can't stop it with the crap I have to work with out here, dammit. Didn't any of you fucking guys notice her going downhill? Jesus Christ Almighty, I can't believe none of you uther jerks saw her going downhill."

"No way in hell man, you know how she is, she wouldn't let any of us check her out during the operation, man." One of the worried soldiers replied to Blood Clot's bitch at them.

"You shoulda fucking kicked her in her lovely little ass and checked her out on your own whether she liked it or not, stupid. I shoulda been informed that she was getting bad on us, dammit. She needs fucking blood double quick or I might lose her. Check out the rest of the troops, I need anyone with O Positive blood to report over to the damn medical tent on this fucking base, real quick like man. I gotta get some stinking blood in her right now dammit." Blood Clot growled at the two large soldiers as he again checked Ice's dog tags, to make certain what type of blood she had, and he wanted to be absolutely positive of her blood type.

"I got O Positive blood, Blood Clot. You can take all the shit you fucking need from my stinking ass for her buddy, just so long as Ice fricking makes it through this crap, man." Mother Flanagan grumbled as he lifted the stretched along with Buckethead, and the two soldiers nearly ran for the medical tent with Ice lying on it.

Ice was sort of drifting in and out of consciousness, and she looked up at Mother Flanagan and mumbled in a very weak voice at him. "I know what you're doing to me Mother. You'll do anything to get yourself inside me one way or the other, mister." She gave him a painful, half hearted smile, and a loving warm look.

"You know that for sure there, little sister. You hang in there for me baby girl. If you go and die on me, I'll kill ya honey." Mother Flanagan replied as they quickly entered the medical tent. Once the soldiers dumped Ice out on an examination table, Mother remained in the tent as Blood Clot entered, and informed the two doctors what was going wrong with the wounded female soldier. As Buckethead took off in an attempt to try and locate any other soldiers who might have O Positive blood. Buckethead spoke to other soldiers, and none of them had O Positive blood. Giving up, he headed for Walker and Colonel Leadbetter to complain at them.

Colonel Leadbetter and Captain Walker walked up to No Neck and the Japanese soldier called McNip, still holding the Iraqi prisoner on his feet. At the same time, Buckethead caught up to the two soldiers and then he watched as the Colonel spoke to the Arab prisoner.

"Take this fucking scumbag's blindfold off his lousy ass, dammit. I want to look the rotten sonofabitch in his fucking eyes when we talk. Does the fucking Iraqi prick understand English, Walker?" the Colonel asked as he watched Neck release the grip he had on the drugged out Iraqi prisoner's arm, and then he attacked the duct tape holding the hat in place over the terrorist face and eyes. It was the easiest way to blindfold any prisoner, just stick a hat over his face and then tape it in place with the briggin or heavy duct tape.

Once his face was uncovered, Neck savagely shook the prisoner by his shoulders until Colonel al-Adwani's eyes flickered opened, and he focused them on his face. When Neck saw the prisoner register his presence, he turned to the

Colonel and announced. "The dumb shit's all yours sir." Neck made certain he did not give the Colonel's rank out to the prisoner out of habit.

Colonel Leadbetter nearly pressed his face up against the shaky prisoner's face, as he snarled at him, sending his spittle flying over the prisoner's face. "Well will you look at your punk ass now buster. So you slimy motherfucker you, you think you can try and assassinate our fucking President in his own damn country and get a fucking way with the damn crime, huh buster?"

Colonel al-Adwani did not reply to Colonel Leadbetter's growl, he was still mostly out of it and was stunned by what happened to him, and he was not registering the officer's words.

The angry Marine Colonel suddenly reached out and he roughly grabbed the still very groggy Colonel al-Adwani by the hair and savagely shook his head by it. When he was certain he had the terrorist full attention, he growled again at the stunned prisoner. "So you fucking lousy little prick you, you think you can try and assassinate our President here in the United States, and get away with it and think you'll live to brag about what you tried to carry off, buster?"

"Take your filthy hands off of me at once. I am a Colonel in the Iraqi Army, and I have no idea what the devil you're talking about, infidel soldier. I didn't try to assassinate no one, especially your infidel of a President of your hated country. All I know is a number of you lowly jackals saw fit to invade Iraq again, and take me out of my country for reasons I don't understand. I demand to have legal representation over this matter you're threatening me with..."

Colonel al-Adwani's words were cut off in mid sentence when Colonel Leadbetter lost his temper, and he balled up his fist and smashed it in the Arab's jaw, knocking him out cold.

"God damn Colonel! You sure do have a way with carrying out a stinking interrogation of an A-rab prisoner, sir." Walker smirked as he stared at the officer, as Colonel al-Adwani's body sagged between the two powerful soldiers still hanging on to his arms. The two soldiers laughed and then they let him go, and watched Colonel al-Adwani fall to the ground. Colonel Leadbetter was so angry at the terrorist he gave the Arab body a kick in the guts out of hatred for the man.

"For fuck sake Walker, if I had my damn way with this little motherfucker, I'd tie his sagging ass to the tail end of the Carrier, and allow that ship to drag his ass all the way back to the United States underwater. I'd give him the mother of all water boarding. I hate this motherfucker that much, the lousy bastard cost me one helluva good soldier, and another one wounded and possibly dying on my ass. I hate all stinking A-rabs in sand land." Colonel Leadbetter growled at the new Captain, and then he happened to notice Buckethead standing behind him and felt embarrassed.

Because he just manhandled the prisoner before the rest of his troopers. The Colonel looked around until his eyes locked on Buckethead, and he looked at the big man and snarled at him at the same time. "Well motherfucker, what the hell do you want for fuck sake? You don't have anything else useful to do but watch what we're doing, mister? This mission isn't completed until we're back in the States. If you don't have any work to perform, I can send your ass back into I fucking raq, and you can hunt down more of these sand swimmers to interrogate, buster."

"No sir, I have plenty to do with myself Colonel Leadbetter Sir. But I was sent out on a special mission by

Blood Clot, Colonel. Ice is going sour on us real fast sir, and he needs fucking blood to pump into her body so he could try and save her life, sir. I never saw the Clot man so damn upset and angry as he was, Colonel Sir." The soldier stared at his commanding officer.

"Well why the fuck didn't you say that in the first place, stupid. I can't believe you were just standing behind me like the Statue of Liberty with your fucking mouth shut, asshole." The Colonel snapped then added. "Did you find anyone with the same type blood she has, mister?"

"Yes Sir Colonel, Mother has her same type of blood sir, but no one else from our teams has the same type blood, and I don't think he can drain enough blood outta Mother to make the difference in saving Ice's life for her, sir." Buckethead reported to his commanding officer.

"Who is with Ice now, Bucket?" Walker asked the massive soldier.

"Mother is with her, he won't leave her side for nuthin, and so are Raz and Three Martines."

"Hey stupid, what type of fucking blood are you looking for mister?" The Colonel asked.

"Blood Clot said he needs O Positive blood, Colonel Leadbetter Sir." Bucket replied.

"Why the fuck didn't you say so when you first started spitting out words from that hole of yours instead of standing there like a stinking shitbird and saying noting, asshole. That's my blood type stupid. Where the hell are they working on Ice? I'd be proud to give that soldier some of my fucking blood. It'd make her a helluva better soldier for it as well to get some of my blood running around inside her, stupid." The angry Colonel roared at the huge soldier.

"Because you didn't ask me Colonel Sir." Bucket replied as he spread his hands apart.

"Because I didn't ask you, damn you tree trunk. I have a good mind to plant my foot up your ass all the way up to my fucking knee, stupid. Get me over to this damn medical tent A-SAP. You two secure the prisoner and hold him until I get back to you guys. Walker, you're with me."

Walker, the Colonel and Buckethead rushed for the medical tent. The new Captain had a double reason to get over to the tent, first he wanted to check on Ice's condition, and he also wanted to be with his lover. It took the three soldiers a few seconds to reach the medical tent, and they plowed right in it. The three soldiers saw Ice lying on a table, and the doctor was working on her shoulder. Ice was out of it, and the doctor was cutting into her with a scalpel. Blood Clot moved over to the Colonel's side and he reported to his commander. "Colonel Leadbetter, even though I flooded her wound with sulfa, the wound was getting infected, sir. We got a pint of blood in her so far from Mother, and that seemed to stop her from going in shock on us, sir. We placed an emergency call out for O Positive blood to be shipped out to us immediately, sir. She needs more if she's gonna pull through. Any cut in this god forsaken land will get infected..."

"Look Blood Clot, I have O Positive blood mister. If the big monkey over there spoke up sooner than this, I would've been here a helluva lot sooner. I'll fix his ass good and proper when I get him back to the States, Blood Clot. Where the hell do you want me, and take as much blood as you need for her. I want, no, I demand she lives through this shit, mister."

"Out fucking standing Colonel, your blood will more than likely make the difference if she makes it or not, sir. Come on over to the table and I'll prepare you for the transfusion Colonel Leadbetter Sir. Captain Willard, we have another blood donor here sir."

"Great, I have her wound cleaned out get him over to the table so we can get more blood into this young lady STAT, sir. With his blood, I think she'll make it over the damn hump."

Colonel Leadbetter was led over to the table, he already had his sleeve rolled up and was quickly pumping his fist like a madman by the time he was seated.

Blood Clot swabbed his arm with a cleaner, and then he stabbed him with the needle connected to a rubber hose leading into Ice's arm. Almost immediately, the Colonel's blood started to get into Ice's veins. It took a few more moments, but Ice's color started to come back, and her blood pressure started to slowly climb up at the same time. The concern doctor let out his breath as he announced to the concerned soldiers gathered in the tent with him. "This is good, very good indeed, her blood pressures climbing, and her colors coming back. I believe this young female warrior is going to make it okay because of the quick actions of her fellow soldiers."

Ramirez, still holding onto Walker's hand for dear life, let her breath out in a rush and she finally relaxed, and then she rested her head against Walker's shoulder for some added support.

After Colonel Leadbetter was released from the transfusion and medic, he stood on rather shaky legs and then he stomped his way over to Captain Walker and barked at him after catching his bearings and breath. "Okay mister, I had my little bit of fucking fun for the fricking day. First off buster, I have steaks and beer for all your troops, sir. I want you to eat a good meal for a change and suck down some suds and get a little buzz on for a job well done, sir. While your people are doing that, I have vehicles coming out here. I'm going to throw you people inside the damn things, and then we're going to drag this fucking asshole through Kuwait like a sack of damn rotten potatoes, and then get on a board C-17 trash hauler, and get flown out to Joint Andrews Air Force Base where this mess first started. Military police will be waiting there, and they'll take this damn jabonie in custody, and stuff him in a fucking birdcage to wait his trial.

"Then my war wackie bastard, you're going to be placed in front of the President, and he's going to give you a sloppy wet kiss right on the fucking lips for a job well done by your gang of shitbirds and fucking criminals, Walker. Then we're going to throw you all the hell out of Washington and then you can go and rot on your tiny little Island of Marathon in the fucking Florida Keys, until we have further need of your services again, mister."

The shaky Colonel Leadbetter had to stop speaking, and he took a deep breath and shook his head slightly, he was feeling the loss of blood. After a few seconds, he began to speak again. "By the way Walker, I got a little something in my pocket for your fucking ass, mister." The Colonel went fishing in his pocket with a shaky hand until he found what he wanted. He pulled the small blue box out, and looked at it for a few seconds, and then he passed it to Walker as he added. "Here you go shitbird. Don't let it be said I never gave you anything of real worth, Walker.

"Err... Walker, all horn busting set aside for a moment sir, this was given to me when I first made the rank of Captain, sir. I give it to you now that you made Captain rank for yourself, sir. May God forgive the President of the United States for giving the order to make you a fucking Captain in the Marine Corps, shitbird. If this shit keeps up, dammit I might have to start respecting your ass a little bit better around here, soldier. Once again you did real good work on this mission Captain Robert Walker Sir. You and your troops did well, real well soldier."

"With all due respect Colonel Leadbetter..." Walker started, but he was cut off by the officer.

"Stop pulling my fucking pud will ya mister. You don't have respect for anything living on the face of the earth but sex and booze, buster. By the way Captain Walker, I happen to know the President wants to raise you up to Captain himself, sir. He has his own insignia he wants to give you for your ass, but I was hoping you'd honor me by wearing my old Captain insignia, mister. It's that important to me that you use my old Captain's insignia, Captain Walker Sir."

"I'd be very honored to wear your old insignia, Colonel Leadbetter Sir." Walker replied as he carefully fingered the Eagle holding a set of arrows. Sergeant Ramirez moved a little closer to his side, and she took his hand in hers and gave it a squeeze as she looked at the Eagle with him.

He looked at his lover and she smiled as she offered him. "Well, it's about time the government finally recognizing all you're doing for her and the citizens of this country, Bobby."

"Exactly Sergeant, by the way Ramirez, how are you doing with making the little Walker in your gut, sister?" The Colonel asked as he gave her a quick look.

"Okay I guess Colonel, thank you for asking about the little one, sir." She replied pleasantly.

Colonel Leadbetter shook his head and then smiled as he added. "Don't thank me for anything Sergeant. I don't know whether or not to congratulate you, or fear for my life another fucking Walker is about to be born to this crazy ass world. I sure hope we're ready for such an event."

Both Ramirez and Walker smiled at the well respected Colonel, they both knew he was fond of them, and he would never wish either any ill will.

"Why the hell don't you two birds go and get some real food in ya and a little rest, the damn vehicles I sent for should be arriving within a few hours, and we'll be on the move again as soon as they get here. We won't stop moving until we're back in the United States once we head off, Walker. So go and have some fucking fun for yourselves before we shove off again. Err..., by fun I don't mean for you two to go and fuck on every square inch of this stinking base either, buster." The grinning Colonel added as if an afterthought to the two soldiers standing before him.

All three soldiers gave a last look at the severely injured Sergeant Diane Morrison, they could easily see that she was doing a lot better already, and her color was good and getting better with every second, and her breathing was near perfect now. She even opened her eyes, and she gave a weak smile at the concerned group of specialized soldiers hovering so protectively over her.

"Hey Colonel Leadbetter, wait until Ice finds out she has some of your stinking blood running around inside her body, man. She's not gonna know how to react to it sir. I sure hope she don't end up with your shitty disposition, sir." The new Captain smirked at the military officer.

"Fuck you and the horse you rode in on, buster. Walker you'll never learn how to properly respect a fucking Officer. And let me tell you something else while I'm at it, mister. Now that Ice has some of my blood in her. She's going to be a helluva lot better soldier, and she might even start kicking her own asses around here for a change, and shaping the rest of you damn misfits into better fucking soldiers. God, how that gets stuck in my fucking throat, you a damn Captain in this man's service, Walker. Go get some damn food and beer in ya ass before the vehicles arrive, and we shove off again you two. It won't be long before we're all back in the United States, sir. I have the rest of the Unit heading back on the Aircraft Carrier as we speak, Captain." The Colonel smiled as he watched Walker and Ramirez leave the medical tent together.

The medical officer who was working on Ice, called out after the Colonel as he prepared to leave the medical center of the base. "Say Colonel Leadbetter, I took a lot of blood out of you a few moments ago sir. So I suggest you take it a little easy for the next two days sir. I think they have some orange juice somewhere on the base, if not, find yourself some damn candy sir. I want something in you to help rebuild your strength so you can keep doing what you do, sir."

"Yeah right, I have a fucking A-rab prisoner I have to look after first, sir. I'll take care of myself when I'm back in the good old US of A, sir. That's when it all gets better for my ass, sir." With that said, the shaky Colonel turned and left the medic. He headed right for the two soldiers the Neck and McNip, and the prisoner they were ordered to be in control of. The Colonel was so pleased that Captain Walker and the elite soldiers were able to get this terrorist for him, and he could not wait until he could drag the prisoner before the President of the United States. So he could piss in the bastard's face if he so chose to do so. The wise Marine Colonel quick marched himself over to the other soldiers and he glared at the still out of it Iraqi terrorist prisoner.

"Wake up the motherfucker for my ass you two shitbirds, and prepare his ass to be tossed in a fucking vehicle, we're getting the hell out of sand land toot sweet. I'm sick and tired of getting another sand enema in this land of endless sand and scorpions. Once you guys have this bum revived and under control, I'll have you relieved so you can have some steak and beer. Bring this prick out of queer street cause I want to speak to him before we leave this fucking dump."

Neck pulled out a bottle of water and poured it over Colonel al-Adwani's face. Instantly, the terrorist took a deep breath and then he shook his head and opened his eyes.

The instant Colonel Leadbetter saw Colonel al-Adwani was awake and alert, he ordered the two soldiers. "Get this lousy sonofabitch on his fucking feet! I want to look him dead in his eyes while I ream him a new asshole for what he had tried to do to our Boss here in the States."

Neck pulled the Iraqi Officer up on his feet and then he locked his arms in his hands and held him before the Colonel. Colonel Al-Adwani was handcuffed and he struggled with the soldiers the best he could who were manhandling him so roughly. Both American soldiers watched as Colonel Leadbetter bent his head forward and looked him deep in the eyes for a moment.

The still slightly shaky Colonel took a step forward and he glared at Colonel al-Adwani and then he hissed savagely at him. "Look here you lousy motherfucker you, just give me a fucking reason to off your stinking ass, any fucking reason at all will do just fine, and I'll enjoy myself at your expense in doing ya ass in nice and slow like. I'll have a ball with stomping a fucking mud puddle in the middle of your damn puss and then walk it dry. This is what's going to happen to your ass in the next few hours, asshole. First off; I'm going to pitch your fucking can inside a vehicle, and then I'm going run your ass through the desert to Kuwait, fucker. Once we're there, I'm going to toss your ass in an aircraft and shoot you to the United States, where you'll be placed under fucking arrest for your crimes committed again my Boss, man.

"Once the people of the United States find you guilty of trying to assassinate their President, I'll tie the fucking noose around your slimy little neck myself, and then I'll watch you as you drop six feet, and your scrawny little neck snaps under your own fucking weight, asshole. The reason I'm telling you this crap is because, if you give me any damn trouble while in transit. I'll snap your fucking neck with my bear hands and save my government a shitload of money and time trying your ass for those crimes you have committed. Are you feeling me here buster?"

The wise Iraqi Colonel did not understand many of the American's angry words that were being aimed at him by the irate American Officer, but what he did not understand, he figured out for himself. He stared defiantly at the fuming American Officer and he refused to reply to any of his angry words. In his mind, Colonel al-Adwani knew the American Officer was governed by the certain laws of conduct, and most of his threats were empty and meant nothing to him.

"You better get the fucking glare out of your damn stare if you know what's good for your damn ass, buster. I know you believe you're safe in my hands, pal. Allow me to warn you in no uncertain terms here buster, we're not in the fucking States yet, buddy. Here I can treat your ass like you lousy bastards treat everyone else around here, Mac. Right now, you're in my little fucking world, and in my world I can rip you apart with my bare hands, and I can fuck your wife, rape your daughter and kill your fucking dog at my pleasure, buster. I can even cook you in an open fire and eat you right here, buster. So keep that in mind at all times my new friend."

Colonel Leadbetter had to stop speaking because he was starting to feel a little dizzy, and then he started again on the terrorist when he caught his breath and got some of his strength back. "Are you fucking reading anything I'm fucking telling your slimy little ass, shithead?" The Colonel suddenly reached out, and he took Colonel al-Adwani by the throat, and he began choking him with the real effort of ending his life in his mind.

As the Iraqi Colonel al-Adwani desperately struggled to breathe and began to realize this wild military officer was not fooling around with him, and he nodded yes to him.

Instantly, Colonel Leadbetter released his death like grip from around his throat, and then he asked the Iraqi Officer in no uncertain terms. "What was that head shake for buster? Does that mean you understand what I'm telling your slimy little ass, and you ain't going to give me or any of my troop's any further fucking problems, buster? Speak asshole, I know you understand and speak English, you lousy pig eater." Colonel Leadbetter was cursing up a storm before the Iraqi Officer because he understood the Arabs hated cursing as much as they protested they did not want to see naked women, and he was trying his best to insult this Arab in any fashion he could.

The fuming Marine Colonel wanted to demoralize the Iraqi Colonel al-Adwani in any way he could, to start to soften him up for when he was finally interrogated by the higher ups back in the States. He knew damn well the President wanted to know if President Saddam Hussein was the one who was behind the attack on his life. The American Colonel further understood if his Boss found out this was true, he was more than likely going to hit Iraq, and bomb

Saddam Hussein and the rest of his thugs back to the days of Ali Babba and his forty thieves.

CHAPTER FOUR

Colonel Abdulaziz Majd al-Adwani took a few quick breaths in and then replied to the angry American Military Officer. "Yes American invader of my country. I have nothing to worry about in your foul country mister. Because I'm free of any crimes others have committed in your land of sin and lust. So I'll give you no further trouble until I had a chance to speak with one of your worthless American lawyers. So then I can begin my own law suits aimed against your hated soldiers, military, and your foolish government, lowly camel eater from the land of sin."

"Man, you fucking people know all the stinking ropes of my country already, don't ya buster? You want to damn lawyer up on me huh? Good, but I got sad news for your ass, buster. Because you were classified a fucking terrorist, and you stand accused of committing a terrorist act aimed against my government, and my President, buddy. The usual laws that protect a true soldier or civilian, doesn't protect your ass one bit, bud. We can do anything to your damn body and mind we want to extract any fucking information we need from your lousy ass, buddy. You might even find your ass cooling off at down at Gitmo with the rest of your fucking terrorist buddies." Colonel Leadbetter warned the Iraqi terrorist by hissing his words at him in no uncertain terms.

The lackluster acting Iraqi Colonel al-Adwani dared to smile smugly at the fuming and extremely angry looking American Colonel.

"Don't fucking smile at my ass motherfucker! Look pal, I wouldn't piss in your fucking mouth if your stinking teeth were on fire, buddy. The first rule of combat is, know the difference between your friends and fucking foes, asshole. And, in case you don't understand it yet, I'm your worse fucking nightmare you ever crossed swords with, pal. So don't go and try and act like my fucking best friend, buster. You two, get this piece of shit ready to go while I light a fire under the rest of the damn soldiers from this miserable operation. I'll have you two birds relieved when I free up some other soldiers from the Unit. So you two shitbirds can go and get something to eat and relax for a little while, before we pull the hell out of here dammit." Colonel Leadbetter stormed away from the Iraqi prisoner, and the two soldiers left guarding him.

Both Walker and Ramirez were just finishing choking down their steak and sucking down some suds when the still fuming Colonel Leadbetter walked up to them and barked at his new Captain. "Walker, I need two fucking soldiers to relieve the Neck and McNip with our fucking prisoner, so those two shitbirds can eat something and relax for a few moments. Get someone over there to watch the damn prisoner for them, and then get the rest of the assholes up and on the damn move. The extraction machines should be here any second now, sir."

Walker gave the upset Colonel a quick smile and then he barked orders at his fellow soldiers. "Boot Camp, you and Hunter get over there and relieve Neck and McNip with the damn prisoner for a little while. The rest of you people saddle up. The Colonel just informed me the stinking extraction vehicles are bout here and we gotta get the hell outta this damn sand parking lot."

Boot Camp, (Sergeant Fred Moorehouse) got his tag name because he was held back at Boot Camp for a mess up he committed during training for the military. The Hunter, (Sergeant Frank Whitcomb), got his tag because he was the second half of the usual pointmen for the Unit. The Ghost was the other pointman for Walker's soldiers. The two got up and headed for the prisoner.

Colonel Leadbetter stared at the two soldiers because they were barely moving after Walker ordered them to saddle up. Then he bitched at Walker. "You know something Captain? It's at fucking times like this I wish I was a damn octopus, that way I could put my feet up eight different asses at the same time. I don't think these damn Squids heard your order correctly. You want to bark at them again, or do you want me to do it for your ass this time, mister?"

"I handle my people myself Colonel Leadbetter Sir. They'll be ready to head out by the time the damn machines finally get here..." Just as Walker said the words, ten desert movers came roaring up to the camp, and they slid to a stop where some of the elite soldiers were gathered.

"You were just saying something to my butt, smartass." The Colonel smirked at Walker as he drew his Captain's attention towards the machines that just pulled up to their position.

The lead vehicle pulled to a stop right before the two officers, and a Marine Sergeant jumped out and he instantly saluted the Colonel and asked. "Sir, are you Lieutenant Walker, Sir?"

Colonel Leadbetter looked at Walker, and the soldier instantly shifted his eyes towards him and he asked again without missing a beat. "Sir, are you Lieutenant Walker Sir?"

"If it's not me then I'm some lucky little bastard who looks a helluva lot like him, Sergeant. What's up your stinking ass pal?" Walker stared at the Sergeant while waiting for his reply.

The Sergeant offered to the officer. "Lieutenant, err... Captain Walker Sir." The Sergeant immediately corrected himself after spotting the insignia on the officer's collar. "I have orders to take your damn prisoner in custody, sir. From this moment on Captain, my people and I are responsible for his person, sir. Where's the prisoner being held at, Captain Walker Sir? The rest of your soldiers are ordered to mount up in my machines, and let us get you the hell out of sand land as quickly as possible, sir. I heard about your mission sir, you people did damn good out there Captain Sir." The proud young Sergeant saluted the new Captain sharply.

"Shove the fucking salute up your damn ass Sergeant. The stinking prisoner's being held over that way Sarge." Walker pointed at the three men standing by one of the sand buggies.

"Got ya Captain Walker Sir, we'll take charge of him for you from here on out, Captain Sir."

"Fine then get to it then Sergeant." Walker growled, and then screamed at his troops. But to his surprise, the soldiers were standing and staring at him. "What's this shit about, you pack of sand slugs? We ain't got time for more fun and games. We gotta get the fuck outta the desert."

Baby Tee, and Six Pack, (Sergeant Joseph Jesposito) stepped up and looked at his collar.

Now Walker knew what was bugging the rest of his troops, and he shot back at them. "Okay you people, you had your little fun and laughs with my stinking ass. Now let's get a move on it."

The elite group of soldiers quickly packed up their stuff, and then they went over to the new military vehicles. When they were loaded up, the drivers started the motors and headed out in the desert. It was just starting to get dark out, and it was planned this way. So the exhausted elite soldiers did not have to deal with the heat of the desert at the worst possible time of day.

Captain Walker, Colonel Leadbetter, Sergeant Ramirez, and Buckethead, Neck and the Mutt were riding in the first vehicle, and they were talking, mostly it was Colonel Leadbetter doing all the barking. "Captain Walker, when we get back to the real world, you're all going to be brought up before the President, but not before General White speaks to you people first. Then you pack of screaming squirrels are going to be placed on extended leave until the next time we have any need of you puke's services. I hope to hell and back that we have no further need for you people until Sergeant Ramirez here has her baby, and she's back with the unit at full power, Captain Sir." The Colonel then glanced at Ramirez for a quick second. He was trying to get used to calling Walker by his new rank of Captain by using it every time he spoke to the new officer.

Walker offered to his commander after he finished his little speech. "Say Colonel, I don't think Raz is gonna stay with the outfit once she has her baby, sir. We've been doing plenty of talking bout it sir. We believe it's a betta idea if she drops out and takes care of our baby, Colonel."

"What the hell are you two trying to spoon feed my damn ass now, Walker? You want me to believe for one second that Raz is actually thinking about hanging them up, just because she's going to have a stinking kid. I thought both of you stupid people knew better than that load of shit you're trying to hand. You two know the only way out of this outfit is feet first or tits up, or you're too old to cut the mustard any longer. You know for a fact Walker, there isn't enough aspirin in the damn world for the headaches you give my ass. And you Raz, what the hell makes you believe for one second that I'm going to allow you out of the outfit just because you're craping out a baby? It ain't going to happen I can assure you, Sergeant. You're stuck with the outfit until I say you had enough of this shit, and the outfit is stuck with you as well, girl."

"I just want to be happy Colonel Leadbetter." Ramirez replied as she tried a smile on him.

"They make a fucking pill for that kind of feeling you're after, Sergeant Ramirez."

"Funny Colonel." Walker fired back at the commander as he glared at the officer.

"Colonel Leadbetter, I'm a girl and all I want to do is raise a family and live the rest of my..."

"No you're not Sergeant Ramirez. You're just a cool guy with long fucking hair, little sister."

"Thank you for that kind remark sir, but I want to raise a family and enjoy being with Walker and our children for a change, sir. I really want him to leave the Unit along with me, Colonel Sir. We want to make a home for us and our children," She added as she smiled at the Colonel.

"Now I know you have to be losing your mind, Ramirez. There ain't no way in unholy hell I'm ever going to allow you to get out of our damn Unit, sister. And, if I won't allow you to drop out of the Unit then I'm sure as hell not going to allow Walker to dip out on me either, sister. In case you two shitbirds don't realize it by now, I need the both of you ball sacks to make this Unit click like a fine tuned machine. Without you two standing at the helm of this outfit, it'll go down the shitter in a fast hurry it up, dammit. Look, I have no further interest in prolonging this upsetting conversation any further with you, and that's that about it, for crap sake. I order both of you to get the idea of leaving the damn Unit out of your fucking minds forever, period."

"But Colonel Leadbetter..." Ramirez began to offer, but she was cut off by the colonel again.

"But Colonel Leadbetter nothing Sergeant, I said fucking period and that's what it means! And you Walker, if your hair gets any longer on your ass, I'm going to buy you a pair of fricking tits to go along with your long hair, mister. Get a damn hair cut and look like the fucking Officer you're supposed to be, buster. You're a Marine, not some damn hippie type asshole sliming his way through life at the government's expense, mister." The angry Colonel barked at Walker, trying to change the subject of their upsetting conversation. As if in answer to his, the Colonel's radio went off it was General John White, the current Chairman of the Joint Chiefs of Staff back in Washington D.C. He was demanding to speak to with Colonel immediately.

Colonel Leadbetter let out his breath in an angry sigh, and then he took the radio from the driver and replied. "Colonel Leadbetter here, go with your traffic General White Sir."

"What the hell is this shit Colonel? I have to make connection with you in order to find out what the hell's happening on this damn operation, mister? You were under strict orders to report to me the first moment you made contact with that hard ass soldier of yours you call Road Kill, Colonel. What the hell's happening out there and was the damn operation a success or what, Colonel! Report the condition of this damn operation, and if it was a success or not, Colonel! I got the damn President standing on my dick waiting to find out if your elite troops were able to pull off this damn operation successfully, mister." The General growled into the radio.

"General White Sir, the operation was a complete success and we just left the old Operation Desert Storm military base stationed in Saudi Arabia, and as of this moment sir. The entire Unit is heading for the Joint Military Airbase stationed in Kuwait, General Sir."

"Great, by the way Colonel, do you have the damn package with you, and is that package still in one piece or what, sir?" The General asked his Marine Officer with concern in his voice.

"Yes Sir General White, the package has arrived safe and sound sir, and is with me at the time, General White Sir. We should be hitting the Kuwaiti Military Airfield in, err... let me see sir." The Colonel quickly checked his watched and then announced to the anxious General. "At Zero, Five, Thirty Five Hours at the latest sir, and that means we should be reaching Washington by sometime around Eighteen Hundred Hours your time in the States, General White Sir."

"Outstanding Colonel Leadbetter, I can't believe that crazy ass live wire of yours was able to pull this damn thing off successfully, Sir. You tell that wild ass sonofabitch that I said he did well on this one sir. Even though he went past the allotted time for the damn mission to be completed, nevertheless, he carried it off. Err... Colonel, were there any casualties taken on the mission sir?"

"Yes sir, I must report that we took a few hits on this damn operation, General White Sir. We have one soldier down for the count; Sergeant Clifford Saldinger, General White. We also suffered three wounded, Sergeant Diane Morrison is the worse wounded of the three injured soldiers, she was hit in the shoulder and she's struggling for her life, sir. I was forced to leave her behind and if she makes it through it, she'll be shipped back to the base as soon as she's able to be moved safely, sir. The other soldier was Sergeant Robert Abbott, he was..."

"You mean that Neck soldier thing, Colonel Leadbetter Sir?" The General asked.

The Colonel was surprised that the Chairman actually remembered the Unit name of any of his soldiers, especially the one called No Neck as he added with a smirk. "Yes Sir General White, he was wounded on his right arm, nothing more than a fat shot though I believe sir, not much to worry about there, sir. It's so small you almost can't call it's a damn wound at all, sir. He'll be fine sir. The other wounded soldier is nothing to speak of, just a slight nick to report General."

"Damn, I'm upset about losing one of my Sergeant's to this damn operation, Colonel Sir. Worst, I have one of my female soldiers wounded and in danger of death dammit. I'll make damn certain she's receiving the very best of medical treatment on that damn Saudi base you left her on, Colonel Leadbetter. Arrr... I guess it could've been a helluva lot worse for us than those few injuries though, sir. Colonel, I'll meet the aircraft when it lands at Andrews. I want to see this Arab package, before he's moved to the Brig at Andrews, sir. That's where we're planning to keep his ass until we can convene a Federal Court Judge set up to hear his damn trial, sir. I see it happening within the next six months or so, but first we're going to interrogate the sonofabitch and see if that maniac, Saddam Hussein was behind the attempt on the President life and then..."

This time the Colonel interrupted the Chairman by asking him. "By the way General White Sir, how is the Vice President doing with her wound, sir? I've been out of the loop so long on this last mission I lost word on her condition, General White Sir. I haven't heard much about her condition sir. I hope she's doing okay, and she's out of the hospital by this time, General White."

"Ahhh... thank you for asking about her condition, Colonel Leadbetter Sir. She's doing fine Colonel, and the Vice President's already back in her office and carrying out her usual duties of office. She's a real trooper here Colonel, but I have to admit she took the death of the National Security Director rather hard, sir. She even had the CIA Director make it possible for her to attend his wake the other day, Colonel. The President was really pissed off over the fact that she showed up, especially because she didn't inform him about her planned visit to the wake before she showed up. What the fuck, this shit doesn't concern us in the least, Colonel. About the damn Iraqi prisoner sir, how the hell is his health, Colonel? I don't want the lousy little sonofabitch clocking out on us half way through the damn interrogation and then trial, Colonel Leadbetter."

"He's doing real fine, General White Sir. But the little bastard must do a helluva lot of TV watching I believe sir." The Colonel offered with a trace of anger in his tone of voice.

"What the hell do you mean by that remark Colonel?" the General growled in the phone.

"Because General White, the stinking prick's denying any complicity in the assassination attempt against the President, and he's also demanding to speak to one of our damn lawyers, and the asshole is also threatening us with a shitload of fricking law suits, sir."

"It figures, all these sonofabitches know the damn ropes when it comes down to getting them a mouth piece to get their asses out of trouble, Colonel Leadbetter. Did you explain to the asshole he falls under the label of terrorist, and as one he's not entitled to have lawyers protecting his ass, sir? He gave up his legal rights when he went against the laws of nature and God, Colonel."

"I explained that and a little more to his dopey ass when I had me a little chit chat with the bastard when I first got my hands on his ass, sir." Colonel Leadbetter offered with a smirk.

"What do you mean by that last fucking remark Colonel Leadbetter Sir?" the instantly upset General snarled at him, angry he was forced to ask the officer another question.

"Well General White Sir, you see it was like this sir. The little prick began to run his mouth on me, until he tried to break my damn fist with his jaw, sir. He was suddenly taken with a slight dizzy spell, and that made him take a little nap for a while sir. Since that little talk we had, he's rather easy to deal with, General White Sir." The Colonel offered to his commanding officer.

"Look here Colonel Leadbetter I want to reiterate my orders so you fully understand them, sir. Again Colonel, I'll inform you of this demand sir. I told you before you began this operation that I didn't mind if this rotten sonofabitch was bent up a little, just so long as he was still alive and kicking when he gets back to the United States, sir. But I'm going to modify that order as of this moment with you, Colonel. Since we have the lousy bastard in custody, and he's in relatively good condition sir. I want to keep him that way until we take him from your hands, sir.

"So this new order states there's to be no further hands on against the sonofabitch until we have him back here in the United States, and the special interrogators handle his ass from that point forward for us, Colonel Leadbetter. I'm going to allow civilian personnel to examine the prick, Colonel. That way there can be no complaints by the sonofabitch later on that we used our military peoples to question his ass only, and he tries to change his testimony, Colonel Lead..."

"General White Sir, you're going to allow the damn CIA Operators to question our damn package, did I just hear that right, sir?" The surprised Colonel Leadbetter said with his voice dripping with sarcasm, because he loved when the higher ups used such phrases with him. Civilian personnel meant nothing more that the CIA Agents, and he knew he would rather be interrogated by military personnel governed by some form of conscious. Rather than to be interrogated by just the damn CIA Operatives who had no conscious whatsoever, and they would get information from their target they want and need for future operations in the field.

"Look Colonel Leadbetter, you keep your smart ass remarks to yourself, sir. You and I both know the damn Spooks are going to handle this fucker until we find out everything about the terrorist mission to assassinate our President, and who was truly behind it with the sonofabitch and the rest of his rat pack, sir. I assure you that Director Raincloud is going to have a field day with interrogating this sonofabitch. I heard he has pulled up the old Native American book of torture out from under his desk, and he's been going over the damn thing ever since he first heard your people were hunting the sonofabitch down on this mission, Colonel Leadbetter Sir. Quite frankly Colonel, I hope the Director strips the terrorist skin from his damn body, one thin layer at a time Colonel, and he takes his time with the sonofabitch while he's doing it, sir."

"Gees General, I wouldn't want that one mad at my ass for a minute sir. I heard stories about the Director in the past, sir. They weren't very pretty ones either I assure you, General White."

"Colonel Leadbetter, allow me to assure you in the Director's line of work, pretty is left sitting outside his office, he's good at his chosen field of operations, sir. So I know we'll get everything about this sonofabitch's mission before we bring the lousy prick to his final justice, Colonel."

"Err... General White Sir, we're getting close to the border of Kuwait now sir. Do you have any further orders for me at this time, sir? I don't want to be caught flatfooted at the border, General." The Colonel asked his commander in a concerned voice as he looked ahead of his vehicle, and picked up the lights of the first border checkpoint they were about to go through.

"Colonel Leadbetter Sir, I have no further orders for you at this time sir. You're to follow your original orders as received, and you're to get that sonofabitch back here to the States in one piece while you're at it, sir. So he can stand trial here, and then the President can pull the damn switch on the sonofabitch himself, Colonel Leadbetter Sir. He really wants his revenge on the lousy bastard." General White snapped at his officer, not liking the way he was speaking in the least.

"Will do General White Sir, we're starting to slow down for the damn checkpoint inspection, General White Sir. I see three Kuwaitis troopers along with two American Advisors moving out to intercept our convoy at this time, sir. We should be arriving at the Kuwaiti Airfield within the next half an hour at the very latest, General." Colonel Leadbetter warned his commanding officer as he went fishing for the special orders he had tucked neatly away on his person.

"That's good to hear Colonel Leadbetter, break off this communication then and the next time I see your ass, sir. I'm quite certain you'll be back on United States soil and we'll have that sonofabitching terrorist here with us and working his ass over thoroughly, sir. Report to me the moment your feet hit United States soil, Colonel." General White offered to the Colonel.

The Colonel did not reply to the Chairman's last words as he broke off the connection with his commander, and then he handed the American Advisor standing outside his machine, the set of orders he was operating under in the nation of Iraq. The moment the security guard picked up the Presidential seal resting on the first page of the Colonel's orders, he stepped back away from the military vehicle and then he saluted the soldiers sitting in the idling machine. Then he waved him and the other soldiers and vehicles right through the Kuwait border checkpoint. Although the soldier wore the uniform of a United States Marine, he was definitely a CIA Operative helping to patrol the Kuwait border along with the other nations of Saudi Arabia, and Iraq.

"Well I'll be a dirty name that was fucking easy enough to accomplish, Captain Walker. I guess when you flash the Presidential shield around here people react to the damn thing, Captain. From this moment on sir, we'll heading straight for the damn Kuwaiti Airfield, and then we're heading home, and we're going to dump our Iraqi prisoner off at CIA headquarters, and the CIA Director is going to be speaking to Colonel al-Adwani personally, Captain Walker. Damn, I wouldn't want to be standing in his shoes when the Director gets his hands around his scrawny little neck, sir." Colonel Leadbetter mumbled to Walker more for the benefit of Colonel al-Adwani who he understood, was listening in on every word he was speaking to the Captain as their convoy drove through the border checkpoint, and then they entered the Kingdom of Kuwait.

"You got that right Colonel Leadbetter Sir. How long before we're back in the States, sir? I'm kinda looking forward to getting back to my home, and start licking some of my little nicks and wounds, and start living in the real world again, Colonel Leadbetter Sir?" Walker offered with excitement showing in his voice as he looked at Ramirez, and then smiled warmly at her.

"Yeah Captain Walker, who the hell are you trying to snowball around here, mister?" Colonel Leadbetter was having a little fun with calling Walker 'Captain' as he continued with his words to his young soldier. "You just want to get back home to lick a helluva lot more than just some of your fucking little nicks and wounds you received in this latest mission, buster. I know damn well what you and the rest of some of these crazy ass war wacky assholes are going to do down on that damn Island of yours in the Keys, Mr. Walker." The Colonel grumbled with a smirk, as he cast a quick look at Ramirez, sitting behind the new Captain in the back seat of the humvee.

When the Marine Colonel's eyes met Ramirez, she ran her tongue provocatively over her lips. She also gave the commander that certain look a woman always gave a man when she was planning to do something real evil to her lover's body, when she was alone with her soldier.

Colonel Leadbetter could not hide the look he allowed to slowly cross over his eyes, as he continued to stare at Ramirez as he digested the look she was giving him at the moment.

By the time the small group of special operation soldiers finally reached the huge transport aircraft scheduled to take the troops back to the United States. The specialized troops were so thoroughly exhausted, they wanted nothing more out of life than to just rest they heads on something soft, and then catch up on some of their much needed sleep. Sergeant Dorothy Ramirez was hanging onto Captain Robert Walker's arm for dear life, because she was afraid if she let him go, she would lose him again and maybe for the last time. The twenty male soldiers including Colonel Leadbetter, and the five American woman fighters, not including Ramirez or the wounded soldier Ice. Boarded the special aircraft and dropped they in the seats like sacks of potatoes, and before the aircraft even left the ground, most of the soldiers were sound asleep.

The flight back to the United States from Kuwait was a rather uneventful endurance run for the specialized mixed batch of soldiers, with the massive C-17 Globemaster aircraft being forced to go through four separate in flight refueling situations. Before the sleeping soldiers knew it, the aircraft was soon circling Joint Andrews Air Force Base for the third time, while the aircraft was waiting final clearance to land on the huge Airforce Base.

EIGHTEEN HUNDRED HOURS ON SUNDAY,
AUGUST 8th, 1999.
JOINT ANDREWS AIR FORCE BASE

Colonel Bruce Leadbetter, the only soldier awake on the aircraft, looked behind him and saw his exhausted soldiers were asleep. He smiled proudly when he noticed Ramirez, sleeping with her head resting peacefully on Walker's shoulder. He shook his head as he remembered leaving the soldier branded Ice, Sergeant Diane Morrison behind in Saudi Arabia because of her life threatening wound, and he wondered how she was making out and if she was still alive.

Then the Marine Colonel looked out the window of the aircraft, when he felt it starting to slow down while in flight, and the landing gear began to lower under him. This informed him they were about to land. At this time of the year, it was still light out, and he could easily see a number of parked vehicles, and a few military type vehicles waiting for the transport aircraft to land. As the plane continued to lower in the air, the Colonel could see the large black Chairman of the Joint Chief of Staff, General John White. He was standing before one of the parked cars, and he was being flanked by the equally as large CIA Director, John Raincloud. The Native American Agent was sucking on a cigarette and speaking to the General while hanging onto his hat with his hand threatening to blow off his head on the tarmac of the airport. Two other military types were also standing by the General's side, but he could not make out who they were, nor did he really care who they were, his commanding officer was his only concern at the moment.

The huge military transport aircraft continued to land, until its wheels finally touched down on the tarmac, and then the brakes locked up and the engines were immediately thrown in reverse. The screaming engines and bumping of the landing woke up most of the still exhausted soldiers inside the aircraft, and then the griping started between the troops.

"What the fuck was that shit all about for the love of the good Christ Child? Are we under fucking attack again and from who this time around, dammit?" the Mutt roared as he made a wild attempt to get out of his canvass chair, while reaching for a weapon that was not anywhere near him, because all the troop's weapons were stored safely on board the aircraft.

"No stupid, we're landing I guess, Mutt." Three Martines replied as she tried to rub the sleep from out of her eyes, and then she attempted to focus them on what was happening around her.

"Who the hell are you fucking calling stupid here, bitch? I got your fricking stupid right here on my stinking ass, sister." The Mutt fired back at the female soldier who he was still angry as hell at, because she caused him such grief a few months back when she first joined the outfit. She thought he was trying to molest her in the showers and almost created a riot in the barracks against him with the other women from the Unit, and he added. "Why the fuck don't you come over here and get yourself some throat yogurt by sucking on the end my dick, girl. If you wanna flap your damn gums like you're doing at my ass, back it up with some fucking action will ya."

"Uh-oh, it looks like the stinking Mutt woke up horny as always, girls. I think we better start watching our backsides, before he tries to ram his half black dick up it on us. Some of you male soldiers better watch yourselves as well I', afraid. When he's this horny, no man, woman, or beast is safe anywhere near him." Baby Tee offered as a warning to the rest of the soldiers now.

"Yes, I hear about horny American foolish soldier all time since joint this crazy Unit in United States, who want woman suck on his Khui (Russian for Cock) all time every day please." Caviar, the Russian Sergeant Lana Dostoyevsky, one of the three Russian female soldiers on loan to the Milti National Rapid Response Force from Russia, said as she got involved on the attack against the Mutt. She was always looking for any reason to hit on any of the American male soldiers from the outfit any chance she or the other two female Russian fighters got.

"I told you before, pissoffsky you fucking Russian bitch. If I want any more shit outta your Russian ass, I'll squeeze your Gorkie noggin for it, girl. Why the hell ain't you out there eating someone's fuck wand, and get the fuck offa my stinking ass for a damn change, bitch?" the Mutt snarled at the pretty Russian fighter, as he shifted his weight in the small and uncomfortable metal and canvass chair, to try and see the Russian soldier he was arguing with a little better.

"Woooo boy, did the Mutt ever wake up on the wrong side of the bed this time, ladies. I never saw him so horny, yet so angry at the same time, girls. We better really watch ourselves girls, I think he's out for a vengeance fuck or something like that." Blind Date, Sergeant Regina Raphael offered, she was the new love life in the Mutt's future. He lost his girlfriend, Fun Bags, Sergeant Barbara Meyerhoff during the Operation Sandstorm action that took place in Iran quite a while back, when the special operations soldiers went after Iran's nuclear ambitions.

The specialized troops destroyed the secret nuclear development base constructed deep in the Iranian desert, where they were developing nuclear warheads, and the vehicles to get the warheads to target. It was a hard hitting operation that cost the group of elite soldiers a few of their own before they were finally able to end the operation successfully.

"Yeah girl, keep piling on the big dumb jerk's ass again bitch, you snail eating surrender monkey you. You wanna flap your fricking gums at my ass like Baby Tee? Then why the hell don't you put some lipstick on my dip stick, girl?" The Mutt was really into it as he snapped angrily at his new lover, but when he saw the sad look she put on her face because of the ugly phase he aimed at her and her people, he felt bad and he lowered his head. The rest of the soldiers saw the look from them, and they got on the two soldiers to get them happy again.

"Hey Mutt, you betta back offa the girls a little man, or you're gonna find yourself taking your pen in hand, and taking care of yourself for a change asshole. The next time you want some loving from the girls from the Unit, they're gonna remember how you just dumped on their asses, and they're not gonna allow you a tumble with them, man." Mother Flanagan offered as he grinned at the Mutt, trying to get him to lighten his mood up some with the girls from the Unit.

"Yeah, I hear you there Mother. Hey Blind Date, I'm really sorry for the nasty slug I just took at ya, girl. I guess I'm a little more tired than I first thought I was, baby. Do you forgive my stupid remark, little sister?" the Mutt asked his new lover as he shot her one of his best smiles.

Instantly, Sergeant Raphael smiled at him and the two were good to go again.

"Knock off the shit so I can hear myself fucking think around here for a second, dammit." Colonel Leadbetter growled at the soldiers having fun picking on each other, but his gripe was cut off when the tail ramp of the huge C-17 Globemaster slowly started to lower, and the aircraft's massive interior was instantly flooded with a rush of fresh and reviving air.

"Okay you pack of war wacky bastards and bitches, get your asses the fuck outta the damn aircraft. We have some top brass hanging around out there, so I want you people to look sharp while leaving this damn trash hauler (the transport aircraft). Buckethead, you and Neck, take charge of our damn prisoner here. Weird Bill, (Sergeant William Molinari), you and Four F, (Sergeant Frank Ferraro), you two are still on GRREG (Grave's Registration) duty. So you two take good care of Sergeant Clifford Saldinger's body." The Colonel would no longer call the dead soldier by his nickname of Sun Tan, because the soldiers would never mention the nickname ever again. As far as the specialized soldiers were concerned, only the nickname of the trooper died but the soldier, he was still alive in their eyes, their minds and hearts.

"Captain Walker, you take charge of your troops, march them out of the damn aircraft, and I want a good formation when the soldiers are debarking from this fucking damn thing. General White's lurking about out there with who knows who else with him, sir. So we have to look our fucking best in front of them lousy pukes. Even the President might be hanging around out there for all I know, so act accordingly Walker and the rest of you people." Colonel Leadbetter watched as the soldiers stood and formed a pair of sharp lines, and marched proudly out of the plane. Once outside the aircraft, the soldiers quickly formed up and stood at full attention.

Colonel Leadbetter walked out of the aircraft last, and he marched his way to the front of the formation of soldiers and then looked at the troops. To his left stood the two largest soldiers, Buckethead and Neck, and they flanked the still very groggy Iraqi prisoner. The Colonel saluted the troops then waited for the General to approach him, and the soldiers standing in formation.

Likewise, General John White, and two other officers marched up to Colonel Leadbetter, and the three officers saluted the soldiers, with the General growling. "Stand at easy troops."

The soldiers took a step sideways then they locked their hands behind their backs.

The Chairman of the Joint Chiefs of Staff and the Commander of JSOC or Joint Special Operations Command, stared at the sharp looking troops still dressed in their filthy uniforms for several seconds, and then he began to address the troops. "Soldiers of the Multi National Rapid Response Forces, you people have done an outstanding job for your country, your President, and God. I thank you troops for your diligence to duty in carrying out this latest mission you were sent out on by your government. To be quite frank with you troopers, a mission the military combat computers place at a thirty percent successful completion rate to. You soldiers have proved the damn computers wrong, along with the brain thrust I placed on this latest mission.

The General turned his attention to the commander of the operation and announced. "Colonel

Leadbetter Sir, the actions of your elite troops is a glowing testament to the training program you have them undergoing, before any and all missions these specialized soldiers are assigned to. Outstanding work there Colonel, and I see a promotion in your near future sir. Err, Lieutenant Walker, front and center mister." The General waited for the young Lieutenant to leave the formation and step up to him. Instantly, his eyes narrowed as he glared at his collar.

"What the fuck are those damn eagles doing pinned on your fucking collar in front of me, mister? Who the hell gave you permission to place those damn things on your blouse, mister?"

Walker reached to his collar and ripped the two eagles from him, and then he snapped back at the excited and angry General. "What Eagles are you talking about sir?"

"Exactly mister, dammit, I wanted to be the one to break the news of your damn rate increase to your ass, buster. I see we have a big mouth somewhere in our outfit, Lieutenant, err Captain." The General shot a hot look right at the Colonel standing to the side of him, before he continued with the Lieutenant. "Now you that know you're in for a rate increase, I'll leave it at that for the time being, buster. But you won't wear the insignia's until the President pins the damn things on your ass himself, mister. Well I called you forward, because you were the Commander out in the field on this operation. True, you had higher ranking Officers on the mission with you. But you were the one assigned as the Commanding Officer of the entire operation out in the field."

The General looked at Captain Wilson this time, and nodded slightly at him and then he went on with his words aimed at the young Lieutenant again. "The reason you were placed in the command of this, err... Unit of soldiers and I use the term soldiers loosely mind you sir. Was because it was believed you were the only one who would, or could control these, err... soldiers. And, that was the only reason you were placed in command of these elite troops for this operation, soldier! Evidently, I was correct in that decision I see, mister. You and your troops have done an outstanding job on this mission. Glad to have you home Lieutenant, and the rest of you soldiers also." The General saluted the troops, and then he offered his hand to Walker.

Walker took the General's hand and then he shook it proudly with him.

The General then glanced at the Iraqi prisoner as he angrily asked Walker. "Is that the lousy little sonofabitch over there who masterminded the attack against our President, sir?"

"Yes Sir General White and he's still in one stinking piece as ordered, sir. Not that I wanted to bring him here in that kinda condition I assure you, sir." Walker gave the General a sneaky smirk.

"Understood Lieutenant Walker, I assure you sir, I don't like the fucking idea of him being in one piece myself, Lieutenant. I'll continue referring to you as Lieutenant until the President gives you that rate increase you so richly deserve, soldier. Anyway, if I had my way about it, I'd talk to him for five minutes, and then I'd give you troops what was left of his damn ass, to do with what you will with it, sir. But the big Boss Man wants him in one piece, and that's the way he's going to stay, Lieutenant." The Chairman complained as he turned on his heels, and then stomped his way over to the Iraqi terrorist and prisoner, and he stared him dead in his eyes.

Colonel Abdulaziz Majd al-Adwani stared defiantly back at the angry looking General.

"That's it stupid, mad dog my fucking ass like that and see where it gets you, buster. In case you don't realize it yet buster, I have your fucking life in my hands. If I decide to close my fist, your damn eyeballs will pop out of your head, mister. Right now, you're alive only because my President wants it that way for the time being. If I had my way with your ass, I'd stick your can inside a wood chipper nice and slow, and see what shit comes out on the other side. You two!"

General White barked at the two officers who had accompanied him before the group of elite soldiers. "Take command of this damn marmaluke here, I don't want him soiling the fucking hands of my soldiers for a minute longer than is absolutely necessary, dammit. Get him inside the damn vehicle and then get his ass over to the damn Brig of this base. I have four Marines already standing guard duty over there, and they'll take him off your hands at the Brig when you people get this one over there. From this minute forward, this here prick is going to be guarded better than our President. And you, you lousy little bastard you, you better be damn well prepared to look into the eyes of the man your group of flaming assholes tried to assassinate, buster.

"I only hope my President allows you to live just long enough, so you can stand trial for your crimes committed against my President, fella. I warn you asshole, you better hope to Allah that my President doesn't drag the Vice President along with him on this visit to you, pal. Because if Mary ever gets her hands on your scrawny little neck for even one damn moment, your ass will be heading for Paradise minus your dick and balls, buster. Get this piece of shit out of my sight before I forget I'm a Gentleman and an Officer, and I go back to Africa on his rotten ass."

The two officers stepped up and they placed their hands roughly on Iraqi Colonel al-Adwani's arms, and then they waited until Neck and Buckethead released their hold on the Iraqi prisoner. The two large soldiers smirked at the prisoner, as he was being lead away by the two officers. They continued smirking until the officers released their prisoner to two other soldiers. The two Marines manhandled the prisoner in the back of a closed humvee, and then the machine took off, heading for the structures constructed on Joint Andrews Airforce Base.

General White watched the soldiers and prisoner leaving the area until the humvee was completely out of sight, and then he turned to the two soldiers and barked at them. "Well, now that that's handled, what the hell are you two popinjays doing still standing here like that, when the rest of your troop are standing in formation. Get back to your ranks and stand tall before the man. You, the big one, I want to talk to you for a moment mister."

The two soldiers replied at the same time. "Me sir?" Because they both were large soldiers.

"Not you asshole, the other tree trunk with you. Yes you, I want to speak further with you."

Neck pointed at his chest like he just got caught doing something wrong.

"Yes you, you're the soldier the other soldiers from your Unit have branded No Neck? Am I correct in this assumption, soldier? I'm certain I remember that name with you, mister."

"Yes sir I am General White Sir." The soldier replied while trying not to smile.

"I want to ask you a few questions about this damn operation if you don't mind Sergeant Abbott." The powerful General growled at the extremely large soldier.

"Hey General White Sir, I don't know nuthin sir. I'm a fucking high school dropout sir."

"Funny, you're a walking joke on two tree stumps I see, aren't you mister? Look soldier, I heard you were wounded on this operation and I want to know how your wound is doing, and that's all mister. I guess everything with you has to be a debate though I see doesn't it buster? You'll answer my questions as I put them forth to you, and you will add nothing else to your remarks soldier. Or I'll pull your tongue out of your mouth, and stand on it until I get the correct answers that I'm looking for from you, soldier. Do you read me loud and clear mister?"

"Yes Sir loud and clear General White Sir!" Neck barked out as he went to full attention.

"I just asked you, but I'll repeat my question because I know you're not the fastest dog in the damn race, mister. I know all about you buster. How is your wound doing soldier?" General White asked the massive Neck while displaying serious concern for him.

Neck slowly moved his arm for a second and the General noticed the blood soaked bandage as the soldier replied. "Sir, it's doing real fine General White Sir, thanks for asking bout it sir."

"How the hell did you get wounded on this damn operation anyhow, Sergeant Abbott? I heard you seem to always get tagged when on a mission. Was it rough back there soldier?"

"Well you see it was like this General White Sir, I got shot because I was stuck with fighting off fifty crazy ass acting Iraqi soldiers charging at me all at the same fucking time sir, with evil intent locked within their eyes and hearts, sir. All I had to fight back with was a fist full of sand in one hand, and a hand full of shit in the uther hand General White

Sir, and I wasn't gonna allow any camel riding sand swimming camel jockey sonofabitches get the best of my stinking ass…"

"That's got to be the stupidest thing I ever heard in my entire life, mister." The General snarled back at the overexcited young soldier.

"Not yet sir, I'm not quite finished with my story for you yet, General White Sir." Neck replied with a smile as he went to continue with his words, but he was cut off by the General.

"You really believe what you're telling me, soldier? God dammit, I don't know why in unholy hell I ever wasted my time trying to have a decent conversation with the likes of you, Soldier. What the hell's the use, the more I try and talk to you the dumber you seem to get mister. I should've had my head examined before I tried it, mister. Get the fuck out of my sight, and get your ass over to the Infirmary and get that arm looked after properly, soldier." The General growled and then he watched the large soldier head over to the med-center of the Andrews Base.

Once the Neck was gone from his sight, the General turned back to the rest of the troops and offered to the commander of them. "Lieutenant Walker, there are five vehicles here for you and your troop's use while you people are stuck on this base, sir. There are six barrack type structures on site as well. You and your troops are to make use of them until you're finally sent for by the President, sir. For some unknown reason to me, he wants to pin a mess of ribbons on your group's asses, make you all look real pretty with the new color on your chests. He probably won't send for you pack of nuts for a few weeks, so get comfortable while visiting this installation, but this place better look the same as it does now, before I release you fools on the complex. The rest of your soldiers will be arriving in the next day or so sir, depending on how long and when the Aircraft Carrier Washington will return to her home port in West Virginia, Lieutenant Walker.

"The Carrier was ordered to weigh anchor the moment you reported that you had successfully caught this missing terrorist, sir. As of this time, your entire group is going to be restricted to this here base for the duration you people are visiting Washington under your President's request. If you think for one second I'm going to allow any of your criminals to roam free around the streets of downtown Washington, you have another think coming to you, Lieutenant. Just because you birds did an outstanding job, it doesn't mean my opinion changed about you people.

"Okay troops, again, you people did an outstanding job for your country and President, and you people look thoroughly beat out at that. So why don't you people do yourselves a favor here, and get your backsides over to the barracks and catch up on some of your needed rest and then enjoy a decent meal for a change, soldiers. By the way people, there'll be MPs stationed around the barracks at all times, armed with orders to protect the damn civilians of Washington from you people. Anyone caught roaming around outside the barracks, will be dragged over to my ass, and I'll ring your necks for the lot of you people for the infraction. Lieutenant Walker Sir, move your troops out. By the way soldiers, be aware these MP's have standing order to shoot you people on sight if you leave the barracks without permission."

The extremely concerned General watched as the group of specialized but exhausted looking soldiers quickly piled into the waiting vehicles, and then they were moved off towards the buildings on the base where the troops were to use as the makeshift temporary living quarters, until they were finally released back on leave. The General then smiled as CIA Director John Raincloud walked up to him, and then he rested his hand lightly on his back and offered calmly to the powerful and respected military officer.

"That's some great bunch of crazy ass soldiers you have yourself there, General White Sir." The grinning CIA Director offered to the soldier.

"Don't I know that for a fast John, but they'll never hear that coming from my lips though sir."

"Err General White Sir... I hate to be the one to tell you this, but I just received a call. It seems the President is up and he wants us over at the Big House ten minutes ago, sir." The CIA Director mumbled to the General as he let out his breath and then smiled at the General.

General White looked at his watch and discovered it was twelve thirty in the morning, on Monday, August 9th, 1999 and he replied to the CIA Director with a slight snap in his tone of voice. "What the fuck is he doing up this early in the morning, dammit?"

"I believe he was waiting up until the troops along with their prisoner made it back to the States, John." The Director informed the Chairman of the Joint Chiefs of Staff.

"Christ sake Director then I guess we had better get our asses over there and report to the President on the success of the operation in Iraqi. Then I'll let him chew on our asses for a little while until he gets it all out of his damn system and then we can share a drink over the success of the operation, and also salute these damn kids for the mission they have just pulled off for us."

CHAPTER FIVE

It took the Chairman of the Joint Chiefs of Staff, General John White, along with CIA Director John Raincloud a little longer than first expected to get over to the White House, because of the unusual amount of heavy traffic they had to battle through at this time of the day. They parked the staff car before the double main doors of the building, and they walked into the building like they owned the world. The White House aide met them by the doors, and then escorted them to the doors leading to the Oval Office, and introduced them to the seated President.

"Well, it's about time you two decided to get here, sirs. I was about to send the dogs out after the two of you. What took you so long getting here and deliver a report on how this operation went down with our troops, gentlemen?" the President growled at the Director and General at the same time, he was still dressed in a bathrobe because he was relaxing in his private quarters of the White House. When he was informed the General's soldiers had touched down at Andrews, and he moved to the Oval Office to meet with the General and CIA Director.

General White spoke up right off. "With all due respect Mr. President Sir, I was attending to my troops, sir. I had one soldier killed, and three wounded in this action sir. At the time sir, I thought they were more important than to be sitting here chewing the fat, Mr. President Sir."

"Yes, yes, quite right General White Sir. I'm terribly sorry to hear you lost one of your fine young soldiers due to this operation, because some asshole tried to assassinate me in my own backyard, General White. How are the wounded soldier's doing, sir?"

"The two soldiers are fine, both received minor flesh wounds, and they'll be up and running at full speed by tomorrow morning, Mr. President Sir. Though I do have to report one female soldier was badly wounded, and she's still in Saudi Arabia fighting for her life I'm afraid, sir."

"I'm pleased to hear two of the wounded soldiers will be fine in a short period time, General White Sir. I also want a constant update on the condition of the wounded female soldier still in Saudi Arabia, sir. I'd hate like hell to have her die on me because of one of my orders, General White. This damn thing has me going and angry as hell over the damn situation, General." The upset President reported as he looked down for a quick moment.

Their conversation was suddenly interrupted by the still suffering Vice President, Mary Hirshfield. She walked into the Oval Office and looked well under the circumstances. Looking at her one could hardly tell she was severely wounded over a month ago, during the attempted assassination on the President's life. The Vice President did not say much as they waited until she took her usual seat in the room. She remained in the White House the entire day, because she wanted to be with the President when he first met up with the General and CIA Director and received the report on how the operation in Iraq went down. No one spoke until Mary was comfortably seated and she nodded politely at the three men and smiled at them.

"You look well today Ma'am. How are you feeling Ms. Hirshfield?" the General asked her.

"I'm doing quite well I guess, General White Sir. I thank you for asking about my health, sir." Mary replied in a scratchy and strained voice. That was the only slight handicap that the Vice President visually displayed from the injuries she had received in the attempted assassination of the President while he was boarding Air Force One nicknamed Eagle's Nest. That and the slightly bandaged neck area still covered from where the bullet left her body during the attack.

"Your troop's General White Sir? How are they? Have all of them returned safe and sound." Mary asked politely. She was waiting at the White House to find out how the troops made out.

"They're doing quite well, and I thank you for asking about them, Ma'am. I have the troops settling down in the barracks over at Andrews, Ma'am. It's good to have the soldiers back in the States safe and sound, Ma'am." General White refrained from informing the Vice President of the wounded and dead from the mission. He felt she did not need to know anything about the bad side of the operation, and he did not want her feeling bad over the death of one soldier, or the wounding of the female fighter.

"And, what about this Iraqi terrorist that I was led to believe you have in custody as your prisoner, General White Sir? I believe his name is Colonel Abdulaziz Majd al-Adwani, sir." The female Vice President asked the military officer.

"Madam Vice President, the Iraqi prisoner's here in the States safe and sound, Ma'am. I have him cooling his heels off in the Brig over at Andrews. He's being held under twenty four hour guard, and nothing will happen to the lousy sonofa... Err... excuse me please Ma'am." The General quickly corrected himself, before he cursed in front of her.

"Please relax a little because I assure you sir that you're among friends here, General White Sir. Believe me General, I have a lot worse names I'd like to call the sonofabitch than the word you were about to use on him, General White." Mary retorted with a beautiful smile.

"Quite right Mary." The President replied, and then he added. "General White, I can't tell you how proud I am of your fine soldiers for getting this terrorist, and bringing him back to the United States alive, to stand trial before the public of our great nation, and the world, sir."

"Thank you for the kind words Mr. President Sir. I'll relay those complements to my soldiers when next I speak to the troops, sir." The General smiled proudly at President Albert Cole.

"Yes, please do that for me General White Sir. By the way General, I want to know as soon as I can have these troops invited over to the White House, sir. So I can display my feelings before the soldiers, sir. It'll be a supper, and after the supper, I'll be giving them the medals the soldiers so richly deserve for carrying out this operation successfully for us, General White Sir." The President announced proudly to the military officer.

"With all due respect Mr. President Sir, I have the rest of the elite troops attached to this operation who were held back in reserve incase the original mission went sour on us, arriving here in Washington within the next two days. These troops too will be stationed at the Andrews Base until you had enough of my troops hanging around Washington and you get rid of them, sir. Let me see, today's Monday Mr. President Sir. Why don't we set the supper date up for next Friday, and that would be August 13th? I sure hope that'll do for you pleasure, Mr. President."

"It does fine for me General White, as long as none of your soldiers are superstitious, sir." The President replied as he allowed a slight smile to cross his lips over his last remark.

"Superstitious Mr. President Sir? I assure you sir, none of my troops are afraid of anything natural, or unnatural, or manmade or invented sir. I'll have the troops here on the thirteenth at say around four p.m., Mr. President Sir. I believe we're only speaking of the few troops who made the penetration of Iraq to arrest the terrorist we wanted, sir? I don't believe you want the entire MNRRF Unit coming to the White House at the same time, sir. I'd fear for the building and Washington's sake if they were all here at the same time, Mr. President Sir."

"Quite right General White Sir, I just want to honor the soldiers who went in, and they took this Iraqi Colonel prisoner for us, sir. I know there are too many of these elite soldiers attached to the specialized Unit to bring them all here at the same time sir, and yet try and maintain a good control over them, General White." The President responded with a smile.

"General White, I have a question for you if you don't mind sir?" the Vice President asked.

"Yes Madam Vice President, you may ask me anything you so please, Ma'am."

"General White, I believe we're speaking about Lieutenant Robert Walker, and his girlfriend Sergeant Dorothy Ramirez? Am I correct in my assumption, General White Sir?"

"Partially Madam Vice President Ma'am." The General responded kindly.

"Partially, what the hell do you mean by that remark, General White?" She asked him.

The General knew perfectly well why the concerned Vice President was asking this question of him. That was because both Lieutenant Walker and Sergeant Ramirez were the two soldiers who rescued her while she was being held hostage by the group of terrorist who attacked the Trump International Hotel and Tower in mid-town Manhattan over a year ago. If it was not for these two young soldiers, she would have surely been killed in the takeover of that building either by the terrorists or the fighting to eliminate the terrorists.

"Madam Vice President, Lieutenant Walker was indeed involved with the inserted soldiers for this operation, Ma'am. But Sergeant Ramirez was forced to be held back from the mission for certain reasons, and she..."

"Why was Sergeant Ramirez held back from the mission, General White Sir?" Mary snapped at the officer, feeling she might have been held back because she was a female soldier.

"Madam Vice President, Sergeant Ramirez was held back from the mission because she's pregnant, Ma'am. That was the only reason she was held back on the mission, Ma'am."

The Vice President smiled at the officer, relieved she was wrong in her assumption of him as she added painfully for her to speak as much as she was doing because of her injuries. "General White, that's such wonderful news to hear that she's pregnant, sir. Are we going to do something special for her when she gives birth to her child, General White Sir? I take it the baby belongs to Lieutenant Walker, General White? And, I believe that was a good reason to hold back this young woman from the dangerous mission and I approve of your action, General White. I also believe because she wasn't involved in the ground action in Iraq. She's not going to be invited to the White House sir, with the other soldiers involved in the operation General White Sir."

"That's right Madam Vice President, unless you have another idea in mind that is, Ma'am? And yes Ma'am, I'm certain the child is that of Lieutenant Walker, Ma'am. But I wasn't planning on anything special for the birth of the child, Madam Vice President. I don't usually get involved in such things with my troops, Ma'am."

"I certainly have some other plans in mind for the birth of this child, General White Sir. I'll find a way to get some particular gifts over to Sergeant Ramirez, General White. You know I've been wanting for quite a while to thank these two fine young soldiers for saving my life, General. But I was forced to wait until this mission in Libya sir, and now this one in Iraq was completed first, General

White. Now that it's been completed successfully General White, and Sergeant Ramirez, and Lieutenant Walker are trapped here in Washington. And, we're planning to honor Lieutenant Walker then I suggest, no correct that please, General White. I demand that Sergeant Ramirez be included in this special supper we're planning for these outstanding troops of yours, sir." The Vice President replied as she sharpened her look at the General.

"Madam Vice President, I had a sneaky feeling you were going to make this suggestion to me, Ma'am. So I was already planning to include her in with the invited soldiers to the White House, Ma'am." General White announced proudly to the waiting female Vice President.

"I should've known you were planning this, General White Sir. What with the way you take such good care of your young troops, sir. And, I'd have it no other way, General."

"I too am as proud of the way you take care of your soldiers, sir. As well as I'm pleased Lieutenant Walker and Sergeant Ramirez are finally going to make it to the White House, sir. So we can thank them properly for all they have done for the United States, and also for my Administration, General White Sir." The President added kindly to his officer.

"Mr. President, General White, I believe I'd like to meet with this damn terrorist. I want to ask him why he did what he did, and who put him up to it. I want to look him in his eyes, and see if he can lie to me straight faced. I want to show him what he did to me, and tell him he killed a great man. And, he almost killed the greatest President the United States ever had. I want..."

"Oh noooo. Now you look here Mary, you know damn well that I have always value you opinion in any situation facing us, and I have allowed you to go forward with many of your own ideas in the past. Even with some of them that I didn't fully agree with I don't mind telling you, young lady. But this request is one helluva humdinger I don't mind telling you. No, I think you're way off base with this latest request of yours, Mary. What the hell makes you believe that you're going to get any kind of a straight answer from this terrible man? This man is nothing more than a hired killer, a killer and a damn thug who'll kill anyone just to satisfy his damn need for blood and hatred, to be quite frank with you Mary.

"I also want to meet face to face with this terrible man, but after thinking about it young lady. The only way I want to see this man ever again, is when he's hung up and swinging from the end of a damn rope. So I have to deny your request with meeting this terrorist face to face, Mary." The President said as he shook his head no towards his shaking Vice President.

The Vice President went to protest, but she was instantly cut off by the General.

"I'm afraid I'm going to be forced to agree with the President on this one and against you, Ma'am. We don't know very much about this evil man. All we know of him, is he's more than willing to order the death of anyone he wants dead plain and simple, Ma'am. No matter who that person might be. Until we know a little more about this evil man, I don't think he's going to be receiving very many visitors, Ma'am." The General warned the Vice President.

Again, the female Vice President went to add something to the conversation, and once more she was immediately cut off in mid sentence, but this time it was by the CIA Director who for the first time, spoke at the special meeting.

"Madam Vice President Hirshfield Ma'am. I'm taking any decision of you possibly meeting one on one with this terrorist out of everyone's hands here. This Colonel al-Adwani is in my custody, and being he is, I'm the only man on the face of this earth who'll allow anyone to visit with this nut in any way, shape or form. My power over this terrorist supersedes that of even the President, Ma'am. Right now, I'm classifying this man as a national security risk to our country and all of us, Ma'am. I further branded him as a terrorist, and as such, he's not allowed any of the usual protections we normally offer to any alleged criminals in this country. Not even a mouth piece is going to get to speak to this man until I allow it, Ma'am."

"Until you allow it Director Raincloud! Now you look here Mr. Director. I'm not used to having anyone tell me what I can, or cannot do while I'm the Vice President of this country, mister. And, since this man injured me! I believe I have the legal right at anytime I want it, to confront this evil man on my terms, sir. Unless I'm informed otherwise, I do believe I woke up in the United States this morning Director Raincloud Sir." The Vice President grumbled at the CIA Director while she stared angrily at him.

The President and General White were more than pleased to allow Director Raincloud handle the always feisty and firry female Vice President. Both men knew when she turned on them they would sooner or later give into her demands or requests. But in Director Raincloud, they both felt Mary Hirshfield might have met her equal in any argument they were engaged in. They sat back and smiled as they watched Director Raincloud and Ms. Hirshfield go at it.

"That's quite right Ma'am. I assure you Madam Vice President that you surely did wake up in the United States this morning. I further assure you Ma'am, all your legal rights are attached to that great privilege, Ma'am. But I also assure you Ma'am, they don't apply to this terrorist and my control of this man, Ma'am. He has forfeited those rights the moment he stepped over the line, and he took it on himself to go against the laws that govern the civilized world, and all her peoples, Ma'am. I'm afraid I'm going to be forced to maintain my denial of anyone visiting with this terrorist, until I had the chance to interrogate him over the matters that we're concerned with, over this situation we're working through Ma'am."

"Your denial to me do you Mr. Director Raincloud! I heard much about you and your steadfast and one-sided opinions Director Raincloud, and I always respected the bravos you always displayed before me and anyone else you were dealing with, sir. But now it's my turn to assure you, Director Raincloud Sir. I'll have my way this time or..."

"Pardon me for saying this to you Madam Vice President, but I don't think so Ma'am. I'm still going to stay with my not allowing you to speak directly with this damn killer, Ma'am."

"Jesus Christ Director Raincloud! I can't believe what I'm hearing coming from your lips, sir. You're daring to tell me, the Vice President of the United States, no I see! Albert, do you hear what this man is telling me sir? I want you to put him in a headlock and pound him in his mush for me, sir. And, if you don't do it Mr. President, I'll do it for myself, sir. How dare this man tell me, the Vice President of the United States, no Mister!"

President Albert Cole laughed over Mary wanting him to place CIA Director Raincloud in a headlock. He smiled because he never witnessed Mary this angry in her life before. It further pleased him to see the fires of hell burning so brightly in her again. He was afraid she might have lost some of that fire when she was so severely wounded by the assassin attempt aimed against him. He shook his head no, and replied calmly to his extremely upset Vice President. "Mary, I can't put the Director in a headlock, young lady. Look at the size of the man will you please. He'll fold me up and stuff me in an envelope, and send me to wherever the hell he wants to. C'mon Mary and think of what you're asking for. Director Raincloud's correct in his…"

"If you're afraid of the Director, I'll help you with him sir. I'll get him in the headlock, and you can pound on him for refusing my request, Albert." This time, Mary said her words with a slight smile. She really did not want the President and Director to get involved in a fistfight.

"Well Mary, if anyone can get the Director in a headlock, I'm quite certain it's you, young lady. But once again honey, I find myself being forced to agree with Director Raincloud on this one against you and your wants to meet one on one with this evil killer, young lady. The CIA Director's absolutely correct that his control over this Iraqi prisoner overrules even my command of this evil man, but I'm just as certain sometime in the near future, you'll have the opportunity to meet with this killer face to face if you truly want to see him that is, Mary." The rather concerned President offered politely, but with some concern in his tone as he slowly separated his hands apart, and he shrugged his shoulders back at his Vice President. Then the President waited for any further response from his Vice President.

"Well, never let it be said that I didn't know when to retreat in a war I was fighting, sir. I don't mind fighting one of you guys, and even taking two of you head on. But when I have to fight all three of you thick headed knuckle draggers at the same time, even I know when I'm trying to push a wagon uphill with a rope. I give up. Err… Director Raincloud

Sir, you'll keep it in mind I want to meet with this terrorist, the first chance I can get sir." The female Vice President said, as she smiled at the powerful CIA Director.

The President released his breath because he was in fear he was going to have more trouble than this from his always feisty Vice President. President Cole turned to the CIA Director and asked the man. "Do you think we're going to have any trouble with the UCLA over keeping this Iraqi prisoner locked away from any legal assistance, while he's waiting to be tried, sir? I don't need them pain in the asses camped out on the front lawn of the White House and throwing rocks at me all day long, sir. You know how they hate Republicans, Director Raincloud."

"Mr. President Sir, I don't give a flying fuc... Err... excuse me please Ma'am I'm sorry for that slight slip of the tongue, Madam Vice President. I don't care what the hell those damn people have to say about this damn situation, sir. This man is not a normal prisoner, or even a prisoner of war, sir. He's nothing but a miserable lowlife terrorist, and as such, he's not offered any protections usually offered to normal prisoners in the United States, sir. Let them come at you sir. As far as I'm concerned about the UCLA, they're nothing but a bunch of out of work lawyers always pushing the dumb issues, so they can make tons of money off the lousy situation, sir. Going after that poor judge down South sir, just because he had the Ten Commandments displayed in the county building, is just plain nuts if you were to ask me sir.

"Since when did we get so damn ashamed about religion, and what religion stands for in our lives, sir? I think we'd all be a helluva lot better off if we remembered our religions a little more, and use it in our daily decisions as well, sir. Maybe nuts like the one we holding at Joint Andrews wouldn't find the platform he stood on, if we remembered God ever once in a while in our daily lives, sir. By the way Mr. President Sir, all you have to do is direct them people at me if they come after you, and I'll happily handle it from there for you, Mr. President. I'm in the right frame of mind to tangle with them bastards, sir." The upset CIA Director offered in a positive tone to the President. Director Raincloud had about enough trouble from the UCLA in the past years, and he was ready to confront them in any fashion he was forced to over this manner.

"I shall do as you have just offered Director Raincloud, because I hate like hell to have to deal with anyone from that organization, and I thank you for offering to handle that situation for me, if and when it arises over this matter we're discussing here today, sir. Please allow me to get back on the subject of the soldiers who carried out this mission, Director Raincloud." The President turned to General White, and asked the military officer. "General White, I trust these soldiers are being made as comfortable as possible, under the present circumstances at Andrews, sir?"

"That they are I can assure you Mr. President Sir. I have the soldiers taking over five of the barracks type buildings usually reserved for soldiers or VIPs visiting Washington, to engage in any celebrations we might have going off here, sir. These barracks are air-conditioned, and have other modern day facilities to make visiting soldiers as comfortable as possible. They have a gym, a large rec room, and even a movie hall if I'm not mistaken, Mr. President. I do have the wild ass soldiers under armed guard though, as long as they're visiting the base Mr. President Sir. I have to keep some form of control over these wild ass soldiers, or they might destroy the entire base, sir." The General offered shyly to the concerned looking President.

"Gees General White, is that really necessary to place armed Military Police standing guard over these specialized soldiers of yours, sir? Having these soldiers placed under armed guard kind of goes against what I have planned for these fine young troopers in the near future, sir."

"Let me assure you Mr. President, it's absolutely necessary I have these soldiers placed under armed guard at all times while they're stationed at the Andrews Base, sir. These troops are the civilized world's worst nightmare, sir. And, if these troops weren't held under armed guard, I'm quite certain a few of them would try something stupid, and end up being taken in by the police departments, sir. The other reason I have decided to place the soldiers under armed guard is, sir. These soldiers are far from a dumb lot of troopers, and yes they're extremely dangerous at that, sir. But right now sir, the soldiers know they're in Washington to be honored by you for a job well done, sir. I'm afraid some of them might take a notion to think we might owe them something special for what they have done on this latest operation, sir. These few soldiers in question might try and push the envelope beyond all good measure, Mr. President Sir."

"Ahhh... I see where you're coming from with this damn situation, General White Sir. I guess I'm kind of forced to agree with the precautionary steps you're taking with these elite soldiers of yours, sir. Err... let's say with protecting these soldiers while they're visiting Washington as my guests, sir, even if that protection is going against the soldiers while they're here, General White Sir. Rather good thinking on your part I believe, General White Sir. Yes I like that very much sir." The President replied to his military officer while smiling.

A strained smiling Vice President cut in and she offered to the powerful Chairman of the Joint Chiefs of Staff. "Then I take it we're talking about Lieutenant Walker, and the man I was told was his terrible sidekick that's been reported is always with the Lieutenant on any mission he's dispatched on sir. The Dog or something like that, am I correct, General White Sir?"

"By all means we're talking about Lieutenant Walker here, Ma'am. Among other soldiers, and the other soldier you're referring to Ma'am, is Lieutenant Frank Hall. He's known to his Unit as the Mutt, Ma'am." The General offered with a smile.

"The Mutt, now that's a name if I have never heard one used around here, General White Sir."

"And, it fits the wild soldier very well at that, Ma'am. The Unit calls him the Mutt because he has a white mother and a black father, Ma'am." The General smiled again at Mary.

"Hmmm... General White. I don't believe I like what I'm hearing sir. I could take the name of the Mutt as a sort of ethnic slur the other soldiers are aiming at this poor soldier, General White." Ms, Hirshfield remarked, as she held the military officer in her gaze, waiting for his reply.

"Madam Vice President Ma'am, I can assure you the name wasn't bestowed on this one soldier as any form of punishment or disrespect aimed at him, Ma'am. One thing my soldiers will never do, and that's to disrespect any other soldiers from their specialized Units. Besides Ma'am, this soldier is reported to be rather proud of this name the other soldiers had bestowed upon him, Ma'am." The General offered, as he shifted his weight from one foot to the other.

"I see what you are saying here General White, and I don't mind telling you sir. I can't begin to try and figure out how your specialized soldiers think, let alone how they live and act with one another and fight our nation's enemy, sir. But I thank my God I don't have to figure them out, General White Sir." Mary returned the General's smile with one of her own.

"Believe me Ma'am I went to sleep more than once in my life while trying to figure out how some of my soldiers think and act, and believe as well, Ma'am. These young kids are a most confusing lot to be in command of, Ma'am. They're always pushing their limits and fighting our control over these soldiers." The General smirked at her as he flashed one of his best smiles at the Vice President of the United States.

"Never mind that for the time being General White Sir. I wasn't quite finished with you just yet, before my Vice President chose to interrupt our conversation, sir. Now that I know your elite soldiers are comfortable at Joint Andrews Airforce Base, I want to know what you plan to do with them once we're finished with the soldiers here in Washington, General White." The President snapped as he glared at the General for the moment.

General White drew in his breath and then he began to explain to his Commander in Chief. "With all due respect Mr. President Sir, once you have no further need of the troops. I plan on sending them home on leave until the next time we have any need for them sir..."

The Vice President interrupted the General for a second time as she offered him in a slightly upset tone of voice. "General White, to be quite frank with you sir, I hope to the good Lord in Heaven that we never have another need of these fine young soldiers of yours, sir."

"I do as well Ma'am, with all due respect Madam Vice President I'm not as romantic as you obviously are, Ma'am. I know as well as I know I'm going to draw in my next breath, that somewhere along the line we'll have further need of these fine young soldiers again, and in the near future at that, Ma'am. What with the present condition of the world, and that nut still running Iraq, I believe it's only a matter of time before we send these soldiers out on another such mission as they have accomplished yesterday, Ma'am." The General replied proudly, and then he continued with his words for the President of the United States.

"With all due respect Mr. President Sir, I want to get these kids back home and out of the limelight for a while, as soon as I possibly can at that, sir. Well before any nosy damn ass reporters discover their presence over at Andrews, and they try to start interviewing any of the soldiers, sir. I want the troops to step back, calm down and fit in with society again sir, until we have further need of them sir. I can't wait for Lieutenant Walker..."

"Who is soon to be made Captain Walker if I remember right, General White Sir?" The President corrected as he interrupted the General's words.

"Quite right Mr. President Sir. I'd like to get Lieutenant Walker and the rest of his screaming squirrels back to his tiny Island of Marathon down in the Florida Keys, sir. That way he can disappear from public view, and stagnate on that little Island until his kid finally arrives, sir. I hope this child will serve to calm him down some while he's stationed in the States, sir. Of course Mr. President Sir, I'll have the usual watchers keeping a close eye on him, and the rest of the highly trained soldiers, all the while they're on leave in the United States, Mr. President.

"If we discover any of these specialized soldiers displaying any sort of possible threats against the civilians of this country, or to themselves for that matter. I'll order that one soldier no matter who he might be, naturalized immediately sir. I can't take the chance of one of these highly trained soldiers to go off the handle while he or she's on leave here in the States, sir. There's no telling how many civilians they might hurt or kill, before the police stop them, Mr. President."

"God how I truly hate the thought of being forced to take out one of our specialized soldiers like that General White, because he loses it and reacts in the way we have trained him while he or she was in our service, General White Sir." The President moaned as he slowly ran his hands through his hair, and shook his head sadly.

"I assure you Mr. President that I'm not very fond of the practice myself sir. But it's something that we have done from time to time, ever since the Korean War had ended, sir. And, since the training of these elite soldiers has drastically improved over the passing years, and we're making much more dangerous soldiers out of these kids we're training to carry out the orders of the Presidency and those of the..." The General was going to go on with his words until he was interrupted for the third time by the stunned looking Vice President.

"And, we made better killers out of these poor kids, General White. We should be ashamed of ourselves over this situation, sir." The Vice President added as she shot a hot stare at the officer.

The Chairman of the Joint Chiefs of Staff gave the female Vice President a look of hurt and deep concern as he went on with his words to the President, as if she did not say what she did to him. "Since the soldiers are so much better trained in the art of warfare and use of weapons, we have been forced to keep a much closer eye on many of the special operations soldiers, Mr. President Sir. It's a rather shitty practice we have adopted, but one we must carry out during these times of guerrilla warfare and terrorist actions and attacks against us, sir. Which are usually carried out against the civilian population of many other nations of the world, sir?

"Mr. President, make no mistake about it sir. So far, we've been extremely lucky not many terrorist attacks have been successfully carried out against the United States, sir. That's why we have developed this Multi National Rapid Response Force, Mr. President Sir. In order to have the damn terrorist actions carried out on the other person's land because they're well aware we'll either stop them, or get them before they can flee the country for the safety of their ratholes, sir. But sooner or later sir, we know damn well the United States is going to be hit and hit hard, and it's only a matter of time when, and where this attack is going to take place against us, sir."

"General White, I happen to agree with you we're on the verge of again being hit by some sort of terrorist action, and soon at that sir. Do you have any idea where and when that hit might occur against us sir? I hope to hell if a terrorist attack is coming, we'll be able to discover the plot before they hit us successfully, General White Sir." The President replied as he suddenly shifted his weight in his chair to get more comfortable.

"Mr. President, I believe when the terrorist attack takes place against us, sir. The attack will take place somewhere in New York City, which offers the most in the way of an environmentally rich target for any terrorist action played out against the United States, sir. Washington would be the second target I'd suggest, and then perhaps maybe even somewhere in Florida, like Miami or the Tampa Bay area, Mr. President Sir. Then probably the West Coast might find itself locked up in the terrorist crosshairs, and maybe a city like Chicago might be hit as a secondary target by these lousy bastards, sir. But it's going to happen in the near future as sure as the sun's going to rise in the morning, Mr. President Sir. Though I hate to offer, that much you can be assured of sir, and we will be hit and hit soon might I add sir."

"General White Sir, since you're that certain we're about to be hit by another terrorist action taking place somewhere in the United States, sir. What the hell have you been doing about trying to protect the civilians of our great country, General? There has to be something we can do to try and put a damn stop, or even prevent this possible terrorist attack you seem certain being planned against the United States, General White Sir." The overly concerned female Vice President offered as she cut into the conversation between the General and President.

"Madam Vice President Ma'am, we, and by what I mean is my office has been working closely with Director Raincloud's office, along with the FBI, and National Security Advisor, or the NSA, Ma'am. We've been comparing notes and trying to figure out any possible terrorist target in certain States the terrorists might try and hit us with, Ma'am. I have to offer Ma'am. There's no way in hell we can actually prevent a possible terrorist action aimed against us, we can only react against it once it has taken place, Ma'am. By that I mean as follows Madam Vice President: The damn terrorist have the luxury of unlimited time on their side in which to work their evil deeds against the nation they have leveled their evil eyes upon, with the least amount of support in personnel and money at that, Ma'am. These terrorists can take all the time they want to work out their attack against their intended target no matter how well protected it is.

"So it's almost impossible to discover this impending terrorist attack, unless it's by just dumb luck or from a possible informer who wants to rat out the damn terrorists. Or we might even pick up some of their communications on their cell phones, or the computers the terrorists employ, or though a simple conversation going on between two terrorists, and is happened to be overheard by an informer who offers us the suggested target. The best defense against a possible terrorist attack aimed at the United States is Intelligence, Ma'am.

"And, that includes wiretaps, money transfers, and computer E-mails, along with cell phone communications or any other form of communications employed by the terrorists that we can possibly tap into successfully, Ma'am. Yes Ma'am, we're keeping a close eye on all known terrorists and their organizations who entered the United States either legally or otherwise. And, every once in a while, one of these damn persons we're keeping under constant surveillance is accidentally ran down by a car, or they find their deaths in another accidental way.

"But there are so many damn terrorist cells operating around the globe Madam Vice President Hirshfield that it's nearly impossible keeping up with all of them at the same time, Ma'am. No sooner do we destroy one known active terrorist cell operating within the borders of the United States, than five more of the damn things crop up to replace the ones we were successful in destroying before they can attack us, Ma'am.

"The one terrorist cell we're trying to keep the closest eye twenty four seven on is the one operated by the king of rats himself, Usama bin Laden. He's the largest and most serious threat against the United States and all our allies or interests both home and aboard, and yes, he was once one of our closest allies. But ever since President Clinton made the failed assassination attempt on his worthless life, the lousy bastard has vowed to take his revenge out on all the United States and our interests spread throughout the rest of the world, Ma'am."

The General suddenly turned his attention towards the American Leader and offered him in a rather calm tone of voice. "Mr. President Sir, from many of the reports and intercepted cellular calls, wiretaps, faxes and computer E-mails we have intercepted on this evil man and his terrorist organization. We're quite certain that he's going to try and hit against us sometime in the near future, somewhere here in the United States, Mr. President. It's absolutely imperative that we train most of our assets on this one man and his god damn terrorist organization.

"Who we have proof are operating out of Afghanistan sir, along with the support and help of his damn Taliban cohorts, Mr. President Sir. The Taliban are offering bin Laden their protection and complete backing, and the two groups of radicals about control all the lands of Afghanistan, and they're tightening their strangle hold on that poor nation every second of the day, sir. This is why I'm extremely concerned about this terrorist organization and the serious threat they pose to our interests both here in the United States, and abroad, Mr. President Sir."

"There's not much we can do about this serious threat coming from Usama bin Laden and his terrorist organization at this time, to end the threat this group of yahoos hold against us and this country, General White Sir?" the President asked with concern.

"It's like I just offered Mr. President, there's not much we can do to the terrorist organization, until they act out against us anywhere throughout the world, sir. Unless we declare war on all known terrorist organizations, and I know for a fact Congress would never go along with that request, sir. All we can do for the time being until the terrorists finally show us their hand, is to keep the bastards under constant surveillance twenty four hours a day, every day of the week and every week of the year, and pray to God we're able to discover where and how they're going to hit us before they do, sir. Then we'll react accordingly against the attack and the terrorist organization at the same time, sir. Unless, you want to try another surgical such strike like the one President Clinton tried against bin Laden, sir. You saw how far that move netted us against this man and his shit filled group of crazies, Mr. President Sir."

"No, no General White, I'm not going to get involved with lobbing a few useless missiles at another country like President Clinton was forced to do some years back, sir. Unless I know for certain that the damn things are going to hit the target we want taken out, sir. If we're going to act, I demand that we act with the full intent of destroying the entire terrorist organization giving us these fits, or we don't start any action against them until we know we can get the lot of them in one action, no matter how long it takes us to get them all, General White Sir." The exhausted American Leader offered as he stared at his military officer.

"Exactly the way I feel about the damn situation, Mr. President Sir. I feel we have to get them all with one action, sir. We can't keep popping off a horde of god damn missiles unless we know for certain they're going to do the job we demand of the damn things, sir. We have to go after the head of the damn snake and destroy their leaders and the rest of the body will quickly die, sir. If we can possibly eliminate the brain thrust of bin Laden's terrorist organization. Then the surviving terrorists will be looking to protect their asses from our further attacks against them. You can bet the back that the surviving terrorists will be hunting holes in the ground where they can hide until the heats off the bastards, Mr. President." The General replied to the President.

Vice President Mary Hirshfield suddenly let her breath out in a deep sigh as she added to the conversation again. "Albert, General White and you too Director Raincloud, I can't believe that we're going to be forced to sit on our rearends, and wait for the next terrorist attack to come that just might kill hundreds and even possibly thousands of innocent American men, women, and children, civilians, dammit. Before we finally do something about this terrible evil man, and his god damn terrorist organization, I guess I'll aim my gripe at you General White."

CHAPTER SIX

Lieutenant Robert Walker was speaking with Sergeant Dorothy Ramirez about the child she was carrying. The rest of the elite soldiers were taking care of last minute business and ignoring the two other soldiers. Although they knew the rest of the soldiers from the group were scheduled to arrive later today. They had no idea the other troops had already arrived on the airbase, and the MPs were leading them to the barracks. The Aircraft Carrier Washington docked two hours ago and the troops on board were transferred from Norfolk Virginia to Andrews Airforce Base.

Walker was sitting on his bunk, and Ramirez was standing and leaning against the post of his rack while speaking with him. Mother Flanagan was lying in the upper bunk minding his business. The Ghost was standing by the front of the barracks, speaking with McNip when the first of the other troops arrived in front of the barracks, and he yelled out to the rest of the troops inside the barracks. "Holy shit the rest of us are here, guys."

Fifty five special operations soldiers tried to pile into the barracks as the other troops inside were trying to get out so they could welcome the other soldiers back. It was pure mayhem at best, with each soldier talking at the same time. None of the conversations were able to be understood because so many troops were speaking at once. Colonel Bruce Leadbetter stationed in another barracks set aside for the officers of the group, came storming out of his building. He started to scream at the troops as they made a helluva scene before their barracks. He was followed out of the structure by Captain Wilson and Sergeant Kirkpatrick.

"What the fuck's happening around here, dammit! You shitbirds are making enough noise to wake the fucking dead. You soldiers don't bother settling in. Transportation's coming out to the base in five hours, and the rest of you slugs will be transported down to Camp Lejeune..."

A flood of gripes cut the Colonel's bitch off in mid sentence, until he barked again at the excited group of specialized soldiers. "Okay you fucking pack of shitbirds, you want to keep griping and not hear what I have to say to you pack of flaming assholes. Keep fucking talking, the longer you jackasses talk, the longer you asses will remain confined on this installation, and you fools will stall your leave from beginning for you asses. Now you poor excuses for soldiers, do you want to keep flapping your damn gums like y7ou are, or do you want to listen up to my damn words so you know what the hell's coming down the chute at ya dumb asses?"

When the Colonel's words sank in on the troops, they quieted down and stared at him.

"I want you shitbirds who just arrived on this base to form up in fucking lines, and when I say eyes, all eyes better be looking at my ass if you people know what's good for you. Or I'll be taking numbers and asses. Anyone I single out will not be going home on leave for a long time to come I can assure you pack of assholes. Form up the damn lines, and let's look like what we are, professional fucking soldiers around here dammit. Move it people."

Colonel Leadbetter and Captain Wilson smiled as the soldiers broke their necks forming lines. When they were ready, the Colonel moved to the front, and began addressing the troops.

"Okay troops, I don't know why in their infinite wisdom that the big shots over at Fort Fumble, (The Pentagon) had you asses transferred over here in the first place, but they did. You people were so close to our home base it wasn't funny, but that's how it goes for us soldiers in the service. Don't ask any damn questions and just do as you're ordered. Now I have to send you people down to Camp Lejeune, and once you're there, you'll be going on your extended leave as soon as possible. Remember to keep your damn portable radios on your person at all times while on leave, in case something comes up and you Squids have to report back to base, dammit. Anyway, your leave will start as soon as the paperwork's completed at Camp Lejeune, people.

"Transportation will be supplied for those who need it; the other soldiers will drive to where you live. Make damn certain you people put down on your paperwork where you'll be staying while you're on leave, and list anything changes with your living situations as well. You're ordered to call the base immediately, and then correct your addresses on the existing paperwork. We have to know where the hell you soldiers are at all times, for fuck sake. Any of you pack of misfits have any fricking questions so far over these orders, ask them now?"

One hand shot up and the Colonel let his breath out in a hissed as he snarled at the soldier. "Identify yourself stupid, and state your fucking gripe mister."

"Hard Luck, Sergeant Henry Butterman, Colonel Leadbetter Sir. And, I'd like to know what the hell's going on with the rest of our soldiers that are going to remain on this damn airfield, sir. From what I'm picking up in the scuttlebutt sir, Lieutenant Walker and his group seem to be being forced to remain at the Andrews Base for some reason not shared with the rest of us soldier, sir. What the hell's going down with the rest of our troops, Colonel?"

"I'll explain it to you, even though it's none of your business what the hell's going on with the other soldiers from our Unit, Sergeant Hard Luck. Now I know why they call you Hard Luck soldier, because you never know when to keep your damn mouth zipped up. You should be more worried more about what you're doing and the hell with what the rest of the soldiers are doing, around here that doesn't concern you buster. True, Lieutenant Walker's group was ordered to remain behind for a few days. It seems the President wants to speak with the soldiers who were involved with the Iraqi mess. But when the President's done with them, they'll likewise be sent home on the extended leave. No one's going to pull any extra duty while you troops are waiting to leave this damn airbase. So for now, your time is your own to screw up anyway you see fit.

"But a word to the wise, if any of you jackasses screw up while you're on this base, I'll have you stopping the landing aircraft with your wasted bodies. No one is allowed anywhere near Eagle Nest. (Air Force One) Try it, and you'll be shot dead by the security guards protecting the fucking thing. There's a good mess stationed on this base, and I suggest you people take full advantage of it while you're stuck stacking pencils here. That's all I got for you Squids, you're dismissed, stay near, your transportation's coming and I don't want to be forced to hunt any of you people down so I can get rid of you people. If I'm forced to go looking for any of you assholes, I'll order you shot just for the hell of it. You people are dismissed."

The Colonel and Captain watched as the still rather excited soldiers broke ranks and then the trooper's pair up with the other soldiers on the base. "I guess that's about it for now Captain Wilson. We better get away from this load of riprap before they corrupt us as they did with each other." The Colonel said to the Captain as the soldiers turned and headed back for the barracks.

The soldiers who did not go on the mission with the other troops who entered Iraq, were stuck sitting it out on the Aircraft Carrier Washington, those soldiers were held in reserve for possible backup support. In case the mission in Iraq went sour on the invading troops, and the other soldiers had to be inserted to the field of battle as reinforcement and support troops, began asking the soldiers who went on the mission all sorts of questions on the operation and how it went for them. All Walker and the other soldiers did, was answer their questions. Then some of the troopers let it be known they wanted to have a party with the female soldiers of the barracks. But that decision was quickly voted down by the rest of the group, because they did not have the time for that kind of pleasure, before the other troops were to be pulled out on the rest of the troopers.

Little by little, the group of elite soldiers started to quiet down some, and then they started keeping their eyes opened for the vehicles that would get half the troops down to Camp Lejeune.

Walker who was still going by the rank of Lieutenant, grabbed hold of Ramirez and led her away from the rest of the soldiers. As usual, the Mutt noticed Walker take off with his girlfriend, and he and Blind Date began to follow them. They headed for the main landing strip area and Walker and Ramirez watched as a pair of sleek F-18 Hornets landed on the runway. Then they glanced over at the Eagle Nest aircraft, the plane was lit up like a Christmas tree, and there were a number of armed special agents hovering around the massive aircraft at all times. A number of military jeeps and regular soldiers were also standing guard duty by the President's aircraft.

The special agents looked like they were just daring anyone to try and come anywhere near the sequestered Presidential aircraft. Lieutenant Walker could see a few civilian workers still working on the jetliner which was slightly damaged during the terrorist attack and attempted assassination on the President of the United States while he was boarding the aircraft when the attempted assassination occurred. Sergeant Ramirez looked at her lover and soldier, and she noticed that he was deep in thought for the moment and she offered in hopes of breakup his trance and get him in a much better mood to be with.

"A penny for your thoughts Bobby?" Ramirez asked, and smiled at her worried soldier.

"Huh? Whatdaya say?" Walker said, as if he was just caught doing something wrong.

"You seemed to be a million miles away from me tonight, and I wanted to talk with you Bobby. Oh look, here comes the pain in the ass Mutt and he has Blind Date with him. Now we won't be able to talk in private any longer, Robert." She complained as she put a slightly hurt look on her face, as the other two soldiers came near them.

"Why not? What can't we say we can't say in front of those two shitbirds? Besides Raz, it looks like the stinking Mutt has something else on his mind rather than talking to us, baby. Look at the crazy ass sonofabitch, he has his hand buried down the front of Blind Date's shirt, he's working over her tits with both hands." He bitched as he shook his head at the two.

The Mutt and Blind Date walked up to the new Captain and Ramirez. The Mutt never removed his hand from Blind Date's blouse as he said. "Hey Walker, what the hell gives wit ya man? You two people seem so fricking serious here, buddy. We came over to see if we could cheer you two birds up any, man."

"Arr... I was just thinking that's all. Man, I can't take a fricking moment for myself, without causing a stinking stir with the rest of you jerks. Raz and I were talking and I'm thinking about leaving the service when Raz has the baby, man. That way I can help her raise the kid and we can start living our lives together like most normal people do. I don't think she's gonna stay in the service when the baby comes, and I know it'd drive her crazy if I stayed in, friend. I think I'm..."

"Come the fuck on and cut the shit out will ya man. You two birds know neither of you will ever leave the damn service, man. Walker, the only way either of you two birds will leave the stinking Unit, is tits and feet up, or you're too friggin old to lift a weapon and defend yourselves properly any longer, buddy. Besides man, you can't leave the Unit now, not after talking me into sticking in after Barb was killed in the damn Sandstorm Operation, Homes. Walker, the Unit will fall apart at the fricking seams if you dump out on us, man. Do you know how many uther guys will check out if you bailout first on the rest of us, pal? Hell man, I'd even get the hell out..."

"So would I, Lieutenant Walker." Blind Date added to the Mutt's words.

The Mutt waved his arm at the rest of the troops at the barracks then told Walker. "Hell man, I bet more than half them slugs back there would dump outta the service with your ass, man."

Walker looked to where the Mutt, (Lieutenant Frank Hall) was pointing and saw many of the other soldiers were staring at them and he replied. "Yeah Mutt, I see what you mean buddy." He looked at Ramirez and she offered. "I don't know where you're going, but I'm not going to leave the service after the baby comes. I don't see how I could possibly live with myself without that pack of soldiers being part of our lives, Bobby. If we leave the service, I'd feel like we're abandoning them, and I'm certain they'll feel the same way about it, Walker."

"Now is not the time to enter this kinda fricking conversation, baby. From the looks of it, we might be home for quite a while anyhow, and we'll have plenty of time to discuss this crap later on Raz. Right now baby, I want to enjoy the night with you. It's turning into a great night for us, so let's have some fun for ourselves while we're stuck here in Washington. I love being on a stinking airbase in the middle of the night, there are so many damn lights, and I love watching the aircraft taking off on afterburner. What the hell are you two turds gonna do tonight man? I think I might want to be left alone with my lady for a little while. After all, I hadn't seen her for the duration of the last mission in sand land, and I want to get to know her again." Walker looked at his love of life in the eyes and then smiled at her.

"Hey Walker, don't go worrying about us any man. We're out here looking for some neat private little place to be alone as well, Homes. I need me some trim for myself man." The Mutt drew Blind Dates right breast out of her blouse, and then he kissed her nipple.

"Ohooooo Mutt baby, you do that so well. You're turning me on once again mista."

"C'mon Blind Date, a stinking fart in the damn wind will turn you on, little sister." Walker fired back at the young and very beautiful French female fighter.

"You two guys wanna join us for some great fun and games? We can have a four way real easy like you know man?" the Mutt asked Walker.

"Like hell man, we're gonna have enough trouble finding a place for the two of us to be alone on this damn base. Let alone finding a place large enough for the four of us to go at it in."

"What's that Bobby?" Ramirez asked as she pointed to a stream of light entering the base.

"I think it's the vehicles that's gonna take the rest of the guys back to Camp Lejeune, honey. Looks like we might be forced to delay our little tête-à-tête till after the rest of the grunts are on their way back to our home base, baby." He grumbled at his lover.

"I knew it was too good to be true we were going to spend some private time together, Bobby. I guess we better get back to the barracks, the other soldiers will never forgive us if we don't see all them off while they leave the base and the rest of us, Bobby." The four soldiers walked back to the group in silence, just as Colonel Leadbetter came charging out of his barracks, and he began bellowing at the elite troops as they watched the convoy of vehicles coming at them.

"Get inside them damn vehicles and get the hell off this god damn Airforce Base you slugs. Move it people, saddle up, we can't keep these people waiting all fucking day for your asses to get a damn move on it for them. They have their own orders to follow and the way you people are moving arou8nd here, you're holding them up from completing their orders."

Walker, the Mutt, Ramirez and Blind Date walked up to the Colonel and stood by his side. Then the four soldiers watched as the other troops quickly climbed on board the waiting military buses. The soldiers started to filter onto the buses, cursing all the way.

"I'll be damn glad when I finally get my troops back to Camp Lejeune where they belong, and they won't be so easily getting in any trouble on this other base, dammit." The concerned Colonel remarked as he kept his eyes on the soldiers filing on the buses.

"I feel ya there Colonel Leadbetter Sir, I won't rest easy until the bulk of our people are heading back to our home base, sir." Walker replied proudly to the Marine Officer.

When the last of the soldiers got on the buses, the jokes began with one soldier dropping his pants, and he mooned the three military officers, and two female soldiers standing outside the bus. The Colonel saw this and bitched at his new Captain. "These fucking people will never learn anything no matter how much time we waste on trying to train the assholes, Walker."

Both Bouncer, (Sergeant Carol Burnheart), and Overnight, (Sergeant Sarah Crowley), worked their way over to two side windows of the bus, and they whipped opened the front of their blouses and they stuck their ample breasts up against the bus windows, flattening them out against the cold glass, and making their breasts look even larger than they were. The girls were calling Colonel Leadbetter's name out, and making all sorts of terrible noises and crude hand movements at him. This caused many of the other soldiers packed on the bus to start to clap and laugh at the two girls and the officers outside the bus glaring at them. Now, it was a challenge for the soldiers on the buses to insult the troops outside the buses.

"Jesus H. Christ, will you look at those two fucking nuts of yours Walker. God dammit man, I wish to hell and back again that one day you'd try and get some kind of damn control over these flaming assholes of yours, buster. One of these days, they're going to do this crap in front of some hot shot brass man, and he's going to lower the fucking boom on all these war wacky wingnuts, mister." The Colonel complained as he backed off and enjoyed the show the female soldiers were putting on, but it did not stop there either. Other soldiers joined the two women at the windows, and all of them were showing off different parts of their bodies. It did not take long for the rest of the soldiers on the other buses to get caught up in the all fun and games, and they started to do the same thing at the officers outside.

Some of the female air persons of the airbase saw what was going on the buses, and they started to gather around them and make their own calls back at the fooling around soldiers on the buses. Everyone was starting to get caught up in the great mood.

"There you go Colonel Leadbetter Sir. It doesn't look like they're upsetting the female population of the airbase in the least, sir." Walker smiled at the still grinning Colonel.

"Yeah stupid, but those two bitches aren't brass, Mr. Wiseass. All I need is for some fucking Colonel or General to come walking along, and catch these flaming assholes of yours doing this crap, and the lot of them will probably end up getting shot, or maybe keeping our Iraqi prisoner company in the damn Brig. Naw, bullshit on that crap Walker, if any of these damn soldiers are arrested and brought over to that Brig then I don't give al-Adwani a long time to remain alive, if they ever get their mitts on his fricking ass, Walker." The Marine Colonel laughed as he continued to watch the soldiers goofing around on the buses.

Finally, the first buses were full with soldiers enjoying themselves on the buses, and they slowly pulled away from the side of the curb. This sudden movement seemed like it calmed the specialized soldiers down a bit. And the fun of flashing the officers quickly ended, and now the soldier's attention went to their drivers of the buses, and each of the special soldiers started to egg the drive of their bus to take the lead, and beat the other buses back to Camp Lejeune.

"Say Colonel Leadbetter, since you're remaining here with us sir, who the fuck's going to be in charge of these soldiers when they get down to Lejeune, sir? Someone has to keep an eye on them or they might take the damn base apart on us, sir." Walker asked the Colonel.

"What the hell do you think I am around here, stupid or something mister? I might have been born at night, but I assure you Lieutenant Walker, it wasn't last night sir. While we were in flight, I ordered Colonel Joseph Salsiccia to be cut away from this pack of rabble of yours, and I had him flown back to Lejeune yesterday, mister. He had nearly a full day to prepare the base and barracks for the arrival of these so called specialized troops of yours, Walker. So the troops are well covered when they get back to the main base, sir."

"That was a good call on your part, Colonel Leadbetter Sir. I'd sure hate like hell to have some strange Officer trying to get control of those fucking guys, until we got back to base, sir. If that happened there might not be much of a base we could return to sir."

"You got that right Walker." The Colonel said as the last bus started up and pulled away.

TWENTY TWO, FIFTY THREE HUNDRED HOURS. JOINT ANDREWS AIR FORCE BASE

By the time the other soldiers left Andrews it was late, but Walker did not want to go in the barracks quite yet. He was dying to spend some private time with his lady. He led Ramirez towards the main landing strip of the massive airbase again. There was a small military leer jet building up power for takeoff, the flames spewing from the twin engines feet behind the aircraft. In the dark it was romantic to see the flames mixing with the landing lights. Ramirez wiggled her body under Walker's powerful shoulder as she watched the plane takeoff in the dark sky. A closed in humvee pulled up to the two soldiers, and two MPs got out and challenged

Walker and Ramirez. After checking their IDs, the MPs told the two to leave the landing area immediately.

The two young specialized soldiers walked away because he was searching for a secluded area to be alone with Ramirez. As they headed back to the barracks, he noticed an area that must have been setup for when soldiers stationed on the base, went to eat outside. There were three large thick concrete tables and six long cement benches, along with a small stand of trees and some thick bushes. Walker led her over to the benches and she sat on the table. He stepped between her legs and started to kiss her, first on the lips and then on the neck as he suddenly pulled her blouse off her shoulders and kissed her there.

Her motor was instantly running on full speed, and she opened her blouse and offered her breast to his searching mouth. He drew her nipple in his mouth and sucked, nibbled, and licked it, causing a moan to escape her lips. Her hand searched for his belt buckle, finding it she quickly undid it, and then she opened his pants and forced them down around his ankles with her feet. He picked up her passion and removed her blouse and was pawing at her breasts. She had to push him a little away from her, and then she turned him around and made him sit on the table as she wiggled out of her pants. She pushed him on the powerful shoulders with her hands, forcing him to actually lie down on the hard table.

She leaned over him and kissed his neck and then his chest, all the while she slowly lowered herself down his body until she ended up resting between his legs. First, she caught his rock hard member between her breasts, and then she began to slide it between her breasts for a few seconds. When she had his full interest, she slid further down his body until his member brushed the side of her cheek. She licked it, and then she ran her tongue over the very tip of it, and then she drew it in her mouth and started working over it with her mouth.

With a passion she did not know existed in her body, she quickly worked over his shaft with her mouth. She was enjoying bringing her lover such pleasure, but she caught herself when she felt him grab her hair with both hands, and he started trying to control her actions. He always did this when he wanted her to finish him off with her mouth. Instantly, she pulled off him and complained at her soldier. "Oh no you don't mister I'm looking to make love to you, not just giving you some head, Robert." She smiled at her lover and he released his hold on her.

She placed her knees on the table on each side of his body and inched her way up his strong body until she straddled his face. He understood she wanted him to return the favor and he started to lick what she was offering him. In no time, he had her moaning and wiggling her hips all over his face. While she was doing this, she reached behind her and played with him with her hand. She could feel him getting harder in her slight grasp. When she could not take it any longer, she moved off his face and slid down his body a second time, until she was in the right position to mount him. Then she guided him in her and began to ride him. Slowly at first, but getting caught up in her passions she increased her speed in which she used on him. She enjoyed making love to her man, it made her feel so close and loved by him, and she needed that.

The MPs stopped by Colonel Leadbetter's office in the barracks, and one of them informed him he had two of his soldiers roaming around the base, and they wanted him to call the two troopers in before they mistakenly walked into a restricted area of the base, and they got themselves in some serious trouble for the mistake. The MPs informed the Marine Colonel he was still responsible for his troops on base, and if they came across the soldiers again out of the barracks, they were going to be forced to bring them in, and he would have to get them released.

"Yeah, yeah right, I know what my fucking responsibilities are around here for crap sake without you having to repeat them to me like I'm some kind of damn asshole, buster. Where the fuck did you say you saw these two asses heading for, Sergeant?" the upset Colonel growled at the MP Sergeant as he glared at the younger soldier.

"Colonel Leadbetter Sir, the last time we saw the two troopers, they walking around out there, and it seemed like they might be heading for the small park like area about seventy five yards to the right side of your barracks, Colonel."

"Fine, fine, I'll get the pains in the fucking asses and order them back to their damn barracks. This bullshit bugs the living shit out of my ass though. We ask these soldiers to lay their lives on the line for us. But yet while they're on this here military base, they're restricted to barracks like we don't trust the damn soldiers. It makes one believe he's not really appreciated by the lousy motherfuckers he's out there protecting, dammit." Colonel Leadbetter snarled at the two MPs as he began to search for his cover in the office. The hat was sitting on a chair right behind him. Captain Wilson, who was sharing the makeshift officer with the other officer, asked him if he wanted company, but the Colonel replied. "No thanks Captain, there is no telling what these two asses might be up to out there alone, sir. I don't want anyone else with me, in case they're breaking some regs as usual, and they're screwing their damn brains out in the dark, sir."

The MPs left the barracks as Colonel Leadbetter walked out of the building, and he slammed his cover on his head. He immediately noticed the small dark picnic area the MPs told him about from the steps of the barracks, and he headed right for it at a rapid pace.

Ramirez was so into making love to her soldier that she would not have realized if the entire world was standing next to her, watching them while she was making love to Walker.

The upset Marine Colonel made enough noise to wake the dead as he approached the dark break area. He wanted to warn the two soldiers first, in case they were doing what he was certain they were up to in the darkness. But neither of the young lovers paid any attention to the slight commotion he was making, and the Colonel walked up to the two of them as they continued making love to each other on the concrete table.

"Jesus H. Christ, as I live and breathe, I knew you two fricking animals in heat were taking care of business out here in the damn dark." Colonel Leadbetter complained as he walked up to the two and then he glared at them in the darkness.

"Not, now, Colonel!" Ramirez grumbled between panting and moans, and not upsetting her rhythm as she expertly rode Walker like he was a stud horse under her.

"What the fuck do you two shitbirds expect me to do, dammit? Stand here like an asshole and watch you two animals going at it like dogs in heat, dammit. I got a mind to get me a damn fire extinguisher and turn the damn thing on you two to try and cool you two pigs down a little."

"I, don't, care, if, you, join, in, Colonel. I, am, not, going, to, stop, until, I finish, making, love, to, my, soldier, sir." Ramirez replied between her heavy breathing and pants.

"I can't believe the two of you jaybirds in the least. I should call the rest of the troops in the barracks out and let them enjoy the damn show you two animals are putting on, Ramirez."

"I, don't, care, what, you, do, Colonel. I, will, only stop, when, I, am, finished, making, love, to, Walker, sir. Not, before sir." She said this time with her chin drilled in her chest as she straightened up while still sitting on top of Walker. Suddenly, her entire body shivered and shook and she let out her breath in a rush and moaned. "Ooooooo." As she joined Walker as they came together. Then she collapsed on his chest and hugged him to her.

"Good God and miracles, I can't believe you two just popped off in front of me during this conjugal visit of yours, Sergeant. Have you no shame about yourself Ramirez?"

She swung her leg off Walker's lap, and then she leaned against the side of the concrete table, naked as the day she was born and proud of it as she rested her hands on the table behind her, and then she stared at the Colonel before replying. "Look Colonel Leadbetter, I'm pregnant, and right this minute I'm suffering from a shitload of PMS, and I'm not in a very good mood either I warn you, sir. Yes, I just made love to my soldier and if you have a bitch about it, sir. I suggest you write it down on a slip of paper, placed it in an envelope and mail it to who gives a shit, sir.

"For three days now, I didn't know if I'd ever see Bobby alive again in my life Colonel, and then I had to wait three more days before I could find a place to be alone with him for a little while, sir. And, what do I find when I finally get him alone, dammit. My god damn nosy ass Commanding Officer standing before me watching us make love to each other, and then having the balls to bitch at me because we gave him the show of his life, sir. If you didn't like what you were looking at, you could have always just walked away from us, and left us alone until we finished making love to each other, sir. But evidently you must have like what you were watching, so don't bug my ass about it will you please, Colonel Leadbetter Sir."

"It was a damn good thing you added the 'sir' at the end of your bitch at my ass, Sergeant Ramirez. Or I might have gotten angry with you, girl. Look Ramirez, I know what you went through on this last mission girl, and how disappointed you were with not going along on the damn operation with the rest of the soldiers from our Unit. But them are the fucking breaks, little sister. If you didn't do what you were just doing then you wouldn't have been fucking pregnant in the first place, and you would've been allowed to go along on the mission. So can the damn complaint at my ass, girl. Dammit it to hell, I can't believe I'm about to say what I'm going to say to you two shitbirds, Sergeant. Sergeant Ramirez, can you put your clothes on please?"

"Why? Whatsumatter now with the fearsome Commanding Officer Colonel Bruce Leadbetter, all of the sudden you don't like looking at my tits, mister?" She said as she moved her chest and made her breasts sway slightly to the motion she was doing. Then she cupped her breasts in her hands and pushed them out towards the staring Colonel's face, and then she smiled as she stared back at her commander.

"No, it's not that at all, Sergeant Ramirez. But I'm so fricking horny myself I just might jump your bones myself, girl. If you continue to stand in front of my ass like you're doing, and keep sticking your damn tits in my face like that, pretty lady." The smirking Colonel mumbled as he continued to stare at Ramirez's breasts, and then he reached out and pinched her nipple lightly.

"I'm terribly sorry for you Colonel Leadbetter, but you had your chance to play with me before, sir. I told you to join in on the fun and games while I was making love to Bobby, sir. Now you can't play with me because you might start my motor running again sir, and I don't think Walker will be up for the job for a second go round any time soon, sir." She said as she glanced at Walker's soft member, and then she smiled at the Colonel and added to her gripe. "You know something Colonel Leadbetter Sir? That was the first time you ever touched me since I first joined this special operations Unit, sir."

"It's been quite the chore to keep my hands off your body, Sergeant. Get dressed please, we have to get the hell out of the area before the damn MPs come back, and they bust all three of us for being out of the damn barracks without an escort. Dammit Ramirez, you have some nice tits there girl." The Colonel said as he watched her dress.

Walker was dressed first and he moved over to the Colonel's side and said. "She's a beaut."

"You got that right Walker. Let me ask you a question mister? It didn't bother you at all that I was watching you make love to your girl, Captain Walker?"

"Not in the least Colonel. Many times there's always someone watching us doing it, sir." Lieutenant Walker grinned at the other officer mostly because he addressed him as Captain, and that rate increase would not take place until the President pinned the rate on his collar himself.

"And it didn't bother you she told me to join in on the fun and games, Walker?"

"No sir, it was your loss for you not jumping on her bones when you had the stinking chance to do so, Colonel. She's more than enough to have screwed the crap outta the both of us at the same damn time, and want some more after we were done out by her, sir." He retorted, again with a smile aimed at the Marine Colonel.

"Arr... you two kids are going to send me right over the motherfucking falls yet, mister. You two shitbirds better get back to the damn barracks before you guys get yourselves in some serious trouble on the damn Airbase, Walker. Your presence out here is causing the base security people some real fits I tell ya, Walker." The Colonel warned the new Captain.

"I noticed it, the damn MPs were on our asses even before we knew where the hell we were going on the stinking base sir, or what we were gonna do when we finally got there, sir. You'd think they'd cut us some stinking slack not flack for once in our damn lives, sir. We just did one helluva mission for these slobs, and yet they wanna treat us like the fricking criminals in this act when we returned to the civilized world, sir. That's bullshit and bad manners if you ask me Colonel." Walker bitched at his commanding officer.

"Don't I know it as the damn truth Captain? I just pitched the same exact bitch at the MPs of this base when they came in my barracks, and complained about you and Ramirez was out on the field looking for some damn trouble, Walker. They threatened to arrest you asses for the minor infraction you two birds committed out there on the lousy tarmac, mister." The Colonel growled at the soldiers as he watched Ramirez finish getting dressed in front of them.

"One of these days the brass is gonna get it straight for once in their worthless lives, Colonel. They're gonna have to finally realize they're gonna hafta start trusting us here in the States, as they do out in the fucking field, Colonel Leadbetter Sir. The brass hats let up play with their million dollar toys on any mission they send us out on, but then they treat us like we don't know enough to blow our own damn noses for ourselves when we're back here in the States, sir. I really hate the way we get treated when we're back in the States by our Commanders, Colonel." Walker grumbled as he lit up a cigarette, and then he offered one from his pack to the Colonel.

"Walker, you know as well as I do because of the way we have to fight on any mission they send us out on, has the top dogs scared shitless of us and our capabilities. So I can't blame them for keeping a close eye on us while we're stateside, my lover." Ramirez said as she held her shirt in her hands and stood topless as she complained at Walker and the Colonel.

"Yeah Raz, but I still don't like the death order hanging over our stinking heads if we get a little out of line here in the States, girl." The Colonel snapped right back at her as he continued to take in the lovely view of her breasts she was offering him.

"Death order, Colonel Leadbetter Sir? I don't know what you're talking about, death order Colonel?" She asked her commanding officer as she struggled in her shirt, and when she was finished dressing she stared at the Colonel while waiting for his reply.

"Never mind the last remark Ramirez you don't need to know what it means at this time. You kids have enough shit to worry about as it is, without my adding any more stress on you guy's backs for Pete's sake." The Colonel replied to the female Sergeant.

"The hell with that line of bullshit Colonel Leadbetter, I should know about everything that pertains to my possible death while I'm here in the States, or anywhere else on the face of the earth for that matter, sir. You made a statement and I want to know what you meant by it sir." She complained at the good looking Marine Colonel, as she stared at him dead in the eyes again.

"The hell you say to my ass Sergeant, you only need to know what the fuck I tell you, and nothing more than that is all I owe you little sister. So let's get back to the damn barracks before I give you two birds something else to really worry about around here, Sergeant. We have to start to prepare for the hot shot supper with the President in a few days, girl."

CHAPTER SEVEN

It was showing the first signs of the sun preparing for its night sleep by the time the requested soldiers arrived on the grounds of the White House. They were scheduled to be there by seven p.m., and Colonel Bruce Leadbetter had the soldiers arrive half an hour early. The special operation soldiers were greeted by General John White, the Chairman of the Joint Chiefs of Staff, and he was with CIA Director John Raincloud, and one of the President's aides from the

White House. The elite soldiers looked great, and were dressed in their finest class A uniforms.

As the soldiers got off the buses, they immediately setup in formation at attention. General John White waited until the soldiers were in good formation, and he then walked up to them and saluted the soldiers and addressed them before he allowed the soldiers to enter the White House building. "It's good to see you people again, and I must say you soldiers look great. You're doing me justice before the Big Man. But I want to take a few minutes to address you people first. I have to warn you because I know how you people act when any of you are around Politicians and the likes. I saw a few of you people in action and it wasn't a very pretty site I tell you."

The General cast a harsh look right at Walker and Ramirez, and then he continued with his warning to the elite troops. "You people are going to share a meal with the President of the United States, along with the Vice President and a number of other characters from his Cabinet, Senate and Congress. So I'm expecting each of you soldiers to be on your very best behavior in there. I don't want any cursing and I want you people to watch how you eat, your manners I'm talking about here. I don't want you volunteering up any unasked for information to anyone in there about this damn operation, or anything else concerning us or our operations. Just answer the damn questions put directly to you as simply and as quickly as you possibly can.

"I then want you people to clam up tighter than Kelsey's damn ass. I don't want any of you to engage anyone in there in idle conversations or bullshit of any kind. The more you people keep your mouths zipped tight, the less likely you asses might get yourselves in some trouble in there. When you're dismissed from the supper, I want you people to get up and leave the building as quickly and as politely as you can. Once outside the building, get back on the buses and get back to base. Once this supper's over with, I'll have you transferred down to Lejeune, and once there you'll all be sent on extended leaves. Do I make myself perfectly clear on my fucking wants and desires during this damn supper with you people in there?" The General placed his hands on his hips, and then he waited for the soldiers to reply to his threats as he glared at them.

A chorus of "Yes sir," was repeated by the gathered soldiers to the General, as a good number of the soldiers were grinning at the powerful Chairman.

"I can't hear you god damn people. Speak out like you got a fucking pair!" The General suddenly roared at the soldiers, as he glared at them this time angrier.

"Yes sir!" Was roared back at the General.

"That's much better. Okay, this young man standing to my left, is the White House Presidential Aide, and his name is Mr. Peter Waters, and he's to be addressed as such and treated with the greatest of respect from you young flaming assholes, once you people are inside the building at all times. Remember his name, Mr., and I repeat for you mentally handicapped assholes here. It's Mr. Waters Sir to you people and nothing less or else will be accepted. He'll be your personal escort while you're inside the White House. If you people need something, want something, have to go to the head or anything else like that, you'll politely get his attention and then you will tell him what you need or want. And, you'll ask him politely for it.

"Anyone I see screwing up in there will answer to me when this damn supper thing is over with. No one moves in there without Mr. Waters by their side assisting them. I have Marine guards stationed inside the building, and they have orders to shoot anyone of you people they see roaming around the place without Mr. Waters by your side, and ask questions afterwards."

The elite group of soldiers let out a nervous laugh over the General's last threat as they waited for the officer to finish addressing them.

"Okay troops, you had your fun with my ass, and you think I'd never have any of you shot for disobeying my orders. You keep thinking that mistake, and when I bury your ass for screwing up in there. You'll know I wasn't fooling around with that threat against you people in the least. All joking aside, you people are about to be honored like very few other soldiers have been honored before. It's not every day the President of the United States wants to break bread with common grunts of our chosen field of operations. So take it for what it's worth to you, an honor, and react accordingly to that honor. Huh, what was that mister?" The General mumbled as he turned to the young White House Aide, and then listened to what he had to say for a second.

The General turned his attention back to his troops and announced in a harsh tone. "That's our cue. The President's in the dining room and he and his people are waiting for us to come in now. Remember what I just told you people. I want you on your absolute best behavior in there. Colonel Leadbetter, you'll take command of your troops, sir. When we enter the building, I'll introduce each soldier to the President, and then they'll take their chairs and keep their mouths shut tight Colonel, or it's your hide I'll take out their mistakes on, sir. Shall we get on with it?"

General White entered the White House, followed by CIA Director John Raincloud, and they entered the room with the President first. They both nodded politely to the seated President, and they remained standing at attention until advised otherwise. As each soldier came in the dining room, the Chairman of the Joint Chiefs of Staff introduced the soldiers to the President and others in the room. The Vice President made certain she was sitting where Sergeant Dorothy Ramirez and Lieutenant Robert Walker were scheduled to be seated, and throughout the meal, she spoke mostly to these soldiers. The Vice President began by offering to Sergeant Ramirez.

"Sergeant Ramirez, I can't tell you how pleased I am to see you again. You see young lady I told you one way or the other I was going to get you to visit me over here at the White House. By the way Sergeant, I understand you're with child? When is he due to arrive?"

"Yes Ma'am, I'm in my forth month Ma'am." She announced proudly.

"Congratulations Sergeant Ramirez, and how is your proud soldier over there taking the news?" The concerned Vice President asked her.

She looked at Walker and shot him a smile that would have melted his heart, as she replied to the Vice President. "I believe he's thrilled to death over the news, Ma'am."

"That's good to hear Sergeant. I want to know your exact due date, and when you're going to have a baby shower, young lady. I warn you Sergeant don't be too surprised if I show up at the shower on you. You're still living on the Island of Marathon in the Florida Keys I take it, Sergeant Ramirez?" the Vice President asked the female soldier.

"Yes Ma'am and it'd be an outstanding pleasure to have you visit me down in the Keys, Ma'am. I'll truly be looking forward to it if you can visit us there, Ma'am." She was following orders to the letter about watching her conversation, and keeping it short and right to the point.

Mary Hirshfield gave Walker a quick glance, and then she leaned a little closer to Ramirez and whispered so only she could hear her words. "How is your livewire doing? Has he learned to calm down a bit, or is he still looking to take a chunk out of anyone he speaks with, Sergeant?"

She smiled at the Vice President who was still smarting from the wound she had received from the assassination attempt against the President's life as she said. "No Ma'am, you know how Walker is Ma'am. He's always looking for any bit of trouble he can find anywhere, Ma'am."

"Yes I certainly remember how your young soldier is, Sergeant Ramirez. Although I have only had to deal with him on the one occasion, I thank God he and yourself were there when I needed you the most, young lady. I truly hope that you two and your new child will be very happy together for the rest of your lives, Sergeant Ramirez."

"Please Ma'am you can call me Dorothy if you'd like Ma'am. I'd really like it Ma'am."

"Yes, yes of course, I remember now. Yes, and I'll make a deal with you young lady, I'll call you Dorothy, but only if you call me Mary like we agreed before, Sergeant. After all we have been through together I believe we both have earned the right to be a little friendlier with each other whenever we're speaking together like this, Dorothy." The Vice President said as she suddenly reached up and rubbed the side of her neck.

"Yes Mary, oh, by the way, I never asked you how you're healing Ma'am. I see you're suffering some pain as we speak, Ma'am. I can't tell you how angry Robert and I were when we first heard you were wounded in the attempted assassination against the President, Ma'am. Walker was in a rage and fit to be tied for a week, and he wanted to rip Washington apart looking for the terrorist who dared to harm you, Mary." She offered.

"Oh, I guess you can say I'm doing as well as can be expected, young lady. My throat still hurts me quite a bit, and the wound to my neck is still opened and it's messing up my speech a little, and I still have the drain in my neck. But other than that I'm doing fine, and I thank you for asking. And yes Dorothy, I can only imagine how you and Robert must have felt about that incident. I mean, after seeing you two in action and how you protected my life in the past. I'm pleased you were able to control Robert though, Sergeant. I still can't believe you soldiers were able to locate and take prisoner this remaining terrorist. I want to tell you one more thing while we're speaking together Dorothy, as soon as this meal is over, I plan to..."

The conversation was brought to a quick end when the President rose and took a glass of wine and lightly tapped it with his spoon. Then the American Leader looked at everyone seated at the table until they all quieted down.

"Thank you ladies and gentlemen for your attention I wanted to let you know why we're all gathered here tonight. I, and my Vice President, Mary Hirshfield, wanted to thank you specialized soldiers who under my direct orders had entered the nation of Iraq to take the Arab terrorist, Colonel Abdulaziz Majd al-Adwani prisoner, and bring him back to the United States. So he could stand trial, and receive his just fate at the hands of our judicial system. I'm extremely pleased that you elite group of soldiers were able to complete your mission as ordered. General John White, would you please stand sir."

General White rose, he was taken off guard because he was unaware the President was going to call on him like this for whatever reason there was in his mind.

"General John White, as the current Chairman of the Joint Chiefs of Staff, I commend you on the outstanding training program you have instituted for your fine young troops visiting here tonight, sir. Without your wise guidance for this mission, I'm quite certain it would've never worked out as well as it had for us and your troops, sir. I also want to thank Director John Raincloud for his fine ability to locate, and then keep this terrorist under constant surveillance until our soldiers were able to capture him. General White, you may sit down sir. And, now for the soldiers who had successfully carried out their orders to the letter. To each of you, I say this.

"You young warriors have done an outstanding job for country and for me as your Commander in Chief and for my Vice President. And, for this I'll be forever beholding to you fine soldiers sitting at this table with me and my staff. Your Mothers and Fathers must be very proud of the job they have done bringing you into this world. We should not forget as we move forward that we have suffered the loss of one fine man, Normal Griffin, and his death though tragic as it was, is one of the motivators for getting our problems correct. As the leader of the most powerful nation in the world, the treasures we have are the sons and daughters, mothers and fathers, nieces and nephews of the American populace. There's a covenant and a special trust: families provide their treasures to us in the form of our military troops, and our job is to defend the homeland here in the United States, and our assets aboard with these treasures loaned to us for this purpose.

"We owe it to these families to make certain we take the proper care of these outstanding treasures entrusted to our hands. I thank every one of you soldiers for your diligence to duty and your country. Now that part of this meal and meeting is over with, I want to tell you that I'm not done honoring you soldiers quite yet. I have some special awards to give you all." The President waved his hand and another aide instantly rushed in the room carrying a tray. He placed the tray down before the President and quickly disappeared.

"Yes, I just started honoring you young soldiers for a job well carried out. Now this is the part of my job I truly enjoy the most. For your duty to the United States and my Administration, each of you soldiers has earned the Silver Star for Gallantry in Action. And believe me, you troops have earned this medal, and I'm extremely proud to have the privilege to bestow this great award on you young soldiers. As I call out your name, please come up and I'll pin the medal next to the rest I see you all wearing today."

After the medals were given out, a second aide rushed in without being given a signal and he placed a small box before the President, and then he quickly disappeared.

President Albert Cole picked up the box and fingered it in both hands as he went in thought for a brief moment. Then he began scanning the faces until he locked eyes with Lieutenant Robert Walker. The President gave him a slight nod and then announced. "You know, with the many duties that come with the office of the President of the United States. None of them can possibly compare with the sheer delight I get out of honoring the fine soldiers of our great country. But on this one special occasion, I'm going to bow out and allow my Vice President the honor of giving this next tribute to one of your outstanding soldiers, General

White Sir. Please excuse me while my Vice President takes over for me at this time, sir."

All eyes went over to the Vice President who looked stunned that the President was addressing her. She was not prepared for this honor.

"Mary Hirshfield, will you come up here please." The President waited until she rose and walked over to him. When she was standing by his side, the President offered her the box and said. "I'm sorry for putting you on the spot like this, but I believe as sure as the soldiers earned their medals. You have earned the right to hand this one out yourself. What with everything you went through over the past year, just because you were picked to be my Vice President, young lady. Here you go Mary, please enjoy the honor."

Ms. Mary Hirshfield had to wipe at a tear that had escaped the corner of her eye as she looked at the blue box locked so tightly in her hand. She knew what it was and was deeply honored to be picked to accolade the soldier who saved her life at the mess that happened in the Trump International Hotel and Tower in New York City months ago. She smiled bravely as she looked at Lieutenant Robert Walker, and then she called out in a commanding voice to him, even though it hurt her so to talk that way. "Lieutenant Robert Walker, front and center please, soldier."

Lieutenant Walker got out of his chair and he walked around Sergeant Ramirez as he headed for the Vice President. When he was standing before her, she opened the small box and proudly announced to the young soldier. "Lieutenant Robert Walker of the United States Marine Corps sir, you have no idea what a great pleasure and honor it is for me to give you the rank of Captain in the Marine Corps you so proudly serve, sir." Vice President Mary Hirshfield removed the gold insignia that signified Captain, and she proudly pinned the golden Eagle on the collar of Walker's uniform after she removed the two bars that branded him Lieutenant, and then she went on with her words aimed at the new Captain. "Captain Robert Walker, will you please allow me the honor of keeping your Lieutenant Bars, sir?"

"By all means, please do Ma'am." Captain Walker replied kindly, making General White beam with pride over the way his soldier acted before the Vice President of America.

Suddenly, Mary Hirshfield leaned a little closer to Walker, and she whispered in his ear so only he could hear what she was saying. "Captain Robert Walker, I want to thank you again for saving my life, sir. I wish you nothing but the very best in your fine young life, sir."

Walker nodded at her there was no need for any words from him.

All the soldiers at the table clapped for Walker as he marched back to his chair, everyone though the medals were given out and the party was about to end.

But President Cole had different ideas about that thought. He removed another box from his breast pocket and then called out his military officer again. General John White will you please step forward again sir." The President waited for the Chairman to walk up to him.

"General John White, when you were first offered to me as the replacement for General William Weidenbacher as the new Chairman of the Joint Chiefs of Staff after his sudden death, sir. I'm afraid I didn't like the idea very much sir. But you have proved to me that you're the right man for this most trying job sir, and Director Raincloud was quite correct to offer you up for the job as well, General White. Throughout the history of the United

States, there has been but a very few Generals who made it to the rank of a Five Star General, sir. Well sir, I'm proud to announce that you have just joined the ranks of those few well honored Five Star General's, General White. I'm deeply honored to be one of those favored President who had the honor to raise his General up to the Five Star Rank, sir."

General White was stunned to his soul because he never dreamed he was going to receive the fifth star for what his specialized soldiers had accomplished in Iraq. The beaming military officer took the five star bar and looked at the rack of five stars, he was thrilled to death over his rate increase. Now, he made it as far as he could possibly go in the military service. His wife seated by him was crying, and so were Sergeant Ramirez, and the few other female soldiers at the table. Everyone rose and clapped for the General.

"Well General White Sir? What do you have to say for yourself now, sir?" the President asked as he stared him in the eyes.

"With all due respect Mr. President, I don't know what to say but thank you sir." The Chairman was fighting tears himself, he was that honored by the President's gesture, and he knew it was given to him because of his elite troops actions on the mission.

"Well General White, I think that says it good enough sir. This is my little way of thanking you for a job well done, sir." The President offered proudly to his soldier.

With the last rate increase given out to the soldiers, the party started to break up. But Vice President Hirshfield was not going to allow Ramirez and Walker get away from her that easily on this night. She walked the two to the main doors of the White House. Where she shook hands with Walker and kissed Ramirez on her side of her cheek and then whispered. "Dorothy, I had a special reason to keep your man's Lieutenant Bars, Ma'am. Because when I come down to Marathon to your baby shower, I'm taking the bars with me, and I plan to give you a field commission to Lieutenant myself. I believe you have earned the right, young lady."

Ramirez was stunned, she never dreamed of being bounced up to the rank of Lieutenant in the Marine Corps. All she could think of doing was smile at Hirshfield.

JOINT BASE ANDREWS AIR FORCE BASE

As the specialized group of soldiers got back to Andrews Airforce Base from the dinner and awards with the President, they were all in great moods. General White trailed the two buses back to the base because he wanted to address the soldiers further before he lost them on their leaves. His staff car pulled up to the front of the buses as they parked before the barracks. He got out of the car as the soldiers quickly poured out of the buses and rapidly assembled before them in formation. The soldiers knew the new Five Star General was behind them, and it did not take a college education to realize he was not quite done with them for the night. Colonel Leadbetter stood at the front of the formation and waited for the Chairman.

General White walked over to the Marine Colonel and shook his hand and then turned to the soldiers and spoke. "Listen up I wanted to take this time to thank you people again for a job well done on this last mission. I never was so honored in all my life because of the actions and abilities of my special soldiers out in the field, like I was tonight. I'm proud of you soldiers and all the troops of the Special Forces stationed at Camp Lejeune as we speak. Since I sent them back to Camp Lejeune so those warriors can be cut free on leave from there as soon as possible, I changed my mind because of you and your actions in this latest operation."

There was a groan from the soldiers because they figure they were not going home now.

"I'll give you people that one, but it wouldn't have been necessary if you would've allowed me to finish my words to you asses first, before you interrupted me and my speech. Originally, I was going to cut the other troops free before you warriors returned to Lejeune. But then I had a fancy, and I decided to hold the other troops in check until you people can join them back at Camp Lejeune. In that way, all you soldiers can be cut free at the same time, troops."

Now, the soldiers were beaming from ear to ear as they listened attentively to the General.

"I thought that'd get the attention from you people. My further orders are as follows: Since we finished with the President and Vice President and that pretty supper they offered you people and we got all our shinny little trinkets. I come to the conclusion that I'm going to get you soldiers on your way to Camp Lejeune the first thing in the morning. And, this I promise to you troops, you'll be heading home by Friday morning, August 29th at the very latest

"That order should get everyone home by Saturday, or Sunday morning at the latest I believe. That's about all I have to say to you outstanding soldiers. You people done an outstanding job on this last mission, and I'm damn proud of all of you for accomplishing that feat for God, country, and her citizens. You' soldiers are dismissed from formation." The Chairman went to turn from the soldiers, but he was stopped when Colonel Leadbetter bellowed at his troops.

"Hold in your formation troops, the General might be done with you but I'm not quite done with you people yet. You soldiers will remain at formation until I dismiss you from duty, period. Is that understood by you criminals?"

The General looked at Colonel Leadbetter with confusion etched in his eyes, and the suddenly grinning Colonel remarked in a low voice to his commanding officer. "General White Sir, you have failed to inform me when my troops have to be ready to set out for Camp Lejeune, sir. I need this information so I know how to prepare these troops for their trip back to base, sir."

"Right, right you are Colonel Leadbetter, I was informed their transportation's scheduled to arrive at Zero, Eight, Thirty, Hours. Thank you for holding the troops back until I was able to clear that up for you sir." General White gave the Colonel a slight nod and a quick smile.

The proud Colonel Leadbetter saluted the General sharply and the Chairman responded with a salute equally as sharp and rushed off for his staff car. In a second the new Five Star General was heading off the base, and left the soldiers staring at their commanding officer.

"Okay people listen up, I need your ears paying attention to my next orders, this is important. You'll be prepared to saddle up in the damn buses at exactly Zero, Eight, Thirty Hours. The buses will be parked right in front of this damn barrack. It looks like we're heading home by bus this time around, troops. Be there or you'll be left behind then you'll be forced to find your own way back to Lejeune. And, if any of you slackers arrive after we head off on leave, any missing personnel will be marked as AWOL, and you'll then be shot on sight just for the hell of it, troops. You're dismissed so I suggest you jackrabbits start packing your crap for immediate transit!" The Colonel bellowed out at his troops and then he watched them quickly disperse from formation. He walked away shaking his head and smiling as he marveled over his trooper's abilities of carrying the war to their enemy to get any job done for their country.

ZERO EIGHT THIRTY HOURS
JOINT ANDREWS AIR FORCE BASE

At the exact time specified by the general and colonel, the buses pulled up in front of Barracks Five, and the group of elite soldiers quickly piled in them. In no time flat, the troops were on their way to their home base of Camp Lejeune. But this time, the soldiers were not as wild as the first batch was when they left Andrews for home base the other day. This group was quiet and calm on the buses, and it took nearly six hours for the buses to make it back to base. As usual, the foot soldiers on base knew before the brass that the second group of soldiers was arriving on base. They met the returning soldiers at the buses parked on the base with hoots and hollering.

The now official Captain Robert Walker's specialized troops spent the rest of the week stuck on base stacking pencils and just killing off their time by looking after any last minute details and on Friday morning, all the troops got their separation papers from the special service people. The soldiers then headed for the Paymaster of the base, and they drew their back pay, so they had plenty of cash on them to start them over in their civilian life. Then the elite soldiers left for the surrounding civilian airfields and boarded planes that would take them home at long last. Captain Walker, Sergeant Ramirez, Mother Flanagan, whose parents did not care if he was alive or not, along with No Neck who lost both his parents in a terrible car crash, were going to follow Walker and Ramirez down to their place in the Florida Keys.

Buckethead, (Sergeant Vincent Lambardo) who did not care much about his family because he and his parents went their separate ways, along with the three female Russian soldiers with Baby Tee, the Mutt and Blind Date, joined the others as they headed to the tiny Island of Marathon in the Keys. It took these soldiers nearly eight hours to get to the Keys from Camp Lejeune.

Half the group was going to stay at Walker and Ramirez's home on the Island, while the other half was going to stay at the Mutt, and now Blind Date's home. By the time the soldiers got to their homes, they were so exhausted the elite soldiers simply dropped down in beds and sleep for ten hours straight, without even waking for food or using the bathrooms.

The next and first day of their extended leave, some of the specialized soldiers drifted over to Walker's backyard, and there they settled down and stared at the peaceful Atlantic water softly lapping in the canal and against the boats moored at the homes of their owners. The soldiers were that happy to be back in the United States and breathing in the air they had worked so hard to keep free. The weather was absolutely beautiful on the Island as usual, and they relaxed and enjoyed the slow and great lifestyle that made the Island lifestyle on Marathon.

None soldiers staying at the Mutt's place showed up at Walker's home for the entire day. Most of the thoroughly exhausted soldiers rested at both homes and they took it easy for the rest of the day. But the girls from the group of elite troops were active as always, and they headed out early to see what was new on the beautiful little Island of Marathon.

The women warriors noticed plenty of small pleasure boats heading out to do some fishing on the bluest water the girls had ever seen in their entire lives. The female soldiers stayed out all day, and only returned to Walker's home when they started to get hungry, and they also wanted to check on the male soldiers they left behind, to make certain they were up and had something substantial to eat.

The men were already busy cooking up a stack of burgers and frankfurters for the rest of the people that Walker bought when he left the home for a few moments to pick up the food. The girls from the Unit were doing the shopping for other groceries they would need for later on in the day, and get some real food in for the elite soldiers on the Island to enjoy. Life was good for the soldiers of the Special Forces enjoying the Island of Marathon. They were home in the United States, and they were comfortable, and they were with the only ones who loved them as much as their parents did. The still extremely exhausted soldiers took the rest of the day off to enjoy the weather, burgers and franks, and watch the fishermen and women catching fish and enjoy the outstanding weather conditions of the Island.

Captain Walker stayed very close to Sergeant Ramirez for most of the day, when the girls returned to their home from their exploring the Island and stores. He noticed Ramirez was hanging on him since returning home from their shopping excursion, and he did not mind all the attention she was lavishing on him in the least from her. Like it or not, he had to admit that he needed her closeness as much as she needed his. He needed her reinforcing her need of him, and he returned the need just as much which pleased Ramirez to all ends.

The days quickly turned into weeks, and then weeks to months. Captain Walker was keeping a pretty close eye on the continuing talks of bringing the Iraqi terrorist Colonel to the courts to start his trail going. But as of yet, the judge was not ready to start the trial for the lone surviving terrorist they brought back to the United States. He was aware he was scheduled to be called as a witness as well as a number of other soldiers from his group who had helped capture the missing terrorist, to testify against the Iraqi Colonel turned terrorist.

It was November 5th, 1999, and the soldiers on Marathon were preparing for two events. The Millennium was fast approaching, and the birth of Walker and Ramirez's first baby. Every soldier on the Island was betting, and hoping that Ramirez would have the baby at the turn of the century. But her due day was January 15th. There was concern because Usama bin Laden's terrorist organization was making more noise of late again. Everyone involved with the security of the United States was concerned, there might be another terrorist attack aimed at the day of the great celebration. For the past few weeks, Walker was receiving many reports on the preparations New York City was carrying out, in order to protect the massive groups of partiers scheduled to show up in the center of Times Square to watch the ball drop.

He read about the military units ordered out in the streets of New York City, for some added protection of the civilians, and help guard against any possible terrorist attack aimed against them or New York City. Although he never received any orders to report back to Camp Lejeune for ready deployment in the United States. He could not help but feel it was only a matter of time before his Unit was finally reactivated, and the soldiers were pulled in for special duty in New York City during the New Year's festivities. Even though he never brought his fear out before his pregnant lady, Ramirez was reading the tea leaves, and she felt the specialized troops were also going to be put in action, and she would not be able to be with them on another mission.

Walker could not shake the ill feeling that he was going to be forced to miss the birth of his child. Some of the specialized soldiers were feeling the pressures as well, and they were starting to get a little edgy. Their moods were changing, and some of the troops were starting to snap at other soldiers near them. It got so bad one day that Walker had to actually stop the Neck and Buckethead from going at each other for real, and it was over a fish that got off Neck's line.

QULBAN-LAYYAH, IRAQ.
WEDNESDAY, NOVEMBER 17th, 1999

It was seven thirty in the morning in Iraq when the first of Colonel Hamoodi al-Qaysi's troops started to filter into the small Iraqi Village of Qulban-Layyah. The village was situated about fifteen miles away from the Kuwaiti and Iraqi borders, and another twelve miles away from the natural zone on the borders between Saudi Arabia, and Iraq. The extremely cautious Iraqi Colonel picked out this well secluded village, mainly because of its strategic location for his future needs. The village was situated close to the Kuwaiti border, and his want to use the International Airport in that nation as means to get his troops onto the Bahamas Islands, and the other tiny Island he was going to use to get his troops transferred to the United States safely.

The other reason the wise Iraqi Colonel picked this village to stage from, was mainly because it was so near to the so called natural zone. Nether Saudi Arabia or Iraq would dare send any of their troops into this extremely dangerous region of vast desert between the two nations. Mainly because the neutral zone was well noted as the main resting area for the exceedingly dangerous Nomad Tribe wanders who prowled the deep deserts of the Arab lands in the Middle East. No military personnel from either nation wanted to tangle with these fierce desert fighters. Although the Nomad Warriors were thought to be the world's greatest light attack cavalry units, they were also well known for their tenacious foot soldier fighting abilities on the soft sands of the desert.

Colonel al-Qaysi picked this small village out very wisely in the event any trailing Iraqi troops still loyal to their foolish President Saddam Hussein, caught up to them. He knew if the other troops trailed his soldiers to the village of Qulban-Layyah, he could engage the now thought to be enemy troops into a running battle, while his troops quickly made their way for the neutral zone between the two nations, and the safety that lawless area offered to his wanted troops. Not even the troops from the United States would dare step foot in the so called neutral zone set aside especially for the Nomads use and expected to live.

Although Colonel al-Qaysi was fuming because it took his troops so long to travel the distance from the village of Dawral over to Qulban-Layyah, because he and his troops were forced to go off in a different direction than heading directly for the village. This was because he had to avoid a number of well known Iraqi patrols he was certain, were out searching the vast desert for his rebel troops. The concerned Colonel thought his troops would have surely been placed in the United States by this time, and he could have started to stalk the hated American troops who had invaded his country, and they took Colonel al-Adwani their prisoner, and the enemy troops then removed him from the safety of his own country of Iraq, after they had killed General al-Zahar. He was extremely angry, because he was not able to start stalking the American judge soon to be picked to try the terrorist Iraqi Colonel in the America court system.

Colonel al-Qaysi had the rest of his troops stroll in the village at different intervals. Before he had his soldiers enter the Iraqi town, he made certain the village was not compromised by any possible trailing Iraqi troops he classified as enemy troops, by his entering the village first. The extremely cautious Colonel was surprised to see so many feared Nomad Warriors hanging around the small village. He though he was far enough away from the deep desert and natural zone, not to see any of this lowly desert trash hanging around the small village in plain sight.

The still rather upset Colonel dressed in his military uniform, went in the old abandoned military building constructed in the village. After kicking down the dilapidated and crumbling front door with his foot, he was pleased to see many weapons were still stored safely inside the old rundown armory. The building for the most part, was not touched by any of the wise local inhabitants of the village. It did not take long for Colonel al-Qaysi to figure out that the military building was left in a hurry by the Iraqi troops, once the Coalition Forces stormed across the Saudi Arabian border, when they began their attack against Iraq nearly eight years ago during the disastrous Desert Storm Operation. The Iraqi Colonel was quite certain the villagers left the building alone for fear of what he was trying to make look like was happening. The soldiers were returning to the old building to take command of it and the village and occupy it again.

Colonel al-Qaysi went about checking out the building and found quite a few still working handheld radios along with a number of canned food rations, full bottles of clean drinking water, and very detailed maps of both Kuwait and Saudi Arabia. He also found a number of maps that clearly showed where the Iraqi soldiers were stationed in the desert, and their preparedness to open their invasion against the Kingdom of Kuwait years ago. There were also some faded maps displaying Iraq's planned attack on the nation of Saudi Arabia, once the attacking Iraqi soldiers completely destroyed the nation of Kuwait first.

As he read over the maps, he found himself wondering why the Coalition Forces did not attack the building, and the invading enemy remove the wealth of information the building held in it. He had no way of knowing the Coalition Forces were moving so swiftly in their invasions of Iraq, by the time they passed through the small village of Qulban-Layyah, they were not the least bit interested in any intelligence this small military building might offer them.

Colonel al-Qaysi brushed the maps to the floor, and then he went outside and signaled, ordering the first batch of his troops to enter the village. When he saw them entering, he went back inside his new headquarters after breathing a deep sigh of relief. Now he felt he was free with trying to get his troops into Kuwait. So he can then get them heading for the Island chain of the Bahamas Islands. His driving force was to attack the American soldiers who had dared to invade his country and killed his commander.

The first five Iraqi troops cautiously entered the village like they were prepared to kill all the people living in the small town. Major Serena al-Shaya led the soldiers to the building, and she entered it and found them staring at their commanding Colonel. He seemed angry as he glared at the first few soldiers who entered the building.

For the first time in quite a while, the female Major saw the Colonel smile, as he offered. "Major al-Shaya, as soon as the rest of the soldiers are here, I want you to set them working on cleaning this filthy mess up. Then I want a complete inventory carried out on the weapons they find stored inside this god cursed building. Also, I want to know about food, check around and look for any fuel also. We lost one of our foul vehicles because it ran out of fuel, and we had no more to put into the worthless thing. If you find any extra fuel, order one of the vehicles to run out to the other machine and refuel it, and then drive it to the village and store if for future use.

"I want the cursed vehicles we have at our disposal, fully fueled up and ready for immediate action to get us into Kuwait. If you find no fuel in this god hated building then you will check out the rest of the worthless villagers and if they have any fuel, you'll confiscate it from the fools and get it into our machines. I want you to find the village leader of this foul hell hole, and inform the fool he's responsible to feed us until we get our supplies from elsewhere. If necessary, find a few of the fools to kill in order to set the stage for the rest of them, and make certain these foolish camel eating fools know we're here to take over the foul village, Major."

Even though Colonel al-Qaysi wanted to get out of the Middle East as soon as possible, he fully understood he had to secure his position in the village of Qulban Layyah first, so he could better organize his troops. Establish him here, and then he would be free to make plans to get his troops out of Iraq safely. As Colonel al-Qaysi began to tighten his vice like grip on the small Arab town and its civilians, the days slowly turned into weeks, and weeks to months.

By June of 2000, the Iraqi Colonel felt that President Saddam Hussein's troops must have finally stopped searching for him and the rest of his troops. He was pleased the Iraqi President was constantly drawing the eyes of the rest of the world aimed on him, and his extremely dangerous actions he was carrying out against the other nations of the world. First, the foolish Iraqi President threw out of Iraq all the United Nation's inspectors looking for his hidden catch of weapons of mass destruction. This move caused the United States to remove their attention and interests from trying Colonel al-Adwani as a terrorist in their country. It also forced the American President to go to the United Nations, and then demand much harsher sanctions be leveled against the nation of Iraq and their foolish President and his people.

President Saddam Hussein's response to the new threats from the United States was to make it look like he was pushing his production of weapons of mass destruction further along. He also fed misinformation to the spies he knew were operating in Iraq for the hated American soldiers, by making them believe he was developing the so called mobile chemical processing plants stored in the back of tractor trailers, to forward his development of these cursed weapons that went against all human beliefs. But in reality, Saddam Hussein made a secret pact with Syria when he started to pack up his biological and chemical catch of weapons, and had them secretly moved to the Iraqi town and chemical plant workings at al-Qa'im, and then he had them moved over the Syrian border to the heavily protected airbase stationed at Dayr az Zawr for safe keeping, and not allow them to be discovered by the hated United Nations inspectors.

Colonel al-Qaysi found himself pleased that President Saddam Hussein was enjoying giving the United States, and United Nations structure new problems over these supposed weapons of mass destruction. The wise Colonel was well aware Saddam made further secret pacts with the nations of Russia, France, and Germany, and in these pacts, Saddam was giving these nations oil deals for military weapons and contracts. These oil deals were agreements between the United Nations and Iraq, for Iraq to sell oil for food and medical supplies so desperately needed by the poor innocent people of his country. But President Hussein did not care one grain of worthless sand from his vast deserts for his poor and terribly suffering civilians of Iraq.

The heartless Iraqi President was more interested in rebuilding his military forces secretly, with the help of these few countries going against the deals set in place against Iraq by the rest of the United Nations members. Every military mind in Iraq knew it would only be a matter of time before their foolish President finally forced the American military to come and destroy their entire nation this time. This knowledge gave the hunted colonel the belief President Hussein had to remove the troops he sent out to capture, and then destroy him and the rest of his loyal troops. Saddam had to be forced to pull the troops back to protect his military installations from further attack by the American and Coalition Forces when they come.

Colonel al-Qaysi was beginning to feel a little more comfortable with his present situation in Qulban Layyah, he even began to send his soldiers out on short scouting patrols. Some of his patrols invaded other Iraqi towns and villages surrounding his village, and his troops stole much needed provisions for his troops from the poor civilians of these towns. The Iraqi Colonel was able to raid a number of small Iraqi military patrols, and stole monies and weapons from these troops who did not have the stomachs to stop the attacks against them. Slowly, he was building up his war chest, and the monies he needed to forward his future attack against the Americans in their own country. He even had his soldiers do a few minor raids over the border of Kuwait from Iraq. These troops were able to hit a bank, and they ended up with plenty of Kuwaiti, and even some American cash to enhance his future operations.

Colonel al-Qaysi had no idea other terrorist forces were hard at work on their own plans to attack prime American targets within the United States. The al-Qa'eda terrorist organization was fast becoming a serious force to be reckoned with by the rest of the world, with the help of the Taliban regime in control of the terribly poor and fractured nation of Afghanistan. During the past few years, Usama bin Laden developed a number of large terrorist training camps spread throughout most of Afghanistan, and he was busy training his Arab troublemakers on making certain attacks against the United States interest at home, and abroad. Bin Laden was incensed with his desire to hurt American interests, no matter where they may lay on the face of the earth.

As the days passed for Colonel Hamoodi al-Qaysi, and Usama Bin Laden, they both pushed forward their ideas to harm the United States by any means they had available to them. But bin Laden's plans were much more further along, because he had four terrorist cells already inserted into the United States, and the terrorists were already working on their attack plans.

Even more weeks and months passed for Colonel al-Qaysi and his troops, and he was still afraid to move any faster along with his attack plans against the United States. The Colonel did make two trips over to Kuwait, and on the second trip, he made contact with a few Kuwaiti civilians who hated the Americans as much as he did. And at the moment, they were getting him and his soldiers Kuwaiti passports and legal identification papers.

Usama bin Laden had twenty terrorist operating in the United States, and fifteen of the terrorists were Saudi Nationals. Bin Laden wanted and in fact, he demanded Saudi terrorists to be used on the attacks because not only did he want to harm the United States, but he also wanted to destroy the relationship established between Saudi Arabia, and the United States. He even wanted to hurt Saudi Arabia for turning their back on him and his supporters, and his wants to destroy the United States. So once his attack on the United States was completed, his revenge would then begin between the two nations he hated the most.

CHAPTER EIGHT

SEPTEMBER 1st, 2001. AFGHANISTAN

Usama bin Laden was at his headquarters in the Afghanistan capital of Kabul, when the first word came in that some of his terrorist assault teams were finally set in place, and the attackers were scheduled to make their opening attack against the United States on September 11th, 2001. Usama Bin Laden congratulated his officers, and then he prepared for the long awaited attack against the United States to begin. He smiled because he had planned this attack for a number of years, and it was finally going to come and then he could get on with planning his next attack.

The next few days went by at a snail's pace for the terrorists concerned with their attack against the United States. The FBI was picking up the increased cell phone calls going down between Afghanistan, and certain people they were keeping a close eye on in the United States. But nothing positive was able to be picked up, so the FBI began partitioning the federal courts for permission to place a number of wiretaps, and computer invasions on the suspected terrorists cells known to be operating within the shores of the United States. The FBI even tried to get some help from the CIA, and NSA (The National Security Advisor) offices, all three divisions were reluctant to trade information with the other offices assigned to the protection of the civilians of the United States. The three offices went to a higher alert status.

On September 4th, 2001. Colonel al-Qaysi received his false but official passports and identification papers he needed for his troops from their Kuwaiti helpers. Now, he wanted to make contact with his Cuba friends, and see if they could direct him to one of these American pleasure boat Captains who made their extra money by smuggling anyone who fled Cuba into the United States safely. Immediately, the Iraqi Colonel was connected to the Brothers of Freedom, who worked with the Cuban refugees who wanted to flee Cuba, and make it to the United States. Their dream was to be brought together with their relatives who went to America through legal connections. The Kuwaiti passports made it rather simple for the Colonel to cross the border to Kuwait, and he used his Iraqi passport to reenter Iraq when he had to return to his village.

Finally, Colonel al-Qaysi felt his plans were taking shape, and he could finally get his troops inserted into the United States, and make his selected attacks against the federal judge supposed to try Colonel al-Adwani as a terrorist, and also get his revenge against the American troops who had invaded his country to capture Colonel al-Adwani. Even though his driving forced was to attack the United States, he was operating under a smaller scale than planned by Usama Bin Laden and his terrorist cells operating within the borders of the United States.

Colonel al-Qaysi planned to make his next visit to Kuwait on September 9th, 2001. He had a meeting scheduled with a Kuwaiti Operative who he was informed, had certain connections with Cuba that would be able to direct him to a man who could make it happen, for him and his troops to linkup with American Captains, and get his people safely into the United States within the month. Colonel al-Qaysi could not be happier with this latest information as he waited for the days to pass. He was to cross the border at ten thirty a.m. American time in his efforts to meet with his Kuwaiti helper. When the day came, and Colonel al-Qaysi found himself waiting by the border to enter Kuwait, he saw something strange happening at the crossing. It seemed everyone wanting to enter Kuwait was being turned away from the border. The more he watched, the more he was positive the border was closed to all civilian traffic coming from Iraq.

Suddenly, he believed Saddam Hussein had finally done something to upset the United States, and the America's soldiers must be attacking his country again. He was fifteen vehicles away from the border guards. He allowed the vehicle before his, to open the gap until he was able to pull out of the line. Then the Iraqi Colonel pulled his car out of the line and turned around and drove away from the Kuwaiti, Iraqi border at a high rate of speed. His actions caused the border guards to turn their attention on his vehicle, and at first the Iraqi guards thought about firing on the fleeing car, because they did not get a chance to inspect the drive or the vehicle. But the guards decided against it, because the soldiers felt if this driver was a terrorist going to Kuwait, he had their blessings to be there and hurt another enemy of Iraq.

When Colonel al-Qaysi left the border, he opened up his car and shot back to his small village of Qulban Layyah. He wanted to prepare his troops for attack by American troops, in case the United States was attacking his country again. He had no idea what had transpired in the United States that would change the world, and to cause all Arab nations along with Israel, to close their borders with other nations of the Middle East.

SEPTEMBER 11ᵗʰ, 2001. 7:58 A.M. NEW YORK CITY

At exactly seven fifty eight a.m., on September 11ᵗʰ, 2001. A United Airlines Flight marked as Flight One, Seven, Five, departed from Boston's Logan International Airport, the flight was bound for Los Angeles, California. The airliner had fifty six civilian passengers, and two pilots and seven female flight attendants on board the flight. The Boeing 767 was hijacked by five Arab terrorists who acted as passengers on the jetliner after ten minutes into the flight. The terrorists were armed with simple box cutter razor blades and cans of mace, and held the passengers at bay with these few minor items. When the Arab terrorist were able to take over the airliner and hold the passengers hostage, two Arab terrorists took command of the cockpit of the civilian aircraft, and then diverted from the plane's original flight path, and the aircraft was now headed directly towards the very heart of New York City.

At seven fifty nine a.m., a second American Airlines Flight, One, One, departed from the same Boston's Logan Airport, and this flight was also bound for Los Angeles, California. It was likewise hijacked by a small number of terrorist, this time by only four Arab hijackers also armed with simple box cutters and cans of mace, and they held the passengers at bay with the few weapons. The Arab terrorists on this flight were forced to kill a female flight attendant with the razor blade by cutting her throat, and then taking a second female flight attendant hostage to take command of the flight, and control the civilians on board the aircraft.

Flight One, One was another Boeing 767, and the aircraft was carrying eighty one civilian passengers, along with two pilots, and nine flight attendants, mostly females, on board the cross country flight. Once the Arab hijackers attacked and removed the pilot and co-pilot from the cockpit of the aircraft, the two hijackers took command of the aircraft and began flying it. This Boeing 767 flight was likewise diverted from its original flight path, and the aircraft was now aimed directly towards New York City.

At eight, oh one a.m. on the same morning, a United Airlines Flight Ninety, Three, a smaller Boeing 757 carrying just thirty eight passengers, two pilots, and five female flight attendants, left the Newark New Jersey Airport, heading for San Francisco, California. Once the airliner was hijacked by another five Middle Eastern terrorists, the airliner was diverted towards Washington D.C., and its target there. At eight, forty six a.m. the American Airlines Flight One, One, from Boston, crashed into the North Tower at the World Trade Center in the heart of downtown New York City, after tracing its way to the city using the Hudson River as guideline for their attack.

At one point, the hijacked aircraft came within a hundred yards of the Nuclear Power Plant and the twin reactors of Indian Point, constructed on the shore of the Hudson River. It was unknown to the terrorists, but they passed a more devastating target than the one they were heading for. If the terrorists crashed their plane into the nuclear facility and large Butler building constructed on the site. They would have crashed into a storehouse of over fourteen thousand tons of spent control rods of Plutonium pellets encased in a zinc metal jacket. Zinc burns at a much high rate of temperature which would have caused the Plutonium pellets that measured a mere one and one half inches long, and one half inch wide stored inside the spent control rods, to burn rapidly and unstoppable, and start the long feared meltdown situation, or the so called China Syndrome.

Thus causing a massive nuclear explosion, and placing over one million tons of highly radioactive contaminated materials and dust into the air that would have contaminated one hundred square miles of New York State and City, and the surrounding States expanding from the epicenter of the explosion on out, and destroyed this prime land for over one hundred and fifty years. It would have also caused the deaths of over three, to eight million American civilians, and continued to cause even more death of any surviving civilians for another fifty years to come, because of many different diseases caused by the released radioactive.

When the hijacked airliner crashed into the North Tower of the Trade Center, the citizens of New York City thought they had just witnessed a terrible aircraft accident, and immediately New York City's finest, along with scores of fearless and proud firefighters, instantly descended on the

North Tower of the World Trade Center. All the emergency responders were treating this incident as an accident, but the Arab terrorists knew what they were doing, and the second plane was held back from its attack on the second, South Tower of the Trade Center for twenty minutes. All civilian workers in the South Tower of the Trade Center were told not to panic and to remain in the second Tower building and go back to work.

The delayed terrorist attack on the second Tower was carried out to allow the emergency responders to get in the area, so when they crashed their second aircraft into the South Tower of the Trade Center. It would kill many of the emergency responders as well as the trapped civilian workers of New York City, during their continuing attack against the United States. As emergency responders watched helplessly, many trapped civilians who made their way to the top of the one hundred and eighth floor of the North Tower, were forced to jump off the building in an effort to escape the roaring flames raging below them. The civilians rather lose their lives in the fall, than be burned to death in the out of control fires of the Tower.

A mass of news reporter and police helicopters tried in vain to pick up some of the trapped civilians that made their way to the roof of the North Tower. But because of the thick black bellowing smoke, and the out of control flames devouring the massive structure's upper floors, along with the strong updrafts and heavy wind currents, made it completely impossible for the helicopters to get close enough to the burning building to complete a successful rescue attempt of any of the civilian workers trapped on the roof of the first burning Tower building, before it was too late to save them.

Upon the impact of the airliner into the North Tower, the Boeing 767 airliner's ten thousand gallons of JP-8 aviation fuel ignited in the crash. The first seven thousand gallons of fuel was instantly vaporized in the beginning blast, burning its way through the heavy fire retardant material protecting the steel support superstructure of the building from the roaring flames. The remaining three thousand gallons of fuel burned hot and out of control, and slowly melted or otherwise twisted the heavy supporting steel of the structure left intact in the area from the forced of the crash on the affected floors of the Tower, thus weakening the building from within. Burning aviation fuel also flowed down the elevator shafts of the building, causing explosions on floors seventy seven, twenty five and a fireball to ignite in the lobby of the damaged Tower.

At nine, oh, three a.m. September 11th, 2001 the second hijacked United Airlines Flight, One, Seven, Five from Boston, crashed into the South Tower of the World Trade Center with a bellowing fire ball of an explosion. The South Tower was never ordered to be evacuated because it was believed the first plane crash was an accident. But the instant the second airliner crashed into the South Tower of the Trade Center, it was understood by civilian and military and emergency personnel alike that the United States was under attack by terrorists.

Hundred of fearless firefighters and responding New York City police officers and other first responders to the affected area, were showered then buried under tons of debris tumbling from both crippled Towers. Many other firefighters and police officers were burned to death in both flaming Twin Towers. The area between the two burning Towers was flooded with thousands of fleeing, scared to death civilians as they wildly ran out of both attacked structures, further hampering the arriving emergency responder's efforts to aid their fellow brothers and sisters.

When the second Tower was hit by the airliner, Fire Captains ordered all surviving firefighters to pull away from the area so they could regroup, and attack the situation with a working plan. But many responders refused to leave, their concern was to save lives, and in doing so they gave up their lives in the effort. Heroes them all, firefighters, police officers and Port Authority police alike, along with many civilians who instead of running, turned and tried to help their fellow workers getting out of the building. They gave up their lives in the effort to help other people live. All these brave people show the world what the people of New York were made of.

The President was caught out of position during the terrorist attack on the Twin Towers, but was informed of what was taking place in New York City. His commanders knew what to do, and reacted properly until the President was able to break free of his prior comment, and take over command of the terrorist situation taking place in New York City.

The United States government went in rapid action, and the Federal Aviation Administration ordered the complete shutdown of all New York area airports. Directive Sixty was transmitted, where all one hundred and three Nuclear Power Plants operating in the United States, were ordered to scram their reactors and go into an emergency hot shutdown of all units. It was feared these were the next targets to be hit by whoever hijacked the aircrafts, and crashing them into the two buildings. At nine twenty one a.m., all bridges and tunnels leading in and out of New York City were ordered closed by the Port Authority Directors.

As all heads that control air traffic flying over the United States, realized the United States was under attack by a number of unknown terrorists and their aim were civilian airlines. At nine, twenty five a.m., the government issued the special ATZ (Altitude To Zero) order, directing all domestic flights grounded in the United States by the Federal Aviation Administration. Any civilian flights in the air, or if they ventured off their preordained flight path for any reason while waiting permission to land, ran the risk of being shot down by attack aircraft taking off from every military airbase throughout the United States, ready to kill any civilian airline that made a wrong move. The military aircraft picked up all civilian flights, and escorted them to the nearest airbase, whether civilian or military in nature.

Air traffic controllers all over the United States picked up countless aircraft on their scopes, as they headed for the nearest base to land. In the confusion, Flight Seven, Seven, went unnoticed until it was too late to stop this aircraft from doing what the Arab hijackers wanted. Even though two F-16s were dispatched to intercept this one out of flight path aircraft, the military aircraft could not catch up to it quick enough to shoot it down before it crashed into its target.

Then, at nine, forty five a.m. September 11th, 2001, the American Airlines 757 Flight Seven, Seven, crashed into the side of the Pentagon Building with a thunderous explosion and massive fireball. Out of control fires instantly consumed the side of the damaged building with hundreds of military and civilian personnel running out of the crumbling structure. Again, America's TVs were filled with flames, and brave actions of firefighters and police responding to the terrible carnage. Special military personnel showed up at the Pentagon, and began to secure the site, and the soldiers rush the scared civilians and reporters away from the damaged building. Tanks and Bradley Fighting machines showed up, and closed off all roads heading for the center of the United States military mind thrust building.

At exactly ten, oh five a.m. the severely damaged South Tower at the World Trade Center burning less time than the equally as damaged North Tower, grumbled, and then collapsed in a domino effect in on herself. With the damaged upper floors falling on the undamaged floors, and the undamaged floors unable to support the extreme added weight, and one after the other, floor after floor of the South Tower failed, and then collapsed onto the next lower floor until the entire building crumbled to ground level, crushing to death any civilian workers still trying to escape the crumbling building.

At ten, ten a.m. in Washington D.C., a large section of the severely damaged side of the Pentagon building collapsed because of the out of control raging fires, burning jet fuel, and terrible destruction the aircraft caused to the support structure of the building. A horde of firefighters continued to try and get the fires under control, as a horde of police and Military MPs and personnel went in the Pentagon, to make certain everyone made it out of the building that was not killed in the initial attack on the building. These great heroes were also looking for any injured and dead who might have been left behind.

At the same exact moment the Pentagon building began to collapse, at ten, ten a.m., United Airlines 757 Flight Nine, Three crashed in a secluded section of a heavily wooded area in Pennsylvania. It was suggested to the President this aircraft's target was either the White House, or it could have been aimed at the Capital Building, which had been evacuated by emergency personnel and the brave Capital police.

At the same instant, many civilians trapped on Flight, Nine, Three decided to act and take back the aircraft from the terrorists. The first two reports came in about Flight, Nine, Three, the first was from the pilot of the F-16 who reported he was trying to catch up to the runaway civilian airliner. The pilot was instructed if he was able to catch up to the airliner, he was to stop the aircraft from reaching its intended target by any means necessary.

The stunned young American pilot of the F-16 realized the unspoken order he had just received from command. He was silently ordered to pull on the civilian airliner and destroy the plane with missiles stationed on the wings of his attack aircraft, before the supposed hijacked aircraft could reach its assigned target in Washington D.C.

As the civilian passengers trapped on Flight Nine, Three tried to attack the cockpit. The terrorist flying the aircraft increased power to his port engine which caused the engine to backfire and flame out. The last report from the hijacker as he questioned why the American military planes were firing missiles at them, the terrorist thought the backfire of the engine was caused by a missile attack on the aircraft. One cellular phone conversation from a husband trapped on board the doomed plane was placed to his wife. Informing her he thought he saw the right wing of the plane hit by something he described as a possible missile. He then asked his wife why the civilian aircraft was being shot down as other civilians continued their attack on the cockpit of the plane. Before his wife could explain why, his phone went dead.

These mistaken reports were immediately squashed by CIA Director John Raincloud, who overrode the reports about Flight Nine, Three. Then the powerful Director announced the miss information report the civilian passengers of the hijacked airliner revolted once they were informed by their loved ones on the ground communicating with them. What took place in the heart of New York City, and at the Pentagon Building. The passengers tried to take back control of the civilian aircraft from the hijackers, and their actions caused the plane to crash in the open field in Pennsylvania.

Director John Raincloud remembered what happened to Russia when she attack, and shot down the Korean Airlines Flight dubbed Double Oh Seven, when it was believed the civilian airliner was running a special spy flight for the United States. The Director also remembered how the then President of the United States beat the Russian's over the head for what the Russians had done to the civilian airliner that went down with all souls lost in the sea to their attack.

CIA Director Raincloud knew no matter what the circumstances was, he was not going to give the Russians this hammer to beat his President over his head with. Because the misinterpretation of the aircraft engine backfire, and the thought the aircraft was being fired on by the trailing attack aircraft the passenger reported to his wife. This thought was the only reason for the CIA Director to make the announcement the passengers on board Flight, Nine, Three, confronted the hijackers, and their heroic actions caused the airliner to crash in the field. Thus stopping the aircraft from killing who knew how many innocent civilians on the ground in Washington.

It took the rest of the day before the President was finally allowed to return to the White House, once it was determined all civilian aircraft were resting safely on the ground, and the only aircraft still flying, was his military aircraft flown by loyal pilots. By the time the President returned to the White House, his Cabinet members, CIA Director, and Chiefs of Staff and all who mattered, were present for an emergency meeting of the President's staff. The President wanted to know what happened on this day, and who was responsible for the terrorist attacks on American land, and of her defenseless civilians.

The thoroughly exhausted and extremely upset CIA Director Raincloud was the first one to address the members of the meeting, but he directed his replies mainly at the American Leader. "Mr. President Sir, with all due respect, from what I was able to construct so far from these two incidents, two hijacked aircraft took off from Logan International Airport in Boston. We gone over all the surveillance tapes at the airport, and were able to pick out two known terrorists wanted for the past three years, sir. They were boarding the airliners with a number of other people believe supporting their hijacking. So it's believed all the terrorists in this action, were that of Arab in nature and it's further believed..."

"Who the hell do you think might have masterminded this damn operation? Do we have any idea who it might have been this early into this mess?" the angry President demanded from the CIA Director in a harsh tone as he looked at the Director with anger locked in his eyes.

"Everything I've been able to put together so far on the four incidents Mr. President Sir, clearly points their fingers straight at our old friend hiding in Afghanistan, sir. Usama bin Laden, Mr. President Sir." Director Raincloud replied in a flat tone of voice.

"I can assure you Mr. Raincloud, that sonofabitch is anything but my friend, sir. Okay, now you gave me a name to aim my anger at, I'll order you Director Raincloud, to make this man the most hunted man in the history of mankind. General White Sir." The President turned his attention towards the Chairman of the Joint Chiefs of Staff.

General White rose and replied the instant he got the nod. "Yes Sir Mr. President Sir."

"General White, I order you to activate any and all our special military assets you have at your disposal, sir. We're going to strike back and strike hard at this sonofabitch, no matter what rathole he decides to hide his ass in, sir. Even if we have to destroy every damn Arab nation who tries to hide or offers any form of help to this filthy man. Nothing on the face of this earth is going to stop me from destroying this bastard, and his terrorist network he established, sir. General White, I want this man more than I wanted that other bastard we captured in Iraq, that Colonel al-Adwani fellow, sir. You'll get this man for me, right General White?"

"Mr. President, do you want me to activate the Rapid Response Force as well, sir?"

The President thought for a few minutes and then mumbled. "No General White, I don't think so at this time sir. I believe we're going to need a much larger military force than theirs, to destroy this devil a man and his evil aims, General White Sir. I further believe we're going to be strained to place ground forces in strength in Afghanistan, to bring this sonofabitch of a man and his evil regime down around his ears. And teach any future would be terrorists, along with the nation they're operating from, what would happen to them if they fuck around with the United States. They're the ones who'll end up getting killed in the long run General.

"Besides General White, I want these special soldiers held in reserve in the United States, just in case any of these terrorist attacks haven't been completed by this nut. At least I'll know we have the right people stationed here in the United States, sir. In case we might have to let them loose in the streets of the United States to hunt down any other of these damn terrorists who might still be hanging around Washington, General. Am I right in my way of thinking sir?"

"Absolutely the right way to think on this one Mr. President Sir, if we're going to put so many ground forces in Afghanistan. Holding Captain Walker and his specialized crew back as a sort of security blanket and defensive group in the States seems like a damn good idea, Mr. President Sir. That way we can release him and the other special troops on whoever tries to hurt us in the States, while the heavier ground forces work over the assholes in Afghanistan, Mr. President. We know the bulk of bin Laden's soldiers are held up in that miserable country, sir." The General offered to his Commander in Chief as he used one of his best smiles on the upset President.

"That's a very good way to be thinking as well General White, and to finish your answer sir, I want a warning sent out to these elite troops of yours that they're placed on military standby and alert of twenty four hours, but they're not activated as of this time, sir. I want the specialized soldiers foaming at the mouth for revenge against anyone who was involved in this damn terrorist attack sir, but I want them held in reserve for the time being, General White Sir. Keep the soldiers appraised on everything that is taking place with the hunt for the attackers, and keep the troopers ready and nothing more for the time being, sir. General White, I'm going to hold you to that proud boast you just gave me that you can have these elite troops activated within three hour's time, sir. Do you still stand by that statement to me, General White?"

"I certainly do Mr. President Sir. You give me the word and I'll have my troops in downtown Washington before that time." The General replied proudly.

"Very well then General White, I need input everybody. What are we going to do next?" the President asked his staff as he looked from one concerned face to the other.

"With all due respect Mr. President Sir, the first thing I think you should do over this situation sir. Is for you to make your way to ground zero, and make your presence known to the emergency responders working there sir. Sort of give them a shot in the arm so to say. From there, you can always announce we're going to get those lousy bastards responsible for this unsuspected terrorist attack on the United States, Mr. President Sir. It'll be a great platform to make this announcement from." Director Raincloud offered the President confidently.

"Outstanding, that's what I want to hear from my support people. One other thing I want to know, is there any way we might be able to get some kind of a number on those innocent civilians killed in this sneak attack that was aimed against us, anyone?" the President replied as a spark of life showed in his exhausted and aching body.

"Yes Sir Mr. President, I'll answer that question for you if you don't mind sir." General White offered as he stood and nodded at the shaken American Leader, as the President turned his attention back on his military officer.

"Please General White let's hang the usual formalities for this meeting sir. Please everyone there's no need to stand up when replying to one of my questions of you people. Right now, I'm only interested in hearing what we intend to do about these damn terrorist attacks that just occurred against us." The President offered as he looked at the many staring faces again.

General White smiled at the President as he took his seat, and then continued with his offering to the American Leader. "Mr. President, as of this moment sir, there has been no exact numbers set on the fatalities that we have and will suffer in these terrorist attacks, sir. But one thing I believe we should adopt sir, is keeping the death rate artificially low, sir. In this matter, if we keep them low, and by low I say we cut the actual death rate in half at the least, Mr. President Sir, because if we make the terrorists believe they killed fewer civilians than they did, sir. Then they won't think their attack was so great a deal for them and their damn followers, sir. Furthermore Mr. President, I want them to get excited and upset at the low number of dead we'll offer them. That way they might start communicating with each other so we might be able to pick up their traffic, and find out exactly where these bastards are hiding in Afghanistan"

"I think that's a very wise decision on your part, General White Sir. We'll do as you have just offered, sir. I'd love to say no one was killed in this damn sneak attack, but we all know that's impossible to say after all that has just transpired people. But General White, I believe you have failed to reply correctly to my last question though, sir. I know how you people are, and you can figure through your computers, how many people lost their lives in this attack, General White Sir. I want to know what you have come up with at this point, sir." The President snapped at his military officer as he held him in his harsh stare waiting his reply.

"You're absolutely correct Mr. President Sir. When I was first informed of the terrorist attack against the Twin

Towers at the World Trade Center in New York City, and the terrorist hit on my building here in Washington sir, the first thing I did was to run a worst case scenario on the suspected deaths caused by these three terrorist attacks, sir. The numbers are quite staggering to realize, and my first figures are base on the low side as it is, and that's because I only went with the least amount of figures I could, from the lower end of the death rate scale I worked out, Mr. President Sir. I'm afraid I'm forced to wait for more information to come to my office, and the true numbers placed on the civilian and emergency responder's death, before I can make a more educated guess as to the total of civilian and emergency responder's who lost have lost their lives during this terrorist attack leveled at our..."

"I knew you'd do that, so please General White Sir. Give me what you have worked up so far for me, and stop all this dancing me around in a corner." The exhausted and rather upset President offered as he interrupted the General for the second time.

"Very well then Mr. President Sir, I'm certain you're not going to like the numbers I have worked up and again sir. I have to remind the President that these numbers are rather under inflated for this situation, sir." The General tried a smile on the President, but it was wasted. Because all the President did was sharpen his harsh glare on the military officer, until he went on with his information. President Cole had to nod at the General to make him speak again.

Letting out his breath in a deep sigh, General White offered. "Mr. President Sir, with all due respect sir, the total death of the Nine, One, One, attacks was placed at around..."

"Wait a second here General. Is that what we're calling these terrorists attacks, Nine, One, One, General

White? Hummmm, I wonder if the sonofabitches had this in mind to rub our faces in the shit, by hitting us on such a special time as Nine, One, One General White. Everyone in the world knows we fashioned our emergency calls on this Nine, One, One number, General. I wonder if these lousy bastards were trying to slap us in the face by hitting us on this day, sir. Dammit, I believe that's why the terrorists hit us on this day now, sir." The President mumbled to his military officer because he was still suffering the shock of the terrorist attack.

"Probably, thinking about it for a moment Mr. President Sir. I'd be forced to say yes, positively sir. It was an added slap in our faces to hit us on this day, sir." The General replied, surprised he did not pick up the meaning of the attack as he cocked his head to the side, and then smiled at the President again, and this time it was returned by the President as he offered.

"Very well General, if these sonofabitches thought it was funny to hit us on this date to drive their attack home, sir. I believe we'll have to force the asses that attacked us to cry out their own call of Nine, One, One General White, when we start to pound their miserable asses in the damn ground, sir. I'll teach the bastards not to rub the faces of the United States in the dirt, because I'll place every last one of them who had a hand in this terrorist attack, under the dirt we walk on, General White Sir." The President growled as he stared at the faces in his office.

The Chairman of the Joint Chiefs of Staff did not know what to do, the President got off the subject of the death toll in this terrorist attack he wanted. And he was not looking forward to bringing the subject back up to his boss either. He felt he had enough problems and hurt heaped on his shoulders because of the terrorist attack in New York

City, and he did not want to twist the knife in the open wound, by announcing the staggering death toll his computers offered. He remained in his seat and quiet as the President seemed like he was thinking a second. Suddenly, the President turned back to him and grumbled.

"General White, we were going over something before this Nine, One, One, thing came up sir, what was it again? I forgot what we were talking about, sir. Err... hold on a second General White yes I remember now, I believe you were going to give me below fugues on the death toll projected by your computers, sir. Do you mind going over them again, General?" the President asked as he let out his breath then shook his head sadly over the terrorist attack on his country.

"As you will Mr. President Sir, I believe it's not necessary for us to discuss the future death this attack has caused us, sir. I feel we've been through enough on this day sir, and why ask for more pain to suffer, Mr. President?" He offered, hoping to end this discussion where it stood.

"General White, it should be more than enough for you that I just asked this question of you, sir. And I expect a direct answer to that question from you at this time, sir. I shall repeat my request I want to know what we're looking at in the way of a death toll for this damn mess. And I want to know what it is this minute, General." The President snapped at the military officer.

"Very well Mr. President, if you insist sir. I ran a quick mockup of the attack, and the possible loss of life, and my computers came up with the death toll placed at around three thousand and thirty civilian deaths in the Twin Towers attack alone..."

"Jesus, Mary, and Joseph, General White, I want to know the low end of this damn death toll sir. But I also want you to place the true number on the deaths expected here, General White Sir. Dammit, I don't know what I want any longer from you about this request, sir." The President ordered his military officer as he continued to stare him dead in his eyes as he waited his reply.

"Yes Sir Mr. President Sir, at the Twin Tower site, the real death toll will be fixed at between five to six and one half thousand civilians, Mr. President Sir. We know many of the deaths will never be recorded for a variety of different reasons, sir. Before you ask me Mr. President, we're aware some of the civilians were actually vaporized in the initial blast and fires, sir. There's going to be complete families wiped out because they were visiting the Towers at the time of the attack, and there'll be no one left who'll report them missing. We also have no idea how many foreigners were visiting the Towers at the time of the attack sir, and how many of them came from other countries who under no circumstances, will admit they lost people to this attack, sir.

"Another reason for this much high a number of deaths I'm reporting is, there are countless homeless people who always sneak into the two Towers on a regular basis every day and night, and these homeless people hide in the elevator shafts, the duct work, and in bathrooms on many of the lower floors of the buildings who'll never be discovered and accounted for in this attack. So no matter the number we release to the world, the death toll will be well over three thousand more than the numbers we'll publish for public consumption, Mr. President Sir. We know for a fact that there were three hundred and forty three firefighters killed in the damn attacks, and over two hundred injured during the attacks against the Towers alone, sir.

"The police suffered far lesser causalities than the firefighters did during the damn attacks, but that's because the police weren't taking the same chances the firefighters were taking by going into the burning Towers and trying to fight the fires, and save lives of any civilians, sir. Yes, there were many police officers who did enter the two Towers before they fell. The police are reporting at least seventy five of their police and Port Authority Officers were killed in the attack, and another two hundred police injured to various degrees, sir.

"The total injured between the Two Towers, and the civilian workers estimated as walking wounded in the streets of the area of the attack, was set at two thousand, two hundred and sixty two, Mr. President Sir. There has also been reported another two hundred and twenty civilians, police and firefighters were killed in the massive cloud of debris that rumbled through the streets of lower Manhattan when the Towers collapsed, Mr. President Sir. The number of dead at the Pentagon was set at one hundred and twenty four souls, sir. And the injured at that incident are known to be seventy six as of this time, sir.

"If I was to add all the deaths together, the truer figure I would come up with will be placed at around six thousand, seven hundred and forty nine dead, not counting the dead that was caused by the debris cloud because all the numbers aren't in as yet, Mr. President Sir. Also adding at least another six thousand plus injured in the damn attacks, sir. But we're going to release the number of the dead we set at just three thousand thirty civilian, police, firefighters and military personnel dead, for the same reason I had previously stated during this conversation, sir. And before this mess is over sir, I'm quite certain we might revise the death toll numbers down to try and take the sting out of the attacks, sir. So we can remove a small part of the prize away from the damn terrorists responsible for this attack against us, Mr.

President Sir. Mind you were not including the dead terrorists in these numbers, sir."

The upset military officer stopped speaking because he noticed the President slowly shaking his head. The President seemed to be thinking, and when the General stopped speaking. It made the President look up at him, and then remark.

"I see what you meant by not wanting to visit this horror on me, General White. Dammit sir! I had no idea the death toll would be so staggering, even at the lower numbers that you have just offered me, sir. General White, if we do nothing more for the rest of my Administration, sir. I want you to get the lousy bastards even remotely involved in this terrorist attack aimed against the United States, sir. You have to promise me this if it's the last thing you do in your lifetime, General White Sir. I want all of them in their graves for what they have done to the innocent civilians of this country. I demand the heads of all of them involved in this damn attack, sir. All of them I tell you General White, all of them dammit!"

"Mr. President, I'll get every mother's son involved in this damn attack, sir. And it won't be the last thing I'll do in my lifetime sir. I intend to get the host nation who is sheltering these criminals, and destroy that country as a whole, Mr. President. We have to hit both these entities at the same time, if we ever want to stop any further attacks against our country, sir." The Chairman of the Joint Chiefs of Staff said to the President proudly as he stared in his eyes.

"Errr...." The CIA Director offered and he instantly drew the President's attention as he snapped at the man. "Director Raincloud Sir, you seem like you have something else you want to add to this extremely troubling conversation? What is it you have on your mind, sir?"

"Yes I do Mr. President..."

"Well let me have it, maybe it'll end this miserable day for me at long last, Director."

"Yes Mr. President and I knew the question of the number of the dead at both incidents would come up during this conversation, and I did a number of run ups before I reported to the White House. This is what I was able to construct for your information, Mr. President Sir. We know for a fact there were Nineteen Arab hijackers and four fuel loaded U.S. commercial aircraft bound for West Coast destinations involved in this terrorist attack. I was able to place a good number of people killed in New York City, Washington D.C., and outside Shanksville, Pa. at Two Thousand, Nine Hundred Seventy Seven people. Two Thousand, Seven Hundred Fifty Three people were killed at the attack against the World Trade Center site in lower Manhattan, sir.

"I was able to place a number of Three Hundred Forty Three New York City firefighters died in the initial attacks and subsequent collapse of the WTC Towers from reports I was able to put together at this point, Mr. President Sir. I was also able to place a number of twenty three New York City police officers who died in the same attacks on the Twin Towers. There were thirty three Port Authority officers who died in the initial attacks and subsequent collapse of the Twin Towers, Mr. President. I was able to pick up the youngest death was that of a two year old child, and the oldest death was placed at eighty five years old, sir. Now turning my attention towards the attack that occurred against the Pentagon Building here in Washington, Mr. President Sir.

"It was reported to my office that one hundred eight four people were killed when the hijacked American

Airline Flight 77 crashed into the Pentagon Building, Mr. President Sir. I'm sorry to report the death toll at both New York City and the Pentagon Building is expected to increase as the emergency responders get to digging deeper into the tons of rubble produced at both sites, sir. Mr. President, it's estimated it cost Usama bin Laden a mere five hundred thousand dollars, to plan and execute the 9/11 attacks against both sites, sir.

"Keeping with the costs these terrorist attacks could cost us in the future, Mr. President Sir. We're looking at one hundred twenty three billion dollar estimated economic losses during the first two to four weeks after the World Trade Center Towers collapsed in New York City, as well as suffering a steep decline in commercial air traffic over the next few years. I have also worked up an estimated cost of the World Trade Center site damage, and this estimate includes the surrounding buildings, the City's infrastructure along with the damaged subway facilities at some sixty billion dollars, sir. Now looking at the enormous clean up expenses of just the World Trade Center site, we'll most likely experience as the clean up begins at both incident sites. I worked out it'll take three million, one hundred thousand hours to clean up the over one point eight million tons of debris created by this attack on the two Tower structures at a staggering cost of over seven hundred and fifty million dollars at the least, sir.

CHAPTER NINE

THE ISLAND OF MARATHON, THE FLORIDA KEYS

As true to form, Captain Robert Walker was on the horn the moment he saw the first airliner hit the Twin Tower building. He knew straight off it was a terrorist attack and he was calling the General at the Pentagon, to give him his opinion on the attack. He got the usual run around, and was still on the phone when the second aircraft hit the second Tower. Now he was positive it was a terrorist action. He was still hanging on the phone when it suddenly went dead on him, and Sergeant Dorothy Ramirez rushed into the room, and she announced that a third plane had just crashed into the Pentagon Building. Walker dropped the phone and rushed to the living room and watched as the pictures showed the raging fire engulfing the military command building.

Mother Flanagan who was visiting Walker's home, asked him with concern lacing his voice. "What the fuck are we gonna do now about this crap man?"

"I'm gonna try the fucking General's private cell phone number he gave us a while back. One thing I can tell you for sure is we're hot as of this moment, man. The General's gonna want some fucking heads for this one, and we're gonna be the ones who'll bring them heads to his ass, man." Walker went fishing in the drawer by the phone and found the General's private number. He showed Ramirez holding their son in her arms. She looked great, she already lost the weight she put on carrying the child, and her muscle tone was back on her taught body. She again looked like the hard body soldier she was before getting pregnant.

Walker smile and then he dialed the phone. Almost immediately, the Chairman answered after excusing himself with the President and the others attending the meeting. "Yeah, this is General White." He growled into the phone, angry someone dared to bother him at the meeting.

"General White, this is Captain Robert Walker, sir. Where do you want us and when sir?"

"Walker, why am I not surprised you chosen to bother me at this so damn important time, sir." The General grumbled at him as he turned his back to the President so he could speak with the young Captain as privately as he could, as he went on with his gripe at him. "I was sort of expecting a call from your ass. Why did it take you so long to communicate with me, mister? It's good to know you're keeping your damn eyes opened on what's happening in the

States, sir. I have information for you and your pack of war wacky bastards down there in Florida. It looks like you people are going to miss this one for the time being sir. The President wants to hold you people in reserve in the States, in case these attacks against us are not done with, Captain.

"We're sure as hell going to go after the damn throats of the rotten little bastards who had any part to play in this one, and we're going to go after them in fucking force I tell you, soldier. You and the rest of your specialized troops are ordered placed on an eight hour standby order and a twenty four hour alert status, sir. This order will be lowered down to a two hour standby order, once we know for certain what the fuck's happening around here sir. Keep your damn people hot and ready to trot at a moment's notice, mister."

"We're always hot and ready to work on a drop of a stinking dime, General White Sir. General, November, Foxtrot Whiskey, (military slang No Fucking Way) on missing all the fun and games when we go after that sonofabitch in Afghanistan, General White Sir. Me and my troops want a part of his lousy ass, sir." Walker growled in his phone at the Chairman.

"Now you listen here to me, Romeo Foxtrot, (Rat Fuck) you'll do as you're fucking ordered and you'll like it mister. Look, I'm busy as hell with the President as you can well imagine Captain. I'm attending a private meeting with him and his staff, so I'll be back to you the first chance I get, personally, or though your main control Colonel Leadbetter, sir. And who the hell are you calling that sonofabitch?" General White snarled at the young Captain, he was interested in who the Captain thought they were going after in the next action coming up.

"You know the little prick I mean General White, that fucking Usama bin Laden dude. We all know he was the bastard behind this terrorist hit against us, sir. We were waiting for the fuck to make his move against us, and now he done it sir. But one thing he didn't know was gonna happen to his ass, the fuck got my ass mad as hell at the bastard now, General. So he betta hunt a fucking rathole to hid in, and pull the stinking ground in over his ass while he's at it, sir."

"You know something mister? You're smart, perhaps you're a little too smart for your own damn good, buster. You heard my orders, and you'll carry them out as received, mister."

"I'll be waiting for any further orders at a moment's notice from you, General White Sir." Walker replied to the dial tone.

"Well, what did the General have to say Bobby?" Sergeant Ramirez asked as she placed Robert Jr. on the floor so he could crawl around while she spoke to Walker.

"The General said we're gonna miss the big show for the time being baby. But we might get stuck playing a little patty cake with any assholes that might still be in the States. The President wants us hanging around for any possible payback action. The hot shot General said we're going after the bastard's big time, which means we might do a little nation stomping while we're at it. Mother, Raz, we have to get in touch with the rest of the guys on the stinking Island. The damn General wants me to place them all on an eight hour standby for possible immediate action. I'm gonna issue a two hour alert myself, I wanna be damn ready if we're called on for action."

THE WHITE HOUSE, WASHINGTON D.C., SEPTEMBER 10th, 2001

The meeting with the President went through most of the night, and everyone returned to the office it seemed like they just left a few minutes ago. The President was preparing to leave for New York City the next day, and wanted to be brought up to date on the terrorist attacks, and see if his staff was able to find out more about the attacks. The Chairman walked in the Oval Office at eight a.m. speaking on his cell phone. It was Walker again, reporting to his commanding officer he alerted his troops, and they were ready to report on a minute's notice to their home base. General White could tell his military officer was chomping at the bit to get after the attackers. He almost felt sorry he was forced to hold back his favorite soldiers.

When the powerful Chairman of the Joint Chiefs of Staff, General John White finished with the call, the President immediately got his attention and then asked his military officer. "It's good to have you back with us, General White. May I ask you who you were just speaking to sir? It seemed like you were having a rather animated conversation with someone sir."

"Sorry Mr. President Sir. Good morning sir. That was my pain in the ass Captain Walker, sir. It seems like he's standing on his feet because he wants to get after the prick who masterminded this attack against us, sir. He picked out the same man we have leveled our eyes on, sir. He's a real smart young soldier there and he placed the blame for this attack square on bin Laden's shoulders, sir." The General offered with a smirk.

"That soldier again huh General White? I'm surprised it took him so long before checking in with you over this situation, General White." The President replied in a calmer tone this time.

"I'm forced to disagree with you Mr. President Sir. The Captain called yesterday when we were having the meeting, sir. I feel he's on the ball as always." The General offered to the President.

"I see, and I'm relieved he was concerned about us, General White Sir. Did you inform him I ordered his troops held back on this one, sir? If you did General, how did the spitfire take the holdback orders, sir? Knowing him, he must not have liked the order in the least, sir."

"You have that right Mr. President Sir, he was fit to be tied but he's a soldier and being such, he'll do as ordered, and he'll like it sir. Err... Mr. President, Captain Walker brought up a good point, sir. One I feel I should run by you before we take any actions against Usama Bin Laden, and the rest of the pack of nuts who follow the asshole, sir." The General offered as he took his seat after acknowledging the rest of the members attending the meeting with the President.

"Oh." The President said more to himself than to the officer as he settled back in his chair, and then he stared at the General. Then the President asked. "General White Sir, if this soldier has something on his mind, sir. I at least owe you that much sir, to hear what Captain Walker has suggested to you, sir. And for you to bring it up to my attention, I feel you think it was that important to hear, sir. Please General tell me what the Captain had to offer you, sir." The President shrugged and spread his hands apart and offered them to his military officer.

"Thank you for respecting my soldiers like you're doing, Mr. President Sir. Well sir, I know this conversation's going to piss off many of us attending this here meeting I'm afraid, sir. But I think my Captain offered up some very intriguing suggestions in our conversation, sir. The most important one he discussed with me, was we know we're going to Afghanistan to destroy this guy's terrorist organization, sir. Mr. President Sir, Captain Walker asked me if we go in with the thought of killing Usama Bin Laden, and if we do kill the lousy sonofabitch then we might be opening ourselves up to more trouble than this man gives us now, sir."

"Exactly what the hell did this Captain mean by that remark, General White? What is he afraid of from this man, General?" The new National Security Director, Bill Blaylocke, who took over for Norman Griffin killed in the attempt assassination on the President, grumbled.

The powerful Chairman looked at the new man and barked at him to keep him in his place at the meeting. "Director Blaylocke Sir, my Captain meant if bin Laden is killed by our soldiers then he'll be turned into a damn martyr for any jackass who can pick up a damn weapon and aim it at one of our soldiers or civilians, sir. We know damn well there are thousands of Muslim's standing on the fence, and killing bin Laden will push many of these assholes off the fence, and they too will become terrorists, sir. My Captain has pointed out if we were able to capture bin Laden then every one of these nuts will try something to get his ass out of our custody, sir. If anything happens to bin Laden by our hands, we'll give birth to thousands more terrorists, sir. And as I speak my Captain's words sir, I believe them more now, Director Blaylocke Sir."

"Hmmm General White Sir, I certainly see what your Captain means by this suggestion, sir. This is something we never took into consideration during our conversations. Did this Captain of yours give you any suggestions on how we should handle bin Laden and his horde of damn terrorists, General White Sir?" The President asked as he looked at his military officer.

"My young Captain didn't have all the answers for this problem, Mr. President Sir. But between the two of us, we did come up with a few ways to deal with this terrorist organization, sir. Mr. President, we feel if we place a bounty on bin Laden's head, maybe some damn Arab nut would come along and kill him for us, thus the heat will be off our damn backs with him being killed, sir. Also Mr. President Sir, we know bin Laden is skipping back and forth over the borders between Afghanistan and Pakistan at will, sir.

"If we can force bin Laden over the border to Pakistan, and that government kills bin Laden then that government would field the full heat for his death. In the meantime sir, we can keep pushing him all over Afghanistan, until we uncovered his terrorist cells and their links, and then destroy them all while allowing bin Laden to escape our traps with the skin on his damn ass, Mr. President. Once we have destroyed all his terrorist networks and training centers inside the nation of Afghanistan, we can then beat the bushes and force this damn nut over the damn border to Pakistan, and as I just offered, allow that government to kill him for us sir."

The Chairman of the Joint Chiefs of Staff stopped speaking so he could hear the complaining from the other members attending the meeting. To his surprise everyone there were nodding in the affirmative to the General's suggestions. General White was surprised to see even the CIA Director seemed like he was agreeing with him also.

"This seems like a simple solution to our problems, General White. To be quite honest with you General, I too was a little worried about killing this man outright, for fear of what might be released on us, once the Muslim world discovered we killed him, sir. I like this suggestion General White, and I feel we'll follow them as you suggested. Well done General White."

COLONEL HAMOODI AL-QAYSI'S HEADQUARTERS AT QULBAN-LAYYAH IN THE DESERT OF IRAQ

The Iraqi Colonel al-Qaysi returned to the Iraqi village on the same day the attacks on the Twin Towers in New York City and Pentagon took place. When he stormed into his makeshift headquarters, he was met by Major Serena al-Shaya, and she immediately began speaking excitedly to him. She informed him of what took place in New York City.

"Ahhh... now I see why the worthless fools closed the cursed border between Iraq and Kuwait, foolish woman. For a minute I feared the worthless Americans were again attacking our country. By the sacred Hand of Allah, do you know what this means to our plans, Major? We can no longer dare think about invading the hated United States now this great fool has attacked America on her own land. This is going to set our cause back many months against us I believe. I hate that cursed fool who dwells in the worthless lands of Afghanistan. If only he could have waited until we were safely in the United States. Then I wouldn't care what the devil he and his band of worthless fools did to the hated American criminals, Major. We have to get our hands on more information from the hated United States.

"Major al-Shaya, we have to know what the United States is going to do, and who they're going to seek their revenge against what nations, and how they're going to accomplish this feat against their intended target. Major al-Shaya, I fear the hated American eyes will sooner or later, be leveled against our foolish country of Iraq again, woman." Colonel al-Qaysi snarled, already taking it for granted that it was Usama bin Laden and his terrorist organization that was guilty of attacking the Twin Towers and Pentagon Building in the United States.

Major al-Shaya announced there were three homes in the village that had large satellite TV sets; they were the wealthiest of civilians who dwelled within the small village.

"Major al-Shaya, I order you to get out and steal one of these evil satellite TVs for our use. I need more up to date information on this situation, so I know exactly what is going on in the world. Have you been able to pick up any information from our military radios about this attack against the United States, Major?" Colonel al-Qaysi demanded to know from his female Major.

"Colonel al-Qaysi that is how we have discovered about the terrorists who just attacked the two phallic symbols that once adorned the skyline of New York City, sir..."

"What do you mean they have once adorned the cursed skyline of New York City, foolish woman? What has happened to these two god cursed building you speak of, woman? I know well of these buildings and have even seen them more than once in my life. I believe the fire departments would save the buildings from total destruction, woman."

"Colonel al-Qaysi, it was said the attacks have successfully destroyed both great buildings, and they are nothing more than massive rubble piles lying in the narrow streets of New York City at this time, sir. The foolish terrorist attacked also destroyed the Pentagon Building once resting in the heart of the land of Satan, Washington D.C. Whoever these terrorist were, they carried out a great attack against the evil lands of our enemies, and blackened the eye of Satan. I applaud the actions of our fellow Arab brothers who attacked the buildings, sir." The Major announced.

"We'll see how proud you are of these great fools who carried out these attacks against the land of the great Satan, when you realize what terrible horror the American soldiers shall visit upon the foul heads of these fools who were involved in the attacks against their lands. Major al-Shaya. You seem to believe you don't know who had carried out these attacks against the hated United States. If you don't know who it was then you're a greater fool than I first believed you were, foolish woman. You know as well as I do that it was Usama bin Laden who gave the order to destroy these two great buildings of the hated Americans.

"I cannot believe he and his warriors were able to destroy these two great buildings. I fear how the worthless Americans are going to react against the rest of the Arab nations of the world, because of this foolish attack against their worthless lands. I fear for the lives of every Arab brother and sister in the entire world. To fill the American people with such a great resolve will forever force their revenge upon anyone who even resembles an Arab. Are you still so foolishly proud of this lowly jackal who hides his foul arse in the cursed wastelands of Afghanistan, woman?" The extremely upset Colonel al-Qaysi growled at the female officer.

Major Serena al-Shaya shifted her weight from one foot to the other nervously, as she stared at the angry Iraqi

Colonel. She was afraid to dare reply to his angry words for fear of his anger being released against her person.

"I didn't think so foolish woman, be off with you and get me one of these hated satellite TVs from one of the worthless fools of this miserable little village. So I can see firsthand what's happening in the great land of Satan. Then maybe I can figure out what their next step might be in their coming revenge aimed at these fools for these attacks against them." The angry Iraqi Colonel let his breath out in a form of a hiss as he glared angrily at the young female Major until she finally left the building to carry out her last orders.

It took the female Iraqi Major a half an hour to return to their headquarters in the village, and in her arms was the TV, in Sergeant Muhammad Mushtaha's arms was the other equipment needed for the satellite dish system to operate properly. He set out to setup the equipment and Major al-Shaya had to stand by the window, until the Sergeant had the satellite dish properly aligned with the satellite that fed the information to the set. As Colonel al-Qaysi stared at the TV, the picture slowly came in clearer and clearer until it was as near as possible, perfect. Then he glared at the tube as the camera slowly when over all the terrible carnage that was once the massive North and South Towers of the World Trade Center, and what the emergency responders were currently doing to try and discover possible survivors of the terrorist sneak attack.

Colonel al-Qaysi was stunned by the amount of the damage he was witnessing as the camera slowly scanned the massive piles of rubble once two magnificent buildings of glass and concrete. He could not believe an airliner could possibly bring down such a huge building and two of them at that. Suddenly, the cameras turned on the Pentagon. A helicopter hovering over the building showed the massive damage done to this odd shaped structure. Colonel al-Qaysi could not believe the lack of damage to this building, when the same type of aircraft was able to destroy the two Towers. He cast an evil look at Major al-Shaya, because she told him the Pentagon Building was destroyed. But as he looked at the many pictures of the building, he saw only a small section of the structure was destroyed by the terrorist attack against it.

The more the fuming Iraqi Colonel saw of the attack, the more it upset him. Because each devastating image showed him he was going to be forced to put off his mission against the soldiers who had dared to invade his country, for longer than he wanted to wait. Under his breath he cursed the Arab terrorists involved in these attacks against the hated Americans.

All the other Iraqi soldiers made themselves busy. The soldiers did not want to be captured under the harsh glare of their angry Colonel for doing nothing to forward his plans. Most of the worried soldiers left the building and they searched outside their headquarters for something to do. Even Major al-Shaya left the headquarters and soon, only the Colonel was the last person still inside the building and he was still watching the stolen TV set.

Even the civilians of the village seemed to know something wrong was happening in the headquarters of the building. They noticed the heavily armed soldier hanging around outside and trying to look busy. Many of the civilians knew of the terrorist attack in the United States, and they seemed to be waiting for the American soldiers to take their anger out on their nation for a second time. It seemed even the children, were afraid to make any noise on this day. Many civilians were standing around outside their building doing nothing but watching the soldiers.

THE UNITED STATED, SEPTEMBER 12th, 2001

The President of the United States made a big thing at showing up at what was classified as the ground zero area in New York City. He stood along with a number of the brave firefighters, police, and many of the vast army of workers looking for survivors and bodies trapped under the mound of rubble of the two buildings. Then it was reported the President returned to Washington to make his plans to attack those responsible for the terrible terrorist action against the United States. The Arab world found itself holding its breath for fear of where the American anger was going to be aimed. Even the Iraqi President, Saddam Hussein condemned the attack on the American civilians, but he quickly recanted his condemnation of the terrorist attack.

At another long meeting between the members of his cabinet, the President began to go over his future planned response to the terrorist attack. He ordered General White to prepare his troops to hit Afghanistan in force. The President warned Saudi Arabia, Jordan, Egypt and Israel he was planning to hit the Arab nation Afghanistan, and destroy the terrorist network freely operating there, and place a quick end to the control the Taliban regime held on the poor people of Afghanistan. All other nations the American Leader spoke to, immediately offered their blessings for the United States to attack the nation of Afghanistan. They were more than happy the United States' anger was not being leveled against them. Many nations, mostly the ones always backing the United States in her times of need or troubles, offered their own elite troops to help the United States destroy the terrible regime of the Taliban radicals and of Usama bin Laden's terrorist organization group operating in the terribly poor nation of Afghanistan.

It took the American Commanders days to prepare their troops and military equipment needed, to invade and then destroy the terrorists operating in Afghanistan. Russia, who had received a bloody nose and black eye in their war with the Afghanistan nation, remained standing on the sidelines smiling. The Russian Command believed the Afghan fighters would do to the American soldiers, what they had done to their prized Russian Warriors. They were about to be proven wrong that the American soldiers are the best fighters in the world.

At an unbelievable rate, military Unit after Units reported they were ready to begin their opening attack against the rebel controlled Arab nation of Afghanistan. The United States was able to stun the world at how quickly they were able to mobilize their massive military forces, and have the soldiers prepared to make war with any nation who harmed Americans, especially in their own country's borders. The clouds of war were thick over the horizon, and the world knew it was only a matter of days before the United States attacked the Afghanistan nation.

OCTOBER 7th, 2001

On October 7th, 2001, the President of the United States ordered an all out air and land strike aimed against the terrorist organization of al-Qa'eda. The terrorists were to be attack no matter where they were organized in Afghanistan. The American Leader issued orders for his air and ground forces to destroy all terrorist training camps and military installations of the Taliban regime and the al-Qaeda terrorist installations discovered in Afghanistan. The military forces were joined by specialized troops, aircraft and naval ships from the usual friends of the United States. As always, the United Kingdom stepped up and committed her nation's specialized SAS troops. They were joined by special troops from Canada, Australia, Germany, and France.

Within a mere three week's time, the combined forced of allied troops completely destroyed the control the Taliban regime once held over most of the nation of Afghanistan. All the terrorist training camps were likewise erased from the face of the earth as soon as they were discovered by any of the attacking allied forces.

Russia, even though she never let on to the fact, was fuming the American troops so easily destroyed the ground forces of the Afghan fighters. Russia was looking forward to the United States getting involved in another Vietnam type endless war in the troublesome Arab nation.

Slowly, the overwhelming war in Afghanistan began to wind down, true the search for bin Laden went on with many of the caves he used as his operational command centers were being destroyed one after the other by the so called American bunker buster bombs. Also, many small skirmishes occurred between the fleeing terrorist fighters and Allied troops, but most of the heavy fighting was concluded in the nation. Thousands of American and Allied soldiers continued to search the mountain areas for the known leader of the terrorist organization. Countless stories surfaced they had bin Laden trapped, and after the fighting ended, it was released that the hunted terrorist leader was able to escape the trap set out against him.

It was happening just as the America Leader ordered. They were pushing bin Laden from one hiding place to another, and once he left this group, they were immediately destroyed by the American Forces. Hundreds of once terrorists were killed in these attacks, and soon, bin Laden found himself with no safe place to hide in all of Afghanistan, and he was forced over the mountains into the lawless regions of the nation of Pakistan. Now, he found himself being hunted down from both sides of the border. The Pakistani government was no fool, and they took to hitting the terrorist camps in their own nation once they were certain bin Laden left the area to be attack. They too, did not want any part of being responsible for the feared terrorist's death, for the same exact reason the United States was worried about it.

MARATHON ISLAND, THE FLORIDA KEYS

Even though Captain Robert Walker and the rest of his specialized troops were not activated after the Nine, One, One nightmare attacks, many of the elite troops showed up at Walker and the Mutt's homes. A few of the soldiers even brought homes on Marathon, or the other surrounding Keys. The soldiers wanted to be around Walker when the call for duty came in. Walker's attention was being torn between his new son, his wife, and the soldiers, and what was going on in Afghanistan. He was keeping a close eye on the troop's actions being carried out in the Afghan nation. If he could not be there physically, he sure was going to be with those soldiers in spirit. Every other day, he made a call to General White, to make certain they were not activated.

The Chairman of the Joint Chiefs of Staff was beginning to feel sorry for his young Captain, because he knew why the calls were being placed to him. Captain Walker was chomping at the bit to get involved in the war against the al-Qa'eda terrorists. But the General did not want his troops going out on a revenge mission, because he understood the soldiers would be brutal against any enemy troops these soldiers came across. He even went so far as to bring this situation up to the President. But President Albert Cole would not budge from his original orders of keeping these specialized troops held back in the United States, in case he needed them here. For the first time since the attack on the Twin Towers and the building Pentagon, the American Leader brought up the terrorist Colonel still being held in the Brig at Andrews Airforce Base.

General John White was relieved the President was turning his attention away from all the mayhem caused by the other terrorists group, and he was pleased to get on with this problem and said. "Mr. President Sir, has there been a Judge appointed to try this case yet, sir?"

"As far as I know, I don't believe a Federal Judge was appointed to the trial yet, General. What with all that has transpired in the past few months, I don't think there was much attention given to this Iraqi Colonel we're still holding. Tell you what I'll do, I'll bring it up to Director Raincloud, and sic him on this situation. I want to start trying this man, and maybe we can get the public's attention away from this expanding war, and turn it towards the court system, sir. It's time we settle this one's hash once and for all sir, before some damn lawyer comes along and starts crying we're holding him and not giving him his day in court." The President said as he ran a hand slowly through this thinning hair, and then he let out his breath in a rush.

"Mr. President Sir, I have a meeting scheduled with Director Raincloud for later on this afternoon, sir. I'd be please to breach this subject with him, if you'd want me to sir."

"Yes please, that way this much crap would be lifted off my shoulders, General White Sir."

"Fine, consider it done then for you Mr. President." The General replied, already showing the first signs he wanted to leave the President, and get on with his own work for the day.

"General White, I can see you have one foot out the door already on me sir. So you might as well get on your way before you hurt yourself here, sir." The President said with a grin.

"Thank you very much for that offer, Mr. President Sir. I sure will take advantage of the offer, sir." The Chairman fired back and then he was up and out the door before the President could possible change his mind. When he was in his staff car and the driver pulling away from the White House, General White placed a call out to the CIA Director, John Raincloud. The excited military officer wanted to speak with the Director for a while, but he was so pressed for time he had not had a chance to speak with the Native American for the past two days. The phone rang three times before it was finally answered by the Director's secretary in a pleasant voice.

"CIA Director John Raincloud's office, how many I direct this call for you please?" Mary, Director Raincloud's private secretary purred sexily into the phone politely.

"Good afternoon Mary is John hanging around in his office. I need to speak to him if it's at all possible." The Chairman announced for the Director's secretary.

Mary immediately recognized the General voice and she replied. "Why good afternoon General White Sir, yes sir, Director Raincloud's in his office sir, and he has an opened afternoon schedule, sir. Would the General like to speak with the Director himself please, sir?"

"How well you know me Mary. No, I don't really want to speak to him over the phone. Do me a favor though and don't allow him to leave the office before I get there. I should be arriving by, err..." He stopped speaking and then looked at his watch, and then he looked out the car window and realized where he was, and then he offered back to the secretary. "I should be hitting his office within the next fifteen minutes or so, young lady."

"Very good General White Sir, I'll inform Director Raincloud you're on the way, sir."

"Please Mary and thank you and good bye Ma'am." General White replied.

"I will and you have a good day at that General White Sir." Mary's words ending up speaking to a dial tone. She smiled as she hung up and hit the Director over the intercom.

"Yes Mary." Director Raincloud replied as he heard the buzzer on the intercom go off.

"Director Raincloud, General White just called the office sir, and he asked me to inform you that he was on his way over to your officer to speak with you privately, sir. The General sounded rather excited in his want to have a conversation with you sir. I informed the General I wouldn't allow you to leave the office before he arrived here to meet with you, sir."

"Very good Mary, would you show him in when he arrives. This is strange we had a meeting scheduled for a little later on in the afternoon. Something must have come up for the General to want to push up our meeting like this, Mary."

"I certainly will the moment he arrives at the office Director, with all that just happened in the past few months in the United States, I'm quite certain something mush have came up to bring the General here earlier, sir. Should I have coffee and cakes waiting for him, sir?"

"No, I think this meeting might need something a little bit stronger than just coffee and some cakes, Mary." Director Raincloud said with a giggle to his secretary.

"Why Director Raincloud, don't tell me General White and you might want to tie one on today, sir?" Now it was Mary's turn to giggle slightly. She loved being around the two powerful men when they started to drink together. That meant she would hear more funny stories the two men engaged in while they were younger men. Even though she was told they would not need any coffee, she decided to brew up a pot ready anyway. In case they drank more than had planned, and they needed some strong coffee to help sober them up a little.

"Me, drink too much young lady. Naw, never happen I assure you Mary." Raincloud retorted.

"Don't try and pull the wool over my eyes, mister! You seem to forget how long I have been working for you now sir And how many times I had to actually pick both you and the General up from the floor, and pour some hot coffee into you two fools. Then I had to have the poor security guard's pitch you two in your cars so your wives wouldn't kill you for spending the night away from them again, sir." Mary replied, openly laughing at her boss now.

"True, true, you have me there I'm afraid, Mary. Thinking about this a little longer young lady, I think you might want to stick around until the General leaves the office. You know, in case the General talks me into drinking too much like he always does." John snickered in the intercom.

"Oh, and now you're going to try and blame it all on the General, Director Raincloud."

"Blame what on me Mary? What the hell did I do wrong now? That old grouch of a boss of yours is always blaming me for something going wrong around here, young lady." General White asked and offered with a smirk as he entered the office.

"Oh, nothing General White Sir, I was just teasing the Director a little, that's all, sir. It's good to see you on this day, General White Sir." Mary smiled pleasantly to the large military officer.

"Mary, is that the grumpy old goat out there honey?" Director Raincloud asked his secretary.

"Who the hell are you calling an old, buddy?" General White replied for the pretty secretary.

"C'mon in John, I've been meaning to talk with you for the past few days myself, sir."

General White nodded to Mary as he walked past her desk and opened the door to the Director's office and entered. Director Raincloud stood and offered the General his hand. They shook then Raincloud offered the General a chair. "Something to wet you whistle with, John?" He smiled at the large, black military officer as he waited for his reply to the offer of a drink.

"Please, I really need one right about now, John. The President has me running around in fucking circles lately I tell you." He said, and then he got down to business with the lead CIA Agent. "Director Raincloud, the Boss sent me here to bring up the subject about the rat we have locked away over at Andrews. He's a bit concerned we're holding the lousy prick a bit too long without bringing him to trial. He's more than worried about some bleeding heart wiseass lawyer going to pick it up, and file a complaint on behalf of this jackrabbit we're holding in the Brig. You know Director, the speedy trial thing and other crap like that, his civil rights Director."

"I hear you there General White." Director Raincloud replied with a smirk as he poured the military officer a good hit of Rye. Then he handed him the glass and asked. "What do you want me to do about the situation you just brought up to my attention, General White? To tell you the truth General, I completely forgot all about this bastard for the time being I'm afraid, John. What with the terrorist hit against us and our troops currently stationed in Afghanistan, sir."

"The President wants me to see if you can possibly hurry up the pick of the Federal Judge who'll put this lousy bastard under the damn ground for us, Chief. He wants this man as bad as he wanted bin Laden, sir." General White said as he downed the drink.

"You need another drink General White? Did you even taste that first one sir?" Director Raincloud asked because of the way the General just downed the first drink as quickly as he put his hand to his chin, and then he began to think of what the Chairman told him.

"Yeah, I need another hit at that John. This damn mess in Afghanistan has me running around looking for terrorists hiding behind every fricking bush I look at, dammit. Now that the main fighting has concluded in Afghanistan, we're constantly being probed by these assholes too fucking stupid to realize they're defeated in that damn nation. The dopey bastards should disappear back in the hole they crawled out from under, before we get our hands on their damn asses. And we plant them in the ground and send them on their way to Paradise, dammit."

"I hear that, any luck with your troops locating bin Laden anywhere in Afghanistan, General White Sir?"

Director Raincloud questioned as he poured the General a second glass of Rye, and then he pulled a file from his desk drawer and dropped it down on the surface of the desk, as he listened to the General's words.

"You should know about the fuck better than I do, Director. We know where he is at all times, and before we hit the next dump he's hiding in, we start to buildup our forces in the area. To inform the ass we're coming for his damn backside, and then we allow him enough time to bug the hell out of the area, and we trail him to his next lousy rathole, and once we destroyed the one he left. We start the same procedure on the next one sir. We got the asshole running all over the damn place, between Afghanistan and Pakistan. Right now, he don't know if he's coming or going, but it's impossible for him to take the time to set up another terrorist attack against us here. He can't even take a damn crap in peace, John. We have all his cellular phone and computer communications fucked up on him." General White reported to the CIA Director.

"I think you're employing a pretty good course of action against the damn terrorist leader I believe, sir." Director Raincloud offered as he quickly went thumbing through the file he had lying on his desk after he finished off his second drink with the General.

"What do you have there for me John?" The military officer asked the Director this time, as he cast his eyes down on the Director's desk and noticed the file on it.

"It's the file on all the Federal Judges who work in the Washington District that I've been considering asking to try this damn terrorist bastard we still holding over at Andrews, General White. I guess I should've gotten on this damn problem long before this time and you were forced to bring it up to my attention again, General. I wanted to find just the right Judge to try this fucker though, so things don't get out of hand on us, John. A Judge who'll drop the boom down hard on the lousy bastard's head when the jury finds him guilty as charged, my old friend."

"You better pick out the hardest nose bastard of a Judge you have in that damn file, John." The slightly tipsy military officer remarked to the Director, egging him ion with picking out the strongest Judge he had in his file.

"Don't I know that for a fact General, ahhh... here we go here's the right man for the damn job I'm looking for General." The Director announced proudly as he quickly scanned the names of the judges in his file folder. "Judge William Karlanderson. From what I know of the man, everyone who walks in his courtroom is guilty as charged until he's proven otherwise to the man. And, he's rarely proven wrong at that sir. Would you care for another drink while we're at this?" Director Raincloud asked as he pulled the sheet with the judge's name printed on it out of the file, and laid it on his desk.

"Naw, my head's spinning as it is already John. One more will put me over the damn edge, and I'll be messed up for the rest of the entire day I believe, sir. Are you going to get on this Judge's backside for me John and bring him up to speed what we want done with this damn case? So I can report back to the President that this thing's being handled for him?" The General replied as he fired off a quick smile at the concerned looking CIA Director.

"Sure will General, by nine a.m. tomorrow morning, Judge William Karlanderson will know he's going to be conducting the trial against this damn terrorist assassin, General White Sir."

"Outstanding, say John I have to get on the run, what say over the weekend we get together and really tie one on for ourselves. I surely do need some R and R." Rest and Relaxation.

"Sounds like a plan to me. I'll be back to you after I notified this Judge he was just selected to run the trail." Raincloud offered as he picked up the sheet with the name printed on it.

CHAPTER TEN

Judge William Karlanderson just walked into his office behind the old courtroom he held his trials in. It was eight twenty a.m., and the elderly judge dropped his newspaper on his desk, and then he was going to get a cup of coffee from the secretary area down the hall from his office. He hung up his jacket and turned up the heat in the office. The judge was about to head out for his morning coffee when his phone rang. He wondered why his secretary did not answer because he rarely had to answer his phone. On the fifth ring, he decided his secretary was not in her office, and reached for the phone and grumbled. "Yes, this is Judge Karlanderson. Who is this please?"

"William, how the hell are you doing sir? This is Director John Raincloud, sir."

"John, it's great to hear from you again sir. What do you know, what do you say sir?"

"Everything's going real fine for the moment, William. The war in Afghanistan is going better than first expected. And we're considering removing some of the ground forces from that area, your Honor. Err... William, this is the reason I'm placing the call to you sir. Since the war is going so well for us, President Cole decided to push up the trial of the Iraqi Colonel, Judge."

"Who the hell is he John?" The judge asked, not remembering the terrorist's name.

"Sorry William, but he's the Iraqi Colonel who masterminded the assassination attempt on the President's life a few months back, sir." The Director reminded the judge on the phone.

"Ahhhh... yes, I remember him now John. Why are you bringing this up to my attention?"

"Well William, as I told just told you sir. The President wants to move forward with the trial of this man, and I suggested you be the Judge who'll try him, sir. If you happen to agree with the appointment that is, William. I really could order you to try the bastard and let it go at that, sir. But I wouldn't want to do that to you, I'd rather you make up your own mind to try this damn terrorist for us, sir." Director Raincloud held his breath as he waited for the judge to reply.

"I'd be honored to try this man for the President, John. To try and kill our President will he, the dirty bastard he is. I'll see to it he's hung up by his laurels for that one sir. When do you want me to start the trial against him, John? It'll take me at least two weeks in order for me to clear my docket, Director. I have a trial scheduled to end tomorrow afternoon when I pass sentence on the prisoner, and then I was scheduled to being another trial by the end of the next week. But I can always shift that one over to another Judge, after that, I'll be free from then on John."

"The President really wanted the trial to begin yesterday, but that timeline you have just offered to me will do just fine for my needs, sir. Glad to have you overseeing this damn case for the President, William. I don't think another Judge could possibly handle it like I'm certain you can, sir. I have great faith in you sir." The Director announced proudly to the Federal Judge.

WEDNESDAY, NOVEMBER 14th, 2001. FEDERAL COURT DISTRICT SEVENTEEN, WASHINGTON D.C., OFFICE OF JUDGE WILLIAM KARLANDERSON

Ever though the judge was nowhere to be seen, his private secretary was busy fielding all the endless questions the news reporters were throwing at her one after the other in rapid succession. Some of the questions asked almost nastily by the excited reporters and she resented them.

"How does the Judge feel now that it's been announced by the Administrative Judge that he was just picked to preside over the trial of the terrorist who had masterminded the assassination attempt against our President, Ma'am?"

"The Judge is honored to be picked to preside over the trial of this suspected terrorist, sir. I can assure everyone here that the Judge is looking forward to sit on the bench for this trial. He's already preparing for the trail, and he's brushing up on the law covering such actions, sir."

"Is there any increase for the Judge's security because of the terrorist attack, Ma'am?"

"Now why in the devil would the Judge want to increase the security he chooses to surround himself with, sir? Judge William Karlanderson is quite comfortable living in the United States without fear of being attacked by anyone, sir." The judge's secretary announced with a snap in her tone of voice as she placed her hands on her hips, and then she glared back at the reporter.

"Well Ma'am, this Arab man he'll see over this case is accused of masterminding the assassination attempt of the President of our nation, and that's why the question of the Judge's security was brought up to your attention. Everyone attending this here press conference knows the President is better protected than any Judge is in this country, Ma'am. Has anyone taken the time to speak with the Judge about his having some extra security surrounding him for the duration of the trial of this terrorist? Under the circumstances that is, Ma'am."

"I can assure you and everyone else attending this press conference, the subject of any added security around Judge Karlanderson has been brought up to his attention. But the Judge has refused to employ any additional security while announcing he was living in the United States of America, and if he couldn't walk down the streets of America safely. Then he's prepared to retire from office and hide in his home." The secretary remained with her hands angrily resting on her hips as she continued to glare at the young reporter who just asked the two insulting questions of her. The young secretary was well aware that the CIA Director had offered the judge some extra security, but the old man had refused it. Offering he would never allow himself to be intimidated by any thugs like this terrorist was while living in his own country.

The questions continued to be asked of the judge's secretary in rapid succession by the horde of overly excited reporters, and both Judge Karlanderson and Director Raincloud listened to the endless questions being fired at his secretary from the judge's private chambers, as his secretary answered the questions from the almost insulting reporters.

"Whew, I'm damn glad you talked me into allowing my secretary answer the reporter's questions for me, John. The damn reporters are being extremely brutal on her, Director. I never expected them to be so aggressive while asking their questions of my secretary. It seems I have a lot to learn whenever dealing with the reporters of our country, Director Raincloud."

"I'm pleased you listened to my suggestion, sir. After all Bill, I've been thought my fair share of these damn interviews with these damn reporters driving me absolutely crazy sir, to know what I'm talking about when it comes down to any of these damn press conferences, Judge." CIA Director Raincloud replied to the judge with a sheepish smile on his lips.

The two men remained sitting in the judge's chamber until the press conference had finally ran its course, and the terribly shaken secretary walked into the judge's chamber still in an upset state. The moment she sat down she began to complain at the judge and CIA Director for forcing her to handle the nasty reporters for the judge at the conference. She was still very upset the horrible reporters had hit her with so many ugly and endless questions. With each one a little more insulting and aggressively asked of her than the other against her boss.

One of the reporters went so far as to dare suggest that the judge might have pulled in some favors behind the stage, to be awarded the high profile trial of the captured Iraqi terrorist. This question instantly made the secretary see red because she knew Judge Karlanderson was well beyond any possible reproach of his character. Here this disgusting reporter was, questioning the integrity of her boss before the world. She wanted to leave the dais and walk across the room and slap this ugly man right across his face, she was that angered by the question.

The overly concerned Judge Karlanderson poured the secretary a glass of rum to help calm down her rattled nerves a little. Once the secretary finished her drink and complaining, the judge gave her the rest of the day off because of all the trouble the reporters gave her at the press conference. Once she was out of the office, both John and William laughed over the way the reporters had attacked his secretary, as they both shared another drink together.

THE WHITE HOUSE

The President was sitting in the Oval Office with General White, and they were going over how the war still raging in Afghanistan was going for them, when the conference for the judge came in over the TV. They both stopped what they were doing and watched the young woman answer most of the excited reporter's questions aimed at her in a professional way, while still maintaining her temper while dealing with the horde of news reporters.

"Hmmmm… I wonder why the Judge didn't hold the conference himself, General White."

"It was on my orders that Judge Karlanderson's secretary was ordered to field the reporter's questions Mr.

President Sir, mainly because the Judge is currently meeting with Director Raincloud in his private chambers, and we have discussed this situation beforehand. We decided it might not be a good idea to allow the Judge to be attacked by the reporters certain to show up at the press conference, sir. Although he's a wise and very intelligent Judge, he has no real experience speaking with reporters, and John and I felt it wasn't a good idea to give him his first experience, before a bunch of hungry for news reporters, Mr. President Sir." General White offered as he watched the conference until it broke up, and the secretary disappeared in an office.

"Ahhh... I see what you're saying General White, and I believe you might have saved our poor Judge's life for himself with those kind thoughts, General. I hate any of these press conferences, the damn reporters never seem to mind the insulting questions they ask at these meeting, General." The President smirked at his military officer as he held him momentarily in his gaze.

QULBAN-LAYYAH IRAQ. WEDNESDAY,
NOVEMBER 14th, 2001

Iraqi Colonel al-Qaysi listened attentively to the report on the TV, because the reporters were interviewing some woman about the judge elected to handle the trial concerning Colonel al-Adwani. Al-Qaysi wrote down the name of Judge William Karlanderson on a slip of paper. He was smiling at the female Major standing at his side then began bragging to her proudly.

"There you see Major al-Shaya; it is like I told you, woman. Be patient my sister, and the foolish American animals will spread their arse cheeks wide. Now we know the name of the infidel Judge who'll try one of our brothers, something no American Judge has the right to do, Major al-Shaya. We also know the cursed trial will be held in their Federal Superior Courtroom in Washington D.C. We further know this Judge refused any added security personnel around him, which will make it easier for us to kill the old jackal, when we get to America. I thank Almighty Allah for the wonderful gift He has bestows upon our worthless heads, my sister."

Colonel al-Qaysi was in a good mood, it was filled with great news. First he found out the American Judge's name and then he was informed by Lieutenant Bashar al-Maluk, who he assigned to keep an eye on the border between Iraq and Kuwait. Al-Maluk was to find out when the border was going to be allowing vehicles back in Kuwait from the Iraqi side of the border. The Lieutenant reported earlier in the day the border checkpoint was finally opened again.

The Colonel was receiving other news from the United States, and Iraq. For the first time in years, President Saddam Hussein was not trying to agitate the Americans and English further. Since the American soldiers and military machines attacked Afghanistan, President Hussein was keeping a sort of low key in his country. Al-Qaysi felt this was so the Americans did not level their eyes on him. The United Nations inspections were going along as ordered, and the President of Iraq even lowered his hate filled words aimed at the United States and any of her Allies.

The United States likewise was forgetting about Iraq, now that she had her hands full with Afghanistan and the war taking place in that country. Even though most of the heavy fighting ended in the rebel nation, there were still some strong remnants of the Taliban regime intact, and members of al-Qa'eda was carrying out guerrilla attacks against the American and Allied Forces there. This was keeping the United States attention aimed at that nation, and she was not looking so much at what was going on in Iraq. Only the Allied warplanes who attack any of Iraqi's missile installations when the Iraq war machine lit up the United States or United Kingdom planes of war with their aiming and attack tracking radar, was the only military actions still taking place inside Iraq from the American and Allied warplanes.

It was getting so calm in and around the nation of Iraq that borders from all sides leading into Iraq was relaxed. The only thing still bothering Colonel al-Qaysi was the fact he was being forced to place his future attack against the United States off until this time. Because of the terrorist attacks carried out by al-Qa'eda with the Taliban help in New York City, and the Washington D.C. area. But all in all, it was better he was forced to wait this added time, before he and his soldiers could attack their intended targets in the United States. He now knew the judge's name, and where the court trail against Colonel al-Adwani was going to be held.

Colonel al-Qaysi though for a while, he was pleased at what was happening around him. He decided to leave the small Iraqi village and head to the border to speak to his contacts in Kuwait. The Colonel wanted to get his people out of Iraq, even though so much was going well around him. He understood it was only a matter of time, before the Iraqi President did something foolish against the world that would force the Americans and her Allies to attack Iraq in force for a second time in the same decade. Now, with the strong patriotism the American public was displaying since the Nine, One, One terrorist attacks against that nation. He understood the American public would stand behind their President if he decided to look at Saddam again.

Major al-Shaya interrupted the Colonel's thoughts as she offered to him. "Colonel al-Qaysi Sir, this is a good time to think about getting our people out of Iraq, and move them in position to invade the United States, sir. I believe if we continue to wait, there's much more of a chance that something will happen in the Middle East to cause the American soldiers to come again to our land. If it does not happen between Israel and the Palestinians, it's going to happen because of our foolish President, when he again tries to test the resolve of the American fools and their Allies. As sure as the winds will blow in the deserts tomorrow, something will happen that'll surely cause the American troops to attack our lands again." She smiled at her commander.

"Huh woman of the desert sands, you're a mind reader I suddenly fear. It's strange because I was thinking the same thoughts. I intend to leave this foul sewer of a village later today, and go to the border to Kuwait. Once there, I'll make contact with our brothers there, so we can buy the foul airline tickets that'll take us to the Bahamas, and then we make our way to the worthless Island we need to be picked up at, once I have successfully made contact with the loathsome American civilian pleasure boat Captains who'll smuggle us into their god cursed land of sin…"

"Colonel al-Qaysi Sir, with the attack on the United States by the terrorists from al-Qa'eda, do you still believe these fools will be so willing to smuggle our terrorists into their god forsaken country safely for us, sir?" the female officer asked her commander as she waited his reply.

"Foolish woman, I have no doubt in my mind that the foul American Captains will still be just as willing to get us into their hated country safely, woman. Major al-Shaya, the United States is a land that is governed purely by greed, want and loathing. And I Major, will pay any increase these hated fools born of a camel's arse will demand of me, in order to get our people into the United States safely, foolish woman." He hissed at the female officer staring at him.

"When will the Colonel be heading for the Kuwaiti border then, sir?" She asked, as she diverted her eyes from his. She feared his answer and his anger even more over her question.

"I guess now is as good a time as any to leave, Major al-Shaya. Order my car be brought around while I get the American cash I need. I have to be rather generous to our foul Kuwaiti brothers, my sister." The Colonel demanded as he rose then stretched his arms over his head.

Major al-Shaya went outside their headquarters to carry out her new orders. While Colonel al-Qaysi went to his room and removed five thousand American dollars they stole from the Kuwaiti bank weeks back. He came down dressed in an expensive civilian suit, and went outside and jumped in his car without speaking to the grinning female Major. Then he gunned the machine and was off like a shot. It took him seventeen minutes to reach the border between the two nations of Iraq and Kuwait. First the officer showed the Iraqi border guards his Iraqi military passport, they checked it and waved him through the checkpoint without concern.

His car did not go another fifty feet before he was stopped a second time, this was by the Kuwaiti border guards. Colonel Al-Qaysi flashed his Kuwaiti passport at the border guards and they automatically waved him through the Kuwaiti side of the lightly guarded checkpoint. The Iraqi military officer headed directly for the town of Khabrat

Umm al-Hiran. It was a small city, but it had an international airport, and the security was reported very weak there. The Arab Colonel drove for another half an hour until he finally pulled into the heart of the Arab city.

He hit the main road, and then he followed it until he was on the west side of the city near the home of the two Kuwaiti citizens helping him and his troops leave the Middle East. He pulled up to the home and parked and got out of his car and walked to the front door of the home and knocked on it as if he owned the world. Instantly, the door opened, and Colonel al-Qaysi saw the face of Yasir Ahmed Tafish, and his friend in the home, Zakaria al-Achhab. Tafish invited the Iraqi Colonel into his home with a smile. He gave a quick look around to make certain no one was following the Iraqi Military Officer, and only then did he closed the door as he offered.

"Ahhh... Colonel al-Qaysi Sir, it's good to see you once again, my faithful Arab brother. May Allah hold His hand above your head for protection, I feared you might have changed your mind about leaving your foul country, and seeking asylum safely in the United States after all that has happened within the borders of the United States. All is ready for you and your fellow troops to leave Iraq through Kuwait, as soon as you chose to leave your homeland sir. The plane that'll carry you to your freedom will land in the Grand Bahamas Island chain. Please Colonel, don't look so concerned sir. It is not uncommon for citizens from Kuwait, to visit the small Islands of the Bahamas for a vacation. It's a most pleasing place to visit my Arab brother.

"It's very good for Arabs to be surrounded with some water for a change, rather than being always surrounded with a sea of unending sands of the desert once in a while. Brother al-Qaysi, everything is ready for you and your friends when you are ready to leave us. When will you bring the rest of your people fed up with your foolish President and his foul actions, and want to go to the United States to enjoy the freedom they offer, sir?" Tafish asked the Iraqi Colonel as he put out his hand, and waited for the Iraqi Military Officer to give him the money he asked for.

"I believe I'd like to leave this foul land of sand by next week at the very latest, my faithful fellow believer of Allah and His great words." Colonel Hamoodi al-Qaysi said as he removed the five thousand American dollars from his pocket, and handed it over to Tafish. Tafish instantly passed the money over to al-Achhab, and he quickly counted it in front of both men, and then he announced in a flat tone of voice to them. "Tafish, it is all here, like we have agreed to."

"In that case Colonel al-Qaysi let me see, today is Wednesday so shall we say you should consider leaving Kuwait on Wednesday, the 21st of November, sir? That way you can begin your trip over to the United States by the end of next week at the latest, Colonel Hamoodi al-Qaysi."

"That sounds like a good time for my soldiers and me to begin our trip to our freedom waiting in the United States, Tafish." Colonel Al-Qaysi replied in a calm tone while carrying out the deception he was displaying before the Kuwaiti citizens. When they first met through a mutual friend, these two Kuwaiti citizens could not do enough for the Iraqi soldier once they were informed he and twenty of his fellow soldiers wanted to defect to the United States from Iraq. These two men would do anything to hurt the nation of Iraq, and their hated President.

"Colonel al-Qaysi Sir, I'd like you and the rest of your followers to arrive at my home on Tuesday night at anytime of the night you can make it here safely, sir. I'll be home all day and night waiting for you, and your friends will spend the night here in the safety and comfort of my home. I already have the airline tickets brought for you and your friends, and the plane will leave Kuwait on Wednesday afternoon; at two thirty p.m. our time and that means you'll be landing in the Bahamas Island chain at twelve thirty a.m., also our time, sir. You'll be arriving in the Bahamas at ten thirty a.m. the Bahamas time, Colonel al-Qaysi Sir." Tafish offered to the Iraqi Military Officer as he waited for some kind of response from the Iraqi soldier.

"This is good for me to hear, because I don't want to arrive in the Bahamas in the middle of the night, my wise Arab brother. I'll have my people here by say, ten p.m. on Tuesday night, and then we'll wait to leave this endless land of sand, sir." He grumbled as he took a quick breath.

"That is a good time indeed to arrive at my home, Colonel al-Qaysi Sir. I'll be waiting for you and your fellow soldiers to come, along with the other five thousand American dollar payment you owe me, Colonel al-Qaysi." Tafish reminded him with a sneer on his lips, and a warning of a harmed look in his eyes, if the Colonel failed to bring the rest of the money.

"I'll have the final payment in full as we have agreed to, Brother Tafish. Again I thank you and your friend here for all your kind help with my leaving our homeland before our foolish President is the cause of the death of Iraq as a nation, Tafish. Allah shall reward you kindly for your help of his faithful Arab brothers in need, and we're true believes in his sacred faith of Sunni who are in need of your help, my Arab brothers of the sands." The Colonel offered politely, but he was still having trouble believing the words he was saying to these two fools.

Tafish did not reply to the Colonel's words. Instead, he nodded as he watched the officer stand, and then quickly leave his home. In no time, the Iraqi Colonel found himself stopped at the checkpoint by the Iraq, Kuwait border. It took him twenty minutes to cross the overcrowded border to his homeland of Iraq. He drove at breakneck speed back to his village, because he wanted his soldiers to get ready to leave Iraq for the last time in their lives. He knew if any of them survived this mission in the United States, and if they were lucky enough to escape the United States with their lives. None of them would ever return to Iraq again in their lives.

Colonel Hamoodi al-Qaysi made plans to live out the rest of his life in secret in the nation of Jordan, and then maybe return to Iraq if and when the United States forces finally kill Saddam for him, and a new government gets installed in his severely fractured Arab country. Then, depending on who was elected to control Iraq at that time, he might consider returning and offering the new President of Iraq his services and connections and military knowledge.

The days could not go by fast enough for Colonel al-Qaysi to be comfortable with. He did nothing but yell at his fellow soldiers, making certain they looked like anything but soldiers for their trip to the United States. He had them dressed in civilian clothes and the women of the group had to get used to the rather reveling clothes he ordered them to wear from this point forward. He even had them cut and make shorter their dresses, and get used to wearing no bars, and leaving their blouses opened, exposing a lot of their breasts to anyone who looked at them. The male soldiers had to look like sex starved Cubans. From all he knew of the United States, Cuba, and the Bahamas Islands, everything there was meant to expose their bodies for all to see. Colonel al-Qaysi found himself even enjoying seeing so much of his female soldier's skin being exposed in this fashion. His only weakness in life was that of the female flesh, despite what the Arab world always believed in. He loved to see the body of a female naked.

Even though they were still trapped in Iraq, Colonel al-Qaysi understood it was expected of all Arab visitors to another nation, to dress and fit in like the locals of the nation they were visiting. Especially since the terrorist attack on the United States, all Arabs or Arab looking people were being attacked in many nations mainly because they were Arabs, and guilty of nothing more. Tuesday, the day they were scheduled to leave for Kuwait, the dangerous Iraqi Colonel had his group disable the weapons they were forced to leave behind in the small Iraqi village. He hated being forced to travel to Kuwait unarmed, a soldier was supposed to be armed every second of the day to be that true soldier. A soldier without a weapon was just another civilian.

In order for the Iraqi group to get out of the Middle East alive, they had to go and travel without any weapons on their person, or hidden within their luggage. All day long, his small group of soldiers prepared to leave Iraq and soon, everything not going along with them was buried, disabled, or given to the needy civilians of the poor village. The Colonel even ordered the satellite dish and TV returned to the people he had it stolen from.

At nine p.m., Colonel al-Qaysi ordered his people to get into the civilian cars they had at their disposal, and then they head for the Kuwait, Iraqi border at the posted speed. He staggered the cars in case any of them ran in any trouble along the way, or at the checkpoints at the border. Then the trailing soldiers could come to the aide of their fellow soldiers. Colonel Al-Qaysi left his military vehicles behind in the village. In no time flat, the Iraqi soldiers were sitting in a short line of civilian cars and trucks waiting to cross the border into the Kingdom of Kuwait. At this time of night, there were not very many vehicles waiting to enter the small kingdom nation.

His Iraqi soldiers had their Kuwaiti passports at the ready in hand, and this made them get over the border quicker without any problems. Once they reached Khabrat Umm al-Hiran, the Colonel had his soldier's park their vehicles in the town in different locations, and then they were to walk alone or in pairs over to the safe house in Kuwait. He and the female Major were the first ones to arrive at the safe house. He knocked on the door and was immediately invited in the home. The first thing he did was give Yasir Ahmed Tafish the other half of the money he owed the two men. Little by little, the rest of his group started to show up at the safe home.

Once the money was counted, Yasir Ahmed Tafish handed out the airline tickets to the Bahamas Islands to the soldiers, and then they settled down to wait for the time to pass until they were to arrive at the airport that was just fifteen minutes away from Tafish's home. At no time, were the Iraqi soldiers offered any food or drink from the Kuwaiti's, and none was expected from them either. Finally, the time to leave arrived, and the Colonel al-Qaysi ordered his people to start showing up at the airport in groups of twos and threes. Each Iraqi had at least one female soldier with them, to help throw off any suspicion of them. With all the people leaving Iraq and Kuwait of late, Colonel al-Qaysi's group raised no special interest. The passports and tickets were examined, and then they were allowed through then they waited for the plane to takeoff.

Wednesday, November 14th, 2001, Colonel al-Qaysi's team boarded the airliner at two twenty p.m., and they had to wait for the aircraft to takeoff at its scheduled time of two thirty. Even though they took up a good proportion of the plane, the Iraqi soldiers acted like what they were supposed to be, vacationers going on vacation. The airliner took off, and only then did the Colonel started to breath normally. He was traveling with Major al-Shaya, and she was acting like his wife. He kept glancing down the front of her blouse, enjoying what he was seeing.

Thursday, November 15th, 2001, at ten thirty p.m., the airliner finally landed on the Grand Bahamas Island as scheduled. The Iraqi soldiers departed the plane and quickly spread out on the small Island as ordered by their commander. From here the soldiers were going to take a quick trip out to the Bimini Islands, and visit the famous undersea highway, and then one by one, they were to get provisions and make their way out to one of the deserted Islands too small for any homes to be constructed on them. It was common practice for visitors to Bimini to head out to one of these small rocks for a day of basking in the sun in the nude.

It was almost expected for most visitors to Bimini to head out for one these small Islands for the privacy they offered all visitors, and the fun the Arab soldiers never allowed themselves to indulge in while they lived in their Arab homelands. Colonel Al-Qaysi knew of this practice and warned the women what was expected of them, once they were on the rock they searched for. If they were nude, the American Coast Guard ships or Bahamian patrol boat passing them on the rock would think the visitors were there to enjoy themselves and the sun, and they would not challenge them. He was actually prepared to order his people to do whatever was necessary to get his people into the United States safely, so they could then carry out their mission.

Colonel al-Qaysi walked the small Bahamas Island for hours, at his side as always was Major al-Shaya. She was starting to get into the laid back and rather quaint Island lifestyle, and the Colonel noticed the Major even opened another button on her blouse. Now, as she swung her arms as she walked, her breasts were able to be seen easily by anyone who happened to glance at her. Throughout the four hour walk, they came across other members of their group but they both ignored the others of their group. At the end of the forth hour, the Colonel and al-Shaya made their way over to one of the small pleasure boats docked at the marina. The concerned Colonel Al-Qaysi spoke to three separate Captains until he finally found the one he was searching for, who would take all his people out to the Bimini Island with no questions asked.

After an hour trip out to Bimini and exploring it for a few minutes from the boat, Colonel al-Qaysi, and Major al-Shaya got off the power boat, and they both walked the Bimini Island and they enjoyed what the Island had to offer them. Beggars, mostly young boys and girls, followed them wherever they went with their hands out, but the Colonel completely ignored the kids. The pair of soon to be Iraqi terrorists visited the popular undersea highway from above the water, after they hired the boat he was instructed to hire by the other Captain.

While they were on the water, Colonel al-Qaysi informed the Native Captain that he wanted to go to one of the small Islands for a little private time with his wife. The Captain smiled and then glanced at al-Shaya nearly hanging out of her blouse, and she smiled at the men staring at her treasures. Then the Iraqi Colonel informed this Captain he was a Cuban refuge, and he and his wife wanted to get in the United States, and he had plenty of American cash for his want. Now, the Captain's smile turned into more of a sneer, as he offered he had a friend, an American Captain on the Island who was known to bring Cuban refugees to the United States for a fee.

Colonel al-Qaysi did not reply to the Captain's remark, instead he patted his bulging breast pocket, informing the Captain he had the cash needed on his person as he spoke with him.

"Ahhh... this is good to hear from my new friend, because this American Captain we speak of is currently visiting the Island, sir. I'll introduce you to him when we return to the main Island, for a fee of one hundred American dollars of course, sir." The Native Captain smiled as he put his hand out, and then he waited until the Iraqi placed a crisp one hundred dollar American bill in it. Then he smiled a sneer again at the Iraqi Colonel.

When the two returned to the Island of Bimini, the Captain walked with the two strangers he believed to be Cubans, and he led them to one of the local bars. Here, the native looked around until he noticed an American drinking one beer after the other at the bar. He left the two at a table and approached the American Skipper. After speaking to the Captain for a few minutes, he led him over to the two strangers, and then he introduced them to the American.

"Yes Santo Trafficante, I'm Captain Richard Livingston, sir. And this young lady here is?"

The Colonel looked at Major al-Shaya and announced proudly. "This is my wife, Rita Diaz Trafficante. We have family living in the United States, and we long to see and to be with..."

"You mean live with them is that not right, Mr. Trafficante? Look friend, we don't have to beat around the bush here. We both know why you requested to speak with me. I know you want to be smuggled into the United States, pal. And I'm the Captain who can get you there safely sir. Err... how many of your family are you going to be bringing into the United States, sir?"

"Mr. Livingston, I have my entire family on the Island of the Bahamas, sir." The Colonel's Arab accent had been altered, and it made it seem like he actually had a Cuban accent.

"That's not what I just asked you buddy, and I'd like you to forget my name from this minute on, my friend. There are no names needed between you and me and the rest of your family when they finally show up here sir. I'll get you into the United States with your entire family, but I have to know how many people you want to smuggle into the United States, my friend?" the American Captain said as he carefully eyed the strange looking Cuban.

"Yes friend, I too feel we have no need for names between us after this point, sir. I have twenty one of my family members who want to go to the United States with me, sir. This number includes me and my wife, sir." The Colonel nodded at al-Shaya and smiled. The female Major smiled at the American as she moved her arms forward on purpose on the table, which caused her blouse to open more than it was, exposing her charms to the American's gaze.

Captain Livingston smiled at the young woman whose skin bore the tan he was mistaking as Cuban, and he made no bones about it as he looked at her ample breasts until they disappeared back inside the blouse. Then he added to his words. "Twenty one people you say. That's going to give me a little bit of a problem, my friend. Look Santos, I can get a few other Captains to come out and pick up the rest of your family, but it's going to be rather expensive for you. Usually, we get the Cuban refugees into the United States for two thousand dollars a head, paid in American cash before we leave for the States, sir. But ever since the Nine, One, One mess, it's been harder for us to get any Cuban refugees into our country safely. So naturally, the price has gone up some. So if you still want to go to the United States, you have to pay the new going price, sir."

"Naturally, I figured the price had to go up under the circumstances, sir. I'm well prepared to pay for the added increase. What is the price you new charge for this service, Captain?" The Iraqi Colonel replied as he put a look of little concern over the money matter on his face.

"We're now getting three thousand dollars apiece for each person we bring into the United States illegally, and the price must be paid in American cash before we leave the Island, sir. I'll have you and your family to wait my return to the Island with the other Captains and their boats. I'll leave for the United States after I finish speaking with you, and it'll take me at least six hours to return to Big Pine Key. Then I'll locate the other Captains I just spoke of that I'll need to get your entire family into the United States. Of course I'll have to sleep, so I won't return to the Island until Saturday morning at the latest. Then I'll get you out of here real fast like. By that time you have to get the rest of your family out to the Island anyway you can, my friend.

"I'd suggest you use the same Captain who brought you to me. He'll get your entire family out to the Island for a mere hundred dollars a head. I'll not be returning to the Island until Saturday like I just told you, that's the 17th of November. I'll be back by seven a.m., so I suggest you have your entire family ready and waiting my return on the Island by that time. If one of your family members is missing, I won't wait for him or her to show up. I'm only going to stop by the Island just long enough to pick you people up, and then we're getting out of here as quickly as possible. If we leave anyone behind, he or she will have to find their own way into the United States, and you'll still have to pay for that missing person on this charter, sir.

"Oh, one other thing I gotta tell ya about, all of you will be given fishing poles while in my boat, and you and everyone else better make like you're fishing all the while we're heading for the United States. If the damn Coast Guard spot and they stop us on the water, I'll do all the talking for you and the others on board. Do you have papers on you, I mean passports?"

"Yes my friend my family have American passports, and they're good. We paid a lot of money to have them made up for us." The Iraqi Colonel offered calmly to the American Captain.

"Great, does the rest of your family speak English as good as you do, buddy?" the Captain asked as he looked at Serena al-Shaya again after catching another glimpse of her breasts.

"I'm afraid I and my wife are the only ones who speak the best English. The rest of my family is not as educated as we are, Captain." The Colonel announced as he stared at the American.

"Shit, okay, yeah, I guess we'll have to work around that problem if the situation comes up. I'll take you on my boat, your wife will have to go on another one, and anyone else who speaks any English, has to be on the other boats. I need at least one of your other people able to speak and understand some English on each of the boats. Once I have you on the boats, we'll take off at staggered times, and travel a thousand yards from each other. It's not uncommon for the Coast Guard to see so many pleasure boats this far from shore. Because the bill fish are running pretty well, along with good size schools of tuna and the fish are known to be running way out.

"I'll tell you this much though, the closer we get to the American shoreline, the less likely we'll be bothered by the Coast Guard. Also my new friend, once I get you out on the water, we'll be heading for the Island of Marathon in the Middle Keys. I'm going to throw you people out of my boat as quickly as I can get rid of you guys once we reach the damn Island.

"Once you're back on land, tell your family to split up and walk around the Island like you people are not visiting it, but you live on the Island. Don't bunch up any, and don't look like you're looking for any kind of trouble, or you might be guilty of anything you can be arrested for on the Island. There are plenty of Cubans living legally on the Island of Marathon, and they'll spot you right away, and they'll take good care of you people until you can make contact with your family living in the United States. Look Santos, as soon as I'm rid of you and your family, I'm going to forget I ever even met you people. So I suggest you do the same with me and my fellow Captains. I can get in some serious trouble for getting your people into the United States, especially at this time after the damn terrorist attacks on my country, sir."

"I understand all you have stated to me well Captain, and I know of the great risk you're taking for my family, to reunite my family with the rest of my relatives living in the United States. We'll do as you have just instructed Captain. I believe I forgot your name already, sir." The crafty Colonel al-Qaysi offered, as he smiled at the American and then he nodded slightly at the man.

"That's good and keep it that way, my friend. Err.., Santos, I do request a down payment for my services at this time sir." The American Skipper smiled at the Colonel.

"Yes, by all means, I understand this request, and how much are you seeking from me at this time, my friend?" Try as he might, the Iraqi Colonel could not stop sounding like a military soldier, while he was speaking to this American Captain.

"Well friend, you said you had twenty one of your family going to the United States on this trip. I did tell you of the new price, and you agreed to it. Are you still willing to meet the new price sir?" The American replied after feeling this man was more than some dumb Cuban refugee looking to make it to the United States to live with the rest of his family. But the smell of this much cash made him not care who, or what this man and his family was about.

"Yes Mr. Captain I have more than enough American cash on my person to meet your demand. I carried this vast sum so I could pay you for the trouble you're taking on my family's behalf, Captain. Here, see how much money I have..." The Iraqi went to reach in his pocket, but the suddenly concerned Captain immediately grabbed his hand and snarled in low voice at him.

"For the love of Christ man, don't pull any fucking money out here, you asshole you. If you flash a roll of cash like that around here, you'll end up being arrested on the spot, or someone will cut your stupid throat for it. Dammit, I thought you people were supposed to be some smart man. Okay, now I know you have the cash on you, I want one third of it up front. That way I can hire the other Captain's and their boats that much easier that I'll need to get your family into the States. The rest of the cash will be paid to me before you're allowed on board any of the boats. One other thing I have to tell you about my friend, you're not to tell the other Captain's how much money you're paying me for this trip under any god damn circumstances, sir. Do you understand if you open your mouth, I'll pitch your ass over the side of my boat?"

"I understand what you are telling m sir and I'll speak to no one on the other boats, and my family will be ordered to do the same, Captain." Colonel Al-Qaysi replied as he smiled, knowing what this greedy American was up to. He was going to swindle his own friends out of their fair share of the money he was going to pay this man, to get his soldiers into the United States.

CHAPTER ELEVEN

Captain Livingston had a problem not smiling at the stranger who is going to pay him to get his family into the United States, because he was going to tell the other Captains he was only receiving two thousand dollars a head, and he would spilt the money with them evenly. But he was going to end up with forty two thousand dollars while the other four Captains spilt up twenty one thousand between the five of them. Not a bad pay for one day's quick work.

The Captain stared at what he believed was a Cuban and offered the stranger in a calm voice. C'mon my friend, we'll take a quick walk over to my boat. We'll get on board, and once on board you'll go in the head, excuse me, the bathroom. Once in there, you'll place twenty one thousand dollars you're to pay me in the covered wooden box sitting on the side of the sink. Then you'll come out and I'll go to the bathroom, and once I counted the cash and I'm certain it's all there. You'll leave the boat and I'll take off for the United States, so I can get the other Captains and boats I'll need to come out and pick you and the rest of your family up."

The suddenly deeply concerned Iraqi Colonel Hamoodi Al-Qaysi's eyes narrowed to mere slits and he knew he had to ask. "My friend, how do I know once I have paid you this great sum, and you leave the Island that you'll ever come back for us? I don't mean to question your integrity my friend, but..." The wise Colonel paused for effect, and then smiled at the large man.

"That's just it my friend, you don't. All you have is my word I'll return for your family and the rest of the payment you'll still owe me my friend. That's the risk you're taking, but it's not nearly as much of the risk that I'm taking for you and the rest of your family, offering to smuggle the lot of you people into the United States safely. But if you think I'll turn my back on this much money for one second then you're a very foolish man. Shall we leave for my boat now, so we can seal the deal and then I can get on my way, and you can return to your family, my friend?" the Captain rose, and then he waited for Hamoodi al-Qaysi to do the same.

The Iraqi Military Officer stood slowly to draw no added attention to him, and then the Arab growled at his supposed wife. "My dear, you'll stay here and wait my return to you. Don't get yourself in any trouble while I'm gone from your side, and keep your breasts inside your shirt for a change please. I'll be back shortly I believe, my love."

Captain Livingston smiled at the man's supposed wife and then he waved his hand out before him and the Iraqi lead the way for them. As the two men walked over to the docks, Captain Livingston informed the Iraqi Military Officer where the boat was docked. It took them ten minutes to reach his twenty eight foot Mako boat with the small cutty cabin. The American Skipper showed the Colonel around the boat and fishing gear. He was making it look like he was being hired to take this man out on a chartered fishing trip. After about ten minutes of exploring the boat, the Iraqi soldier loudly announced that he had to go to the bathroom for the benefit of anyone who was observing the two men and what they were doing.

Once he was in the head of the boat, he quickly removed twenty one thousand dollars after counting it out very carefully, and then he placed the cash in the small wood box sitting right where the American pleasure boat Captain told him it would be. Colonel al-Qaysi took a leak while he was in the head as a sort of an insult against the American and his boat. Then he came out while fixing his pants, and smiled at the waiting Captain.

Captain Livingston took a few minutes to go over the rest of his boat with the foreign Colonel, and then he also disappeared into the head. Once he was in the small bathroom, he quickly counted the money after examining it to make certain it was real. Then he hid it under the sink in the special place only he knew of, because he built the hidden compartment when he started to smuggle the Cubans refuges into his country. Then he walked out of the head and announced loud enough for anyone who might be listening, or even watching them he needed to go back to his

Island to get some different gear for their upcoming fishing charter. He was no fool because he knew the American Custom Agents has also tightened their security on many of the out laying Islands surrounding the American coastline.

"My friend, I have a charter already booked for tomorrow morning. It's an all day charter at that. But I'll return to the Island on Saturday morning with my new gear, and then I'll take you and your family out and catch you some good eating fish. It's going to be a good day for fishing, and the tuna are running strong, and some dolphin are starting to show up in the area as well. One way or the other, we'll catch some fish while we're on the water on Saturday morning, sir."

Colonel Hamoodi al-Qaysi shook hands with the slightly taller American boat Captain and then he quickly left the boat. But he waited on the dock until the Captain started his boat, and then he removed the mooring rope lines, and then the charter boat shoved off from the dock. The cunning Iraqi soldier remained standing on the dock until the boat was completely out of site, and then he returned to the bar to collect the Major, and then get the rest of his troops out to the small Island so they could wait for the American fool to return with his boat.

Colonel Al-Qaysi met with the other officers from his Iraqi unit throughout the rest of the day in different locations on the Island, as if he just happened across them by accident. He placed Lieutenant Aziz Abdel al-Atrash in command of five troops, with one female soldier in each group of five. The Colonel's group was going to be comprised of six members, because he was going on the largest pleasure boat coming out to bring them to the United States safely.

He placed Major al-Shaya in command of the second group. He then placed Lieutenant Bashar al-Maluk in command of the forth group, and Lieutenant Miranda al-Mutaa was to be in command of the fifth batch of his soon to be terrorists. Each group was ordered to speak to the Native Captain who brought the Colonel to the American pleasure boat Captain. They were to make deals to hire him to bring them out to the small pickup Island, where they were to wait for the return of the American, and the other boats he was going to bring with him. All five groups of Iraqi soldiers were going to be brought to the small Island, but the Colonel had to give each commander enough American cash, being he was the one controlling the cash for the group.

The Iraqi Colonel had to make certain the commanders of each of the groups had enough cash to buy some food, water, and also pay the Native Captain what he demanded to get them out to the small Island that was no more than a large rock. One hundred dollars for each soldier he was taking out to the secluded Island. The groups of Iraqi terrorists brought towels and umbrellas with them, because they understood they had to look like tourists visiting on the Island, and not like they were waiting for the pleasure boats to pick them up and get them to the United States.

Colonel Hamoodi al-Qaysi held back some of the soldiers he trusted the most, and they remained at the bar where he could keep his eyes on the dock area where the American Captain always moored his boat. He watched as the first group of his soldiers boarded the small boat of the Native Captain. They were quickly whisked off for the Island more like a rock, where they were to wait for the American Captain to return the next day. The Colonel stayed with his group, and they nursed their beers, so he could see his other soldiers were moved out to the rock successfully. After the last group of Iraqi's left for the Island, Colonel al-Qaysi checked his watch and was surprised it was after five p.m. already. If it took the Native Captain the hour to get out to the rock, and return, by then it was going to be well after six p.m. before his entire group would finally head out, and they linkup with the rest of his soldiers already our on the Island.

The waitress of the bar was sort of hanging around the table trying to force the men to either leave the place, or order another rounds of drinks for themselves, or maybe something to eat. She was only interested in making money for the bar, thus making her pay for the night, and hoping for a good tip from this group of people. The Colonel noticed her actions, and he finally called her over and ordered some food and beers for the group. This made the waitress smile, because the Colonel tipped her ten dollars to appease her attention. The Iraqi Military Officer felt the slight kick under the table and he started to look around the bar.

Colonel Al-Qaysi was shocked when he noticed two Americans casually walk into the place and sat at the bar and started to look at the faces of everyone in the place. The two were dressed in American Naval Military Uniforms, and they seemed to be looking for anyone who might look out of place in the overcrowded bar. The Colonel waited for their food as he whispered at the four men and one woman he was with. "Fools, don't look so guilty or you'll draw their attention to us. They have no idea who we are, so act like I ordered you to act in this cursed bar. Khalaifa, open another of your foul buttons, and walk out of this filthy place as if you're going to the bathroom. Allow these two fools to get a good look at your body before you leave, woman.

"Once you're out of this foul establishment, I'll send Damerdji out another door to the bar. You have to get the

American military men's attention glued on your foul breasts, woman. But don't leave the bar until you ate your foul food first."

The beautiful young female Sergeant nodded then did as ordered and opened another button on her blouse, and her face immediately flushed. As soon as she opened the button, both her breasts were easily seen by anyone sitting in the bar. She was thoroughly embarrassed by the way she was forced to expose herself to everyone who seemed to be staring right at her, as she remained seated at the table surrounded by the men. She started to keep her arms close to her chest in order to try and protect her body from their gaze.

"Move your foul hands away from your breasts, stupid woman. Why the devil do you think I had you open your god cursed button for, woman? You need to show the lust filled cursed American fools what a true Arab woman's breasts look like, woman. You must do this for our mission and for the sake of Allah. Do as I have just ordered and remove your foul hands away from your worthless chest, woman. Be proud you're a young, pretty Arab woman, and a dangerous weapon for Allah's faithful cause, worthless woman." Colonel Al-Qaysi hissed in a whisper as he glared at her as soon as he realized what she was doing trying to cover herself.

Slowly, the upset female removed her arms, and both her breasts showed out the opening of her blouse. Every man in the bar, along with some of the women as well, was now staring at the Sergeant's breasts sticking out of her shirt. The Colonel thanked Allah that the female Sergeant was so well endowed, because the effect was exactly what he was looking for, and from the reactions of the males in the bar. He knew the foolish Americans believed no Arab woman would ever dare expose herself in the manner the Sergeant was doing in the bar. The two Coast Guard Officers turned their attention away from Colonel al-Qaysi's table. But they kept sneaking quick little peeks at the Sergeant's breasts, and smiled to one another as they continued to sneak their little peeks at the good looking female who was almost completely topless in the bar now.

When Khalaifa finished eating her hamburger and drank her beer, the Colonel lightly tapped her foot with his under the table, and she knew what he wanted. She stood, drawing every man's attention in the bar to her body. She smiled at the Colonel as she announced in flawless English. "My dear, I believe I'll take a quick dip in the pool and then I'm going back to the apartment, and I'll wait for you there. I warn you dear, don't keep me waiting too long for you to arrive, or I'll start without you as I have done before when you kept me waiting too long for you to come to me, my love." The female Sergeant sexily wiggled her hips at the Colonel, which caused both her breasts to come completely out of the opening of her blouse for a second.

The Colonel could swear he heard every man in the bar suck in their breath, as the Sergeant slowly wiggled her hips and breasts in front of his face.

The young and pretty Iraqi female Sergeant sexily walked away from the table, but since she was forced to act like the common whores of the United States, she planned to make the most of it. She walked right by the two obvious Naval Officers, stopping by the chair of the first one. She had the guts to place her hand on the back of the chair, drawing the attention of the two Americans right to her. She stopped moving, lifted her left foot and checked the bottom of her shoe. Doing this exposed her close up to the stare from the two men. She saw them looking right down her blouse, but she did not move as she offered the younger man in a low tone. "If my stupid husband would rather drink at this bar than share what I have to offer him. Then you two are more than welcome to visit my apartment, and keep me company for tonight."

The younger officer laughed and replied. "Ma'am, I assure you, it'd be my pleasure to spend the night with you. But I'm afraid I'm still stuck on duty, and I can't get away at this moment. Besides, I believe your husband will be coming along quickly if he's a smart man. But I thank you for the kind offer, Ma'am. Where do you live in the States, Ma'am?"

"New York City, Manhattan why, are you planning to visit New York in the future, Officer?" The Iraqi Sergeant purred sexily at the young and good looking American Officer.

"I am now." The officer replied as he turned and began to speak to the Lieutenant again, sitting by his side. Both men waited until the lady left the bar and then the one she was speaking to, said to the other. "Well Eddie, what the fuck do you make of that one, man?"

"Paul only in New York City are the women that fucking sexy, dog. I'll tell you this much, if you didn't make her shove off when you did. I was going to jump her bones right here in the fucking bar. She was making my teeth melt I tell you. Man, was she ever a good looker. Things are starting to really pick up around here I see."

The two officers gave the female Iraqi one last look over as she walked out of the bar. Neither noticed the male sitting at her table a few minutes ago, get up and leave the bar as they spoke to the female. They were busy watching the woman walk out of the bar so sexily and slowly. Nor did the two Naval Officers notice the second man leave the bar once sitting at the table with the lady, as they continued to joke about the good looking woman who just walked out of the bar.

Over the next hour and a half, Colonel al-Qaysi had the two remaining Iraqi soldiers seated with him leave his table, and when he was sitting alone in the bar, one of the Naval Officers cast a quick look in his direction, and then he remarked to his partner. "Well will you look at the stupid bastard still sitting over there sucking down the damn suds, while his hot to trot wife waits for his stupid ass in their apartment? Man, if I had something that fucking hot waiting for my ass at my room. I wouldn't be wasting my time slugging down beers and pulling my pud in this bar like he's doing. I'd be back in the apartment doing the U turns in bed with my lady. The asshole must be brain death, or his dick doesn't work right or something like that, man. I can't believe he's still just sitting there like that with his lady waiting for him to go to her."

"Maybe the damn fool can't get it up any more, who the hell knows and who gives a shit, man. We're not here to worry about the asshole's sex life, buddy. We're here to see if anyone hanging around here looks like he doesn't belong, or suspicious, man. This place is getting boring, what say we walk down to the shore and see if we can find anything happening around there more exciting than this dump is, Eddie." The First Class Petty Officer finished off his beer, and stood and paid for the drinks for the both of them, while he waited for his partner to finish his drink.

"I know what you want to see by the shore, man. You want to see if that hot little hen got tired of waiting for that asshole of a husband of hers to come home. I don't think you're going to find her hanging around on the beach this time of the night, but there's that one chance in a million we might come across a chick skinny dipping, or fucking on the beach like the last time we went down there. So let's see what we can see there. I'm with you this time, this place is beat out tonight something hopefully has to be happening by the water." The Lieutenant dropped a five dollar bill on the bar, and then he gave one last look at the man still sitting at the table by himself, and then they left the bar laughing at the ass sitting at the empty table.

By the middle of Friday, the Iraqi soldiers attached to Colonel al-Qaysi's Unit were out on the tiny Island, waiting for the next day to arrive. The soldiers were the only people on the entire Island that was no more than fifteen hundred feet long, by three hundred feet wide. It was five feet higher than high water line. The day was beautiful and the small group of Iraqis were getting caught up in the fun a fine day such as this causes. The males swam, and dove under the water from the rocks. The women were taking the Colonel's orders to heart, running around the Island topless while sunning themselves. Twice since the group landed on the Island, a plane passed over them. One time the plane actually dipped the wings at the group of young people enjoying themselves. The Colonel was sitting and speaking with Major al-Shaya, and she was sunning herself and al-Qaysi was enjoying looking at her fine shape and making small talk.

The Iraqi soldiers took along enough provisions to last them for two full days or longer, and one of the soldiers started a fire and cook some hamburgers and frankfurters for the others of his mixed group to enjoy. They had plenty of beer and sodas with them as well. The sun was strong and the group of Arabs was used to it, so they did not get sunburned. The Colonel leaned back on the sand and locked his hands behind his head and he mumbled while looking up in the sky. "You know al-Shaya; I believe I could get used to this kind of lazy lifestyle. I'm finding it easy to get caught up in the way these worthless Americans live their loathsome lives. I find it most pleasurable to lie in the sun, and I don't mind telling you. I enjoy seeing a woman being around me half naked, other than only in the foul bedroom. How are you feeling about it?"

"I'm afraid to offer Colonel al-Qaysi, but I too am enjoying the freedoms the Americans enjoy. I must admit I'm not finding it hard to lie about without my top on." The Major glanced at her breasts, and found her liking the way her breasts were glimmering in the sun and sweat. She smiled, until she looked at the Colonel and saw him staring at her breasts also.

"Hummmm... I see you're enjoying this also, Hamoodi." The Major grumbled pleasantly as she crossed her arms over her chest.

"Yes I am, and please don't cover your breasts on me woman. I mean, in case the foul American Coast Guard comes by and sees you covering up, and they enter the Island to see why."

"That has to be the lamest excuse I have ever heard in my entire life, my dear Colonel al-Qaysi." Major al-Shaya replied as she smiled, and then she removed her arms from across her chest, as she added with a smirk to her words. "I'll remove my arms in case the hated Americans come by as you have just offered to me, Colonel." Then she gave him the look that informed him she knew what he was doing and what he wanted to see from her.

The wise Iraqi Colonel was enjoying the view and smiled because he was just caught in a lie. The soldiers ate and then continued fooling around in the sun, but as it got later in the day and the sun went down, it got cool on the small Island. Every one of the soldiers dressed in their clothes, and then they started to look for anything made of cloth to cover them with. For the rest of the night, the soldiers shivered and two of them kept the fire going all night and this helped, but not enough to warm them completely. As the Colonel laid on the sand dreaming about getting his troops to the United States safely, he suddenly heard the sounds of lovemaking. He knew some of his soldiers were taking advantage of the pleasant situation.

The group of Iraqi soldiers was up early, and the sun was already blazing and warmed them from the long night's chill. In a short time the women were out of their clothes again, and they were playing a game of catch with the male soldiers. It had the makings of another beautiful day and there was no breeze, and the sea was calm and flat as a board. It was already eight five degrees, and it was getting warmer with every second that past. Colonel al-Qaysi checked his watch, it was seven ten a.m. and the American Captain was already late arriving to pick his soldiers up, and he found himself looking out to the sea, trying to locate the Americans coming out to pick them up and bring them to the United States. By a quarter after seven in the morning, he was beginning to become concerned. He was worried maybe he was taken by the worthless American boat Captain. He covered his eyes with his hand and continued to stare out to sea.

He ordered each woman out of their clothes, because he wanted the American fools to be staring at them more than looking at his male soldiers. He was just about to call Major al-Shaya over to his side, when he happened to notice a fast moving small pleasure boat coming directly at their small Island. As he stared, he noticed four other boats following the one in the lead. He let out his breath and then he bellowed out at the rest of his soldiers.

"Get ready, the great fools are coming for us. Take only our clothes and leave everything else behind us. We have no further need of these worthless items from the worthless land of sin. The women will remain without their tops until the five Captains get a good look at you. I want them to be kept off guard until we're safely in the United States. They're almost here so be ready."

SATURDAY, NOVEMBER 17th, 2001.
SEVEN TWENTY A.M.

Captain Livingston's small pleasure boat traveled right up on the small sandy beach of the little Island, and he shut the motor down. The American climbed out of the boat as the Iraqi soldiers looked over the craft. Everywhere he looked, he saw a fishing pool sticking out of the watercraft. The Captain walked up to the Iraqi Colonel and growled at him. "Mr. Trafficante, shall we get on board my boat? I believe we have some further business to conduct first, before we can leave this Island." The American waved his hand out before him.

The smug looking Colonel Al-Qaysi did not reply as he followed the American Captain on the boat, and they both went in the small cabin together. Once inside, the Arab handed him the rest of the cash, and the Captain counted it right in front of the Iraqi Officer this time. The smiling Captain Livingston made two separate piles of cash, and then he folded one and moved it away from the other pile. Then he removed another four thousand dollars out of the other pile, and folded that and stuffed it in his other pocket. Once he was done, he asked the Iraqi to leave the boat for a second. As soon as the Colonel was out of the cabin, he went in the bathroom and opened the small hidden compartment and hid his share of money in the hiding spot. He placed the extra four thousand dollars in the compartment also.

He decided to leave the extra thousand American dollars to be split between the other Captains. Once he had the money hidden, he went out of the cabin and moved to the back of the boat, and a second craft steamed right up on the sand covered beach on the Island.

Captain Livingston handed him an envelope with money this Captain was going to spilt up the way he wanted to split it with the rest of the other Captains from their group. Then the two American Skippers walked their boats back in the water and Captain Livingston called out to the Iraqi leader of the group. "My friend, six of you will have to walk in the water and get on my boat, and then we're leaving here as soon as you're on board my boat. Once we leave, five of your family will go in the second boat, and when that boat is full and takes off, the third boat will come in and pick up another five of your family. We'll do this until all your family is in the boats, and we're heading for the United States. Sir, within the next six to seven hours depending on the water conditions, you'll be stepping foot on American soil. C'mon people, we have to get a move on it before any of the local authorities come out here snooping around to see why we're landing these five boats on this damn rock. Get a move on it please."

Colonel Al-Qaysi waved his hand to the five soldiers to be on board his boat, and they waded out in the water. Shurug Kahalaifa was still topless and she tried to climb on the boat moving on her because of the slightly rolling water. The American had to lend her a hand to get on board the boat, and his hands were not very careful where they landed on her exquisite body. The Colonel noticed the liberties the American fool was taking with his female

Sergeant and he smiled. He wanted to do the same to the pretty woman himself. When everyone was on board the pleasure boat, it pulled away from the Island heading out to the open sea.

For most of the Colonel's soldiers, this was the first time they were ever on the water, and it did not take long for many of them to become seasick, and heave over the side of the bobbing boat. The Colonel would not leave the American's side, and they watched as his people got sick one after the other. The only one fishing was the female Sergeant, she was actually enjoying herself. Captain Livingston's boat was well out to sea by the time the second boat was loaded with the others, and then it left the Island as the third boat came in to pick up his people.

Captain Livingston's boat was the furthest one out in the sea, and he was the first one to be approached by a Coast Guard Cutter working over this section of the sea. The cutter closed in on the Captain's boat, and when the Seaman began to hail him to heave too. The pleasure boat Captain slowed and waited for the larger ship to catch up with him. By the time the two boats were near, the small craft was twenty miles from the Island he picked up his stowaways from.

The smiling young Coast Guard Seaman who hailed them was hanging over the side of the cutter, and he was speaking to the Captain. "What the devil are you doing this far out to sea, Captain Livingston Sir?" the Seaman asked as he took the Captain's papers and glanced at the two people heaving their guts out over the side of the boat.

"I have a charter scheduled and I passed you my Captain's license, these people wanted to catch some damn dolphin, sir. I told them they weren't running anywhere near land just yet, but we might be lucky enough to catch a few if we went far enough out as I'm doing, sir." The Captain looked over his shoulder and complained at the grinning Seaman. "As you can see for yourself Lieutenant, I have a bunch of greenies on board who can't take a bit of rough water, sir." The Captain laughed at the people on his boat heaving their guts out over the side.

"I see what you mean Captain. Looking at the mess they're making on board your craft sir, I don't think I'm boarding ya to check them out, sir. Everything seems to be in order with your papers and charter, Captain Livingston. I take it everyone on board are Americans, right Captain?" the young Lieutenant replied as he handed the Captain back his papers back.

"Yes Lieutenant, I picked them up on Marathon for this charter earlier this morning, sir."

"Great, well Captain Livingston Sir, I guess I wasted enough of your time, sir. Have a great day fishing sir, and good luck with your charter and greenies on board, sir." The Lieutenant smiled again and then he saluted the Captain and waved his hand at his Captain at the same time. The Coast Guard Cutter ship immediately powered up and slowly pulled away from Livington's small boat, and then the Cutter increased speed and began to move further away from the small pleasure craft. The concerned Captain of the pleasure boat watched as the Coast Guard Cutter picked up speed and then headed in the direction where it would not intercept the rest of his boats heading for the shores of the United States.

When the Coast Guard Cutter left his side, Captain Livingston called to the second Captain trailing his boat the nearest, and he warned him about the Cutter prowling the area in the code they had worked out before they left the Island of Marathon. Immediately, the Captain of the other pleasure boat started to drift a little further south to make certain he did not cross the path of the Cutter this Captain was able to see on the water.

The small flotilla of pleasure boats did not have any further trouble from the Coast Guard, and none of the five Captains breathed properly again until they picked up the tall metal tower from the old Sombrero Lighthouse in view off the coast of Marathon. Seeing the lighthouse meant the five boats were within twelve miles of the tiny Island of Marathon. The Captains of the other boats sped and easily caught up with the lead boat, and they were now sailing just a few yards away from each boat in almost a formation. The five pleasure boats kept coming until they found the mouth of Boot Key Harbor, and they had to slow down until they were making no wake. One boat suddenly peeled off from the rest and moored up by Burdines which was a fuel dock and restaurant. Here, the Captain pulled in to fuel up and allowed his thought to be Cuban passengers to get out of the boat after telling the one who spoke the best English of the group. To walk out of the dock area and keep on going until they came across Highway One, and then they were to go anywhere they wanted on the Island after that and he assured them someone would approach and offer to help them on the Island.

The other four pleasure boats kept going until they came across a second dock, where another boat peeled off, and this Captain unloaded the passengers in the same way as he fuelled up his boat, to make it seem he had a reason to be at the dock. The third boat landed at a beach area on Boot Key, and it let his passengers off there. The other two boats kept going until they came up to Dockside. It was a local bar on Marathon, and the two Captains docked in the designated area for the bar, and everyone got out. The two

Captains headed for the bar, and the Iraqi Colonel's soldiers started to walk down the road heading for Highway One. The Captains headed for the bar to share a beer and laugh about the amount of money they just made. There was not many people hanging around the bar this early in the day. So the Captains that had money, enjoyed a second beer, and continued laughing over the easy money they made for the one day's work.

The Iraqi Colonel and the rest of his group of soon to be terrorists headed for the main and only highway on the Island of Marathon, he was intending to get on a greyhound bus, and then make way for Miami. He had to ask someone on the Island where the bus stop was located, and he was informed it was at the small Marathon Airport. He was told he could purchase the tickets for the bus director from the driver of the bus. Colonel al-Qaysi's group quickly worked their way over to the airport before his other soldiers did. He was forced to miss one bus until all his people finally showed up gathered by the airport. The next bus was not due in until eight p.m., and the driver he spoke to, informed him that bus was usually empty, so his friends should be able to get on it at the same time.

At eight p.m. sharp, the almost empty bus pulled up, and the driver got out and asked the Iraqis for their tickets and luggage. Colonel al-Qaysi smiled at the driver as he explained. "You see sir, one of my friends had an argument with his wife, and she left him on the Island. The rest of our wives left with her so we were forced to find our own way off the Island. We were visiting from Miami. Some of our daughters stayed with us while the wives when with the hurt lady. They took our luggage with them, so we could travel light while we return to Miami, and keep our angry friend here company, sir. It was a terrible end to a good vacation I'm afraid to say sir."

"Say no more about it. This isn't the first time I heard this same story told to me, sir. I take it you people don't have tickets for the bus, sir?" the driver asked as he smiled at the talker.

"No sir, I'm afraid I have not sir. How do we get a ticket for your bus, sir?"

"That's easy enough, all you have to do is give me twenty four dollars and fifty cents apiece, and I'll get the lot of you home safe and sound sir." The driver replied with a grin.

"That's fine." The Iraqi Military Officer answered as he quickly counted out the money he needed, and handed it over to the driver. When the driver was certain it was correct, he issued the group their tickets. Then he waited until everyone was on board the bus, and then the driver climbed on the bus and drove off Marathon. The Colonel sat with Major al-Shaya, and he settled in the comfortable chair and closed his eyes. He could not believe it was so easy to get his people into the United States so safely, especially after the terrorist attack on two cities. In no time flat, he was snoring away, warm and comfortable.

Major al-Shaya smiled at the Colonel as she watched him sleep. She hated to admit it, but she was falling in love with him, and it was pleasing her she was able to run around in front of him topless, teasing him as she did on that small Island. She was thrilled with all the attention he was showing her with, when they were waiting to be picked up by the American pleasure boats.

Two and a half hours later, the bus slowly pulled in the terminal in Miami near the airport. When the Iraqi Colonel woke and stood, his soldiers automatically rose with him and the group quickly left the bus. When the Iraqis were walking down a road, Major al-Shaya asked the officer with much concern in her tone of voice. "Al-Qaysi, I hate to bring this up to your attention. How are we doing with the American money? Although I don't know how much we took from that worthless Kuwaiti bank, the way we're going through it, it must be getting low on us by now."

"We're doing just fine with the money, al-Shaya. Do not concern yourself with anything involved in our efforts. Allow me to worry about all the cursed details, woman."

"I'm pleased to hear that, Colonel. Now, all you have to do is tell me where we're heading, and I'll be quiet." The Major added with a slight smile.

"Woman, you're full of worthless questions aimed at making me angry, and those questions don't concern you in the least I warn you worthless woman. You'll follow me with your mouth shut before I have hot sand packed in it. I know where I'm going at all times, al-Shaya."

"To hear your words is to obey." The Major replied sarcastically to the Colonel.

The group of Iraqi soldiers cautiously walked down the roads following their commander, without question or complaint. Once while they were walking, did they get the interest of a police officer who passed the small group in his squad car. But since the group was creating no problems, he had no real reason to bother them. The police officer did circled the block three times until he felt this group had someplace to go, and then left them.

It took the group of foreigners an hour to walk to where the Colonel was taking them. Three times, the officer was forced to check a map and instructions to the safe place he was looking for. When the soon to be terrorists were on the block he wanted. Colonel Al-Qaysi ordered his people to break up and stroll around the area. Each one of them were ordered to come down the same road, and if the safe house was still safe, the Iraqi Colonel would enter and when he saw the others walk by the place, he would call them in the house one by one. The Colonel left the group and headed for a building that looked like it was just built, and someone with a lot of money owned it. He walked up to the building like he was an old friend visiting the owners. He lightly knocked on the door in the special tap sequence given him by the Kuwaiti helpers, after they discovered where the Colonel's sister lived in the United States.

When the Colonel saw the woman standing at the door, he replied. "My sister from the vast desert, it is I your brother Hamoodi al-Qaysi. I come a long way to visit you."

When his sister saw him, she immediately flung opened the door and invited him in the home, after placing him in a breath robbing bear hug and kissing him on the both cheeks while crying. "Hamoodi, it has been six years since I last saw you." As she pulled him into her home, she asked. "How were you able to leave Iraq? What with the terrorist attacks against the United States and all that, my foolish brother. I cannot believe you're here with me at long last Hamoodi, how is mother's health? I haven't seen her since I left Iraq after the Desert Storm War. I never dared to believe you'd ever leave Iraq, my foolish brother. Are you still with the Republican Guard Unit, and if so, how did you get permission to enter the United States?"

"I'll answer all your questions, but first I have to ask you where your new American husband is at, dear sister?" the Colonel knew the only way his sister was able to leave Iraq, was when she married the young American Marine Lieutenant, and he took her out of Iraq when his tour of duty was completed in his country. He believed he would never see his only sister again in his lifetime, after she left Iraq with the American Marine. At first he hated her for betraying Iraq by marrying a hated American soldier, but now he found himself pleased she did. It was only through the Kuwaiti's help that he was able to locate his sister living in Florida.

"Hamoodi, my husband's away from home until tomorrow afternoon, and then he'll be returning home for three weeks, my brother. Why do you ask me this question? I don't think I like the way you're talking all of a sudden, my brother. Are you truly in the United States legally, Hamoodi? Are you here to do a terrorist attack against the United States? I know that President Saddam sent Colonel al-Adwani to the United States to do harm against their American Leader a few months ago. Are you here for the same foolish reason as he was, my foolish brother?"

"I'm here so allow us to leave it at that for the time being my wayward sister. I have a number of other soldiers with me, and we need a safe place to stay until I can make contact with my friends in Washington. Ilham, sister are you still a true Iraqi Agent, or has this foolish marriage to a god cursed American soldier changed your loyalty away from our country?"

"I'm still a loyal Agent for our country, what do you want me to do, Hamoodi?" Ilham al-Qaysi replied as she looked deep in her brother's eyes.

"I have to get my soldiers off the god cursed streets, before the worthless fools are picked up by any of the local police officers, sister. Once they're safe, I'll further explain my plan to you. We'll have to kill your husband when he returns home to you." The Iraqi Colonel offered to see her response that he planned to kill her American husband.

"So. If my actions help my country, I'd be most pleased to give up my life for my country's sake, and for Allah, my brother." Ilham al-Qaysi offered proudly.

"Ahh... spoken like a true Iraqi soldier. I'm so pleased that you remember your allegiance to our country. My sister, I have some sad news I must inform you of. Mother is dead she was killed by an American attack when they dropped their god cursed bombs on a missile site in Iraq a year ago. I'm still a member of the Republican Guard, and yes, I'm here on a special mission for our country's sake, sister. I'm here to free Colonel al-Adwani from the hated American fools, and kill the god cursed soldiers who have invaded our country, when they came for the worthless spy of a Colonel al-Adwani. I have need of more American money, and then I have to get my soldiers up to Washington. Can you help me with both problems I have my sister of mother desert?"

"Yes I can easily help you with plenty of American cash, my brother. Getting the troops up to Washington is going to be a further problem that faces me I fear. I'd suggest you place some of the soldiers on a train and send them up to Washington that way, and the rest of the fools should be placed on buses. That way they shouldn't arouse very much interest from the security people watching over this loathsome country, ever since the terrorist attack on this god forsaken country. I must offer you my faithful brother, you have accomplished the worst part of your mission already you were able to get you and your soldiers into the United States safely. The rest of the mission should not be too hard for you to accomplish. Their American security people are not yet looking for us inside the borders of the United States. They're only interested in keeping us out of their god cursed country. So I'm going to have to get..."

"Wait a minute, here comes one of my people and I have to get her off the cursed street as quickly as possible. She is Major Serena al-Shaya, I want you to walk outside and speak to this woman, and then you must invite her into the home like you have done for me my sister." The Iraqi Colonel said as he looked out of the window and picked up his female soldier slowly walking past the home alone, like she was just out for a walk around the neighborhood.

For the next two hours, the highly concerned Iraqi Colonel al-Qaysi and his sister invited the rest of his soldiers in her home as soon as they were spotted by the home. One female soldier was already busy cooking some steaks and potatoes for the soon to be terrorist group as they got comfortable in Colonel al-Qaysi's sister's home. Ilham knew a number of these soldiers from her past dealings with the Iraqi military back in Iraq. Most of them were so tired after they ate they immediately fell asleep, some of them never bothered to get out of their street clothes as they slept right on the floor, in beds, and on couches.

Colonel al-Qaysi and his sister stayed up most of the night, as they talked about their past lives in Iraq, and who and how many of their family members were still alive in their country. The Colonel had his soldiers move upstairs so they could rest a little easier, and he stayed with his sister and together, they waited for her husband to come home. He knew he had to get the drop on the large American soldier because if he was a Marine. He would be a very hard man to kill, especially in a hand to hand combat situation.

It was nine thirty Sunday morning, and the Colonel's people were still asleep, all but the Colonel and his sister. Her husband was due home in the next half an hour. In order to get her husband off guard, she was going to tell him her brother was her uncle from New Jersey, who she begged to visit when they talked, since she first came to the United States as his wife.

At ten a.m., her husband came home and parked his Ford Explorer SUV in the middle of the driveway, and then he walked into the house carrying the Sunday paper, and some pastries he picked up at the local bakery for breakfast with his wife. He smiled as his wife opened the door for him and as he entered, she began speaking in a rather excited voice. The husband was half listening to her words as he stared at the stranger sitting at the kitchen table. He was taken back to see a stranger in his home while he was gone.

"Honey, you'll not believe this for a moment I fear. But my favorite uncle from New Jersey has decided to pay us a little visit, my dear. He arrived a few hours ago and he said he wanted to meet you at long last, John."

The husband let out is breath as he smiled and lowered his guard, and then asked the Arab looking man how he was, as he offered his hand once he placed the pastries on the table. He still held the newspaper in the other hand. Colonel al-Qaysi rose so the American could not take it as a threatening move aimed against him, and offered his left hand, and as he went to shake hands with his sister's husband, his other hand stabbed the Marine Lieutenant right in the center of his chest with a bread knife. Then the Colonel place the injured American in a bear hug as he pulled the knife out of his chest and stabbed him a second time, this time in the right lung, without giving the American soldier a chance to react against his attack on him.

Then the Iraqi soldier pulled the knife out and he stabbed the American soldier in his left lung after he wrapped his arms around his body again, and stabbed him from behind this time. Almost instantly, the Marine

Lieutenant started to sag down to the floor while still locked in al-Qaysi's powerful arms. As he dropped to the floor, the Marine was continuing to struggle to breathe, yet his military training was ordering his mind to fight back against his sudden attacker. With no strength left in his arms or body, he struck out with his last breath at the man who just stabbed him, and ended up lightly punching the Colonel on the side of the face.

The Colonel waited for a few moments before he would dare release his death like grip on the body of the larger Marine Military Officer until he knew for certain that the man was dead. Then Colonel al-Qaysi released him, and the Marine fell completely to the floor. There was a slight trace of blood where the husband had struck him in his face, and as he wiped at it with his hand. He knew he was right to kill this extremely dangerous man so savagely and outright. Because just from the slight blow he received from the American soldier, he understood if this man was able to get his hands on him. He would have surely been the one who would be dead. The Iraqi looked at his sister and noticed she was near tears and staring at him.

"I'm terribly sorry I had to kill your husband like this, please forgive me sister."

"Never mind him, the only reason I married the worthless fool in the first place, was so I could get out of Iraq and live in the United States. We have to hide the body, put him in the garage. Once he's taken care of, we'll get on with your mission. Tomorrow, I'll go to the bank and remove the money that you need to see you through this operation you are here to accomplish, my brother. We have thirty five thousand dollars in the bank, and then I'll go with you..."

"No one will miss your foul husband, sister?" Hamoodi asked of his pretty sister this time.

"No not for quite a while, this was his last day on active duty in the service, and he was coming home for a six month leave. The fool had no job planned, and we were intending to travel around the United States for a little while and visit our relatives and see some of this worthless land. When we returned home, he was going to call the service and see if he could go back on active duty again rather than go and get himself a real job."

"Good, tell your neighbors that both you and your husband are leaving home for..."

"Don't trouble yourself with this foolish concern. That was all we talked about with the neighbors for the past three months or so." Ilham informed her brother.

"Good, I'll wake up my worthless soldiers from their sleep, and they'll take care of this man's body for us. I think we should shove his body in the attic of the garage. That way it'll take a long time before someone finds it. I have much to do and little time to do it." The excited Colonel offered his sister, and there was a sudden sound behind him and they both spun around and found themselves looking at three of his soldiers.

"Good, I'm pleased some of you three fool's who call yourselves soldiers of Iraq, woke on this worthless day. We have to hide this cursed body, and then we'll stay here for a week. In that time, my faithful sister will get us the needed cash. During that week's time, some of you will buy train tickets for Washington, while others will buy tickets for the cursed bus, heading for the same destination as the others from our unit. Once you soldiers turn up in Washington, you'll report to the Roland's Motel where our other soldiers used for their headquarters to assassinate the American Leader. It's a foul and very evil place right in the heart of the black section of the worthless city. There'll be three of you to each god cursed filthy room.

"I'll give each of you the address of the worthless motel when I have you all standing together before me. Right now, I want this body of the loathsome American soldier moved out to the garage, find a way to get it in the attic and stuff him up there. But first I want you to find some heavy plastic, and wrap his body tight in it and use plenty of tape to seal every opening in the foul plastic. The longer we keep the god cursed body from stinking, the longer we'll be safe to operate in the United States from this foul home. Once we get up to Washington, I'll send my sister out of the country. I'll send her to Egypt, where she'll stay until we leave this cursed country of sin and lust, after we have carried out of operation successfully against the hated soldiers who had invading our country for a second time. Then I'll find her and take her to Jordan, until we can return to our country of Iraq. Get this foul body out of here, now."

The angry Colonel watched as three soldiers struggled with the heavy, limp body of the dead American soldier, and he turned to his sister and complained at her. "By Allah's all wise and great wisdom, they sure do grow them large in this foul country of sin, sister."

"You should only know what it was like to lay under his loathsome weight, as he snorted like a filthy pig while he did what he called making love with me. How many times I have cursed myself for allowing me to live and marry this worthless pig. I should've died in the rubble of my country, rather than to ever allow this evil man to ever take me away from my country. If I was there, I would've stopped mama from dying."

"Dear sister, nothing you could have done would've saved mother's life when the cursed American warplanes attacked our country again. Where she was, was in the worst possible place for her to be. You see my little sister, our once thought to be wise President of Iraq, had a number of missile sites moved to different, highly populated civilian areas in the cities. This move enabled the missile sites to harass the loathsome American warplanes as they tried to maintain the two no fly zones they have installed over our country.

"It would have worked for a little while, just as long as the missile sites aimed only their tracking radar systems at the hated American planes of war. But when the worthless fools received new orders and they started to fire their worthless missiles at the enemy warplanes, the American aircraft replied with missiles of their own.

"Our fool of a President was the catalyst that caused many of our civilians to be slaughtered in the continuing attack by the hated Allied warplanes on our country, my sister. So you see, even if you were still living in Iraq during this time, you would be dead just like mother, and you wouldn't have been here in the United States helping us gain our revenge against the hated and cursed infidels of this cursed country."

Colonel Hamoodi al-Qaysi words of pain did what they were intended to do to his sister. They calmed down his young sister and stopped her from hating herself so much.

CHAPTER TWELVE

WASHINGTON D.C. TUESDAY, DECEMBER 11th, 2001

An article printed in the Washington Post reported Federal Judge William Karlanderston planned to begin the jury selections by the third week of the New Year, for the start of the trial of the terrorist who had masterminded the assassination attempt against President Albert Cole. The terrorist was also responsible for the murder of the National Security Director, Norman Griffin, and the severe wounding of the Vice President of the United States, Mary Hirshfield.

The elderly judge announced that he planned to begin the trial against the terrorist by Wednesday, March

20th, 2002. The article further stated the trial was thought to be a twenty week ordeal, with the government calling up to thirty witnesses for the United States, against the Iraqi terrorist. It also stated the government was planning to call the commander who led the American soldiers that entered Iraq, and was responsible for taking the wanted terrorist, Colonel Abdulaziz Majd al-Adwani into custody, and brought him back to stand trial in the United States. There were a few other soldiers who had also invaded Iraq scheduled to testify at the trail.

President Albert Cole was seated in the Oval Office with General John White, the Chairman of the Joint Chiefs of Staff, along with CIA Director, John Raincloud, and Vice President Mary Hirshfield. The well respected Chairman was briefing the President and others attending the meeting of the many continuing problems President Saddam Hussein was creating for the United Nations inspectors. The General was offering his opinion that he felt it was only a matter of time, before the usual trouble making President of Iraq, stopped the inspectors from looking for his catch of weapons of mass destruction hidden throughout Iraq all together. The General let it be known he believed Saddam was going to stop the inspections, and possibly even throw the inspectors out of his nation. The CIA Director agreed with what the General offered.

The President was about to respond to what the Chairman was saying when an aide came in and she quickly informed him of the article printed in the local newspapers. The President was relieved he was going to be able to get off the subject of the Iraqi President. He turned to Mary and announced. "Mary, Judge Karlanderson intends to place Colonel al-Adwani on trial in mid March. Dammit, maybe we can finally handle his hash. This trial was too long in the making."

"I'm pleased Albert, I can't tell you how many times in the middle of the night I woke in a cold sweat. Remembering poor Norman's eyes as he lied on the steps of the aircraft with half his head missing, I want this man dealt with so bad I can actually taste it, Albert." The noticeably suddenly upset Vice President gave the President a weak and trembling smile, and then she shivered and crossed her arms over her chest in a protective manner.

"Dammit, you're still having nightmares over this bastard, Mary?" the President snorted.

Mary did not reply she just nodded yes to the President's last question.

"Well Mary, the only thing I can offer you is Colonel... Wait a minute if I keep referring to this evil man as a Colonel, I feel I'm talking about a soldier, not what he truly is, a damn terrorist. Mary, this al-Adwani's nightmare is about to start for him, this much I can promise you."

"I know, and I truly hope once he's on death row, my nightmares will stop Albert." Mary offered as she continued to hug herself.

The General interrupted the conversation between the two American Leaders by clearing his throat loudly, and then he stared at the President. Informing him he wanted to address him, and the conversation he was having with his Vice President was interfering with his conversation.

"Yes, yes General, I know we were having a conversation about this other thorn in my side, sir. What do you suggest we do about him, General White Sir?" The President snapped because he was upset he interrupted his conversation with Mary.

"Mr. President Sir, I believe we should think about increasing the pressure on Saddam and his military machine. I feel we should increase the no fly zone flights in both sections of Iraq, sir. I'm of the notion that we should also allow the Coalition aircraft to hit every target they detect radar emitting from, even if they're not under attack by said radar installations, sir. I think we should hit these targets with evil intent, no matter where he has them setup throughout his country, even if they're in the middle of the civilian sections of his nation. We have to keep his nose bleeding, or he's going to become a larger problem to us in the future, Mr. President Sir.

"One I fear is going to become so large it's going to force us to invade his nation for a second time and finish the job started by President Bush. Don't get me wrong Mr. President I believe President Bush was absolutely correct to stop the war where he did. It's a good thing for any President to display a heart and conscious, especially because he had the power in his hand to close his fist, and Saddam would've been crushed. He was a great President, sir. But the job wasn't done, and President Bush's actions proved to the world you can't show any mercy to a tyrant. You can't get respect from someone who doesn't respect his own civilians, Mr. President Sir. The man's plain outright nuts and he's going to force us to invade his country for a second time, to end his weapons of mass destruction programs, and to stop him from slaughtering the innocent civilian in his own country once and for all. It's coming sure as hell sir."

The President sat back in his chair and let his breath out in a rush, as ran a hand slowly through his thinning hair. He was stunned at what he was hearing coming from his powerful General. He knew the military officer long enough to understand he wanted to use a military application to end any possible threat against the United States. He further understood the Chairman had a marvelous military mind, and was not prone to see ghosts hiding behind every headstone in the graveyard. If his military officer informed him there was going to be a problem in Iraq then he could bet the bank it was going to happen as the he just suggested.

The American Leader also understood he was involved in a heavy ground war still raging in Afghanistan, and he did not think he could possibly afford a second war in Iraq. He was worried if he allowed the General to attack Iraq, that would be two Arab countries his nation would be at war with at the same time, and he felt the other Arab nations of the world would complain the United States was going to war with every Arab nation. He looked back at the powerful General.

"I'm terribly sorry for suggest this pending course of action for you, Mr. President Sir. But I see it coming in the near future and if we continue to ignore it, it's only going to come up behind us and this constant problem is going to end up biting us right on the ass again, sir. We have to react and react powerfully against the President of Iraq, before it's too late to react at all against him without a massive military operation, Mr. President. Then we'll find ourselves involved in another massive ground war with the madman of the Middle East, Mr. President Sir."

"Dammit to hell General White, every damn time I see you lately, all it seems to me is you want to beat on the Iraqi President..." The President started to complain at his General.

The military officer went to defend himself, but he was waved to silence by the President as he added to his words. "Please General I'm not attacking you here sir. If you offer me a problem is coming over the ongoing situation taking place in Iraq then the problem is real and serious, sir. Christ sake, okay General White Sir, if you see this problem and you suggest we increase the no fly zone flights over the two sections of Iraq, and you want to hit all discovered targets in Iraq. Write it up and I'll sign the order for you, sir. I can ill afford Iraq giving us any further problems, not with the mess we have still taking place in Afghanistan."

"Will do Mr. President, you'll have the paperwork on your desk by later this afternoon sir."

TUESDAY, DECEMBER 11th, 2001.
MIAMI, FLORIDA

Colonel Hamoodi al-Qaysi also read the article printed in the Miami Turbine about the judge, and his want to place Colonel al-Adwani on trial in mid March. The Iraqi Military Officer was upset over the fact he was being forced to stay so long in Miami. His sister had to handle a lot more items than he was lead to believe. It was getting noticeable in the garage something was wrong. No matter how well the Iraqi soldiers wrapped up the body of Ilham's dead Marine husband, the smell from his body was beginning to be noticed inside the home. But reading this article in the newspaper, gave a new purpose to the Iraqi Officer aims. He had to get his soldiers up to Washington as soon as possible, if he intended to try and free Colonel al-Adwani, or kill him so he could not bring Saddam Hessein's name up in the assassination attempt.

Colonel al-Qaysi had to make a connection with the Libyan Operative who had worked out of the Libyan Embassy, Captain Badawlhmed Nabih Kamis. He needed to linkup with this Libyan soldier and let him know Iraq still had operatives working in the United States. There were also plans in the offerings aimed at freeing Colonel al-Adwani, and for Iraq to seek their revenge aimed against the American soldiers who had recently invaded his country. He wanted to inform the Libyan Operative if they were unable to get the Iraqi terrorist Colonel out of the United States, he was going to kill him. So no possible connection with Libya could be divulged by anyone. Colonel al-Adwani was the last surviving terrorist who took part in the assassination attempt on the American Leader. With either his release or death, all names of anyone who even might have been involved in the attack would never be known to the world.

Colonel al-Qaysi picked up one of his soldier's bus tickets and read it. Even though it was dated, it was an open ended date which meant the owner could use it once, for the full year before it voided itself out. He smiled, at least this much of his plan was looked after properly.

Major al-Shaya walked in the living room in a great mood, and he sat down on the couch with the Colonel. The Major was dressed in a bathing suit, and she was beginning to like the skimpy American clothes, and she also liked looking like a woman before the men of her group. She enjoyed it when a soldier looked at her as something other than a soldier. When she sat she looked at the Colonel who had troubled eyes and said. "A penny for your thoughts, Colonel?"

"Ahhh... Major al-Shaya. You always seem to be by my side whenever I'm deeply troubled. The loathsome American Judge is going to start the cursed trial of the great fool Colonel al-Adwani in March of next year. So we have a little more than three months to kill this worthless Judge, and to free this failure of a Colonel or kill him. We're beginning to be pressed for time, and we have to get our plan in motion or fail it like the foolish al-Adwani failed his orders."

"Colonel al-Qaysi, I can have the troops immediately head for Washington, and we can always join them when your sister finishes all she has to look after in this foul city. Or we can all leave now for Washington, and have your sister leave the United States and have her go to Iraq until we return to the Middle East. She's of no further use to us in our operation." The female Major said as she turned to see the Colonel's face a little better. By turning like she did, it caused the top of her bathing suit to pull away from her breast, and he found himself viewing her treasures. The Colonel was getting turned on by the exposed nipple and how erect it was. Without thinking, he rudely slid his hand in the top of her swimsuit. This caused the Major to purr at him.

"What is this foul woman? You don't mind my taking foul liberties with your body?"

"Mind my Colonel, I've been doing everything in my power to try and make you take notice of me in a way other than my being a soldier. Excuse me Colonel al-Qaysi Sir." Major al-Shaya said as she stood by the couch and then she reached behind her back and untied the top of her suit. She threw it on the couch and stood before the interested Colonel topless. Then she straddled his legs and sat down on his lap. Instantly, the Colonel's hands were all over her breasts, rolling them slowly in his hands, lightly pinching the nipples between his thumbs and pointer fingers. Everything he was doing to al-Shaya made her purr all the more at him. Her hands went to the Colonel's lap, and found the rock hard bulge in his pants and she smiled.

"Major al-Shaya, you don't know how much I need this tonight, how much I need you. It has been a year since I have last shared my tent with a fine Arab, woman."

"Ooooooo Colonel, you suckle my breast like a hungry new born looking for the offered teat. Please, get out of your pants while I get out of the rest of my swimsuit. Then I'll make all your troubles leave your worried mind. I waited so long to be with you Hamoodi." Al-Shaya offered as she stood up again and removed the rest of her bathing suit.

Major al-Shaya stood before the grinning Colonel as he quickly unbuckled his pants, and then he pushed them down his legs until his pants were off. He worked on his shirt as al-Shaya began to wiggle out of the bottoms of her bathing suit. When she was naked, she placed her hands on her hips and allowed the Colonel to view her exquisite body.

The grinning Iraqi Colonel was shocked because for some reason al-Shaya had shaved all the hair from her body except for her head. He found himself staring at her womanhood. He never saw a woman without hair in her private area before in his life. She wiggled her hips slightly, and this got his attention but quick. Then she stepped forward and knelt before his legs, and started to play with his manhood. When he was standing at full attention, al-Shaya lowered her head and drew his member into her mouth.

As experienced as the wise Colonel was, this was only the third time in his entire life he had a women take him in her mouth. It was an experience he always longed for, and al-Shaya knew what she was doing. In no time she had him wiggling all over the couch. When she felt he was about to cum, she pulled off him and looked him in the eyes. She wanted him to calm down a little before she brought him any further pleasures. When she felt she waited long enough, she stood and straddled him and skillfully guided him in her. Slowly at first, she started to ride him, her pace rapidly increased when she was getting in the act of making love to the man.

Major al-Shaya was going wild and about to cum herself, and when she did. She stopped her movement and then she collapsed on the Colonel's strong chest. She laid there for a few seconds trying to get her breathing under control. When she had it, she slid off his lap and moved down his body until her face was leaning against his swaying member. She licked it and drew his shaft back in her mouth. She licked and nibbled on his member with her teeth, and pulled off him and blew her breath on his shaft. Then she took him back in her mouth.

Quickly, she ran her mouth over his shaft, and this caused Colonel al-Qaysi to grab her by the hair and then help her head go up and down on his growing shaft. Al-Shaya knew when he was about to cum and she pulled off him in time and allowed the first stream to shoot on her lips, cheeks and chin. Then she opened her mouth and took the second stream in it. With her mouth dripping with his essence, she took him back in her mouth and kept sliding it over his shaft until he was drained. When she knew he was done, she pulled off and moved his cum from her face and mouth with her fingers. The Colonel could do nothing but merely stare at her while she did this act before his eyes.

Suddenly, there was someone standing behind her clapping by the door leading to the living room, and both Colonel al-Qaysi and Major al-Shaya turned to see who was watching them make love to each other. They both saw his sister standing in the doorway clapping, and then she announced in a rather sarcastic voice. "My, my, Major al-Shaya, I must say I didn't know you were so well educated in the art of how to bring western pleasures to my foolish Arab brother. I say, I believe I might have learned new ways of pleasing a man from you. One day, I'll have to share a man, not my brother of course with you. Then I can see how well you use your mouth and tongue on me, sister. Maybe we can teach each other of some new ways on how to please a man, and each other while we're at it." Ilham sexily walked into the room and she looked at her brother and then she reached out pinched the major's nipple. When al-Shaya did not move away from her hand, Ilham began to fondle her breast right in front of her brother.

"You see my foolish brother who still dreams of the vast land of sand, when living in the United States and married to an ugly American soldier, one learns many different ways to please that man she's married to. He has taught me much in the art of making love to him. Some I have enjoyed and others have disgusted me." Ilham began to play with both of al-Shaya's breasts, and she was getting turned on by her actions, but not as much as Major al-Shaya was getting hot. This was not the first time she had another woman's hands on her body.

"Enough of this cursed foolishness you're displaying before my unpleased eyes, my wayward and foolish sister. Don't make me believe you have become so ugly living in this foul land of sin and lust, you daughter of the scorpion." The Colonel grumbled as he found his pants and put them on. All the while he was dressing, Ilham continued to play with Major al-Shaya's breasts, and al-Shaya did not stop her because she was enjoying it that much.

"I said enough of this madness you're engaging in before my disgusted eyes before I beat you for your sins, Ilham!" The upset Colonel suddenly roared as he took his sister roughly by the arm, and he pulled her away from his Major savagely, actually sending her falling to the floor. All of a sudden he found himself actually hating his younger sister. He decided to send her back to Iraq like al-Shaya had suggested.

"We have to leave! Major, send the troops on their way by bus and train to Washington. We'll stay behind for two more days and then we'll take my sister's SUV and drive to Washington. We'll lose the cursed vehicle there. I have another vehicle Lieutenant Elmasry will drive to Washington, woman. Ilham, you'll report to the Saudi Arabian Embassy in this city, and tell them you have to get out of the United States fast. Tell them some American tuffs just killed your husband because you were Arab. That'll make them get you out of this foul country quickly. I have to get to Washington before the Judge starts his foul trial of Colonel al-Adwani."

The still angry Colonel growled at the two young Arab women staring at him with questioning eyes. More anger quickly filled Colonel al-Qaysi's chest and he snarled at his sister. "What is this foolishness you're aiming at me? Is there sand filling your foul ears, and it is stopping you from hearing my words? I ordered you two to move, and that's what you will do! Now!"

The two young women jumped over the force lacing the fuming Colonel al-Qaysi's words. Both women ran from the living room, with Major al-Shaya finishing dressing as she ran from her commander's view. He brought his hand down he threatened the women with, and then he smiled because he was still able to instill such fear in people with mere words and harsh looks, and a quick raise of his hand.

Major al-Shaya ordered the remaining Iraqi soldiers to assemble in the living room, and then she ordered them to head to the bus and train stations they had the tickets for. The soldiers were then to head for Washington. Ilham packed up two suitcases and set them out in the hall, and then she placed a call to the Saudi Arabian Embassy. Once she finished with the representative, she called a cab. She took two thousand dollars and prepared to leave her home for the last time in her life. Ilham walked to her brother and kissed him.

It took several minutes for the cab to arrive, and Ilham was out of the house and gone.

The Iraqi Colonel Al-Qaysi watched his sister leave the home, and the rest of his soldiers followed her out. When everyone but Major al-Shaya, and Lieutenant Elmasry and himself were out of the house, he addressed his Lieutenant. "Elmasry, you'll get in my foul car and drive up to Washington. The Major and I will leave in two days, and we'll meet with the rest of you soldiers on Sunday, December 16th, at the worthless Roland's Motel. Then we can start our mission. Lieutenant, be extremely careful about yourself at all times, don't get involved in a car accident, or get a traffic ticket. I cannot have the cursed police authorities investigating any of my people. Leave me and be very careful as you drive to Washington, fool."

"Yes Colonel, I'll arrive in Washington safely as ordered Colonel al-Qaysi Sir."

"You better, if you're stopped by police for any reason, you're not to be taken alive. Don't fight the fools just kill yourself so they don't capture you. I cannot allow any of us to be taken prisoner and be questioned by the hated police of this evil country. The mission is more important than all our worthless lives are." The Colonel stared at Elmasry until he finally left the home. He gave each of his Arab soldier's five hundred American dollars for their trip up to Washington. Just before he sat in the living room, he checked his remaining store of American cash. He had over forty thousand dollars left. He knew once he spoke to the Libyan, the cursed fool would give him additional funds his group would need to pull off his mission successfully.

Once everyone was out of the home, and al-Shaya and al-Qaysi were alone again. Major al-Shaya pulled her shirt off and she stared at the Colonel.

"Huh al-Shaya, all of a sudden you have no shame about you I see any longer, lowly woman." The smiling Iraqi Colonel said to his female Major.

"And I believe you love it Hamoodi. It took me so long with acquiring your attention, and if you think for one moment that I'm going to allow you forget me, you're sadly mistaken you old camel rider desert dweller you. One thing I want to ask you though Hamoodi, how did you feel when your sister was playing with my breasts in front of you? Did it turn you on any?" Al-Shaya asked with a wicked smile, and concern lacing her eyes as she stared at him.

"It didn't turn me on to see my foul sister playing with you like she was doing, al-Shaya! Anything sexual about my sister would never turn me on, wicked one from the vast hot desert sands." He snarled angrily at her. He did not want to be thinking of getting sexually aroused by his sister and her foolish actions, and become even worse of a sinner.

"I hear in your voice that you have misunderstood my question of you, Hamoodi. Forgetting it was your sister doing what she was doing to me, did it turn you on to see another woman playing with a woman's breasts before your non-believing eyes? Who is so proud he doesn't know what question is truly asked of him, Hamoodi." The female Iraqi Major Al-Shaya smiled at the concerned looking Arab Colonel as she moved her upper body to make her breasts sway slightly at the foolish soldier staring so intensely at her.

"If you must ask me such a foolish question Major, I'll answer it, bitch born from the slim of the desert. I answer the question because you asked me, evil woman. Yes, I was turned on by the foolish event, loathsome woman." He snapped at the Major then he reached out and began to play with the Major's breasts in the same manner his sister was doing a short while ago.

"Hmmm... my most inquisitive Hamoodi, I see that you truly have learned something from that brief encounter I had with your evil little sister. If it'll please my lover, when we leave the hated United States and end up in Jordan, I'll seek out a woman and we'll play with each other in front of you. So we can add to the great pleasures I intend to shower you with in the future. For now I have your attention my dear, I'll never allow it to wan again. Sometime in the near future, I intend to make you my husband, desert fool." The pretty female Major purred at him as she ran the tip of her finger slowly along the side of the Colonel's face.

"Oh, you intend to make me your husband do you, evil woman who thinks she can tell me what she's going to do with me. I believe you might have placed the wagon before the foul horse I believe it is how that is said. If I remember how it works properly, I believe it's usually the man who makes the woman his wife and he tells her what to do, and not the other way around as you seem to believe how it works, my foolish Major." He gave al-Shaya a smile as he continued to play with her breasts as she stood before him.

"Ahhh... yes that's the way it works in our country, Hamoodi. But since you chose to drag me to this foul land of sin and lust, it has changed some of my faithful ways, and I think I like the change it has caused in my heart. And that change gave me the right to make you my husband, fool." The female Major grinned at the Colonel.

"Enough of this foolish bantering back and forth, we have other things that I must attend to. There'll be plenty of time for us to explore each other's bodies once we're out of this god cursed evil country, Major. Right now, we have to concentrate on getting everything we'll need, and then getting up to Washington. I want to be ready to kill this cursed Judge by the end of January, or the beginning of February. If we kill this worthless Judge, it'll delay the trial of Colonel al-Adwani, and it'll give us the time we need to make our preparations to free him from jail, or kill him to silence his lips forever." The Colonel took a quick breath then let it out slowly.

"It'd be a shame if we're forced to kill al-Adwani. After all the effort we expended getting to the United States to free the worthless fool, Hamoodi. To kill this man makes it seem wrong. I know if we have enough time to work on our plans, we can free al-Adwani, and get him out of the United States alive. So we can bring him back to the Middle East as what he is to us, a hero to the Muslim needs, and the sacred teaching of Allah." Now it was al-Shaya who took a breath, as she stared at her lover. She could not remove the love she felt for this man, from her eyes.

"You're correct with your choice of words, Major. But I assure you we'll do whatever is necessary for the good of our honorable country and cause, and for the sake of Allah. I, like you my sister, would hate to be forced to kill the terrorist Colonel al-Adwani. He has done so much for our just cause I feel we own him to try and free him from the hated Americans. Even though I hate all what the man stands for, we have to get him from the lowly infidels. The longer they have him in their custody, the more likely it might be that this god cursed spy will break under their constant questioning, and he tells the fools the names of everyone involved in his evil work.

"We cannot possibly allow the fact that President Hussein was involved in this failed assassination attempt against the worthless American President. Mind me my sister of the desert sands, it's not for Saddam's worthless head, but for the sake of Iraq I say this. I fear what the hated American soldiers will do to our country if they ever discover that President Saddam was truly behind the assassination attempt of the American President. Bah, I hate what we're being forced to do. I'm an honorable soldier trained to fight my enemy face to face on the battlefield. Not to roam around in their foul country lowing myself to the standards of a common and hated terrorist. The only reason I seek revenge on the loathsome American soldiers, is because they have dared to invade our country, and in doing so they have insulted every honorable Iraqi soldier. For that terrible insult I shall wreak my revenge upon their cursed souls and foul bodies." Colonel al-Qaysi bitterly complained to the beautiful Major al-Shaya.

The female Iraqi Major did not reply to the Colonel's angry words, she knew better than to speak when he was in this type of mood. She also knew deep in her heart he would do whatever was necessary on order to free Colonel al-Adwani from the evil American authorities' custody. That was the only reason for the Iraqi soldiers coming to the United States. She understood the problem with the American troops invading Iraq, was only a side car for Colonel al-Qaysi's seeking revenge against them. She turned and put her blouse on, and then she went about her business leaving the safe house and loading up the SUV, and then leaving Miami.

The rest of the day passed quickly, and soon the excited Colonel wanted to leave the safe house and head for Washington. The smell of the body rotting in the garage attic was starting to get to him. The soon to be terrorists climbed into the SUV and he started the vehicle and then they left the home, but not before locking every window and door, and turning the air-conditioning real low. This was to help keep down the odor from the body hidden in the garage. The drive up to Washington was done at a slow pace, because he did not want any trouble with what he called the road police. They had plenty of time to get up to Washington, so they stayed in Georgia on the first night of their traveling.

The two Iraqi soldiers enjoyed the night in the motel and they shared the bed for their first serious bout of lovemaking. On Thursday morning, the two military officers left by ten thirty a.m. and they drove Highway I-95 at the exact posted speed. The drive was rather pleasant, and the still tired Colonel ordered the Major to stop in Virginia for their next night's rest. Colonel al-Qaysi wanted to enter Washington on Friday morning, well rested and refreshed from a good night's sleep, for his visit with the Libyan scheduled for later in the afternoon.

Colonel al-Qaysi had no intention of staying at the filthy Roland's Motel with the rest of the troops, not after what he had heard about the filthy place. He and Major al-Shaya were going to stay at a hotel in downtown Washington. He was silent as he saw the sign for Washington on the side of the road, and when the traffic got heavier, he grew angry. They had a nice night, spending it at a chain motel with al-Shaya sharing her bed with the Colonel for a second time, exploring each other's bodies. By the time they got to downtown Washington, the traffic was madding.

They were passing a McDonalds diner, and Colonel al-Qaysi ordered Major al-Shaya to pull into the restaurant so they could get something to eat. While he was waiting for al-Shaya to bring him the food he knew he was not going to like. He placed a call to the Libyan Captain at the Embassy by cell phone. The phone rang three times before it was answered by the secretary of the Captain who was the Ambassador's security chief also.

"Yes, you have just reached the office of Captain Badawlhmed Nabih Kamis, who is the head of security for the Libyan Embassy and Ambassador, please. How may I direct this call for you please?" A voice that sounded more like he was angry at the world than asking a question, nearly snarled in the other end of the phone.

"Yes, this is the Captain's old friend and I wish to speak with him, if you don't mind." The Colonel said, he did not want to identify himself to the lowly secretary.

"Yes, and the Captain has many old friends living in the United States who always wish to speak with him, sir. What is the name of this old friend who wishes to speak with the Captain, so I know it and I can inform the Captain who it is who wishes to speak with him, sir?"

"You tell your Captain that I'm a friend who went to school with him in the land of the sand who wishes to speak with him, foul fool who uses up my time like this on the phone."

"You're an old friend who went to school with my Captain? But I see that you have a serious problem with mentioning your foul name to me, sir. So I may inform the Captain of who wishes an audience with him. No name and no talk with the Captain, old friend. If you continue to refuse to inform me of your name, I'm afraid you will soon be speaking to a dial tone, sir."

"You fool who chances to anger someone who might have his worthless head removed from his foul shoulders by the edge of a sword. You just tell him what I have told you to say to the Captain and be done with it!" The Colonel growled low in the phone.

"You can get as angry as you dare want with me sir. I will not dare bother my extremely busy Captain, unless I have a name of the foul one who wishes to speak to my Captain to offer him, to the voice who insults me so over the phone as if you have me in fear of your threats, sir."

"Desert fool, you just tell him Hamoodi al-Qaysi wishes to speak with him. If he doesn't remember my name, you tell him he helped my brother last year when he came to the United States, looking for certain tools for the chosen work he was in, fool."

Now, the security guard realized he was right. This person on the other end of the phone was an operative wanting to speak to his Captain as he replied in a huff to the voice on the other end of the phone. "Mr. Al-Qaysi, please hold the line while I see if my extremely busy and exhausted Captain wishes to speak to his old friend as you call yourself." Instantly, the angry voice left and soft Arabic music instantly filled the Colonel's ear.

The male secretary quickly informed the Libyan Captain of the man's name asking to speak with him on the phone, and he offered the Captain that he believed the man on the phone was an operative from Iraq, or another Middle East nation. The secretary watched the Captain suddenly rub his chin as he tried to place a face with the name. Finally, he barked harshly at his servant. "Ahmed, have the call transferred over to my private line immediately. I don't remember who this man might be, but his name sounds Iraqi. I wonder if General al-Zahar has sent him to us for reasons I am unaware of at the present time you fool. Maybe he's going to try and finish the job of killing the American President. Yes, I'll speak to this man on the phone."

Colonel al-Qaysi was getting angrier as he waited to speak with the Libyan Captain. Suddenly, the voice was back on the phone and it snarled in his ear. "Old friend of my Captain you call yourself, he'll speak to you sir. Hold the line while I transfer the call to his private office. If we get disconnected for any reason, call back immediately. Hold on."

In seconds, a new voice filled the phone. "Yes, this is Captain Badawlhmed, sir."

"Yes it's good to hear your voice this is Hamoodi al-Qaysi. An old friend of ours has instructed me to make contact with you when I entered America on my first visit to this..."

"Who is this old friend of ours you speak of? I'm afraid I don't recall your name, sir."

"I'm sorry you don't remember me, sir. Our old friend was General excuse me, a gentleman who told me you have once helped his brother when he first arrived in the United States, sir. Al-Zahar, please excuse me again it's a far land that I come from, my old friend. I'm sorry, but my English is not so good I fear." The Iraqi Military Officer was trying to speak in code, and he was hoping the Libyan fool would pick up what he was trying to say.

Instantly, the Libyan Captain pulled the phone away from his ear and put the two words this stranger just offered him together. General al-Zahar. But something the stranger said shook him to his very soul, it was one word but it still shook him though. The Libyan looked at the phone and then spoke again. "Hamoodi, your old friend was most correct to tell you any friend of his is a friend of mine, sir. Where are you at this moment?"

"I'm in Washington, Captain." The Iraqi offered in the phone.

"How long will it take for you to get to the Embassy, Hamoodi?" the Captain was trying to repeat the name as many times as he could, in hopes of remembering who he was speaking with.

"I should be able to arrive at your Embassy within a half an hour at the very latest I believe, my old friend." The Iraqi Colonel offered the Libyan Operative.

"Good, then begin your journey here, I cannot wait to see my old friend once again." The wise Libyan Captain hung up without further words to the Iraqi warrior.

Major al-Shaya came to the eating booth carrying a tray with their food as Colonel al-Qaysi placed his cell phone back in his pocket. They ate quickly and then he told al-Shaya they had to leave. He never told her where they were heading. A half an hour later, the Ford SUV entered the Libyan Embassy gate, and parked in the open lot designated for visitors to the Embassy. The Colonel was driving the vehicle this time. They got out of the car and an escort instantly picked them up and walked them towards the main doors. They were met by two guards from inside.

As Colonel al-Qaysi and Major al-Shaya entered the Embassy Building, they were immediately ordered to stop in the middle of the hall and place their hands away from their sides. The two Libyan guards expertly padded them down for any possible hidden weapons on their persons. The guard checking Major al-Shaya, as usual took liberties with his search of her body. Once it was determined neither visitors hand any weapons hidden on their person. One guard pressed a button on his desk, and a door leading to a private office slid opened, and Captain Badawlhmed came strolling out of the office with a smile plastered on his lips.

He immediately offered the Iraqi Military Officer his hand and as they shook the Libyan operative leaned a little closer to Colonel al-Qaysi and he whispered to him. "I believe I have heard you mention General al-Zahar had sent you to find me. Am I correct to believe this is true, stranger to my Embassy? This is the only reason why you were granted entry and you and your female friend stand before my door like this, my faithful Arab brother?"

"That's correct Captain Badawlhmed Sir. I have much to inform you of, is there a place where we can speak in private and secured? We need help from you and your government, sir."

"Please, let us go to my private office. By the way, who is this lovely young woman standing to your side, Hamoodi? I pray to Allah she's your lovely wife, she's beautiful." The three entered the office. The secretary who answered the phone was waiting inside the room for them to enter. When Captain Badawlhmed looked at him he ordered. "Ahmed, bring some tea for my new friends." Then he nodded to the secretary also his personal bodyguard.

When the angry male secretary saw the slight nod, he knew instantly these strangers were safe. The secretary/bodyguard left the room to get the tea as ordered. Once the secretary was out of the room, Badawlhmed waved his hand towards seats in his office and sat behind the desk.

When they were seated, Colonel al-Qaysi began speaking. "Captain Badawlhmed Kamis Sir, I'm afraid I carry some bad news for your honorable ears to hear, sir."

"Please Hamoodi; I fear my ears have not grown unaccustomed to bad news strangers bring. What with the sorry shape the Arab world is in lately, bad news seems to be all I'm hearing from my brothers of late who pay me a visit. What is this bad news you bring on your shoulders for my ears, my Iraqi friend?" the Libyan grumbled at the stranger as he held him in his gaze.

"First Captain, I was General Hassan al-Zahar's second in command, sir. The bad news I bring to you is the General is dead, sir..." The Colonel stopped speaking the moment the Libyan rose from the desk and he began to pace the room. Colonel al-Qaysi watched as the obviously upset Libyan Captain paced back and forth for a few moments. When he returned to his seat and stared at the Iraqi for a few moments, Colonel al-Qaysi spoke again.

"Captain Badawlhmed, the General was killed by the Americans who have invaded my nation when they arrested Colonel Abdulaziz Majd al-Adwani, and remove him from Iraq, sir..."

"Yes, yes, I have heard of that surgical strike the American commandos had carried out in Iraq against your troops stationed at a small village I cannot remember the name of, Colonel." The Libyan Operative offered as he interrupted the Colonel, and then went on with his words. "Colonel al-Qaysi, you made mention that you were in search of some needed help from my government when you first entered my office, sir. How may we be of service to you? I take it there are more than just you two in the United States, Colonel? Are you and your, err... friends on a special mission here in the United States am I to believe? And if so, what is the nature of this mission? I must know of this, if I'm to offer you any of my help, Colonel."

"I know this and have need of help myself, Captain Badawlhmed Sir. I, we're not alone in the United States. I have twenty one well trained soldiers in all in Washington, including the Major at my side and myself. Yes, we have a special mission in mind, but it's a self appointed mission, and is not sanctioned by my government I might add. My group is not terrorists we're here to kill the Federal Judge who was picked to try Colonel al-Adwani. Once we have killed this evil American Judge, we plan to break the Colonel out of jail, and then get him out of the hated United States still alive, sir. There is a second part of my mission also, sir. I intend to kill the foul American soldiers who had invaded my country.

"If I cannot kill them then I'll kill the one in command of the soldiers who had attack my nation. I heard his name mentioned over their radio numerous times, his name is seared into my memory. His name is Lieutenant Robert Walker. If I kill no other American fool for the rest of my worthless life, I'll not leave the United States until this one man, this one soldier is dead, Captain. That's my driving force to this selected mission. What I need from you is, I need more American cash to carry out my mission, and I have need of assault weapons. Any help you have that could assist me on this mission, sir. I'm sorry I come to my brother with problems at hand. I have to do this special mission for my country, for General al-Zahar, and for myself, Captain."

"Colonel al-Qaysi, I remember you well now, we have met once when I was in Iraq, visiting with the General. I'm stunned that the hated American soldiers were able to kill such a fine Commander. Another thing Colonel, you don't have to feel bad coming to me for help. If you and your soldiers are going to free Colonel al-Adwani then you can count on all the help I'm able to offer you and your fellow warriors. The Colonel is a dear friend, and I'd do anything to get him out of the evil hands of the lowly Americans, Colonel al-Qaysi." The Libyan offered with a smile then added. "Colonel al-Qaysi, do you have a place to stay for the night in Washington?"

"No, the Major and I were planning to rent a room here in Washington..."

"Nonsense, nonsense, I'll not allow you to stay in a worthless motel here in Washington, sir. You'll stay in the Embassy for your stay here, so we can talk more at our leisure, Colonel. Should I make two rooms available to you or just one, Colonel?"

Colonel al-Qaysi turned to the Major, and then he smiled when he noticed her shaking her head no, and then he replied to the Libyan Operative while still wearing his smile. "Captain Badawlhmed Sir, one room will do very nicely for our needs, sir."

"Ahhhh... I see the Major is more to you than a mere fellow soldier, my Arab brother. It is a very good idea to travel with someone who you can lay with at night." The Libyan mumbled as he gave Major al-Shaya a long and leering look.

"Major al-Shaya is what she has to be for the betterment of our sacred mission for Allah, sir. Captain, we'd be most honored to spend the night in the Embassy. Will you be staying in the building as well, Captain Badawlhmed Kamis Sir?" the Colonel asked the Libyan.

"Yes Colonel, no visitor is allowed to stay in the Embassy unless the one who had invited him, also remains inside the building sir. I have a room I use when I happen to, or am forced to stay in the building for the night. I'll have my secretary have one of the spare bedrooms setup for you. I'll make certain you have some food to nibble on, unless you find yourself something else to nibble on, Colonel." The Libyan added in a sarcastic tone when he leered at al-Shaya.

The Iraqi gave the Libyan a nasty look, but did not reply to his stinging words.

"Colonel al-Qaysi sir, it's getting rather late. I'm of the mind to put off any further speaking together until tomorrow morning when you're better rested, sir. You made mention that your troops are here in Washington, do they have need to hear from you sir? Or do they know what is expected of them, and how they're to act in the capital of this evil land, Colonel?"

"Captain Badawlhmed, my soldiers are well trained and they know what is expected of them at all times, without my being forced to watch over the fools. I don't have to waste time holding their foul hands, or speak to them before I can turn in for the night. They're truly well trained Iraqi soldiers in my Unit." The Iraqi Military Officer snarled at the Libyan as he glared at him.

"I'm sorry if I made you believe I felt you had to look after your foolish soldiers like little children, Colonel al-Qaysi." The Libyan smiled at the other military officer.

The Iraqi Officer slowly rubbed his chin because he felt he barked at the Libyan because he was tired as he offered. "Captain Badawlhmed Sir, perhaps I'm more exhausted than I had first realized I was, sir. I believe it's a very poor friend who snaps at the hand that offers him the help he needs to complete his mission here in Washington, my wise Arab brother."

"Say no more my brother, your words are not necessary, Colonel. Ahmed, you'll escort Colonel al-Qaysi and Major al-Shaya to the third bedroom in the East Wing of the Embassy. You know which room I mean, the one with the bathroom. Once they're comfortable, you'll return to my office and we'll speak further. I have letters that need posting, and other needs of you on this night, Ahmed." The Libyan shrugged at his male secretary to get him moving.

The Libyan secretary and bodyguard Ahmed led the two Iraqi Officers to the ordered bedroom, the secretary knew what the Captain was up to, and once he deposited the two Iraqis in the room, he rushed downstairs. The secretary went through the Captain's private office and into the secret closet, and took the stairs up. He came out in a narrow hall that went by the three bedrooms in this section of the building. He saw the Captain already looking through a small peephole.

Ahmed smiled as he looked through another peep hole and watched as Major al-Shaya slowly undressed by the side of the bed, and then she went to shower. The Iraqi Colonel sat on the bed and relaxed. The two Libyans waited for the female to come back. They wanted to see what the two were going to do in the bedroom once they were along together.

As Major al-Shaya came back in the bedroom with just a towel wrapped around her exquisite body, the Libyan Operative mumbled just loud enough for Ahmed to hear his words. "Come on whore of the hot desert sands remove that worthless towel away from your fat body for me. I want to see your cursed body, and see what you'll do next, desert pig."

As if she heard his words, Major al-Shaya pulled the towel from her body, and then she sexily approached the exhausted Colonel still resting on the bed, and the Libyan mumbled. "Look Ahmed I knew she had perfect breasts."

"What is the filthy pig going to do to the foul Iraqi Colonel, Captain?" Ahmed asked as they both stared at the naked women in the room.

"Look at the filthy Sharmoota Haygana (horny Bitch), she pulled the Colonel's pants down and she is rubbing his filthy kisich (penis) between her fat breasts, Ahmed. Now, she's taking his member in her foul mouth to compound her crime. This Sharmoota can Mos Zibby (suck my dick) anytime she cares to, Ahmed. Oh, the nasty Sharmoota, (bitch) she allowed the Colonel to release himself in her filthy mouth, and she is lapping it up like a hungry jackal. I think this pig has visited the United States before in her foul life, Ahmed. Come, we must leave the two lowly infidels before we become as polluted as they are. I saw all I wanted to witness on this foul night between those two fools. I'm tired, and I want to turn in for the night myself, Ahmed. I'm remaining in the building for the entire night." Kamis announced to his aide.

"Captain Badawlhmed Sir, do you want me to order Samia to visit your room tonight, sir?"

"You mean the Ambassador's private whore is going to be staying in the building overnight, desert jackal?" the Libyan Captain asked his aide with excitement in his tone.

"Yes Captain, the Ambassador ordered her to remain in the Embassy because of the Iraqi visitors, sir." Ahmed replied with pride, pleased at what he offered the Captain.

"Yes fool who has feasted on sour breast milk. Of course I want you to order her to my bedroom for the night. That way while I teach the foul one the correct way to respect an honorable Arab male, I can also question her and find out what the devil the fool of a worthless Ambassador was up to today. I'm pleased the fool has ordered his private bitch to stay for tonight. Ahmed, I thought this was going to be a most boring night to endure, but you and Allah have seen fit that I'll enjoy myself on this endless night. Tell Samia I want her in my room in twenty minutes. I have to shower before she comes to me, that way I'll be prepared for her." The now excited Captain allowed an ugly smile to cross his lips, as he stared at Ahmed.

CHAPTER THIRTEEN

THE ROLAND'S MOTEL, WASHINGTON D.C.
FRIDAY, DECEMBER 14th, 2001

Colonel Hamoodi al-Qaysi's soldiers followed their orders to the letter, and they entered the small motel in groups of three, and each group signed in and asked for a room on a weekly bases. The manager of the filthy pig sty was grinning from ear to ear, because this would be the first time in years that his motel would be filled for the night. It looked like these strangers were going to rent the rooms for a little while. The manager walked each group out to their rooms. Some of the trio's had a woman in the group, but the manager made notice it seemed like none of the stranger knew each other. He did not care what the groups were about, he was dying to return to his office and report to the owner that he had rented the whole motel out, and it was just before Christmas. He was hoping to find something extra in this paycheck for filling the motel.

As each group entered their rooms, they turned up their noses at what greeted them in the apartments. Besides the terrible smell, the chamber was filthy and some of the rooms actually had broken windows. Sergeant Aicha Said Damerdji drew in a breath, and then he announced proudly to Corporal Bashir al-Beidh and Sergeant Yussa Shahid. "Phew, the cursed stink and foul dirt of this ugly room reminds me so much of Iraq, and how we were forced to live since the loathsome American soldiers had destroyed our country on us. I cannot wait to begin our revenge against the foul fools for their crimes committed against our country."

Sergeant Shahid, the only female member of this group, growled at the Sergeant. She was insulted by his crude remark that the smell and dirt of the United States, reminded him of his country. "Sergeant Damerdji, how dare you say such a foul thing about your country, cursed fool? Fear Allah's great wrath for daring to insult His sacred land with your worthless words."

"I once feared Allah's great revenge that should've been aimed at the cursed American soldiers, when they first invaded our lands, pig. I also feared Allah's anger with our President who allowed the war to destroy our country. Then I feared Allah's hatred for the way His children are being treating, and changing the meaning and words in the Holy Book of the Qur'an. But seeing these terrible insults to Allah and yet He restrained his revenge against these loathsome people, I no longer fear Allah's anything, foul pig. If it's as written in the Great Book then the Arab's who shed another Arab's blood, should be dead by Allah's revenge, woman."

"Blasphemy! You speak Blasphemy to the Holy Qur'an and against the Almighty Allah, fool! Shame on you Sergeant, I should kill you for the foul words you just spoke, evil one."

"I only speak what is in my heart and mind and what my eyes have witnessed fool. Once this mission is over, I intend to remain in the United States and begin a new life here. I'm done with living in a land always at war with the other nations of the Middle East. I'm extremely tired of all the cursed bombs constantly falling out of the sky at the will of the loathsome American soldiers. If we cannot stop them I might as well live with them. That's what's going to happen to Iraq. The foul American leaders will not be finished with Saddam until he's dead and buried in the sands of our land, and they own Iraq and all our oil fields. I'll not die in bed when American made bombs wake me. I'm going to remain in the United States and disappear."

"Sergeant Damerdji, to hear your unholy words spoke by your cursed lips, makes me believe that you can no longer be trusted, and carry out our plans for Allah against the hated Americans. If this is true then speak the words and I'll dispatch your worthless life as we speak, desert rat. We cannot have anyone not totally behind Colonel al-Qaysi, and all of what he's trying to do for our country, and for the honor of Allah." Shahid hissed as she glared at the angry Sergeant, and removed a knife she picked up when they ate at the diner. She was prepared to kill the man she felt was more of a threat against their mission, than he was of help for it.

"You foolish foul sharmoota, how dare you threaten my life with a god cursed knife, woman! No matter my foul feelings about my life and what I have witnessed happening to my beloved country, worthless bitch of the desert. I'm a proud and loyal Iraqi soldier first, and as a true soldier of Allah, I'll obey my Commander's orders with my life without hesitation. Or I'll go to the gates of Paradise because I died following those orders. Witch I warn you, I'm still a faithful member of this unit, and I'll carry out my orders to my death. I'll do to my..."

"Enough of this worthless madness that spills forth from your worthless mouth's, fools! We have enough problems facing us and scores of evil doers wanting to kill us, without our fighting and threatening to fight and kill each other. We're ordered to wait here for the Colonel to arrive no matter how long that wait may take us. Once he arrives, he'll tell us what to do next for our mission's success. Sergeant Shahid, if you don't understand Sergeant Damerdji by this time. I fear you'll never understand he constantly complains about everything, even when a woman sucks on his limp zib (Penis) he complains. If I thought for one second he could no longer be trusted with this mission, it would've been I who ended his foul and wasted life, woman.

"Calm down my sister of the desert sands. All is as it should be between our faithful soldiers of Iraq, unless you can no longer control yourself and it's you who have become a serious danger to our unit and mission. I said calm down woman, and put away that foul weapon away. Though I'm pleased you thought to arm yourself with a weapon, woman. We need weapons, woman!" Corporal Bashir al-Beidh growled at the two angry Sergeants. Even though he was of lesser rank than the other two soldiers, he was making the most sense out of the three of them.

"You fool who displays the great wisdom of Muhammad. Your words are wise and I bow to you for speaking them to us so wisely. It's as you have just offered me, Sergeant Damerdji would complain about everything, but his loyalty is not to be questioned by any of us. Sergeant Damerdji, please forgive this lowly woman for threatening to kill you."

Damerdji bowed slightly towards the female Sergeant, and offered her a quick smile.

There was a sudden knock on the outer door of their room, and the three Iraqi soldiers immediately went into a defensive posture while Sergeant Damerdji turned to the door to see who wanted entry into their room. The Sergeant walked near the door and he growled through the door. "Yes, who is seeking entry in my room? Speak, or you'll not have the door opened for you, and you'll stand outside until you leave my door or die of age, you great fool you. We're a peaceful lot of people in this room who only want to live in peace."

"If you're of peaceful people in there then you wouldn't be in there in the first place, you worthless fool. It's I, your neighbor from across the hall, and I'd like to meet with you for a few moments, sir." Sergeant Muhammad Mushtaha announced from the hallway.

The Sergeant opened the door and then he grinned and invited him in the room.

"Ahhh... it's good to see your room is in the same filthy condition as ours is in. We have found a number of used things the cursed American fools cover their foul Zibs with, when they don't want to make a woman with child, lying on the floor of the room we rented. I don't know how people of so great a worth and intelligence, could possibly spend one second in a foul building as filthy as this one is, and I thought the living conditions in Iraq were bad to deal with. Do you think all the cursed hotel rooms in the United

States are kept like these foul and filthy ones are, my Arab brother?" The Sergeant asked his fellow Sergeant as he cautiously entered the room.

"I don't know and I care even less about that thought. All this filth makes me hate the foul land of Satan all the more. Are the other fools settled in their rooms yet, my brother?"

"Yes Sergeant al-Beidh, all but Lieutenant Malika Nabeel Elmasry. He's driving the Colonel's car up to Washington. I was informed he'll be in command of us when the Colonel and Major are away from us. By Allah's great breath, this foul room smells even worse than ours. I wonder if the filthy Americans are able to piss in the foul bowl they're so proud of in this country." The Sergeant complained to his fellow soldiers as he brought his hand to his nose and held it.

"Young fool born from a camel's arse. Do you think for one second that Colonel al-Qaysi and Major al-Shaya will stay in a room in this foul cesspit, fool?" Sergeant al-Beidh asked.

"My brother from the desert, we've been warned never to use our military rank when we speak to each other while in the United States. The Colonel doesn't even want us to use our Arab names in the United States. I'm certain once we linkup back with Colonel al-Qaysi, he'll give us the American names we'll use while on this foul mission. But for the time being, I suggest that we speak to each other without using our names or our ranks in the service." Sergeant Mishtaha offered kindly to his fellow soldier.

"True, I guess we'll wait in our cursed rooms until our leader finally arrives to tell us what to do next." Sergeant al-Beidh replied because he had nothing else to offer the other soldiers.

SATURDAY, DECEMBER 15ᵗʰ, 2001.
THE LIBYAN EMBASSY IN WASHINGTON D.C.

Both Colonel Hamoodi al-Qaysi and Major Serena al-Shaya had a great night's sleep, and they would have still been sleeping if Ahmed did not knock on the door and offer them some food. Al-Qaysi got out of bed and took the tray in the room. The two Iraqis ate while staying in bed, with al-Shaya allowing the sheets to rest below her breasts while she enjoyed her meal. They made love twice last night, and she was looking forward to make love to the Colonel again before they started their day's work. But Colonel al-Qaysi's mind was worrying about his troops at the hotel. His mind was too busy to thing about making love to al-Shaya on this fine morning.

The Libyan Operative Captain Kamis also had a fine night of lovemaking with the Libyan Ambassador's beautiful secretary and personal little play toy. The Captain was not the least bit interested in his two visitors at the moment, while the Ambassador's private secretary made love to him with her mouth. He made her do it in the same fashion as he watched al-Shaya do it to the Iraqi Colonel, when they watched the two making love through the spy holes in the room.

It took a while for Colonel al-Qaysi and Major al-Shaya came down from their room, and they sat down in the large waiting area. They were waiting for the Libyan Operative to come to them. The Iraqi Military Officer wanted to speak to him a little further, before he left to be with the rest of his troops staying at the filthy Washington motel. There was a newspaper lying on a table and he picked it up and began to read it. It was the Washington Post and the front page was donated mostly to the war still raging in Afghanistan, but there was a highlighted box that mentioned Iraq, and it stated the story began on page three of the newspaper.

As Colonel al-Qaysi read the article he grew angry. It reported how the allied warplanes carrying out the no fly zones in his country came under increased testing by the attack radar's from the SAM (Surface to Air Missile) sites in the two declared no fly zones over Iraq. The paper further explained Iraqi's increasing pressure and threats aimed against the allied warplanes, forced the American President to increase his attacks on these troublesome sites. He knew what this meant it was telling him Saddam was again testing the United States will and commitment to the no fly zones. He knew this was an extremely foolish move on his foolish President's part, what with the way the American public was reacting to the war in Afghanistan, he knew anything Arab in the world was fair game to the United States planes of war and anger.

Major Serena al-Shaya noticed the angry look on the Colonel's face, and she cautiously asked him. "Colonel al-Qaysi Sir, is there anything wrong sir? You seem suddenly upset I'm afraid."

"I am the great fool in control of our country is at it again I fear. And, his foul actions might cause us to be forced to delay our attack against the hated American Judge. What he's causing, are the attacks against our land to be increased by the cursed Allied warplanes. We might be forced to see what actions the god cursed American military is going to adopt against Saddam, before we go after this hated Judge." The Colonel hissed low.

Major al-Shaya shook her head sadly in response to the Colonel's words.

Captain Kamis came downstairs and found the Iraqi Colonel and Major sitting in the waiting room and he said to the Colonel. "Ahhh... Colonel al-Qaysi I trust that you had as enjoyable a night's sleep as I had enjoyed for myself, sir?" The Libyan did not bother to even acknowledge the female Major sitting to the right side of her Colonel.

"Yes Captain Badawlhmed Sir, I trust we might speak so I can get back to my people, sir."

"Yes, yes of course, will you follow me into my private office again Colonel al-Qaysi Sir?" The Libyan remarked as he waited for the two Iraqi soldiers to stand and follow him.

The three entered the office and took seats, the Libyan sitting behind his desk. He clasped his hands together and then rested his elbows on the desk, as he stared at the Colonel then offered. "Colonel al-Qaysi Sir, when you first entered the Libyan Embassy, you made mention of needing any help I might be able to offer you and your Iraqi warriors. What is this help you seek from me and my government, Colonel? If it's within my power, I'd be proud to help you sir."

"Captain Badawlhmed Sir, my most important need at the moment is more American cash. Although I have enough to see my troops through with their living expenses, I have no extra in case of an emergency I didn't consider. I also have need of a number of weapons to carry out my attack against the Federal Judge and the foul American soldiers I'm here to destroy, sir."

"And this is all the help you seek from me on this foul day, Colonel al-Qaysi Sir?"

"Yes, everything else of the mission I'll handle for myself, Captain Badawlhmed Sir." The Iraqi offered confidently to the Libyan Operative.

"Very good Colonel, as I have done in the past, I'll make the weapons stored in the Embassy, available for your needs, sir. The American cash is no problem for me to produce either sir. I can have a draft cleared, and the cash will be delivered to you by my aide here, Ahmed. When will you need the cash? That much is the easiest part of the help you seek from me, Colonel al-Qaysi." Again, the Captain was completely ignoring the female Major.

"Captain Badawlhmed, I don't want to begin my activities too quickly, for fear of drawing some attention to myself, or my troops. I have enough money to see us through to the beginning of the New Year sir. After that time, I'll have need of this extra money you offer me sir."

"That's fine and I'm rather pleased to help Colonel al-Qaysi. I'll have a draft cleared for one hundred and fifty thousand American dollars this week, and store the monies in my office. In that way, when you have need of it, just place a simple call to me and ask how the weather is. I'll know you have need of money, and I'll send Ahmed to bring it to you. Colonel, I think this is the last meeting we'll have between us in person. Once your mission starts in the United States, you'll not be allowed back in this Embassy. When you're ready to accept the weapons, you'll call and I'll have the weapons delivered to where you can get at them easy enough, sir.

"I'm sorry and concerned for these much needed precautions I must adhere to, Colonel al-Qaysi Sir. I can ill afford to have my Embassy and country thought to be involved in any manner in this mission of yours, sir. I assure you before you leave the Embassy, I'll give you a number that cannot be traced by the foolish American authorities. Although I'll not stay on the phone long, it'll be private conversations we'll engage in. I'll also offer you all support for this adopted mission of yours, sir. Anything you need, place a call and I shall have what you need, delivered to you immediately. This is the best I can offer you, especially because you're in the United States without your country's blessings for this new operation, Colonel."

"Yes Captain Badawlhmed, I understand why the need for these precautions is needed by you. Anyway Captain, I'd be most honored for any help you can possibly offer to me and the rest of my troops, sir. Sometime in the future I assure you Captain that I'll find a way to thank you properly for all the help you shall give my mission. I have a long memory and remember all those who have helped me in the past, sir." Colonel al-Qaysi nodded to Captain Kamis.

"Thank you for your understanding of my situation, Colonel. By the way sir, I heard the Americans are going to increase their attacks against your country in the near future. Do you think if they do, this action might hamper or change your mission's aims, Colonel al-Qaysi?"

"That'd depend on how strong the hated American Military responds with these new attacks aimed against my country, Captain. I also read the reports in the newspaper earlier. But I'll do what I have to in the way I have to do it when the time arises. I have no intention of doing anything before the end of this year anyhow, sir." The Iraqi control replied to the Libyan.

The two Arabs spoke until they covered just everything they had to go over. Then the Colonel and Major left the Libyan Embassy, knowing they would never be allowed back inside the building again. He had the cell phone he would use to speak to the Libyan Captain further.

THE ROLAND'S MOTEL,
WASHINGTON D.C.

The Iraqi Colonel Hamoodi al-Qaysi and Major Serena al-Shaya arrived at the rundown and dilapidated small motel, and they were rather appalled at the terrible condition of the building, and the lowlifes who hung around outside the filthy establishment at all hours of the day and night. Lieutenant Malika Nabeel Elmasry arrived the night before at the motel, and he moved into the room along with Lieutenant Bashar al-Maluk and Lieutenant Abdel al-Atrash.

The Colonel and Major went to their room first, in order to speak with those other officers. He wanted to make certain they had the other soldiers from his group of soon to be terrorists all settled in, and he wanted to be absolutely certain none of them got in any kind of trouble with the Washington police authorities. The area around the motel was flooded with the obvious down and out riffraff, drug addicts, prostitutes, and the young ones looking to get in some kind of trouble for the night. He felt extremely threatened by the dangerous group of people hanging around the motel as they walked towards it.

Many better areas in Washington were richly decorating their homes with strings of Christmas lights. It was cold and damp, and the temperature was in the low thirties, and it was scheduled to snow by Sunday night. His soldiers were looking forward to this event, because most of them had never seen snow before in their lives.

Colonel al-Qaysi gave Lieutenant Elmasry five thousand American dollars, and then he told him he was to use it for his group's needs and food. Then he and Major al-Shaya left the motel without speaking further to the others from his group, and the two of them decided to drive around

Washington in the car the Lieutenant brought up to Washington for him. He parked his sister's SUV in a mall parking lot the night before, and never gave the car another thought. Even though the abandoned car was going to point an accusing finger at his sister when the authorities finally found her husband's body stuffed in the garage, and her car parked in Washington.

The two Iraqi Military Officers found a clean motel a half a mile away from the Roland's Motel, and they rented a long term larger room. This place had a pool, even though it was too cold to make any use of it. The two Iraqi's settled down for the rest of December of 2001, to wait it out when they would finally be able to kill Judge William Karlanderson.

The days slowly turned into weeks of time wasted, and the small group of Arab terrorists enjoyed the countless decorations for Christmas in Washington. Christmas came and went, and now everyone in Washington was waiting to celebrate the coming of the New Year. Colonel al-Qaysi was starting to enjoy the lifestyle of the United States and her people. The many stores, anything he wanted or needed, he found easily in the countless stores and shops. He even enjoyed the many different dresses the women of the United States wore.

Things were so peaceful in the United States at this time of the year because of the holidays that Colonel al-Qaysi almost forgot there was a war still raging in Afghanistan, and the American warplanes were continuing to attack his country more over the past few days before the holidays started. But the reality of these events was going to come roaring back in the Colonel's face, shortly after the end of the holidays. The American President announced his

State of the Union Address was going to occur on January 15th, 2002.

TUESDAY, JANUARY 15th, 2002.
WASHINGTON D.C.

At exactly eight p.m. Tuesday night, the President of the United States State of the Union Address started. Colonel al-Qaysi, along with Major al-Shaya sat in front of the TV staring at it intensely as was the rest of his soldiers were doing at the small Roland's motel. They stared at the set until the American President finally walked on the floor before the members of Congress, and began to speak. He reported on how the war with Afghanistan was going. Then he made some comments on the economy and covered a number of other matters that did not concern the two Iraqi soldiers. Towards the end of his speech, the President got to his plans for Iraq.

The President announced that Saddam was constantly probing the allied aircraft patrolling the two no fly zones, in the South and North over Iraq. He further stated that the probes were fast becoming more serious with each attack aimed at the Coalition aircraft. He also warned the Iraqi President in no uncertain terms not to press his luck or the patience of the United States or her people, or he was going to come out on the short end of the stick. The American Leader even hinted at much stronger steps was in the offerings for the misguided Iraqi President. This threat left no doubt in al-Qaysi's mind that the United States had plans to attack Iraq again, and all they were looking for was a reason to carry out the attack against his terribly weaken nation.

Colonel al-Qaysi was correct about the United States, and what the Americans were going to do to Iraq. Throughout the year of 2002, the United States military started to change their tactics over the skies of Iraq, and dealing with the always troublesome Iraqi President. He had no idea there was a new order given to the Allied Commanders. The order came under the code name of Operation Southern Focus. This order was a direct response tactic structured to disrupt, and destroy the command structure of the entire Iraqi Airforce. The communication and missile control systems of Iraq where selected target in Southern Iraq, and they would be immediately attacked the instant when they were located by the allied aircraft enforcing the no fly zones.

No longer, did the Coalition warplanes have to come under a direct radar attack by Iraqi ground units, before they could attack those forces. Now, the warplanes were free to hit any radar or missile installations when they came across them anywhere in Iraq. These attack plans were designed to open Iraqi's southern section to the future invasion of Iraq. This second invasion was going to be the one that would completely destroy Iraq's military machine once and for all.

After hearing these latest threats coming from the American President leveled against Iraq and their foolish President. Colonel al-Qaysi started to think about putting his attack against the American Judge off for another few months or so. The Iraqi Commander wanted to see what other steps the United States military would take against his country, before he finally committed his forces to forward his mission. He felt if the United States went after Iraq again then there might not be any further need to carry out their attacks he planned against the United States. What would be the reason if the United States went after Iraq, and their soldiers completely destroyed his nation, he would have no country to continue to fight for its honor.

He thought he might think about changing his way of thinking. If Iraq was destroyed then he might speak to his soldiers and see if they would might want to defect to the United States, and put all this hatred behind them. He did not know which way to go, because it all hinged on America's response to his foolish President's actions in Iraq. All he knew was he had to wait and see what happens first. He ordered his people at the Roland's Motel to standby.

For the next five days of the first month of the New Year, the Iraqi Colonel and female Major did very little in the way of exploring Washington. He too, was trying to stay out of the vision of countless Washington police. The two for the most part, remained staying in their room taking advantage of the down time they had together, by exploring each other's bodies. Lately, anytime they were alone, Major al-Shaya was walking around the apartment topless. Again, al-Qaysi found himself liking the lifestyles of the Americans he was not hating as much as he did, when he came to the United States to carry out his self imposed mission against them.

On the sixth day of their waiting, al-Shaya could not stand it any longer, and she demanded they go out and visit some of the local bars in the area. Not to drink, but to more or less see some of the nightlife of Washington. The wise Colonel al-Qaysi easily picked up the angry look in his female Major's eyes, and knew she was about at the end of her patience and endurance with their mission. He too was getting a little edgy from the lack of doing anything but just sitting around the hotel room. After thinking about it a little further, he agreed with his Major's demands. He offered to take her to a bar near their Best Western Hotel they were staying at.

The Libyan Operative stayed good to his word, and now Colonel al-Qaysi had plenty of American cash at his disposal. The one hundred and fifty thousand dollars was hidden in his hotel room. Little by little, the two Iraqi Military Officers were picking up more and more of the mannerisms of the Americans, and they were fitting in well with the local population, to the point where no one paid any special attention to them when they walked around, or visited any bars in the area. The two even dressed in American style clothes, and headed out for the bar.

Major al-Shaya was dressed to kill, because everything she wore for this trip to the local bar accented her exquisite body perfectly. Her breasts were about popping out of her blouse, and her dress was so short that it did not leave very much for the imagination. The rather excited Colonel was proud to walk the streets of downtown Washington with the beautiful Major hanging on his arm. The two Iraqis entered the bar that he had no idea was a topless one until they entered. He wanted to leave right off, but al-Shaya stopped him from leaving. She wanted to see one of these bars she had heard so much about in Iraq. Besides, if anyone was looking for any possible Arab terrorists in Washington, they would never dream of looking for them in a topless bar.

Colonel al-Qaysi's accent was hard to place now, sometimes when he spoke he sounded Arab, other times he sounded more European. Major al-Shaya spoke perfect English with not a trace of her Arab accent, so she was telling everyone they met in the bar that her husband was Italian and they were taking a vacation in Washington.

The very overcrowded bar was really hoping by the time the two young Iraqi soldiers settled in and they ordered their first drinks. There were three young women on a raised stage dancing up a storm. One woman was completely naked and she had a great shape, while the other two women were just topless, and they were making their breasts bounce to the sounds of the extremely loud music. There was a small group of men surrounding the stage, and they were waving dollar bills in the air before the three dancing women. When one stripper saw it she would move a little closer to the men with the money, and she allow them to fondle her breasts for a brief moment. Then the women would move their rearends right in the men's foolish face, until they slid the bills in their g-strings, or in the top of their lace panties.

Major al-Shaya suddenly lightly squeezed Colonel al-Qaysi's hand, and when he looked at her to see what she wanted, she offered barely over a whisper. "This is a rather novel way for these foolish women to make some money. Allow a stupid man to rub her breasts for a second and they get paid for it. My lover, would you like a few dollar bills so you can enjoy having a woman's rearend shoved in your foolish face like that sir?" She snickered at her words.

Colonel Al-Qaysi glared at her for a moment, and then he went back to watching the dancers.

The bar was filled to overflowing with young American soldiers stationed somewhere in and around Washington. There was everything from Army to Naval personnel hanging around in the bar, and the soldiers were having a great time with drinking and bothering the naked and near naked female dancers. Three American soldiers dressed in uniforms that Colonel al-Qaysi did not recognize, walked up to them and they sat down at their table uninvited. It was Major al-Shaya's fault that these few soldiers decided to walk over to them and their table. This was because of how her breasts were constantly peeking out of the top of her blouse, and the interested soldiers wanted to get a better look at her.

The loud and extremely obnoxious soldiers sat down next to the beautiful young Iraqi woman without being invited, and then they started to speak mainly to al-Shaya. "Hey girl, I'm called Moonshine by my fellow grunts, I'm Sergeant Calvin Cobb, honey." The large black soldier offered, and then he introduced the other soldiers with him to the two Arabs. "The utter guy over there is called Gunny Sack, he's Sergeant Francis Singleton, and the utter guy is called Nose, he's a stinking ginny (Slang for Italian), and his real name's Sergeant Billy Constatino." The large black and obviously very drunk soldier openly leered at al-Shaya, and made no bones about his trying to look down the front of her blouse.

The extremely angered by the American soldier's intrusion and just sitting down at their table without being asked to join them, Colonel al-Qaysi allowed the soldiers to pay attention to his female Major as planned. This was to keep them off sort of guard, and to make them more talkative about who they were and what the soldiers were doing in Washington as he asked the soldier doing all the talking for the others with him. "Those are rather strange names for young soldiers to have? Do all you soldiers have such strange names?"

"Hey man, if you wanna get along a little betta with my stinking ass then you betta start using my stinking Unit name, so I know you're fucking talking to me, pal. We all got these names because we're all part of the Special Forces, man."

"Why are there special soldiers stationed in Washington, Moonshine?" Al-Shaya purred sexily as she gave the soldiers what they came to see, a little peep show. She leaned forward on the table, and this caused her left breast to come completely out of her loose fitting shirt.

"That's because we just got back from a special act we did for our stinking government, and we're sorta hanging around Washington until we're finally allowed to go home on leave." The black soldier announced proudly.

"A special act you say, soldier?" Colonel al-Qaysi asked the man with concern.

"Hey pal, you sound like you're a fucking ginny too, man. Yeah, we did an act in I fucking raq a few months back man. We picked up some stinking bad ass dude who did a real no no in my stinking country, and we brought the lousy little bastard back here to the States to stand trial for his fucking crimes the stupid asshole did here, man." The soldier branded Moonshine proudly boasted to the male stranger he was speaking with in the bar.

The stunned Iraqi Military Officer just leaned back in his chair while desperately trying to keep control of his suddenly rampaging emotions. The fuming Colonel could not believe his luck with just stumbling over some of the hated soldiers who had obviously invaded his country, so easily in Washington. Colonel al-Qaysi shook his anger out of his mind and he smiled at the American soldiers and added to their conversation. "Yes, I believe I have read something about your act, as you called it in the local newspaper a few days ago. So you soldiers were the ones who stepped foot on Iraqi soil I guess. I think that was very brave of you, Moonshine."

"No man, you got me all fucking wrong here my friend. Yes, although I was with the soldiers who went in Iraq to capture the lousy dude. I was stuck with cooling my stinking heels off on the Aircraft Carrier. We soldiers were part of the backup forces for the mission in Iraq, man. We never got a chance to stomp on some stinking Iraqi assholes in the lousy action, man."

"I see Moonshine." Major al-Shaya said as she tried to keep the conversation going, to find out more about the special operation soldiers and their mission in Iraq. Colonel al-Qaysi ordered more drinks for everyone sitting at his table as al-Shaya spoke more to the large black soldier.

"I'd love to know the names of the other brave soldiers who entered Iraq along with you Moonshine. That way if I ever meet them in Washington, I can thank them properly for the brave thing they did for our country, sir." Al-Shaya was trying to make the soldiers believe they were Americans, as she slid her hand in her blouse, and started to play with her breast.

"Hey girl, if you're in the mood and wanna thank any fucking soldiers for our service, you can always start with thanking the three of us fucks, lady. We're more than game to help you thank us properly for what we done for our country, baby." Moonshine offered with a wide grin as he waved his hand out before him at the other soldiers with him in the overcrowded bar.

"Although you soldiers are obviously very brave, I'd like to start at the top of the soldiers who had actually entered the nation of Iraq. Once I thanked them then I can work my way down the list until I thanked all of you special operation soldiers." Al-Shaya purred sexily at the three soldiers enjoying the show she gave them.

CHAPTER FOURTEEN

The American soldier branded Moonshine grinned at the stranger as he remarked. "In that case honey, you're gonna hafta start off with the main man from the stinking outfit, the new Captain Robert Walker, baby. He was the soldier who was in command of the ground forces who entered Iraq. Then you have to think about thanking the Mutt, Lieutenant Frank Hall then Neck, Sergeant Robert Abbott, and then Buckethead, the Ghost, Wacko, hey honey, the list goes on. But if you linkup with Walker, he'll tell you the rest of the utter guys and dolls who were involved in the fun and games in Iraq, and you can thank them all at the same time while you're at it, baby."

"You're not placing these soldiers in any danger by mentioning their names like this are you, Moonshine. I mean by offering their names and what they have done for the country to us?" Major al-Shaya asked as the Colonel paid for the drinks as he listened to the two of them talking.

"Hell no sister, I ain't giving away any stinking state secrets around here, kid. All the names of these soldiers were listed in the Washington Compost paper just yesterday in fact, honey."

"The Washington Compost, I'm afraid I'm not familiar with this newspaper the list of soldiers was printed in." Major al-Shaya offered as she moved, and again gave the soldiers a show.

"Sorry sister, the Washington Compost is the fucking Washington Post rag, all the soldiers branded it the Compost cause of all the stinking shit the paper is constantly printing about our stinking President, and everything he's trying to do for the good of the damn country, sister. The paper is a real liberal rag, baby. It sucks the big one honey."

"Oh, I understand what you're telling me." Al-Shaya replied in a sexy voice to the soldier. "Look friends, I'm afraid I have to leave this bar. I'm getting tired, and besides, seeing all these naked women have turned me on, and I want to bring my boyfriend home, and thank him in the way I want to thank Captain Walker, for what he done for our country, soldier."

"Cool deal sister, but don't forget about us poor fucking foot sloggers back here either, baby."

"I assure you, I'll not forget you soldiers." Suddenly, al-Shaya leaned across the table and she whispered in Moonshine's ear. She was giving the soldiers a good look down the front of her blouse as she spoke. "Moonshine, are you soldiers going to be in this bar tomorrow night?"

Cobb nodded yes to the foxy looking lady as he stared at her breasts.

"Good, I'll come back to the bar tomorrow without my boyfriend. Then I'll leave with you, and show you what I intend to do with this Robert Walker, and the other soldiers brave enough to invade Iraq, and take the other man in custody and bring him to this country for justice. I assure you, none of you will be disappointed in what I'll do for you soldiers, Moonshine." Al-Shaya allowed the black soldier to slide his hand in her blouse and play with her breasts for a moment.

Cobb was grinning from ear to ear, as he replied in an excited voice to the beautiful young woman who was bent over in his face. "Hey honey, we'll be here with fucking bells on tomorrow. Don't fuck us over by not coming back to the bar tomorrow night now, baby."

"I'll not let you down soldier. But I'll not be wearing bells, in fact when we get to where we're going, I believe I'll not be wearing a thing, until tomorrow night soldier." Al-Shaya removed Cobb's hand from her blouse and she kissed it. This made the black man smile more as he gave her a quick wink of the eye, and then the soldiers watched the hot number leave the bar with the other guy. As soon as they were out of ear shot, one of the soldiers grumbled.

"Man Moonshine that fucking guy must be a stinking turd pusher (queer) or something, man. He didn't even react when you stuck your stinking hand down the front of her fucking blouse, and you started to play around with that bitch's tits right in front of the stupid dude, Homes. What the fuck did she whisper to your ass anyhow a few moments ago, fucker?" the Nose, Sergeant Billy Constatino asked the large black soldier.

"She told me she was gonna dump the zero and get herself some fucking heroes, namely us, asshole. She said she'll come back to the bar tomorrow night without her boyfriend, and fuck the shit outta all of us at the same time, man." Moonshine boasted as he watched the two leave.

"You fucking believed her man. I don't think we'll ever see her pretty little ass again."

"Who the hell gives a shit, at least I gots me a hand full of tit before she left, Homes."

As the Iraqi Colonel and Major walked back to their hotel room together, al-Qaysi grumbled at al-Shaya. "I never wanted to slice someone's god cursed throat more than I wanted to kill that black bastard who dared to put his hands on your breasts, Major. I'll have my revenge on his worthless shoulders yet before I'm done here in the United States for that insult, woman."

"It was a small price to pay for the valuable information we were able to receive from the great fool, lover. Besides Hamoodi, I was having a lot of fun teasing these foolish American soldiers. They're so easy to manipulate. All a woman has to do is show these fools a little skin, and they'll say or do anything for you. They're so easy to control with just my body, Hamoodi." Al-Shaya smiled at her commanding officer, but she was trying her best not to use Colonel, when she spoke to al-Qaysi, so she was not mentioning any name when she spoke to him as she added to her words to the officer. "Do you think we might be able to get our hands on yesterday's Washington Post paper? If what the worthless soldier said is true, we'll have the names of the cursed American soldiers who were involved in the capture of Colonel al-Adwani, sir."

"Of course we will, in America you can get whatever you want or desire at any time you need it from the great fools, lowly woman. Come with me, because I feel we have exposed ourselves enough on this foul night to many staring eyes of the cursed Americans, al-Shaya. We'll ask the man at the front desk of our hotel, if he could get us yesterday's newspaper. I'm certain he'll be able to get one before we return to our cursed room in his foul establishment, woman."

As they entered the hotel lobby, al-Shaya walked to the front desk and asked the man if he could get her yesterday's newspaper and he happily replied. "Sure thing young lady, you can have mine. I'm finished with it. I was going to toss it in the garbage anyway, Ma'am."

He gave al-Shaya his newspaper and got quite a show for it. Once she had the paper in hand, she rushed back to the Colonel standing by the elevators waiting for her to catch up with him. They were the only ones in the cab, and Major al-Shaya opened the paper. She found the article she was searching for, and discovered the names of the American soldiers who were involved with the invasion of Iraq, and the arrest of Colonel al-Adwani in Iraq. She read Walker was lifted up to the rank of Captain, and informed Colonel al-Qaysi of the fact as she smiled at him.

The article further informed the reader that the Special Forces soldiers involved in the attack in Iraq were scheduled to visit the Special Operations Training Group at Camp Lejeune, North Carolina. The soldiers were to be stationed at Camp Lejeune in April of 2002 to sharpen their operational skills, and learn any new tactics to be employed against any and all enemy of the United States. The Iraqi Officer smiled because he felt the reporters always gave away too much information when it came to their military, and what that military was doing with protecting their civilian's lives. He also believed if he wanted to know anything about the United States or her foolish troops, all he had to do was read one of the local newspapers, or watch the news on the TV, and everything he would be interested in, he would know immediately.

Now, the Iraqi Commander was torn between two different thoughts. He really wanted to kill the Federal Judge and stop Colonel al-Adwani's trial, but he also wanted to kill the cursed soldiers who dared to attack his country. Both situations were going to come to a head about the same time. He was wondering which one he wanted his revenge to fall upon first and the most, the soldiers, or the judge. The answer was going to be made for him in the next few weeks.

As the days slowly turned to weeks, the Washington newspapers were beginning to carry more articles about the American and Coalition planes attacking military installations the aircraft discovered in the no fly zones over Iraq. It was beginning to become very intense because Saddam again threaten to end allowing the United Nations inspectors from carrying out orders in his nation. With each article printed, the angry Iraqi Colonel leaned more towards hitting the soldiers before he killed the judge. Every time he read the newspapers, he was looking for when the judge was going to begin his jury selection. He never found any articles about the trial, and the jury selection never took place at the time it was scheduled to begin.

TUESDAY, FEBRUARY 5th, 2002.
WASHINGTON D.C.

The first article about the trial of Colonel al-Adwani showed up in the paper. Major al-Shaya pointed it out to Colonel al-Qaysi. Because of the continuing war raging in Afghanistan, and the widening tensions in Iraq, the Federal Judge announced the jury selection for the case against Colonel Abdulaziz Majd al-Adwani has been held off. It would now take place the second week of February, which would cause the trial to be pushed back until Wednesday, April 17th, of 2002. All citizens in the Washington area can be called in for jury duty. The case was expected to last up to twelve weeks. The jury pool was expected to number five hundred prospective juries, and twelve will be picked, with another ten being picked as back up juries for the trail of the terrorist.

"That's no good Major al-Shaya. It gives us many problems we'll be forced to deal with. The cursed American soldiers are due to report back to their base for added training in mid April. This is the same time the trial of Colonel al-Adwani is scheduled to start. I don't know which target to go after first, my desert sister. If we kill the Judge then they might tighten the security around the entire country against us. On the other hand, if we chose to kill the hated American soldiers, they might not increase the security. That way we can always get at the Federal Judge later, after we have successfully killed the loathsome soldiers who had invaded our country. What do you feel about the foul situation I speak of with you, Major al-Shaya?"

"I have a good idea, we can always split up our forces, leave some of our warriors here in Washington to kill the Federal Judge, while we and a picked few other soldiers

Page 344

go to North Carolina and kill the hated American soldiers there, sir. That way we can take care of both situations at the same time, Colonel al-Qaysi." The female Major offered with a grin.

"That's no good either, because I have to be with the hit team that kills the loathsome Judge. That way, we can go after Colonel al-Adwani at the same time we kill the Judge and rescue our terrorist and fellow soldier, or we kill the fool Colonel, either way we'll stop this foul trail."

"You're correct and most wise in your thoughts of our future plans, Hamoodi. I forgot about trying to rescue Colonel al-Adwani first. But if their military is anything like ours, the American soldiers will start to report back to base before their ordered time. We can always watch the Judge through the jury selection process, so we can figure out his routine, and what is the best way to slaughter the great fool. So by jury selection we can make our plans on how we can kill the old man. Once we have established this routine, we can head for North Carolina to this American Military Base, and wait for the cursed soldiers to show up at their base, sir.

"We can hang around the bars and speak to other soldiers stationed at the base, we can get known and when the soldiers we want to slaughter finally show up, we can wait until they go on leave and then kill the fools. Then we can leave here before anyone knows what happened, and make our way back to Washington. Kill the worthless Judge, and then get Colonel al-Adwani out of the hands of the hated Americans, or kill him. Then we can get out of the United States and go to Jordan, and live our lives in peace there together, Colonel al-Qaysi Sir."

"You have everything worked out very well in your mind, Major al-Shaya. I cannot argue with your logic, I believe it's absolutely perfect. You come up with what we're going to do for our attacks on the ones we want to kill. I think I'd like to make a trip to North Carolina, so we can see what we might be up against there. Then we'll come back to Washington and wait until the jury selections start, and observe the Judge's routine and discover how we're going to kill him, and get al-Adwani out of their custody. I wonder al-Shaya, does the fool Colonel al-Adwani have to be in the courtroom while they're picking out the cursed jury?" the Colonel asked the Major.

"From what I know of the hated American court system, Colonel al-Adwani has to be present during any of the jury selections, sir." The female Major replied proudly.

SATURDAY, FEBRUARY 9th, 2002.
NORTH CAROLINA

It took Major al-Shaya and Colonel al-Qaysi three hours to drive down to North Carolina from Washington. They drove right by the main gate of Camp Lejeune. The massive military base was staggering in size, and the Colonel was able to see an ocean of military equipment of parked tanks, fighting machines, armor vehicles, and countless large jeeps known as Humvees, parked in neat rows on the massive base. The two Iraqi Military Officers were stunned by the amount of war making equipment parked on the Marine base. On their way to the base, they passed four bars within a mile of the military compound, and figured these bars were the in spots for the soldiers to let down. Two were topless; the other two were common bars.

Colonel al-Qaysi offered to Major al-Shaya the bar called Bare Parts was the likely one most of the young American soldiers would head for when they were allowed off the base. It was the largest bar in the area, with the most parking spaces for cars. To make a point, there were only seven cars in the parking lot, and as al-Shaya drove through the parking lot of the bar, the Colonel noticed four cars had military stamp on the windshields. So the soldiers could drive onto, and off the Marine Base when allowed.

The female Iraqi soldier suggested to her commanding officer that they should remain in North Carolina for the rest of the night, and see if any of the soldiers who showed up at the bar at night, wore the same insignia of the skull with the snake woven between the eyes. Along with the Marine sword driven in the skull, and the snake's head resting on the handle of the famous Marine sword. The Iraqi Colonel readily agreed with the Major's suggestion as he turned and looked her in the eyes as he went deep in thought for a few moments.

The two hung around the area of the massive military base for the entire day, and entered the bar with their eyes set on seven p.m. on Saturday night, and the bar was in full swing. There were five women dancing completely naked on a stage, two were sliding around on a brass bar that went from ceiling to floor, and the bar was filled with male soldiers in various stages of drunkenness. They took a table against the wall, and then they watched the soldiers make first class fools of themselves with the women of the bar, or the strippers they got to come anywhere near their tables by waving money and calling out at the women.

Major al-Shaya pointed out seven soldiers in the bar with the same Special Forces patch they were looking for on their uniforms. The two Iraqi soldiers remained in the bar until nearly midnight, and they saw many American soldiers come and others leave the bar. The Colonel had the Major counting all the soldiers she spotted with the special patch on their shoulders. By midnight, the two Iraqis counted seventeen soldiers with the fearsome patch. This made the Colonel believe they truly discovered the bar the soldiers he wanted, would likely be at night. They got up and walked out of the bar with al-Qaysi being in a great mood.

The Arab Colonel enjoyed the naked women dancing during the night, and sitting with the very beautiful female Major. She wore a blouse that mustered almost the same amount of attention from the horde of soldiers hanging around the bar, as did the naked women dancing on the stage. What made him most pleased was the fact he was certain he found the bar where the soldiers he wanted to kill, would surely be hanging out in. By the time the two foreign soldiers left the bar, Colonel al-Qaysi was not only happy, but he was horny and looking forward to sharing his bed with Major al-Shaya, when they returned to Washington and their hotel room.

The first thing Major Serena al-Shaya did when she got back to their room at the hotel was to shower. It was four a.m., but neither one of them were really tired. The Colonel waited for al-Shaya to finish her shower, and then he took one. He came out with a towel wrapped around him and found al-Shaya lying on the bed naked. She called him to the bed, and when he was near she pulled the towel from his body. That was all he need, and they made love and then gave into their bodies need for sleep. They slept wrapped up in each other's arms for the rest of the night. Neither Iraqi gave a thought as to the other soldiers living in the pig's sty of the Roland's Motel.

Both al-Shaya and al-Qaysi took Sunday off, and they enjoyed the freedom of not having to worry about anything on this day. They stayed in the room and enjoyed room service deliver food, and al-Qaysi enjoyed the TV while al-Shaya sort of lied around the rest of the day. Both officers took a couple catnaps because they were still exhausted from their trip to North Carolina.

By Sunday night, the two Iraqi Officers were starting to get tired enough to turn in for the night. There was not much on TV, and the Colonel was not very interested in basketball, mainly because he did not understand the game. He turned the set off by nine thirty and they made love again. They slept with the curtains opened because it was lightly snowing, and the Arabs could not get enough of the snow, how it felt, how cold it was, and how it looked on the ground.

Major al-Shaya was the first up and she showered again. It seemed she could not get enough of the warm water, and beautiful smelling soap and hair conditioner and shampoo. She was getting caught up in all the traps of the lifestyle the Americans took for granted. She talked to herself and admitted she was not truly looking forward to returning to the harsh conditions of the desert life in the Middle East. She found herself wishing Colonel al-Qaysi would say never mind their mission, let's ask for political asylum in the United States, and live their lives here.

Monday, it was cold out and the Iraqis were ill prepared for the freezing weather, and they stayed in their rooms all day. The Iraqi Colonel met with the rest of his people, and he issued them the same orders, stand by and wait. Today, he and Major al-Shaya were going to go to the Federal Courthouse, where Colonel al-Adwani was scheduled to be tried. They had no idea who they were going to bump into on their short trip over to the courthouse. By eight thirty a.m., they both were sitting in the coffee shop directly across from the ancient courthouse.

Major Al-Shaya noticed the elderly man enter the coffee shop and he seemed like a kind old man who nodded at everyone he looked at, he even shook hands with a few of the people in the place. The old man was smiling all the time he was in the coffee shop. At one point the good looking old man looked directly at Major al-Shaya and he smiled and nodded to her.

The Major leaned closer to al-Qaysi and said. "My lover, do you see that old man there?"

"Yes, so what. He's just another worthless old man who flirts with all the young women."

"My lover, perhaps your eyes might have lost some of their sharpness due to many years living in the sand of our vast deserts. That old man there is Judge William Karlanderson. Look at how easy it'll be for us to kill the old man where the fool stands in this place. He walks around with no security surrounding him. Not even the police give him any added security. He seems to be a pleasant old man, and it's going to be a shame to be forced to kill him, just because he had the misfortune to be picked to judge the actions of one of our people. Fate is the lonely hunter."

"You make a mistake with your foul words to me woman. This old man has been picked to die by his own cursed people. He'll die because the United States leaders believe they have the power and right of life and death over the sacred Arab lands of the world. Al-Shaya, we're in the United States to prove to the hated American fools they're not on par with Allah and His great wisdom. Allah is the only force in the world that holds the power of life and death over His faithful desert children. It's time the worthless Americans find out they're not the guardians of the Arab world. The United States has to be taught that we Arabs are more than capable of ruling over their own fate and justice in this world. The hated United States must be forced to learn to keep their foul noses out of the world's affairs, especially in the Arab world. It's been too long the hated Americans think because they say something, the world is going to believe what they have to say, and they live their foolish lives according to what America decreeds."

The Major listened to the Colonel's words, but she kept watching the old man as he slowly walked around the coffee shop. He paid for his coffee and left the shop as quietly as he had entered the establishment. They watched the old man as he crossed the street like he had no fear of the day, or what it might bring. Once he was on the sidewalk on the other side of the street, the judge stopped and he spoke with a few people he obviously knew as he sipped his coffee. He took his time as he walked into the building. He was followed in by the people he spoke with.

Colonel al-Qaysi witnessed enough of the elderly judge, and made like he was going to stand. Major al-Shaya suddenly grabbed him by his arm and she stopped him from moving any further. Something just caught her eye and she wanted to check it out before they left the place. The Iraqi Colonel picked up her concern and he instantly stopped moving and looked in the eyes of the Major. She smiled and shifted her eyes, and he followed them until he noticed the two men sitting at another table in the shop. He caught what they were doing, they were checking out everyone in the coffee shop. He picked up they were obviously some kind of special police or military type. He relaxed and held his fingers up and the waitress came right over to his table.

He smiled and said in almost perfect English, "Young lady, we have changed our minds, and we will have breakfast after all I believe." He ordered and the waitress looked at al-Shaya, and she ordered the same meal. As the waitress left, Major al-Shaya's hand moved to the buttons of her blouse and opened two. In her mind, she knew the Americans would never believe they were Arabs, if she exposed enough skin to them. Colonel al-Qaysi caught her actions and smiled as he noticed what she was doing. The way her shirt was opened, he was able to view her charms and nodded his approval to her. As they spoke together, he kept glancing over at the two men, and he noticed an immediate change in their attitude towards them. At first what he took was suspicion, quickly changed into an attempt by the two men to see more of Major al-Shaya's breasts.

Their food came, and they took their time eating. He decided they were going to stay in the coffee shop until the two men left the place. The Iraqi Colonel felt if they displayed no interest in what was going on about them then these two men would quickly lose interest in them and leave. Major al-Shaya got up and sexily walked past them on her way to the bathroom. Both men watched and one actually nodded to her and she smiled back at him pleasantly.

"What do you make of them two over there?" One agent asked of the other.

"I'd say they're either lovers, or one, or both of them are married and they're meeting for a little tête-à-tête. Either way, I don't think they're any threat to anyone but themselves."

"I agree, but I'd like to have a few minutes alone with that one, she a real beaut."

"Jim, you'd like to be alone with a female cat if you thought you might score with it."

Jim laughed and then he added with a smirk. "What say we get going?"

"Sure thing, but I'm not leaving until I get one last look at this pretty girl. I never saw a woman walking around showing off so much of what she has to offer, Jim."

"And you say I'm the one who's only interested in fucking sex, my friend." The agent said.

"Yeah, but you're not married like I am my friend. I don't have the luxury of seeing a different woman every night of the damn week. I see the same pair of tits and ass every day of my life, so I'm going to take advantage of this act for as long as I can, man."

The two young special agents waited until Major al-Shaya came sashaying her way out of the bathroom, and she slowly walked past them for a second time. This time the two agents nodded as she passed by them and she smiled and gave them both a slight and sexy wiggle of her hips. Then the two young agents got up and they paid for their meal and then gave Major al-Shaya one last quick look, and then the two left the coffee shop smiling.

The two Iraqi warriors allowed themselves to relax a little, once the pair of obvious special agents left the coffee shop. They spoke and ate for the next fifteen minutes, and then they decided to leave the eatery. Colonel al-Qaysi was pleased it was going to be so easy to kill the elderly Federal Judge when they turned their angry attention against him. At first he thought about using a simple car bomb to kill the old man, now he could just use one of his people as a sniper, and kill the old man from a good distance away. The Iraqi Commander did not even think if his shooter might not be able to get away from killing the judge alive. The only thing they still had to discover was they had to find out was how the American authorities were going to transport Colonel al-Adwani over to the courthouse, and see if they were going to be able to free him. Or was he going to die in the same sniper attack as the old judge was going to die in. He was overwhelmed with the desire to kill the American judge and free his Iraqi Colonel.

The two Iraqi Military Officers continued to scout out the area around the courthouse for a half an hour, before finally returning to their hotel. Again, they made love together as they settled in for the rest of the day, to wait for the next time they had to go out. That next time was going to be when the jury selection began. This was going to be the first time the Colonel was going to be brought over to the courthouse in person. Colonel Al-Qaysi wanted to see how the police were going to transport him over to the courthouse, and what type of security was going to be around him at the time of his transportation. Then he would make the final decision if al-Adwani was going to be able to be freed, or if he was going to die alongside the American Judge.

THE WASHINGTON D.C. FEDERAL COURTHOUSE, FEBRUARY 12th, 2002.

The Iraqi Colonel Al-Qaysi and Major al-Shaya were hanging around the courthouse since seven a.m. on this day. This time al-Shaya did not wait until they came under the eye of any of the special agents or police authorities hanging around the ancient building. She had her blouse opened below her breasts, and she was dressed like the rest of the women in the area. They ate at the same coffee shop, but this time it was a little different. There were many wooden police barricades set up outside the courthouse, and there seemed to be a lot of civilians hanging around the building and many were angry. At eight twenty a.m., the elderly judge entered the coffee shop as he did the last time they saw him. But this time he was being trailed by two obvious special agents. The judge was his friendly old self, nodding and smiling and speaking to anyone he knew. The two agents stood behind him, and they followed him everywhere he moved.

Outside on the street before the courthouse, over a hundred civilians lined up behind the police barricades. They were very loud, but not out of control. Many of them carried signs asking the judge to sentence the assassin to death for his assassination attempt against the President's life, and for the killing of the National Security Advisor and the wounding of the Vice President in the same attack. There were other signs asking the judge not to have the assassin killed.

No matter all the extra security suddenly surrounding the judge, Colonel al-Qaysi still felt he was an easy target for death. He exposed himself to a kill, especially when he crossed the street to the courthouse. There were plenty of Washington police officers stationed just outside the building, keeping the civilians under control and behind the barricades. The judge walked between the opening the barricades created, and the civilians cheered him as he slowly crossed the street. Many posters were waved at him. He smiled at them as he walked to the building.

Suddenly, three black Chevy vans pulled up in front of the buildings with blacked out windows. The courthouse was surrounded by other buildings, and that made it impossible for the police to bring Colonel al-Adwani into the building through a backdoor of the courthouse. The three trucks pulled right in front of the courthouse, and six heavily arm police officers dressed in black stepped out of each truck, and they immediately surrounded the center vehicle. When the security officers were closed and tight, Colonel al-

Adwani was then pulled out of the vehicle. He was handcuffed and shackled and dressed in orange coveralls. It was obvious to Colonel al-Qaysi that he had a bulletproof vest on his body under the coveralls.

Once the Iraqi terrorist was out of the vehicle, he was immediately rushed inside the building. Every one of the civilians gathered in front of the building, cursed and booed the Iraqi Colonel, as the police officers literally dragged him inside the building. Many of the protesters shook their fists in the air at the haggard looking terrorist.

Major al-Shaya and Colonel al-Qaysi followed the judge out of the coffee house and actually joined the civilian hordes lining the barricades, they even cursed and raised their fists in the air and shook them at the Iraqi Colonel quickly being lead into the building. This action from the two Iraqis was carried out to remove any possible suspicion against them that they were there to attempt to free or kill the Arab Colonel. Once the heavy circle of police and Colonel al-Adwani were inside the courthouse, the civilians quickly grew bored and they started to slowly disperse. They walked away still cursing and talking about seeing the attempted assassin. The two Iraqi Officers followed many of the angry Americans as they walked away from the courthouse area. No one paid any special attention to the two strangers walking with them.

As Colonel al-Qaysi walked down a side street with Major al-Shaya, he spoke low to her. "Well, that settles that much for us. With all the extra security they have surrounding Colonel al-Adwani. I feel it'll be totally impossible for us to get anywhere near him, to gain his release from the cursed American authorities. I see no way to stop Colonel al-Adwani from being put on trial before the hated American public than by killing him before the trial starts. Allah knows what the American fools might have done to his body and mind, to gain the names of any other of our people who were involved in his mission to assassinate the evil American President.

"Al-Shaya, we have to stop the worthless failure of a foolish Colonel from being made the spectacle for the American fools. And to possible imply that President Saddam was the one who gave his blessings to the operation to kill the hated American President. If this were to come out then the American military would be absolutely ruthless in dealing with our country and our innocent civilians in Iraq. No, there is no other way to react than to just kill the foolish Colonel, and that way silence his lips forever. I don't mind telling you that I'm pleased it'll end this way, as much of a soldier as I am. I just don't approve of our government employing lowly assassins and spies in their service. Soldiers are bred to die on the battlefield, not to be hung like common criminals, like this foul fool will be if he's allowed to be tried by the cursed American fools."

"After seeing the security surrounding Colonel al-Adwani, I'm forced to agree with what you are suggesting to me, Colonel. I'm afraid that Colonel al-Adwani must die if we're to silence his lips. Who'll make up the sniper team that'll kill the elderly Judge, and Colonel al-Adwani?"

"Hmmmm, who are the best shooters we have from our group, Major? You'd know the answer to this question far better than I." Colonel al-Qaysi stared at al-Shaya while waiting her answer.

"If I was to pick the sniper team we wi..." The female Iraqi Major began to offer the Colonel.

"In case you're unaware of the fact as yet, woman of the hot desert sands. You are the one who is going to pick out the sniper for our needs for this mission. I shall leave this decision entirely within your foul hands to deal with, Major." The two soon to be terrorists stopped walking, and were now sitting on a park bench seven blocks away from the courthouse. The park was nearly empty, and there was no one within a hundred yards of the two as they spoke together.

"In that case Colonel al-Qaysi, I'd pick Lieutenant Aziz Abdel al-Atrash and Sergeant Said Damerdji as the sniper shooters for the two hit teams. They're our best shooters, and they'll get the job done for us, even if they lose their worthless lives in the attempt. I'd also add Corporal Mohammed Oveidat, and Sergeant Muhammad Mushtaha as their support team and backup for the two snipers. The reason I picked these two soldiers as support for the hit teams is because they're the next best shooters we have, and if anything happens to the two original snipers. These two soldiers could pick up the weapons and complete the mission as ordered, Hamoodi."

"Those are very wise picks for this mission you offer me, woman. I'll inform the fools and the next time we come to see the cursed Judge, and how they bring Colonel al-Adwani over to the courthouse. I'll bring those fools along with me. I'll not bring the support soldiers though I don't want too many fools hanging around the courthouse. The two support members will have to go it by ear, and if anything happens to the snipers, they'll be forced to complete the mission. Even if they have to pick up the weapons and charge the Colonel and Judge in order to kill them both.

"Thinking about this a little further al-Shaya, this is what we shall do. Once I'm certain these four foul fools know exactly what is expected of them. We'll head back to North Carolina and then we'll stalk the god cursed American soldiers I want to die for invading our country. The snipers can scope out the area of the courthouse, and when they feel they're ready to attack, they can kill the Judge and al-Adwani while we're in North Carolina. We'll not return to Washington once the worthless Colonel and this foolish old Judge are dead. We'll remain in North Carolina, and kill the hated American soldiers. Once they're dead, we'll get out of the United States and then make our way to Jordan where we'll live our lives in peace."

"Hamoodi, there's one thing we have never discussed..." Major al-Shaya offered her commander, but she was immediately cut off by the Iraqi Colonel.

"What is it you feel we have failed to discuss in our many conversations of what we are doing here in the United States?" the surprised Colonel growled as he interrupted her question.

"Hamoodi, we have never gone over how we were going to get out of the United States safely, once we have successfully completed our mission, and the lowly Judge, Colonel al-Adwani, and the foul American soldiers you want dead, have been accomplished, sir." Al-Shaya asked the Colonel with much concern in her tone of voice.

"Yes, you're correct with your question of me, my sister. It shows me you're keeping your mind on what we planned and this pleases me greatly, woman. I must ask you this so you can see how simple it'll be for us to leave this foul land of sin and lust, al-Shaya. I'll not expect an answer because I shall answer my own question I put forth to you. Al-Shaya, what simpler way to leave the hated United States then by the same way we have first entered this god cursed land?

"Once we killed all who must die to set the scales of justice in balance, we'll make our way back to the Island in the Keys. Once there, I'll contact the same American pleasure boat Captain who brought us to this worthless land. He gave me his phone number if I had any further need of him again, al-Shaya. Once we're back on that rock of an Island, we'll follow the same path we took when we first entered the United States in reverse. But this time, instead of landing in the foul nation of Kuwait, we'll board a plane to land in Jordan. I have Jordanian passports for our use. They'll make it easy for us to enter Jordan." Colonel Al-Qaysi stopped speaking and took a quick breath. This pause in his words opened the way for al-Shaya to ask another question.

"Hamoodi, you mentioned you have Jordanian passports. But we have nineteen soldiers with us. What's to become of them if we're only concerned with us getting out of America alive?"

"Huh! It's just like a foolish woman to worry about the other fools under our command. I suggest you start to worry about yourself, and your own safety, and stop worrying about everyone else for a change, lowly woman. But to explain to you what I feel is not needed to be explained by me. I'll inform you of everyone else's plans for leaving the loathsome United States, once our mission has been completed successfully. First Major al-Shaya there are many of the foul fools who let me know they wish to remain in the United States after the mission has been completed.

"I gave these foolish soldiers permission to do just that. The others who want to remain Arabs, and live in Arab lands have their own passports and means of travel and the money to get them there safely. Some of the foul fools will make their escape through Canada. The other fools will make their way down to Mexico and leave for Arab lands through those means. I'm afraid some of them will surely die in our efforts before we can leave this cursed land. Al-Shaya,

I assure you, I don't intend to be among the ones who'll die on this foul mission. That's why I have selected the safest possible route of escape for us to employ. So you see my sister of the desert, your worries are most unfounded. All is looked after, without your worry over them, woman."

Major al-Shaya show by her body language she relaxed as she replied to her commander's words. "It seems you have covered just about everything to worry about, Hamoodi. I had no idea some of our fellow Iraqi soldiers wanted to remain here in the United States. To tell you the truth Hamoodi, I was hoping to remain in the United States with you at my side, and live our lives in this land of plenty in peace." The pretty female Major smiled at the angry looking Iraqi soldier.

"How romantic you truly are to offer that foolish a suggestion to me woman, but I assure you that I have no intention of remaining in the hated United States any longer than I have to. I have further plans for my country, and to carry out those plans I have to be near Iraq, when the great fool in control of our nation is finally sent on his way to dwell with his cursed ancestors. That is why I'll be returning to the Arab lands of my ancestors. But you Major al-Shaya, you are more than free to remain here in the United States if that is what you truly desire, woman."

"There'd be no sense in my remaining in the United States if you were not with me, Hamoodi. I believe I have fallen in love with you, and the few months I've been in the United States gave me more ways in which I'll fulfill your wildest dreams and desires. My future is in your fate my lover." The pretty Major smiled lovingly at the Colonel.

"And you al-Shaya are my future as I see it myself. So we're in agreement then and we're both heading back to our Arab lands, woman?" the Colonel stared at her, waiting for her reply.

"I'll go wherever the sands of the desert decree as long as you're by my side, Hamoodi."

"Good, I believe it's time we head back to our apartment. I feel we have exposed ourselves long enough to the gaze of these hated American fools who walk about this city of hatred and commands." With that said, he rose from the bench and they both walked to their apartment. Although they had a car, al-Qaysi was walking wherever he went, because he was saving the vehicle for their trip to North Carolina, and use the vehicle to get them to the Keys, and their release from America. He could not wait until his mission is completed, and he could leave.

The two special agents that spotted the Arabs the other day in the coffee shop watched them from a distance. They decided the two strangers were harmless visitors to Washington, and they allowed them to walk off. This decision was cast mainly because of the way the woman was walking around the streets of Washington. Both agents knew no Arab woman would ever walk around and allow so much of their breasts and legs to be seen as this woman was doing.

The two Iraqis walked around their apartment, in case they were being followed. It took them an hour to return to the hotel. They stayed inside the room for over an hour before Colonel al-Qaysi announced he was going to walk over to the filthy Roland's Motel, and then inform the others from his group who they had picked out to head the sniper teams. He ordered al-Shaya to remain behind because he wanted to speak to the soldiers alone.

The Colonel walked over to the Roland's Motel, and by the time he got there he was freezing. He entered the dump of a motel and headed right for Lieutenant Aziz Abdel al-Atrash's room. Upon entering he was forced to actually hold his breath for a moment because of the terrible smell instantly assaulting him inside the filthy room as he offered. "Lieutenant al-Atrash, how in the name of Allah's grace are you putting up with the foul smell of this filthy room?"

The Lieutenant laughed as he replied. "Colonel al-Qaysi, after a few moments of being in the room, your nose will quickly get used to the horrible smell, sir."

"As long as Allah allows me to live on earth, my nose will never get used to the foul smell inside this cursed room, fool. Lieutenant al-Atrash, I have come here to inform you of what we have decided about the cursed Federal Judge, and Colonel al-Adwani's foul fate. We have witnessed the fool of a Judge on this day, and saw how the police are handling Colonel al-Adwani's custody. I decided it's out of the question to try and free Colonel al-Adwani. So I come to the conclusion that I want two sniper teams to be set up by you. You'll be one of the snipers, and you'll be in command of the other sniper team, led by Sergeant Said Damerdji I demand.

"You two are our best shooters of the soldiers we have to work with, and you'll be assigned to kill the Judge, while Sergeant Damerdji will be given orders to kill the foolish Colonel al-Adwani. You two will be supported by Corporal Mohammed Oveidat, and Sergeant Damerdji will be supported by Sergeant Muhammad Mushtaha. No matter the outcome of your orders, your teams must kill the foolish American Judge and Colonel al-Adwani. You may pull in the rest of our troops in order to accomplish your orders successfully. You'll move the other three soldiers into your room, and you'll keep the sniper teams together until they're needed.

"I'll take Lieutenant Elmasry and Sergeant Khalaifa down to North Carolina with me. The four of us will kill the cursed American soldiers we're hunting. Once you have killed the foul Judge and Colonel al-Adwani, you and the rest are free to do whatever you have to do to live in the United States, or leave it. Lieutenant al-Atrash, if only one of your targets is killed on your mission, that one has to be Colonel al-Adwani. He is the most important target to kill. The foul Judge is to be considered a secondary target. Both your teams must make certain the Colonel is dead, before turning your attention on the hated Judge. Once Major al-Shaya and myself and the others head for North Carolina, we'll never be returning to Washington. So I leave the two important deaths in your hands, Lieutenant. Don't let Allah and myself down." The Colonel snarled at the young Lieutenant as he stared at him for several long moments until he replied.

"Colonel al-Qaysi, now you trusted the death of these two fools in my hands, you need not worry about them any longer. As we speak, they are both as good as dead, and once they're dead, the rest will be free to work out their way to live in the United States, or leave it as you have suggested, Colonel. I heard my orders and I'll carry them out to their completion, or I and everyone with me will die in the effort of killing these two you demand dead, Colonel al-Qaysi."

"This is exactly what I wanted to hear from you, Lieutenant al-Atrash. I'm sorry we have to split our ranks like this. But the American soldiers we want to kill will be arriving in North Carolina at the same time the great fools here will begin the jury selection against Colonel al-Adwani. So we're forced to carry out both our actions at the same time. I'm leaving the bulk of our soldiers here with you, it's more important the worthless Judge and especially Colonel al-Adwani die on your sacred mission, Lieutenant. Than it is for the hated American soldiers die for their evil invasion of our country." Colonel Al-Qaysi never told Lieutenant al-Atrash that he wanted the soldiers dead more than he wanted the Judge and Colonel al-Adwani dead. He was seeking his own revenge against the brazen American soldiers who dared to attack his country with so few soldiers, and embarrass the country of Iraq and his troops.

Colonel al-Qaysi went over all he had witnessed when he checked what was happening by the courthouse today. He informed Lieutenant al-Atrash where he was to station his snipers in the area, and at what time the judge usually arrived at the courthouse, and when the police brought Colonel al-Adwani to the building. He ordered al-Atrash to collect Sergeant Hanan al-Wazir, and they were to scout out the area of the courthouse twice, before they went on to kill these two men. He further ordered the Lieutenant to make certain nothing about the judge and his security changed, before they began their attack against the old man. He also ordered the Lieutenant to take al-Wazir with him, because she was the youngest female soldier they had in their Unit, and she had the best shape of the rest. He told the Lieutenant to have al-Wazir wear a blouse that exposed much of her breasts to anyone's view while they were scouting out the area.

Once he finished his orders with Lieutenant al-Atrash, Colonel al-Qaysi walked out of the room, and he did not stop until he was out of the filthy hotel. He never spoke with the other Iraqis staying at the motel. His driving force was to get as far from this section of Washington and his soldiers as possible. In case he was being trailed by the police or special agents. If he stayed away from the others then they had a double chance of completing their missions. But if he kept coming around the other soldiers, he could cause both missions to be discovered and fail.

For the next two weeks, the group of Iraqi soldiers remained hidden inside their one room suites, with Lieutenant al-Atrash making quick little excursions over to the courthouse, so he could check on the security precautions still surrounding the old Federal Judge. Even though Colonel al-Qaysi informed him he was to start his mission during the jury selection of the trail. The rather concerned Lieutenant knew the Colonel wanted him to make his hit against the judge and Colonel al-Adwani at the same time as his commander made his attack on the American soldiers stationed in the other state of North Carolina.

The Iraqi Lieutenant knew why Colonel al-Qaysi wanted the hits to happen at the same time. With the two murders happening at the same moment, the police would not know where to start their investigations first. He understood the top priority would be given to the death of Colonel al-Adwani, then the old American judge. The death of the American soldiers would cause little concern to anyone investigating those murders in North Caroline. So he understood the Colonel had the best chance of getting away with his life after the attacks were carried out.

The weather in Washington was a mix of light snow and or rain mixed with sleet and chilly. It was cold but not freezing, which forced most of the civilians to remain in their offices and homes most of their time lately. This made the streets of Washington nearly empty, especially at the time of day when the Iraqis were going to make their kills against the judge and Colonel al-Adwani. Everything about the attack on the two targets seemed to be working out very well for the future Iraqi attackers. The security around the judge never increased much, and the Iraqi Lieutenant saw how well the security guards were trying to protect Colonel al-Adwani's life from a possible sniper who wanted to assassinate the man who tried to kill their President.

The Lieutenant knew it was going to have to be a head shot to kill Colonel al-Adwani. So al-Atrash decided he would do the kill on the Iraqi terrorist, and allow Sergeant Damerdji to kill the judge and support him during his attack against the terrorist. Lieutenant al-Atrash understood his kill was going to be the important kill, and he had to make certain he killed Colonel al-Adwani so the investigators could not link Saddam to the assassination attempt on the American Leader.

Since Lieutenant al-Atrash was placed in command of the Iraqi troops operating in Washington. He decided to release the rest of the Iraqi soldiers who wanted to remain in the United States. The young Lieutenant felt there was no need to expose them if he did not need them for his part of the mission, needlessly. He knew he would never need all the troops he had at his disposal, to carry out his assassination against the American Judge and Colonel al-Adwani. He understood when Sergeant Damerdji killed the judge, he was going to disappear in the maddening streets of Washington, and then quickly lose himself in the crowds.

Lieutenant al-Atrash was aware Sergeant Damerdji was planning to make his way to Montana and hide and make his living in that state. He remembered laughing when the Sergeant first announced in Montana, he felt he could disappear in the vastness of the state, and no one would think to look in that state usually covered with snow for him or any of his friends.

The days passed slowly for the Iraqi assassination teams. Both Major Al-Shaya and Colonel al-Qaysi were enjoying staying at the much better and cleaner hotel in middle of Washington. The two Iraqi Officers were making the best of their down time. They visited the better eateries of the area, stopping at some of the local bars at night to share in the wild nightlife Washington had to offer the visitors to the state. For the most part, everyone they met at night on their excursions to the bars, were pleasant and kind and they shared their time with them, and brought drinks at night as they told jokes and shared many good laughs.

The two Iraqi Military Officers shared drinks with many of the young American soldiers they met in the bars they visited on those occasions. The two Arab Officers made friends with a few of the American troopers, and they took their phone numbers down with a promise of making contact with them later, so they could carry on with their developing friendships. Soon, Colonel al-Qaysi and Major al-Shaya made friends with the soldiers hanging around Washington.

Many times in the past few days, the two Iraqi Officers made a number of dates with some of the soldiers to meet up with them at bars they were visiting the next day. The two Arab Officers were easily accepted by the excited soldiers, mainly because of the way al-Shaya was dressed at night. And the show she offered the young soldiers more homesick then they realized.

The selecting of the jury to try the Iraqi terrorist went on without a hitch for the judge. It also caused CIA Director John Raincloud to relax his guard some. The Director was well prepared for a problem, so he had the area flooded with special agents and SWAT teams from the Washington police and FBI, and his own paramilitary units. None of the agents and officers noticed the male and female Arabs, watching everything going on during the Jury process. The two from al-Qaysi soldiers were in the middle of the civilians cursing the terrorist as he was led in the building.

Director Raincloud and General White were in constant communications over this case, and they were speaking on the phone over some of their concerns. "John, I'm beginning to believe Saddam doesn't give a crap about this lousy sonofabitch we took out of his country, right out from under his damn nose." General White smirked at the full blooded Native American.

"I'm beginning to believe that myself, John. I had police and special FBI and a number of my own Agents surrounding the Federal Building, not even a damn fly would've been able to get at the Iraqi Colonel terrorist if they wanted to, General White. No police or agents reported anyone out of the ordinary or suspicious, watching the mess going down at the courthouse. I think we might have dodged a fucking bullet on that one, John." Director Raincloud mumbled.

"Yes sir, even though nothing has happened this time around, Director Raincloud Sir. I trust you're still going to maintain a constant ring of protection surrounding Judge Karlanderson, and this damn Colonel al-Adwani bastard, John? I don't want anything going wrong that might upset the damn trial on us. You know it's not going to be very long before we finally go after Iraq for a second time and the big Boss Man wants this trial over with long before we jump off on Iraq again. I'm already making my plans of attack against Iraq in the coming days, John."

"I understand the orders General. I'm going to keep two Washington SWAT teams and twenty FBI and my Agents at the courthouse during the entire trial. That way I'll know no one's going to get at the Judge or that lousy sonofabitch, until we have his damn ass ready to swing from a fucking tree, sir." The CIA Director replied to the powerful Chairman of the Joint Chiefs.

"That's a damn good idea there Chief. I have Captain Walker's group of war wacky bastards reporting to their main base at Camp Lejeune in a few weeks for some minor refresher courses in counterterrorism. I want to keep my elite troops as sharp as their K-bar knives. Even though the war in Afghanistan's going quite well for us at this point, I want to be well prepared for anything in case things go tits up on us over there. They'll be in the area at the time the trial starts, John. That's the reason for the refresher courses I just ordered up sir. That way the soldiers are just two hours at the longest away from Washington. I want them around, just in case someone tries something against the Judge or the Arab terrorist. There's so much hatred for the slimy little bastard that I'm seriously worried about one of our own people trying to take the sonofabitch out on us." The General leaned back and took a drag off his cigar as he stared at Director Raincloud.

"You say my idea was good as the way I have things laid out. I think your idea is a great one there, General. I was wondering why you were screwing around with your troop's liberty, until you explained this to me, sir. I don't mind telling you General, I'm more than pleased over having the extra special operation soldiers around in case." The Director replied confidently.

WASHINGTON D.C., APRIL 2nd, 2002.
THE BEST WESTERN HOTEL

Major Serena al-Shaya was busy checking out of the hotel and paying their bill. As Colonel al-Qaysi was supervising Lieutenant Malika Nabeel Elmasry, as he removed the few belongings they had from their hotel room, and placing them in the back of the Mercedes. Sergeant Shurug Khalaifa was helping the Lieutenant with the Colonel and Major's stuff. When they had the car packed up, Colonel al-Qaysi settled in the passenger's seat, and then they waited for the Major to come out of the hotel and drive the vehicle for them. The other two Iraqi soldiers took over the rear seats of the vehicle, and they remained silent as they waited for the Major.

Al-Shaya rushed out of the hotel and spotted the vehicle, it was running with the heater on full blast. For the first few days of April, Washington was caught in what was being called the last cold spell of the winter. The temperature was in the lower forties for the high of the day. She frowned when she saw the Colonel sitting in the passenger's seat. She was hoping he would drive so she could catch up on her rest. Being they knew they were leaving Washington, neither slept very much, and they were exhausted. They made love once last night, but that was all.

Major al-Shaya jumped in the driver's seat and shot the Colonel a quick smile, as she let out her breath and then she blew on her freezing hands. She then released the brake and put the Mercedes in gear, and then slowly pulled out of the parking lot of the hotel and headed for I-95. It was the quickest way to get down to North Carolina.

"How did it go in the foul hotel, Major?" Al-Qaysi nearly barked at the female soldier.

"I had no problems, I paid the bill and they thanked us for staying at their filthy establishment, and then I left. I wish we took some time to eat before leaving for North Carolina though, sir."

"We'll eat somewhere along the way. If you get hungry, you're free to pull off the highway at the first sign you see for food. Make certain you don't take me to that foul clown place again. I was sick for two days after eating the worthless food there." Colonel al-Qaysi snarled at her.

"What's bothering you today? We're heading to begin our mission and then we'll be free to leave this foul land of sin and lust. I'd think you'd be pleased we're moving out, to be involved in an action again, Hamoodi." Again, Major al-Shaya tried a smile on the angry looking man.

"I'll not be happy again until we finally leave this foul land of Satan for the last time, foolish woman. What has me upset the most on this foul day is, I spoke to Lieutenant al-Maluk, and he informed me Lieutenant al-Atrash allowed many of our foolish soldiers to leave the motel, so they can begin to find their new lives here in the United States. He took it upon himself to release these god cursed soldiers from their duty, and I don't know how to react to his orders.

"I have questioned Lieutenant Elmasry about this foolish and cursed decision, and he has informed me he knew nothing of this order. He stated he rarely saw Lieutenant al-Atrash since I placed him in command of the mission to kill the Judge and Colonel al-Adwani. I don't know what to do about it. The fool, suppose something goes wrong with the mission, and the camel's arse needs more of our soldiers to help fight his way out of a situation with the police. Now, he'll not have them available to him. I'm concerned about the mission in Washington, woman."

"I believe it's a little too late for you to start worrying about this now, Colonel al-Qaysi Sir. Unless you want to put off us going after the worthless American soldiers and head back to Washington, and take command of the mission from the fools there again, sir. That's the only solution I can see to help you with your concerns." The female Iraqi Major replied with caution lacing her voice as she read the first sign, giving the exit off the highway leading to Virginia. She could not believe they were out of Washington so quickly.

"No, I'll allow the worthless fool to run that mission as he sees fit, the cursed fool he is. I don't care if the foul scorpions are killed on that foul mission in Washington, woman. As long as Lieutenant al-Atrash completes his orders and kills those two people, or at least the worthless Colonel. We'll continue on with our part of this mission and then leave this miserable land." The Colonel closed his eyes and put his head against the seat. Then he smiled, he knew he gave Lieutenant al-Atrash the worst part of the two missions. He believed if al-Atrash took the shot at the judge, the police authorities were going to find and kill him and the others of his hit team with him. He did not care about anything any longer but his own revenge aimed against the hated American soldiers, and then getting out of the United States safely.

Colonel al-Qaysi padded his pocket lightly and felt the budge created by the stack of American cash he carried on his person. He had money stuffed in every one of his pockets, and the rest of the cash was packed away in his overnight bag stored in the trunk of the car. Another smile slowly crept across his lips, and this was because he knew he had over one hundred and twenty thousand American dollars in cash with him. He was aware if he entered Jordan with this much money. He would be able to live like a king in that land of lowly infidels, until the fate of Iraq was cast upon the vast pure sands of the desert. Then he would know if he would be allowed to return to his homeland, and assume some kind of power over his fractured country.

The two Arabs sitting in the back seat of the car remained quiet. They knew the other soldiers of their group were going to die on their part of this mission, and were silently happy they were no longer part of that mission back in Washington. Elmasry discussed with Khalaifa, and they both agreed once the mission in North Carolina was completed. They were going to leave Colonel al-Qaysi and Major al-Shaya, and remain in the United States forever. Lieutenant Elmasry was quickly falling in love with Sergeant Khalaifa, and he wanted her to share life with him. They had it with the military lifestyle they labored through in the Middle East.

Major Serena al-Shaya kept her eyes glued to the road and when she saw a sign for a Roy Rogers Restaurant in the distance, she asked the Colonel if he was hungry yet.

The exhausted Colonel al-Qaysi opened his eyes and waited until his eyes focused, and then he replied. "I told you before that you were free to stop anywhere you want to get something to eat. We have no set time to arrive in North Carolina, as long as we arrive in daylight. So we can pick the next foul hotel we'll stay at. Do as you were told and leave me alone! I have much weighing heavy on my mind, and I don't want to be disturbed by you or anyone else again, Major."

"I see you're still in the same foul mood that you were in when we first left the foul hotel property back in Washington, Colonel al-Qaysi Sir." Al-Shaya said, her being intimacy with the extremely dangerous Iraqi Colonel gave her the power to tease him in this manner.

"Take better care in the way you address me before the other two fools in the back seat of this vehicle, evil woman. Just because you're sharing my bed, it doesn't mean that the deadly sting of this scorpion has lessened as a threat against you and your worthless life, if you're foolish as to anger me further. I want to be left alone until we finally reach North Carolina, lowly woman."

"Fine Colonel Grouch, I'll not bother you even when we stop to eat, if you really mean the angry words you aimed at me in such harshness." Al-Shaya snapped her words at the Colonel, showing him she did not like the way he just spoke to her.

Again, Colonel al-Qaysi opened one eye this time, and he gave the Major a terrible look. But he was forced to smile when he saw she stuck her tongue at him in reply. He again settled in his seat, but this time the smile did not leave his lips. This was because he was beginning to feel he was lucky to have the heart of Serena al-Shaya. She was a beautiful and well respectful Arab woman and loyal soldier, and any man in Iraq would consider himself specially blessed by Allah's hand if she were to just smile at them as she walked by.

Al-Shaya glanced at the Colonel and noticed the smile, and wondered what he was smiling about. She did not care what it was, as long as his foul mood left. She hated it when he was angry. She saw the exit with the Roy Rogers restaurant and pulled off the highway, and drove to the end of the exit and picked up the place she was looking for. She crossed the street and pulled into the parking lot, and then she whispered. "Hamoodi, we're here and food waits us, sir."

"It's about time you got us here woman, I'm starving. I hope the foul place that you picked out for us this time to eat is better than that clown place that tried to poison us when we were first coming to Washington? Also, I believe we have to drop our military titles whenever we speak to one another while we're on this mission. I don't want these hated Americans realize we're Iraqi soldiers. We have already decided to drop the military title and we have to get back to that idea."

The small group of Iraqis ate, with Colonel al-Qaysi complaining about the terrible food. Nothing was going to please him on this day, so the other Arab soldiers ignored his complaints. After they ate, the group was on their way again. They reached North Carolina and it was just after one thirty in the afternoon. Immediately the Major began to search the area near Camp Lejeune for a hotel to stay at. She was looking for another Best Western, because she enjoyed staying at the place. After twenty minutes of driving, they found one just off the highway. She pulled into the parking lot, got out and following the Colonel's orders, she rented two rooms on the third floor of the establishment. They were both connected by a door between the rooms.

The four Iraqi warriors went to the rooms and crashed, they were thoroughly exhausted from the quick drive down to North Carolina, and the terrible stress the Colonel caused them by being in such a bad mood for the entire drive.

CHAPTER FIFTEEN

MARATHON FLORIDA, THE KEYS

It was April 7th, 2002, and the special operation soldiers living and staying on the Island of Marathon, Captain Robert Walker, Sergeant Dorothy Ramirez, Lieutenant Frank Hall and Sergeant Regina Raphael and the other soldiers visiting them. Things were going great now that Sergeant Ramirez had her child and little Robert was already a year old. But today was a rather somber day for these troops, because the soldiers only had little time left to enjoy their remaining leave time, before having to report back to Camp Lejeune for added training.

The massive soldier branded Buckethead, (Sergeant Vincent Lambardo) sat on the dock along with the equally as large soldier known as No Neck, (Sergeant Robert Abbott). They both were enjoying watching a number of small pleasure boats heading down the long canal towards the opened sea for a day of fishing and fun out on the water. Neck saw a beautiful girl sitting on one of the boats and he called out to her from the dock. "Hey baby, make my face the happiest place in the damn country by sitting on it for a little while will ya, honey."

The boat stopped and turned around and came back by the dock. A fairly large man himself bitched back at Neck. "Hey you stupid bastard, you better watch what you say to my wife. You look like a fucking flaming asshole to me, pal. Next time you say something to my wife like that, I'll kick your fucking ass all over the god damn Island, big shot."

"Hey Neck I wouldn't let him call you that even though you do slightly resemble an asshole, man." Buckethead grumbled as he put his hand on Neck's shoulder, and together they glared at the big mouth driver of the pleasure boat. Neck thought about starting some trouble with the rude dude, but then thought better of it. The husband was angry only because he disrespected his wife, and the soldier did not blame the civilian dude in the least for being angry at him.

Instead of barking back at the angry acting guy, Neck sort of just waved his hand at him, and the boat took off like a car that would have spun its tires on the blacktop. The two men laughed as the pleasure boat sped away at a high rate of speed on the water.

Mother Flanagan, (Sergeant Richard Flanagan) was sharing a joint with the Ghost, (Sergeant Walter Casper). They were staying more to themselves for the time being. This usually happened every time just before the Special Forces soldiers were ordered to report back to a military base. Most of the elite soldiers that invaded Iraq along with Walker were staying or living on the Island with him and his lady. They were enjoying all the Island had to offer them, great weather, great fishing, and many things to enjoy on the tiny Island.

The soldiers had another seven days of freedom left to them, before they were scheduled to report back to Camp Lejeune on the 15th, of April for their added specialized training. Walker was the brunt of many questions from the concerned and some upset elite soldiers.

"Hey Walker, what the fuck's this new bullshit all about, man? I thought we weren't gonna be called in unless there was a fucking emergency or something like that? Did things suddenly get hot on us or what, man?" the Hunter, (Sergeant Frank Whitcomb) bitched at the Captain.

"Beats the fuck outta my stinking ass buddy, I was lead to believe the same shit myself man. I was assured by the fools over at Fort Fumble (Pentagon) they'd be no more call ups unless the world was coming to a fucking end, and we were the glue ordered to hold it all together."

"You think this crap about calling us in for this so called special training tripe is a load of shit then, Walker?" Wacko, (Sergeant Salvatore Tomassi) griped at the young Captain this time.

Walker merely shrugged at the soldier and then grinned at him.

"Man, you're just a fucking wealth of stinking information on this one I see, Walker. What the fuck good are ya if you don't know shit why the brass is pulling our leave on us, man?" Mother complained angrily. He did not want to report to base, he was having too much fun on the Island.

"You betta watch your fucking ass when you're addressing me, because you're walking into a first class fucking headache talking like that, bubby. I'll show you what fucking good I am when I kick your ass all the way back to god damn Lejeune, buster. Look man, you see I'm the type of guy who doesn't believe in the proverb of a damn eye for a fucking eye, I take both fricking eyes, asshole. You wanna keep breathing right, you betta watch the fucking way you talk to me, friend or not, pal." Walker hissed at Mother Flanagan, he was surprised the usually meek soldier popped off at him like he did. It was out of character of the usually calm and easy going Mother.

"Hey man, Mother's here because his mother forgot her pill on the day he was conceived." Baby Tee always ready to get on Mother's can, called out as she joined the group.

"Keep it up sister, and I'm gonna start sucking on your tits until I can pull them out of your damn chest, that way you'll finally have a real pair of tits, Baby Tee." Mother fired at her.

"Oooooo baby, that could be very interesting Mother." Baby Tee purred at the Mother.

"C'mon and get offa it will ya. You know damn well what the fuck you signed on for. You guys know the brass can pull our leave for any fucking reason they feel like. So can the bitching. Hey Blood Clot, you have any fricking word on when the Ice lady is gonna link back up with us? How is she doing anyway Homes?" Walker asked about the female Sergeant who was severely wounded in their recent action in Iraq, when the troops kidnapped the terrorist and brought him back to the United States to stand trial for attempting to assassinate the President.

"Yeah Walker, from what I was told about her condition, she's doing pretty well man. I believe she's supposed to be heading down here as we speak. I know she wants to speak with you, to show you she's A number One and fit for fucking duty again, man. The last time I spoke to her, she was a little worried that you were gonna bounce her out of the damn Unit because she was that bad hurt, man. I told her she was pipe dreaming that you'd never bounce her outta the Unit unless she was dead, or too old to hold a weapon and fire it properly any longer, Walker." Blood Clot, (Sergeant Richard Brumbach) reported to Walker. Blood Clot was the Unit's medic.

"Out fucking standing man. The Unit's gonna be complete for this so called tune up crap. Raz is back, Ice is coming back in time for some retraining crap." Walker announced proudly.

"Hey Walker, how the hell are we getting up to Lejeune, man?" the Mutt asked his friend.

"The brass is gonna have a C-130 land on the Island. Them fly boys are gonna get us back to base. I guess that's the least the brass can do for cutting our stinking leave time short on us."

"You think we might be finding ourselves being shipped off to Afghanistan, Captain Walker?" Blind Date asked Walker with a little concern in her tone, as she stared at him.

"No way in hell baby girl. Not with the way the Special Forces and rest of the uther troops are handling shit over there. They don't need us going over there and screwing up the chip dip on them guys. Why Blind Date, you seem like you don't want anything to do with that damn Arab country?" Walker asked the pretty female French fighter on loan from France.

"I don't want to go anywhere near that backwards country if I can help it, Captain. I heard so many terrible stories they still eat their young over there, Captain. Besides sir, I like staying on this little Island of yours sir. I think I want to get married, maybe even have a child or two, and then live in the United States with an American husband for the rest of my life, sir." Blind Date replied, showing she was concerned about heading there, and she had something else on her mind, rather than heading out fighting in another war someplace.

"Hey little sister, now you're talking my kind of talk. Living in the United States is the best, girl. Who do you have your eyes aimed at as this husband you want, as if we didn't know the answer to that one, little sister?" Baby Tee said as she smiled at the French soldier.

Blind Date did not reply, instead she grabbed the Mutt in the crotch and tugged on him.

"Hey pretty girl, it looks like you got the big dummy right where you want him by the short hairs. Maybe if the stinking Mutt finally gets married and settles down and has some kids, he might calm down a bit and start acting like a real human being. Not!!!!" Mother Flanagan retorted as he calmed down and got in the bickering going on with the rest of the group.

Blood Clot's cellular phone went off and everyone quieted while he answered it. "Holy shit girl, you won't believe this shit, but we were just talking about your ass. How you doing girl? Where the hell are ya sister?" Blood Clot covered the mouth piece and mouthed Ice to Walker.

"It's nice to know one is missed by the ones she loves the most in life, Blood Clot. Have you talked to Walker for me like I asked you to do, Richard? I'm just passing over the Vaca Cut Bridge, so I believe I'm about ten minutes away from Walker's place now, Blood Clot. I don't want to come there if he's going to cut me from the group."

"No way in hell will he ever do that to you, little sister. You're still part of the damn Unit until you're too old to fuck. Hey girl, Raz had her baby, it was a boy, but thank God he looks more like Raz and not Walker. You get you pretty little ass over here on the double quick, we're all waiting to see ya again, girl." Blood Clot offered in an excited tone on the phone.

"I'm on my way Blood Clot, and thank you for talking to Walker for me. I owe you honey."

As soon as Blood Clot hung up with Ice the questions started, but the medic held up his hands and told everyone at the same time. "Ice is on the Island and she's heading right for here, man. She's really worried you're gonna dump her ass from the Unit. I can't wait to see her again man."

"The hell you say to my ass, let's all get out front and wait for her to get her lovely little ass over here." Walker said and started out of his driveway in a rush, followed by the rest of the soldiers. When they saw her car coming down the road, the soldiers started to call out her name. By the time Ice parked her car, she was crying because of all the attention her friends and fellow soldiers were showing her. When she was out of the car, the soldiers immediately closed in on her and actually lifted her over their heads, and then they carried her to the back of Walker's home. They kept walking until they were all standing on the wood dock. Then the soldiers lowered Ice until one soldier was on each of her arms and legs, and they started to swing her at the water as another soldier called out. "One, two, three, heave ho man."

By the time Ice hit the water, she was some ten feet away from the dock. She hit the water with a splash, and then the other soldiers followed her in the water. They swam around her and began kissing and touching her. Most of the excited soldiers wanted to make certain she was back with them at full strength. The water was a little cool, so the soldiers swam back to the dock and got out of the water. Sergeant Dorothy Ramirez ran in the home and she came back with a bunch of bathrobes and towels. The soldiers stripped on the dock and when Ice got out of her clothes, the soldiers as a group stopped what they were doing, and they looked at the terrible scar on her left shoulder, neck, and the upper part of her breast. Ice saw them looking at her and she immediately lowered her head and said barely over a whisper to their concern looks.

"Yes, I know my body is ugly now. I don't blame you people for looking at me like that."

"Like fucking what Ice? All you got is one helluva badge of fucking honor on your bod, baby sister." Walker snarled at the soldier as he walked up to her and kissed her on the scar.

"You mean you and the other soldiers don't find me ugly now, Captain Walker Sir?"

"You, ugly? That'll be the fricking day sister. You're still hot enough to melt fucking ice, sister. So cut out the fucking pity train shit will ya. You're a soldier, and any soldier worth his dog tags got himself a fucking scar or two to be proud of. How are you doing anyway girl?"

"Oh thank you for that Walker. You don't know how much I needed to hear that. I'm doing okay I guess, I still have some pain though, and my neck is stiff every now and then. But the Doc's said this will pass in due time, sir. But other than that, I'm locked, hot, and ready to rock."

"Good fucking deal and you got here just in time girl, because we're all heading back to Camp Lejeune on the 15th of April. We just got word to report back to home base for some kinda special training crap some brass asshole thought up for us. I think it's some kinda fricking ploy to get us back on base, so the lousy bastards can ship us out on another fucking mission somewhere in this mixed up crazy ass fucking world. I'm sure by now some other motherfucker is trying to eat their damn neighbors again." Walker announced to the female soldier.

"Oh no, please don't tell me we're heading on another mission so soon, Walker." Ice cried.

"It's like I just told ya girl, we're going on a special training act in Lejeune. But it's a damn gut feeling I got because every time we find ourselves back at Lejeune, we always end up going on a fucking mission. I guess all we can do is go along with the flow, and find out where we'll end up this time, Ice. It's great to have you back with the damn Unit, sister." Walker kissed her on the cheek this time then he stepped back and Ice wiggled into the bathrobe Ramirez gave her.

The troops on Marathon began to calm down by cutting out the booze and pot for when they were to return to base. Walker was spending much of his time with his new child and lady. But as the days got closer to when they had to depart for base, the soldier's moods became really somber. Sergeant Ramirez had a wonderful woman she trusted who was going to move into their home and care for her child and place while they were gone. As far as the elite troops knew, they were only supposed to be at stationed Camp Lejeune for four weeks at the longest. Then they were supposed to be placed back on leave until needed again. This was the only reason the specialized soldiers were not so upset with this latest call up order.

NORTH CAROLINA, WEDNESDAY,
APRIL 10th, 2002

Colonel Hamoodi al-Qaysi, Major Serena al-Shaya, Lieutenant Malika Nabeel Elmasry, and Sergeant Shurug Khalaifa, were hanging around the bar known as Bare Parts for three nights in a row. The Iraqi Colonel picked these three Arabs, two women and one man because they looked the least like Arabs. The women were ordered to wear blouses designed to capture the attention of the American soldiers in the bar. The women made the men accepted by many, and they brought drinks for the American troops, and in return they brought drinks for the four unknown Arabs. The four Iraqis had been seen by the American soldiers so much that they soon became part of them. Colonel al-Qaysi had to sit through many boring stories the bragging soldiers spoke of, he knew they were talking so much to try and impress his two pretty females.

Every time the Iraqi troopers saw an American soldier with the Unit patch of the soldiers who had invaded his country and took his Colonel prisoner, and they brought him back to the States to stand trial, they made friends with those soldiers. He was friends with four troops from the specialized group of warriors he wanted to kill soldiers from. When the Americans came in, they headed to right al-Qaysi's table and began to speak to the two women. As the Arabs sat in the bar they discovered Captain Walker and the troops that invaded his country were scheduled to be back at Camp Lejeune on April 15th. The Iraqi Colonel was promised the soldiers from his Unit would introduce Walker and the other troopers to them, once they were back on base. Everything was working out real fine for the Colonel and his soon to be group of snipers.

WASHINGTON D.C. SATURDAY, APRIL 13th, 2002

Lieutenant al-Atrash and Sergeant al-Wazir was by the Courthouse, watching as Judge William Karlanderson walked in the coffee shop and picked up his usual cup of coffee. Then the elderly judge crossed the street as he done on the other occasions he watched the man. The Iraqi Lieutenant noticed two security guards walking a few steps behind the elderly judge, and he smiled. Al-Atrash waited until the three black trucks pulled up to the courthouse, and the police rushed Colonel al-Adwani into the building under heavy guard. The Lieutenant never picked up the two sniper teams hiding on the roofs of the buildings surrounding the courthouse.

The soon to be Arab sniper decided to make his hit on the American Judge and Colonel al-Adwani on Tuesday, April 23rd. This was because he wanted the trial to begin first, because he needed the police to feel there was no sort of threat planned against the judge or the terrorist Colonel, so his hit on them might be a little easier to carry off. Once Colonel al-Adwani was inside the courthouse and out of his sight, the Arab Lieutenant left his perch and then he walked out of the area like he had no care in the world, and he headed back for the rundown Roland's Motel, and the other Iraqi attackers waiting his return.

Colonel Al-Qaysi allowed the American soldiers to enjoy looking down the front of Major al-Shaya's and

Sergeant Khalaifa's blouses. He was a little surprised because all these soldiers had to do was look over their shoulders, and they could see a number of completely naked young women dancing before them on the stage. But these fools seem to be more interested in looking at his female soldiers exposing themselves to their ugly gaze. Try as he might, he just could not figure out why the worthless fools would struggle and catch just a quick glimpse of these women's breasts, rather than look at the naked women on the stage behind them. He smiled because he would never be able to figure out how the foolish American's mind worked. He was pleased they were so interested in his women though, because he found out everything about Walker and the rest of his troops he wanted to know, before he attacked and killed them.

At twelve thirty p.m., the Iraqi Commander gave the women the look, and they immediately stood and announced to the Americans that they were tired, and they were going to turn in for the night. The small group of American soldiers put frowns on as they watched the two beautiful young women and their boyfriends leave. Colonel al-Qaysi caught up to Major al-Shaya and he placed his hand on her shoulder and whispered to her. "These very foolish American soldiers would sell out their foul country just to see a woman's fat breast. No matter, we now know when our intended targets are scheduled to arrive here. We'll continue to come to this filthy bar every night until the foul soldiers we want to kill finally arrive, and we can see what they truly look like. From the sound of him, this Walker soldier seems like a one man Army.

"We'll kill them, and then we'll quickly leave this god forsaken country for good. I believe we'll come back to the bar on the night of Monday, April 15th, when these cursed soldiers are to arrive here. We'll leave the bar before the soldiers do, and then we'll wait outside and shoot two of them and then leave the area at once, al-Shaya."

"Are we going to kill the one who leads the American soldier's first, al-Qaysi?" the female Major asked as she stayed with her orders, and she made certain she did not use their military rank when they spoke to each other where someone might overhear what they were saying.

"No, I want him to die last, that way he'll suffer the most with the knowledge someone is killing all his friends. Then the bullet of fate will find his head last after he suffered the deaths of all his cursed friends. I have no mercy for this soldier." Colonel al-Qaysi snapped at her.

"You have another good plan in mind, al-Qaysi?" Al-Shaya announced because she did not know what else to say to her commander. If she had her way about the mission, she would kill the leader of the soldiers first, and then leave the United States after his death. She knew the longer they played the game of death with these extremely dangerous American soldiers. The more likely one of them would discover them and kill them before they completed their mission.

Colonel al-Qaysi had to pull on Major al-Shaya's hand to break her daydreaming as they headed for the car. This time Lieutenant Elmasry was doing the driving, and Sergeant Khalaifa sat in the front seat and the Colonel and Major sat in the back seat of the car. Once they were comfortable, the Colonel spoke to his female Major. "Al-Shaya, when we get back to our foul room I want you and Elmasry to go over the weapons our brother from the Libyan Embassy gave us, so we can carry out our mission successfully. I want you to make certain that they're all in the proper working condition. We'll have to kill the American soldiers from a far distance, and our shots have to be true. It's your duty to make certain the weapons are good."

"Yes Hamoodi, I'll look after the weapons myself, have no fear of that sir."

The rest of the trip back to the hotel was completed in silence by the future terrorists. Colonel al-Qaysi was not fearful anyone from the hotel would find their weapons hidden in their room. The weapons were stored in their luggage, and they were broken down to where they did not look very much like weapons to the untrained eyes.

The Iraqi Colonel took a quick shower as soon as he entered the apartment. Sergeant Khalaifa went to her room, and Major al-Shaya and Lieutenant Elmasry went to work on the weapons as ordered. In no time, they had the weapons assembled and working properly. Al-Shaya adjusted the scopes then loaded four clips for each M-16, which were accurate weapons at near range, and that was where they were expecting to kill the American soldiers.

By the time al-Qaysi finished his shower, the M-16s were laid out on the bed fully assembled and ready for firing, along with extra clips for the weapons. He picked up a weapon and put it to his shoulder and checked the scope. He pulled back the action of the weapon as if chambering a round, and then he allowed the chamber to slam home with a loud click. The weapons were in perfect working order as expected. Next, the Iraqi Officer checked on the clips for the weapons. He was aware the M-16s still had the slight problem with jamming every once in a while, but that was when the weapon was used on full automatic.

The Commander of the Iraqi terrorists was planning to squeeze one round off at a time, unless they came under attack by the police authorities. Nevertheless, he ordered Major al-Shaya to place eighteen rounds in the twenty round clips. He read about the Americans stopping the jamming by placing just eighteen rounds in the clips, the other thing he did not realize, he was using the five point five six mm Colt M 4 version of the M-16s. This weapon never jammed, and it was extremely accurate from far greater distances than the original M-16 weapon.

After checking out the weapons, he gave Lieutenant Elmasry two weapons and eight clips for them, and then he informed him he was responsible for those weapons. Then the Colonel led Lieutenant Elmasry to the door and almost shoved him out of the room. He wanted to be alone with the Major for a while.

Once the door was closed behind the Lieutenant, he removed the other weapons from the bed and then he stood them up against the wall. He picked up the remaining clips for the weapons and placed them on the night table by the side of the queen size bed.

Al-Shaya watched what he was up to and automatically began to undress while standing behind him. When he had the bed cleared, al-Shaya walked over to it and waited behind him. When he saw al-Shaya naked, he grabbed her by the arms and lightly tossed her to the bed while smiling. Al-Shaya giggled as he lied down on top of her and began to play with her breasts. She purred when he drew her nipple in his mouth and sucked gently. She giggled again when he lightly nipped her nipple and sucked on it a second time.

Just as al-Shaya was beginning to get turned on by his attention, he let out his breath in a rush and rolled off her and lied down on the bed by her side and looked up at the ceiling.

"What is suddenly wrong with you lover? You were doing so well tonight then you stopped."

"It's I cannot get these foul American soldiers out of my mind. My breath, my every thought about them is to seek my revenge against their god cursed souls. I cannot believe they had the audacity to dare enter our country as an invading Army. Carried out a military operation where General al-Zahar was killed, and Colonel al-Adwani was taken prisoner by these cursed soldiers. I have so much trouble believing I'm not thinking like a true soldier, and offer these brave soldiers the credit I should be offering them, by their successfully carrying out such an operation in our country. All I can see when I close my worthless eyes, all I can taste when I swallow is my want of revenge aimed against these worthless American soldiers. Am I going mad with my want for revenge against these soldiers who carried out their Commander's orders?"

"Hamoodi, there is an old saying in our country you should keep on your mind. 'If you seek vengeance, dig two graves'. Is it not a wiser idea to walk away and give these American soldiers a bow for what they have accomplished in our country? Like you said, we should honor rather than seek revenge against them. I'd like to do what some of our soldiers done. I'd seek asylum in the United States and never mind our want for foolish revenge. But what you decide, I'll back you. I only want to be with you, and to be with you I'll do whatever you want of me, sir."

"Al-Shaya, you mentioned this desire before to me, and I let you know my wants. Yes, to seek revenge, one must prepare to dig two graves. But if I have to dig a hundred graves, I'll carry out my revenge against these hated American soldiers. Forgive my moment of weakness and doubt. I don't want to hear more of your want to remain here in the United States. If you want to stay in America, stay! You'll stay without me standing by your side. My place is in the land of sand and my brother Arabs, not sin." Colonel al-Qaysi stared at the Major until she replied.

"Allow my actions to be the answer you seek from me, Hamoodi."

The Iraqi Colonel could do anything but place his hands behind his head, and then he watched and enjoyed the wonderful feeling as al-Shaya brought him the pleasures of the mouth. When they were finished making love, they collapsed exhausted on the bed and soon fell asleep.

MARATHON ISLAND,
THE FLORIDA KEYS

Captain Robert Walker and Sergeant Dorothy Ramirez were making love at the same time Colonel al-Qaysi and Major al-Shaya was. They were making love on the dock. When they finished, the two lovers laid back and stared at the star filled sky. It was a lovely night, with the temperature hovering in the lower seventies. The cool breeze made the sweat covered hard bodies of the two lovers covered with goose bumps. Walker felt Ramirez shiver and pulled her closer. He kissed her on the forehead and mumbled sexily. "You know something young lady?"

"No, what's that my soldier and lover? You know I'm always interested in anything you have to say to me, Bobby." She purred sexily to her man.

"I love you. We have two more days before we hafta leave for base. What say when we get back to Marathon, I make you an honorable woman and we get married?"

"I am an honorable woman, and in love with an honorable man. But if you want to get married, ask and you'll find out my answer." Her smile grew wider.

Walker rolled on his side and got down on a knee and took Ramirez's hand and held it tenderly. He looked deeply into her blue eyes and she saw there was not a trace of a smile as he spoke seriously to her. "Sergeant Dorothy Ramirez, would you please be my wif…"

Ramirez slapped him on the back of his head with her other hand and snapped at him. "You know Bobby it'd be much more romantic if you dropped the damn Sergeant you know."

Walker smiled and struck himself on the forehead and then he mumbled at himself. "Durrrrrrr." Then he wiped the smile from his lips as he started again. "Dorothy Ramirez, Dorothy, Raz, will you marry me and make me the happiest man in the ever loving world? I love you more than I loved anyone in my life, and I want you to be my wife for the rest of my life. Will you marry me pretty lady?" he stopped speaking and then he stared his lover right in the eyes as he waited for her reply.

She started to cry because she was so happy by what he just asked of her. She pulled his head to her, and then kissed him passionately on the lips. Then she pulled away and looked him in the eyes. With tears streaming down her cheeks she replied with the widest smile she ever had. "Yes Bobby, I'll marry you, and this will make me the happiest woman in the whole, wide ever loving world. I love you so much Bobby."

Suddenly, there was clapping from behind the two lovers, and they turned and saw half the guys from the Unit visiting them on the Island. They were standing and everyone was quiet as mice. Now, the soldiers were clapping and grinning at the lovers, happy for Ramirez's reply.

Neck mumbled at them. "Man, I was around when a few of my friends asked their girls to marry them. But this is the first time I ever saw anyone ask his lady to marry him while they were both as naked as a pair of jaybirds. This has to be a stinking first here people."

"You know our fearless leader, if there was a way for Walker to go off to war naked, he'd do it. He does his best work naked like he is." Baby Tee offered as she smiled at the two.

"You should know about that Baby Tee. Hey girl, when the hell are you gonna a grow yourself a pair of real tits?" Walker snapped at her and then he blew her a kiss.

"I'll grow tits when you have another kid, stupid." Tee fired right back at him as she wiggled her slender hips and grinned at the Captain.

"I don't know, I think it was kind of romantic for Walker to ask Raz to marry him when they were naked." Ice, (Sergeant Diane Morrison) offered in a weak voice. Even though she would never admit it to the soldiers, she was still in a lot of pain and her body was weak yet.

"You would baby girl. You're like the big dumb slug over there, that's why you think this was so damn romantic little sister. The two of you birds should start your own nudist camp on this stinking Island, little girl." Mother Flanagan offered as he lit up a joint, and then he passed it on to the Mutt who was grinning from ear to ear for his friend. Mother stared at the Mutt as he took a pull from the joint and then passed it on to the Ghost.

"What the hell's up your stinking ass all of the sudden, Mother? You suddenly look pissed off man." The Mutt asked the soldier with concern.

"You, that's what's up my ass man. This piece of upchuck over there on his knees asking this good looking Spanish chick to marry his big dumb ass is your best fucking friend, man. And here you are, not saying a damn thing to the pretty lady about to make the biggest ever loving mistake of her life, and take Road Kill as her hubby for life, man. C'mon Mutt, you have a fucking door opened where you can get back at both them crazy ass shitbirds at the same damn time, man. All you're doing is sucking on the wet end of a dope stick, and not dumping on these two shitbirds in the fucking least, buddy. What the hell gives with you anyhow man?"

The Mutt took his eyes off Mother and then leveled them on Walker now standing, and helping Ramirez up to her feet. His smile grew as he looked at his two best friends. He was amazed Ramirez was able to get her shape back so quickly after just having a baby. She looked as good as always. He could not help but stare at the both of them. All his staring made the Mutt's girlfriend call out to the other soldiers in a warning.

"Uh-oh, look at the dogman, he's looking at them two fools standing there naked as the day they were born with lust burning in his evil eyes. You better watch your ass Walker. I don't know if that look's aimed at you, or at Raz, but the both of you are in danger. I believe the both of you better get dressed in a quick hurry it up, before you have the mad dog drooling all over himself and going into heat at the same time. I saw the look in his eyes before, it wasn't a pleasant sight to see I tell you." Blind Date walked up to the Mutt and she slapped him on his rump. The slap was so loud it sounded like a gun shot, and it made the Mutt jump at the same time.

"Hey Mother, I don't know what to say to them two birds. The only thing I can say is, it's about fucking time the dumb friend of mine came to his senses, and he finally asked Raz to marry him. If he didn't ask her, I was gonna. I love you two shitbirds. Congratulations."

"Here, here." The rest of the soldiers offered to the Mutt's words.

Ramirez started to cry again as she walked up to the Mutt and she kissed him. Instantly, his hands were all over her breasts and she shoved him away and then complained at him. "Dammit dog, I should've known you'd say nice words, only so you could play with my breasts, stupid. I can't get over you buster, is there nothing but sex on your evil mind, mister?" she complained at the Mutt as she stood and allowed her friend to play with her like he was doing again.

"Hey you should know betta than to come anywhere near me naked like that, baby girl. You forced me to do this to your bod, sister. Next time you wanna come near me and not have me play with your tits, wear clothes." He said as he rolled Ramirez's nipples between his fingers.

"Hey Raz, if you came anywhere near the stinking Mutt wearing clothes, you'd only force him to rip the damn things offa your body, girl. He'll still be playing with your tits one way or the other you know, baby girl." Buckethead called out from the group.

The soldiers laughed as they watched the Mutt going at Ramirez's breasts with both hands. When he leaned forward and drew a nipple in his mouth, she immediately pulled away from him and grumbled at the dangerous soldier. "No you don't mister! You're not going to get my motor running and call for a party tonight, buster. I'm not going to get stuck making love to all you swinging dicks from the outfit at the same time on this night. I was just asked to be married by the only man I love in the whole world. If I'm going to make love to anyone tonight, it's going to be my lover only, mister. Stop that will you please, what the hell are you trying to do, give my nipple a damn hickey, stupid?" She pushed the Mutt's mouth from her breast.

The Mutt released Ramirez's breasts and the mumbled while placing the sad look on his face. "Hey girl, you can't blame a guy for trying. I was only trying to get you turned on so you'd dump the dopey slob and come looking for a good ride on space mountain here, girl. Walker's getting too old to keep up with a dish like you. You need me to take care of ya needs for ya."

Walker came up behind Ramirez and cupped her breasts from behind and then he fired back at the Mutt. "Let me tell you something, asshole. You're space fucking mountain died from lack of oxygen many years ago, man. These tits here belong to me and me alone, buster." He rolled Ramirez's breasts in his hands as he grinned at the Mutt and then he added. "Thanks a lot man, it's good to have you on my side as always, buddy."

"I don't know about the rest of you slugs watching these two fools having all the fun here. I'm starting to get turned on watching Walker play with Raz's tits like that. If he doesn't stop pretty soon, I'm going to jump on someone's bones, and have him make good loving to me. I'm getting hot as hell watching these two going at it like this. The Mutt was bad enough, but Walker looks like he's trying to prove a point to someone here." Baby Tee offered as she started to play with her breasts through her blouse as she stared at what Walker was doing to Ramirez.

"Hey baby girl, if you're getting that hot about this shit. I got the water hose hanging right here for ya that'll cool you down good and proper, little sister." The Mutt roared at Baby Tee, and then he grabbed his dick through his pants and began to shake his member at her, as he placed the hugest shit eating grin on his lips.

"You're a little too damn willing and you're not going after any other woman in the outfit with that half ass black snake of yours, mista. At least not until you satisfied me with the damn thing first, big boy. Come on mista and bring that thing on over here and give me a little whirl, because what Walker is doing to his girlfriend is getting to me at the same time." Blind Date offered as she started to play with the Mutt by rubbing his dick through his pants, as she smiled in the eyes of her lover.

"C'mon people, this thing's starting to get a little outta hand here. I just asked my lady to marry me and she said yes. All I wanted to do was have some fun with her so cut the shit out. We ain't gonna get involved in an all out party and take away from us what happened between us. I'm taking my lady to the house, and we're gonna have a little private time for a while, and make serious love to each other. I don't care what the fuck the rest of you slugs do out here as long as you guys don't burn my home down, but I'm warning the lot of ya fuckers.

"If I see any of you guys again today, I'll know you don't feel like living any longer in this stinking world. You guys feel me, hear what I just said? Do you hear fucks what I'm saying to you people? If not I'll clear it up a little betta for you pack of asses. If anyone of you walking sandbags comes a knocking on my fucking door while I'm with Raz. Those knocks are gonna be answered by five rounds coming through the stinking door, and if you live through that. I'll chase your ass outta my home while still firing at you until I either get ya, or I run outta ammunition. C'mon, I want to talk to you alone for a change, baby." He actually picked Ramirez up while giving the rest of the soldier's one last warning look, before he disappeared in the home.

"Yeah, I bet you two birds are gonna talk in there, buddy. You can't fool me that easily Walker and you know it man. You two birds are gonna fuck like stinking bunnies in there, and you don't want any of us to see you two dogs doing it, man. That ain't fricking really fair my friend, we always let you two birds watch when we fuck around out here, buddy. I'm gonna launch a stinking complaint about this shit to someone who can do something bout this shit, man." Neck called after the two lovers as they entered their home. This caused some of the other soldiers to laugh at the pair while watching them enter the room.

Sergeant Ramirez reached around Captain Walker's back and she gave the Neck the finger as she allowed Walker to carry her to the bedroom.

"Well, that didn't go the way I thought it would go. I thought with all the horn busting we were doing to the two jerks. They woulda invited us in to watch them going at it like two dogs in heat." The equally as massive Buckethead, grumbled at the soldiers standing in Walker's yard.

"Huh, and that's from a guy who sat in front of a stinking slot machine for over an hour and a half while hitting the coin return slot, and thinking he was breaking even with the damn machine. I'm not gonna stand here like a fish outta water all night long, man. I'm gonna go out and find something for me to do." Mother Flanagan complained until he turned around and saw Blind Date giving the Mutt some head in front of the rest of the soldiers. Baby Tee was holding his dick while Blind Date worked the Mutt over good and proper with her mouth.

"Well will you fucking guy's look at these three animals going at it hot and heavy now." The Neck grumbled as he pointed to the three soldiers enjoying themselves.

"There's some room here for a few more of you jerks to come and join in on the fun and games if you want, if any of you guys want to play that is. Like I said fools, I'm horny as hell and I want some, and when I want some, I'm going to get me some one way or the other. So you guys better get on with it if you know what's good for the lot of you pigs. You guys line up in front of me if you want a little before we turn in for the night." Baby Tee announced as she took off her shirt off and threw it at Flanagan who caught it and looped it over his shoulder, and then he started to walk at the pretty female. It was going to be a long night for a few women.

With the soldiers watching Walker asking Ramirez to marry him, placed the rest of the soldiers in great moods. Now, with watching the three other soldiers having some fun then joined them and soon, every soldier was having some fun.

CHAPTER SIXTEEN

Captain Robert Walker and the rest of his special operation soldiers were bunched up at the tiny Marathon Airport, waiting for the huge C-130 transport plane to land. It was seven thirty a.m. and the aircraft was late arriving. The way Walker figured it; if they were in the air by eight thirty, they should land in North Carolina by eleven a.m. He believed they should be settled in their old barracks by two p.m., and the rest of the day would be there's to do what they wanted, and get readjusted with being back on the massive Marine Base.

Most of the elite American soldiers were already talking about visiting the well known titty bar Bare Parts. The place was the highlight of being stuck at the Marine Base at Camp Lejeune in North Carolina. Walker had to admit he was kind of looking forward to seeing the old place again, and enjoying the nightlife of the bar. The last time the elite group of soldiers were at the bar, many of the women fighters from the group got up on stage with the bar women, and they did the greatest strip show for the rest of the soldiers in the bar. It was one helluva night for everyone involved to enjoy with the wild party as it turned out to be at the bar.

As Walker was thinking, Ramirez lightly tapped him on the arm and when he looked at her, she pointed in the air. He looked up to the bright sky and easily picked up the huge C-130 transport coming in for a landing. He pushed himself off the wall of the structure with his powerful shoulders, and barked at the other soldiers. "Okay people, let's look alive our stinking transportation back to Disneyland is coming in. I want everyone to look sharp. Remember, we're fucking soldiers, so let's start looking like them, guys. Move it out you walking sand bags."

Walker's soldiers did as they were ordered and they quickly lined up and prepared to board the incoming aircraft. The group of soldiers went right through the metal detector, because the airport security guards knew the group was soldiers reporting for duty so the X-ray machine was shut down, because they were getting on a waiting military plane. The aircraft landed without a problem, but she was one of the largest planes ever to try a landing at the tight and small airport on the Island. The landing aroused the attention of a number of the locals as they watched the huge aircraft land and complete a careful turnaround at the far end of the runway. Then taxied back down the runway until it was facing the wind for takeoff. The commander had orders to land, pick up the group of troops and then do a quick takeoff again. The aircraft kept its engines running just above idle speed all the time, as it waited for the troops to make it out to the aircraft.

The soldiers walked out the door of the terminal and stepped on the tarmac. Then they hustled down what the soldiers laughed at was the landing strip of the Marathon Airport. There were cracks, and even a number of potholes in the poor runway. Walker found two sheet metal screws lying on the tarmac and put them in his pocket. He wanted to give them to the pilot to show him what he was landing on. He knew the screws were a double edge sword against any landing or taking off planes. If the aircraft got a flat tire it could crash on the next landing, or if the screws were sucked up into one of the engines, it could cause the aircraft to crash.

As the specialized soldiers approached the transport aircraft, the pilot powered the engines up to three quarters takeoff power. The massive engines were screaming as the soldiers began to board the plane. When they were on board, they quickly fanned out and took the canvass seats, and they strapped themselves in for the quick flight back to the base. When it was reported to the commander the soldiers were set and secured, the pilot received permission to takeoff, and he pushed the throttles up until the engines were at full military takeoff power.

The plane then roared down the tight runway and slowly lifted into the morning air. It was a quick flight, and the soldiers were on the ground at the North Carolina civilian airport that served as the main landing area for most of the troops reporting for duty at Camp Lejeune. There were two military buses parked on the tarmac, and the elite soldiers were directed over to them. The troopers were then taken off the airbase, and driven over to Camp Lejeune. As usual, Colonel Bruce Leadbetter was waiting for the group of elite soldiers to arrive on his base.

The always upset Marine Colonel was standing with his hands on his hips, while pacing as the buses pulled up before his headquarters. As the soldiers got off the buses, he started right in on the troops. "Get the fuck off them damn banana boats and stand at attention, you pukes trying to call yourselves fricking soldiers in my beloved Marine Corps. I said move it, and if you people don't move, I'm going to start kicking some asses around here, dammit. Let me tell you people something, your damn pleasure vacation stopped the very moment you slimy asses stepped foot on this military base. You screaming squirrel ass fucking pussy hounds got fat and lazy on my ass, while you were lying around this great land of ours your government allows you people to live in. Dammit, I told you people to get the hell off them damn buses, step on it people.

"Let me tell you war wacky bastards and bitches something, I'm going to work off that baby fat from your milk bodies. You people look like you got real soft on my ass. Shitttt, and you fucks call yourselves Special Forces soldiers. Tighten up the damn ranks, at least try and look like fucking Marines for a little while you're here, dammit. I can't believe you people."

The Colonel stopped his ranting at the soldiers, and then he waited for them to quickly line up before him. No matter what he threatened the soldiers with, nothing made them move any faster. The troops were immune to his moods, cursing and threatening. The Colonel had to fight not to smile as he watched his elite soldiers display every type of disrespect against him. That was what he wanted from his specialized troops. Do what they were ordered, but under their terms, not his.

Colonel Leadbetter checked the faces of his troops as they quickly formed up good lines. It was good to see the soldiers again. This bunch of specialized troopers was the cream of the crap as he always referred to them. The wise Colonel noticed Ice who was wounded on their last mission, and he was extremely pleased to see her looking so well. He was surprised to see her standing in the ranks with the rest of her soldiers. He was certain Walker would have dropped her from the Unit by now because of her wound. Every soldier from Walker's Unit had to be in top notch condition, or he or she was immediately dumped from the Unit. The commanding officer was certain Ice was still hurt and not operating at one hundred percent. The wise Marine Officer had to smile when he spotted Sergeant Ramirez as she stood by the side of Walker as usual.

She looked good as always, and she was one of the Colonel's favorite troopers of the group. He looked at her for a long moment and she seemed to be fit enough for active duty. He could not believe she just had a baby. When the troops were ready for close inspection, he started to walk the line before the soldiers. All the while he was pacing, he glared at each trooper he walked by. Colonel Joseph Salsiccia was walking by Colonel Leadbetter's side, but a new officer was added to his group. It was Major Wilson, who was on the ground with Walker's group as a Captain, when the soldiers were operating in Iraq a few months ago. Sergeant John Kirkpatrick, Colonel Leadbetter's private henchman was also walking with the officers.

"Well, well, as I live and fucking breathe I see you're still leaching a good living off your damn government's expense, mister. Stand at attention before I take a giant shit on your damn puss trooper!" Colonel Leadbetter went off on his favorite target, the Mutt.

The Mutt, (Lieutenant Frank Hall) did not flinch an inch as he stared straight ahead.

"I see you're still suffering from a serious case of fucking brain damage, stupid. I just ordered you to tighten up your damn formation, mister. And that's exactly what you'll do, or I'll shit fuck you to death, buster. Where the fuck is your dignity at, puke? You're a damn Marine, so start looking like one for once in your wasted life, asshole."

"Colonel Leadbetter Sir, we lost our dignity somewhere between Vietnam and Presidential blow jobs, sir." The Mutt flashed one of his well known smiles at the fuming Colonel.

Colonel Leadbetter fought off a smile as he turned his head until he saw Captain Walker and snapped at him. "Walker your fucking idiot here is getting a little smarter I see, mister."

"No offense Colonel Leadbetter Sir but that one was pretty cool sir." Walker replied.

Colonel Leadbetter turned his attention back to the Mutt and snarled at him. "Whatsumatter mister? Were you dropped on you damn head when you were younger, buster?"

"Yes sir I sure was Colonel Leadbetter Sir. But up until now, everyone was polite enough not to mention it to me, Colonel. I'm kinda a little sensitive about that subject and I don't like to be reminded bout it, Colonel." The Mutt fired back as he allowed a grin to cross his lips.

"I give up on you you're going to be a damn disgrace to my beloved Marine Corps until I finally find a way to get rid of your ass, mister. And don't sir me mister, you don't know who the fuck you're dealing with around here, buster. You see people this man standing before you here is why I don't have any children of my own. He's the perfect excuse for why tigers eat their damn young." The Colonel growled as he walked away from the Mutt and returned to the group.

The Marine Colonel walked right past Ice, but he hesitated just long enough to give her a slight smile, and also acknowledge her presence in formation of troops. Ice picked up the smile and she let out her breath in a rush and allowed her shoulders to sag a bit. She knew she passed Walker's eye, but she was holding her breath for fear Colonel Leadbetter was going to dump her from the outfit. Seeing the smile and slighter nod, she knew he just gave her the welcome home signal.

The Colonel walked until he was standing in front of the formation of soldier again, and then he bellowed at the troops. "Okay, you people passed the first test of this new training program crap. You all made it back to my beloved Marine base without getting your fool asses lost for your efforts, or arrested. You're dismissed and you people know where your damn barracks are stationed on the base. Heaven knows you asses were here enough fucking times to know it by now. Get over to your barracks, and settled in. Tuesday's a full day work, so be prepared to sweat your asses off some. You'll have liberty while on base every night, unless you fuck up on my training program, and I pull your damn liberty from you dumb Squids. Captain Walker, Sergeant Ramirez, and Sergeant Morrison, report to my office before you head for your barracks. That's all people.

Tomorrow, I'll start my killing of you pack of so called fucking elite soldiers."

Colonel Leadbetter said no more as he turned on his heels, and then he stormed into his office and private living quarters. He was followed closely by Colonel Joseph Salsiccia, Major Wilson and Sergeant Kirkpatrick, and the three soldiers he demanded report to him.

The group of soldiers instantly broke ranks and then most of them headed for their barracks. Walker, Ramirez and Morrison walked up to the Colonel's office, and Walker pounded on the door like he was angry at it.

"Take it easy on my fucking door out there, dammit! You asses better get in here before I have you shot for no other reason than my wanting to have you people shot. Get in here, dammit!" Colonel Leadbetter snarled from his chair. The moment he finished screaming at the soldiers, he sat back in his chair and then waited. Then he locked his hands behind his head, and stared at the three young and dangerous soldiers. Suddenly, he leaned forward and brought his hands down and rested his elbows on his desk and laced his fingers together as he studied the three soldiers.

"Well, as I live and fucking breath, you a damn Captain in this man's Marines. Christ sake and miracles, Heaven knows why the hell anyone chose to lift you up to the rank of Captain. Jesus, Mary and Joseph, when the hell are you going to start to look like a fucking Officer anyway, mister? Look at you, your fucking uniform's a mess and your damn hair's too long. If your hair gets any longer buster, I'm going to have the damn Docs do some surgery on your ass, and give you a pair of tits to go along with that damn long hair of yours, mister. How many times do I have to tell you about your damn hair anyway, before you cut it like a true Marine...?"

"Hey look Colonel I'm certain you didn't call me in here to bullshit about my stinking hair on me, sir. What's up Colonel? Why the hell was we pulled back to Lejeune, and don't give me any of that bullshit we're here for some special kinda damn training crap either, Colonel." Walker sharpened his hard look at the other military officer.

"You know Walker, one of these days we're going to really go at it, mister. You still don't know how the fuck to address a Commanding Officer do you buster? Arrr... shit, I guess I should level with you at that, Captain. Walker, you know the damn trial of that Iraqi terrorist is scheduled to begin in Washington in the next few days. Well, it seems the President has a wild hair up his ass, and he thinks someone is going to try and do something at the trial to disrupt it on us. He voiced his concerns to General White, and the Chairman came up with the idea of getting you people near Washington. In case something is tried against either the Judge, or the damn terrorist. So the General came up with the thought of running you guys through a sort of a more or less refresher course, to have you people hanging around the area, just in case. Do you have a problem with your fucking orders now, mister?" the Colonel glared at Walker.

Walker allowed himself to relax a bit and then he replied to his commanding officer with a snap in his tone of voice. "That seems like a pretty legit reason to break up our fucking leave time to me, Colonel. Most of us were kinda concerned this damn training bullshit was a stinking ploy to get us back to the base, and once here, we were gonna get stuck going out on another stinking mission, sir. As long as we're gonna stay here in the States, I see no problem sir."

"Well ain't that too fucking bad what you see mister? Let me tell you something, Mr. Walker. Even if you were pulled in to be sent out on another damn mission, that's what your fucking war wacky bastards would do. This damn thing is no democracy. Your pack of son of a bunch of bastards are in the service of your country and President. If he decided to send you people to bum fuck Egypt then that's where you'll go, without any gripes mind you." The Colonel growled.

Walker put the fuck you look on his face and did not reply to the Colonel's angry words.

"I thought so buster, now we have that shit straightened out for us Captain, once your troops are settled in, we'll go over some of the new training ideas for your troops, sir. It starts as of tomorrow morning, so tonight you have for your fucking selves, so burn off some of that energy tonight. This training program will include urban tactics and ideas. Your troops will be taught how to deploy in the streets of any fricking city in the United States or elsewhere, sir.

"You people will learn how to track down any would be fricking terrorists, and how to work with the local police and FBI Hostage Rescue Units. If a hostage situation arises on them peacekeepers, and they need our help in the damn operation. If and when your help is requested, by the time you finish with this new training crap, you and your troops will be put in command of any situation you're called out on sir. Your people will further be taught how to take suspected civilians as hostages, and how to interrogate them properly, to get any needed information that might assist us in finding other terrorist cells possibly operating in the United States.

"You'll also be taught how to intercept radio, cellular phone and computer communications and chatter.

Intelligence is the only proven way to stop a possible terrorist attack before we're hit again, and we'll gather all intelligence, even if we have to bug the President's fucking Office itself. To hell with any need for warrants to carry out our intelligence gathering efforts, it's time the damn bleeding hearts of this country realize. Give up some of their civil rights if they want us to stop the next terrorist attack against our country. You troops will further be taught how to stakeout suspected terrorist cells operating here in the United States or elsewhere in the world.

"You'll also have training courses on how to trail, observe, and collect evidence that'll prove a case against anyone you're tracking and arrest or take out, Walker. The best thing about this new training program is, if you people are set free in the streets of the United States, and you find yourselves involved in a life threatening situation, you'll be free to react with evil intent. Lethal force will be left entirely in your hands, and any damn bleeding hearts will be shut up by General White, who'll respond to any and all complaints leveled against your soldiers, Captain.

"We're not going to have happen to you people, what has happened to the police of this country. If you people are sent out to work in the streets of the United States, you'll be deployed under wartime circumstances. Your hands will not be tied behind your backs for any situation you people are sent out on. Make no mistake about it in the least Walker, when we're dealing with a group of terrorists discovered operating within the United States. You'll be operating under a wartime fucking situation sir. If we miss any terrorists, the civilians of our country are going to pick up the tab for your fricking mistakes, mister. Our President refuses to have another Twin Tower god damn situation happen anywhere within the States ever again.

"The next time we see any damn civilian bodies being pulled out from under destroyed buildings on the boob tube. It's going to be the damn terrorist attackers and not the civilians of our country who'll be dragged out from under the damn debris. I'm telling you Walker, under the present situations facing the American public, we'll be doing a number of military operations here in the States, and they'll be conducted like you people are working on any battlefield in the fucking world. To deal with this new bred of damn terrorists we'll have to react worst than they are doing. If they walk through shit then we'll follow them through it on our damn bellies.

"If the damn terrorists want to act like damn animals, then we'll react like wild fucking animals. If they want to act like nightmares to our civilians then we'll become their worst fucking nightmares hunting them down and killing the lot of them like the dogs they are. If the bastards cook and eat their young, we'll eat them raw dammit. To deal with these fricking animals we have to act like worse fricking animals ourselves, plain and fucking simple mister.

"We'll act accordingly against any possible threat or suspicious moves created by anyone we believe to be terrorists or insurgent groups wherever the hell they are operating form. Sure as hell, there'll be innocent people who might be caught up in our missions and they'll be classified as shit happens targets, but them are the breaks Captain. We have to change our mentality when dealing with these damn terrorists. Instead of believing allowing ten guilty to go free rather than do in one innocent jackrabbit, we have to operate under the impression if one innocent goes down for us to get ten guilty, C'est la Vie. We have to prove to the American public they're safe in their country in their beds, and if we're hit again by any lousy terrorist cells then not only are they going to pay for their fucking crimes. But any nation these fucking terrorists are believed to be operating from is also going to feel the full fucking brunt of our military response, sir.

"We're no longer going to find ourselves pussy footing around with these damn pain in the ass terrorists, or any bleeding hearts who want to try and protect these scumbags at the cost of further American lives. Let me explain how counterterrorism works, Captain. To be a counterterrorist means the counterterrorist has to be worse than the damn terrorists in any actions. They break a few heads then we have to crush a lot of heads. If they break an arm, we bust up their whole damn body. If they destroy a fucking building here in the States, we destroy a whole fucking country on the lousy bastards. That's how counterterrorism truly works. Do you have a problem with your orders so far?" the Colonel snapped as he eyed Walker while waiting his reply.

"Colonel Leadbetter Sir, you said what us damn ground pounders have been bellyaching about all along, sir. Kill them before they kill any of us. We have to make the damn terrorists fear the shit out of our military response, if we wanna cut off any future terrorist attacks leveled against our country, sir. Even if it doesn't stop the damn terrorists in their tracks, it'll surely make any backasswards country backing, or giving these pieces of shit a safe haven to operate from, the fear of God if the terrorists hit us their stinking country is gonna be fricking history, sir."

"Ahhh... spoken like the true killer you are Captain. I'm pleased to see we're working off the same damn sheet of music, Captain. I assume your words go for every swinging dicks and bouncing tits from your entire outfit, mister? That question doesn't need a reply from you mister, if I didn't believe you were speaking for your entire fucking Unit. None of you pukes would be on my base sir. You people would be sloshing your fricking way making a damn living in the United States, without any pay from your government. Err..." The Colonel suddenly turned to Sergeant Ramirez. He wanted her and Ice, because he wanted to speak to them both as well.

"Sergeant Ramirez, I wanted you here because I have a few questions to ask you, and I didn't want to ask them in front of the shit we call soldiers around here, sister. So I might as well start off on your ass at this time, Sergeant. I don't mind saying that you look pretty damn good after shitting out your kid, how the hell are you and the child doing anyway, Sergeant? I still can't believe that we now have another fucking Walker on the face of the earth, Heaven protect us all from that fear, Ramirez." The Colonel complained as he sort of smiled at his female Sergeant.

Ramirez smiled back at the Colonel as she replied to his bitch. "Colonel Leadbetter Sir, Robert Jr. is doing just fine sir, and I thank you for asking about him sir. He's growing like a weed, sir. I have a young woman living in our home, and she's taking great care of Robert Jr. while I'm ordered out on another mission, sir. I trust her completely with my child and our home sir..."

"Is that what you're calling your kid, Robert Jr.? Damn, Walker a Captain and supposed gentleman and an Officer and responsible for popping out a carbon copy of himself at your expense, Sergeant Ramirez." Colonel Leadbetter then smiled at Ramirez. Even though he was gripping about the kid, both Walker and Ramirez knew he was happy for them. Suddenly, the smile disappeared and he snapped at his female Sergeant. "All this shit about your kid is all fine, well and good, but I want to know how my damn soldier is doing after having the kid. You look good, are you at one hundred percent and combat capable? Sergeant, I'm not fooling around with you in the least here, if we're forced to go hot tomorrow. I need to know that you won't double over because your guts are still ripped up from having the kid. No one will deploy unless they're A number One to be in the field and defending our country's demands, Sergeant. I can ill afford to have one of my soldiers drop on me because he or she was not in top notch condition."

"Colonel Leadbetter, I can assure you sir in all certain terms that I'm as fit as I ever have been in all my life, sir. I think having a kid has even made me much stronger than I was before in my midsection, sir. Have a look for yourself Colonel so I can prove to you that I'm in A number one condition and fit for duty." With that said, she pulled the front of her blouse opened and showed the concerned Colonel her washboard stomach and a lot more. While she held her blouse opened, she began to flex her stomach muscles. She was right in her assumption of her present physical condition, but the rather surprised Marine Colonel was not looking at just her stomach.

Colonel Salsiccia was kind of daydreaming because he was not the least bit interested with the Colonel ripping into the soldiers, and he was tired from reporting to the base for the recent call up. He had his elbow resting on the Colonel's desk and his head was resting on his hand, and his face showed he was thoroughly bored to dead with the Colonel digging into his troopers. But when Sergeant Ramirez flashed the Colonel, his elbow slid off the desk and he almost fell out of his chair as his eyes opened, and he found himself staring at Ramirez's outstanding breasts.

Major Wilson was sitting behind the three other soldiers at another desk, but when he saw Ramirez open her blouse. He jumped out of his chair and nearly ran in front of the female soldier, so he could have a good look at what she was showing off to the grinning Colonel.

Colonel Leadbetter sat back and acted like he was stunned by Ramirez's sudden actions. He was enjoying looking at her as he grumbled hotly at her. "For the love of the good Christ Child Sergeant, will you please cover up them damn puppies of yours before we all get in some serious trouble around here, dammit! How many fucking time do I have to tell ya to keep those damn tits of yours locked up in your damn shirt, sister? Cover up will ya please."

"Colonel Leadbetter Sir, I'm not showing you my tits, sir. I'm showing you how good a shape my stomach is in, sir. I wanted to prove to you once and for all that I'm fit for active duty with the rest of the soldiers from my outfit, sir." For a second time she flexed her stomach muscles, while still holding her shirt opened so her breasts were out of her shirt as well.

"You might be trying to show me your damn stomach. But your tits are swinging in the damn breeze, cover them damn guns up will ya Sergeant." Colonel Leadbetter snapped at her again.

"Hey Colonel, this seems like it's not the first time you saw this Sergeant's tits. How many times has this soldier flashed ya, sir?" Colonel Salsiccia asked as he enjoyed the show she was giving everyone in the office, and then he put a frown on when she closed her blouse.

"Very fucking funny you damn Holy Roller you. I thought you'd go to hell in a damn handbag if you ever looked at another woman's breasts, mister? What the hell are you doing looking at this soldier anyway, mister?" The upset Colonel snapped at the other Colonel in his office.

"I might be a holy roller Colonel, but I'm far from being dead I can assure you of that much, Colonel Leadbetter Sir." Colonel Salsiccia said with a grin from ear to ear.

"Well, I'm damn glad you're dressed again Sergeant Ramirez. Seeing your, err... the shape you're in, I'm going to expect everything out of you that I'll get from the rest of these so called soldiers, Ramirez." Colonel Leadbetter warned the Sergeant.

"And you shall have it as well sir. I wouldn't have it any other way myself, Colonel Leadbetter She." She replied with one of her sweet smiles.

Colonel Bruce Leadbetter ignored Sergeant Ramirez's last comment as he turned his attention to the other female Sergeant standing in his office, the soldier branded Ice. She was scared to death the Colonel was going to drive her from the Unit. The moment the Colonel's eyes fell on her face Sergeant Diane Morrison immediately opened her shirt and flashed him. The Colonel noticed the terrible scar from where the bullet ripped into her body, and it was easy to see she was not at one hundred percent. Especially because she was showing him her wound and it was still red and very angry looking. He diverted his eyes and then snapped at his injured female Sergeant. "What the fuck are you doing? I don't need to see your fucking wound, Sergeant."

Again, Colonel Salsiccia's eyes flew opened as he stared at Ice's fantastic breasts. He also saw the nasty wound and felt terrible for the pretty young female soldier.

"Colonel Leadbetter Sir, I'm not showing you my scar. I'm showing you my tits so you won't dump me from the Unit, sir." She said as she held the two ends of her shirt opened.

"Man Ice, you got some nice tits there sister." Walker said as he enjoyed the view she offered.

"That'll be enough shit out of your ass, shithead. If I want anymore shit out of your ass, I'll squeeze your fucking head for it. Ice, will you put them damn things away, dammit. You women soldiers are going to send me right over the fucking falls, dammit." Colonel Leadbetter growled at the female soldier, and then he stared at Ice until she finally closed her shirt. Once she was dressed again, he spoke to her in a much more calm tone of voice this time.

"Sergeant Morrison, what the hell makes you believe for one fricking moment that I was going to drive you out of the fucking outfit, sister? Did that bullet fuck up your head on you or something, girl?" he grumbled at his female Sergeant again.

"Colonel Leadbetter Sir, you just warned Sergeant Ramirez that you didn't want anyone not at one hundred percent in the outfit, sir. I'm afraid I'm still not at my very best quite yet sir. The wound took quite a lot out of me, but the doctor's say I'll get back to my best in a little while, Colonel Sir." She reported as she lowered her eyes and looked to the floor at her feet.

"God dammit, now you're starting to piss me off, when the hell are you pain in the ass fools ever going to grow up for Christ sake? No one gets bounced out of this fricking outfit unless they're carried out feet first and tits up, or they're so old they can fart dust and pump rust. I'm not fucking done with your ass quite yet Sergeant. You're stuck with this damn unit until I tell you other fucking wise sister. Yes, I read you FitRep (Fitness Report) Sergeant Morrison, and I know damn well that you're operating at about seventy percent at the best. But you're still part of this fucking outfit, and if the troops are ordered to report, you'll report as well soldier.

"So I won't send you out in the field until you're at one hundred percent and fit for active duty Sergeant, but like I did with Sergeant Ramirez for this last operation our outfit was involved in. I'll use you in any manner I can use you, until you're fit for duty again. No one pulls any damn slack time in my fricking Unit. I have many other duties you can pull for me, until you're good enough to go hot and full balls ahead. So shut the fuck up and stand at attention, Sergeant."

Sergeant Morrison noticeably relaxed as she let out her breath and smiled at the Colonel.

"Okay, I think I'm about done with you three pukes. Get the fuck out of my sight and you women soldiers, keep them damn tits inside your damn shirts, or I'll cut the damn things off on you girls. If I see any more of them things sticking out I'm going to pour sugar on them, and then I'll stake you bitches out on a fucking ant hill for a coupla hours. Get out of my damn office!" Colonel Leadbetter suddenly roared at the three soldiers as they quickly left his office.

Before Walker turned to leave the Colonel's office he smirked at the other officer. "Colonel Leadbetter Sir, it's a good thing the girls didn't get any special treatment from you for sticking their damn tits out like they did, sir. If they did then I woulda flashed my tits at you also, sir."

"Let me tell you something Mr. Walker. If you keep trying to be a wiseass around here, I'll have your ass drawn and quartered pal. You heard my orders, get the fuck out of my office."

Walker snapped off a sharp salute at his commanding officer, and then he turned on his heels and followed the two young women fighters out of the Colonel's office. As soon as the three soldiers were out, the three officers began laughing over what they had just witnessed from the three specialized soldiers.

"Jesus H. Christ Bruce, I didn't know you hold private little strip shows in your office, sir. I have to start hanging around this office a little more often I see. Man, did you see the tits on the soldier you called Ice, sir?" Colonel Salsiccia grumbled as he laughed again.

"Yeah, and I saw the fucking scar from the bullet that ripped into her body also, Colonel Salsiccia Sir." Major Wilson added as he stopped laughing and shook his head sadly.

"Dammit to hell Major, I thought Joe was the only Holy Roller I had hanging around here. Why the hell would you look at that, when you had a perfect pair of perky tits sticking in your damn face, Major?" Colonel Leadbetter said as he continued to laugh with Colonel Salsiccia.

"Because I didn't think I was here to see our female soldiers standing in front of us with their damn breasts sticking out like that, sir. I was under the impressions we were going to offer these elite soldiers some new training skills, sir." The Major replied to Leadbetter.

"Well my friend, I have some bad news for your sagging ass then, hanging around this lot of war wacky soldiers, sir. I suggest you get a little used to this kind of shit going down in front of you, sir. They're a wild bunch of lunatics who'll do anything in their power to try and get a fucking raise out of our asses. But I'll add this in their defense though these soldiers are the best fighters we have to throw up against anything our fricking enemies throw at us, sir."

Walker and the two female warriors rushed back to their barracks. He wanted to see what the other soldiers were up to. The three troopers entered the barracks and saw the soldiers hanging around and he snapped at them. "What the hell is this shit all about, dammit? You people were ordered to get settled in, not stand around like a bunch of wash women hanging around a water well bullshitting. We got some damn work to do. I just found out what this call up was about."

Instantly, the elite group of soldiers linked to the Special Forces Unit quickly gathered around Walker, and then they waited for him to tell them what it was about. The Captain had a second barracks with a hundred and fifty four other specialized troops in it he had to inform why they were ordered to report to Lejeune. He decided he would do that a little later on. He looked at the soldiers from this barracks and told them what Colonel Leadbetter had informed him about the new training program, and General White wanted them around just in case something went sour with the terrorist trial up in Washington. Walker's words relaxed the soldiers, and now they understood they were not going to be shipped out on another mission, so the elite soldiers went in much better moods. Pot joints began to make the round through the ranks, and one soldier put the radio on. Soon showers started, and male and female soldiers took showers to try and relax.

Sergeant Ramirez wrapped her arms around Walker's neck, and she kissed him and asked in an excited voice. "Hey Bobby, are we still going to get married when we return to our Island?"

"You bet your lovely little ass on it, girl. Why? Are you getting cold feet or sumthin on me, sister? I'm not gonna allow you to back out on me now, not afta you had just agreed to marry my ass, baby." Walker warned his future wife, as he looked deeply in her lovely eyes.

"Not on your life Robert. You asked me to marry you, and I happily accepted. If you think for one second I'll allow you to back out of it now, you have another think coming to you, love." Again, she wrapped her arms around his neck, and she pulled his head towards her. This time she pulled his head to her breasts and wiggled her chest right in his face.

He slid his tongue out and licked the side of her breast, causing her to pull his head away from her body and cry. "Gees Bobby, you're getting disgusting when you want to be a real pain in the ass lately you know mister." She slid her hand in her blouse and wiped the side of her breast.

The Mutt moved over to Walker's side, and he watched as Walker lick Ramirez's breast. When he was free he asked him. "Hey partner, what the hell are we gonna do tonight, man? I'm still all revved up and I wanna do something real wild like tonight, man."

Ramirez looked at him as Walker complained. "I'll tell ya what we're gonna do. We're gonna hit Bare Parts and have one helluva last night of it. Even though the stinking Colonel said we'll have liberty while stuck on the base every night. I think the fuck's gonna pull a lot of night duty shit on us, and we won't be able to get out every night, so we'll make the best of tonight."

The soldiers in the barracks let out a roar of approval of Walker's words.

"It looks like the rest of this mess agrees with you, Walker." The Mutt added with a grin.

"Yeah, but everyone betta be all squared the fuck away, before anyone leaves this damn base on liberty tonight. I'm gonna run a quick barracks inspection, and anyone who doesn't pass the damn muster is gonna pull extra duty for the night. If we all wait to get squared away and old whatisface comes in here and pulls a stinking barracks inspection on us, if one of us fails none of us are gonna get the hell outta here tonight." Walker not only warned the Mutt, he said his words loud enough for the rest of the soldiers to hear his warning. In a flash, every soldier went about stowing their belonging in footlockers, and hanging up civilian and military uniforms. Within an hour there was nothing that should not have been hanging around the barracks loose, seen.

Walker was sitting on his bunk, his legs crossed under him and he was speaking to Ramirez, Ice, the Mutt, Baby Tee, and where Baby Tee was, Buckethead was. He liked the small woman and was trying everything in his power to make her notice him. He was always near, helping her on any obstacle courses, and kept a close eye on her when they were on a mission. Everyone from the group knew he liked Baby Tee, and they were waiting for her to give him a tumble.

As Walker watched his troops quickly square away the barracks, he mumbled at Ramirez. "Who the hell ever said these troops are a bunch of flaming assholes? All you gotta do is threaten to hold back liberty on them, and they'll accomplish anything you put before them..."

"That's real good to know mister." A voice growled from behind Walker.

Walker spun around and saw a grinning Colonel Leadbetter and he immediately complained at his commanding officer. "Jesus H. Christ Almighty Colonel Leadbetter Sir, why the fuck don't you hang a stinking bell around your damn neck for us. That way you won't be able to sneak up on my ass and hear something you're not supposed to hear, sir."

"First off buster, I'll always be able to sneak up on your damn ass, even if I was singing a damn tune coming at ya ass. Why you may ask me, and I'll answer you, because I'm that fucking good buster. Besides Captain, how the hell am I going to get anything on you poor excuse for soldiers, that'll work on you people? I need all the damn inside ammunition I can possible get on this pack of lunatics." Colonel Leadbetter laughed at the angry young Captain.

"Look Colonel Leadbetter, I'm kinda busy here as you can see for yourself sir. So if you have something I need to know bout, how bout you spit it out so I can get back to what I have to take care of for myself, sir." Walker snarled hotly at the Commandant. He was that angry the Colonel just invaded their barracks so soon after they showed up back on base.

Colonel Leadbetter's eyes instantly narrowed and clouded over with anger as he glared hotly at the Captain. His shoulders hunched up and he leaned slightly forward, taking the warning stance of a linebacker about to charge the quarterback. Then he growled at Walker. "Mister, if you keep probing my fricking ass like this, you're going to drive me out of my mother fucking tree. And let me warn you buster. If you're able to get me out of my tree, I'm going to rip the fricking thing out of the damn ground and beat you to death, using the damn roots and all. You better watch the way you speak to my ass mister. I know you believe you're God's gift to the Marine Corps.

"But I'll beat you to death with your own body if you don't start respecting my ass, along with the rest of the Officers on this fucking base, mister. In case you're wondering about it mister, I have a reason for being in your barracks, even though I'm not very thrilled to be in here, Captain. I know I take my life in my hands every time I walk into this mess with you walking nightmares. I wanted to tell you pack of clowns the classrooms won't be ready for use tomorrow morning. So it looks like you people will be pulling another day off, before the work finally starts here. I want you to find a constructive way to keep your troops occupied tomorrow, mister. Run some minor workouts for this pack of flaming asses, and make them sweat a little while you're at it, Walker.

"But you can choose to give the soldiers the day off, but I'll make them pay for it the next day, if you do..." The Colonel saw the dumb look on Walker's face, and snapped. "Oh please, spare me the astonished look, stupid. Walker, I expect you to stand there and look stupid and nothing else, mister. Just make damn certain your troops are doing something worthwhile tomorrow. I warn you Captain, if I see any of these screaming squirrels of yours hanging around base doing nothing, or if they're looking for trouble. I'll find them something to do easy enough. I assure you they won't like what I'll have them doing in the least. Carry on with your orders, butt wipe."

Walker remained bunched up until the Colonel and Kirkpatrick was out of his barracks. The soldiers witnessed the confrontation, and once the officer was gone they surrounded Walker.

"Hey Walker that fricking dude is stuck on stupid and stupid on stuck." Neck complained.

"Yeah man, I'd buy him a parachute if I though it wouldn't open." Buckethead added.

"I didn't see anything wrong with the lousy dude. He was only telling us we had an off duty day tomorrow, what the hell's wrong with that?" Wacko asked Walker as he smiled at him.

"What the fuck's wrong with you, asshole? Do you have both your contacts in the same stinking eye again? Even Helen Keller could have seen the Colonel was looking for trouble, stupid. Since when are you sticking up for the lousy prick anyway, buddy?" Walker growled.

"Say Walker let's look at the bright side of this mess. Right now, we're done with anything we hadta do on the base, man. So we can dump the hell outta here right now, and have some fun for a change. And to give it a better kick in the ass while I'm at it, we got tomorrow off. That means we can get really fucked up tonight, and we'll have tomorrow off to lick our wounds, or anything else we wanna lick here." Neck mumbled as he cast a quick glance at Ice standing near him.

"Hey big man, was that slug aimed at my ass, buster?" the pretty young woman asked.

"You got it you wanna take me up on my offer?" Neck asked Ice smiling at him.

"Okay Neck, you got me, I give up you win. You see, your persistence made me overlook your shallowness, big boy. When we get back to the barracks, I'm going to see if you're as good at making love as you believe you are, mister." Ice sexily wiggled her hips slightly at the big man after she placed her hands on them, and then she gave Neck a smile that made the other males, and even some female soldiers in the barracks raise their eyebrows at her.

"Hey Neck, now you gone and done it, once you make love to that pretty little Tiger, she's gonna know you suck at it and you'll never get another chance with her between the sheets, man. I told you to leave them guessing about ya ass. Sometimes it's betta to let them think you're a fool, rather than opening your mouth and proving you're a fucking asshole between the sheets." Mother Flanagan fired off at Neck, he too had his eyes on Ice, but he was never as forward as Neck was about his feelings towards her. Besides, he was also looking at Baby Tee for a partner.

"Hey Homes, I'm so damn good at making love that I call my own name out when I'm doing the down and dirty with a stinking chick. I ain't got nuthin to worry about. Once I make love to her purdy little ass, she'll never go looking for it anywhere else but from me." Neck bragged proudly to the specialized soldiers in the barracks.

"Look at the big dumb sod will ya, he actually believes his damn line of bullshit guys, and they were spoken by a man who is too stupid to scratch his own fleas. I'm telling you girlfriend. You might want to reconsider parting your legs for this ugly guy here. Look at the size of his ass, he's so big he'll squash you under his weight, and his dick, take it from me little sister. I saw the damn thing once, and that was more than enough to last me a lifetime, he'll ruin you bad girl. It's as thick as two normal dicks, and maybe a foot long, girl." Baby Tee said, getting on the big man as she moved next to the Neck, and she actually bumped hips with him.

Neck smiled at Ice, he knew Baby Tee was just dumping on him, but he would never get angry with Ice because she was still suffering so much pain from the wound she received in their last operation. Besides he really liked her also, so he just smiled as Ice continued to get on him.

"That's why I want to try him on for a little size, ladies. I saw his pin too in the past, girlfriend and I think I can handle him. Nevertheless I'm going to give him a tumble. I'm game for the big guy, especially since I'm going to be part of the unit, even though I hurt. I'll do anything in my power to stay in the Unit, ladies." Ice offered she was always up for a challenge anyway.

"Girl, if you go riding on his pin too then you'll never be satisfied again unless a normal man used his foot to make love to you next time, sister." Baby Tee added, warning Ice as she grabbed Neck through his pants and then she gave his member a little squeeze.

"Look at him will you please hey Baby, you got the big slug panting like a damn goat in heat, girl You keep screwing round with him like you're doing girl, and he's gonna make you take care of him where you're standing, little sister." Buckethead called out the warning to her as he smiled at the smallish and pretty female soldier.

"Hey what say we stay in the barracks and have us a party? We can party here and that way we don't gotta go out and get in any trouble out in the world. It's been a fricking while since the last party we had us with the chicks from the outfit." One male soldier called out in a booming voice.

"On no you don't buddy, I didn't come back to this base just to have a party in the barracks with you bunch of pigs. We girls want to go out and have some fun first, guys. Then when we get back to the barracks after we're turned on and a little drunk, maybe then you slugs will end up with a little party later on tonight. If we want to oblige you dickhead's that is. But we girls want to go out first and have some fun for a change." Ramirez fired back at the grinning soldier.

"Hey girl, I can go along with that easy enuf I guess. I don't mind tenderizing my meat a little before I nibble on it, baby girl." Neck replied as he slid his huge paw under Ice's blouse, and he started to play with her breasts. He was being very careful not to go anywhere near the injured breast on the left side of her body.

"Man, that big jerk is stupider than I thought he was. What do you expect from a jerk who still wonders where his lap goes when he stands up? If he keeps talking like that then the only thing he might be using his log on is his hand for the night. That jerk better learn how to speak to us girls if he wants any of us to take care of him when we get back to the barracks tonight, and we might be turned on and a little high. He's so stupid with the words he keeps aiming at us we get angry at the big sod." Blind Date offered as she got in on the conversation with the others.

"Don't worry bout the stinking Neck, he's from the Planet Stupider. Hey people, let's back up the party train for a second here. Lemme get this right boys and girls, if we guys show you chicks a good time tonight at the stinking gin mill. We're gonna party hardy when we get back to the damn barracks and all you girls are gonna get involved with the party for us right? Am I right in my way of thinking around here, ladies? Did I just hear you girls right, and we're gonna have some real fun and games when we get back from the bar, ladies?" Walker called out as he raised his hands in an attempt to shut everyone up so he could hear the girl's answer. He stared at his girlfriend as he waited for her reply. Walker knew Ramirez spoke for the rest of the female soldiers from the outfit, and if she said they were going to party then there was going to be a party one way or the other. No female soldiers would ever disagree with her on any subject.

The female soldiers to the last nodded yes to Walker's question. But he kept staring at Raz, and only when she finally joined the other girls and nodded yes, did he smiled and announced. "In that case you girls you got a stinking deal. I can sure use a party it's been one helluva long time since we last rocked a stinking barracks with you girls.

First we're gonna show you chicks a damn good time at the bar tonight and then let the games begin in earnest." Walker added and glanced at Ramirez and noticed her nodding yes and he smiled.

The three Russian female soldiers were standing together a little away from the rest of the other soldiers in the barracks by one of the bunks. Siberia, the Russian group spokes person, stepped up to the mixed group of soldiers and she looked right at Walker. The look instantly informed him that she wanted to say something to him.

He gave her a quick smile and a slight nod as he looked back at the Russian babe. Since their last operation in Libya branded 'Operation Bio Level Three'. The new Captain completely trusted the three Russian babes as he asked her with a sort of snap in his voice. "What the fuck's up your purdy little ass now, Siberia? If you got a gripe, now is the time to air it."

"I want ask big dumb American soldier leader if Russian soldier involve in this party time you call for tonight, Captain. We want make sure we part group of what you call America and soldier from world, and as such we entitled take part in some fun rest America and other soldier do all time here, Mista." Siberia asked more than said as she stared in his eyes, hoping the three female Russian troopers were part of the elite soldiers.

"It's up to you three girls if you wanna be part of this party time tonight, if you guys want in all you gotta do is strip down and then just join in on the fun and games. No one has to be invited into the party, all you gotta do is show up, strip down and jump on someone's stinking body." Walker offered to the pretty Russian female Sergeant with a grin plastered on his face.

"Yes big shot American soldier Captain you. We want join fun in barracks right okay with other soldier from Unit please. But first I want make certain we Russian soldier invite join fun with other soldier from you Unit, mista? We want and demand to be part of Unit full time, and join in everything Unit soldier do, no matter what do, fight or have fun we are there. We want to be part of Unit of soldier like all rest are and be true by rest of soldier from Unit, Captain." Siberia snapped at the new Captain as she waited for him to respond.

"In case you didn't realize it as yet, the way you stinking Russian babes handled yourselves in Libya on that last shit filled stinking operation that was a real pain in the stinking ass, made you Russian chicks part of this outfit for life, sister. Some of us even owe our damn lives to you three foreign chicks. So whatever we do from this day forward, we do as a complete Unit, and you three hens are part of it and are included in the action any time it goes down on us, Siberia. You don't hafta wait to be invited, all you gotta do is just jump in and do whatever the hell the other troops are doing, no matter what it might be, sister. Just because we didn't single you Russian birds out to invite you to partake in all the fun and games we plan for tonight, doesn't mean you chicks weren't included to be part of the fun and games that's gonna take place later tonight. So welcome to the stinking Zoo, girls. I hope you three Gorkies know what the hell you're asking for here?" Walker complained at the pretty female Russian soldier.

CHAPTER EIGHTEEN

THE BAR BARE PARTS IN
JACKSONVILLE NORTH CAROLINA
MONDAY, APRIL 15th, 2002.

The Iraqi Colonel Hamoodi al-Qaysi walked into the topless bar like he owned it and was angry at the world, and he was followed closely by Major Serena al-Shaya, Lieutenant Malika Nobel Elmasry, and Sergeant Shurug Khalaifa. The two young and very pretty Arab women were dressed to kill, their blouses and short dresses showed off all their assets to anyone who wanted to view them in the bar. The strip joint was really hoping with four women on the stage dancing completely naked to the extremely loud music. The girls were listening to all the cat calls from the men surrounding the stage and them. The bar was filled from wall to wall with a horde of good looking young soldiers in fantastic shape from Camp Lejeune, and the troopers were hitting on every woman hanging around the bar, whether they were with men or not.

The four Arab soon to be terrorists, headed for their usual table in a corner of the overcrowded bar, but it was already taken by some soldiers from the base. So they were forced to walk around the bar until they finally found an empty table. Major al-Shaya jumped as an obviously drunk soldier actually slid his hand up her dress and grabbed her rearend. Even though she was insulted by the suddenness of the soldier's hand, she was turned on the man wanted to touch her like that.

A second soldier actually bumped into Sergeant Khalaifa's breasts, and by the way he bumped into her, she knew it was definitely on purpose, and she merely smiled at the soldier as he quickly disappeared into the maddening crowd. When the four Arab terrorists were seated, one soldier they made friends with when they were in the bar yesterday, walked over to the group. He sat in the only empty chair at the table, and then he started to talk to Colonel al-Qaysi as if he knew him for many years. As the American soldier spoke, he kept looking down the front of Major al-Shaya's blouse, and she was making it awful easy for him to see all of her he wanted to see.

The American was Sergeant Jerome Rosenberger, and his Unit name was Short Cut. He started his conversation off with the Arab man as soon as he sat down at the table. "Hey Bill, how the hell you doing tonight, man? This stinking place is really fucking jumping tonight man."

Colonel al-Qaysi, who introduced himself as Bill to the American soldier they met in the bar the other night, nodded at the trooper. In his mind, he was going over the other American names he gave the others of his group. Al-Shaya's was Helen, and Khalaifa's was Joan, and Elmasry's was Mark. He smiled and replied to the American. "Yes Jerome, the bar is truly active tonight I see. This is the most soldiers I saw in here since I first started to come here. I wonder why it's so busy tonight. This is not a weekend, but I don't mind the new people coming in the bar, friend."

Short Cut did not reply, he was too busy looking at the two pretty young women seated at the table, when his attention was drawn to his buddies he introduced Colonel al-Qaysi to when they met four days before. Short Cut had to stand and wave at the two other soldiers until they finally noticed him, and then they headed for their table. Each soldier grabbed an empty chair and they carried them over to the crowded table. Shot Gun, (Sergeant Dennis Sassano), and Nails, (Sergeant John LaRusso), slid their chairs to the table and sat. When they were seated they nodded at the Arabs and Shot Gun spoke. "Man, its fucking really nuts in this stinking dump tonight. What's everyone drinking? I'm buying the first rounds tonight. I feel great guys."

After the soldiers ordered their drinks, they engaged in some small talk and watched the strippers doing their act on stage. It was so noise in the bar that one was barely able to hear himself think, and breathing in the place was getting to be a real problem as well. The bar was filled with a thick cloud of heavy cigarette smoke and odor of stale booze, and when anyone opened the door to one of the bathrooms, a powerful stink assaulted everyone in the bar.

The question the Iraqi Colonel al-Qaysi asked Short Cut was forgotten. The Colonel shivered when he tasted his harsh drink, it was stronger than usual. The two Arab girls were starting to really get tuned in with the music, and they were swinging their hips while sitting in the chairs, and moving their shoulders to the rhythm of the music. Every time the women moved, they exposed another part of their exquisite bodies to the soldier's gaze. This was exactly what al-Qaysi had them with him for. Their actions were keeping the American's attention glued to them and their bodies, and they were talking to the Iraqi men without looking at them.

It was early in the evening, but Colonel al-Qaysi wanted to get to the bar so he could be there before his targets finally arrived. He was actually dying too met face to face with the soldier who was called Road Kill, Captain Robert Walker. He wanted to see his face before he killed him for his crime of leading his cursed troops invading his country, and taking Colonel al-Adwani their prisoner. He also wanted to speak to this young American soldier, because he was dying to know what kind of man he truly was, he knew what kind of soldier he was already. He wanted to know so much about the one man, before he killed him.

CAMP LEJEUNE, JACKSONVILLE NORTH CAROLINA

Captain Robert Walker was pushing his troops hard to finish up what they were doing, so they could get out of the barracks and hit the bar for the night. He was looking forward to returning to the barracks so they could have one of their infamous party nights. That was where the women took care of the men. It was a free for all of sex, with some of the girls taking care of two and three men at the same time.

It relaxed the soldiers and brought them ever closer with each other.

The Mutt was hanging around Walker all night, watching the troops moving like they were running while carrying a piano on their backs. He finally griped at Walker after watching the soldiers for a while. "Hey man, will you look how slow our people are fucking moving, man. It seems like none of them wanna go out for some fun tonight, Homes. You want I should yell at the asses, you know, sorta get a fire going under their asses for a stinking change, Walker?"

The Captain looked at his watch and realized why the soldiers were moving so slow, it was only seven thirty p.m. He knew the troops did not usually hit the bar until around nine that way most of the soldiers at the bar would be plenty drunk. And the girls in the bar would be feeling pretty mellow from the booze they drank to put up with his wild bunch of crazies when they entered the bar. He smiled as he turned to the Mutt and said. "Don't you see what they're up to man? It's too stinking early to head for the bar. All the amateurs are still in the fricking place soaking up the suds and prying the chicks with drinks, so they end up as easy marks for our asses. These smart asses are giving the bar time to thin out before we attack the place in force, man."

"Got ya man, I knew it hadta be something that was making the asses stall like there doing tonight man. I was planning to hit the stinking bar early myself then get the girls good and drunk and then get them back here to the barracks so we can party out with them tonight, Walker." The Mutt replied to Walker's words as he grinned at the new Captain.

"Man, you got some real devious stinking mind on your shoulders, friend." Walker grumbled.

"I don't care what you may call me, so long as we party out with the girls tonight, man." The Mutt replied to Walker's bitch as he kept his eyes on the slow moving troops.

Sergeant Ramirez walked up to her lover and soldier and gave him a tweak on his rearend. He turned and then smiled at her as she said. "What's up baby? You look so concerned Bobby."

"Arrrr... it's the guys moving like they have a load of shit in their damn draws. The stinking Mutt wants to get everyone over to the bar early, so we can get you girls good and drunk so we can take advantage of ya later on tonight, baby." Walker smiled at Ramirez a second time.

Ramirez looked at the Mutt and then snapped at him. "It figures, this man has no class about him lately, Robert. He thinks every woman on the earth is here so he could have sex with them. You never stop amazing me dog man. You're so shallow I could walk on your body and not get my feet wet. When are you going to start respecting someone in your wasted life, mister?"

"And your point being what, Raz?" the Mutt asked her with a grin stuck on his face.

"I don't know why the devil I try and talk with you. The more I talk to you, the dumber you get on me, mister. You're really hopeless Mutt. Walker, I checked a little while ago, and it seems everyone from our Unit has arrived on base as ordered. From what I was told, no one was missing from our group, and this made the stinking Colonel get in a pretty good mood for a damn change. Have you see Ice hanging around anywhere in the barracks lately? I haven't seen her for quite a while, and I wanted to check on her again. I'm getting a little worried about her."

"Yeah, I saw her heading for the stinking showers bout half an hour ago, lady. She looked like she was doing just fine to me, Raz." The Mutt offered the female Sergeant.

"You mean she's been in the damn shower for a half hour, and you didn't think to check on her condition, stupid? Dammit Mutt, you have to start keeping your eyes open better than you're doing, if anything's wrong with her, I'm going to plant my foot up your can. I swear you're some damn shitty Officer to this Unit, mister." Ramirez growled at the dog man as she left him and Walker standing by the bunk, and she rushed for the showers in the barracks.

Walker looked at the Mutt and barked at him angrily. "If anything happened to her, I'm gonna skin your damn ass alive, man. Where the fuck's your brains at dog man?" he then took off and rushed after Ramirez and she got in the shower area first and she immediately started to look for Ice. The heavy steam was making it rather hard for her to see where she was going in the shower area, so she called out Ice's name as she moved forward.

"She's over here Sergeant, I was just coming out to get you Sergeant. I think something's wrong with the Ice lady, because she's down and not looking so good any longer, Sergeant." Three Martines, (Sergeant Cheryl Grantham) called out to Ramirez.

She headed for where she was sure the voice was coming from in the shower area. There she found Three Martines naked and resting on a knee while stoking Ice's wet hair. Ice was sitting flat on the tile floor, leaning up against the metal wall holding her injured arm with her other hand against her chest. Ramirez slid to a stop on the floor and dropped to her knees and looked at Ice. Walker and the

Mutt came in right behind Ramirez and watched her working with Ice.

"What's wrong baby? Are you okay honey?" Ramirez asked as she touched her head lightly.

"Oh it's my damn arm again Raz. It's hurting the hell out of me, but the Doctor's told me to expect a little trouble with my shoulder every now and then, and I guess he was right with his warning, Sergeant. Please don't tell Walker about this, or he'll push me out of the Unit if he knew I was still hurting like this, Sergeant. I don't want to be dropped from the outfit I'd die." Ice cried as she looked deeply into the eyes of Ramirez as she waited for her reply.

"I told you the only way you're gonna get out of this fucking outfit, is either tits up, or you're so old you can fart dust and pump rust. What the fuck's wrong with you soldier? Ramirez, get her off the damn floor. None of our people sit on the floor when they're hurting. Do you want me to call for a damn ambulance Raz?" Walker growled at the two women as he stared at Ice.

"I don't know yet Bobby. Give me a chance to check her out first, before we even think about calling for an ambulance. Where the hell is Blood Clot at, for Pete's sake? We need him in here! Somebody better get out there and find him and tell him I got a downed soldier in here, dammit."

"I'm on my way." The Mutt said and he was off and running for the Unit medic.

Walker got down on his knees and he look at Ice's face and shook his head sadly.

"I'm sorry for bothering you so much Captain Walker. All I wanted was to shower sir."

"C'mon and get down off the fucking cross, someone else needs the stinking wood. You're a fricking soldier, so get on your damn feet and lean against the damn wall. The Clot's on the way and you don't wanna let him see you sitting on the stinking floor like this, baby girl. He'll get pissed off at ya." He growled at the downed soldier, he was trying to spark in action.

"Walker, will you get off her ass for a minute and allow me check her out a little better. We don't know if it's a good idea for her to stand or not, Bobby. I don't know what the hell's wrong with her yet and until I do, she's not moving an damn inch, mister." She warned her lover.

"Then get the devil outta my way and let me get a look at her, girl." Blood Clot snapped at Ramirez as he came in the bathroom and went right over to the gathered soldiers. "Will someone turn off these damn shower heads so I can see what the fuck I'm doing in here, dammit."

Ramirez got out of Blood Clot's way and turned off the shower head Ice was using to wash. Walker slapped Three Martines on her bare ass and told her to go get dressed. But the fighter did not move an inch from Ice's side. She was more worried about Ice than being naked in front of the male soldiers. Three Martines remained where she was and this was because she was one of the first soldiers who got to Ice's side when she was wounded in Iraq a few months back.

Ramirez joined Three Martines standing with the other soldiers crammed into the shower area of the barracks. Everyone was worried about Ice's condition, and they wanted to be near her in case they were needed to help move her from the shower area.

"C'mon my favorite girlfriend and move your arms for me please, I gotta see what the hell's going on in there, girl. C'mon, I hafta move your hand so I can see your shoulder a little betta. If you think I'm gonna let anything happen to your pretty little ass after I worked so hard on you out in the field, you got another think coming to ya, honey." Blood Clot, carefully lifted Ice's good arm and slowly moved it out of the way. Once Ice's hand was moved, he moved her legs until her back was flat up against the wall, and her legs were flat out in front of her. When he was certain she was comfortable sitting on the floor, he started to look at her injured shoulder.

He did not like what he was seeing in the least. The area around the wound was angry red and hot, but he knew it was not infected. The medic tried to move her right arm and Ice almost jumped out of her skin, as she straightened her back against the wall and she drew in her breath and he grumbled at her. "Dammit, I'm sorry for hurting you like I just did sister, sit back and catch your breath some. Ice, did I ever tell ya you got the best set of tits I ever saw?"

"You did, don't you remember when I was wounded in Iraq when we went after that damn terrorist Colonel who was behind the assassination attempt against our President, and you started to work on me? You had to cut my shirt away and you told me I had the best tits you ever saw. If it wasn't for you I don't think I'd be here right now, thank you for looking after me like this, Richard." Ice smiled at the medic as she reached up and ran a finger along the side of his face.

"I'm sorry you can't blame me for not remembering, not with all the tits I've seen in my life, girl." Blood Clot replied as he began to examine her shoulder with his hands.

"You mean with all the tits you saw in your life, you still think I have the best, Blood Clot?" This time Ice winced from the pain the medic caused with his probing of her injured shoulder.

"Without a doubt little sister. If I had my way about it, I'd make a mold of them and hang them over my damn rack. What did the Doc's tell you to do and not do with your shoulder, baby?"

"As long as Walker doesn't get mad at me, I'll tell you what he said, Blood Clo..."

"I'll kick you right in that lovely little ass of yours if you don't knock this shit off and answer the medic's damn question, girl. What the fuck do you think he's doing here for crap sake, sister? Taking a damn shower with ya? He wants to help you with the damn pain and what's causing it, girl." Walker warned Ice angrily as he stared at her with concern etched in his eyes.

Ice looked at Walker and then she nodded and replied. "Richard, the Doc's told me not to work my arm too much, and not to lift anything heavy for a month or so. They said to try and stay away from any real cold or hot until I could stand it without feeling any pain. The Docs also wanted me to stay out of the Unit for up to six months. I knew if I was away from the Unit that long, I'd surely be replaced by the Colonel or Walker. I'd just die if I was forced out."

"You mean to tell me that you came back six months fucking early, just to stay with the damn Unit for fuck sake? Girl, even though you got yourself such great tits, you ain't got much in the way of fucking brains working fur your lovely little ass I see. How many damn times do you gotta be told no one is gonna bounce you outta the damn Unit for any stinking reason, sister?" Blood Clot snarled at Ice as he tried to figure out what was wrong with the female warrior.

"Look Ice, I want you to lean against the wall for a few minutes and collect your thoughts. Or at least until you think you can get up and move on your own without much pain bugging ya. I'm not gonna leave your side for a stinking second, so take all the time you need before you try it for me honey." Blood Clot said as he stood and flexed his legs.

Walker moved over to his side and leaned his head close to him and whispered. "What the fuck's wrong with her, blood sucker? Do I hafta call an ambulance for her or what, fucker?"

"I believe she's okay Walker, all she did was overheat the damn wound, and the hot water made it rather tender and hurting her. I wish to hell I knew she was ordered to stay the fuck away from us by the damn Doc's. The damn order shoulda been put in her jacket so we knew she was back too early. I'll tell you this much though Captain, she has to be placed on extra light duty for at least six months, or you could end up hurting her permanently, Homes." Blood Clot warned the concerned Captain, and turned his attention back to Ice and looked after her.

"That puts the icing on the fucking cake for my stinking ass, mister. I know I can't bounce her out of the damn Unit, or the rest of the fighters will eat my ass alive. But I'm gonna put her ass on clerical duty as long as it takes for her to be A number One chips for us. We'll see how she'll like shuffling papers around for a coupla months, Blood Clot. How long before you can get her up on her feet? I don't like her sitting on the damn floor like this, mister." Walker was talking to the medic as if he was angry at him for some reason he was so concerned for his downed soldier.

"I think it'll take her about ten to fifteen minutes before her body finally cools down enuf for her to be able to take the damn pain outta her shoulder so she can start moving around again on her own, Walker. I gotta keep my damn eyes on her though, I don't want her body to cool off too much to the point where she might catch a fricking chill and she gets sick on me, Captain. That would give her another serious problem she'd have to hack. Dammit, if only she woulda told me what the damn Doc's told her when they released her. I coulda stopped this shit before it happened to her, and I coulda saved her a helluva lotta stinking pain at the same time, man."

"Look Blood Clot, we're gonna hafta take it out of her hands, dammit. I want you to pull her stinking FitRep file, and see what the hell the damn Docs wrote out on her ass. Once you know everything, you keep your fucking eyes on her ass and if you catch her doing anything wrong, play with her damn tits. That's an order, mister. Did you hear me Ice? We're gonna find out what the hell you can't do, and if Blood Clot catches you fucking round, he'll play with your tits until he had enuf of them. How you doing anyway little sister?" Walker asked her in a calm tone.

"I know what I can and can't do Walker. I guess I was kind of pushing too hard, that's all, sir."

"That's why you're in this fucking outfit. If you don't push all the time then you're in the wrong place. If the mud ain't flying you ain't trying. You take it easy, and I'll... What?"

"Get out of my way Bobby I have a bathrobe for Ice. I don't want her catching cold sitting on the tile floor on us." Ramirez mumbled as she pushed her way past her lover.

Blood Clot took the robe and laid it over Ice's legs. He wanted the upper part of her body to cool off a little more, before he allowed her to get in the robe. Then he was going to get her on her feet and have her walk around the barracks on her own for a little while.

"Why the hell are you not covering her body with the robe?" Ramirez asked the medic.

"Because I want her to cool off a little more first, besides, I like looking at her tits Raz."

"Richard, you're going to make me blush talking about my tits like this you know, mister." Ice remarked as she winced from the pain still hitting her from her arm.

"Who the hell are you trying to shit around here, that'll be the day when you blush over anything, girl?" Blood Clot replied as he kept an eye on her condition. He knelt and lightly touched her skin and discovered it was getting good and cool to the touch.

Walker looked behind him and he noticed everyone from the barracks was now crammed in the shower area, and he barked at the other soldiers. "Okay you people saw all you're gonna fucking see here for the time being. Get back to whatever the hell you were doing before this shit happened. What the hell do I have a bunch of damn girls on my hands that hafta see what the fuck's going on here for crap sake? Move it people!" Walker warned his fellow soldiers.

The elite soldiers grumbled as they quickly filed out of the area. Most of the concerned soldiers did not want to leave until they were certain that Ice was going to be alright. But they also knew the Captain was right, and they had to get out of his way so they can work in the ice lady better.

Blood Clot checked Ice's skin again and it was a little cooler. He picked up her injured hand and moved her arm carefully. Ice wiggled a bit and winced which informed him she was still in some pain. But he could tell the pain was not nearly as bad as it was just moments before. He checked the wound area again, and most of the redness was gone and her skin was now a rosy pink. "Hey Ice, your skin color's coming back, and you're starting to get some more movement in your arm. It don't seem like it's gonna be too long before I'm gonna allow you to cover up those perfect boobs of yours. Then I'm gonna get you on your feet and moving around some."

"Richard, anytime you want to see my boobs just ask, and you shall receive. You saved my life and I'll never forget it, Richard." Ice smiled one of her best smiles that would melt her name.

"Hey girl, I didn't do nuthin, if you weren't in such good shape, that stinking little piece of lead woulda cashed in your chips. So if anyone saved you, it was you. Do you wanna stand?"

"Please." Ice replied as she pulled her legs up under her, and the robe fell off her. She leaned her back against the wall and then she used the strength in her good shoulder to help her inch her way up to her feet. Blood Clot helped her by putting his hands under her arms, supporting most of her weight for her. When she was on her feet, Blood Clot told her to lean on the wall, and he picked up the robe and helped her get in it. The medic noted the female soldier wince when he helped her in the robe, and he knew she was sucking up the pain to try and bluff him. When she was in the robe, Blood Clot tied the cord for her and said.

"Look girl, I know this hurts like two mutherfuckers, but you gotta get blood going to the wound. I'm worried the longer you don't use it, you might stop using it. How you doing, do you have your sea legs under ya yet? I want you to walk around as soon as you're able to move."

"Yes, I'd like to try and walk around the barracks for a little while, Richard. Then I want to get to my bunk and lie down for a while and take a little rest and maybe a nap, that's all." She replied as she moved away from the wall helping to support her body.

The moment she moved away from the wall, she complained. "Whoa boy that wasn't a very good idea." She got dizzy and Blood Clot had to catch her weight in his arms again, or she would have gone down to the floor in a heap and possibly hurting herself worse.

"That's it Blood Clot, I'm calling a fucking ambulance for her! I'm not gonna wait until she gets hurt by falling, dammit. Hell, I shoulda done it long before now for crap sake. I'm not gonna wait until she hurts herself falling and cracking her noggin on the damn floor. I'm talking the decision outta ya fucking hands right now, Clot." Walker snorted at the Unit's medic.

"Calm down Walker, she's gonna be fine in a few minutes. It was to be expected she woulda got dizzy, give her a few minutes and she'll be walking like a champ." The medic snapped.

Ice quickly caught her breath and bearings and then she cried to Walker. "Please don't call the ambulance on me, sir. If you call one then Colonel Leadbetter's going to find out about this, and he's going to scrub me from the Unit, whether I like it or not. Please Captain Walker Sir."

Captain Walker saw the look in her eyes and he knew right off he could never do anything that would hurt this female fighter. He shook his head and said to her. "Okay little sister, I'm gonna give you enuf stinking time to get your friggin sea legs under ya little ass. The longer you take, the more I'm gonna get pissed off at ya though, sister. I want you to get back to your bunk and rest up and get some of your stinking strength back, and then..."

"Hold it Walker. I don't want her lying down right away man. I want her to walk around the barracks for a few times so I can make sure she's alright, before I allow her to lie down and rest any sir. If I get her moving, that's great but she hasta keep moving once she starts, man." Blood Clot warned the concerned young new Marine Captain.

"Okay, whatever you say goes around here, you're the fucking medic, Blood Clot. You ready to try it again girl?" Walker asked the injured good looking female soldier.

"Yes sir, so get out of my way and eat my dust, Captain. I'm going to show you two that I'm Number One A One Chips again." She warned the two worried soldiers as she pushed off the wall and started to walk. At first she was moving on very shaky legs, but she quickly got her strength back and by the time she left the shower area, she was moving pretty well on her own. Both Blood Clot and Walker walked behind her ready to catch her if she lost her balance. By the time she got out to the middle of the barracks, she was walking like nothing happened to her. But she did walk and supported her injured arm with her good hand. As she passed by the other soldiers in the barracks, some of the soldiers called out to her.

"You go girl, looking good baby sister." A female soldier said as Ice passed her.

All this concern made her feel proud to be part of this elite group of specialized soldiers. In no time flat, she started her second walk around the barracks. One of the Russian female fighters joined her in her second walk, and soon, Three Martines joined her. By the time she finished her second walk around the interior of the barracks every woman from the group was walking by her side and keeping a close eye on her movements at the same time.

Walker was with Blood Clot and asked him with concern in his voice. "How many stinking times is she gonna hafta walk around this damn dump, man? I don't like her walking around in that stinking bathrobe like that. She looks like she's fricking ill, buddy. I can't afford to have Colonel

Leadbetter come marching in here and catch her walking around like that, he might send her down to medical. You know damn well them fricking bone crackers might red flag her stinking ass, and cause her to be bounced from the damn unit whether we like it or not, man."

"She's gonna walk around the barracks until I feel she's well enuf to lie down and that's that, Captain. I'm gonna miss going out tonight with the rest of the guys, Walker. I think I'm gonna stick around the barracks and keep a betta eye on her. I didn't like the reaction of the hot water hitting her injured shoulder. I almost called an ambulance myself for her, but she was so dead set against it so I didn't dare, Walker. I don't need to party tonight, and I'll make it like I was too tired to go out. I don't want her to feel bad." Blood Clot offered to his commanding officer.

"Shit, I forgot all bout going out tonight, what the hell time is it anyway, dammit?"

"It's already ten of nine, almost time for you people to shove off for the titty bar, Walker."

"I almost wanna stick around the barracks myself, I wanna keep an eye on her too man."

"It's not necessary for you or anyone else to stick around here. I can take care of her betta by myself. Besides, you'll end up getting in the way if she might go sour on us, Walker." Blood Clot offered his commanding officer as he looked over his shoulder to check on Ice again.

"You sure bout that crap, I think Raz is really looking forward to going out for a while tonight, Blood Clot?" Walker offered as he looked for Ramirez who was walking with Ice.

"You think so? Have you looked at her lately my friend?" the medic replied.

Walker located Ramirez and saw her hovering by the side of Ice, as she walked through the barracks again and grumbled. "Dammit, I betta make sure she still wants to go out I guess, man."

Walker headed for Ramirez, and got her attention. When she came over to his side he asked her. "Hey Raz, you still wanna go out for some fun and games tonight or what baby?"

"What about Ice, she's still in a lot of pain and I really don't want to leave her until I know she's doing okay, Bobby. I'm really worried about her you know." She replied with concern.

"Raz, Blood Clot just volunteered to remain with her all night. He told me he thinks we might be in the way if we hang around, in case anything goes wrong with her again. I think he's right, and this might be the last time we get out for who knows how long and enjoy ourselves some. Besides girl, if we don't go out tonight then Ice is gonna feel real bad bout us worrying so much about her condition, baby. She's looking good and I think we should get out for a little while."

"I don't know Bobby." Ramirez offered as she looked at the injured female soldier again.

Blood Clot got in the conversation and he offered the worried Sergeant. "Hey Raz, I'd rather everyone gets the hell outta the damn barracks. I know once I'm alone with the Ice woman, she'll come out with what's really happening to her body. I think she don't wanna say much in front of the rest of you shitbirds here. I gotta see what's really wrong with her ass, because if she's still bad hurt then I'm gonna hafta request the Colonel sends her home until she's good to go at a hundred percent. She'll never tell me the truth, not with you guys hanging around the barracks."

Ramirez glanced at Ice, even though she looked better than she did she could tell by the way she was walking she was still not herself yet. She turned to Blood Clot and replied. "I know what you're up to here mister. You just want to be alone with her so you can see her tits again, buster."

Even before Blood Clot could react to Ramirez's last words she just fired at him, she immediately smiled and then she took his hand in hers and added to her words. "I happen to agree with you at what you are saying to us Richard. But the only way I'll let you send Ice home, is if she's in danger of hurting herself worse then she already hurting, mister."

"Look Raz, I won't request her to leave the outfit unless it's a matter of her life or death, sister. I assure you that I'll take damn good care of her purdy little ass while you people are gone for the night enjoying yourselves. Go out and have a good time will ya please, and don't worry about Ice. I got her okay and I won't allow anything to happen to her while you people are gone. C'mon Raz, you guys will only be in our stinking way if you stay so bug out for a while will ya."

"Okay Blood Clot, I'm not going to ruin the night for the other soldiers. Look at them they're standing there staring at Ice like they're waiting for her to fall apart on them dammit. I think it might be a good idea to get the pack of fools the hell out of the barracks, so they can get their minds off Ice, and you can take care of her better, Richard." Ramirez offered to the unit medic.

"That's another reason I want everyone outta the damn barracks. Raz, if everyone stays behind then they're not gonna leave her alone for a damn minute. When I finally allow her to rest for a while, that's exactly what I want her to do, rest. So you'll be doing me a big favor here to get the rest of these slugs the hell outta here for the night." Blood Clot replied to the Sergeant.

That was all Walker had to hear. He walked out to the center of the barracks, and then he bellowed out at his troops. "People, people, people, we have a titty bar to check out. I don't know bout the rest of you people, but I'm going out and having myself some stinking fun tonight."

Now, the soldiers were stuck between two wants. They all wanted to stay behind and make certain Ice was alright and back to her old self, but they also wanted to go out and have themselves some serious fun. Walker saw the mixed looks and he added to his bitch at the soldiers. "People, Blood Clot said he's beat out, and he's not coming along with us to the titty bar tonight. So anyone who doesn't wanna get wild is more than welcome to hang back with the blood sucker here and the pretty looking cripple here, and keep them both company for the stinking night. But as for me, I'm heading out and I'm gonna have me some fun tonight."

The injured Ice looked at Blood Clot the instant she was told he was not going out with the rest of the other soldiers. She knew why he was staying behind instead of going out with the rest of the soldiers. The concerned troops also knew why the medic was staying behind in the barracks. They knew if Blood Clot was going to stay back with the Ice lady then there was no need for any of them to miss out on the fun. The soldiers were revved up for going out and tying one on because they knew tonight was a free night and once they started training, going out is off.

Now, the troopers were moving like they had a real purpose in mind, everyone was looking after their last minute details. Stowing their loose gear and splashing after shave lotion on, and combing their hair. The female soldiers were as excited at their male counterparts were.

THE BAR KNOWN AS BARE PARTS

The Iraqi Colonel Hamoodi al-Qaysi allowed the American soldiers drinking with him to bore him to death with their constant bragging about their past military deeds they were involved in. The Arab would be terrorist was on his second beer, and he thanked Allah the Americans were more interested in the female Arabs than talking to him or Lieutenant Elmasry. He glanced at his watch and was stunned to see it was ten after nine already. He surveyed the interior of the bar, fearing Captain Walker and the rest of his troops who had invaded his country he was certain to have with him, might have somehow entered the bar without him noticing them come in.

Hamoodi al-Qaysi turned to the American soldier called Short Cut, and then he announced. "Jerome, it's getting late and I'm growing tired. It's a shame, I was looking forward to meeting this soldier you called Road Kill. I heard many fascinating stories about him from the rest of the soldiers in the bar. But I can barely keep my eyes open any longer, so I must go home and rest."

"Oh C'mon man, you're not gonna crap out on me this stinking early in the night are ya pal? The night hasn't even started for us yet man, and besides I know Walker and his group is gonna show up any fucking minute now. I'm telling ya Bill; if you leave now you're gonna miss the all the fucking fun when he finally gets here, buddy. I don't know what's keeping them uther stinking guys from getting here. They're later than usual when they're stationed on the stinking base, Bill. He'll be here soon enuf man, you just gotta hang in a little while longer man.

"C'mon man and have another stinking beer and get in a fricking festive mood, pal. You don't wanna have the uther guys think you're a pussy, and you couldn't take a night on the damn town. Man, look at your girlfriend, her motor's running in high fucking gear. You pull her outta here now, she'll never forgive ya man." Short Cut was almost begging al-Qaysi to stay, because he did not want to lose the show the two Arab girls were giving him as they hung around the table.

The wise Colonel Al-Qaysi got what he wanted from the American soldier, reassurance that Walker was coming to the bar tonight. The Iraqi Military Officer knew he had the weapons he needed hidden in the car, and he was not worried about anyone seeing them. It did not matter, because about all the pickup trucks he saw in the parking lot, had long guns hanging in racks in the vehicles. He was told most of what they called ridge runners or red necks, carried rifles because they were hunters, and there was plenty of deer in the hills of North Carolina.

The American soldier branded Short Cut was not going to allow Colonel al-Qaysi and his other friends to leave the bar this easy. He wanted the girls to stick around until Walker finally showed up. He was certain once the other soldiers came in, there was a good chance they would get these two women out of their clothes one way or the other, and he could see what they both really looked like. Short Cut grinned at Iraqi Colonel al-Qaysi, and then he held up three fingers and a waitress immediately came over to the table with three beers, and placed them on the down and then she waited to be paid for the drinks. Short Cut paid for the beers and opened one for al-Qaysi and said to the man. "Drink up buddy, you can't fly with one stinking wing man."

Colonel al-Qaysi had no idea what the American soldier meant by his last remark, but he took the beer and then he saluted him with the cold bottle, and then he took a sip.

"That's better, join the friggin party." Short Cut offered as he joined al-Qaysi in his drink.

The two Iraqi women were doing what they were ordered to do by their commander. They were trying to keep the attention of the few American soldiers with them glued to their bodies. Every time it seemed like they might get up and leave the table, both al-Shaya and Khalaifa would move and then expose more flesh to the young and wild soldiers, and they place their attention back on the two women. The women were beginning to really enjoy all the attention they were receiving from the good looking group of American soldiers.

The Iraqi Colonel tapped his foot on the floor while waiting for Walker and the other soldiers accompanying him, to come into the bar. The Iraqi Commander kept glancing at his watch and then staring at the door, like he was actually trying to will Walker to come into the bar. Short Cut was making a real pest of himself, because he was trying to get the stranger to stay longer in the bar. He knew they were going to kill one of the soldiers who would be in Walker's group on this night. This was because he wanted to see how the Americans were going to react to the sniper attack aimed against them. If they reacted too strongly against the attack then their next hit would have to be made against Walker. Then they would get out of the United States as quickly as possible and make their way to Jordan, and live there until they saw what was happening in Iraq.

A noise caught the attention of the Iraqi Colonel, and he looked around until he saw a woman on the dance floor take off her shirt to the call of the horde of drunk soldiers surrounding her. She started to swing the shirt over her head, and making the soldiers go wild with her crazy actions.

CAMP LEJEUNE, NORTH CAROLINA

Captain Robert Walker was waiting for the women to say their goodbyes to Ice, Sergeant Diane Morrison. He could easily see Ice was really exhausted and she was still in considerable pain as well, and all she wanted to do was rest. He finally barked at the stalling women he felt were just dragging their feet because they wanted to make certain the injured soldier was doing well. "If you girls don't leave Ice the hell alone, I'm gonna order her to go to the other barracks so she can get some fucking rest for crap sake. C'mon girls, it's starting to get late, and by the time we get over to the stinking bar and have some fun tonight, it's gonna be too fricking late to come back here and party out a little. C'mon will ya and let's go, dammit."

Ice perked up and she announced in a weak tone to the group of women warriors surrounding her. "You slugs better count me in on this supposed party. I'm still part of this outfit, guys."

"Yeah sure right, you're gonna party with us tonight, huh girl?" Walker bitched at her.

"Damn Skippy Walker. And if you don't like it, don't bother with me tonight mista."

Walker headed out of the barracks shaking his head. The rest of the soldiers followed him.

When everyone was out of the barracks, Blood Clot walked Ice over to her bunk and ordered her to sit. Ice smiled and asked the medic. "Are you going to check out my wound Richard?"

"Naw, there's not much I can do for it now it's well healed on the outside. The pain you're suffering is because it's still raw inside the wound, Ice. I'm afraid your body has to do all the stinking work, I can't do for you I'm afraid, honey."

"I think you should check it again anyway Richard. I mean really, because it's hurting me like the devil again." Ice said as she removed the robe and threw it on the floor.

Blood Clot checked the wound again and discovered it lost all the redness and remarked to the concerned young female warrior. "Everything looks real fine to me honey."

"That's all you want to look at Richard? I mean the wound stupid." Ice added and she moved her hands and cupped her breasts. But she let go of the right breast because it hurt her arm and breast so much. Then she looked up at Blood Clot with smiling eyes.

"C'mon pretty lady, you ain't gotta do that shit for me, honey. I love you like a sister and I'd do anything to make it better for you, sister. I didn't wanna stay behind so I could take advantage of you, baby girl. You ain't gotta prove anything to me or the uther guys of the group for that matter. You're part of this outfit until the day you die you know. You better put the robe back on and I want you to lie down for a little while and catch up on some of your rest, sister. But I don't want you to fall asleep, because I want you back on your feet and get dressed, and then we're gonna take a little walk around the base. I want you to get all your strength back. I'm warning you sister, I'm gonna watch what you eat. You lost a bit of weight after you were wounded you know. In case you don't know it, I kinda like my ladies with a little meat on their bones."

Blood Clot picked up the robe and he handed it to Ice. She looked at him with tears building up in her eyes and she said. "Thank you for understanding what I was trying to do Richard. I really needed that and your kind words of encouragement. I love you so much mista."

"Hey pretty lady when the hell are you ever gonna learn? You ain't gotta prove anything to anyone from the stinking group. Baby, once you're accepted into this close knitted group, you're part of it forever. So you betta get that through that thick head of yours, baby. C'mon and lay down for a few minutes and then we're going on our little walk about of the damn base, Ice. Did you eat anything tonight you know you hafta keep up your strength? You're body's still healing, and not eating your normal food is gonna prolong your healing a bit, sister."

"You're starting to nag me again Richard." She complained at him with a smile.

"Someone has to nag you, the way you're going with not eating properly, is gonna extend your healing process quite a bit, little lady." Blood Clot replied to the injured soldier.

Walker and his group piled in the eleven suburban extended carry all vans, and once they were loaded up, the trucks took off for the local bar. The excited soldiers were singing, or talking up a storm. Everyone was looking at Blind Date and Sergeant Ramirez, because they were dressed to start a riot in the titty bar. Even Three Martines was dressed to kill tonight, showing a lot more skin than she ever showed since the first time she linked up with them. The soldiers were still concerned with this soldier though, because of the ton of trouble she started with the Mutt, when she went nuts on him in the showers. Sergeant Cheryl Grantham had them believing the Mutt touched her when she did not want to be touched in the showers, and the female soldiers wanted to lynch him from the yardarm because of what she accused the Mutt of doing to her.

Walker was pleased Three Martines was starting to fit in well with the group. She changed that day when Ice was wounded, and she saw how the medic had to cut away her shirt and expose her breasts while he worked on trying to save her life out in the field. She also noticed how the male soldiers diverted their eyes and they did not stare at her breasts as the medic worked on saving Ice's life. It was on that day she understood what Ramirez meant by having to worry about exposing a woman when a medic had to work on them out in the field. Three Martines realized she was being very foolish. She made up her mind on that day she was going to fit in with the rest of the elite soldiers, no matter what she had to do to find her place with them.

It took the eleven trucks just over fifteen minutes to reach the bar after the soldiers checked out of the main security gate of the massive Marine base. When the trucks stopped by the bar, the soldiers quickly piled out of the machines and they gathered in the parking lot until everyone was assembled. Then they attacked the bar like it was an enemy position and they were the invading soldiers going against the structure.

Hamoodi al-Qaysi immediately noticed the new influx of soldiers just entering the bar. Even though none of them were dressed in their usual military uniforms, it was easy to tell all these men and women were soldiers just by the way they walked, or held themselves and moved. It was quite a commotion when Walker and his group entered the bar.

Short Cut (Sergeant Jerome Rosenberger) turned and saw the soldiers come in and announced to the Iraqi Colonel in an excited voice. "Here you go Bill, I told you Walker and his group was coming to the gin mill tonight, man. Now the party will start for sure my friend."

Colonel al-Qaysi stared at the new soldiers he was trying to pick out Walker by himself.

Short Cut knew what al-Qaysi was doing, and he offered to who he thought was a civilian. "Hey Bill, Walker's the one with the good looking dish glued to his stinking arm man. The chick with him is Sergeant Dorothy Ramirez. That's Walker's main squeeze and they just had a kid a while ago. They're really good for each uther man. I heard they're gonna get married real soon."

"So that is the great Captain Robert Walker huh? You'll remember to introduce me to him some time on this night, right Jerome?" Al-Qaysi asked while he held Walker in his glaze.

"Yes sir and I don't mind telling ya Bill. You're describing him to the damn tee man."

"He's that good a soldier you believe, my new friend." The Iraqi Colonel remarked as he kept his eye trained on Walker and his girlfriend, as they walked through the horde of soldiers in the bar. He never saw so many people slap another man on his back and make all sorts of remarks to the man as he moved through them. If he did not know any better, he would swear that some powerful politician had just entered the bar. There was another soldier who seemed like he was shadowing Walker's every move, and he too was with a pretty looking young woman.

"Short Cut, who is the other soldier who seems like he's with the one you said is Captain Walker?" Colonel al-Qaysi waited until the soldier looked again at Walker.

"Oh that one, he's about as wild as they come I'm afraid, Bill. You don't ever wanna get on the wrong side of that soldier. You'd never be dead enuf for him to stop beating on ya ass. His name's Frank Abbott and his Unit name is the Mutt, and that's because he has a white mother and a black father, man." The soldier called Short Cut offered to the man seated at the table.

"That is something I find very strange about the American soldiers..." As soon as he said 'American soldiers', he wanted to bit his lip because he feared he might have aroused suspicion from this soldier. He looked at Short Cut and when he saw no facial change he continued with his words. "Your soldiers seem to get along very well with white and black soldiers alike."

"Man, I guess you were never in the fucking service Bill? That's the only place in the whole world where everyone is fucking color blind, man. You never have time to worry about the color of someone's skin standing next to your ass when your life or their life depends on the soldier near ya, man. When crunch time comes a knocking on ya door, and you're so fucking scared you're shaking in your stinking boots like a fricking turtle trying to dry hump a stinking bone dome. (Helmet) You don't give a flying fuck if the guy next to you is a Jew, Catholic, or Muslim. You don't care what his lifestyle is, if he fucks a man, woman, or beast. All you are is damn glad to have someone you can trust standing next to you at this time. Each soldier knows he can trust his brother or sister to be there when he or she is needed, man."

"You are correct Short Cut I was never in your military, Jerome. I came over to the United States three years ago from Italy. I'm afraid to offer I have a physical ailment that had stopped me from joining any military organization. Not that I never tried to serve my new country, friend." Colonel al-Qaysi was lying through his eye teeth, but he knew he made a terrible mistake when he was speaking to the American soldier, and now he wanted to correct it before this soldier became a little suspicious of him.

"I thought you were a fucking foreigner man. But you got an American wife, so that makes you A number One in my fucking book, Bill. You look like you need another stinking beer, Bill."

"Yes I do, but I'm buying the next round of drinks for everyone at our table, friend." Al-Qaysi raised his hand in the air and in a few seconds a topless waitresses came over to the table with a pad, and she wrote down the drinks everyone wanted, and then she smiled and left.

The waitress was back in a few moments carrying the requested drinks. Everyone was having a great time watching the naked women dancing on the stage, and the rest of the active and fit soldiers moving around the bar. Even some of the women fighters were giving better shows on the dance floor than the strippers were doing on stage. The bar was so noisy and overcrowded it was giving al-Qaysi a pounding headache. He could not believe so many people could fit in such an overcrowded bar. The soldiers made the bar feel very confining and small.

Walker and his group worked their way deeper in the bar. It was a madhouse in the jamming place. Short Cut tried to get Walker's attention twice, but they could not connect up. But Short Cut was able to get Ramirez's attention though, and she waved at him and shot him a quick smile. Short Cut pointed to Walker and made a hand signal, informing her he wanted him and her to come over to his table. She nodded once she realized what he wanted from her, and then she tried to get Walker's attention so she could direct him over to Short Cut's table.

Ramirez closed in on Walker's side and when she caught up to him she grabbed his arm, and when he looked at her, she pointed towards Short Cut's table. Walker knew what she wanted from him and he started to cut across the dance floor and headed for Short Cut who he liked. He was with Walker ever since he first entered the service over ten years ago.

Walker had to shove and push his way through the mob of drunken soldiers and civilians, because the bar was so overcrowded and hoping. He was trying his best to get over to the table and other soldiers who wanted to speak with him. He kept glancing over his shoulder to make certain that Ramirez was following him the best she could move through the crowd. He was suddenly hit by an elbow from someone who was dancing crazily on the dance floor and he almost slugged the dude because he hit him so hard. He rubbed his eye while still glaring at the soldier dancing like an asshole with some chick that seemed like she was three sheets to the wind, and only going through the motions of dancing.

CHAPTER EIGHTEEN

By the time the four soldiers finally worked their way over to the already crowded table, they looked like they walked through the fires of hell. Sergeant Ramirez's shirt was pulled and twisted up so bad one of her breasts was practically sticking out the opening. Walker had his shirt pulled on so much that two buttons were ripped off his shirt, and his hair was a mess. The Mutt looked fine, but Blind Date looked just as bad as Ramirez did. Her shirt was pulled on so much it was actually torn slightly on the shoulder, and her skirt was twisted around until the zipper was resting on her hip instead of her rearend. This was because as the women walked across the dance floor, any male soldiers they passed by grabbed a hand full of their body's wherever the soldiers could reach them.

Short Cut stood as Walker got to the table and they smacked each other on the shoulder. Ramirez gave Short Cut a peck on the cheek she did not like him much. Mutt hit Short Cut in the guts and then grinned at him. Blind Date was behind Mutt because she didn't know the soldier.

When Captain Walker came up to the table, Iraqi Colonel al-Qaysi and Lieutenant Elmasry both stood in anticipation of being introduced to the very popular soldier al-Qaysi could easily tell, was an extremely dangerous man, just by the way he moved his body and walked. The two young Arab women remained in their seats, but they made certain they were exposing much of what they were there for the new soldiers to their table. The Mutt already zeroed in on the two women and he made no bones about looking down the front of al-Shaya's loose fitting blouse. Even Ramirez gave the women a quick look over, and then she smiled at them pleasantly.

Walker looked at the two men standing and pointed to them with his chin to Short Cut and he replied. "Hey Walker, these two stinking dudes are friends. They moved to the area from New York. They're real cool dudes. We've been partying with them for the past few days, Homes."

Walker looked at the largest of the two men, sizing him up for a fight. Short Cut hit Walker's arm and knew what he wanted and offered his hand to the Iraqi as he grumbled, not trusting the stranger in the least. "Hey pal, I'm Robert fucking Walker, buddy. Who the fuck are you man?"

Colonel al-Qaysi put out his hand and took Walker's hand and they shook, as he introduced himself to the very dangerous looking and nasty acting man. "Hello Mr. Robert Walker, I'm Bill Paterson, and this is my lovely wife Helen sitting to my left. We've been married for three years now and we are still getting to know each other I guess." The foreign Colonel was trying to speak correctly while also trying to covering up his Arab accent.

Walker cautiously eyed the stranger for a few seconds, he was trying to place the slight accent he detected, and then he snapped at him harshly. "I didn't ask you for your whole fucking past life history, man! You sound like you're a stinking A-rab to my fricking ass, buster. What the hell are you doing in my country, man?" Hearing his accent and thinking he might be an Arab, already made the new young Captain dislike the dude.

Al-Shaya spoke this time as she moved in front of her Colonel instead of standing by his side. She had no trace of an accent any longer, and when she spoke, everyone there thought she was a true blood American. She knew she had to say something to protect her commander, and she snapped angrily back at Walker. "Mr. Walker, my husband is not Arabian he's Italian, and he has been living here in the United States for over ten years with me now. He has his proper papers, and by marrying me has made him a full American citizen as you well know, Mr. Soldier. I don't think I like the way you're talking to my husband in the least sir.

"If you don't like us that's fine with me mister, just leave us alone and we'll not bother you, and please don't bother us either. We're here to have a good time and meet new and interesting friends and that's all. We don't want any trouble with anyone in the bar, especially soldiers who we respect so much for the sacrifices they're making for our country." Al-Shaya placed her hands on her hips out of habit, and in doing so she exposed more of her breasts than she planned.

Walker stared at the young woman with the fire burning in her eyes, and then he glanced at her chest and fired back. "Calm the fuck down little lady, I was just trying to get to know your old man a little betta, that's all. Don't go and get your stinking tits in a fucking uproar, and get the glare out of your damn stare. Look sister, any friend of Short Cut is a friend of mine."

With his mentioning the word tits, made al-Shaya look down at her chest. When she noticed how exposed she was, she took her hands off her hips and slowly button one of her buttons.

This action made the Mutt grumble at the Captain. "Arrr... shit Walker, your always in a bad fucking mood just cost us a pair of tits to look at, asshole. I just want a fucking drink."

With that said everyone at the table finally relaxed a little. Then the Neck stepped away and found an empty table and he easily carried it over his head to Short Cut's table. He put it down next to his, and the other soldiers found a number of empty chairs in the bar, and they brought them over to the second table. When everyone who could sit was settled in, the drinks started to flow between the specialized soldiers, and the unknown Iraqi terrorists. Sergeant Ramirez leaned near Walker and told him to make peace with the stranger, and then she started to speak with al-Shaya. He watched Ramirez and saw how quickly she had accepted the girl, and he decided to make peace with the new guy in order to try and keep the peace between him and Ramirez.

Walker learned over the table and said to al-Qaysi. "Hey Bill, your lady said you were in the States for some ten years now, whatdaya do for a stinking living buddy?"

"I work with computers, I write programs from military applications to certain games. So their instructors can teach their soldiers in the classrooms rather than on the field of battle, how to correctly react to certain situations on the battlefield, sir. What do you do for a living, Mr. Walker?" The wise Iraqi Colonel asked while he was trying to sound dumb.

"Hey look pal, if you wanna be friends with me, dump the stinking Mister crap when you're talking to me, friend. I'm a soldier, and I do it real good man." Walker grinned at al-Qaysi.

"You're a soldier? I believe Short Cut had already told me you were a soldier before Walker, but I did not believe him when I first met you..."

Walker cut off the Arab Colonel's words in mid sentence as he nearly barked back at him this time. "Yeah? And why the fuck was that for? I don't look like a fucking soldier to your stinking ass, bud?" He snorted angrily at the stranger at the table.

Ramirez reached out and she grabbed Walker's hand and gave it a quick little squeeze, she saw him in action many times before. The way he was speaking to this man made her believe he was really looking for some trouble with him. When he turned to look at her, she smiled and said. "C'mon Walker, he seems harmless enough to me, why don't you give him a little break here. He doesn't look like he's trying to give you any trouble. Besides Bobby, I like his wife."

Walker stared at Ramirez for a long moment and when she smiled a second time at him, he smiled and turned back to the Iraqi Military Officer and waited his reply. He still did not trust this guy in the least and wanted to move away from him.

Major al-Shaya spoke pleasantly to Ramirez. "I don't believe your husband likes mine very much, is he always so combative? Bill was sorry he couldn't get in the military. It really bothered him that he was unable to do his duty for Italy or the United States. He's a real good man, and I thank you for allowing me to call you Raz. I hope our two husbands can get along a little better. I'd like to get to know you a lot more. Maybe you can show us around town."

Ramirez smiled at al-Shaya and replied. "I'm sorry Bobby's being so mean to your husband, Helen. He never trusts anyone right off the bat when he first meets them. First he has to get to know him a little better, and once he's accepted by Walker which Bill will be. Your husband will never find a better friend than he'll find in Bobby. He's a good man, and I love him too."

"He's a big man, is he tender with you Raz?" Al-Shaya asked her new friend.

"Helen, Bobby would step on a land mind to protect me. Yes he's big and can tear the head off any man who gives him or his country any trouble with his bare hands. But he's also like a big teddy bear with me. He's the kindest, gentle, and most honorable man you'll ever find in life. But you don't want to cross him, because he's like a badger and he'll never rest until he finds anyone who hurt him, and gets his revenge on that person. I never met a man who could be so savage one second, and yet so kind the next." She smiled and this made al-Shaya smile at her this time.

Colonel al-Qaysi stared at Captain Walker while the two girls spoke with each other pleasantly. The Iraqi Commander was sizing him up in his mind. He came to the conclusion he could not beat this man in any hand to hand combat. He was too large to fight in that kind of manner. The Arab Commander decided if he was going to go up against Walker in the near future, he would have to attack him in a sniper attack. He knew he would never give Walker a fair situation when he decided to take his life. Already, Colonel al-Qaysi feared this man in his mind as he continued to kind of stare at the American Captain's face.

Walker saw the man was off on a short day trip, so he cleared his throat and asked a second time. "Hey pal, you said you didn't think I was a soldier when you first saw me, and I asked you why. I'm asking the same question. I was never taken for anything but a stinking soldier."

The Iraqi Colonel al-Qaysi had to shake his head to try and force his mind to come back to the conversation with this dangerous American soldier. "Yes Miste... Walker, I must admit when I first saw you, I didn't think you were a soldier. I thought you were more of a politician for the United States. That was because of the way everyone was treating you when you first came into the bar. I saw many politicians on TV in the past, and when one of these men was being met by civilians. They were always treated in the same manner as you were when you entered this bar tonight. That was why I didn't think you were a soldier. I'm sorry for my wrong assumption, Walker. But now I spoke to you, there's no doubt you're a soldier for your country."

Captain Walker stared at the stranger for several moments while weighing his words, and then he leaned back in his chair and started to laugh. Al-Qaysi also sat back as he watched Walker laughing. He did not know whether or not to be upset over his laughing.

Ramirez watched Walker, not knowing what he was laughing about. She was scared when he stopped laughing, if he was going to be friends with Bill, or was he going to get in a fight with the man. It could go either way with Walker at this point she felt.

Walker stopped laughing and picked up his beer and took a pull. Then he looked at who he thought was Bill and said. "This is the first time I was ever thought of as a stinking politician, man. I always said my job was fighting, not bullshitting. If you wanna find yourself a politician in the service, find yourself a fricking General. No Bill, I'm everything but a politician. I must admit I can see how you mighta mistaken what these pukes were doing to me when I came in this dump. I haven't seen some of them for a few months now and they were happy to see me."

"Then you're not such an important person as I thought Walker?" Al-Qaysi asked.

"Only to my mother am I an important person, pal. No Bill, I'm nothing more than a common stinking ground pounder for my country. There's no red cape hidden under my fricking shirt I tell ya. But I have to say this you really made my stinking day thinking me a fricking politician, man. C'mon pal I'll buy ya a damn beer." Walker held up his fingers and a waitress quickly headed right for his table. He brought a round of drinks for both tables, and when the waitress was busy getting the drinks, he put out his hand and offered it to Colonel al-Qaysi.

The Iraqi shook hands, this hand shake was different. It was less firm and threatening.

"I like you Bill, you're okay in my book. Hey man will you look at the set of puppies on this hen coming at our table." Walker offered as he spotted Bouncer, (Sergeant Carol Burnhart) coming at them. She had the largest breasts of all the women from his outfit, and she was proud of them and she showed them off whenever she had the chance to show off. Bouncer's blouse was opened to her waist and both breasts were swaying in the open as she walked.

Colonel al-Qaysi did not know what Walker meant by puppies until he looked at her, and he saw her breasts. He smiled as he watched her walking towards the table. All of a sudden, he felt he was accepted by this extremely dangerous soldier he was about to kill.

Bouncer came to the table and stuck her breasts right in Walker's face and he kissed them as she said. "Well Road Kill, why the hell didn't you tell me you were back on base, mista?"

"Sorry sister, I was busy with the uther guys. How ya doing? Have you picked up any new orders from the brass yet?" Walker asked the soldier as he cupped her breasts and rolled them.

Al-Shaya saw what he was doing and asked Ramirez in a confused tone of voice. "Raz, you don't mind what your husband's doing to that other girl right in front of you? If I ever caught my husband fooling around with another woman like he is doing, I'd cut his ding dong off."

"You have a lot to learn about us, Helen. We're soldiers, and we can be killed on any mission at a drop of a hat. So we accept actions that usually go against normal relationships in the real world. Sometimes we party, when any woman from the outfit can make love to any guy. It doesn't matter if that other partner is in a relationship or not. But once the party's over then it's back to normal way of living for us." Ramirez looked at her new friend and smiled at her.

"Oh, I have heard stories about this type of lifestyle, I believe it's called swinging, right?"

"It's sort of like that, but we keep it all in the family, just between us soldiers Helen."

"I see, and I think I can see what you're saying to me Raz." Helen replied.

The women stopped speaking and listened to Bouncer's reply to Walker's remark.

"No Walker, I heard no changes to our orders as yet. It seems the top brass is keeping it real close Zip Lip about the reasons we were ordered back to base, big boy. But I'm doing fine other than that." Bounce replied as she enjoyed what he was doing to her.

Walker told her. "When we get to back base look me up, and I'll tell you what it's all about, so you can clue in the rest of the stinking guys from your barracks. I meant to speak to you uther guys before we left the base for the stinking bar, but we had a slight emergency and I didn't get a friggin chance to speak with you guys before we left for here."

The Iraqi Colonel remained silent while Walker spoke with the female soldier. Once he was done, Walker looked back at the stranger and then held him in his gaze for a few moments. Something about this guy was still rubbing him the wrong way, and he could not put his finger on what was truly bothering him about the guy.

The Mutt asked Blind Date to dance. Everyone watched the Mutt and Blind Date head for the dance floor because they all knew he was a great dancer. They were not disappointed because as soon as he was dancing, he was all over the place. He did some kip ups, and then he spun around on his shoulders, and ended up snapping up and spinning on his feet. He then spun Blind Date in his arms and bent her back and flipped her in the air and caught her in his arms. All on the floor stopped dancing and they watched the two dancing. Even a few of the strippers on stage cheered the two on. They stopped dancing after the song ended and they walked back to the table with everyone clapping at them. The Mutt sat by Walker out of breath and he wiped his face on a rag.

Walker smiled at his friend and the asked him. "Are you finished showing off yet bird brain?"

"No way in hell man. I only started to show off around this stinking dump, man."

"You're gonna have to go some to try and top your last act, buddy." Walker warned him.

"I got that one all figured out in my stinking mind already, my friend." The Mutt retorted.

"Yeah? What the hell are you gonna do to top that one, dog man?" Walker asked his friend.

"I'll tell you what I'm gonna do next in this titty dump, man." The Mutt replied as he pulled Blind Date by the hand on his lap. When she was sitting on him, he pulled her breast out of her blouse and began to play with it as he told Walker. "When I'm ready man, and we're bout ready to leave this stinking dump. I'm gonna bring Blind Date back out on the damn dance floor, and then we're gonna make love right in front of all these lousy little pukes in this stinking dump. We're gonna show them uther stinking pukes the right ways to make love together. Ain't that right baby?" the Mutt said as he drew her nipple in his mouth.

"Mmmmmmmmm... Anything you say to me lover." Blind Date replied in her French accent.

"That's all you gotta do bubble head. If you try that kinda act on the stinking dance floor, the lot of us will be thrown outta this bar for life, Mutt." Walker warned his fellow soldier.

Ramirez slapped the Mutt on the top of his head and he turned and looked at her, and then she bitched at her.

"What the hell didja do that for, sister? I ain't doing nuthin wrong here."

"If you do anything to get us thrown out of this fricking bar, I'll do something that'll stop your sexual pleasures for good, dog man. We're having a good time, so don't do anything to upset that on us mister. And stop playing with that poor girl like that will you please! Have you no shame about yourself any longer, Mutt? Gees, you're worse than a new born baby for Pete's sake." Ramirez could not help it she was trying to keep a straight face. When she saw the look on the Mutt's face when he thought she was really angry, she had to laugh at him.

"Dammit girl, you had me going there for a minute. You wait until I get you back to base, I'm gonna make you suck my dick good and proper, sister. Scaring me like that, shit you should be ashamed of yourself baby. You made my hardon go away on me, dammit." The Mutt rubbed between his legs as he made Blind Date move so he could do it without her sitting on his lap.

"You don't have to worry about your hardon disappearing, lover. I'll make you grow like a might oak tree again, Mutt." Blind Date said in a drunken state as she slid her hand on the Mutt's crotch, and then she began to play with him through the pants and giggled.

"Errr...Walker, are all your women fighters so free with their sexual desires?" Lieutenant Elmasry asked this was the first time he said anything to anyone at the table.

Walker looked at the man and snapped at him. "Yeah, you got a problem with it bud?"

Lieutenant Elmasry immediately placed his hands up and held them out as he shook his head no, to the suddenly angry looking soldier.

Sergeant Ramirez saw Captain Walker was getting angry all over again, so she did the only thing she could think of doing to try and make him stop being so angry while they were out and supposed to be enjoying themselves. She lifted her shirt and flashed her breasts at him.

Major al-Shaya saw a way she could cement her friendship with this young and beautiful female American soldier, and she also stood and flashed Walker. She was determined to have her breasts out for as long as Ramirez's were out. Instantly, the group of elite soldiers sitting at the two tables clapped, some of them even wanted the two women to take off their shirts all together, but they both ignored their requests.

When Ramirez saw Walker was smiling she sat down and closed her blouse some. Al-Shaya did the same and left her blouse opened as much as Ramirez's was. She was not going to allow this American female to outdo her until they finally left the bar.

Walker leaned nearer to al-Qaysi and he mumbled at him while trying to get a raise out of the stranger he still did not like all that much. "Hey Bill, you're lucky man your wife has some nice set of tits there man. Glad she's showing them off for us guys." He knew what he was doing, he was testing this stranger, and he was seeing if he could get him in a fistfight. He was not comfortable with him, and he was only being cool with the guy, because Ramirez seemed to be hitting it off so well with his wife. He knew she would make friends with anyone she met.

The Iraqi Colonel Hamoodi al-Qaysi felt Captain Robert Walker was trying to challenge him for a fight for some reason, and he vowed to himself that he was not going to allow him to win a victory over him by getting him involved in something he did not want to do. So he put all his efforts into making a false friendship with this extremely dangerous soldier, until he finally had the chance to kill him. He smiled at the American soldier as he announced calmly to him. "Yes Walker, she does have nice breasts, and that is one of the reasons I married her."

Try as he might, he was having a pretty hard time with trying to stay angry at the stranger in the bar. He could not put his finger on exactly what was truly bugging him about the guy, all he knew was he did not like him in the least and that was that. He stared at the stranger for a few moments, and then it hit him, he did not like the fact he was a computer whiz guy. He always felt anyone who worked on a computer was nothing but a brain, and he did not know how to make a living with his back or his guts. Realizing this, for the first time since he first sat down at the table, he finally relaxed with everyone there. But he made up his mind he was going to have a little talk with Short Cut, to see how well he knew this guy.

Short Cut was also concerned how Walker was treating his new friend, and was watching everything going on between the two. He kept giving Ramirez a quick glance, and the last one got a slight shrug from her. She was used to Walker not liking someone right off.

Colonel al-Qaysi was struggling with trying to get Walker to let down his guard. He decided to press his adulation of the soldier by offering him. "Say Walker, you stated you're an important man only to your mother. If that is a fact, how come everyone in this bar was treating you like a celebrity when you first walked into this place? I was here, and I saw how everyone was treating you. If I didn't know any better, I'd swear I was in the presence of Royalty, or at least a very popular and important person. Why do the other soldiers respect you so much?"

Short Cut saw his chance to get the anger out of Walker, as he jumped in the conversation and he slapped him on his back and then announced. "Whether you know it or not buddy, you are in the presence of Royalty. Road Kill is the perfect killing machine, man. He's the type of guy if he took a shit and reached around and took a fist full of it and tossed it against the wall, it'd immediately turn to gold. Every operation they send him out on, he comes back the hero with more awards and rate pinned on his ass. He's the only soldier who can be sent..."

"Short Cut, you got a big fucking mouth all of a sudden, buddy. If you don't shut it the fuck up real quick like, I'll shut it for you good and proper, buddy." He instantly hunched up his shoulders and every soldier watching the two, knew he was really pissed about something.

Sergeant Dorothy Ramirez saw the angry act taking place between the two soldiers, and she was on her feet in a flash. She wanted Walker out of the bar before he finally got in a fight with the other soldier he was so angry at and she offered to him to try and calm him down some. "C'mon Bobby, I think I need a little breath of fresh air, it's awful stuffy in here you know." She tugged on his arm until he rose and allowed her to lead him out of the bar.

As they walked out of the bar, some of the other soldiers who witnessed the confrontation, started to sing the song from the old TV show Dragnet. Walker flipped them all the bird from behind his back as Ramirez continued to pull him out of the bar. Once they were out in the parking lot, he lit up a cigarette and waited for Ramirez to get on him. The wait was not long.

"Jesus Christ Almighty Walker." She started as she flung her arms in the air. Her Spanish temper coming to the surface as she went on with her angry words at him. "What the hell was going on with you in there? Dammit to hell Bobby, I came out with you to have a good time tonight, and all you're doing is giving everyone a case of the ass. What the hell's going on between you and Short Cut anyway? You know we don't threaten anyone from our group. Gees Robert, you're breaking your own rules tonight mister. What the hell's wrong with you?"

"All of a sudden, Short Cut got himself a big fucking mouth!" He snarled at her.

"Why is that Bobby? And if he has a big mouth, is that enough for you to want to fight him?"

"He has a big fucking mouth because I felt he was gonna tell this lousy creep what we did in Iraq last year. I don't know anything about this lousy fuck in there, and until I do, I don't want anyone giving away any of our stinking trade secrets to the damn mutherfucker. What the hell do we know about that little prick in there? He might even be a stinking reporter looking for a damn story or attack me because I'm a soldier?" He was so upset about it he shot his half smoked cigarette out in the middle of the lot, as he blew the smoke out of his nose in a sort of hiss.

"Dammit Bobby, why don't you like these new people? I've been talking to Helen, and I found her to be a really nice person. And so what if Short Cut was going to brag a little about your mission in Iraq to capture that damn terrorist, about to go on trial for his life for what he tried to do against our Boss. All that's not top secret you know, if Bill was up to anything and wanted to know about that mission, all he has to do is read the damn newspapers and he'd know everything you guys did on that damn mission, Robert. The entire mission was explained to the letter in the paper. C'mon Bobby and relax tonight will you please. I want to have a good time tonight, besides if you don't calm down they're going to have to bury your ass standing up, mister."

"Arrr… there's no talking to you for Christ sake, especially when you're arguing logic to my ass." He growled at Ramirez, knowing she was right on, and he was really acting like the south end of a north bound horse. All he could think of doing was smile back at her.

When she saw his suddenly smile she rushed into his arms. She kissed him and then leaned her head against his powerful chest and said. "I love you Bobby."

He squeezed her to him so hard it almost stopped her from breathing properly. He released his bear hug and then mumbled to her. "You're right as usual kid. What say we go back in there and finish our stinking drinks and have some stinking fun tonight, baby."

"I'm always right Bobby, and one of these days you're going to realize that. Are you going to behave yourself when we go back in there Bobby? If you do, I'll give you a sugar titty to suck on later on tonight, Robert dear." She smiled one of her best smiles at her lover.

He smiled when she offered him a sugar titty. The last time she offered him one was when they were on board the plane heading to New York to speak before United Nation for the President. He was making so much trouble in the plane when she was trying to sleep she spread her melting Butterfinger candy bar on her breast, and allowed him to lap the candy off her breast.

She took his hand in hers and then led him back inside the still overcrowded bar. They headed back to their table, and the soldiers who took their seats when the two left, got up and gave them their seats back. Ramirez smiled at Bill and Helen and spoke to her again.

Walker looked at Short Cut and gave him a slight nod. Short Cut nodded back and relaxed. Then he looked at Bill and nodded to him. Al-Qaysi grinned, pleased whatever his future wife told him, calmed him down some. The Iraqi picked up his Bud and saluted Walker with it.

He tipped his bottle at Bill and then took a pull and relaxed.

The massive soldier called Neck, came across the bar supporting a red hand print on the side of his face, and he slammed his hand on Walker's back, forcing his body forward from the force of the blow. He grinned at Walker, and he saw the red mark and asked him. "What the fuck happened to your stinking puss, tree trunk? It looks like someone just slapped your face man."

"I did that to the big jerk Walker." Baby Tee bitched as she caught up with the Neck.

"Why didja do that for?" he asked as he laughed at the bright red mark she gave Neck.

"Because he wouldn't take no for an answer tonight dammit, he wanted to fool around a little in the bar, and I'm not going to start balling the big dumb ass in here for no one." Baby Tee snapped as she glared angrily at Neck again.

Neck looked down at the floor and started to move his foot around the way a young child would do, while trying to explain away a bad mark on his report card to his parents.

"By the looks of it you really put him in his damn place, Tee. You know you can't keep beating up the big dope like this, Baby." Walker offered as he stared at the Neck.

"Damn right I did. I warned the big jerk I wasn't going to put up with his shit tonight, and he kept pushing me all night Walker. What else was I going to do with the dumb sod?"

Everyone at the tables laugh at Neck, no matter how big he was, this little lady just did him in. The soldiers knew how Tee got whenever she was angry, and no one wanted to test her anger.

After a few seconds Baby Tee moved against the huge man and snarled at him. "I want another beer go get me one before I lay another one down on your fat ass, stupid."

Neck took off like a shot and headed for the bar to get the drink Baby Tee demanded.

Walker looked at her and then mumbled. "Hey Baby, when the hell are you gonna give the big ass a stinking break around here? You know how he feels bout you honey."

"I know that, but if he wants me then he has to work for me, Walker. I don't come easy or cheap. He also likes Ice, and besides I have my eyes leveled on Buckethead, I like my men big."

"Boy, can I contest to that Tee. At the last party, I tried to make Tee come with my tongue, guys. I couldn't do it man, and I ended up with a paralyzed tongue for my efforts with the little lady. When she don't wanna come, no one living on God's green earth is gonna make her pop, no matter what they try on her, man." The Mutt bitched as he wiggled his tongue in his mouth.

Baby Tee glared at the Mutt this time as she snapped at him hotly. "You looking for a good smack on the damn gob as well, mister? I'm not afraid of your ass either buster."

The Mutt fired right back at her. "Hey girl, you look tired, here let me clear a place for you to sit down." He ran his hands over his face and slid his tongue out of his mouth at her.

"Jesus Christ, you're disgusting Mutt. How the hell do you ever put up with a dirty thing like that, Blind Date?

He's nothing more than a slimy pig!" Baby Tee complained, as she walked over to the Mutt, and she laid one down on the back of his head for his rude remark.

Everyone laughed as Neck returned to the table carrying a Bud beer for Baby Tee.

Colonel al-Qaysi could not help it and he found himself laughing over the bickering these soldiers were doing with each other. He was beginning to find the American soldiers very amusing, and wondered how these young men and women could be so friendly towards one another. Yet if they were put on a battlefield, he would feel sorry for the other soldiers these troops were sent against. He knew if they could joke with each other in this manner then the Americans had to be quite the unit of warriors to fight with, or against for that matter.

Another soldier turned up at Walker's table, and he started to babble, Sergeant Abdullah al-Saleh, better known as Ali Baba to the rest of the elite soldiers. Colonel al-Qaysi paid close attention to this soldier because he was obviously Arabian, and he was stunned the Americans allowed him to be part of their supposed specialized unit. But he did not act anything like a faithful Arab, as al-Qaysi found out the moment he opened his mouth to speak with Walker.

"Hey hey man, it's fucking Walker, the best known stinking warrior we have. People, this man here is getting to be better known than any other soldier in the history of modern warfare."

"You got a big fucking mouth too, you little fucking A-rab bastard you." He snarled at the happy young man speaking to him.

"My my, I see the visit you made to my land of sand did nothing to make you any more pleasant to be around, brother. C'mon Walker, you're a stinking famous person, so why not enjoy the damn fame a little you're getting for being the best fucking soldier in the damn Unit, man." Ali Baba said as he ignored the way Walker was growling, or even looking at him.

Walker looked at who he thought was a guy named Bill. He shook his head as he let out his breath and then moaned as he put a sort of a smile on his lips and he offered. "Look Bill, it seems no one around here is gonna get offa my stinking case for a damn minute, until you find out why these stinking popinjays are sucking up to my stinking ass like this, man."

"I was going to ask you why everyone who comes up to you, act like you're someone very special to them, Walker." Al-Qaysi replied as he grinned back at the new soldier.

"For some strange reason, I knew this shit was gonna come up again tonight. So I might as well tell you bout it so you can understand why these damn pains in the asses keep coming up to my stinking ass, trying to pick my fucking pocket on me. If you were in the States as long as you told me you were then you gotta know bout that group of A-rab terrorists giving us a shitload of fucking trouble lately, buddy. Last year there was a fricking attempted assassination carried out against our President. It didn't happen, but in the attack one dude from our government was killed, and the Vice President was wounded in the stinking attempt.

"Well man, a number of soldiers from my Unit were picked to take the terrorist who escaped our country back to his stinking little rathole in Iraq. Either a prisoner or if we couldn't get him outta his rathole, we were ordered to kill his ass plain and simple. I was picked to lead the mission to find the missing terrorist. We found the stinking dude lurking in Iraq and tracked him down, and then we made a grab and scoot with his ass, and once we had him in our custody. We took off outta Iraq like our asses were shooting sparks. We went in Iraq with orders to take this lousy dude and bring him back to the United States so he could stand trial for his crime.

"Well man, we were operating under strict orders to keep all the damn killing down to an absolute minimum while we were out on this mission, and not engage any Iraqi soldiers we came across unless we were attacked by them first. We did get in a quick but little firefight with the Iraqi soldiers protecting the stinking dude we wanted. We were forced to shoot it out and as is the fact in all battles between warriors, soldiers die for what they believe or were ordered to do. But we didn't go to Iraq to kill Iraqi soldiers, man. In fact, when we were leaving the village where we found this lousy little dude hiding, we were trailed by more Iraqi soldiers who musta came to help the Iraqis we were fighting against. We didn't want to kill anyone not a serious threat against our mission, so we just disabled the vehicle and didn't kill them soldiers."

Captain Robert Walker had no idea he was speaking to the Commanding Iraqi Officer who was in the second vehicle that entered the village his troops had attacked, as they were leaving the small village with their captive, Colonel Abdulaziz Majd al-Adwani. Colonel Hamoodi al-Qaysi was trying everything in his power to try and hide his rage over what this young American Commander was telling him. The Iraqi soldier wanted to jump to his feet and slap Walker across the face, and tell him he was with the soldiers forced to stand by and watch his soldiers leave his country. Then he would kill the man for what he had done to his country, and the Iraqi soldiers his invading team had killed in their firefight with his soldiers in Iraqi.

Walker did not want to get involved in telling this stranger about the mission. He was not into blowing his own horn. All he wanted to do was drink, and watch the naked women around him.

The three other Arabs seated at the table with Colonel al-Qaysi, were staring at Walker as he spoke to their Colonel. Major al-Shaya was kind of respecting this young American soldier for what he and his fellow soldiers had accomplished for their government. She knew she would be very proud if she went on a mission to avenge some insult delivered against her President. She was starting to like this young Captain Robert Walker.

Walker ignored the other strangers at the table for the most part. He was only interested in finishing his story with this guy named Bill and getting back to enjoying himself at the bar for the rest of the night. In fact, he was hoping some other soldiers would come by and invite him over to their table, so he could dump this guy he still did not trust or like very much.

Ramirez could see he was still rather uncomfortable with the new people, and she decided to end his torment as she stood, and then she told him she wanted to dance a little.

The Iraqi Commander watched as the two American soldiers danced up a storm on the floor. His mind was caught between many emotions. His first instincts were to hate this man for what he done in his country, and for what he stood for with the other American soldiers in the bar. Then he wanted to like him because he was so much the soldier, so much like himself, and he too would do anything for his country, whether or not it was right. Then he wanted to kill Walker more than he wanted to kill anyone else in his entire life, and he also wanted to spare Walker's life and get to know him a lot better, and maybe become friends with the dangerous American soldier. He was suffering through the troubling thoughts of wanting to hurt him.

The Arab watched them dance, and decided before Walker died by his hand, he would have the honor of watching his girlfriend, wife, or whoever she was to him, die right before his worthless eyes. He found himself mumbling at his back in sheer anger. "May the womb of your foul mother cry out in shame and sorrow for what she is about to lose." Right there and then, Colonel al-Qaysi decided he was going to kill this woman known as Sergeant Dorothy Ramirez, to hurt Walker beyond all pain and sorrow and suffering.

Buckethead was enjoying his drink when he looked at Walker and Ramirez going at it on the dance floor. Then he mumbled to Mother Flanagan. "Man Mother, the way Raz is jigger bugging her little ass out there, she's not making milk she's making fucking butter, Homes. Look at her go will ya man. I never saw a woman shake it up like she's doing out there man."

Mother laughed as the drink was starting to get to the soldiers that came in with Walker.

The song ended and they returned to the table out of breath. He plopped down in his chair and took a slug of his beer. The Mutt, (Lieutenant Frank Hall), moved over to his side and looked at him. Walker picked up the look and asked the Mutt with a snap in his voice. "What the fuck's wrong with your stinking ass now for crap sake. You having a damn fit or sumthin, Homes?"

"No way man, I always look this way when I'm getting me a fucking idea, Walker."

Ramirez piped in and offered. "Are you drunk Mutt? You look drunk to me, dog man."

"Naw, I ain't that fucking drunk yet baby sister, but I'll tell you this though. The two of you look hot enough to eat right here and now, girl." The Mutt slurred his words slightly.

Ramirez knew the Mutt meant he was seeing double and she laughed at him. Then she gave up trying to speak with him, because she knew he was out of it. She also knew when he was like this he was soon going to start to look for some trouble in the bar.

The cunning Colonel al-Qaysi tried to engage Walker in yet another conversation. But he completely ignored him, because every soldier with him was trying to talk to him, or some of the other soldiers in the bar. He turned to Sergeant Khalaifa and gave her a slight head movement. At first she did not understand what the Colonel wanted from her, so he moved his hand down his chest, stopping at his breast and made a move across his chest with his hand. The female Arab Sergeant instantly caught on after that move.

Sergeant Khalaifa easily caught Buckethead's attention. She liked this big American soldier, probably because he was so large and seemed so foolish and so easy to insult. When she was able to lock his attention on her, she pulled one side of her blouse opened, and then she flashed him. Buckethead arched his eyebrows, and then he gave her a huge smile as he enjoyed the lovely view she was offering him. Sergeant Khalaifa wanted the big man to ask her to dance, because she was dying to show off her dancing skills before everyone else drinking in the bar.

Lieutenant Malika Nabeel Elmasry, introduced to the soldiers as Sergeant Shurug Khalaifa's husband, noticed what she was doing to the big soldier. He made like he either was not very interested in the action, or he did not see her give the American soldier a quick flash.

Now, Buckethead would not take his eyes off the pretty Khalaifa for a moment, because he thought she was interested in him romantically. Already in his mind he saw himself making love to this good looking young firecracker of a woman. He grinned back at Khalaifa and nodded slightly, and then he shrugged. He knew she wanted something from him, but he could not pick up the subtle message she was sending, so all he could do was to continue to stare and grin at her.

Sergeant Khalaifa knew she was not getting her message across to the big man, so she took the next step forward and she put out her hand. Then she twirled her fingers from her other hand across her palm, and she moved them like her fingers were dancing in the center of her hand.

Buckethead's eyes flew opened and then he nodded excitedly back at her, as he allowed a huge smile to cross his lips. Then he stood and walked around the table and put out his huge paw, as he asked her husband. "Hey Mark, you mind if I borrow your wife and have a dance with her?"

Lieutenant Elmasry, who was going by the name of Mark, waved his hand at the big man. Already, Khalaifa put her hand in his, and Buckethead so easily pulled her up to her feet.

Walker watched the two head out for the dance floor and he warned Lieutenant Elmasry in a joking manner. "Hey Mark, you betta keep your fucking eyes on that big one out there with your lady, man. He might try something on your pretty lady you know, man."

The Iraqi Lieutenant Elmasry remembered the words from the female with Walker when she told them they swung, and he replied in a matter of fact tone of voice to him. "My wife is a grown woman and she can make up her mind what she wants to do and with who. All I care about is she comes home after she has done with what it was she wanted to do. I can no more control my wife as any other man married, has control over their wives."

"Ahhhh... spoken like all married men afraid of their fucking wives, buddy." For some reason, he kind of liked this smallish guy more than he cared about Bill.

Everyone watched Buckethead with the woman on the dance floor, and it was like Walker warned. When he could make a move on her, Buckethead slid his hand in her blouse. Khalaifa purred as she allowed this big man to have a free hand with her body. As much as she was appalled at what the American soldier called Buckethead was doing to her, she also found herself enjoying the attention he was giving her while out on the dance floor.

When the music stopped, Buckethead tried to keep her out on the dance floor until the next song started. But Sergeant Khalaifa stop him, she was afraid to have another dance with him, because he almost had her topless with the first dance, and she was worried he might have her naked during the second dance, and that was too much for her to accept even if her commander ordered her to do what the large American wanted from her. The order she received, even covered having sex with them. Although she agreed to follow his orders, she was going to stop it short of being forced to make love to one of the American soldiers in front of the other soldiers in the bar. Besides, she wanted to save herself for Lieutenant Elmasry, for when they leave the

Colonel and the rest of their team, and they remain in the United States to start their life over.

Everyone seated at the table was picking on Buckethead and the young female as they returned to the table. Walker was getting sort of antsy because he wanted to get away from these people, and spread himself out a little more in the bar with the other soldiers. As he sat at this table, other soldiers kept calling his name out. They wanted him near them, but it was not until Three Martines, (Sergeant Cheryl Grantham) sashayed over to the table. She looked like a train crash because she was so drunk she was barely able to walk properly, and her clothes were a mess, hanging in complete disarray on her body.

It was quite obvious some of the other soldiers were playing with her. Her shirt was buttoned all wrong, and her shirt was much shorter because it was pulled high up on one side. She came up behind Walker and almost collapsed right on his shoulder. She was hanging onto him for dear life while trying to tell him to come over to their table and visit them for a little while. She suddenly belched and then almost heaved, making Walker jump out of his chair, because he thought she was going to get sick all over him. He tried to make her stand and she actually slid out of his arms. He ended up holding on to what was left of her shirt and she was sitting flat out on the floor, topless. Ramirez got up and snapped at Walker.

"Give me that damn shirt, man is she gone over the falls without a stinking net, Robert." Ramirez struggled to get Three Martines back in her blouse and once she was dressed, she helped her up to her feet. Then she tried to lead her back to the table where Neck, Baby Tee, Mother Flanagan, Snatch, Just Bob, Four F, and Weird Bill were sitting. The three Russian female fighters were also at the other table right next to the soldier's table.

Walker saw his chance to get away from the table and the four strangers he really did not care for, and he followed Ramirez over to the other soldiers. More chairs showed up, because it was after twelve midnight and some of the soldiers left the bar because they had early duty back on base. Walker with Ramirez sat once they dumped Three Martines back in her chair. It did not take long before the Mutt and his girlfriend, Blind Date left the table with Colonel al-Qaysi and the rest of his Iraqi soldiers, and they joined Walker at the other table. The other soldiers that came in with Walker left the Arab's table also, and they quickly joined the other table.

Soon, Colonel al-Qaysi and the three Iraqi soldiers with him, found themselves sitting with the original American soldiers they were sitting with, before Walker and his group came in the bar. He gave a quick head movement to the two women, and they immediately closed their blouses. Now, he was trying to get rid of these American troopers so they could talk amongst themselves in private. Once the women were covered up, the soldiers lost interest in them.

Short Cut started to look around the bar and when he spotted two women sitting alone, and she gave Short Cut the look and Nails picked it up also. He stood and offered the Iraqi his hand as he announced he noticed a few other friends he wanted to talk with for a while.

CHAPTER NINETEEN

The Iraqi Colonel Hamoodi al-Qaysi smiled as he shook hands and thanked the soldier branded Short Cut for introducing him to Captain Robert Walker and the other few soldiers with him, and then all four Iraqi troopers watched as the three American soldiers left them. When he felt no one from the bar was paying much attention to them, they began speaking to each other. "Elmasry, what do you think about this god cursed soldier who is named Walker? I must admit that I was deeply impressed by him and his military skills and commands. But what I have to talk with you three about is, we have to pick out one of these soldiers who is with

Walker, and we have to kill him or her tonight. I'm starting with you Elmasry, but I'll also speak with our two desert sisters as well. All four of us have to agree on the one who we'll kill tonight. Al-Shaya, and Khalaifa, I must admit that you women have carried out your orders very well on this night.

"You have done your duty for our country, above and beyond all normal duty, sisters. But we're far from being normal soldiers. I believe we're much like the soldiers we're hunting tonight. They're evil soldiers who'll do anything their cursed government puts before the foul fools. But they'll find out soon enough we're made from the same metal, because we'll do anything our government and President requests of us, for the good of our country, and for Allah's sake, Elmasry." The Iraqi Colonel was careful not to call his fellow terrorists by their military ranks as he spoke with them barely over a whisper in the bar.

The Iraqi Officer sat up straighter in his chair, and then he leaned forward as he spoke low to his commanding officer. "Colonel al-Qaysi Sir."

The Colonel instantly cut Elmasry off in mid sentence, as he barked at the man in a low and extremely angry voice. "Foul fool of fools, how many times do I have to remind you not to employ our military rank while we're speaking in this cursed establishment."

"I beg your pardon al-Qaysi, I'll not repeat my mistake a second time. As I started to say, I must admit I was highly impressed by the American Commander. It'll be a shame when we kill him. But that is all I'll say about this soldier. I've been watching the other Americans in the god cursed bar, most of these very dangerous soldiers seem like they were all with Walker during his attack against our country. Al-Qaysi, I picked up one soldier who seems to be almost as popular as this Walker is. I think if we're going to kill any of these worthless American fools one at a time until we kill the head of the cursed snake, we should hit this one soldier first."

Iraqi Colonel Hamoodi al-Qaysi started to search the interior of the now less than crowded bar, in an effort to try and pick out this one soldier who his Lieutenant was speaking of. He could not locate the one, and he finally turned to his Lieutenant again and groaned at him. "Elmasry, I don't see any other soldier in this foul establishment commanding near the respect this Walker does. Who is this other soldier you have leveled your cursed eyes upon? Tell me in a hurry Elmasry! I must see his foul face, to see if I agree with your interest to kill this man first."

"Col..." Elmasry almost called the Colonel by rank again, before he caught himself and he continued with his words. "Al-Qaysi, if you were to turn to your right and look at the table the third from the front window of this establishment. You'll see the soldier who has aroused my interest. The one I feel if we kill, would hurt the American soldiers the most we wish to harm."

The upset Iraqi Colonel turned in the direction he was directed by his Lieutenant, and his eyes fell on a soldier seated at a table and two women were all over him, and a few other soldiers were trying to speak with him at the same time. The table was covered with empty drinks and beer bottles, and other soldiers were hanging around them also. He maintained his eyes on this one soldier, and it was apparent he was a very popular man with the other soldiers. But the Iraqi had no idea this American, Sergeant Ralph Cavavagh known as Me Do, was at the bar to celebrate his birthday. That was why he was receiving the extra attention from the other soldiers.

After watching this soldier for a short while, he was forced to agree with his officer's pick for their attention. The Iraqi Colonel looked at Elmasry and then he offered him in a calm tone of voice. "My foolish brother of the endless sands, you have done a service locating our first target to kill, to begin our revenge against these cursed American invaders to our country. Do you two women agree with our selection for death, and our start of revenge against these foul soldiers?"

The women watched the target for a few moments, and then they nodded in agreement with his want to kill this one soldier first, and he added. "That is fine, we have decided, this man will die tonight. But since we're here, I want you to look at the other soldiers in this cursed bar, and then pick out our next target for another night to be dealt with. I want all the soldiers we pick to be the most popular of these foul fools until we finally kill their leader, Walker. I understand we cannot possibly kill all the cursed American soldiers, but I want to kill the most important ones first, before we kill Walker. Has anyone picked out another soldier to destroy on this night?"

Major Serena al-Shaya went to speak, but she was instantly cut off by Sergeant Shurug Khalaifa as she offered to her commander. "Al-Qaysi, I saw another soldier in this foul bar that seems pretty popular with the rest of the American fools. She's the female soldier standing by the fifth table on the same side where we have located our intended target for the night. She seems almost as popular as Walker and this other soldier we have leveled our eyes upon."

The Iraqi Commander turned slow to hide he was searching the bar for future targets. This time he made like he was looking at a beautiful blonde lady who was in the process of taking off her bra while dancing on the stage to the music. He watched her for a few moments until she was naked, and then he turned the rest of the way around. He stopped his gaze on the fifth table until he noticed the young woman who had every soldier's attention at this table. Again, he did not understand why all the attention was turned on this one woman. She was telling the males a nasty joke, and they were laughing and joking with her as she continued to speak with them.

He turned back to Sergeant Khalaifa, and then mumbled at her. "You're correct with your pick this foul woman fighter seems to be popular with the other soldiers. This is what we shall do, we'll kill the first target tonight, and then we'll wait for two days before we return to this cursed bar. If they didn't make too big a deal of the death of this first fool by the authorities, we'll kill this woman two days from tonight. Errr... al-Shaya, you were going to offer someone before you were cut off by Khalaifa. Who have you leveled your foul eyes upon on this endless night?"

"Hamoodi, the soldier I picked for death, was an easy one to decide on. He was visiting our table while we spoke to Walker. At first, I was eyeing the soldier they called the Mutt for death. As good a friend as he is with Walker, I had a feeling not many other soldiers were very pleased with this foul young man and his ugly actions. This is why I kept searching this bar, and when I spotted this one soldier. I knew if this one was killed, it'd hurt the unit as a whole working with Walker. I decided and offer to kill the soldier they call Neck. He's so big and stupid, it caused the other soldiers to want to look after him while he was drinking and stumbling around."

This time the Iraqi Colonel did not bother to search the bar, because he knew who the soldier was al-Shaya was speaking of. He liked her pick for the one they were about to kill, and he offered her in a slightly excited voice. "Al-Shaya, you have picked very wisely, and we'll do the same with this foul soldier. We'll wait two days after we have killed this female soldier tonight. But we'll wait only one day, to change our way of working, and I offer to destroy the foul female Sergeant Ramirez. If this worthless woman is soon to be Walker's foolish wife then she must die before we kill this loathsome American Captain and her foul lover.

"We'll kill the fearsome Captain Walker on Saturday at this loathsome bar. I believe once his foul wife is killed, the worthless fool will be looking to drown his sorrow in this cesspit they call a place of pleasure. This will force us to remain in North Carolina for another week I fear. Once Walker is destroyed, we'll make our way to the Florida Keys, from there we'll wait until the foolish al-Atrash kills the Judge and the useless Sergeant Damerdji kills the terrorist al-Adwani, if the fools were not able to win his release from the authorities. Once this part of the operation has been completed, we'll have finished our mission in America, and that'll free us to leave this land of Satan. I cannot wait until we leave this land of hatred. I witnessed enough naked women tonight to last me my life. Does everyone agree with my idea as I stated it for my followers?"

Major al-Shaya agreed with her Colonel, but both Elmasry and Khalaifa hesitated for a brief moment. The ever alert Iraqi Colonel instantly picked up the uncertainty in their response, and he questioned them as he held the young pair of soon to be murderers in his angry glaze.

The Arab Colonel's harsh stare sharpened, as he looked at the two. After a few seconds, he snarled at them angrily. "What is this foul hesitation you are offering me? Why do you two fools hesitate to answer the question I have set forth before your foul feet? Do you two fools wish to tell me something that I'll not enjoy hearing, especially from you Elmasry?" he directed his question right at the male warrior as his Arab customs demanded of him.

Lieutenant Elmasry straightened in his chair as he drew in a huge gulp of air, and then he reply. "Al-Qaysi, I fear that Khalaifa and myself have been speaking together, and we request to ask you if it'd be alright for us to remain here in the United States, once our mission against these hated soldiers is completed. We wish to get married and live in this evil country of plenty. We feel the United States has so much to offer the young of this world, sir."

After a few moments of strained silence, he finally responded to his fellow soldier. "Oh the young of our world of sand so ready to throw away all their learning and ancient customs, for the want of a better way of life from the bosom of their motherland. Yes young ones, I understand what you're requesting of me. Perhaps, if I were a little younger myself, I and al-Shaya would join you in this evil land that offers more than just sin and lust to their foolish children. Elmasry, when this mission we chose has ran its course and we're successful. We'll part ways, and you and Khalaifa are free to remain here in the United States if you so chose and I know Allah will protect and provide for a true follower of His great words and wisdom."

"You and al-Shaya would stay in the United States also?" Lieutenant Elmasry asked the Colonel, he was stunned by what he heard his commander offering him.

"Yes Elmasry, I fear that the same strong emotions that have captured both you and Khalaifa in its foul embrace, had also wrapped its tender arms around us as well. We too have been blessed with the grace of falling in love with each other. But alas al-Shaya and myself will return to the lands of our honored ancestors, and there we'll wait for the winds of fate to cleanse all wrong with the Arab lands of our ancient past of the Middle East. My lust to kill this foul American soldier is so overpowering in my mind. Why you may ask of me and I'll tell you why I have such passion to see this one soldier dead, because we're both students of war and honor."

"Al-Qaysi, I thank you for understanding of our desires and wants, sir." Elmasry replied.

"I assure you Elmasry I understand your desires more than you'll ever know. But these desires come with a terrible price tag attached to them I fear. If I leave you two fools behind to live out your lives in the United States, I must have your assurances that both you and Khalaifa will stay with me until our mission has been completed. And all of who we discussed tonight is dead and our revenge is complete. If you promise this much to me on the sands of Mecca, I'll give you and Khalaifa my blessing to remain in the United States, to live your lives hopefully in peace, my brother." The Iraqi Commander was no fool, because he planned to kill Khalaifa and Elmasry after they completed their mission, and he was going to leave the weapons he used to kill the Americans with them. That way the authorities would think they found the murderers.

All along, the Iraqi Colonel was planning to take Major al-Shaya out of the United States through the way they had first entered the country. Now, with the two of them wanting to stay would be a small matter for him to have Captain Kamis from the Libyan Embassy, give the American authorities their names. That way, it would remove any possible suspicion Libya assisted the murderers of the American soldiers, and give the authorities the killers. Al-Qaysi knew Elmasry, no matter how much he wanted to stay in the country, would never give up if the authorities cornered him and his girlfriend. He would fight them to his death.

"Al-Qaysi, I give you my sacred word as I hold my hand over the Holy Book of the Qur'an, I'll never leave your side until our mission has been completed successfully."

"And this boast covers the promise from Khalaifa as well I take it, Lieutenant Elmasry?" Hamoodi asked of his young Lieutenant as he looked him dead in the eyes.

Elmasry looked at the beautiful Shurug Khalaifa for a moment. The Sergeant was practically hiding behind his back, shaking like a leaf. She feared the Colonel would have been extremely upset with them, if he knew they wanted to remain in the United States. She slowly came out from behind Elmasry's body, and she looked at the Colonel as she nodded in the affirmative.

"Very well then, you two fools have my permission to stay in the United States. If that is what you two fool's truly want to do with the rest of your worthless lives. But first we have further work we need to accomplish, before we can get on with our lives, no matter where we want to spend our closing years. It's getting late on this never ending night, and I believe we should leave this pig sty of an establishment. Then we must set ourselves up outside the bar, to prepare for the worthless soldier we want to kill, to come out of this foul bar. That way we can hide for two days, before we strike again." Al-Qaysi offered the young assassins working with him.

He held his hand over the table to keep the other in their seats while he did one last survey of the bar's interior. The concerned Colonel Al-Qaysi picked up Walker and the rest of the soldiers with him sharing some good times. It seemed like all the action still taking place in the bar, was happening at or around his table. Then he shifted his eyes and located the other soldier that they had picked to die. It seemed the action at this table was starting to die off, and he felt it would not be long before this group of soldiers finally left the bar, and the elite soldiers head back for this military base they were stationed on. Once he was satisfied no one was paying much attention to his group. He pulled out a twenty dollar bill and left it resting on the table as a good tip to their waitresses. Then the small group of terrorists walked out of the bar nodding at the soldiers who introduced al-Qaysi's group to Walker and his fellow soldiers earlier in the night.

He turned towards Walker's table before he and his group walked out of the bar. He was surprised to see the soldier looking at him as his people left the bar. He nodded to Walker and to his amazement he gave him a half ass salute with his beer. He was further surprised when he noticed the warrior flash him a quick smile and slight nod as he watched his group leave.

This move committed by the man he hated the most in the world, made the Iraqi Colonel feel more confident he was beginning to be accepted by this dangerous Walker as his friend. In his mind's eye, he could see Walker lying on the ground in a pool of his blood, and the soldiers he was going to allow to live, gathered around his dead body shaking the soldiers to their soul.

Walker was not making any kind motions towards this man to be friendly with the dark skinned stranger and his three friends leaving the bar. He was using them more as a sign for them to get the hell out of his bar, and leave him and the rest of his soldiers alone, or he was going to beat the crap out of him and all his friends, males and females. Once the small group of strangers was out of the bar, he flipped them the bird as his last act of insult, and then he went back to paying attention to Ramirez, and the rest of the soldiers seated around the table. No one else from the bar paid any attention to the people walking out of the bar like they had no cares in the world.

OUTSIDE THE PARKING LOT OF
THE BAR BARE PARTS

The angry Iraqi Colonel Hamoodi al-Qaysi drove the car for the group again, the one they rented in Miami when they first arrived in that city from the rock they were picked up by the American Captain of the pleasure boat. Major Serena al-Shaya was in the passenger's seat and Lieutenant Malika Nabeel Elmasry and Sergeant Shurug Khalaifa were in the back seats of the vehicle. He drove over to the spot they had picked out earlier, to shoot the soldier they were going to kill as he left the bar. It was a rather secluded spot with a stand of trees and a thick growth of brushes surrounding the location for the Lieutenant to hide in and wait to kill the American soldier. Colonel Al-Qaysi stopped the car and then he got out of the vehicle with the Lieutenant, and he opened the trunk to get at the weapons they would need to kill the American.

Lieutenant Elmasry removed the M-16, and he immediately checked the clip for the weapon, and then he quickly disappeared in the heavy underbrush. He had orders to kill the soldier and then run to the other end of the stand of tree and brush, and his commander would wait there with the trunk opened, and the car running. As the young Lieutenant disappeared into the darkness of the night, the still angry Colonel got back in the vehicle and put the car in gear, and then he drove three blocks away from the bar and then parked where Elmasry was sure to come out of the bush. From this position he had a clear view of the main door of the bar and most of the parking lot. The two women in the car remained quiet as they waited for the death shot to be fired. The M-16 was silenced, so no one should be able to hear the round as it was fired at the man.

Inside the bar, the soldier branded Me Do, (Sergeant Ralph Cavavagh) was starting to feel the drinks the soldiers brought him all night to celebrate his birthday. By this time, the bar was down to just one stripper still dancing on the stage, and everyone was either too drunk to enjoy the woman, or they were just too tired to keep on with the partying they were doing all night.

Most of the drunk soldiers partying with Me Do, were likewise starting to slow down their celebrating and drinking. Now, the troops were sitting at the table while nursing drinks and pounding headaches, still too stupid to call it a night just yet. None of the soldiers wanted to give up the ghost, and return to their base to sleep it off, so they could do the same act all over again the following night. The few women fighters still hanging around in the bar with the soldiers, were sleeping in their chairs, or staring off in space. No one ordered another drink for the past hour. Even the waitresses were too exhausted to push any more drinks on any of the remaining customers still in the bar. At this time of the night, everyone who worked at the bar was praying that the diehard drinkers still hanging onto the ghost would give it up and leave the bar, so they could start to clean up and then lock up the bar and go home for the rest of the night.

Finally, Me Do stood on shaky legs and swayed as he finished off his last beer, and then he announced that he was going back to base. His car was parked in the lot in front of the bar, and he was going to drive back to the base. It was only fifteen minutes away and he knew most of the local police who worked this area of North Carolina, and they kind of gave the soldiers a little leeway to drive back to base while they were drunk, so long as they went right back to the military base from the bar, and did not go off driving around the area and they were careful.

The soldiers branded Poncho Villa, (Sergeant David Lopes) and CoCo-G, (Sergeant Milton Pettibone) who hitched a ride with Me Do, remained in their seat as he left the bar. They were too drunk to get up with him. They were going to go back to base with someone leaving the bar a little later on. After the soldier branded Me Do saw his friends were not going to leave with him, he shrugged and then stumbled towards the door. As he walked out the bar, he fished around in his pocket for his car keys so he had them ready by the time he reached his vehicle.

Hiding in the stand of trees, Lieutenant Elmasry took up a position standing by a wide oak tree surrounded by heavy brush. He leaned against the tree, and trained his weapon right on the front doors of the bar and then settled in and waited. The area was well lit up by the parking lot spotlights, so he had a clear shot at anyone exiting the bar he wanted to kill. It was three a.m., and no one was hanging around the outside area. Elmasry went over his orders in his mind. He knew when he took the shot, if someone saw him do it he was to run in the other direction of the parked car. He was prepared to give up his life if he was discovered by the police authorities.

It was warm this time of year, and sweat ran in his eyes as he stared so intensely in the sniper scope. Twice since he took up his position, a flood of other American soldiers came out of the bar and got in their cars and then left the lot. Each time he spotted the soldiers leaving, his blood pressure went wild. Elmasry just removed the weapon from his shoulder and looped the strap around his arm again, and placed the weapon in a better firing position, did the main door of the bar opened for the third time. This time it was his target stumbling out of the bar, moving liked he was stuck in slow motion. The Iraqi Lieutenant took three quick breaths to help calm down his breathing, and then he began to track his target in the scope of his weapon.

The Iraqi shooter did not want to kill this soldier right at the doors to the bar, because his body would be found too quickly by the soldiers remaining in the bar. He tracked his target until he was standing by the side of his car. When the target was trying to unlock the door of the vehicle, Elmasry lined his head up in the cross hairs, and then he held his breath and fired. With the sound of a spitting Cobra, the weapon bucked against his shoulder as he fired.

He kept the target's head locked in the scope until he saw it shatter from the round hitting it square in the face. The Iraqi shooter watched as the American soldier's body was violently pitched backwards and then it fell between two parked cars in the lot and he lost sight of it. The instant the soldier went down, Elmasry took off and ran for the waiting car. He came out of the woods right where he was supposed to, and he flung opened the unlocked trunk and tossed his weapon inside and then he slammed the trunk closed, and he jumped in the car.

Colonel al-Qaysi slammed the vehicle in gear and then left the area with no great haste. He drove slowly by the front of the bar and spotted no one moving around with any alarm. He was certain no one in the area had witnessed the murder, or even heard the shot being fired. He drove away from the bar as he asked Elmasry with a snap. "Are you certain the fool is dead, fool?"

"Yes Colonel al-Qaysi Sir, I saw the bullet hit his head and he went down in a heap."

"You're certain no one saw you shoot the cursed American fool, Lieutenant?" He asked.

"Yes Colonel, no one from the cursed bar saw me kill the foul soldier. He was alone in the lot, and no one came out of the structure as I left the area, sir." Elmasry let out his breath.

"Good, good, you have done very well my Arab brother from the vast sands of our honored ancestors. We'll be back at our hotel soon enough, and then you can get some sleep. As I have stated, you have done very well tonight, and our mission has started, and soon it'll be completed and we can get back to enjoying our lives as is should be in the Middle East."

No one in the bar heard what happened outside the saloon. The soldiers were drinking and talking to one another, and it was still pretty noisy in the bar. At three fifteen a.m., the bar tender announced last call, and waited for the diehard soldiers to belly up to the bar for their last drinks. Everyone in the place knew they had fifteen minutes to finish off their drinks and leave the bar.

Mother Flanagan, drinking with Neck, Buckethead, and Baby Tee, suddenly stood and said he was heading outside to catch some fresh air and take a leak. The others laughed as he staggered towards the door. Once outside, Mother lit up a joint and headed for the few cars parked close together. It was the only place outside to take a leak without anyone seeing him. As he walked past the first few cars, he did not see anything wrong, as he past the third parked car he noticed a pair of feet of someone lying on the ground. Mother smiled as he thought someone must have passed out as they went to their car. He kicked the foot as he grumbled at the downed person. "C'mon shithead, the floor's no place for a stinking soldier. If Walker sees you passed out like this, he's gonna tear you a new fucking asshole, stupid. C'mon, I'll help you... Holy Shit!"

Mother Flanagan jumped away from between the two parked cars and his military training immediately kicked in. He ducked down behind the car and quickly scanned the entire parking lot area, as he picked up Me Do's arm and checked for a pulse. Seeing the condition he was in, he knew he was shot in the head and dead. When he felt no pulse, he headed back for the bar in a low crouched run. He hit the doors and bellowed out at his commander. "Hay Walker, I got a fucking soldier down out here man." All traces of his drunken state left his body.

Walker was up in a flash, his high left him and he rushed towards Mother and the double doors of the bar. He glanced at the bar tender and then he snarled at him. "Call Nine, One, One you fucking asshole. Mother, who's down out there for fuck sake man?"

"Me Do, he's shot in the fucking head man. He's down for the damn count Walker."

"He's dead?" Walker asked Mother in an excited tone as he looked out the doors.

"Is he dead? Walker, half his fucking head's blown all over the fricking place out there man. It looks like someone was waiting for him, and they took him out as he headed for his damn car man. It fucking looks to me that Me Do was set up for the stinking kill out there, Walker."

The rest of the elite soldiers still inside the bar quickly gathered around the Walker by the doors, all of them losing their highs from drinking as they prepared for a fight outside.

"Didja see anyone hanging around out there, Mother?"Walker asked the excited soldier in an angry tone, already they could hear the sirens from the police coming at the bar.

"No man, it's as naked as the damn chicks from the fucking stage, Walker. I saw no one out there man." Mother Flanagan reported to his commanding officer.

"Okay, let's get out there and check the area for the fucking sniper. You people are Tier One soldiers, no fail teams, so you know how to do the act. I want flanking positions to protect us in the lead. Anyone have any fucking weapons on them? Where's Me Do's car parked, Mother?"

Two soldiers announced they had pistols, and Walker told them to protect their flanks as they moved out to get to Me Do's body. Flanagan pointed out where Me Do's car was parked.

"Okay people, let's get the fuck out there, we got one soldier down, and I don't want him lying on the fucking ground out there without us surrounding his ass. Let's do this thing like we were trained for people." Walker instantly charged out the doors and made his way towards the cars parked in the lot. The rest of the concerned soldiers fanned out and followed Walker lead towards the vehicles. Sergeant Ramirez and the Mutt were by Walker's side as he moved out of the bar.

By the time the soldiers rushed to the three parked cars, the first police cars came screaming in the lot. The officers spotted the group heading for the cars, and they figured that was where the shooting happened. Walker just got to the body when the first cop jumped out of his car and pointed his weapon right at him and barked. Stop where you are buster or I'll blow your fucking head off your damn shoulders. Put your hands over your head and stand there, mister."

"Hey man, calm the fuck down a little buddy. This stinking dude was with us, we're fucking soldiers from Lejeune, sir." Walker growled at the cop as he did as ordered.

More squad cars roared into the parking lot from the other side of the building. Two fire trucks and an ambulance also came up and parked in the lot away from the incident. The police stopped the soldiers from nearing the body as they ran crime scene tape around the three cars parked together in the lot. One look and the police knew the dead man was shot in the head, he was a mess. Some of the police officers started to interview the soldiers, and when the officers were told that Mother Flanagan was the one who found the body. They immediately separated him from the rest of the soldiers surrounding the few cars still in the parking lot.

Detectives showed up next in the lot. By the time the coroner arrived, Walker and a few soldiers were allowed to approach the body. Military Police arrived and they took over the investigation from the police. They took Flanagan in custody for questioning, and a military ambulance showed up, and the medics took charge of Me Do's body from the police officers.

Walker saw what someone done to Me Do and the first thought he had, was Sergeant Ralph Cavavagh must have done something wrong to a woman and she was probably married, or might have had a boyfriend and the rude dude avenged the insult for his girlfriend by killing him. It looked like a crime of passion to him because of the way he was shot and left for dead.

The Marine Commandant, Colonel Bruce Leadbetter was the next person to show at the crime scene, and he was as angry as a wet dog. He ordered his troops to line up, and then he laced into them. "What the fuck's wrong with you sacks of shit out here for fuck sake? You people see that fucking mess lying on the god damn ground over there. That was once your brother, your blood, your friend. He was a member of your fucking family and yet he's lying on the fricking ground like a pile of shit. I want to know why the mutherfucking scumbag who killed him is not lying on this same ground, and why the fuck his body isn't being ripped apart by you pieces of shit standing in my damn face. None of you shitbirds know what happened to this, your brother your blood here, dammit? I better hear someone fucking talking real god damn fast around here."

When no one spoke up, the fuming Colonel ordered the soldiers to get in their trucks and had the MPs escort the troops back to base, after he warned them he was calling a muster at Zero, Six Hundred Hours on the grinder. Then he spoke to the police and military investigators doing their act in the parking lot. It seems like they were of the same mind set as Walker was, they were already leaning more towards believing this was a crime of passion. That the soldier was killed because of some indiscretion he might have committed against one of the local females and the partner of the insulted woman took matter in his or her own hands, and settled the argument in their own fashion. It was not a rare occurrence at any of the strip joints in the area.

By the time the still fuming Marine Colonel headed back to base, that was the assumption the police and military investigators assumed, and he was forced to agree with for the time being. The topless bar was not going to be allowed to open until six p.m. By then the investigation should be completed and life around the mainstay bar would be back to near normal again.

Walker was roaring that he just lost a man, and it was not due to any military operation. When the soldiers entered the barracks, he went in a fit and he began to rip the place apart with his bare hands. The other soldiers were equally as angry, but they allowed him to vent their anger for them. When he finally calmed down to be talked to safely, Sergeant Ramirez walked over to his side, and she rested her hand lightly on his shoulder as she offered him. "Walker, you can't take it to heart man. It's not your fault Sergeant Cavavagh was killed tonight. This is the bad part of life, and there's crime in the States, as well as overseas. You have to let it go now honey."

"You're right Raz, but I'm gonna place the fucking titty bar off limits to all our damn soldiers for the rest of the time we're on this fucking base, dammit. Someone out there has a damn hardon for us soldiers, and I'm not gonna feed him any more of our people to kill."

"Walker, I think you better reconsider that order. If you put that bar off limits to our troops while they're stuck on base, they'll be dry humping the bunk posts in two days, if they can go out to the strip bar, Robert." She was trying to make light of the death of the Sergeant as she added. "Let it go and see what the police come up with, before you react to anything, honey."

THE HOTEL ROOM AT THE BEST WESTERN HOTEL

Colonel Hamoodi al-Qaysi was the first one up the day after the death of the American soldier, and he rushed out of the room and headed for the lobby of the hotel. He went to the newspaper stand in the hotel, and he looked at the different papers until he found the one with the headlines that read. 'A soldier was killed at the local bar' he was looking for. He took this paper and paid for it, and then he rushed back to his room. By the time he got back there, Major Serena al-Shaya was up and waiting for his return to the room. He read the paper with the Major leaning over his shoulder while trying to read the same article at the same time. They both smiled when they read the police thought the murder was a crime of passion, and they were not going to order the bar closed for any length of time. What they did not read was the bar was going to be allowed to remain opened, because of the revenue it brought to the local residents.

Major al-Shaya offered to the military officer and her commander in a calming tone of voice. "You see Hamoodi, you were absolutely correct to believe that the cursed police authorities of this worthless country would read what they wanted to believe into the death of this filthy American soldier, sir. This opens us up to be able to kill the second hated soldier at the foul bar that you want dead. But I'm quite positive that once we kill the second soldier, the police authorities will surely take other precautions after that one's cursed death. I'm positive the hated authorities will close the evil bar down for who knows how long, while they investigate the next killing we shall commit. Or they'll increase their presence there, which will make it nearly impossible for us to kill any other loathsome American soldiers who visit the filthy bar, Colonel. I believe if this takes place the weary I see it, we'll have to stalk one of the other soldiers, like the one call Neck, until we can kill him next, Colonel al-Qaysi Sir."

"Foolish woman who offers me her guidance that I didn't request, this large soldier called Neck is not the one I truly want to have death visit him, so his death is not that important to my desires, Major. The only reason I want him to die next, is to cause as much pain and confusion as possible to this Captain Walker and his filthy girlfriend. Once he's dead, we'll see how great this so called soldier who everyone thinks he is deals with his tragedy in life. We'll see how he acts with the death of his loathsome girlfriend weighing heavily on his cursed mind. I believe it'll make him an easy target for us to kill, careless in his foolish actions and thoughts. That's what I believe and hope's to take place for us, Major."

"No matter the outcome of this mission, we'll kill this one soldier called Walker. Then we'll leave this loathsome country and go back to our home of sand. I'm tired of all this killing and living the way we're forced to live while carrying out our orders. I pray Allah to place an end to it for us, Hamoodi." Al-Shaya complained as she let out her breath and shook her head sadly.

"Major al-Shaya, I assure you that all the foul death in this worthless country we're so concerned with, will finally come to a conclusion with the death of this one worthless American soldier who is named Walker, and the hated Federal Judge, and of our Arab brother and failure, Colonel al-Adwani. Once these three people are walking with their lowly ancestors in the land of forever, I'll finally be able to lay my head down on the soft sands of our vast deserts, and I can finally rest comfortably again. I too am growing very tired of all this constant killing and causing death to visit strangers we have no knowledge of who they may be. It seems that I have wasted my entire life in the hunt to kill innocent people in the name of Allah and my country's wants, woman. Yes, I'm as tired as you are obviously tired of all this killing we are constantly being forced to carry out, woman."

CHAPTER TWENTY

Captain Robert Walker and his troops hung around the barracks for most of the day, they were visited by Colonel Bruce Leadbetter and he informed them what the police decided about the death of their fellow soldier, Sergeant Ralph Cavavagh who was better known as Me Do. But his Unit name was no longer allowed to be used, because as far as the elite soldiers were concerned, his nickname was killed, but not the soldier's memory. Since it was determined it was not an attack aimed directly at any of the specialized soldiers, the restrictions on base were canceled. Walker decided he was not going to allow troops anywhere near the titty bar for the night. No soldiers seemed interested in going out on the approaching night. They were quite and somber.

The next day was another day off for the elite group of troops, and this was because of the death of one of their own. But today was different, the soldiers were restless and hot to start their new training program, and since it was canceled for the day, they wanted something to do with their time. Walker fielded their complaints and knew he had to do something, so he gave them menial jobs to complete to use up their time. As the soldier's workday ended, the young Captain was able to see the troops were still tight, so he bellowed once they were in the barracks.

"Okay shitbirds listen up we're going out for the night, and we're gonna tie one on while we're at it. We need to relax, and going to the titty bar seems like the only way we're gonna be able to do it. But this time I want anyone with pistol permits to carry the damn things on them tonight. Anyone who doesn't have a damn weapon, take your fucking service revolver with your ass. If there's some jackass who has a hardon for anyone from the service, let's show the asshole we're hot, and we fucking bite back." He stared at the group as his words breathed life in them.

As the four large civilian Chevy trucks left the huge military base and they pulled into the bar parking lot, the soldiers saw the bar was alive and cooking already. But the four strangers that Walker met in the bar two days ago were nowhere to be seen this time. He did not miss the strangers, and did not think about them as his group piled into the topless bar. He was only interested in getting the stress off his troop's shoulders. It did not take very long for the excited soldiers to let down as soon as the first three strippers came out on the stage, and they started dancing and stripping. Instantly the elite soldiers were back to their old selves again.

One of the strippers walked over to Mother Flanagan who was busy sucking on a beer, and she purred sexily at him as she actually bumped him lightly with her hip. "You know something mister I really love a big man dressed in a military uniform."

"Okay bitch then let me stay in it for a little while will ya? What the hell don't you shove off and come back after I had a drink and get a little buzz on from the stinking suds. Then you can see what you can do bout getting me outta my damn uniform, baby."

"You think I might come back to you later tonight, hot shot. You just dissed me, asshole. And now you want me to come back and beg to be with you later on, fat chance of that happening, asshole." The stripper walked away wiggling her rearend at him as an insult.

"Looks like you just blew that one big time, Mother." The Mutt smirked with a grin.

"Now if she woulda offered to blow my stinking ass then she woulda got me out of my uniform that fucking quick man." Mother offered at the Mutt, but the cautious mood of the soldiers was on full display and their usual good moods were nowhere to be seen.

Walker ordered the soldiers to leave the base dressed in their uniforms in case the shooter did not know Sergeant Cavavagh was a soldier when he killed him. He was betting on with so many troops hanging around the bar in uniform, any shooter might think twice at taking a shot at them.

It was nine twenty by the time Walker's group finally arrived at the bar, and he ordered the soldiers they were leaving the place at midnight, because they had work to do the next day, and he did not want any of the troops to get too drunk tonight. He did not want anyone to stay at the bar until closing time, in case the shooter was looking for another target to kill.

At ten thirty, Colonel al-Qaysi's car made the first circle of the bar. He easily spotted and recognized the vehicles that brought Walker and the rest of his troops out to the bar the other day. This time he and Major al-Shaya were going to enter the bar by themselves. Lieutenant Elmasry was going to remain outside, and he was going to be set up in the same location as when he killed the soldier called Me Do, Sergeant Ralph Cavavagh. He was ordered to stakeout the place until the female soldier they were after on this night, left the bar and he killed her.

The Iraqi Colonel and Major were going to stay in the bar after Walker and the rest of his group left for the night. He wanted to be there to see the action once Lieutenant Elmasry killed the female American soldier. He was using this action to help remove any possible suspicion the Captain might have against him. He knew Walker did not like him in the least, and he wanted to see his face when the woman fighter was killed almost right in front of him.

Everyone inside the bar was having a great time, and when Major al-Shaya and the Iraqi Colonel walked in and she was dressed to kill. Sergeant Ramirez immediately drew Captain Walker's attention to the two as they entered. His anger instantly heated up and he harshly glared at Colonel al-Qaysi until he noticed the look, and he and the female with him took a table at the other side of the bar well away from him and the rest of his soldiers.

Sergeant Ramirez picked up the angry look and she remarked to her lover and soldier. "What's with you and that guy anyway for Pete's sake? How come you don't like the man, Robert? He seems nice enough and his wife is a nice person. You have to learn to relax a little my dear."

"Relax you say to my ass Raz? The last time I was around that scumbag and relaxed, we lost Sergeant Cavavagh." He snorted as he kept his glare plastered on the face of the man.

"You don't think he had anything to do with the death of the Sergeant, do you Bobby?" Ramirez asked as she stared at her lover while waiting for his reply.

"No! I just don't like the lousy motherfucker and that's it in a stinking nut shell, sister." He replied hotly as he turned to Ramirez and the other soldiers with him at the tables.

Sergeant Michelle Soloman who was known to the rest of the soldiers from the elite Unit as Jail Bait, was dancing up a storm with a second soldier on the dance floor. She was so good looking and had such a great shape that she was always the center of attention to many of the male soldiers, whenever she was out on the town with them.

Blind Date saw Jail Bait having a good time and she drew the Mutt's attention to her. He griped back at Blind Date. "Yeah, Jail Bait can have a stinking party all by herself, baby."

"Do you want to join them?" Blind Date asked the Mutt, hoping to dance with him.

He refused, not many soldiers from the group Sergeant Cavavagh was with, seemed very interested in partying out tonight. The Mutt did not tell Blind Date that he and the two pointmen, the Ghost, (Sergeant Walter Casper) and the Hunter (Sergeant Frank Whitcomb) were ordered by Walker to remain on the full alert for the entire night, which meant these three soldiers were not drinking and they were watching everyone moving going on around in the bar. He knew the wise Captain was trying to set up a trap for the shooter if he was around on this night. He had a plan and was hoping the shooter who killed his soldier, was stupid enough to return to the scene of the crime. That was why he wanted his people to be armed, just in case they were hit again by the sniper. If he was, the soldiers were going to hit back, and they were going hit back hard.

Even though he did not believe the strangers had anything to do with the death of his Sergeant. He kept finding himself shooting a look of anger at the two strangers sitting at the table some fifteen feet away from his. He never wondered where the other two who were with these two the other day were, because he liked them other two people.

The concerned Iraqi Colonel al-Qaysi kept picking up the harsh looks aimed at him from Walker, and at one point he thought about cutting the next killing off, before his Lieutenant killed the female soldier when she left the bar on this night. He knew all he had to do was walk out the bar before their target did, and Lieutenant Elmasry would see the signal and pull back from the ordered kill. But he was so obsessed with wanting to punish Walker that he refused in his mind to stop Elmasry from killing the female soldier. Every time he looked his way, al-Qaysi smiled and nodded at him, and this caused Walker to get even angrier with the rude dude.

As the night went on, the soldiers picked to watch everyone in the bar, slowly let down their guard. No one in the place seemed like a threat against them. Nevertheless, Walker and the three others kept watching, keeping an eye behind them, to see if anyone followed the other soldiers out of the bar. The on alert and cautious Marine Captain was working under the assumption if the shooter was stalking his soldiers. The shooter had to be in the bar in order to pick out his next target. He also knew if his specialized troops stayed close with one another, it would be less likely anyone would dare to try and hit them again. Even though it was believed Sergeant Cavavagh was killed by someone he might have bothered somehow. The Captain was not taking anything for granted he wanted to be ready for anything coming his way tonight.

By eleven thirty, things were staring to slow down in the bar, and some of the soldiers started to drift out and head back to base. Walker saw two soldiers leave the bar one at a time, and he nodded to the Ghost and Hunter, and they followed the soldiers out. The two extremely dangerous pointmen returned and shrugged, informing him nothing happened outside the place.

Jail Bait stopped dancing and she was sitting on Snatch's (Sergeant George Weaver) lap, and Snatch was trying to slide his hands up her blouse. The two were laughing and carrying on. Jail Bait was drunk enough to think anything the other soldiers did, was funny at this point.

Walker smiled as he watched everyone hanging around the bar. Nothing he saw gave him any alarm. Even Ramirez let down her guard and was speaking with Baby Tee. Ice was still in the barracks and Blood Clot would not leave her side. Ramirez was beginning to think the two were going to become an item in the future, with all the attention Blood Clot was giving her lately.

At ten minutes to twelve, Jail Bait suddenly stood and she got off Snatch's lap like something was suddenly wrong with her. She seemed to be in some sort of distress and she was acting like something was bothering her. Her move instantly drew Walker's attention to her, and he stared at what was going on at her table. He picked up Snatch say something to her, and Jail Bail shook her head no at the worried looking soldier. Walker let out his breath in a hiss as he got up and walked over to the table to speak to Jail Bail to find out what was bothering her all of the sudden.

"Hey sister, what's up honey? You seem like something's really bothering ya."

"Walker, I have a problem and I have to go out to my car for something, and Snatch wants to come with me and I don't want him to." The female Sergeant complained at Walker.

"Hey kid he's only following my fricking standing orders, sister. I don't want anyone walking outta this stinking dump alone, girl. We might have a stinking hunter staking us out there someplace. When I saw you jump up I thought Snatch did something to ya, and I was gonna hop him in the ass if he did. Why the fuck do you hafta go out to your damn car for, Jail Bait? I want two soldiers together at all times tonight." Walker asked the woman fighter as he stared at her.

"It's none of your damn business why I have to go out to my car for. I have to go to my car for a second, and I don't want anyone following me either, sir. It's rather personal you see Walker." Jail Bait snapped angrily at Walker as she rested her hands n her hips and glared at him.

"I don't give a flying fuck how frigging personal it is to you, sister. I wanna know why you gotta go out to your damn car for, and unless you tell me, every swinging dick in this lousy place is gonna follow you outta the place to your car, sister."

"Jesus Christ Walker, I hate this shit. We women can have no secrets from you filthy pigs."

"Look, I'm not gonna get in a pissing contest over this crap with ya, Jail Bait. If whatever you hafta do outside is so personal you don't want anyone to go with you. Then I'll send one of the uther women outside with ya purdy ass, so you can do what you gotta do out there. If you need some pot, we have some shit at our table." Again, Walker glared at the female soldier.

"Dammit Captain, if you must know why I have to go out to my car, Mr. Nosy." Jail Bail leaned a little closer to him and she hissed barely over a whisper at him. "Walker, it's that time of the month, and I have to get something from my car. There, are you happy to know what's bothering me, you pig you. Now you know what my problem is. Or do you want to watch me put my tampon in, maybe that'll turn you on a little, My Nosy." Jail Bait glared angrily at Walker while resting her hands on her hips again, and she was angry as hell.

"Hey girl, that almost hurt my stinking feelings, little sister. I must admit I was a little turned on by ya offer though, nevertheless it did hurt my feelings. Look honey, I know this shit sucks the big one, but until I know for certain there's no fucking hunter stalking any of us troops. I'm gonna keep a tight fucking rein on everyone from the damn outfit."

"If you believe I need someone to escort me to my car parked thirty feet from where we're standing, I'll take Snatch with me, Captain. Does that satisfy your need to be a soldier twenty four hours a day, every day of the week Captain?" Jail Bait placed her hands on her hips again.

"Yeah, it'd make my stinking boat float alright, sister. Take Snatch out with ya so I can sleep tonight. We're all heading outta here pretty damn soon anyhow, so if you'd rather wait for all of us to leave this dump." Walker shrugged at her and waited for her reply.

"I can't wait that long Walker, unless you guys want to be slipping and sliding in puddles of blood around here.

God I hate to have to be talking to a guy about this kinda shit, mister."

"I'm embarrassed as hell about this shit myself, girl. The next time just give me the damn nod and I'll send Raz over to talk to you if that'll make it any stinking easier for ya." He replied to the angry female soldier who was red faced because of their conversation.

Jail Bait did not respond, she just reached behind her and she pulled Snatch up to his feet, and then they both quickly started out the bar. The instant Colonel al-Qaysi noticed his target head for the door he stiffened up. Major al-Shaya saw the Iraqi Colonel get nervous and she also tense up and ordered another round of drinks for them. She wanted it to look like they had no interest in leaving the bar yet, or they might be concerned with what would soon happen outside the establishment in the parking lot. She was trying to make it look like they were having fun.

As Walker headed back to his table, he picked up the female with the person he thought was Bill, order drinks and he ignored them. When he got back to the table he plopped down and Ramirez asked him what was wrong with Jail Bait. When he explained what the problem was, she got angry because he forced her to explain the problem to him. But she was also pleased he moved Jail Bait away from the other soldiers before they spoke together.

As Jail Bait and Snatch walked over to her car, they had no idea a weapon was trained on them all the way. Lieutenant Elmasry kept the woman fighter locked up in his sights, as the pair slowly walked across the almost empty parking lot. Snatch kept up the pressure trying to play with Jail Bait's breasts, and she was laughing at him and slapping his hand away from her body. When the two reached the parked car, Snatch stood by the trunk to give her some privacy, as Jail Bail walked between the cars and then as she fumbled around looking of her keys in her purse.

Snatch griped at her she should have had her keys out before they reached the car. Jail Bait turned and stuck her tongue at him and was about to reply when suddenly her head exploded. Snatch immediately dropped down to the deck and drew his pistol. He thought he caught a muzzle flash out of the corner of his eye, and he fired two rounds in that direction, as he struggled down between the two vehicles to check on Jail Bail's condition.

The soldiers still in the bar heard the rounds go off, and they instantly poured out the bar like a pack of crazy people with weapons drawn, ready to fight back at the shooter now obviously stalking them. The bar tender immediately called the police as the soldiers charged out the bar. Walker stayed real low and he bellowed at the soldiers who left the bar with him. "Jail Bait, Snatch, where the fuck are you two birds at? Are you hurt man?"

"Over here Walker, by the second overhead light to your left. Jail Bait's down and out of it man. The prick hit her square in the fucking head, and I think I picked up a flash to our left. I put some lead in that direction and took no return fire from the shooter. The sonofa fucking bastard has a silenced weapon, and the shooter seems to know what the fuck he's doing, man."

"You said you picked up a muzzle flash to my left. You stay where you are with Jail Bait and don't leave her side for a fucking moment, the rest of you slugs with me. We're gonna get this fricking shooter right now, dammit!" He had no idea, but the flash Snatch picked up came from a tractor trailer windshield as the rig went by on the highway some fifty yards to the left of the bar, and it reflected a set of head lights from an oncoming car. The group of elite soldiers left the front of the bar and quickly fanned out and headed in the direction Snatch sent them off in.

Lieutenant Elmasry quickly left his perch and headed across the wooded area, and was wondering why the foolish American soldiers were heading in the other direction from where he just fired at the target. He did not care, as long as he got out of the area safe and fast. He spotted Colonel al-Qaysi's waiting car and jumped in it and Sergeant Shurug Khalaifa pulled out of the area like any normal driving person would drive in the area. The Iraqi Sergeant drove back to the hotel and then hunkered down and waited for the Colonel and Major to arrive.

When Colonel al-Qaysi heard the shots fired outside the bar, he feared the wise American soldiers set them up in a trap, and when he saw the soldiers charging through the bar, and many of them had weapons drawn and headed for the parking lot. He was certain it was a set up against them. But he also knew he had to react or he would surely draw some suspicion against himself. So he and al-Shaya got up and they charged out of the bar, along with the rest of the soldiers in the place. Walker saw the two strangers come out and he snarled at them. "Hey Bill, this is no fricking place for any damn amateurs out here, buddy. You two assholes betta get your stinking asses back inside the fucking bar where you two will be safe, man."

"If there's trouble, I want to help Walker." The crafty Iraqi replied to the Marine Captain.

"If you don't get your stinking ass back inside the fucking bar this minute, I'm going to rip your frigging head offa your damn shoulders asshole, get back in the damn bar." Walker roared as the first of the police cars screamed into the parking lot. This time the bar tender said there was a sniper outside his bar, and the SWAT teams responded to the call along with the regular police officers. The police tried to stop the soldiers from acting on their own, but once they saw it was impossible, they used the soldiers to help in the search for the sniper.

Al-Qaysi and the female Major went back in the bar as more police came to the scene. But the Colonel was in a good mood, he saw the police and soldiers heading in the wrong direction which informed him Lieutenant Elmasry was able to get away safely.

Colonel Bruce Leadbetter was notified about the second shooting and he arrived at the bar with the MPs again, and they immediately took over the investigation from the local police. Slowly, his soldiers came out of the area once they came across the highway, and they did not find any sign of the shooter. Now they felt the shooter was using the main road, taking his shot and then driving away before they could get at him. Colonel Leadbetter was looking for Walker, and when he saw the Captain he headed for him as he bellowed.

"Walker, I want to see your stinking ass right now soldier. Jail Bail is fucking dead and she was hit the same way Sergeant Cavavagh was killed in this damn parking lot. It looks like the same weapon was employed by the shooter as far as I can tell. I want you to round up our people and get them the fuck off this damn property. As of this moment, this place is condemned and any swinging dicks or bouncing tits that get caught on this fucking property again until further notice, is going to wish to God the fricking sniper got to them before I do, dammit."

Walker saluted the Colonel he felt the same way that there was a sniper on the loose in North Carolina. Now, all that had to be determined was if this sniper was after just soldiers, or was these two killing random hits. Walker ordered his troops outside to line up, and he went back in the bar to make certain the rest of his soldiers were out of it. He didn't want to leave anyone behind when they left the parking lot. When he entered the bar he spotted Colonel al-Qaysi and his supposed wife, they were standing by the front windows trying to see what was going on outside. He headed for the two and when he was near them, he snarled.

"Hey man, that was pretty fucking stupid on your part, buddy. There was a stinking shooting outside, and there you two asses were, standing out there like a stinking fish outta water. You coulda gotten yourself killed just because you were being fricking nosy out there, man. That wasn't good thinking on your part, man." Walker bitched at the man he still did not like much.

"I just wanted to help you guys that is all Walker. I knew you were having a problem outside, and after the other soldier was killed a few days ago. I was worried another of your soldiers was hurt outside, Captain." Al-Qaysi replied as he tried a quick smile on him.

"Yeah, right, okay, anyway stupid, it was a bad idea on your part to come outside this stinking dump like you did, man. Look, you keep doing this kinda shit around here, and I might get to liking ya ass a little betta, fella. That took some guts to come out there after you heard the fucking shots fired, man. Next time I'm in the bar and you show up, I owe you a stinking beer, man. Well, I gotta get my people the fuck outta here ten minutes ago, before one of them get in any more trouble tonight, man." Walker nodded at the two strangers and then he was gone.

He quickly got his troops back to base, but the Colonel demanded a night time assembly, so the floodlights on the massive parade grinder were on, and the elite group of specialized soldiers was standing at attention in formation while waiting for the Colonel to address them. The body of Jail Bail was on the base, and the inspectors were going over her body with a fine tooth comb, looking for any possible evidence and what damage the round did to her body.

The steaming Marine Colonel Leadbetter came charging out of his office across from the grinder training field like he was angry with the world. He was hatless and heated and glaring at the gathered warriors. The officer stood on the platform leading to his office, and he screamed at the soldiers as soon as his eyes fell on their faces. He was being flanked by Colonel Joseph Salsiccia, Major Wilson and Sergeant John Kirkpatrick.

Colonel Leadbetter started reaming his troops. "Okay you bunch of fuck ups, we just lost another one of our damn soldiers to this sonofabitching sniper, and that's two too many if you were to ask me. As of this moment, I'm ordering each one of you motherfuckers to be armed to the teeth at all times when you're off this fucking base. No one from this base is to be off base without at least two soldiers with you at all times, until further notice from my ass.

"We have a flaming asshole out there, and so far he has not shot anyone other than fucking soldiers, our soldier's people. So it's believed at this point that we're his main targets, until the damn shooter proves otherwise to our asses. If any of you come under sniper fire, you'll fucking respond accordingly, a round for a round, a death for a death. We find ourselves at war right here smack dab in the middle of the United States. There'll be at least one long rifle and shooter in any vehicle, military or civilian leaving this base and that shooter will fire back on any motherfucker shooting at our damn asses. You people are on full alert as of this moment, but I'll not stop any liberty time at this point. I won't allow this miserable asshole to stop you people from enjoying yourselves while stationed on this base, period, dammit. We owe you troops that much while you're in the service of the United States government.

"We might use you people for fucking bait out there, as long as this damn nut is singling out our soldiers. Then we stand a greater chance of getting him before he turns his attention to any fucking civilians of this State. I want this sonofabitch as much as the President wanted his damn sniper. We got his, so I want you people to get our fucking sniper. You guy's been bitching ever since you first arrived on base that you asses wanted some serious action. Well spudheads, it's waiting for you out there so go get some. I'll tell you troops this much, if another soldier is killed by this asshole, and that prick isn't lying on the ground by our downed soldier. I'll be taking numbers and asses. You people are allowing some fucking nut to kill you people off, and that's not in our fricking play book of military training. In case you people aren't aware of it yet, we just lost Sergeant Michelle Soloman to the damn sniper tonight."

No soldier replied to the Colonel's angry words, all they knew and wanted was to be turned loose and find the sniper killing some their own. But the wise military officer knew he had to clear his words up, or some of his elite soldiers were going to interpret his orders in the way they wanted to hear them. He understood he could not have a pack of wild ass vigilante troops running all over the place thinking they were doing God's work, armed.

"One thing I must clarify for you damn horde of misfits. When any of you are off this damn military installation, you aren't free to shoot anyone who looks at you the wrong fucking way, dammit. We have a stinking sniper working us over like a damn professional hit man. I don't need a bunch of angry soldiers doing the same fucking thing this asshole is doing. You people better make damn certain your fucking target is the target you're out there after, if you have to fire at anyone while you're off this base, dammit. I'm going to make contact with General White, and I'll see how he wants to handle this damn mess, and if he has any other ideas.

"Until that time, you people will walk around like you're going on Noah's Ark, and you're waiting for it to start fucking raining on you people, two at a damn time. You don't go anywhere off this stinking base, unless you're walking around in god damn pairs, I can't make it any clearer than that for you pack of war wacky bastards. Remember your damn orders, okay, you people are fucking dismissed at this time!" The still fuming Marine Colonel glared at the elite group of soldiers until they finally broke ranks and headed off to their barracks.

Colonel Leadbetter remained standing as most of the troops left the area, because he was waiting for what he expected next to come at him. Walker headed directly at him and he was not very happy, as the Colonel barked in a sharp voice before the young Captain could even get one word out of his mouth. "What the fuck can I do for you, Captain Walker?"

"I want fucking blood Colonel Leadbetter Sir! And I want it right now dammit! I want to hunt this miserable little prick down like the fucking dog he is, Colonel! I want my people out there hunting this prick just like he's hunting us. We can't possibly allow a stinking civilian sniper to have us battle harden troopers bunching up on fucking base like we're even the least bit scared of this lousy mutherfucker, sir." Walker snarled angrily at his commanding officer.

"It's a damn good thing you stuck 'sir' at the end of the fucking bitch at my ass, mister. Captain Walker, I know damn well you want blood, and I assure you so do I, sir. But you have to maintain control over yourself and your fucking troops at all times over this present situation, or we might find ourselves placed in a blood bath right here in middle of the United States. I have to be square with you Captain. As of this moment, we're not certain this lousy shooter is just working on us soldiers. Remember Captain, the soldier we branded Me Do, Sergeant Cavavagh wasn't dressed in his military uniform when he was killed by this fucking sniper two days ago, mister. But I'm more than willing to error on the side of caution Captain. That's why I gave the order to arm all the soldiers leaving this fucking base for any reason whatsoever, mister.

"One other thing I must commend you on Captain, that was a very wise order on your part to have your people armed when you fools headed for the damn titty bar tonight. I see we're both thinking along the same line, Captain. We have to make certain we have everyone armed at..."

Sergeant Kirkpatrick walked up behind his commander and interrupted the Colonel and Captain's conversation, informing the Colonel that General White was on the horn, and he wanted to speak with him immediately. The Colonel turned back to Walker and looked at him, and then said in an angry tone of voice. "C'mon mister, you might as well be a part of this fucking conversation as well, Captain. I'm quite certain General White has to know what the fuck just happened down here tonight by now, and the death of one of our troops. I'm just as certain he wants to ream me a new asshole over the damn situation, and also wants to find out what the fuck I'm doing about finding this damn sniper and putting out his lights, sir."

When the two military officers were in the Colonel's private office, Colonel Leadbetter picked up the phone, and moaned in it in an exhausted tone. "Yes General White Sir, this is Colonel Leadbetter here sir, good evening General and how are you sir? General White, I'm pretty certain you're aware we have a slight problem developing down here in North Carolina sir, and I'm trying my damn best to get a damn handle on the situation before it gets..."

"What the fuck is so damn good about this evening, Colonel? I can't believe my damn ears and what I'm hearing about this damn sniper operating down there, and killing two of your special troops, Colonel Leadbetter! What the hell do you have happening down there for love of the good Christ Child, Colonel? What the hell is this shit I heard about you having some damn lunatic working over our elite troops, and taking your specialized people out one at a damn time, and this is the second soldier he got on us down there, dammit?

"Look Colonel Leadbetter, I hate like hell to lose one of my damn soldiers out on the field of battle, sir. But I'm sure as hell not going to start losing my highly trained specialized soldier's right here in the middle of the United States, without taking some heads in return, sir. You better pay strict attention to my next orders if you know what's good for you, Colonel Leadbetter. I want this damn sniper taken out ten minutes ago, mister. Do you read me loud and clear on this last order I just issued to you, Colonel Leadbetter? Ten fucking minutes ago I repeat Colonel." The Chairman of the Joint Chiefs of Staff stopped yelling so he could hear the Colonel's reply.

"General White Sir, I can assure you sir that we're acting on the same orders you just issued to me, sir. I just issued orders for all troops leaving the base for any reason whatsoever, to be armed to the damn teeth at all times, and ready to attack anyone who tries to attack them. And, those troopers aren't to leave the damn base at any time alone, General White Sir. I further ordered a long rifle shooter to be installed in every vehicle leaving the base with the other troops, sir. I was planning to call you in the morning to see if you wanted to increase the response I have ordered for the troops on base, General White Sir. Furthermore General, I have also issued all military bases in both North and South Carolina, to be likewise protected with weapons and a sniper in each vehicle leaving any military base in both States until further notice, sir."

"Hmmmm you seem to be making all the right decisions so far over this present situation, Colonel Leadbetter Sir. I agree with all your orders as you have issued them at this time, sir. I don't want another one of our soldiers getting hit by this damn nut down there, sir. Colonel, I think I'm going to increase your orders, and order every military base on the entire eastern coast of the United States to be likewise protected as you have stated, until further notice. Hummm... is there any possibility that this act might be being carried out by an unknown terrorist cell operating in the States? And, these possible terrorists are going to keep pecking away at our soldier's asses like this, until they get their fill of killing our people, Colonel Leadbetter Sir?" General White barked angrily at his lesser officer over the phone.

"I don't believe this is an act committed by a possible terrorist cell, unknown or otherwise at this time, General White. Mind you General this question did come up between the local police and our own, but it was voted out as a possibility, sir. I think we have some wounded husband, or possibly a damn jilted lover who might have lost his wife, or his or her other half to an active duty soldier, sir. And this flaming nut has a hardon for anyone dressed in a military uniform, or supports a military hair cut, or even just happens to just look like a soldier on active duty and attached to a military base, sir. And since he or she has hit a male soldier first even though he was not dressed in a military uniform, but he supported a military type hair cut, and then the shooter hit a female soldier on this second hit in the same fashion as he had killed the first soldiers and…" The Colonel's words were instantly interrupted by the General.

"This last killing was one of our female soldiers, Colonel Leadbetter Sir?" the stunned General offered over the phone communication angrily.

"I'm afraid to report so General White, and that's why we feel we're likely dealing with some nut that might have lost his love to a soldier on active duty, sir. Besides General White Sir, we're not that certain this damn sniper is just working over soldiers at this point, sir. The first killing was leveled against one of my soldier's who was dressed in civilian clothes at the damn bar, sir. So we might be hunting some damn shooter who is singling out the local titty bars surrounding our military base, and this shooter is waiting for anyone thought to be a soldier to come out of the damn place, so he could pop them off in a sniper's fashion on us, sir."

"Dammit, okay Colonel Leadbetter Sir you gave me a few other things that I must look at here, sir. I'm going to meet with CIA Director Raincloud tomorrow morning, and run this shit by him, and see what he thinks about this crap. Be back to you Colonel." General White broke off the communication without any further words, and he left the Colonel listening to a dial tone.

CHAPTER TWENTY ONE

THE BEST WESTERN HOTEL, NORTH CAROLINA

The Iraqi Colonel Hamoodi al-Qaysi and Major Serena al-Shaya were ordered out of the bar by the police as they started their investigation of the latest murder at the bar. Both Iraqi Military Officers were forced to hail a cab and be driven back to their hotel. Once in the room, the Colonel was sitting at the table and Major al-Shaya was lying on the bed wearing a Best Western nightshirt and nothing else. She was watching the upset Colonel who seemed to be locked deep in thought. She remembered their lovemaking last night and smiled pleasantly. But nothing she could do would break the hard trance he was currently locked in at the moment.

"The concerned Arab Colonel was staring at the newspaper, he was disappointed to see the police ordered The Bare Parts bar closed until further notice, or the authorities were able to capture the sniper working near the topless bar. Again, he found himself wondering if he should go after Captain Walker next and kill him, and then leave the United States before they were finally captured by the local authorities currently searching for his hit team.

The worried Iraqi Commander looked at the calendar and saw it was Friday, April 19th, 2002. He remembered the trial of Colonel Abdulaziz Majd al-Adwani was scheduled to start on April 20th that was next Wednesday. He understood his hit team still operating in Washington, was going to make the assassination attempt on the Federal Judge and Colonel al-Adwani on Tuesday, April 23rd. So he had to be done with his killing of the American soldiers by that date, and then he and the female Major would head for the Florida Keys soon after that time. He also knew once the Federal Judge was killed, the American authorities would automatically close down all the borders as they had done after the Twin Towers terrorist attack. The swift Colonel wanted to be set in place by that time, and at lease be on his way back to the Island in Bimini they used when they first entered the United States, which seemed like a lifetime ago to him.

The happy Major al-Shaya was able to get the Colonel's attention, and he looked at her. "Hamoodi, you're being much too serious today I feel. We're doing well with what we have planned for the hated American soldiers. We have successfully killed two soldiers so far, and our time in the United States will soon be concluded. I can't wait until we're back home sir."

"We might be home a lot sooner than I first expected, desert sister. Lieutenant Al-Atrash is supposed to kill Colonel al-Adwani, and the fool Damerdji is to kill the worthless Judge on Tuesday morning. I plan to have Captain Walker and his filthy girlfriend dead before this time, and we'll be at the least, in the Florida Keys before the cursed Judge and our worthless Colonel are dead. I'm hoping to be safely on the foul Island waiting to get to the Bahamas before their deaths. That way we'll not be blocked from leaving this cursed country on these pending deaths. The reason I'm having Lieutenant Elmasry do the killing of the American soldiers. When the foul fool remains in the United States with Sergeant Khalaifa, I'll make certain the loathsome Libyan Captain, ends up with the worthless weapon he killed the soldiers with, al-Shaya.

"In that order, the American authorities will end up with the murder weapon with Lieutenant Elmasry's fingerprints all over it. And the hated police authorities will search for him, and the fool will die in their attempt to capture him, and the worthless female Sergeant sure to be with him. Thus ending the fear of a sniper stalking the streets of the United States, and the authorities will believe they have successfully captured all the snipers involved with our hit team, between Lieutenant Elmasry, and Sergeant Khalaifa. And, the foolish Americans will end their foul search for any further cursed snipers involved with the two killers. It's a simple plan in which to protect ourselves, while giving the hated Americans the animal they're searching for, Major."

Al-Shaya slowly lowered her head and let out her breath in a deep sigh. She was unhappy Colonel al-Qaysi was going to throw the lives of Lieutenant Elmasry and Sergeant Khalaifa to the officials to protect their lives, and allow them to escape from the United States safely. She was of the belief if soldiers were sent out on a mission then it was the responsibility for those soldiers to live, or die trying to protect each other's lives, or their mission was for naught.

"Foul woman, I see by your face that you disagree with my plans as I have just laid them out before your worthless eyes. Major, in the world in which we dwell, sometimes it becomes necessary for the common soldiers to lay down their lives to protect the soldiers who command them. In that way, the commanders will live to carry on the fight for their country it's a fact of life Major al-Shaya. You'll do as you're told and nothing more, lowly woman. Our concern is to carry out the death sentence we have bestowed upon the American soldiers we want dead. This Neck person is the next one on the hit list. I want him dead by the end of the foul day."

"But what if we can't get at this foul soldier you seek to kill, sir?" the Major asked.

"We'll spend this entire day with keeping the military base under constant surveillance, and if we can't get at this Neck soldier. Then we'll get any other cursed American soldier who comes off the military base. Go next door and wake the two fools there, Major. I want to leave as soon as possible on our next mission. I'll plant Lieutenant Elmasry near the military base along with his foul weapon, and we'll setup and between the four of us, one of us is bound to kill another American soldier. We have to keep the pressure on the worthless fools. We're doing Lieutenant al-Atrash and his group a service. We're attacking the hated Americans here, so the security in Washington will not be improved around his intended targets. Go wake them two up Major."

In a matter of moments, the two other Arab terrorists from next door were standing in Colonel al-Qaysi's room. He gave them their orders and they instantly headed for the car. It took the shooters fifteen minutes to get near the massive Marine Military Base, and Colonel al-Qaysi let out the three other soldiers in the selected areas where they would be able to shoot at any military vehicle or civilian car or soldier leaving Camp Lejeune.

CAMP LEJEUNE, JACKSONVILLE NORTH CAROLINA

Captain Robert Walker's group was up since five a.m. and they went through their daily exercises and then they ate mess. Now, the specialized soldiers were back at the barracks reading over a number of papers the Colonel gave them. It was the beginning training on how to better cover all urban counter terrorism tactics, and what was expected of the elite soldiers, if and when they were deployed in any civilian streets of the United States, or in any other allied nations. Colonel Leadbetter was in the process of setting up another special training shoot house constructed right on the training field of the base. He was also devising a number of different scenarios on certain situations he was going to place his elite troops in during any possible civilian deployment. Walker's group was informed the field training would not start until the end of the week, so they were on their own until their training started in earnest.

Wacko, (Sergeant Salvatore Tomassi) came over to Walker's bunk, and he sat on the edge of the bunk. Walker looked up from his paper and snapped at him. "What's up with you Wacko?"

"Hey Walker, not for nuthin man, but I'm kinda outta fucking grass and need some, man."

"Then go over to the damn PX and pick up some crap from them, stupid. They always have it ever since they legalized the crap, buddy. What's your stinking problem, man?"

"That's just it Walker, the stinking PX has a sign up stating they're not selling any fricking grass for three weeks. Some big puke is arriving on the damn base, and the lousy dude don't like the crap sold to us soldiers on base, man." Wacko complained at his commanding officer.

"Now that's a fucking serious problem, buddy. Wacko, no one is restricted to base, so go rec a truck and head out and find some for yourself, man. Since no one is gonna leave the base at night until they locate the damn shooter. We're gonna need some crap in the barracks while cooped up on base, buddy. Take Mother Flanagan and the stinking Neck with ya, use Neck as the long shooter and get some crap, only if you know where to pick the shit up without having to hunt for the crap, stupid." Walker cocked his head to the side and stared at Wacko for a second.

"You want me to tell the uther guys they hafta go along with me? Those guys ain't gonna listen to me for nuthin you know, man." Wacko complained to Walker.

"Hey, what the fuck can I tell ya man, if you really want any of the damn shit, go get it and stop busting my stinking horns over the shit will ya. If you don't wanna ask those uther two guys to go along with you then stop bugging my stinking ass about this shit. I'm not gonna order someone to go out on a fricking pot mission for no one, buster. I just as soon keep all you stinking guys offa the damn shit until we're back on the Island in the Keys, and well away from this damn sniper and stinking military base anyway, Wacker."

"Fuck that shit Walker, if you think for one second I'm gonna get stuck on this stinking base for three weeks or more without some damn grass then you're plain nuts, man. I'll talk to the uther guys, and go out and get some shit for us man."

"I'm telling you Wacker, if Neck doesn't wanna go with you as shot gun then no one's leaving the base and that's that. You got it loud and clear friend?" Walker warned the soldier angrily.

"I hear ya loud and clear Walker, he'll come with us, or he won't have any grass either, man."

"That should make him go with you easy enuf, Wacker. You'll report to me when you're back from this damn pot run, stupid." Walker snapped at the soldier then went back to reading.

Wacko rushed over to the Neck and started to speak to him. Sergeant Ramirez, who was resting on her rack right next to Walker's, sat up when Wacko left, and she said to her lover and soldier with some concern lacing her tone of voice. "Walker, you think it's a good idea to allow them three dopes to leave the base for a pot run? With this sniper active out there, I wouldn't want any of my people going out and maybe ending up running into his cross hairs just for some damn pot, Robert. Who knows where the damn shooter might be lurking about, Bobby?"

"C'mon Raz and get a real life will ya. First off baby, it's light out and you know no stinking sniper does his crap in the light of day. The damn night is the real domain of the fucking sniper to operate in. Besides Raz, the soldiers will be riding in a stinking vehicle, and they'll also be armed to the frigging teeth, and they'll also have another stinking soldier riding shot gun for them at the same time. And, you heard the stinking Colonel's bitch, he said he wasn't gonna allow some asshole to hold us hostage on our own base. So I'm just following his orders of having the guys armed and ready for any action aimed at them, baby. What more can I tell ya?"

"It's too late for anymore talking Bobby. The three fools just left the barracks, and I hope they'll be okay." Ramirez warned him as she watched the three soldiers leaving the barracks.

"They'll be just fine so don't worry bout them damn slugs will ya. They're fucking soldiers, and they know how to protect themselves, especially when the asses are armed like they are."

Wacko, Neck and Six Pack, (Sergeant Joseph Jesposito) left the barrack. Mother Flanagan did not want to be bothered going with them. They picked up an unarmored Grungie (Humvee), and the three left the base without telling the Sergeant why they needed to use the vehicle.

The Iraqi Colonel al-Qaysi let Major al-Shaya out from his vehicle, and he was heading back towards the main gate of the massive base of Camp Lejeune. He was looking for a place to turn the car around, so he could find a spot to park, and wait for his people to kill a soldier from the base, and then leave the area. He stopped the vehicle in the middle of the road and was about to start his turn, when he noticed the Humvee driving out of the main gate of the base. He waited for the truck to pass him so he could see who was inside the vehicle. A smile quickly spread across his lips as he saw the huge man he wanted dead, sitting in the rear seat of the jeep.

The Iraqi Commander picked up his radio and keyed the mike and said. "One, Two and Three, our package is in the rear seat of the machine coming at you. Three, I'll pick up One and Two, and you'll pick up the package. By the time we pass your position, you'll have the package in sight, and have it sent by postal to its destination. Click if you understand your orders, Three."

Al-Qaysi counted three clicks over the radio. The heavy military Humvee was well ahead of him when he stopped the car and picked up Major al-Shaya. He moved the car up until he saw Sergeant Khalaifa, and picked her up. Then he zoomed down the road and passed the lumbering and slow moving military vehicle, and headed to the second road where he knew Lieutenant Elmasry would be once he fired at his ordered target. It took him nine minutes to get to this other position. He was going to hide the weapons and then they were going down to the water once the shot was fired, and walk the shoreline. He wanted Elmasry to jump in the water to remove any trace of gun powder residue on his person, in case the American soldiers stopped and they checked them out. He parked his vehicle and waited for Elmasry to accomplish his orders.

Lieutenant Elmasry had the weapon resting against his shoulder aiming it from the stand of weeds he was hiding in. He saw the Colonel's car pass his position and he looked down the deserted road. He picked up the military type machine coming down the road. He aimed the weapon and waited for his target to reach his position. When the jeep was near enough for him to see inside the vehicle with his scope, he singled out the man sitting in the rear seat. He held his breath and fired at the vehicle, it was a straight and easy shot. The second he fired, he picked up and ran like a wanted criminal across the field towards the secondary road and al-Qaysi's car.

Wacko was driving and Six Pack was looking out the side window at a Super Cobra fast attack helicopter doing some fancy maneuvers in the air off to his right. The Neck was sitting in the middle of the seat in the rear of the vehicle, so he could look out the front windshield easily. Suddenly, the side window exploded on the soldiers, and the force of the exploding window caused Wacko to swerve the machine as he cried out to the other soldiers riding in the vehicle with him. "What the fuck was that shit man?"

"Something hit the fucking machine on the left side, stupid. You okay man?" Six Pack asked him as Wacko was able to get the swerving jeep under control.

"I'm fine, but now I gotta explain to that Sergeant how we broke his fucking window."

Six Pack looked in the rear of the machine, he was going to ask the Neck if he was all right. But when he looked behind him, he saw Neck lying across the seats, and he was bleeding from his chest. "Holy shit Wacko, pull this damn thing over man, Neck's been fricking hurt by whatever the fuck hit the damn Grungie, man. Hey Neck, you okay man?"

The Neck had his hand resting on his chest near his shoulder, and warned the other soldiers in san excited voice."I was fucking shot man! We got a stinking sniper out there, you two betta be ready for the bastard taking another shot at us."

Wacko pulled the truck sideways to the road, and the two excited soldiers rapidly climbed out of the machine from the passenger's side of the vehicle. They pulled their weapons out and prepared to shoot at anyone they spotted moving around in the bushes. Wacko reached in the vehicle and pulled the mike out the door and screamed in it. "Base, One, Three, Three this is Rover One. We're on the main road from base and we're taking sniper fire. We need god damn help out here pronto like! I have one fucking soldier down by sniper fire and two soldiers ready to defend position against the unknown shooter. I repeat, we have one soldier down."

The helicopter Six Pack was watching a few minutes ago carrying out maneuvers, did a sharp spin around, and it was heading directly for the Humvee parked in the middle of the road to the base. Sirens instantly went off on the base, and soldiers rapidly piled into all sorts of Humvees and other vehicles revving up to go out and assist the soldiers taking weapon fire. The excited soldiers were heavily armed, and the troops were heading out to help their fellow soldiers under attack. A military ambulance joined the other vehicles as they headed off base rapidly.

Captain Robert Walker and Colonel Bruce Leadbetter were riding in the same Humvee, along with Sergeant Ramirez, the Mutt and Blind Date, and Walker was already screaming on his radio to Wacko. "Who the fuck's hit and how bad is he wounded, dammit? Is the wounded soldier still alive, asshole?"

"Hey Walker, they got Neck this time. He's bleeding from the chest and he's alive and talking and really pissed off at the same time, sir." Wacko replied as he watched the helicopter now hovering directly over their vehicle with the cockpit aimed at where the pilot felt the round was fired from. He had his weapons free, and the weapon's officer riding shotgun on the helicopter was ready to reply to any further shooting from the sniper.

The Iraqi shooter Lieutenant Elmasry quickly made it to the Colonel's vehicle before the attack helicopter arrived on scene of the attack against the American troops, and the terrorists were heading for the area where a lot of lovers go down to the shore for some fun in the water and sun. He slid his car to a stop and ordered the women out of the vehicle, and told them to take off their tops and act like they were having fun on the deserted beach. Once the women were topless, he ordered Elmasry to run to the ocean and get soaking wet. He told him to discard his shirt, and then Colonel al-Qaysi ran to the water with a bucket, and he filled it with cold salt water, and then he rushed back to the car and threw the cold water over the hood of his car. Then he removed the weapons and hid them where he was certain no one would locate them easily.

Next the wise Iraqi Colonel threw a towel over the sand and placed a portable radio on it and turned it on, he ordered the women to dance to the tunes. The Iraqi Commander popped the top on four beers, and he dumped the contents in the sand. Then he popped the tops on another four cans and did the same thing. Then he handed each of the other Arab attackers with him a beer, and ordered them to drink them. Major al-Shaya joined the Colonel sitting on the towel while Khalaifa joined Elmasry in the cold water of the ocean. The Colonel lit a cigarette and then waited for what he knew was coming next at him. The longer it took for anyone from the base or police authorities to approach them, the longer it would seem to anyone who approached them that these kids were there long before the attack on the soldier happened.

In moments after the attack on the Humvee, fifteen other Humvees circled the attacked one. Soldiers, armed and dressed in body armor and ready to kill, piled out of the machines and they immediately spread out into the surrounding area, and they searched for the sniper, or any evidence they could discover on that was attacking them. The angry soldiers were armed with orders to find this sniper attacking American servicemen. Two more attack helicopters from the base came out, and they started to search the area for anyone moving around nearby them.

Walker's Grungie pulled up and he was out of it before it came to a complete stop. Wacko and Six Pack had the Neck lying on the road behind their parked vehicle, they were administrating first aide to him. As Walker rushed over, two base medics took over care of the Neck. Walker snarled at Wacko, fuming at the soldier because of his want for some grass, he almost lost another soldier from his unit to this damn sniper, now obviously hunting the soldiers.

"How the fuck is he stupid? All this shit because of some fucking grass, I want to talk with you when we get back to base, buster. Privately at that mister!" Walker warned the Wacker.

"I don't know how the fuck he is Walker. You gotta ask the stinking medics that question."

Walker looked at the medic working on Neck, and he reported. "Captain, the wound isn't life threatening to the soldier, sir. Your soldier will be just fine in a few weeks of rest, sir. Captain, the bullet went in and came out, and it doesn't seem like it hit any bones or vital organs on the soldier on its way out his body, sir. But the soldier will have a pretty little scar to go along with the others I see on his body, sir. I have to tell you Captain, if the bullet hit the soldier just two inches over and an inch higher. It'd be a different story entirely sir, and we'd be sending for a mummy sack (body bag) for the wounded soldier, sir. Your big man was very lucky with this attack aimed against him, very lucky indeed Captain Walker Sir."

"If he was so lucky then the bullet woulda missed his ass all together, man. This asshole doesn't know how to get the hell outta the way of a stinking bullet. You okay you dumb slug you?" Walker asked Neck as he kicked him on his foot and he stared down at the big man.

"Hey man you can't kick me like that man, I'm a wounded fucking soldier, Captain. I hafta be pampered and looked afta by the chicks from the damn Unit, man." Neck smiled up at Walker.

"Pampered! You just wait until I get your stinking ass back on your fucking feet, stupid. Then I'm gonna kick your ass all the way to Bum Fuck Egypt and back, asshole. When the fuck are you ever gonna learn to duck outta the way of a stinking round fired at your ass, spudhead? I'm getting kinda tired of checking on the bullets that your fat ass body keeps stopping all the stinking time, bullet stopper." Walker smiled back at the wounded soldier.

Colonel Leadbetter cut Captain Walker off as he ordered angrily at the soldier. "C'mon Walker, we got the damn sniper still in the area. We have three Helios up and we stand a damn good chance of finding this rotten fuck this time around, and find out where the fuck he fired the round from. We need to find some evidence on the bastard, get command of your troops and do your act, mister. You know what you have to do soldier, so get it done for me Captain."

Walker gave Neck one last look, and when he was satisfied he was going to live, he headed for the rest of his soldiers. Ramirez was the first to ask. "Bobby, how is Neck? Is he alive?"

"He's doing real fine but he's still too damn stupid to get killed by a stinking round."

"You have that right Captain. The Neck's so stupid he don't know what the hell silver dollars are made from, sir." Baby Tee added relieved the Neck was okay.

"He's the only guy I know who invested in a pig farm in Israel, Walker." A second soldier from the Unit added, relieved the Neck was going to be alright.

When Walker took over command of the other soldiers, one soldier was out hunting and he waved the Captain over to his side. He was standing in the field looking down at something. Walker got over to him and the soldier pointed towards the ground. He noticed several footprints left in the sand, and two snubbed out smokes and one brass casing from a round lying on the ground, and he growled at the soldier. "Good work Danko, protect the stinking area and get the damn CIT (Criminal Investigations Team) out here, so they can secure the damn evidence you just found. We have a good foot trail now to follow, so let's get going, buddy. By the way Danko, the stinking Neck's gonna be just fine, it's more a flesh wound than anything."

"Thank God for that much, Captain." Danko replied with a smile.

Walker signaled to a helicopter hovering overhead, and then he pointed in the direction he wanted the helo to head off in. He and the other soldiers with him continued to follow the footprints in the soft sand. They followed the prints until they came out on a black topped side road, and they lost any further prints in the area left from the shooter. The second helicopter came up and Walker signaled one in one direction, and the trailing helicopter in the other direction. The lead helicopter heading west, and it ended up flying over the highway of I-95. The second helicopter heading east and quickly found itself flying over the ocean that bordered the massive military base, and further up and down the coast. The helo did a run up and down the coastline near and part of the military base. This pilot reported seeing nothing out of the ordinary, but he did report he located four people fooling around by the shoreline. It was believed the sniper made his way out to I-95 and was long gone from the incident by this time.

"What about those mother fucking people you spotted? Do the dumb shits seem like they were there for a while or what?" Walker asked the pilot of the first helicopter in a huff.

"Yes Sir Captain, they have a campsite all set up, and they're having some fun sir."

"Okay, linkup with the other helicopter, I'm gonna head down to the beach and speak to these asshole people. Maybe they might have seen something when they were heading down there to play their fucking games." Walker waved his hand over his head, and the Grungie he was riding in started up, and the machine charged over the sand towards the waiting troops. The fuming Captain turned to the Hunter and Ghost and then he ordered the two soldiers. "Okay you two stinking bloodhounds, I want you two birds out there to do your stinking act, and tell me where the fricking sniper headed off in. This lousy little fucker has the blood of three of our soldiers on his fucking hands now, and I want his ass real bad you two."

"Hey Walker, even though the stinking Hunter has a nose like a bloodhound, the rest of his puss is okay to look at, man." The Ghost offered, trying to be funny.

"Fuck you, get going asshole." Walker snapped as he watched the two extremely dangerous pointmen take off while checking the ground for any possible evidence or further tracks. The Humvee stopped by him and he, Ramirez, the Mutt and Blind Date climbed into the idling machine. The Captain growled at the driver, McNip, (Sergeant David Nirajima). "Get us down to the stinking beach area on the double quick, mister. We got a few assholes fucking round down there, and they mighta seem someone hanging around the damn base when they drove down to the damn beach earlier in the stinking day, McNip."

McNip did as ordered and he pulled on the road and headed east for the beach. He knew the area the

Captain wanted because he brought a few girlfriends there to be alone with them.

Colonel al-Qaysi was the first one to hear the sound of the motor from the Humvee even before he saw the machine heading for his group. He quickly warned the others with him they were about to have company in the form of the American soldiers from the military base. The women went for their shirts to cover up, but the Colonel ordered them to remain without their blouses on, until they saw what and how the soldiers were going to act with them.

Walker was staring straight ahead, and he was the first one to pick up the two people in the water enjoying it. Sergeant Dorothy Ramirez leaned over and said to her soldier, "Bob, it looks like some kids just having some fun in the water."

Walker did not reply as he continued to stare at the people swimming in the water, and then he spotted two more people on the sand and let out with a groan.

"What Bobby?" Ramirez asked, not sure of what was upsetting him this time.

"You won't believe this shit for a fucking minute, but these four jerks are the same flaming assholes from the stinking bar last night, baby. The lousy little prick I hate with a damn passion is there, Raz. I got a good mind to place a cap in his fricking ass just on general principles, because he still bugs the stinking shit outta my ass so damn much."

"You don't really think they had anything to do with the hit against the Neck, do you Bobby?"

"No way, these damn people are too scared of their own damn shadows to attack a soldier who could easily rip their stinking heads off their damn shoulders and shit down their throats."

The heavy Humvee pulled up to the two people sitting on the towel on the sand. Walker was one out first of the machine as usual, and the Mutt got out and immediately headed for the topless woman. He was staring at her breasts as the upset Captain growled at the man they thought was named Bill. "What the fuck are you stinking guys doing down here for crap sake, dammit?"

McNip got out of the Grungie next and he automatically walked over to the parked vehicle, and he slowly ran his hand over the hood of the parked machine. It was cool to the touch which meant the car was obviously parked there for quite a while. McNip had no idea Colonel al-Qaysi had the smarts to cool down the hood of the vehicle with cold sea water, and he also kicked some sand with his foot around to hide where the water landed on it.

"Walker, how nice to see you again, what are you doing out here? We have plenty of beer…"

"I just asked you the same fucking thing and I repeat for your stinking benefit, what the fuck are you shitbirds doing out here, buster? How long have you stinking people been down here screwing round, man?" Walker snarled at the Iraqi colonel as he held him in his angry stare.

"We've been enjoying ourselves here for at least three hours, or maybe even a little while longer. Why do you ask me that for, and why are you so angry at me Walker?"

"I'm asking the fucking questions around here, and you're to answer the damn things as I ask them of you, buster." Walker looked at McNip and he immediately replied.

"The motor's cool which means these people have been here for quite a while, Captain."

"When you guys were coming down the road, did you people happen to see a stinking car parked on the side of the road on the outside of the damn military base, you guys passed by in order to get down here by the stinking water?" Walker demanded from the man named Bill after he returned his attention on the man and continued to glare angrily at him.

"Come to think of it Captain Walker, I believe we did see a car parked by the side of the road when we drove down here. But I'm afraid I didn't pay very much attention to it though. I'm sorry Captain, but I don't even remember the color of the car. Why? And why are you soldiers walking around with weapons in your hands, and you soldiers seem like you're ready to shoot anyone you come across, Captain Walker?" The wise Iraqi Colonel asked as he stared back at Walker, and then he looked at the weapon locked in his hands.

"Because if they must know what the fuck we're doing down here, we just had anuther fucking sniper attack on one of my fricking soldiers, and that's why the stinking weapons and we're damn ready to use them at a drop of a stinking hat, buddy. You can't remember anything about the fucking car you saw parked off the side of the damn road, buddy? Can anyone of you people remember anything about the stinking car you guys passed by coming down here, dammit? The size, the stinking color, or maybe even the damn make and model of the vehicle? C'mon you people, this is extremely important to me man. You're the only people who mighta saw the damn vehicle and the stinking sniper. You gotta remember something about the damn thing?"

Iraqi Lieutenant Elmasry and Sergeant Khalaifa walked up to the other Arabs and soldiers surrounding them, and Khalaifa was still topless and made no attempt to cover her nakedness, as they listened to Walker speaking to Colonel al-Qaysi in such an angry voice.

A second Humvee charged down the road, and Colonel Bruce Leadbetter had the door half opened and his foot half way out the machine as it came to a complete stop. He got out and stomped his way over to Walker and growled angrily at him. "What the fuck do you have going down here, Captain Walker? I should've known you'd find yourself some damn naked women hanging around someplace, even under this present god damn situation, Walker."

"Colonel Leadbetter Sir, we know these stinking people and they're cool, sir. They didn't see a damn thing and they've been down here all morning long, sir." The young Marine Captain refrained from informing the angry Colonel the four saw the sniper's car parked on the side of the road. This was because they said they did not pay any attention to it, and he did not want to be the cause of having the four detained, if they could not really help them out any.

"Well then you're wasting your damn time for crap sake with these damn civilian pukes here, Captain. The helicopter pilots believe our perp made good his escape on I-95, and I want you swinging dicks out on that fucking road ten minutes ago hunting this damn sniper down, and ending his damn life for him, mister. So if you had your stinking fill with looking at these women's tits. I suggest you get back on your damn horse and head out for I fucking 95, and see if you can be of any help with the other searchers out there looking for this lousy prick, Captain. I can just hear the damn Chairman of the Joint Chiefs of Staff going off on my ass when he finds out we just had another hit from this damn sniper, and he wounded one of our people in this latest attack aimed against us, Walker. Dammit!" Colonel

Leadbetter stomped his way back to his Humvee and climbed into the machine, and it was off as quickly as it had appeared.

When the Marine Colonel made a comment about the women, they immediately went to their tops and put them on. It would have been done by any woman, and they did not want to act any differently than anyone else would have acted under the circumstances. Colonel al-Qaysi smiled as he watched as the two women got dressed with their backs to the soldiers standing in a group behind them. He felt the women were acting properly to do this before the other soldiers staring at them with lust in their eyes, as they dressed. He was proud of how his female soldiers were acting and carrying out his orders while the American soldiers were hanging around them.

Of course, the Mutt had to offer his two cents in on what was going on. "Hey Walker, what the fuck did the Colonel mean by, if we had enuf looking at these chick's tits. I never have enuf looking at any woman's tits. If you ask me, I think the Colonel's losing it on us, Homes."

"That's fine stupid, why don't you tell the stinking Colonel what you think of him and his last remark, dog man?" Walker snapped at the Mutt as he put a disgusted look on his face.

"Errr.... no thanks man, come to think about it Homes, I kinda like the way I'm shitting. I keep finding it awful hard to take a dump with his stinking foot sticking in my ass all the time as it is, without my adding to his stinking anger, man." The Mutt offered as he smiled.

The Mutt's words made everyone standing in the group laugh as Walker turned back to Colonel al-Qaysi and his group and told him. "Look Bill, I kinda did you a stinking favor bud, by not telling the Colonel you people saw the sniper's vehicle we're searching for, man. If I did, he woulda took you people in custody, and he woulda sweat your asses for who knows how long, until you admitted to the assassination of JFK, buddy. But if you do remember anything at all about this vehicle you passed on your way down to the water, or anyone who mighta been hanging round the side of the stinking road. I want you to report to the main gate of the base, and ask the gate Sergeant to get hold of my ass. I'll come out and speak to you. Try and remember anything you mighta saw, it's fucking important, man. We can't allow some asshole with a stinking hardon for anyone in the military to hunt our asses down like he's doing."

With this said, Walker gave a quick hand signal, and the rest of the soldiers with him quickly piled in their war machine, and then it shot down the road in a cloud of dust and noise. Major al-Shaya offered to the Iraqi Colonel as soon as the angry American soldiers were gone.

"Well Hamoodi, I believe we pulled this one off very well, sir. I was fearful we were going to be captured on this hit by the American soldiers obviously all over the place. We were very lucky on this one sir. May I suggest our next hit should be carried out against Captain Walker, so we can end our mission and get out of the United States while we still can, sir? I believe if we try and hit his girlfriend before we kill Walker, we're pushing our luck beyond reasonable thinking. I suggest we make our hit on Captain Walker then get out of this cursed country as fast as we possibly can. I don't want to replace revenge with foolishness and rash moves, Colonel. We have successfully accomplished most of what you have dreamed of doing already against the hated American soldiers who have invaded our country and killed our General, sir."

"And may I suggest to you Major al-Shaya, to have the other fools with us retrieve our weapons and then hide them back inside our vehicle. Then we're going to follow this cursed road out to the end. Hopefully, it'll lead us far away from the military base and any police authorities assisting the worthless soldiers in their search for the sniper. Lieutenant Elmasry, I commend you for your very successful operation you have carried out against these hated fools we are here to destroy. Now go and get our foul weapons so we can leave this filthy area." Colonel al-Qaysi knew what he was doing with his orders he was still refusing to touch any of the weapons himself. Without his fingerprints on any of the weapons, the police authorities could never possible connect him to any of the snipers killing the soldiers in the State.

Once the weapons were hidden in the car, the Colonel started it and slowly drove along the beach road for five miles, before he found another side road that seemed to head in the direction he knew the major highway was in. For a few moments he thought about leaving the weapons behind, but he was worried about someone finding them, and he would be without weapons needed to finish his mission against the American soldiers. That was why he took them with him wherever he went. The wise Iraqi Colonel knew the first section of the highway was heading north, and he felt the police would search only the vehicles heading north on the main road.

Colonel al-Qaysi was taking a lot for granted, but he was correct with his assumption. By the time the terrorists came out on I-95, they were six exits below the Camp Lejeune exit. He smiled as he drove over the overpass of the highway, because he spotted a number of police cars stopping all the vehicles trying to enter I-95 while heading north.

The extremely dangerous Iraqi Commander also picked up other police cars, and the officers were stopping vehicles trying to get on I-95 heading south. He drove over the overpass and continued down the road looking for a crossover road. Now, he was prepared to drive wherever this road took them, and if they got lost in the process, he would find some way to get them back to their hotel. He drove for another hour before he finally picked up a secondary road he knew the bar Bare Parts was on. He turned north on the two lane road and drove the exact speed limit all the way. As they drove they passed six other police cars speeding down the road in the other direction, their emergency lights blinking and sirens screaming as they shot by his car.

Colonel al-Qaysi got cold feet and decided to turn into a restaurant to see if he could discover what was happening with the police. Much to his dismay, he turned into another McDonalds. He hated the food here, but nevertheless he parked the car and they got out and went in the eatery and ordered some food. They ate and all the while he watched the road and counted four other police cars speeding by them. The small group of terrorists hung around the place for three hours, and he only got up after he picked up a few police cars return with their lights off, and driving at a much slower speed. Now, he was worried about the weapons he had stored in the trunk of his vehicle. If they were stopped and searched by the police authorities, they would surely be captured and he would find himself in the same trouble as Colonel al-Adwani was in.

The small group of terrorists walked to their car, and the Colonel drove for the group this time. But now he knew near about where he was, and he took a bunch of side roads and ended up coming out right on the same street his hotel was on. He froze in place when he spotted a police roadblock set up right across the road stopping traffic in both directions. But the sharp Arab Officer noticed the roadblock was set up a full block past his hotel, and the road blocked lead onto the south bound lane of I-95 and overpass. He moved out and carefully drove down the road and turned into the nearest entryway to the hotel's parking lot. He pulled up behind the hotel and parked his car facing the empty vast field behind the hotel. He parked here because the hotel building hid his car and them from the view of the road and the searching police officers.

The wise Iraqi Officer ordered Lieutenant Elmasry and Sergeant Khalaifa to stay behind until he and Major al-Shaya were out of sight on the other side of the hotel building. Then they were to go to their room, but he and the Major casually walked down the block and watched as the police stopped all the vehicles heading onto the highway. To the Colonel's surprise, the police were only making the cars with one male occupant pull over, and they were checking their cars out very thoroughly. Now he realized if he had four people in the car, they most likely would not have been searched by the police authorities. He slightly bumped al-Shaya with his shoulder and when he had her attention, he made a quick head movement and then they both headed back to the hotel, walking hand in hand this time like young lovers out enjoying themselves.

CHAPTER TWENTY-TWO

THREE ARMORED HUMVEES GOING NORTH BOUND DOWN I-95

Captain Robert Walker was riding in the lead Grungie, and he had the Mutt, Blind Date, Sergeant Ramirez and the Ghost in his machine. The second vehicle was loaded with the soldiers Buckethead, Mother Flanagan, the Hunter, Caviar, and CoCo-G doing the driving, and the Roach. The third Humvee had Siberia, Snatch, Baby Tee, Boot Camp, Three Martines and Four F. Four F was driving and McNip was driving Walker's machine. They were barreling down the highway at sixty miles an hour and two of the heavy military Humvees were in the last lane, and Walker's machine was riding in the middle lane, and the soldiers were checking out any vehicles they passed. The Captain was fuming and wanted this sniper in the worst way, and he was prepared to keep everyone out on the road until they were finally able to locate the sniper, and either kill him, or take him into custody. The Captain was out for blood.

Colonel Bruce Leadbetter was riding in his Humvee, and had two more machines with his small caravan heading south on Highway I-95. They were likewise checking the drivers they passed on the road. All six Humvees had CB radios set up and on, and they were switched to the police scanner side band. The military were the only vehicles allowed to monitor the police bands. The soldiers were listening to see if any police officers found the sniper. Colonel Leadbetter wanted to communicate with the police in case his teams, or Walker's found the sniper and they wanted the police as backup while they took out the sniper.

Before Colonel Leadbetter left Walker, he gave the Captain the order if they found the sniper, he did not want him brought in alive for trial. He wanted the sniper dead and the situation ended plain and simple. The Humvees opened up the gap between the two search teams, and when Leadbetter's three vehicles came to a sign warning him the Stateline to South Carolina was just ten miles ahead of his vehicles, he gave Walker a call over the radio.

"Captain Walker this is Colonel Leadbetter. Come in sir. Over."

"Here sir, go with your traffic Colonel." Walker snapped in the radio at the angry sounding Colonel as he kept his eyes glued to where his Humvee was heading.

"Captain, where the hell are you and your damn team traveling at right now, mister? We're nine miles away from the South Carolina Stateline sir, and we're going to turn here and head back to base at this point. We have no clearance to cross the Stateline and beside Walker. I don't think this damn sniper is this far away from our damn base. So far, he hit three soldiers and they were all hit within ten miles of base. I think the lousy bastard's working over the area, and he's no more than twenty miles away from the base and hunkered down at this time, Captain. I want to close in and keep the damn area around the base under constant surveillance, right now I want everyone to regroup at the base, and then we'll work out our next plans from there, mister."

"Colonel Leadbetter Sir, we're some twenty miles away from the Virginia Stateline sir, and I was planning to turn round at that line and backtrack, and see what the hell I might be able to discover heading back towards the base, sir. Colonel, I don't wanna come in and regroup at base just yet, sir. I wanna stay on the roads and find this lousy sonofabitch today if possible, sir. He hit one of my favorite turds today Colonel, and I'm not gonna allow him to get away with that for much longer I can tell you sir." Walker complained in the radio to his commanding officer.

"Now you listen to me Walker, I don't give a flying fuck what the hell you might want or don't want to do, mister. I'm the Commander for our damn Units mister, and I just gave you a direct fucking order to turn around and head back to base, buster. And that's exactly what you'll do if you know what's good for your ass. I have two helicopters up and they're watching from the air, Walker. I have something else in mind, and I want to run it by you and we need to talk about it face to face at this point, now Captain! So turn your damn ass around and head your stinking kista back to base, I'll meet you there, period sir!"

Walker did not reply as he punched McNip in the arm and then ordered him. "Turn this damn thing around! The stinking Colonel has a wild hair up his ass and he wants me to pull it out for him. Get us back to base pronto, so I can see what the hell he has on his stinking mind."

McNip kept his eyes opened and soon he came across a turnaround used mainly by the State Police to turn onto the other lane of highway heading in the opposite direction. All three of the heavy Humvees were traveling in the speed lane, and when Walker's machine put on the blinker. The other two machines followed suit and the drivers did the same.

The three military vehicles turned onto the service road and then they got on the southbound lane of the highway heading back towards the massive military base. A State Trooper picked up the soldier's vehicles illegal turn, and he pulled up to the lead machine. The trooper picked up the mike and showed it to the passenger of the military machine. Walker saw him and he took the mike and hit the button to speak to the police officer.

"Soldier, I'm Lieutenant John Smith, sir. What the hell do you people call what you just done on one of my roads, sir? I usually write paper on anyone who uses that road for a turn around."

"Glad to meet ya Lieutenant Smith, we're out hunting the stinking sniper, and we just received orders to turn around and head back to base, sir. My stinking Commander didn't give me any uther choice in the matter, sir. If you wanna tag my ass for the fucked up turn I just pulled off on your road, sir. Then I suggest you put the bad paper on my Colonel's ass, and see what he has to say bout it sir." Walker let go of the button and waited for the officer to reply.

"Understood your bitch Captain Walker, and that's what I'm going doing, Captain. We've been ordered to pull some overtime and stay out on the roads and pull over anyone who even looks out of place on the road, sir. Or the driver looks suspicious, sir. Good to have you people out giving us a hand looking for this guy, soldier." The Lieutenant gave Walker a sort of salute and a good smile, as he pulled behind the three Humvees and followed them to their base.

"You got that all wrong my friend, we're not out here to give you people a stinking hand in the least, Lieutenant. We're out here to get this fucking sniper and that's that, sir. We're armed and have to locate this lousy little prick before he hits another one of us soldiers again, sir." Walker replied hotly over the radio to the State Trooper as he started at him from inside the machine.

"You mean to tell me you people are armed, and you're operating under orders to get this sniper by any means possible, soldier?" the stunned young trooper said as he tried to see Walker's face riding in the machine and yet keep his car under control at the same time.

"You got the word right Lieutenant. We're armed and hunting this damn sniper, and if we find the lousy sonofabitch, we'll need a mummy bag for his ass." Walker fired back at the trooper.

"I don't know about that order, soldier. I have to call in and see if I have any new instructions on how to deal with this order you just informed me about, sir. I'll do this much though for you soldiers, I'll escort you people back to your base, sir. I need orders about this one, and I don't want to be out here with a bunch of half crazy gun happy soldiers, sir." The concerned trooper replied as he glanced at Walker riding in the vehicle. The worried trooper was that concerned about the soldiers being armed, and out hunting for this sniper on the highway. He needed further orders from his command center after he pulled out and moved up to the lead Humvee.

"Look Lieutenant, this lousy cocksucker we're out here hunting for has killed two of my fricking soldiers, and he has also wounded another one today, sir. If this rotten prick wants to take chunks outta us soldiers then we're gonna take chunks outta his stinking ass plain and simple, sir. No disrespect intended Officer."

"Wait a minute soldier I have a call coming in for my Command Center sir. Hang on for a second please, sir." In a moment, the trooper was back on the horn and speaking with Walker. "Say soldier, you said you were Captain Walker, right sir?"

"The one and only, why do you ask me that question for Lieutenant?" he smirked in the radio.

"Because I just received orders from my Command Center to linkup with you and the other soldiers under your command, and I'm further ordered to assist your soldiers in the search for this sniper, sir. This is going to be very interesting to witness, I was told you troops are the special operation soldiers, and you people are supposed to know what the hell you're doing out here, sir. What's the top end of those heavy machines of yours sir?"

"Sixty five miles an hour at best and that's with us pushing the shit outta the damn things so I'm told by the ones supposed know all bout these damn things, Lieutenant. Why do you ask sir?" The Captain replied to the State Trooper pleasantly.

"Because I'm ordered to escort you back to base Captain, and I'll run out front of you with my lights and siren, sir. I'll keep your MPH in mind, and I'll clear any civilian traffic out of your way. I was ordered to run you down to Camp Lejeune, and I was to report in if you people don't follow me to your base as ordered, sir. This seems to be taking on a joint venture, soldier."

Walker did not reply as he looked behind him and said to the Mutt. "Hey dog man it looks like the stinking Colonel's taking things in his own fucking hands against us, man. I guess he doesn't think we're coming in on our own, and he ordered this cop to rain us in, the sonofabitch."

"I guess the Colonel's getting to know us betta than we thought, Walker. It looks like we're gonna hafta change our way of thinking, if we wanna keep screwing round with his mind, man."

Walker laughed at the Mutt's words as he looked at the trooper as he moved his car out before his lumbering Humvee, and when the trooper was in the front of the small convoy, he put on his lights and siren. It worked out well for the elite soldiers, and they got back to base quicker than if the trooper was not in front of his machine clearing the way for them. As his machine followed the police car, he noticed a number of other Humvees parked outside the base. The police car past these Humvees, but Walker's machines stopped by them. He saw the Colonel speaking to an officer and a number of police officers, and he wanted to find out what was going on.

He headed right for the Marine Colonel and saluted him sharply. The still upset Colonel did not return his salute as he introduced Walker to the Commander of the State Troopers and he nodded. Then Colonel Leadbetter said to his officer. "Captain Walker Sir, I called everyone in because we're going to set this sniper up, and if he tries to hit us again. The fuck's going to end up with a face full of lead in return. Everyone but the drivers is going inferred. We have three machines with a turret inferred system mounted on them, and if this sonofabitch is lurking about in damn bushes waiting to get another shot at us, these fucking machines will pick his ass up surer then shit, and then we can give him a taste of his own fucking medicine for a change. These police officers are going to work closely with us Captain, but with one difference though sir.

"If the Troopers locate this lousy prick before we do. They're going to take a backseat and allow us to take this prick in, one way or the other sir. It's believed this is a military operation, and as such we're the ones in command of the entire operation, and the police are backup support units for us. This is a good deal Walker. If you remember why you people were pulled in the first place, it was to learn urban tactics and work with the local police departments.

"Well mister, there's nothing like a little on the job fucking training to make someone know what the hell's expected of them out in the damn field. But I have to warn you and your pack of screaming squirrels of something. This isn't a mission where your weapons are on free fire, Captain Walker. This mission's a search and splatter action against one or possibly even two snipers, and nothing more than that. You people have to make certain of your target, and make damn sure he's the snipe, then and only then he's to be deal with plain and simple. I'm ordering you to keep any SHTs (Shit Happen Targets) down to an absolute minimum, sir. This is extremely important Captain, you people will be solely responsible for your actions out in the field, and make certain your troops are well aware of this order or it's on your ass on the line Captain. (Shit Happen Targets is someone not a target getting hit by military fire).

"I'll not allow any free fire on this operation, and if any damn civilians get caught up in a firefight you people might get involved in. I'll take a strip of hide off each and every one of your soldiers for every damn civilian puke that gets hurt on this operation. I don't give a shit if the civilians are hit by the sniper or your people's fire, sir. Don't engage this fuck if any civilian puds might get hurt in the damn operation, Captain. If any damn civilians are threatened, you'll take command of the situation and wait the lousy fuck out. Time is on our side on this one sir."

The Colonel gave the look that informed Walker he was finished speaking with him, and he was now waiting for the Captain's reply to his last orders. He grabbed a quick breath in and then started off with his words to his commanding officer. "Colonel Leadbetter Sir, I understand my orders and will carry them out as received sir."

"I knew you would Walker, that's why you're in command of this band of lunatics of yours, sir." The proud Colonel snapped back at his Captain.

The young Captain smiled at the Colonel, and then he added. "Colonel, I'm afraid I'm not very familiar with this new inferred system loaded up on the few of the Humvees, sir."

"I didn't think you'd be very familiar with these new machines and their systems, mister. Follow me and I'll explain them and how they work for you in the field, Captain. The new system is a turret type inferred system, which reads out in a three hundred and sixty degree spread, sir. If the system is reading open fields or heavily wooded areas, any possible heat signature it picks up, will immediately show you where it is on the small screen fixed inside the interior of the damn machine, sir. No one has to wear them damn night vision glasses any longer, with this here baby on the job for us, Captain. All you have to do is watch the damn scope and it'll tell you if anyone is lurking about in the fields trying to be invisible. And, if the damn target the machine picked up might be a threat to your ass to boot, sir. Here you go Captain."

The rather pleased Marine Colonel offered as he opened the door to the machine, and then he showed the Captain the scope he would be watching, as his machine drove the roads of North Carolina in search of the sniper. He flipped the machine on and it instantly marked out the small group of soldiers and police officers standing near the machine.

"Damn, this is great because I see the damn machine's also picking up some animal life out in the bush. No one will have a stinking chance to set up on us with this machine in operation, sir. What further orders, Colonel? I wanna get back out there and find this lousy scumbag, before he hits us again, dammit." The excited Captain said as he pulled his head out of the Humvee.

"That's what you're going to do, mister. You're going to get your ass out there tonight Captain, and then you're going to hunt down this lousy prick until you finally get his ass for us. Keep searching, stop at any motel along the way when you get tired, keep the people you have with you at all times and keep searching for this prick. You're getting carte blanche for this one Captain. All you have to do is report in every six hours, and inform me how you're doing. But you're out on a mission, and I don't expect to see you slugs until you find this little pecker and either do him in, or take him in custody and place an end to his threat against us, sir.

"Any bills you make will be charged to me, and I'll take care of them. Use your military credit card for any gas and lodging you need, mister. Walker, I want this damn sniper's ass, and you're going to get him for me, or it'll be your ass I'll be chewing on if you catch my drift, sir. Shove off anytime you're ready to get going again, mister. Keep me informed on your progress at all times and work well with the damn police on this one, Captain. The Commander of the State Troopers is going to stick this Lieutenant Smith with you and the rest of your people, and he'll be your contact with the damn police working with us on this damn case. One thing more you have to know about Walker, I don't want the damn police getting to this fucking man before you do, do you read me and you know what I'm telling you to do on this mission loud and clear, mister?"

"I read you loud and clear Colonel Leadbetter, and I'll bring this sniper's head back on a fucking stick to you, sir. Err... has there been any further word on Neck's condition, Colonel?" Walker asked Leadbetter with concern lacing his voice as he waited for the Colonel's reply.

"Yeah Walker, the last word I had on the lazy ass was, he's doing fine and wants out of medical. The jerk even wants to join you people out on the search. I'm please you understand what I want from you and the rest of your people on this operation, Captain Walker. There's no god damn need to clog up our court system with trying this miserable puke. He's as guilty as sin in my fricking book Captain, and you people are operating under my rules and regulations and my damn laws on this mission, sir. Shove off and get the job done and get our revenge on this sonofa fucking bitch for killing two of our people, and the wounding of that big dumb sod of a soldier, you people branded the Neck." Colonel Leadbetter snarled hotly at his Captain.

The Captain saluted the Colonel then he looked at his people gathered up behind them and he growled at them. "Okay you bunch of walking sand bags, we got us a job to do, and it needs to be concluded immediately. Pile up in these three stinking toys and we're heading out hunting for this damn sniper, soldiers. No one returns to base until we bring this damn sniper in, all trussed up nice and neat and strapped to the front end of our fender like a dead deer, troops. Ghost, you monitor the inferred scope in my machine, you got the best eyes of the group, man. Hunter, you monitor the scope in the second vehicle, and Mother Flanagan has the scope in the third machine.

"McNip, you drive for me as usually, the rest of you clowns chose who is going to be the driver for your machines, and who and what they do in each of the three machines. I don't have the time or crayons to lay out everything for you pack of crybabies. Raz, you, Blind Date, Mutt, Ghost and McNip, are in my machine. Let's shove off we do our best work in the dark. By the way people, Neck's doing fine and wants to join the Unit on the search for this missing shooter. The medics won't let him outta the medical unit this quickly, so he could link back up with us. Let's bring the Neck back a fucking trophy to play around with while he gets betta, people."

Some of Captain Walker's group slapped at the air with their fists over the news Neck was going to make it, as they quickly climbed into the new machines. The State Trooper caught up to Walker before he got in his machine. The trooper assigned to work with him asked him with a snap in his tone. "Say Captain Walker, what the hell do you want me to do on this one, sir? I'm opened for any suggestions you may want or have need for me to do for you, sir."

"Look Lieutenant Smith, I need your cop car to stay out in front of my military vehicles, and I want you to keep monitoring your communications for us, sir. Maybe you can take that much shit offa my stinking ass will ya. I'm gonna use your car to help clear the road for my people and machines. If this damn shooter's discovered by your people before we find the lousy little prick and bring his ass to justice. From the way I read my latest orders sir, it seems like we have complete control of this entire operation, and your police officers are operating under orders to work with us for a stinking change, sir. I wanna head out now sir, and we're gonna stay out until we find this lousy bastard, and place a quick end to his ass, and what he's doing against my troops, sir. Do you have to break off your working with us when your shift ends, sir?"

"No Sir Captain Walker, I was ordered to stay with you people until this mess is over with, sir. They cleared all the overtime for me. So the way I read my orders sir, I too am to be on a twenty four hour call until further notice from my Command, sir. When you people stop for the day that's when I stop along with your troops, Captain Walker Sir. You'll not go anywhere without my being present with you and the rest of your troops, sir. I know you have Command of the entire mission as you just mentioned, but I have the power to stop you and your actions at any time, sir. If I feel your action might get some civilians caught up in the line of fire, sir."

Captain Robert Walker smiled at the sharp looking young State Trooper. It never ceased to amaze him how good a condition most of the State Troopers kept themselves in, and this guy was no exception to that rule. Lieutenant John Smith was young, in his mid to upper twenties, and he was in outstanding soldier's shape. Big chest, small waist, and looked like he had powerful shoulders and a good set of guns (arms) on his body. The wise Marine

Captain could easily see the size of his arms through his neatly pressed uniform blouse. This man held himself correctly, proud, and he saw it in the way he walked and also in his stance. This trooper commanded respect just from his mere posture, and his powerful presence. The Captain understood right off he did not want to cross swords with this man unless he was absolutely forced to. Everything about this trooper showed him he was proud of his profession.

The young Marine Captain weighted his words carefully, and he replied to the trooper. "Look Lieutenant, I feel ya here and hear your words man. I assure you sir we'll not react against this bastard if we get this shooter in our cross hairs, if any stinking civilians might get hurt in any exchange. I know my first duty is to protect the lives of any civilians we come across out there. But the decision has to be mine and mine alone to make, Lieutenant. I'll think before I order a reaction against the sniper when we find him, but if we chance losing the shooter because some damn civilians ended up in the way. I'll hafta make that decision in the field, sir. I'll let you to put in your thoughts, but I'll not allow this shooter to escape if the life of one civilian is on the table, sir. We can't have the shooter escaping because he has a hostage in possession, sir.

"Don't get me wrong for a second here Lieutenant, if the fricking shooter has a human shield, and I have no doubt in my mind the shooter would kill him if we corner the lousy prick. We can't let him use that shield to escape us, sir. We'll do everything in our power to free that possible hostage first, but if it comes down to it, I'm really sorry sir." Walker looked in the eyes of the concerned police officer, and then went silent and allowed his silence to finish his words.

Lieutenant Smith shook his head slowly and then replied. "Look Captain Walker, I know some times a soldier is forced to overlook the life of a civilian, but I have to maintain some kind of control over this situation, sir. I can't possibly allow you to go after what you're calling the damn shooter, if it's going to cost one civilian his life needless in any action we're forced to engage in, Captain. I just can't possibly allow myself to do it, Captain Walker Sir. I have my responsibilities that I must keep in my mind at all times while I'm on the job sir."

"Lieutenant Smith, I don't have the stinking time nor the frigging patience to get involved in a longwinded pissing contest over this shit with you at this time, sir. We're already arguing over fucking shadows here, Lieutenant. If and when the situation arises out in the field, and we have this damn shooter locked up in our sights. Then and only then will we discuss this shit at that time, sir. I'm certain you'll agree with our actions if and when we have to move out against this lousy shooter, sir. Until that time comes a knocking Lieutenant Smith, try and keep up with up our stinking asses, sir." Captain Walker stopped speaking and jumped in his lead vehicle, and ordered McNip to move out. Instantly, the State Trooper's vehicle moved out in front of the slow moving military trucks, and the officer led the way for the elite soldiers.

The Ghost was already glued to the inferred scope and even before they got off the main road leading to the massive military base, he picked up something hot moving around out in the woods and he called out to his Commander. "Holy shit Walker, I got something hot moving around by that small stand of trees at the end of the fucking road, man."

"McNip, slow this fucking thing down right now, dammit!" Walker bellowed at his driver and then he picked up the radio and roared into it. "Nightstalker to Shadow Follower, we have a hot spot picked up some fifty yards from the end of the fricking road just west, northwest our current position. You gotta get out there and check the damn thing out for us, and if it's a stinking person. Let us know and we'll handle it from there on out, sir. Nightstalker out sir."

"Roger that last Nightstalker, confirmed as received sir, am on the target and am picking up same hot spot on my equipment at this time, sir. Will appraise you of our finding if the stinking target's human, and will hover if is until your troops cover said target, sir. Over." The pilot of the Blackhawk helicopter replied as he flew over the stopped military vehicle below his airframe. The State Trooper was surprised the soldiers had a helicopter backup for this mission. He was listening to the military band on the handheld radio Colonel Leadbetter gave him for his use, when he was ordered to be part of Walker's search group for the missing sniper.

The Captain watched as the helicopter quickly took up position directly over the suspected target. When the aircraft was set in position, the pilot reported back to Walker with a smart tone in his voice. "Shadow Follower to Nightstalker, target has been identified as a small dog, Captain. It looks like he's taking himself a damn leak against said trees, sir. Do you want me to sterilize the target so it doesn't become as a serious threat against you and your troops down there, Captain Walker? He looks pretty damn dangerous to me from my present position, sir."

"Funny Commander, fucking real funny buster, you betta be careful we don't sterilize your stinking ass in that metal can you're flying for your ass, friend. This ain't no fucking game we're playing down here, Commander. We have two soldier's dead and one wounded. Resume fucking position over our damn machines, and stand ready to assist us, sir. Nightstalker Out!" Walker snarled into the radio as he looked out of the window and glared at the unseen pilot.

WASHINGTON D. C., SATURDAY, APRIL 20th, 2002

At General John White, the current Chairman of the Joint Chiefs of Staff's office at the Pentagon, the powerful General waited for the CIA Director John Raincloud to arrive. The Chairman was deeply concerned over a shooter killing a number of his specialized troops down in North Carolina. He wanted to speak to the large full blooded Sioux Native American, and see what he thought about the situation, and if they should take other precautions over it. The Director walked in and John offered him. "Coffee, it's behind you, help yourself Chief."

The CIA Director did not take the offered coffee as he smiled and started to speak to the seated military officer. "John, I know why you sent for me sir, and I have to tell you General. I've been on this damn thing all night, and I haven't been able to locate a direct connection with any known, active terrorist groups operating within the borders of the United States at this time, sir. I believe we're dealing with some nut that has a special hardon for anyone wearing a damn military uniform down in North Carolina, General. I'm going to keep after this damn thing until it's conclusion, and I'll have my people working on it until we come up with some sort of a..."

"John, one of my people wasn't dressed in a military uniform when he was hit by this damn sniper, sir. He was hit wearing his civilian clothes while visiting some damn titty bar in North Carolina. He was the first one killed by this nut we're out hunting for, John." The military officer fired back at the concerned CIA Director, knowing he was telling the Director something he was not aware of. He felt this information he found out about when he was speaking to Colonel Leadbetter, was going to change the Director's thoughts over this present situation. He was certain he was going up against a new terrorist cell operating in the United States.

"Shit, I didn't know that crap, so that puts a new light on the mess for my ass, General White Sir. I was quite certain if this guy was hitting just military personnel he was probably after your people for some certain reason, sir. I believed he might possibly be a jutted lover sir, or someone who was dumped by a service person. Dammit."

"I knew this was going to change your mind over this situation once you knew that fact, Director. Do you have anything on new terrorist cells set in operation, or if any new terrorist cells were able to sneak into the United States after the Twin Towers terrorist attack, John?"

"You know something General White Sir. A few weeks ago I picked up some crap about a small group of supposed Cubans coming to the United States a few months back by way of the so called Cuban express down in the Florida..." The CIA Director began to offer to the General, but he was immediately cut off by the military officer as he offered.

"I believe I heard something about that fricking thing going on down there in the Florida Keys as well, John. I've been meaning to speak to you about that shit for quite a while now sir. But I never had the damn time to bring it up to your attention and discuss this shit with you as yet, sir. What with the Twin Towers and Pentagon attack, don't you think it's about time your people finally start to step on that little smuggling act going on down there, sir? If you don't do something about it pretty damn soon then I'm going to step in and do it for you, sir.

"Can you imagine what the damn newspapers would do to the present Administration, if they ever discovered we're kind of closing a blind eye to the smuggling of Cuban refugees into the United States, especially after the terrorist attacks against us, Director? We've done just about everything in our damn power to make the civilians of our country uncomfortable at the airports and border crossings between Canada and Mexico and ourselves, sir.

"Yet we're continuing to allow a nearly constant flow of Cuban refugees get into the United States with us almost helping them to get in our country illegally, John. The damn news reporters would crucify the President over this information, and possibly drive him from office while they were at it, sir." The General growled as he interrupted the CIA Director's words.

"I know, I know and I assure you that I'm working on the damn situation as we speak, General White Sir. I just sent a few Special Agents down to the Florida Keys, and have them speaking to many of the local damn Captains of these small pleasure boats that are bringing the Cuban refugees into the United States illegally, sir. We're warning them time and again we're aware of what they're doing down there, and we're also keeping our eyes on them at the same time, sir. But the reason I brought this subject up to you in the first place John is. About three months ago, some twenty supposed Cuban refugees were reportedly brought into the United States using this small smuggling operation being carried out in the damn Keys, sir.

"It was believed they weren't really Cuban refugees at all, but some people from the Middle East. Since we got word on this one situation, we've been trying to locate the American Captain who brought these few people into the country. There were five Captain's involved in this one smuggling operation, and since we started to snoop around down there, these Captain's clamed up tighter than a moonshiner's cork in the jug, sir. Once we find this Captain then we can determine if a new batch of terrorist was able to sneak into the States that I'm not aware of, sir."

"Jesus Christ Almighty Director, if you knew about this group of assholes getting into the United States beforehand then why the fuck are you just bringing this shit up to my damn attention? I'm not waiting for confirmation on this miserable group of illegal's we're speaking about in this conversation. I'm ordering my troops to react to this damn shooter as a terrorist cell working in the United States, sir. That way, if this fuck turns out to be some sort of nut then that's good for us, but if my troops are up against a group of maybe twenty possible well trained terrorist. Then I want my damn troops to be prepared for any contingency, sir.

"Dammit to hell and back again John, I can't believe you've been sitting on this fucking information for so long, Director. I have to make contact with Colonel Leadbetter, and get him up to speed on this crap you just handed me, John." The General grabbed the phone and quickly dialed it. In a few seconds he was speaking to the Colonel stationed at Camp Lejeune.

"Colonel Leadbetter, General White here sir, I was just informed a possible twenty man terrorist team might have gotten into the States through the Florida Keys. You're to inform your troops of this possibility and have them act accordingly against this new information, sir. They have to know they might be up against some well trained soldiers rather than some nut."

The General slammed the phone down and Colonel Leadbetter went right in action as he picked up his mike and then roared into it. "This is Action Mountain to Nightstalker. This is important, so come in Captain Walker Sir. Over."

The searching troops just stopped at a Holiday Hotel off the main highway, because they searched the entire night for the sniper with no luck. Captain Walker plopped down in the bed along with an equally exhausted Sergeant Ramirez, when his radio growled. He picked it up and snapped in the machine. "Yeah Action Mountain, Nightstalker here sir. Welcome to the half way to hell club, sir. What's up sir? Over."

"Walker, I just fucking received word there's a possible twenty man terrorist cell who might have successfully worked their way into the United States recently sir. You have to go under the assumption that you're going up against a number of possibly well trained enemy soldiers, and your troops are to act accordingly if engaged by them, Captain. The General's going to lift the threat warning up to all States. So that response is going to put a helluva lot of other Police Officers and Special Agents out there on us, Captain. We have to get these lousy bastards before they can turn their attention against the civilian's of our country next, sir."

"Roger that last Colonel Leadbetter Sir. I'll inform the rest of the soldiers of this new possible threat, and what we might be dealing with this time sir."

"You do that, and I'm sending out another three Humvees, and they're going to spread out and check on the areas you people haven't checked yet. Out." Leadbetter snorted at his officer.

When he was off the radio with the Colonel, he informed Sergeant Ramirez about the possible terrorist group this sniper might be part of. Then he left the room and went to the other soldiers and State Trooper, and informed them about the new possible terrorist threat. The elite soldiers wanted to get back on the road no matter how tired or who they had to up go against.

THE BEST WESTERN HOTEL, NORTH CAROLINA

Iraqi Colonel Hamoodi al-Qaysi also wanted to get out and kill his next target of Sergeant Dorothy Ramirez, and once she was dead, he was going to concentrate all his efforts on Captain Robert Walker. Once Walker was dead, he was going back down to the Florida Keys and escape from the United States from there. The upset Arab Colonel went outside the second floor landing to grab a quick breath of fresh air. As he stood outside he noticed a flood of local police and State Trooper cars traveling the roads with their lights flashing and at a high rate of speed. From where he stood, he easily picked up the vehicles setting up new roadblocks in the area.

The Iraqi Commander watched the police stopping every civilian car waiting to get onto the highway, and the officers were checking out the vehicles out very thoroughly, even the trunks of the vehicles this time. Colonel al-Qaysi was stunned when he saw the police stopping random vehicles on the road and having the people get out of the car, and the officers search the vehicles from front to back. Instantly, he felt something was wrong for their operation, and he quickly dipped back into his hotel room. He ran across the room and then snapped the TV on to the local news channel. An excited woman was busy explaining they just received word a new terrorist group might have possibly snuck into the United States. It was further believed the terrorists were responsible for the rash of sniper attacks occurring against the soldiers in North Carolina.

The upset Iraqi Military Officer angrily threw his hands in the air as he suddenly roared at the stunned female Major who was sitting on the bed watching him. "That great fool we have left in command in Washington. He must have done something wrong, and he was obviously discovered and killed, or the worthless fool was taken prisoner by the local authorities, woman. Major al-Shaya, I fear we'll not be able to carry out our attack against Captain Walker and his foul girlfriend, and we must now think about leaving the hated United States at once, woman."

As the extremely upset Iraqi Colonel spoke, an excited Lieutenant Malika Nabeel Elmasry and Sergeant Shurug Khalaifa rushed into their room also upset. They wanted to report of the news warning, and the Lieutenant believed it was being aimed at them.

"Of course the threat was aimed at us you great fool born from a camel's backside. We have decided on not doing another attack against the hated American soldiers. It seems Allah's will deem Captain Walker and his evil girlfriend shall live until he finishes his evil work for his own God he respects. We're going to stop hunting these worthless American soldiers and sit still, until the fools in Washington kill the foul Federal Judge and our worthless spy of a Colonel. Once this has been accomplished, we'll leave the United States and head back to our land of sand and wonderment." The Colonel offered to the concerned look on the Lieutenant's face.

"What is on your foul mind now, young fool?" the Colonel snarled at him.

"Colonel al-Qaysi, I hope you remember the Sergeant and I wish to remain here in the United States, once you ended this operation for us, sir." Lieutenant Elmasry offered to the Colonel.

"I'm well aware of that request, you young desert fool. I'll release you and the cursed female Sergeant you have leveled your evil lust on, the moment we know for certain the other foul attack teams in Washington have successfully killed their assigned targets. We'll stay away from the car and weapons until that time, Lieutenant. Once we're certain the worthless fools in Washington have completed their mission, I'll have you and the Sergeant remove the foul weapons from our vehicle, and then hide them out in the field behind this worthless establishment.

"After that time, both you and your young girlfriend will be more than free to make your living here in the worthless United States, fool. I demand both you and the Sergeant remain with us for a little while longer, just in case we have some further need of your services for this operation, until the foul Federal Judge and our worthless spy are both dead in Washington, Lieutenant." The cunning Iraqi Colonel knew why he wanted the two young soldiers to stay with them until after the murders of the two people in Washington. He was going to use them as his escape goats, in case the American police authorities discover who they were, and what they were up in North Carolina. As far as he was concerned, as long as his and Major al-Shaya's fingerprints were not on any of the murder weapons. The authorities could not possibly prove they had anything to do with the murders of the two American soldiers.

Lieutenant Elmasry wanted to take Sergeant Khalaifa and leave the hotel and Colonel at this moment. He was of the mind the American authorities felt there was a new terrorist cell currently operating within the borders of the United States. He believed it was only a matter of time even if it was only by dumb luck that the searchers would soon discover them, and they would all be killed. He further understood he was an Iraqi soldier, and as long as Colonel al-Qaysi was still alive, he owed him his total loyalty. But the deeply worried young Lieutenant made up his mind he was going to speak to Sergeant Khalaifa, and if she wanted to leave in the middle of the night, he would leave with her without any complaint. He was not that concerned with staying with the Iraqi Colonel until his captured or death.

The Arab Colonel allowed the young Lieutenant his moment of daydreaming, before he barked angrily at him again. "Lieutenant Elmasry, I demand yours and Sergeant Khalaifa's passports, you young fool. I'll maintain control of them until I finally release you and the Sergeant from your duty to me and the Major and our President."

The stunned Elmasry stared at the Colonel like he had just read his mind, and he replied in a low and trembling voice. "I'll go back to my room and retrieve the requested passports for you to retain, sir. I'm no threat to you or your will or operation, Colonel al-Qaysi Sir."

"A threat to me, why in Allah's great name would I possibly think you might be a threat against me in any fashion, Lieutenant Elmasry? I just asked for your passport so I can maintain them safely for you until we finally part company for the last time in our lives. Get the foul things for me, I'm going out for a little walk. You'll give the passports to the Major while I'm gone, and she'll maintain them until my return to this foul room. I want to see what the lowly infidels of this worthless country are doing in the way of security aimed against our efforts.

"We might be forced to remain in this foul country for a while longer then I had first suggested to you, Lieutenant. If the security is too strong, we'll be forced to wait until it relaxes, so go now Lieutenant while I check on the American's security." Colonel al-Qaysi waited until Lieutenant Elmasry and Sergeant Khalaifa was out of the room, and then he turned to Major al-Shaya and announced to her in a gruff voice. "You were wise to suggest I remove the fool's passports from them before they took them and abandoned us and our mission, woman. You take charge of their foul passports while I check out the security the Americans are employing against us."

Colonel al-Qaysi bowed slightly to the pretty female Arab Major, and then he straightened up and walked out of the hotel room to scout out the surrounding area of the hotel. The concerned Arab Commander was dressed in common street clothes and with the way his hair was now cut, he looked everything but an Arab person. He stood on the landing of the hotel and scanned the roads in all directions from the structure. He spotted a number of blinking lights from a flood of police cars in two different directions, and he slowly walked down the steps to the parking lot, and then he headed for the largest collection of police cars blocking the road.

This heavy police presence roadblock was setup three blocks away from the hotel and on his walk, Colonel Hamoodi al-Qaysi stopped and picked up a cup of coffee to go from a small shop, and he continued walking. He was acting like he had no worries on his mind. After a few moments the Iraqi Commander was standing on the sidewalk near one of the parked police cars. When an officer looked at him, al-Qaysi lifted his coffee to the officer and nodded and smiled. The officer returned the smile and the slight nod and checked the next car stopped by him.

Colonel al-Qaysi watched as the three police officers searched a car quickly without making this driver get out of the vehicle this time. The small horde of officers checked his driver's license and looked in the back seat of the vehicle from the outside. Other cars, the officers were making the driver get out of the vehicle and stand on the side while they opened the trunk, and removed many items and checked out the interior of the vehicle. The Iraqi Military Officer noticed the police officers were coming down heavily on some of the drivers that had two and three or more passengers in their vehicles. The police were no longer overlooking any cars with more than one person riding in them. This gave the Colonel a new problem to deal with, and he decided the security on the roads was far too heavy for them to try and leave the United States at this time. Seeing enough, he headed back for the hotel.

The Colonel and his fellow group of terrorists were lucky, this hotel was large enough to offer food and anything else he wanted or needed to survive their wait, without his needing to go out and get any special provisions, or other members of his group. So he decided they were going to hunker down for a while and wait out the police security, and once it was relaxed, they would then leave the hotel and United States as quickly as they could leave.

CHAPTER TWENTY-THREE

WASHINGTON D.C., SUNDAY, APRIL 21st, 2002.
THE ROLAND'S MOTEL

The Iraqi hit team assigned to kill the Federal Judge and the Iraqi Colonel in Washington, was still held up in the filthy and dilapidated motel rooms, while waiting their time to begin their attack against the people Colonel al-Qaysi wanted dead. Lieutenant Aziz Abdel al-Atrash was aware of the heavy security taking place in North Carolina, and it was like Colonel al-Qaysi told him it would be. He would begin his attacks before they hit the judge and Colonel al-Adwani. This would cause security to be placed around them in

North Carolina, and he would still be free to kill his targets as ordered. Al-Atrash's soldiers were down to six remaining Iraqi troops. He allowed the rest of his once terrorist group to leave the motel, when they told him they wanted to remain in the United States, and he felt they were of no longer a need to his operation.

Lieutenant al-Atrash was sitting in his room along with Sergeant Aicha Said Damerdji, the second shooter of his future hit team. Also in his room with him were the two supporters of the shooters, Sergeant Hanan al-Wazir, and Sergeant Muhammad Mushtaha. The two backup supporters were Lieutenant Bahaa Handoni, and with her was Sergeant Mustafa Abdullah. They were sitting on either of the two filthy beds or on the floor, and they were going over how they were going to work their intended targets in order to kill them.

In the back of Lieutenant al-Atrash's mind, he was really concerned that the hated American police authorities might take it upon themselves, and increase security surrounding their two intended targets, because of what Colonel al-Qaysi was doing down in North Carolina with killing the American soldiers he wanted dead. Every time the terrorists were out eating because the motel did not offer any food service. They never saw any increase in the security surrounding the federal courthouse, or the area around the courthouse. So the Lieutenant was going to stay with their original plan and takeover a number of perches they discovered that would offer them the easiest shots and kills at their two targets when the time came for them to go in action.

THE FEDERAL COURTHOUSE, WASHINGTON D.C., SUNDAY, APRIL 21st, 2003

Even though it was a bright Sunday morning, it was two days before the trial of Colonel Abdulaziz Majd al-Adwani was scheduled to begin. The Washington Capital Police SWAT teams were going over their ordered positions to supply added security for the judge, terrorist and jury. The first two SWAT teams were going to be aided by another two teams, and a number of soldiers were added as special shooters to the support teams. The police were walking the rooftops of many of the surrounding buildings near the courthouse, looking for the best possible place to set the sniper teams up, yet have the police shooters remain out of the public's eye.

The last thing the local police wanted was to cause any alarm to the jurors going to decide the fate of the terrorist who was the commander of the assassination team who tried to assassinate the President of the United States. The command knew if the worried jurors picked up any of the sniper team's set up to protect everyone involved in the trial, they might become concerned and this worry could very well affect their judgment over the terrorist.

When the SWAT teams were satisfied with the assigned positions they picked out to protect everyone of concern to them, they quickly left the area. They did not want to hang around and have some news reporter see what they were doing on the rooftops. The entire outside of the courthouse was being ringed with news satellite trucks, chairs, and platforms the over hundred reporters would report to the world on the progress of the trial of the terrorist commander from.

When the police came out of the building in the back, the commander ordered his officers to return to the area of their responsibility at four a.m. sharp, and the SWAT teams were to disperse to their designated areas of protection. Once there the police officers were to watch for anyone acting suspiciously in the crowd expected to arrive to see if they could get picked to enter the courthouse and see the trail of the Arab assassin first hand. The SWAT teams knew there was going to be a flood of plain clothes foot officers mixed in with the crowd. But the SWAT teams were the extra eyes high up, to see what the foot officers could not detect. The SWAT teams were going to be deployed for the length of the trial. There were also two other officers dressed in plain clothes assigned to watch over the judge, and this gave him a total of four bodyguards who had orders to make like ghosts while they were protecting the well liked elderly judge.

THE FEDERAL COURTHOUSE, WASHINGTON D.C. MONDAY, APRIL 22nd, 2002.

The Police SWAT teams showed up as ordered and the officers watched everyone milling about the courthouse to see the judge and terrorist arrive. The Commander of the SWAT teams watched as the judge arrived and went in the coffee house and got his usual cup of coffee. He did everything he had done for the past nine years, without changing a single habit of his. The Commander picked up the four extra police assigned to protect the judge. He cringed when he watched Judge William Karlanderson slowly walk across the street to the courthouse. The unconcerned old man stopped to speak with a few friends he knew standing outside the building.

The SWAT Commander smiled at how the elderly judge completely ignored the flood of posters being shoved in his face from the angry crowd there to watch the trial of the terrorist from outside the building. Although there were no cameras going to be allowed inside the courtroom, every word said in the courtroom was going to be broadcast to the crowds and reporters through speakers set up outside the courthouse. The SWAT Commander was getting a little upset at how the judge was exposing himself to a possible assassination attempt by staying outside the building for so long a period of time while speaking to friends on his march to the courthouse. He made up his mind he was going to complain to see if he could move the judge along a little quicker. Once he was inside the courtroom, the judge was much easier to protect.

All SWAT members were on edge, and the officers only relaxed when the judge finally entered the aged courthouse, and quickly disappeared from view. Now, the police officers were waiting for the van carrying the terrorist to arrive. Everyone was ordered to report to the court building, so the judge could go over any last minute instructions for the lawyers of the terrorist, and the DA team prosecuting him for his crime. It was the last scheduled meeting between all concerned, before the trial was to start on the following morning.

The judge showed up as usual around eight thirty in the morning, and the terrorist was scheduled to be brought over to the building at nine fifteen a.m. sharp. The worried Commander of the SWAT teams was the first one to notice the three large black Chevy vans heading for the courthouse. Again, the SWAT teams tightened up their security, as the officers watched the police rudely pull Colonel al-Adwani out of the center van. Then they immediately surround the terrorist and hustle him into the building quickly. The Commander further noticed the heavy bulletproof vest wrapped around the terrorist's upper body and arms.

All SWAT Officers kept their eyes covering the ever enlarging crowd of civilians starting to shout out a steady stream of curses at the terrorist. The civilians also began to wave posters as the three unmarked black vans pulled up to the building. The police were looking for anyone who looked like a possible threat against the judge, terrorist, police, or any of the gathered civilians. Everything the SWAT members saw taking place on the streets seemed as normal enough as they could be under the circumstances, and the activity surrounding the courthouse.

Once the Iraqi prisoner was moved inside the building, the police started to relax their tension, but nevertheless they maintained their constant surveillance of the horde of civilians still crowding the streets. The police even watched the gaggle of news reporters, in case one of them might be an assassin in hiding. With what was going on down in North Carolina, no police officer wanted to take a chance that action was a ploy to take the attention off the trial, so other terrorists could make a hit on either the Arab Colonel, or the judge.

All SWAT members stayed in place until court was over for the day. The police security did not move until the prisoner was brought out of the courthouse. Then the prisoner was placed in the center unmarked police van, and the three vehicles took off with the overhead police helicopter following the vans to the main detention center in downtown Washington D.C. Police snipers remained set in place until the judge finally came out of the building, and the officers watched as he got in his car, started it up and then headed for home. The SWAT Commander smiled as he watched the two unmarked police cars closely follow the judge to his home. The Commander knew there was going to be two police cars stationed outside of the judge's home both day and night, until this trial was over.

Once the judge was gone from the area, the SWAT Commander held his people set in place for another hour, just in case they were able to pickup someone out of place in the crowd worth watching. No one seemed very suspicious, so after the hour the wise Commander finally broke up the teams after ordering them to return to the same positions at four a.m. sharp on Tuesday, April 23rd, 2002, the ordered start of Colonel Abdulaziz Majd al-Adwani's trial.

NORTH CAROLINA, MONDAY, APRIL 22nd, 2002. TWENTY TWO HUNDRED HOURS

Captain Robert Walker and his specialized soldiers started their fifth drive of the night. This time the soldiers were ordered to head north from the South and North Carolina Stateline. The troopers were going to drive up to the Virginia, North Carolina Stateline and then turn around and head south hunting for the missing shooter, and anyone who might be working with the shooter. The Captain was using his people protected by bulletproof vests as targets, hoping he could entice the sniper to take a shot at the well protected soldiers. The troopers picked up nothing out of the ordinary on their drive, except for a car with three women they passed. One woman flashed the soldiers as their car shot by the much slower moving war machines. Of course, the Mutt wanted to pull the girls over and see if he could score with any of them.

As they hit the Stateline of Virginia, the State Trooper got on the radio with Walker and offered. "Say Captain Walker Sir, what say we stop and get something to eat, sir?"

"Fine with me Lieutenant Smith, you pull off the road anywhere you wanna stop, and we'll follow ya fricking lead sir. I'm getting kinda hungry myself sir, and I think we're wasting our stinking time with searching for this lousy scumbag on the damn highway like this, Lieutenant. With all the police roadblocks you people have set up all over the stinking place. I'm betting the damn bank on this shooter would hafta be a flaming asshole to try anything against us with this much security searching for his damn ass tonight, sir. This is bullshit and bad manners if you ask me, but it still seems like the only stinking way we might get lucky enuf to find this little prick." Captain Walker complained as they passed another highway exit, and he saw at least three more police cars stopping everyone who wanted to get onto I-95.

"What are you saying Captain Walker? Am I wrong or do you want to call it a night, sir?" The State Trooper asked Walker as he tried to look at him and drive his vehicle at the same time.

"At first, I was kinda thinking about doing another run down to the South Carolina line, just in case our fucking shooter might have overslept for the fricking day, and he wants to try his luck again with trying to kill another one of my soldiers, Lieutenant. But I don't think we're gonna get him on this stinking night though, sir. I guess what I'm trying to say is, I'm kinda leaving it up to you on this decision to call it a stinking day or not for all of us, sir. You wanna call it a stinking night we'll go get something to eat and then head back to our hotel rooms and takeoff for the rest of the damn night, Lieutenant Smith Sir." Walker offered as he saw the same sign warning him the soldiers were ten miles away from the Stateline to Virginia.

"Well Captain Walker, since you're leaving the decision up to me, sir. I'm of the same mind set as you seem to be sir. I don't think we're going to be lucky enough to get the sniper tonight, sir. I think he's going to lay low for a little while until we finally relax our security around the state some, and then he'll try and hit us again, sir. The sniper has to know the entire State of North Carolina can't possible pay for all this overtime to the police officers are racking up now, Captain. So I believe he'll sit back for the time being, and then wait for us to step down our security, and then he'll make another hit against us sure as hell, Captain Walker."

"That's the same way I feel about it, Lieutenant Smith. If you wanna, we can stop and eat along the line and then head down I-95 until we get back to our fricking hotel rooms, sir. Then we'll turn in for the night and catch up on our damn sleep sir. Let me call the others and tell them what we're gonna do, Lieutenant. Nightstalker One to Nightstalker's Two and Three, and Shadow Follower, I want you all to copy this transmission." The Captain waited until the two other vehicle operators, and the helicopter Commander checked in with him before he issued his further orders for the other soldiers working with him.

"Okay people, Shadow, we're gonna break off for the night, so you're free to break off the ready air cap over our vehicles. We're gonna get a late start tomorrow morning, and then we're gonna stay out all night in fucking case our stinking shooter gets hungry for some more fricking blood. Nightstalker Two and Three, we're gonna follow the damn gumball machine (police car) in front of us, and when he pulls off the road that's where we're gonna eat. I can sure use me one of them Big Mac's to gnaw on tonight. Then we're heading for the hotel to turn in for the night.

"If any of you people need anything special to see you through the stinking night, I suggest you guys get it before we reach the damn hotel. Once there, I don't want anyone of you puds to leave the dump in case our fricking asshole gets a little antsy and he tries to hit us again, and we're called out in a fucking hurry to find the lousy prick before he gets back to his stinking rathole. The State Trooper has his blinker on, so I guess we're turning here and heading south again. We'll follow the dude until he finally stops to get somethin 'to eat for crap sake. Out."

Every soldier riding in the other Humvees knew what Walker was suggesting, if any of them needed some pot to help them make it through the night. He was ordering them to stop now and score, before they reached the hotel. Even the State Trooper listening in on Walker's orders, realized what the young military officer was telling his soldiers to do, before they reached the hotel rooms. The State Trooper smiled as he turned off the highway and pulled into the turnoff.

The convoy of vehicles and trooper car turned on the service road, and the vehicles pulled back onto I-91, heading south. The group drove for twenty minutes before the State Trooper flipped on his right turn signal and pulled off the highway. Walker looked at the sign and knew the State Trooper was taking them to a steak house for supper. He smiled because he was that hungry he could use a good steak about now. The convoy pulled in the parking lot and everyone piled out of their machines and the excited soldiers attacked the restaurant like an invading army.

A number of Walker's group headed for the bathrooms, as the rest of the specialized soldiers took over a number of tables, and they slid four of the tables closer together. So the soldiers could all sit together while they ate and discussed their current situation and hunt for the missing sniper. People already eating inside the restaurant, stared at the angry looking group of thoroughly exhausted looking soldiers, and the State Trooper sitting with the group of soldiers. None of the soldiers brought their weapons into the eatery, and they left the large soldier branded Buckethead in the parking lot to guard their vehicles and weapons stored in them, while the rest of the group ate. Captain Walker was going to bring him out a meal, and Buckethead could eat in the Humvee as they headed for the hotel rooms for the night.

The soldiers laughed and told jokes and nodded at any kids in the place that looked at them and smiled. Some of the troopers shot the looks that informed the women what they wanted to do to their bodies, if they had half the chance to be alone with them. Women blushed over the leering looks from the soldiers, and others smiled back at them, and others simply turned away after giving the soldiers dirty looks and cold shoulders. No soldiers discussed why they were on the roads on this night. If they had to speak over any problems with their orders, they would do it over their radios, so no one overheard what they were up tonight.

All the while Captain Walker waited for his meal to arrive he was studying the many faces of the civilians eating in the restaurant. His well trained military mind was constantly searching for any possible sign of something or someone acting even the slightest bit suspicious against them. He knew he was not going to rest again until he, or someone else from his group located and killed this missing shooter. The Captain was kind of taking it personal, because the shooter killed two of the soldiers from his specialized Unit, and he also wounded a third and one of his closest friends. His meal came and he was forced to break off his checking of every civilian seated in the eatery. Sergeant Dorothy Ramirez knew what he was up to, so she busied herself speaking to the other soldiers while giving him the peace to check everyone out in the restaurant.

Once the soldiers finished eating, Walker handed the waitress his military credit card, and she took off in a rush. By the time she returned with the slip for Walker to sign, he, Ramirez and the State Trooper were the only ones still left inside the restaurant from their large group. He was taking his time paying the bill, because he knew the other soldiers who wanted anything to smoke tonight, would find it before the rest of them came out of the place. Even though he was aware the State Trooper understood his orders to the soldiers. He was still trying to be careful, because he did not want to rub in the fact that some of his people were scoring on a pot run.

By the time the two soldiers and State Trooper walked out of the eatery, the Captain noticed his people were milling around the three parked military vehicles. He looked at the soldier they branded the Ghost, and he nodded towards him. So Walker headed for his machine while the State Trooper headed for his cruiser. They started up the machines and pulled out onto the roadway and in no time flat, they were heading towards the area around Camp Lejeune and their hotel. All the while the soldiers drove, Walker looked over the Ghost's back as he intensely studied the inferred machine inside their vehicle.

A couple times the soldiers noticed a hot spot in the woods, but the Ghost was so good with reading the heat signatures he was picking up, he informed Walker the heat signals were too small to be human, and the signals had to be a small animal or a bird rummaging around on the ground. Every exit the soldiers passed to the highway, the Captain noticed more parked police vehicles, and the officers were checking every vehicle that entered or left I-95 Highway.

The traffic was light at this time of night, and the Captain felt this was because everyone understood a sniper was working over the road, and they did not want to be killed while driving on the roadway. The Marine Captain did not understand this fear, all three soldiers killed or wounded by this shooter, was not driving a vehicle. But everyone was free to deal with their own fears in any manner they may choose. After another hour of driving, Walker's convoy finally came across their exit and as they pulled off the road, they were ordered to stop by the police manning this roadblock. The State Trooper got out of his cruiser and Walker and a number of his fellow soldiers jumped out of his military vehicle and caught up with the trooper.

The State Trooper with Walker's group walked up to one of his fellow officers, and the police officer said. "Evening George, you guys see anything out of the ordinary on the road tonight, sir? You know we're now looking for upwards of possibly twenty people who might be involved in this shooting action going down lately around here, right sir? We were informed they might all belong to a new terrorist cell and they sneaked their way into our country."

"Sure we do John, and we didn't come across anyone who wasn't supposed to be in the area yet tonight. By the way, how the hell are you making out with this mess of soldiers you were stuck working with lately, John?" the second State Trooper asked as he gave a quick head movement towards the military officer and rest of the soldiers standing at his side.

"Excuse me sir, Captain Robert Walker, this man is Trooper George Greenwood, sir. George, Robert." Lieutenant Smith offered as he introduced Walker to the other State Trooper, as they ignore the rest of the soldiers standing behind their Captain.

The second police officer put out his hand and shook with Walker as he offered. "Glad to meet you Captain. I'm really sorry about the two soldiers killed by this asshole we're out here looking for sir. But I assure you Captain, we'll get the sonofabitch one way or the other, and soon enough for you at that, sir. It's only a matter of time before he messes up and we finally find his ass, sir. They all mess up after a while, Captain. I hope we get his ass before he kills again, sir."

"So do I Corporal Greenwood, so do I sir. I'm damn glad to meet you sir." He replied as politely as he shook the other trooper's hand and smiled at the man.

Captain Walker and Trooper Smith watched the other officers as they stopped another three civilian vehicles, and the alert police expertly searched the civilians and their cars, before they allowed the stopped vehicle go, and the officers headed back to their police vehicles. The Captain and the rest of his people were waved right through the roadblock next. The soldiers continued to drive until they parked in the Holiday Hotel parking lot. The exhausted soldiers removed their weapons and carried them exposed into their rooms. Lieutenant Smith secured his shotgun in the trunk of his squad car, and then he headed for his own room. The soldiers were thoroughly exhausted from their long night of searching for the shooter of their fellow soldiers, and they just plopped down in their beds and in no time at all, most of the soldiers were snoring away.

Captain Walker and Sergeant Ramirez took their time to make love soft and slow, before they finally turned in for the rest of the night. There were four soldiers to each room, so it was not very private for their love making secession. Walker and Ramirez were sharing their room with the Mutt and Blind Date, and the Captain was kind of surprised the always horny Mutt turned in without making love to Blind Date first.

ONE AND ONE HALF MILES AWAY AT THE BEST WESTERN HOTEL

Colonel Hamoodi al-Qaysi and Major Serena al-Shaya were also asleep, but not before they made love. The terrorists slept peacefully, knowing they were safe in the hotel room. The Iraqi Colonel was looking forward to tomorrow morning, he understood Lieutenant Aziz Abdel al-Atrash and his group was going to kill Colonel al-Adwani, and the Federal judge. He was no fool and knew their death would take the heat off their backs and their act being carried off in North Carolina. Then he and the female Major would be free to leave the United States for good.

The exhausted Colonel went to bed wanting this night to end quickly, so he could watch the TV tomorrow and see his hit team go in action and kill their intended targets. He knew he would never be able to leave the United States unless these two targets were killed first. He was more worried about Colonel al-Adwani than the judge. He knew if the police authorities were able to break the Colonel down, he would inform the Americans that President Saddam Hussein was the man behind the orders that sent him and the rest his terrorist cell to the United States to assassinate the American President. Colonel al-Qaysi understood if Lieutenant al-Atrash's team did not successfully kill Colonel al-Adwani, he was going to be forced to head back up to Washington with Major al-Shaya and the other two terrorists with him, and no matter what the outcome to them. He would have to make the hit and kill on the Colonel himself.

Although he tossed and turned all night, Colonel al-Qaysi got a good night's sleep. He woke at five a.m. and he could not fall back to sleep no matter how hard he tried. Once he saw the time, he knew his hit teams up in Washington D.C. were about to set out on their ordered mission. This knowledge stopped him from drifting off to sleep a second time. He was excited, not only was his hit teams going to pull off their mission. But there was a good possibility he was going to be able to watch the attack on TV, alive as it played out. Because every time the police brought al-Adwani to the courthouse, it was a media event, and it was shown live on American TV stations. As far as he knew, this was going to be the first time in history of any terrorist attacks. The trial was going to be televised live and in color before his eyes and for the rest of the world to witness.

This thought brought a sadistic smile to his lips as he got out of bed. Then he started coffee brewing for him and al-Shaya who was still asleep. Then the Arab Military Officer put the TV on without regard for the sleeping female Major. When she heard the TV, she rolled over on her side and saw the Colonel skipping through the channels. All the news stations he found this early in the morning were very boring, with the commentators talking about the upcoming trial against the captured Iraqi terrorist scheduled to begin later today.

The broadcasters were showing file shots of the old courthouse in downtown Washington D.C., but they were yesterday's pictures of the Iraqi Colonel and judge going in the well aged building where the trail was to be held. The Colonel's blood suddenly froze as he caught a quick glimpse of what looked like a police officer hiding on the roof of a building situated directly across the street from the courthouse. Now he understood the police had added to the security surrounding the elderly judge and Iraqi Colonel and courthouse. Anger built up in his shaking and tense body, as the extremely upset al-Qaysi stared at the TV while trying to pick up more of the police officers perched on the roof of the building again.

The female Iraqi Major Serena al-Shaya picked up the change in the Colonel's look and said as she swung her legs off the side of the bed and walked over to him as she asked her Commander. "Hamoodi, you suddenly look very upset sir? I was enjoying watching you being in such a good mood a moment ago. What has happened that changed your mood so quickly on you sir?"

"We have a huge problem with our hit team working in Washington, Major al-Shaya. I just picked up what I believe was a police SWAT team hiding on a roof of a building by the foul court building, where they'll bring the worthless Colonel al-Adwani to for his cursed trial by the hated American government officials. If there's one worthless police officer hiding on the roof then there has to be more on many other roofs of the buildings surrounding the cursed courthouse, foolish woman. I have to make contact with Lieutenant al-Atrash immediately, and warn him over this new threat mounted against him and his fellow brothers and sisters, by these very crafty but hated American police authorities. What's the phone number to that foul motel where the worthless fool is staying at back up there in Washington, Major al-Shaya?"

Major al-Shaya left the Colonel's side and she went to her purse and dug around a few seconds, until she found a card from the filthy motel, and it had its phone number printed on it. Colonel al-Qaysi was standing by the phone angrily waiting, so she read the number to him so he could dial the number on the phone at the same time.

The Colonel dialed the number as she read it, and waited for the phone to be answered by the manager of the complex. He stared at the naked Major as he waited. It was finally answered.

"This is the Roland's Motel in Washington D.C., and we have rooms opened if you'd like to rent a room at my establishment. What can I do for you today sir?" the rather pleasant speaking manager of the motel answered sharply in the phone.

"Yes, this is Mr. Santo Trafficante sir, and I wish to speak to my brother renting Room Seven from your establishment, sir. It's important I speak with him immediately sir. It seems our dear mother in Miami has taken ill, and she's not expected to live through the illness I'm afraid, sir." The wise Iraqi Colonel used the name he used before when they were speaking with the American Captain who brought his terrorist team into the United States a few months ago.

"I'm sorry to inform you sir, but the man and woman renting Room Seven has checked out of the motel earlier today. He paid his bill and said he'd not be returning. They left the motel fifteen minutes ago, along with the other four people renting Room Eight, sir. Look, I can call the police and have them look for your brother if you want me to, Mr. Trafficante. Maybe they're still in the area and once the police find him, they can have him get in touch with you, sir." The manager of the motel said, trying to help the man trying to locate his brother.

"No sir that'll not be necessary. I know where my foolish brother is going, and I'll call my sister in Washington and have her tell my brother to get in touch with me immediately. I'm sorry for bothering you at such an early hour, and I thank you for your time and patience in this manner, sir." Colonel al-Qaysi said as politely as he could as he broke off the connection with the manager and then looked at Major al-Shaya again and offered.

"I can't believe the blessings Allah has bestowed upon these great fools we're trying to kill. He offers them more protection than he does His own faithful follows from the land of the sand of the Middle East. Now, I can only hope Allah will extend His protective hand over Lieutenant al-Atrash's worthless shoulder, and He blesses the great fool with the same protection He offers these lowly infidels of this cursed country of lowly infidels and jackals, woman." Colonel al-Qaysi complained at the major as he looked up towards the heavens for an answer.

THE ROLAND'S HOTEL, TUESDAY,
APRIL 23rd, 2002. 5:30 A.M.

Lieutenant Aziz Abdel al-Atrash paid their bill for the rooms. When this was done, he walked out of the office and headed for the rented car. Sergeant Hanan al-Wazir, Sergeant Aicha Said Damerdji, and Corporal Mohammed Oveidat with Sergeant Muhammad Mushtaha, the original sniper and support team, and the extra two supporting soldiers, Lieutenant Bahaa Handoni, and Sergeant Hanan al-Wazir, loaded their belongings and the broke down weapons in the car. Once al-Atrash was in the vehicle, he drove it the seven blocks to the Federal Courthouse. He drove to the parking lot of the Circle K store, and left it parked in the back of the building and locked it.

The two Iraqi terrorists picked to be shooters for the hit teams, took the bags with their broken down weapons stored inside them, and they headed for their stations to wait for their targets to show up at the courthouse. The supporting two Iraqi soldiers took their modified M-16s with them. They cut down the stocks and barrels so the weapon was easily hid on their person. The two extra supporter members did the same thing, and they also hid their modified M-16s on their person. The two extra supporters for the hit teams were ordered to wait outside the double doors the shooters would use to get up on the roof of the buildings around the courthouse they picked out to kill their targets from.

Lieutenant al-Atrash understood once they killed their two intended targets, the entire area surrounding the courthouse was going to be flooded with Washington and Capital Police Officers, and they would be looking to capture them. This was why he left the extra supporters on the ground to protect their escape route for them.

What Lieutenant al-Atrash was not aware of, there were four police SWAT teams set up for the start of the trial of the terrorist already stationed on the roof area of the same building they intended to use for their assassination attempt of the Federal Judge and Iraqi Colonel. The police were set in position since four a.m. that morning. The Commander of one SWAT team just returned to the roof area of the building, and he was carrying a bag with five cups of coffee and some cakes for his officers. He handed the cakes and coffee over to his officers, and they were sipping the coffees while keeping a sort of eye on the street before the courthouse.

Not even many of the news reporters showed up for the start of the trail this early in the morning. They usually started to come around near about seven a.m., and then the reporters would have coffee and talk amongst themselves for a while. Then they would start to set up their cameras and recording equipment to cover the trial, and be ready for the arrival of the judge and terrorist prisoner at the courthouse.

Not one protester was near the site yet. The protesters usually started to show up around eight a.m. at the courthouse. The horde of protesters was going to be the biggest problem for the police on guard duty to handle and keep under control for the duration of the trial. There were so many angry protesters showing up at the courthouse lately, and the crowd was so thick it was nearly impossible for any of the police officers to see anyone who might be looking to attack any players in the rapidly unfolding drama of a court trial. The SWAT Team Commander suggest to his superior that they should move most of the protesters a little further away from the courthouse doors, but he was voted down by his own Commanding Officer. So he was forced to do the best he could with the situation, and he was not very happy with it or his order.

Today was going to be an extremely stressful and trying day for the police officers involved with the protection of the judge, and the Iraqi terrorist going to stand trial for his crimes against the American President, and his Cabinet Staff and the Vice President. All the police officers knew if anyone was going to try and disrupt the court proceedings, it would surely happen on this opening day. If anything happened at the beginning of the trial, the court would be forced to seat a new jury, and then start the whole mess over again, especially if the attackers killed the judge for the trial. he jurors were ordered to be at the courtroom at nine fifteen a.m. at the latest, and the court was scheduled to begin at exactly ten a.m. sharp for the start of the trail of the Iraqi terrorist. Then the jurors would be sequestered for the rest of the duration of the trial.

The extremely concerned SWAT Team Commander was busy speaking with a young Police Lieutenant, and they were resting against the concrete parapet wall four feet high on the very edge of the building they were using for their temporary headquarters. The two officers were looking at the streets below as they spoke together. The Commander's handheld radio was resting on top of the wall by his hand, and all he was armed with was his service revolver.

The Lieutenant was armed with an M-16 assault rifle with a special scope mounted on the weapon and it was slung over his right shoulder. Two other police officers were armed with MP-5 machine guns for fire support, in case the officers found themselves locked in a firefight with any possible terrorist or civilians trying to take the law into their own hands, and they try and kill the terrorist before he was tried.

On the street below the officers, the six Arabs terrorists walked towards the courthouse. They wanted to get near the building long before any police, reporters, or protesters arrived at the site. They wanted to be well set up to make their hits by six a.m., and then all they had to do was wait for their targets to arrive and kill them, and then leave the area.

The small group of Iraqi terrorists walked the three blocks over to the courthouse with each male member of the hit teams allowing the women to carry the heavy bags with the sniper weapons stored inside them for the shooters of the cell. The group of Arab radicals were trying to look like any other ordinary visitors to the downtown Washington D.C. area, who showed up because they wanted to see the judge and Iraqi terrorist who masterminded the assassination attempt against the President of the United States, as they came up to the age building. The terrorists were trying to look as inconspicuous as possible to anyone who might be looking at them, as they entered the area of the courthouse.

The first SWAT Team Members were likewise enjoying their coffee, and they were the furthest team set out from the courthouse building. One of the officers suddenly noticed the six young people walking into his area of responsibility, and he immediately drew his Commander's attention to the small group of people. The suddenly concerned Police Commander looked over the edge of the building and carefully studied the six people. His second in command was crouched slightly by his side, and he asked his Commander with concern lacing his words. "What do you think about these people sir? Could they be a threat against us or the Judge, sir?"

"I'll tell you what I think about them. This fucking trial is going to draw the attention of anyone nosy enough and want to see this damn terrorist. I guess these six people must get their rocks off seeing killers, sir. Who the hell knows? I wonder why they're here so early though."

"To get the best seats in the house I guess Commander." The second officer offered.

"Maybe so, but I don't like anyone being in the area of the courthouse so damn early in the morning, sir. This is the exact time I'd use to set myself up, if I was going to do something to disrupt the proceedings of the court and trial, Officer. Hey wait a minute, look at the two women carrying those bags, dammit. Christ sake I don't like this shit one damn bit. I think these fucks are up to something no good and I am going to react on the side of better judgment and send out an alarm about them." The SWAT Commander grumbled as he picked up his handheld radio, and then he pressed the button and said in the mike.

"To all SWAT Team Commanders, we have six people entering our area of responsibility at this time. I see two female subjects struggling carrying large bags over their shoulders that seem to weight heavy. I don't like the looks of these few people. We're going to stand by and see what this group is up to. Stay alert people. I think we might have us a little fucking problem building up on our hands here, and I want everyone to stay on top of this damn thing before anything gets out of hand on us. Keep a watch on our lead and act accordingly if we go into action."

The other Commanders of the SWAT Security Teams immediately checked in and notified the lead Commander who just alarmed them that they were on the subject targets. Each SWAT member securing the roof areas picked out the six people penetrating their area of responsibility.

The Commander of the foot police protecting the courthouse structure from the ground, checked in with the SWAT Team Commander. He asked the Commander if he wanted them to intercept the small group of intruders before they became a possible threat against them.

"No Phil, as it stands at the moment sir, we don't have many civilian or damn news reporters showing up in the area of our responsibility as of yet, sir. So we're operating under the best possible circumstances at the moment to deal with any possible suspected terrorist attack in the area. At this point, I think I'd rather see where these few people are going, and what the hell they might be up to, before we react against them in force, sir. I don't want to give away our present positions until we know for certain if this group of people might be people we have to be concerned with, sir. So hang loose for the time being I guess, and I'll keep you advised if and when I want you people to intercept this group, sir.

"These guys just might be a bunch of crazy ass protesters showing up to get an early start to their bitches, and I don't want to give away our position under a non-event situation here, sir. If we react now then all manner of surprise will be eliminated from our security detail, sir. If these damn people are nothing but what I suggested they might be, and we do have other terrorist we're unaware of hanging around out there someplace. Once we react against this damn group, we'll give away our positions and then we'll become the damn targets, as well as the people we're here trying to protect, dammit. No, stand down until needed sir."

The SWAT Commander picked up his field glassed and he concentrated them on one of the females carrying the obviously heavy bags for the two males walking in front of them. He was trying to get a shape on the bag. So far, they were acting like normal visitors to Washington. But when the Commander's Lieutenant pointed out the men were dressed in heavy long coats for this time of the year. The SWAT Commander grew even more concerned and suspicious with the small group of strangers still walking towards the building the police were using for their perch to keep an eye on what was going on below them, as he reported over his radio to the other Commanders of his team again.

"To all SWAT Team Commanders in the field, our people of interest are dressed in heavy coats for this time of the year. Standby, I believe we have something preparing to go down against us over here. Our subjects are vertical and moving, two female and four male subjects are under observation and suspicion at this time. Standby and be ready to lend immediate assistance if this situation goes active against us." The concerned SWAT Commander offered as he watched the group walk until they were standing in front of the courthouse.

The Commander cursed under his breath as he picked up the first news reporters as they started to show up to cover the proceedings at the courthouse, and the people with him entered the satellite truck and started the generator to power their equipment. Even before the people of interest walked by the news truck, the reporter was out with his cameraman, and they were already filming the area before the courthouse. Now, the SWAT Commander realized if these people were really terrorists then their action was going to be televised live to the rest of the world, when they react against them.

The now extremely concerned SWAT Commander was hoping if these people of concern were a serious threat against them or the judge or terrorist. He could have handled the situation before any of the reporters show up by the courthouse for their coverage of the proceeding. The worried Commander cursed aloud again when he saw the reporter walked towards the middle of the street, and then he start to film the area from that position. The Police Commander also noticed this reporter was going to be right in the line of fire from where he was standing, if anything went down on the SWAT team against the people of concern.

As the people of concern continued to move around in the area, more reports came into the Commander in control of all SWAT teams for the security of the trial. One after the other the reports came in and the officers were reporting every movement from their people of interest they spotted moving around the area. "Have the subject targets in my sight."

A second report came in. "Packages seem to be stopped and they're speaking to each other. Requesting permission to challenge subjects and see what the hell they're up to in this area, sir. "

"Target subjects seem to be scanning out the area, better keep your heads down low people. I got a gut feeling these people are up to no good here."

"I don't have a good tag on the moving suspected targets. I have no visual on the six suspects from my present position. I need more input. Over." One of the officers on the ground patrol detail reported to the SWAT Commander over his radio.

"I have a good visual on the six subjects in question. Our packages are definitely scouting out the area surrounding the courthouse. Packages seem to be up to no good from where I'm observing the subject's actions. Over." The third SWAT member reported to his Commander.

The Lead Commander got in contact with the GTCO, or the Ground Team Commanding Officer, and requested him to walk over to the reporter and get him out of the way for them.

The SWAT Commander watched as the six subjects cautiously moved about on the ground, and then they suddenly spilt up in two sets of three, and each set went off in a different direction in the area. The Commander's attention was drawn back to the reporter as an officer walked up to him as if nothing was wrong, and ordered the reporter out of the middle of the street. As soon as the reporter was out of the way, the Commander turned his attention back on one of the sets of three people, as they headed across the street from the courthouse at this point. It seemed like the strangers were heading directly for the building the Commander was using for their operation.

"To all SWAT and Ground Force members attached to the security of the courthouse, this is Field Command Commander. The three subjects in question are coming directly towards our building. Standby people, we have to see what these damn packages are up to. Dammit, they're definitely coming right at our building. All members get low I don't want anyone to be detected by the subjects until we find out what the fuck they're up to. I lost the other three subjects they're no longer in my field of vision. Can someone pickup the other three subjects and report to me what the hell they're up to and where they are heading. Over." The SWAT Command Commander complained in his mike to the other units under his Command.

"CC, we have a positive on the other three subjects in question locked up in our field of vision, sir. The second set of subjects just entered a building near the courthouse, sir. If they went in that building it's a positive this group is setting up a sniper's nest to operate from, sir. We have a second SWAT Team set up on the roof of said building, sir. We got the other three subjects covered as they still walk on the ground, sir. Over."

"Affirmative, keep me apprised of the other subjects in question actions. We have these three subjects covered from our position. Over." The SWAT Commander replied in his radio.

The new reporter spotted some of the movement on the roof of the building directly across the street from his, and quickly realized the movement was from police officers obviously stationed on the roof of the building for security reasons. The reporter understood the police were trying to protect the courthouse from that position. The police seemed to be preparing for some kind of action. Now, his reporter instincts were overflowing, and he had his cameraman keep the building he was watching in his camera's view at all times from that point forward. Then the reporter noticed the three young civilians slowly walking into the same building where he noticed the police stationed on the roof and moving around, and he locked onto the movers. Now he wondered if this small group of young people was the reason for all the police activity.

CHAPTER TWENTY FOUR

Colonel Hamoodi al-Qaysi kept switching channels of the TV in anger, until he finally came across Fox and Friends on the Fox News Channel. There was a report coming in about the courthouse, and it seemed like it was a live telecast. The Iraqi Colonel stopped here and again his anger grew as the camera showed at least two police officers obviously stationed on the roof of the building the camera was now constantly keeping in his view. Then the reporter's eyes narrowed as the camera scanned the ground and picked up the backs of three of his hit team members as they cautiously entered the same building the police were on top of.

Instantly, Colonel al-Qaysi realized his hit team in Washington was heading for the roof of this same building, and they were going to run right into the police stationed on the rooftop. He understood this assassination team was going to be unsuccessful on their mission. Al-Qaysi cursed angrily as he watched the two members of his attack team suddenly disappear inside the building, and the third member who was the elected spotter for his team, take up a position of security just outside the building. Now he wished he had one of the radios the Libyan Captain gave them in his possession. He threw his away, once he shot at the American soldier called No Neck, but not before he completely destroyed the machine first though.

NORTH CAROLINA, THE HOLIDAY HOTEL

Marine Captain Robert Walker was watching the TV. This was the reason he told the other soldiers from his squad, it was going to be a late start to their day. Because he wanted to see what was going to happen in Washington with the start of the trial against Arab terrorist, Colonel al-Adwani. He had a gut feeling there was going to be a problem with the start of the trial, and he wanted to see if he could spot what was going to happen before it went off, and if he was right with his bad beliefs. He easily noticed the SWAT team stationed on the roof of the building across from the courthouse, because he knew where to look for such an action. But when the camera scanned the backs of the three strangers entering the building, he knew he was correct in his assumption. The three people were obviously a part of a hit team operating in Washington, and the group had to be there to start problems at the trial.

Walker did not have a chance to call out the alarm as both the Ghost and Buckethead started to wildly pound on his door. Other members of his group were stacking up in the hallway also while waiting for him to answer the door. Their commotion woke the State Trooper, and he came out of his room to see what all the noise was about with the soldiers he was working with. He was worried something might have happened that he was unaware of with the soldiers.

Sergeant Dorothy Ramirez threw a shirt on and then answered the door as the Mutt got up and he growled at Walker. "Man, what the fuck's wrong with you for Christ sake? Don't you ever fucking sleep anymore man, I want to sleep some more if you don't mind, pudhead?"

"Mutt, drop your cock and grab your socks, we got a fucking possible hit going down in fucking Washington, man." Walker's words were heard by everyone now piling into his room. The State Trooper barked at Walker as he entered the room. "Are you positive about that last statement, Captain Walker Sir? I received no threat calls from my Command Center, sir."

"Hey man, if Walker says it's happening, you can bet your lady's draws on it, it's going down as we speak buster." Buckethead snapped at the trooper as he shot him a nasty look.

The excited State Trooper looked at Bucket and then back to Walker to hear his reply.

"Look at the damn TV and you'll see it for yourself, Lieutenant. I'm positive there's a hit gonna go down up there on us." Walker replied to the officer as he glanced at the TV again.

"I don't need that much proof sir. I have to make a phone call to the Commander up there sir." The trooper left Walker's room as everyone else closed ranks on the Captain and grinned at him.

He smiled and tried to watch the TV over the other soldier's shoulders, and he bitched angrily at the rest of the troops suddenly clogging up his room. "I see you people noticed the same damn thing I picked up on the fricking set. It looks like we just found out what this stinking shooter was doing down here in North Carolina for Christ sake. The fucking shooter was trying to divert our attention away from the damn action gonna take place up there in Washington fucking D.C. I want you people to get ready, as soon as we see what the fuck goes down in Washington we're getting back on the damn road and find this stinking shooter. If they try to hit the damn Judge and free this stinking Colonel al-Adwani dude then they might try and hit us to take some of the stinking heat offa their lousy ass shooters up there for crap sake, people.

"I wanna be ready for anything going down in Carolina. I don't wanna lose another damn soldier to the shit filled hit team working our asses over down here, man. I want some asses, and I want them right now, people. Move it out guys, it looks like we're gonna be plenty busy around here when the act goes down up there in Washington." Walker growled at the rest of his elite soldiers, and then he turned his attention to the TV again.

The soldiers headed out of Walker's room, with Buckethead griping as he walked by Walker. "I don't know why the fuck we were worried about you not knowing what we saw on the damn TV, man. We shoulda knew you'd be watching the same shit we were watching, Walker."

"Hey Buckethead, don't make me get my damn stun gun out again, buddy. Get back to your room and get dressed before you find your face on the back of a fucking milk carton, big guy. We're gonna shove off as soon as I see what the hell happens in Washington, asshole." The Captain growled at Buckethead as he removed his eyes from the TV and glared at the big man.

The Mutt smacked Walker on his back and then he drew his attention back to the TV. It was showing one of the three strangers took up his standoff position just outside the door the other two civilian types just disappeared in, and he said to his commanding officer. "It looks like it's going down right bout now on us, Walker."

Walker looked at the TV when the State Trooper came charging back in his room and he announced in an excited voice to the. "Captain Walker, it seems you're right on target with your assumption of something going down in Washington, sir. When I reported to the Commander, they informed me they were aware of the problem and were handling it, sir. They congratulated me on my awareness though, Captain Walker. Good work sir, we got them dead to rights, sir."

"I knew they were on it Lieutenant, because I saw a number of police officers watching the movers from the roof area, sir. Let's watch how they're going to react against this situation, and then we're getting back out on the road and continue our search for our fucking shooter, sir. Because I think the shooter operating here in North Carolina is working with these cocksuckers in Washington, and they're gonna hit us again to take some of the stinking heat offa the shooters operating in Washington, Lieutenant Smith Sir." Walker, Sergeant Ramirez, the Mutt and Blind Date, along with the State Trooper settled down to watch the action as it went down.

"You know something Walker? One of these fucking days you're gonna fall down and crack your head opened, and nothing but a shitload of empty fricking beer cans and half eaten pussies are gonna come tumbling outta it, man. I don't know where you're getting your fricking brains from, but they sure as hell aren't in your fucking head, my friend. I was told you only think with your small head anyway, man." The Mutt complained at his lifelong buddy.

"You're getting to be a real fucking Jerk Benny lately, Mutt. But if I'm thinking with my little head, at least I'm thinking with something I guess, stupid. Shut up man, we gotta pay attention to what's the fuck's going down in Washington, dog."

"Walker, if you can't eat it, drink it, fuck it, or fire it. I'm not very interested in it, man." The Mutt replied as he smiled at his lifelong friend and fellow soldier.

"You're right on the fucking mark as always I see today, Mutt. Who the hell knew masturbation could make a fellow so fucking witty." Walker fired back at the Mutt.

Everyone turned their attention back to the TV and quieted down as they watched how the police were setting up what they believed to be a group of civilians who were up to something either against the police, or the terrorist standing trial for his crimes.

WASHINGTON D.C., THE FEDERAL COURTHOUSE

The concerned Commander of the SWAT teams growled over the radio at his team members not to intercept the small group of what they believed was civilians. "Shit, I just lost the three subjects heading for this damn building. I need some real time input from the rest of you guys out there. At the moment I'm blind and I need some help to relocate our moving targets, so I know where the hell these three subjects are at and I can react accordingly, dammit."

"Be advised Commander, I picked up two of the three subjects in question entering your building from the ground floor area, sir. It's believed the three subjects are heading for the roof of the structure, sir. One subject in question was a female, and she was carrying a large bag on her shoulder, sir. The second subject in question was a male and was empty handed, sir. The third subject, another male has assumed a sort of guard duty standing by the door the other two subjects just used to enter your building, sir. I suggest you make your people look like ghosts up there and hide, until you know what the hell these two subjects are up to up there, sir."

"Roger that, we'll act accordingly against the threat from the stair area of this damn building. Thanks for the input sir. Over." The SWAT Commander broke off his communication with the other commander, and then he barked at his six officers stationed on the roof area. "Snipers, disappear, support members be prepared to defend our position against any possible purps coming at us from the staircase of this building. It's believed we're about to have two visitors up here, and until we know what the hell they're up to, we'll react as if they're terrorists, Officers."

The two SWAT snipers moved out of the way, their weapons were useless in a close quarter battle, and four other police officers chambered a round in their MP-5 machine guns, and then waited for the two strangers to make their appearance on the roof with them.

As soon as the extremely cautious Iraqi Lieutenant Aziz Abdel al-Atrash and Sergeant Hanan al-Wazir entered the stairway leading up to the six story building's roof. The terrorists stopped moving the instant the metal door closed behind them. The female Iraqi Sergeant placed the heavy canvas bag down on the floor by her feet, and then she quickly opened it and removed the weapon from the bag. As she handed the disassembled weapon to the Lieutenant, he quickly assembled the weapon into a proper firing condition, and then he snapped the loaded clip of thirty rounds home, and then chambered a round in the weapon. Once the Lieutenant was locked and loaded and ready to move out again, Sergeant al-Wazir removed her modified M-16 out from under her dress, and she immediately chambered a round into the weapon. When she was ready to go to work, the terrorist assassination team headed for the roof area of the building, so they could kill the Iraqi Colonel and Federal Judge.

The SWAT Commander listened to his radio as he hid behind a metal roof vent that brought fresh air into the air-conditioning unit constructed on the roof of the building. "Be advised SWAT Commander, I have the confidence target locked up in my sights, sir. Once whatever is happening on the roof is over with Commander, or any alert is issued from the confidence target, and he's aware something's happening on the roof with his two buddies. I'll wound said target on guard duty on the ground, sir." A police sniper from another SWAT team checked in, and he warned the SWAT Commander stationed on the roof of what he intended to do.

What seemed like a short lifetime for the Police Commander, he finally head a slight noise coming from the stairwell area leading to the roof.

Downstairs, the news reporter who came to work early knew something was taking place before him, and he felt he was on the verge of the scoop of the century for his network. He began whispering into his microphone as the cameraman kept his camera trained right on the building, scanning the roof area where the spotted officers were stationed. Now they saw nothing moving around on the roof of the building. In order to keep the audience and Fox New Channel's attention and to stop the broadcast from going to a commercial break. The reporter was making it sound like a possible police firefight was about to take place just outside the courthouse, right in the center of downtown Washington D.C.

It was working out very well for the young reporter, because the News Channel would not dare go to a commercial break with what they were picking up happening at the courthouse. Even the three people who ran the Fox and Friends broadcast were seen now and then, and they were staring right at the same thing their audience was watching on their TVs. Every once in a while, one of the concerned commentators would ask the reporter down in Washington to move the camera back to the roof area of the building, or move it back to the stranger still standing guard at the door leading into the building they were looking at. As they continued to wait for whatever was going to happen, to occur before their eyes.

Slowly, the door leading to the roof opened and the male stranger cautiously walked onto the roof like his life was in danger. The Commander of the SWAT team ducked down when he picked up the first subject carrying a weapon. None of the other police officers reacted until the female subject came out on the roof right behind the male suspect. The second she did, everything happened in less than a heartbeat. The SWAT Commander made his radio snap, which informed the police they had armed people on the roof with them.

Like the deadly spit from a cobra, the sniper on the ground placed a round in the guard standing his post by the door of the building from long range. This subject was not killed because the round hit him high on the shoulder of his right side. But the bullet disabled him enough and the subject dropped the unseen weapon on the floor. Immediately, two other police officers appeared from out of nowhere and they quickly secured the downed subject along with his weapon. Then the police dragged the subject away from the building area.

"Bill, was that man just shot by the police standing by the door to that building?" the female commentator asked the reporter on the ground with concern lacing her voice from the news room at the Fox and Friends station in New York City.

"I believe the man was shot yes, and as you can plainly see from what we're filming here. A number of police officers just dragged the wounded man away from the building, as they quickly disappeared from our view. The man in question was obviously armed, you saw the weapon fall before he did as he was wounded. This is amazing, we have a terrorist situation going down right on live television, and we're witnessing it as it's happening in real time. Please standby, we just detected some other movement up on the roof..."

The police stationed on the roof suddenly showed themselves at the same time the SWAT Commander yelled out from his position for the two intruders to drop their weapons, and then ordered them to place their hands on their heads.

The female Iraqi Sergeant Hanan al-Wazir and male Lieutenant Aziz Abdel al-Atrash nearly jumped out of their skins, as they heard the booming American voice warning them to drop their weapons and raise their hands. Al-Atrash's eyes frantically searched entire the roof area, and he immediately located at least four police officers, and all four of them were aiming their weapons right at him and his female Sergeant. The Iraqi Lieutenant was scared to death to even breathe at this point, because he understood he and his Sergeant were mired in a no win situation, and he did not know what to do next. The Arab Lieutenant did not want to be taken as a prisoner by the police authorities, but he also did not want to die.

A thought suddenly flashed in his mind, and he remembered hearing of turning state's evidence, and the American justice system usually went very easy on whoever gave them any vital information, to stop another situation from happening somewhere else. He went to drop his weapon, but Sergeant Hanan al-Wazir made a foolish move with her weapon. Instantly, two muffled shots rang out, and both rounds striking his girlfriend square in the chest, and she stepped backwards and then dropped down on the roof of the building.

Lieutenant al-Atrash looked behind him as the Sergeant crumbled to the floor in a heap. As he turned, his actions were instantly classified as hostile in nature towards the police, and he was immediately wounded once in the upper chest area. He went down, and the police quickly charged at the two downed subjects. One officer landing on al-Atrash's chest with his knee, knocking the breath out of his lungs, and the second officer kicked the weapon out of everyone's reach. The officer working on the male subject flipped the smaller al-Atrash over on his stomach, and then he forced his arms behind his back and then roughly handcuffed them together.

While the police were manhandling him, Lieutenant al-Atrash tried to see around them to see if Sergeant al-Wazir was still alive. Two other officers were securing her body on the roof. They savagely pulled al-Wazir's body onto her stomach, and then they ripped her arms behind her back and secured her hands with a pair of plastic flex handcuffs. Then the two officers rolled the badly wounded al-Wazir over on her back to allow her to breathe a little easier. Then a third officer started to work on her wounds.

As the group of SWAT police officers were waiting for the terrorists to come out on the roof, a news helicopter from the Fox News station suddenly turned up, and from a good distance away from the building they filmed all the action that was going down on the roof by the police against the invading subjects. Everyone watching the Fox Station, witnessed all that had just transpired as it happened in real time, and the two terrorists get wounded, and the pair then taken in police custody. The helicopter crew kept filming until the police started to rip the blouse off the downed female subject to help with her wounds and make certain she had no hidden weapons on her.

Once Lieutenant al-Atrash was secured, he was flipped on his back, and then another officer checked out his wound. Already, the scared male terrorist was asking the police how his girlfriend was. The police was more interested in what he was doing with the weapons on the roof, and overrode the question of the wounded woman. Al-Atrash announced defiantly that he would not answer any of their questions until he knew how his woman was doing.

Sergeant Aicha Said Damerdji's group of terrorists did not fare very well on their mission either. Lieutenant al-Atrash's team went in action before his, and when it was determined the six people were a threat against them. The police did not wait for the other assassination team to set up whatever they were up to in the area surrounding the courthouse, the judge and the terrorist on trial. SWAT team snipers locked up the three members from the second shooter team in their sights, and then they went into action. "Shooter One, package is in the open. I have a good tag on the target in lead of other two subjects. Subject is vertical and moving under own power at this time. Requesting further orders against subjects in question? Over."

"Shooter One, at your discretion Shooter, you have clearance to naturalize said target, Shooter. You're free to corpse the subject at your discretion. Go postal on his fucking ass Shooter. Over." His Commander ordered the SWAT sniper.

Instantly, Sergeant Aicha Said Damerdji was hit in the head with a silenced round. Sergeant Bahaa Handom watched in horror as Sergeant Damerdji fell to the ground at her feet. She did not know what just happened to him, because she heard no shots fired at them. Just by the way the Sergeant fell she knew he was dead. The female Sergeant did not have a chance to react to her partner's death when she was hit in the head, and she was dead before her body hit the ground. The last member of this second hit team instantly flung his hands in the air, and he dropped his weapon. Then he waited for the police authorities to come out and get him.

Over the radio, it was reported. "Three targets engaged, two dead, one taken in custody alive. All Ground Fire Teams move in and secure the entire area surrounding the courthouse. Someone better stop the Judge and the officers bringing the terrorist over to the courthouse, before they turn up right in the middle of this fucking mess. I want a ten block square ring of security laid out, and no one is allowed that close to this crime scene we have underway. Stop the jurors from showing up at the courthouse as well we don't need them seeing any of this shit. Over."

The SWAT Commander moved the offices out of his way, and he spoke to the wounded terrorist. He was conscious and still able to speak. Lieutenant al-Atrash was so concerned with the condition of the female terrorist that he would not answer any questions. The Commander leaned a little closer and looked at the wounded Iraqi Lieutenant and then asked him. "Who the hell are you buddy? Look pal you're badly wounded, so I'd suggest you start to worry about yourself for the time being. I repeat, who the hell are you and what the hell were you two people up to here? You better tell me everything I want to know, because we'll find it out anyway. We have prisoners from your other group, and two are already telling us everything we want to know from you, pal. So you might as well help yourself out by talking to me, mister."

"I don't believe your god cursed words you lowly lying infidel. I know none of my friends would ever betray my trust in them." Lieutenant al-Atrash snarled nastily at the angry looking SWAT Commander, as he held him in his angry glare.

The swift SWAT Commander knew he had the downed terrorist right where he wanted him, because once anyone replies to the first question of any interrogation, they'll always talk afterwards. He smiled at the wounded prisoner, and then he added to his words. "I see by the way you speak that you're Arab in nature. Do you mind telling me what the hell you and your lady friend over there were up to here, buddy?"

"I am far from your buddy, god cursed lowly infidel. My fate is held in the sacred hands of the Almighty Allah alone, not yours non-believer of the sacred words of Allah."

"Hey look buddy, if you want to continue to be a fucking asshole about this shit you're in. I just as soon leave your ass lying on the roof and let you bleed out until you're fucking dead, sir. You want to talk to me and I'll assure you of the very best medical treatment for you and the rest of your damn group, pal. Especially for your girlfriend over there, and I already told you one of your partners was talking. So I don't need anything from your ass, man."   The Commander remarked, allowing his anger to start cursing at the wounded prisoner.

"I still don't believe the worthless words coming out of your lying mouth, evil infidel. I believe you're lying as all infidels do to anyone they are speaking with." Al-Atrash replied.

"Maybe so pal, but can you take the fucking risk that I'm screwing around with you and your girlfriend, buddy?" the commander snapped as he grinned nastily at the downed subject.

Lieutenant al-Atrash gave another quick glance at the wounded woman lying on the floor some ten feet away from where he was lying. The SWAT Commander saw where he was looking and the concern in his eyes, and he waved his hand at the officer helping the female prisoner, and then he said to al-Atrash. "You see pal, I as soon allow her to die where she's fucking lying. We don't need her ass, and we sure as hell don't need your fucking help either. So if you want your girlfriend over there to get any further medical help from us, I suggest you answer my questions as they're put forth to you, pal. Or the both of you can go to hell, and we'll use the help of your other fucking partner already talking to us." The SWAT Commander was cursing up a storm once he realized the subject was an Arab. He understood how insulted and upset they always got when someone cursed in front of him. And, the Commander wanted this subject as upset as possible to weaken his resolve not to answer any his questions of him.

"You promise me you'll help my female friend if I talk to you, sir?" Lieutenant al-Atrash asked as he stared intensely at the terribly wounded Sergeant Hanan al-Wazir.

"Look friend I don't want anything to happen to you or your damn girlfriend. First off buddy, you and your friends didn't do anything that cost anyone their life, before we stopped you people. So you're not in that hot water just yet. The more you help us and tell us what the fuck you people were doing up here, and who you people are working for, the better off it'll go on you and her when it comes time for you two to go before the Judge. What say you be smart about yourself and help us out some here, so I can help you in return when it matters to you and your girlfriend's fucking ass the most, pal." The swift Commander gave another hand movement, and the officer helping the wounded terrorist went back to work on her wounds.

"You see my friend, you help me and I'll help you and your girlfriend that quick. It's that simple pal. Now, do you want to tell me your name, I don't like disrespecting you by not knowing it." The Commander asked the injured terrorist.

"My name is Aziz Abdel al-Atrash, sir." The Arab replied to the police officer.

"That sounds like you're Arab sir. Am I correct in that assumption, and what country do you come from Mr. al-Atrash Sir?"

"You're correct, I come from Iraq. I'm a Lieutenant in the military service of Iraq, sir." The wounded Iraqi said as he moved in order to try and get more comfortable while lying on the roof.

"What were you doing here sir? What was your mission, and who ordered you to do this, sir? Are there more members to what I want to call you people, a hit team? Are any members scheduled to attack anywhere else in the United States? How many members are there in your teams and how many teams do you have active in my country, Pal?" the SWAT Commander already cleaned up his words now that the Arab terrorist was talking to him.

THE BEST WESTERN HOTEL IN NORTH CAROLINA

Colonel al-Qaysi flew off the edge of the bed as he watched Lieutenant al-Atrash go down from the bullets fired at him from the police stationed on the roof of the building. He was fuming as he snapped the TV set off, and then he ordered Major al-Shaya nastily to go next door and order Lieutenant Malika Nabeel Elmasry and Sergeant Shurug Khalaifa to come to their room. "We have to leave this cursed hotel no matter the circumstances, immediately! The great fool Lieutenant Al-Atrash was just taken alive by the police authorities in Washington, and it'll be only a matter of time before he breaks down and tells the hated police authorities of our presence here in North Carolina, and where we're hiding and what we're planning to do down here."

Major al-Shaya nodded and then she quickly left the room to carry out her last orders. She knocked on the Lieutenant's room, and Sergeant Khalaifa allowed her to enter it. Al-Shaya smiled at the other female from her group, and she started to speak. "Lieutenant Elmasry, Sergeant Khalaifa, Colonel al-Qaysi wants you to come next door immediately. He wants to speak to all of us together. Things are happening in Washington that you must be informed of."

"What happened Major al-Shaya? You seem very upset Major."

"Lieutenant al-Atrash's mission had just failed us in Washington, and he was taken a prisoner by the hate police authorities. The Colonel wants to leave this State and immediately head back for Florida. I believe he has something he wants you to do before we leave this cursed State. Don't worry Lieutenant Elmasry, this doesn't change the fact that you want to remain in the United States along with Sergeant Khalaifa. I know he's only planning to leave this god cursed State with me. You'll be free to remain and do as you please."

The other two Iraqis followed Major al-Shaya back to the Colonel's room without further word. Once inside, Colonel al-Qaysi began to speak in an angry tone of voice. "Lieutenant Elmasry, the mission in Washington is completed as far as I'm concerned. As soon as it gets dark, I want you to remove the cursed weapons from the trunk of our vehicle, and then you are to hide them out in the field beyond this cursed structure. Once this is completed, I'll give you back your passports and enough American cash to last you a long while, until you're firmly established in this land of lowly infidels. It has been a pleasure to serve in our government's service with you and the Sergeant. You both have done everything that was expected of you, and more sir."

THE HOLIDAY HOTEL IN NORTH CAROLINA

Captain Robert Walker and Sergeant Dorothy Ramirez watched everything go down on the TV in Washington, with the police easily getting the upper hand on the small group of terrorists, and stopping their attack dead in their tracks. He smiled as he watched the police take out five of the six suspected terrorists, with two alive and in custody. As soon as the police took the terrorists down from the roof, the news broadcast immediately went in a commercial break. This was his first chance to break away from the TV. He turned to the Mutt and he grumbled at him.

"Well my friend that seems like that up there in Washington, man. I want to get everyone back on the stinking road right now, buddy. I think once the lousy sonofabitch down here sees the other part of his fucking mission failed in Washington. This little prick is gonna do everything in his power to get back at us for their blunder up there, man. I wanna be out there in case this lousy little dude goes wild on our asses, and he tries to take revenge against the civilians of this State because his uther damn attack failed his ass, man. Betta get the rest of the guys moving and tell them were fricking going out in the next twenty minutes, Homes. It's now eleven thirty in the a.m., and I wanna be the fuck back out there on the road again before the noontime traffic starts getting going on us. Get going and follow my orders, soldier."

The Mutt took off and went to the other rooms in the hotel their people were in. He even informed the State Trooper when Walker wanted to be back on the road. It was going to be a long night for everyone involved in the search for the shooter working over the area in North Carolina and killing his fellow soldiers.

Sergeant Dorothy Ramirez was dressed and ready to shove off. She walked up to her lover and purred as she kissed him on the cheek. "I can't believe you Bobby. You hit the nail right on the damn head with the warning some terrorists were going to make a problem at that hearing today. I'm so proud of you honey, I don't know how you know these type of things, Robert."

"It doesn't take much thinking on anyone's part if they really use what God gave them to work with for Christ sake. I think I gotta tell ya this fucking shit, I can see these things a little betta than most of these hot shot big brain thinkers wasting their stinking time up there in Washington. That's because I look at the things in the simplest terms possible. I don't try and confuse my stinking mind down with a load of what ifs and fucking maybes crap. I put myself in the place of any stinking terrorist, and then ask myself how is the best way to hurt our enemy, and then it comes to me real simple, like on how and when and where they might hits us. I don't need any stinking computers to help me map out a terrorist's friggin mind. The terrorists don't use any damn computers to figure out what the hell is their next target. They use this thing I use."

He pointed to his head and then added to his words aimed at his girlfriend. "The stinking trouble with everyone else trying to figure out these simple minded terrorist bastards and their fucked up attacks, they're trying to rely too much on their damn computers, and the simple minded assholes aren't using any damn computers to help them develop their attacks against the civilized world. No wonder they're having so much trouble trying to figure these people out. What is the phrase I keep hearing said, 'Keep it simple stupid'." Walker grinned at his girlfriend.

THE FEDERAL COURTHOUSE, WASHINGTON D.C.

The police took over the interior of the courthouse building, so they could lend medical aid to the wounded prisoners. There was a medical facility constructed in the interior of the building, and the Commander of the SWAT teams wanted to continue speaking with the Iraqi prisoner talking to them. In his mind the Commander knew he had at least another shooter team still active in North Carolina. The Police Commander wanted to see if he could find out more information about the last shoot team working against the soldiers in North Carolina.

Lieutenant Aziz Abdel al-Atrash was lying on his back on a military cot, and a civilian doctor was working on his bullet wound. The male Iraqi was so concerned with the wounded female Sergeant from his hit team that the Commander of SWAT allowed her to be placed on a cot right next to his side. Sergeant Hanan al-Wazir was in real bad shape, and the Police Commander was informed by another doctor working on her that she was not going to make it.

The Commander now understood he was working against time with his prisoner, and he was going to allow her to lie by the side of Lieutenant al-Atrash, and allow him think she was going to be alright for as long as it took to get all the information he needed from the wounded terrorist. He ordered the doctors working on the female attacker to continue to work on her even though there was no chance she would ever pull through her wounds alive. Every once in a while, the doctor would give the Police Commander a false condition report on the wounded woman, who was lying so near al-Atrash, in an attempt to try and keep the young male Iraqi terrorist talking to the SWAT Commander.

The Commander noticed the wounded Iraqi Lieutenant relax more with each report he heard offered from the doctor working on Sergeant al-Wazir. The SWAT Commander was pushing hard on the Iraqi, because he understood it was only a matter of time before he figured out his girlfriend was dead. He was worried if the terrorist found out the Sergeant was dead, he would clam up on him tighter than a drum.

"Mr. al-Atrash, I asked you a while ago why you were brought to the United States. I'd like an answer to that question if you don't mind sir." The Commander asked the Arab man.

"Sir, I came to the United States with the thought of killing the cursed Judge, and then gaining the release of Colonel Abdulaziz Majd al-Adwani from your hands by force, or kill him so he could not answer any further questions for the police authorities. We wanted to gain his release and bring him back to Iraq as a hero to our country, sir. But when it was discovered how well your police officers were protecting our Colonel. Colonel al-Qaysi who is in Command of our terrorist cell, decided to change our orders, and he ordered us not gain our Colonel's release from your Officers, sir. We were then ordered to kill him outright." The Iraqi Lieutenant replied to his police inquisitor calmly.

"Is this a military operation ordered by the President of Iraq, Lieutenant al-Atrash? And why do you want to kill Colonel al-Adwani?" the Commander asked his prisoner.

"This mission was a non sanctioned military operation by our President, sir. Everyone who came to the

United States with our Commander was soldiers in the Iraqi military. But since your soldiers entered my country and they had removed Colonel al-Adwani by force, we became outcasts in our own country, because we no longer wanted to follow a President who couldn't keep Command his own military assets correctly, sir." Lieutenant al-Atrash replied to the concerned police officer doing the questioning of him.

"I can understand that concern easy enough I guess. What was your rank in your government's military service, sir? Also, did you have anything to do with the secret military side of your military in Iraq, sir? I need to know this information, sir." The Commander was trying his best to try and confuse the Iraqi Officer as he asked him his military rank, even though he was well aware of it, and then he continued with his words to his prisoner. "Also Mr. al-Atrash, will you be kind enough to answer this question for me, sir? Was your President Saddam Hussein the one who had ordered Colonel al-Adwani out, and was he behind the attempted assassination of our President, sir?" the Commander held his breath because he knew he was pushing the injured Iraqi soldier real hard now. But time was precious and he was fast running out of that time.

"As I told you a few moments ago sir, I was a Lieutenant in the service of the Iraqi Army, and you even called me Lieutenant when speaking with me before, sir. No, I had nothing to do with the secret side of the Iraqi military. Sir, may I ask you a question before I answer your last question of me, sir?" the Iraqi Officer asked the Commander.

"Yeah sure, as long as you continue to answer my question, Lieutenant al-Atrash." The Commander knew what he was doing he was trying to show this Iraqi Officer he respected him.

"Sir, I'd like to file for political asylum in your country. If I'm offered this request, I'll tell you everything I know of the terrorist cell operating in your country, sir." Lieutenant al-Atrash looked deep into the eyes of the Commander, as he stared at him.

"I'm sorry to say this Lieutenant al-Atrash, but I can't possibly offer you that kind of deal, sir. That's something my government officials has to offer you, sir. But if I go before my officials with enough information from you, and this information stops another civilian in my country from being killed by the terrorist active from your group, sir. I don't see how they wouldn't offer you this privilege, sir. We have rewarded other people from different nations, once they proved where their loyalties laid for my government, sir." The Commander knew he was lying through his eye teeth to the injured Lieutenant, because the wounded Iraqi was already designated as a terrorist even by his own words. There was no way this side of judgment day the Lieutenant could possibly claim to be a political refugee from his government under these conditions, and because of what he and his group of terrorists was up to in the United States.

"You'd do this for me sir? I mean, you'd put in a good word for me with your government officials to allow me to stay in your country in peace, sir?" Lieutenant al-Atrash asked with surprise in his voice as he turned slightly so he could see the Commander's eyes.

"Look Lieutenant, I can assure you I'll do everything in my power to try and gain you special favor with my government, sir. I can tell you this much though, if I'm in your corner then there's a great possibility that you'll be allowed to remain in my country as an invited and protected guest, sir. And, this invitation will be extended to your pretty girlfriend over there as well, and it'll give you every possible protection my country offers to those who help her in her time of need, sir." Now, the Commander was pulling out all the stops as he tried to gather more information he needed from the wounded terrorist, before his time ran out on him.

"You'll allow Sergeant al-Wazir to be with me in your country forever, to live with me as my wife, sir?" Lieutenant al-Atrash asked with great surprise lacing his tone.

"Without a doubt Mr. al-Atrash, as long as you tell me everything I need to know about your damn mission here in the States, sir. Then yes I'll do that much for you and your young girlfriend, sir. I'll get you and her to remain in the United States as a special guest of my government, Lieutenant al-Atrash." The Commander had to force himself not to smile at his prisoner as he spoke the words, he knew this Iraqi Lieutenant was going to be a guest of his government, but not in the manner he believed and hoped for.

"Then in that case sir, I'll tell you everything I know about our mission in the United States, sir. Colonel Abdulaziz Majd al-Adwani was sent to your country by President Saddam Hussein, to seek out and destroy a target of opportunity that'd force your government to lift terrible sanctions slowly strangling my country to death, sir. Although my President never gave the order to assassinate your President directly to Colonel al-Adwani, I know this for a fact that President Hussein wasn't informed of the selected target the Colonel had leveled his eyes on, sir. We came over to the United States as a twenty one person terrorist cell, sir. Many from my group wanted to remain and live in the United States once we entered your country. We saw how well your people were free to live their lives in peace and treated each other, and I released the others of my cell before any action against your people began, by the remaining soldiers from my group sir.

"These Iraqi troops are gone forever I'm afraid to offer, and I have no idea where they might have went in your vast country, sir. They left my presence yesterday afternoon and are gone. There were six of us left to carry out our ordered mission, and we were ordered to kill your Federal Judge and Colonel Abdulaziz Majd al-Adwani for the same reason I told you. So he could not possibly implicate our worthless President in what he tried to do here in the United States, and against your great President. We believed in order to save his life, Colonel al-Adwani was more willing to say Saddam gave him direct orders to kill your President, which would've been an outright lie committed by Colonel al-Adwani. We were extremely concerned with this thought, and that was why we were going to kill Colonel al-Adwani once we were able to get him in our sights, sir. Sir, I can use something to drink if you do not mind."

The SWAT Commander allowed the Iraqi prisoner to take a quick drink from a bottle of water he was offered and when he was comfortable, the police officer started his questioning of the Iraqi again. The Commander had another officer standing within earshot of him, and he was recording everything this Iraqi prisoner told him as he answered his questions.

"Lieutenant, you made mention of this Colonel al-Qaysi. I take it he was the Commander for your entire operation. I'd really like to know a lot more about this Colonel of yours, sir." The Commander refrained calling the Iraqi's operation a terrorist mission, for fear of and causing the prisoner to stop talking to him.

"You're absolutely correct to believe that assumption, sir. Colonel Hamoodi al-Qaysi was the

Commander of the troops who came to the United States, to follow his orders and kill the elderly Federal Judge, the Colonel you have in custody, and the American soldiers who had invaded our country and removed Colonel al-Adwani from the desert of Iraqi, sir. Colonel al-Qaysi was the one who brought us to the United States, and he's the one who gave us orders and money we needed to survive while we're operating here in the United States, sir. He was in complete control of all our movements while in your great country, sir."

"I have another question Lieutenant al-Atrash. This one is extremely important to me and it must be answered by you immediately, sir. Where is this Colonel al-Qaysi hiding at? I must know where he and anyone else operating with him are, sir. Another question I must ask of you, do you know what's happening in North Carolina, sir?"

CHAPTER TWENTY FIVE

"Sir, Colonel Hamoodi al-Qaysi is operating down in North Carolina, along with a female Iraqi soldier named Major Serena al-Shaya, sir. They also have two other Iraqi soldiers working with them, Lieutenant Malika Nabeel Elmasry, and another worthless female soldier, a Sergeant Shurug Khalaifa. Sir, they went down to North Carolina so Colonel al-Qaysi could seek his own revenge against the American soldiers who had invaded our country, and they killed General Hassan al-Zahar, and they took Colonel al-Adwani as their prisoner and brought him to America." The hurting and exhausted Lieutenant al-Atrash stopped speaking at this point.

"I hate to say this Lieutenant al-Atrash, but you have neglected to inform me what this Colonel al-Qaysi and the other three Iraqi soldiers with him are doing in North Carolina during all your words you told me so far, sir. I want to know what that attack teams is doing down there." The Commander was well aware of what the Iraqi soldiers were doing in that State, but he wanted, he needed to hear the words spoken by this wounded Iraqi Lieutenant.

"I'm sorry for not continuing my conversation with you sir. I had to take a stop so I could catch my breath, and try and also absorb some of the pain I'm suffering through. Yes, Colonel Hamoodi al-Qaysi, and the three other Iraqi soldiers working with him are operating in North Carolina. They are there to kill the American soldiers who shared in on the attack against General al-Zahar's headquarters in Iraq, sir. The group in North Carolina is the ones your newspapers are calling shooters, killing your American soldiers there, sir. The Colonel's completely obsessed with the want of death of these few of your American soldiers, sir. He wants them dead, even more than he wants this Federal Judge and Colonel al-Adwani's dead, sir."

Lieutenant al-Atrash kept referring to the Commander of the SWAT team as sir, because the Commander never told him his name. He did not want this vile man to know his name. He wanted to act as his friend, yet he did not want it to get personal between them. The Commander slapped at the air as he said to the wounded Iraqi Lieutenant. "That's what I wanted to hear from you, Lieutenant. Now Lieutenant al-Atrash, I have one more question to ask of you, and then I'll leave you in peace so you can start your healing, sir. Since you know this Colonel is operating in North Carolina then you must know where he's staying at down there, sir? I need to know this information from you sir, where I can locate this Colonel al-Qaysi. So I can stop him before he kills another soldier in North Carolina." The Commander then stared at the Arab.

"Alas, I hate to report to you that I truly do not have that knowledge in my possession, sir. May Allah forgive me for this failure sir."

The Commander let out his breath as he gave the Iraqi Lieutenant a queer look, informing the wounded soldier he did not believe his last words. He continued staring at the injured soldier for several long moments, while trying to force him with just his mind to tell him where this missing Iraqi Colonel and the rest of the killers with him were hiding in North Carolina.

Lieutenant al-Atrash could not take the angry look any longer from the obviously upset looking police officer, and he slowly lowered his head to get out of his harsh glare. This forced the Commander to bark at him once again. "I'm sorry to hear that crap from you Lieutenant al-Atrash. After all you have told me so far in this conversation, I thought you were going to work with me, so I could help you and your girlfriend stay here in the United States, sir. I see I was wrong in my belief of your total assistance, sir. What the hell good was it you told me this Colonel al-Qaysi was operating in North Carolina? Yet you still refuse to tell me where the hell he's fucking hiding at, Lieutenant. You give me little information I can work with, yet you withhold the most vital part of that information I seek from you, and yet you expect me to help you and your girlfriend stay here in the States, and live out the rest of your life here in peace."

"Sir, it's not that I refuse to tell you where Colonel al-Qaysi and the other three Iraqi fighters with him are hiding in North Carolina, sir. I'm sorry, but how can I possibly tell you what I do not know of, sir? I believe Colonel al-Qaysi chose not to inform me where he and the other Iraqi fighters were staying in North Carolina for this exact reason, sir. If I was captured by your police authorities as I have obviously been, I could not possibly tell you where he was staying in North Carolina, sir. I swear by the sacred beard of the Prophet Muhammad, I don't have any idea where Colonel al-Qaysi and the other soldiers might be hiding in North Carolina, sir.

"May the Almighty Allah cursed my body and order it to be staked out on a mount in the sands of the desert of my honored ancestors, and may the lowly desert scavengers feast upon my soul and body, if everything I have told you is not the absolute truth as the way I understand it, sir." The wounded Iraqi soldier stopped speaking at this point and he took a deep breath for himself, and then he let it out slowly as he turned his eyes away from the angry looking police officer glaring at him. Lieutenant al-Atrash wanted to see Sergeant al-Wazir, and see how she was doing. His eyes suddenly opened wide, because the female Sergeant's face was covered over with a white sheet. This instantly informed him that she was dead.

The Commander turned to his next in Command and snapped at him. "You better get me in touch with the Military Officer stationed at Camp Lejeune in North Carolina. I want to speak with the Colonel in Command of the troops searching for this Iraqi Colonel Hamoodi al-Qaysi, and the ones working with this Iraqi Officer that are killing the soldiers stationed in Carolina. I believe the Commander's name was a Colonel Bruce Leadbetter, or something close to that sir."

The Police Commander walked out of the courthouse as the police officer he ordered to get the Marine Commander on the line for him ran up and offered him a handheld radio. He took it and barked angry as hell into it. "This is SWAT Commander Bradford protecting the Federal Judge in Washington, and I wish to speak with the Commander of the Commander stationed at Camp Lejeune working on hunting down the damn shooter operating in North Carolina, sir."

"It's Commandant and this is he, Colonel Bruce Leadbetter sir, and I'm in Command of the troop's down here sir. What can I do for you SWAT Commander Bradford Sir?" the Marine Colonel asked in a rather bored sounding voice.

"Colonel Leadbetter Sir, I just finished interrogating one of the surviving terrorists we were able to take into custody up here in Washington, and I have some vital information to share with you at this time, sir. It's now known your troops are up against a four person shoot team down there in North Carolina, and they're definitely after your soldiers, sir. The Iraqi hit team is being lead by a Colonel Hamoodi al-Qaysi, sir. He's an Iraqi soldier and he has two women and one male member working in his hit team, Colonel Leadbetter Sir. He's out for revenge against the soldiers who did that action in Iraq, who took the terrorist Colonel we have up here standing trial as their prisoner, sir. That was what this mess up here was all about today sir. The fucking hit teams were going to try and kill the Judge and this Colonel al-Adwani terrorist, in their attempt to keep his mouth shut.

"The damn terrorist team has to be working near the area of your military base sir, if they're going to try and continue going after said soldiers, sir. I hope this information will help you and your outstanding soldiers out while searching for this Iraqi hit team, Colonel Leadbetter Sir."

"It certainly does help me out more than you'll ever know Commander Bradford Sir, and I thank you for that information, sir. I'll put this new information to damn good use I assure you Commander. Let me go so I can get in touch with my soldiers operating out in the field, sir. Once again, I thank you much for your help with this damn situation, sir." With what the Commander had just informed the military officer about, did not surprise him in the least. He already believed the shooter was strictly after his soldiers, and now he knew it for a fact. Colonel Leadbetter placed a quick call out to Captain Walker. He wanted to catch him before he went back on the road after the missing shooter again.

The young Marine Captain was about ready to walk out of his hotel room and start hunting the shooter on the roads again, when his radio suddenly squawked to life on him. He picked it up and snarled into it. "Yeah, this is Walker, who the hell wants to talk to my damn ass now, dammit? I'm fucking kinda busy at the stinking moment for Christ sake."

"Jesus good Christ in Heaven Walker, one of these days you're going to finally learn respect for a Superior Officer, mister! This is Colonel Leadbetter, and I have some vital information for you and the rest of your head hunters out there, buster. I should keep it to myself and let you and the rest of your pack of damn criminals take your fucking chances out there with the damn shooters because of the way you just spoke to me over this damn thing mister. But you have other troops in your Command who I have to worry about, and there's no sense with my punishing the whole lot of them, just because you don't know how the hell to speak to your Commanding Officer, Captain. God dammit shithead, one of these damn days I swear I'm going to teach you how to properly respect a fellow Officer, mister."

Walker shifted the radio to his other hand, and then he moved his hand up and down in front of him as if masturbating, in response to the angry words the Colonel was aiming at him.

"Arrr... shit there's no sense with trying to get any fricking respect out of you Walker. Listen up, it has been reported that you have four Arab shooters going against you and the rest of your troops, two males, and two females. Walker, you and your troops are their intended target. The shooters are lead by a one well trained Iraqi Colonel Hamoodi al-Qaysi, and he has a personal hardon for your ass alone, mister. It seems to me this Iraqi bastard was somehow part of General al-Zahar's group of thugs you guys did in back in Iraq, and he's really pissed off at you especially, and your troops for invading his backasswards country. Be advised Captain, the two hit teams in operating Washington have been killed, or otherwise neutralized at this time, sir.

"Captain Walker, I want these four fucking Iraqi assholes operating here in North Carolina in the same damn way, neutralized one way or the other mister. Walker, there's no sense with clogging up the court system by taking these four jackrabbits in custody, and keeping them alive so they can stand trial at our taxpayer's expense. I want you to handle any action taken against these fricking shooters when you finally come across the bastards. I want you to give them a forty five caliber fucking court marshal out in the field Walker, if you know what I mean?"

"I read your orders loud and clear, Colonel Leadbetter Sir. You want me to show these uther friggin shooters that they have run out of fucking world to live in, sir."

"Exactly Captain, so follow your damn orders as received mister. Good luck on this mission sir. Walker, one question before you go on me, do you want any more soldiers to help support you on this mission, sir? Before you answer that question, I want to remind you Captain. Now that we know for certain these damn shooters are aimed at you and the rest of your people, and there are four of them lousy pukes. If I place more soldiers out in the field, we might be offering these bastards more targets to get at, before we finally get their fucking asses down and out for the count. Another thing Walker, now that we know your troops are these shooters main targets, I want any further searches for these pricks to be carried out around our base. If they're sole aim is being after you people then they had to be staying somewhere real near the damn base, sir."

"Colonel Leadbetter Sir, your suggestion is wise, but I feel the same way you do on this one sir. The more soldiers we have out in the field looking for these sonofa fucking scumbags, the more targets we offer them to shoot at, sir. I have enough troops to get the damn job done sir."

"That's want I wanted to hear from your ass, so go and get the sonofabitches and bring them to justice for me, Walker. I want fucking heads to hang in my trophy box, and I'll not be happy until I have them stuffed in there, mister. I have a bare wall in here Captain, and I don't like that one bit sir. I'm going to rescind all leaves for every soldier on this fucking base until further notice, until you people have placed a period at the end of the damn sentence for these fucking shooters operating in this damn State. Walker, the lives of your fellow soldiers are resting in your hands sir, so go and get these lousy bastards and kill them dead, Soldier."

Walker did not reply to the Colonel's last orders, he was already heading out the hotel room. He ran across the parking lot to the three parked Humvees. The State Trooper was with his troops and they were waiting for Walker to tell them where they were heading next.

THE BEST WESTERN HOTEL IN NORTH CAROLINA. FOUR THIRTY P.M. TUESDAY, APRIL 23rd, 2002

As the highly upset Iraqi Colonel Hamoodi al-Qaysi continued to watch everything that was taking place live at the Federal Courthouse District Seventeen in Washington D. C. on the TV, he realized he was fast running out of time for him and the other Iraqi soldiers with him. If the American police authorities took Lieutenant al-Atrash in alive as a prisoner, then he believed it would be only a matter of time before he finally broke down and talked, and betrayed him and the other fighters with him. Again, he stormed over to the TV and snapped it off. Then he looked at Major Serena al-Shaya sitting on the bed in silence, she was afraid to speak to the angry acting Colonel. He glared at her for several long moments before he snarled savagely at her.

"Major al-Shaya, we're out of time to complete our foul mission of revenge successfully, lowly woman! We have to move out quickly before the cursed police authorities move in, and they capture us. I believe the worthless Lieutenant al-Atrash has betrayed us in Washington to the hated authorities, and I'll not sit and wait until the worthless police come and arrest us next. Unlike that great fool in Washington, I'll never allow myself to be taken prisoner by the foul and lowly infidels from this land of sin we travel in, woman."

"What do you want me to do now that our mission has obviously ended, Colonel al-Qaysi? Where and what are we going to do now, sir?" the female Major asked her commanding officer.

"That's a very good question you ask of me, Major. I want you to get the two fools from the next room. I have changed my mind, and you'll order them to remove their foul weapons from the trunk of our vehicle, and then they are to hide them out in the large grass field behind this lowly establishment. I'll move our god cursed weapons to the cab of the lowly vehicle, and then I'll start the foul thing, and wait for the two young fools to return to us before we leave this lowly hotel for the last time in our lives. When they're set in place inside the foul vehicle, we'll then leave this worthless area with haste for the filthy Florida Keys, woman.

"Major, you'll inform the worthless Lieutenant Elmasry and his woman Sergeant Khalaifa we'll let them out of the vehicle, once we safely crossed the Stateline to the State of Georgia. Once the two fools are out of the car, they'll be on their own to sink or swim in this land of lowly jackals and sin. We'll get back to that lowly Island called Marathon, and then contact the same worthless American Captain who brought us to this cursed country of hatred, and have him bring us out to the Island he picked us up from.

"Once back on that filthy little rock of a worthless Island, we'll find our way to Bimini, even if we have to swim to that miserable Island, and then we'll board a plane bound for Jordan. Once we're in that country, we'll forget what happened in this foul land of Satan. We'll also forget about the worthless fools who have let us down on this sacred mission, Major. Once we're back in our own country of Iraq, my vengeance will fall upon the worthless heads of all the members of everyone who has failed us on this sacred mission in the United States, female. Be off with you, I wanted to be on the road in ten minutes. Every second I exist in this foul country of lowly jackals, makes me feel filthy of body and mind, evil woman."

Major al-Shaya left the Colonel's room in a rush to carry out his last orders. Colonel al-Qaysi quickly wrapped up their belonging he wanted to take with them. Then he left the room and walked out of the hotel as if he was angry at the world. He intended to leave without paying his hotel bill, he was that angry with the United States and all she stood for. By the time the fuming Iraqi Military Officer walked over to the Mercedes Benz parked behind the hotel, he noticed Major Serena al-Shaya, Lieutenant Malika Nabeel Elmasry, and Sergeant Shurug Khalaifa were already standing by their car waiting for him to reach them.

The three Iraqi hunters had to wait for him because Colonel al-Qaysi was the only one who had the keys for the car. He walked up to the three other Iraqi soldiers and opened the trunk and gave out his next orders to them. "Lieutenant Elmasry, take your and Sergeant Khalaifa's weapons, and then you're ordered to hide them well out in the field. I'll wait for you to return to us and then we'll leave this foul place forever." The still extremely angry Iraqi Colonel quickly scanned the large tall grass field behind the hotel. He saw a wide tree stump some five hundred yards away from the parking lot, and he pointed at it as he added to his orders.

"Lieutenant Elmasry, do you see that worthless old tree stump out there in the foul field? The one stump about five hundred feet away from where we are standing."

The young and concerned Iraqi soldier looked in the direction he was pointing, and then he nodded in the affirmative as he turned back to the Colonel and waited for further orders.

"Very good, I want you and Sergeant Khalaifa to take an evil weapon apiece, and then hide them behind that foul tree stump. It'd take any searchers half the day of searching to locate them, Lieutenant Elmasry." He lifted the trunk lid so the two Iraqi soldiers could pick up their weapons then they took off running out in the field with the weeds as high up to their knees.

When the two young Iraqi soldiers headed out in the grass field, Colonel al-Qaysi took the remaining M-16 weapons and he carried them to the front door of the car. He opened it and tossed the weapons on the back seat in the open. Then he snarled at the female Major as he slid in the car, and then he started it up after ordering her to close the trunk for him. "Get in the cursed vehicle so we can leave this worthless place at once, Major."

Major al-Shaya ran to the back of the idling car and she slammed the trunk closed, and then she ran up to the passenger door, opened it and then she slid in the front seat. Even before she was able to snap the seat belt closed, the Colonel suddenly slammed the car in reverse and he made the tires squeal as he turned the vehicle hard. Then he placed the car in forward and made the tires squeal again as he zoomed out of the large parking lot as fast as the car could possibly go in so short a time.

The Major's head spun around and she looked out the window back at the two young Arabs who stopped running, and now they were just standing out in the field of weeds watching the Colonel's car zoom away from them at a high rate of speed. Major al-Shaya snapped her head around, and then she stared at the upset Colonel as she yelled at him. "Colonel al-Qaysi, what in the name of the Almighty Allah do you think you are doing here? You're leaving Lieutenant Elmasry and Sergeant Khalaifa behind us sir. They'll surely be captured by the loathsome police authorities, and then they'll be killed or taken prisoners by them. You have to stop this vehicle at once and wait for them to return to us. We owe them a..."

"Bah foolish woman! We owe them two jackals nothing, nothing witch of the desert sands. You'll watch how you dare speak to me if you know what's good for you and your worthless life, woman. I know what the devil I am doing, and I don't have to inform you of my actions, or listen to your incriminations aimed against me, woman. If you want to remain alive until we're safe on Arab lands again then you'll keep your foul mouth shut, and you'll respect me at all times, foul woman. Or I'll kill you with my bare hands, and then I'll leave your worthless bones to rot in this land of sin and lust, forever to be away from the sacred gardens of Allah, lowly woman."

Major al-Shaya knew she had no other choice opened to her over this latest situation, and she took one last look at the two young Iraqi soldiers desperately running to the end of the field towards the large parking lot of the hotel. In a frantic hope of catching up with the Colonel before his vehicle left the parking lot and was gone from them forever. She drew in her breath and then shook her head slowly no, because the two young Iraqi soldiers were still carrying their weapons out in the open as they ran after their speeding car, and the safety it offered them. In her mind, she realized the angry Colonel was leaving them behind to be discovered by the police authorities, and she knew they would never give up to them.

The way the Colonel was spinning the tires of his vehicle on the pavement of the parking lot, caused many of the renters from the hotel to come out of their rooms to see why there was someone speeding around the lot. Ten people saw the Colonel's car speeding out of the lot, and then they noticed the two young people running in the field with weapons in their hands.

Instantly, a number of phone calls to 911 went out, reporting two people running in the field behind the hotel with weapons in their hands. With the threat of snipers loose in the area, the civilians believed they might have just saw two of the shooters killing the soldiers in North Carolina. The civilians wanted the police to do something with these two people with weapons, and hopefully place an end to the killing of the soldiers in their state.

A MERE MILE AND A HALF AWAY FROM
THE BEST WESTERN HOTEL

Captain Robert Walker and his troops were just leaving the parking lot of the hotel, when the first call came in over everyone's radio. "To all cars, to all cars involved in the search for the snipers, it's been reported two people were seen running in the field behind the Best Western Hotel. The two are reported carrying long weapons on their persons. The two subjects are to be considered armed and dangerous, and are to be approached with extreme caution. To all responders, the two subjects could be the shooters killing the soldiers in our State. A late model snow white Mercedes Benzes with tinted windows was also reported leaving the Best Western's parking lot at a high rate of speed, at the time these two subjects were spotted in the field. It's not known if anyone riding in this Mercedes was working with these two possible shooters, or if they were the shooter's targets, and they left the parking lot to survive the attack aimed at them.

"To all special operatives involved in the search for the shooters operating in North Carolina, this report is directed at you responders. You're ordered to move to the Best Western Hotel by Exit Forty Three off I-95. With what has just taken place in Washington, we believe this action is connected with the snipers stopped before they were able to kill anyone in Washington. That is all at this time. Over."

Walker had the soldier branded McNip, driving the Humvee stop his machine as he picked up the radio and placed a call to the State Trooper working with their response group. "Lieutenant Smith reporting, did you copy that last fucking list of bullshit just transmission from your damn Commander, sir? And if you did copy that load of crap transmission, where the hell is this fricking hotel in reference to where we're stopped at this time, sir? How fucking close are we to this dump, and how fricking long will it take for us to get over to this damn hotel from here, sir? We have to assume control of any possible response aimed against the stinking snipers discovered at this fucking hotel they're bitching about, sir."

"Captain Walker Sir, yes I picked up the transmission from my Command Center sir, and I'm reporting we're about a few minutes away from the hotel in question, sir. With any luck sir, we should be the first ones responding to the call, Captain."

"Out fucking standing Lieutenant Smith, I want you to get back on your stinking radio, and then I want you to warn any of the other responders to this call that we're in Command of any fucking operation that concerns these two possible shooters, sir. Lieutenant, all you police hafta do is make damn certain these stinking shooters stay where the fuck they are, and when we get there, we'll take over Command of the stinking operation from that point on from you guys, sir. You hafta warn the other responding Officers that we're on the fucking way over to this reported hotel, Lieutenant Smith."

"I copy that last Captain Walker Sir, and I'll do as you have just ordered sir. If you people will follow me, I'll get you over to the Best Western Hotel before I finish speaking on the radio, sir." The excited State Trooper suddenly floored the gas pedal and a cloud of smoke streaming from his rear tires of his vehicle, and his lights went on and siren screamed its eerie call. Walker's three Humvee war machines followed the trooper, struggling with trying to stay up with the speeding police car, as they sped through the local streets heading for the hotel.

Captain Walker's machines followed the police car as fast as they could drive, until the squad car finally spun into the parking lot of the hotel where the possible snipers were reported active. Three other police cars were already parked in the large lot. The police were out of their cars in a snap and they took up positions hiding behind the open doors of the vehicles, as they tried to pick up the two people spotted with weapons hiding in the weeds in the field. When the first police cruiser pulled in the lot, the two suspects dropped down and they hid in the tall grass. The Humvees pulled in front of the police cars to give them something better to hide behind.

The Humvees were heavily armored, and a bullet could not get through the thick armor hide of the war machines. Walker was out of his machine first, his M-16 held in his arms as he left the doors of the machine opened, and he slowly walked behind his machine while he was tapping out a cigarette and lit it and started smoking like he didn't have a care in the world. The State Trooper parked his vehicle and he went behind the military machines with the

Captain. The two then waited for one of the responding police officers to report on what they had discovered about the situation when they first pulled onto the hotel property.

A Sheriff Deputy came out from behind his parked car and walked over to the one he thought was in Command of the soldiers who had just arrived on the scene. He nodded and Captain Walker asked him with concern in his voice. "Whatdaya got going down here, sir?"

"Captain err..."

"Walker!"

"Captain Walker, I'm Corporal Edward McCollum of the Sheriff's office sir, and we have two purps trapped out in the field about one hundred and seventy yards towards that old tree stump out there, sir. I had a good visual on both suspects, sir. One is a female, the other a male, and they had what looked like military type assault weapons on their person, sir. I'm sorry Captain, but I didn't get a good look at the weapons before the two disappeared in the thick underbrush, sir. So I couldn't tell for certain exactly what type of weapons they were carrying, sir. But they were definitely armed and they looked like they knew how to obviously operate the weapons they had, sir. I don't think they have moved an inch since we spotted the two in the field, sir."

Captain Walker looked in the direction the police officer pointed at, and then he took over Command of the situation and he ordered his soldiers in motion. "Ghost, Hunter, you two know what you two gotta do out there, so get her done for me. Get out there and get these two flaming assholes and naturalize them real pronto like. Say Corporal, what about that fucking car that was reported seen speeding out of the damn parking lot of this damn dump a little while ago, sir? Do you have anything new on the damn vehicle as yet, sir?

"Was the driver of that damn thing part of these two assholes we have trapped out there, sir?" Walker asked as he looked at the hotel structure for a moment, and he noticed everyone was out of their rooms, and they were gathered on the walkways watching them and what they were doing, and he warned the police officer he was speaking with. "Hey pal, don't you think you should get those fucking civilians back inside their stinking rooms, just in case any fricking shooting starts around here, man?"

The deputy did not say a word as he ran for his car and picked up a megaphone and screamed in it. "You people standing on the damn landing of the hotel, you're ordered to get back inside your rooms and stay away from any windows. This is for your own safety. We have a possible terrorist situation taking shape here, and we don't want any civilians getting hurt if things get out of hand on us." When the deputy saw none of the civilians were moving as he just ordered, he barked. "Get back in your damn rooms before you get hurt out here, now dammit!" Once the deputy yelled at the civilians this way, they immediately ran and hid in their rooms.

Once the civilian situation was handled, the deputy reported back to the young Marine Captain. "I'm afraid to report that we don't have very much on the missing car at this time sir, or the occupant or pants as well, Captain Walker Sir. We have two police helicopters up though, and one of them is working along the highway heading south, while the second helicopter is heading north over I-95, sir. They have orders to report any late model white Mercedes Benz they come across, and then we're going to have the car stopped by any police presence in the area of it, Captain

Walker Sir. We also have a third helicopter reporting to this situation, but that helicopter isn't able to be on site for another fifteen minutes or so, sir."

"Fine, but you might as well cancel that third chopper, because this situation will be over well before the fifteen minutes are up, friend." Walker grumbled as he watched his two dangerous pointmen expertly sneak out in the large grassy field and instantly, they seem like they disappeared from sight in the heavy brush. The Deputy Corporal watched in silence as the two soldiers went out to intercept the possible snipers, and then he asked the military officer. "Say Captain Walker Sir, not that I mean to try and tell you your business here, sir. But by the way those two soldiers are stalking those two people with weapons we have trapped out in the field sir. It doesn't look to me like you plan to take them in alive, sir."

"And your fucking point being!" Walker growled over his shoulder as he tried to pick up his two soldiers, or any sight of the missing subjects hiding in the underbrush.

"Hey Lieutenant, what the hell gives around here, sir? Since when do we allow soldiers to take over a civilian situation on us? Then we're expected to sit on our asses while these soldiers hunt down these two people like they're going to outright kill them, who we don't know for certain who they might be, or what they might be up to out there with those weapons, sir. For all we know about these two purps, they could be just two screwball hunters who got lost in the damn woods, and the asses ended up coming out of the woods near the hotel, sir." The concerned State Trooper Corporal complained as he rested his hand threateningly on the heel of his weapon.

Walker saw the action and he snarled back at the police officer. "You move that fucking weapon any further in my fricking direction Corporal and you won't live long enough to complete your stupid act buddy. Look Corporal, in case you don't understand this mess we're involved in here. These reported two fucking shooters killed two of our soldiers, and they wounded a third on us. So that makes this mess a fucking military response. If you don't like us taking over this mess then you're relieved of friggin duty, and you can get the fuck outta here so you don't see what happens to these fucking subjects next, pal."

"I can't believe this bullshit you're going to kill these two suspects even before you know what the hell the two might have been up to out there! I can't believe this shit for a damn second, Captain Walker! You soldiers are going to kill these two people before we can even figure out what the hell they might be up to with these damn weapons and who they might be, sir." The stunned young Sheriff Deputy cried, allowing his voice to raise some.

Walker lost patience with the young deputy busting his horns, and he growled at the other police officers watching the confrontation going down out in the field. "If someone don't get this fucking kid offa my stinking ass, I'm gonna have one of my soldiers shut him down but fucking quick. I don't have time for this bleed heart crap coming from his fricking ass. I have two soldiers in harm's way out in the stinking field, stalking two armed and known to be shooters preying on our god damn soldiers. So someone betta get this fucking guy the hell outta here, dammit! Before I take matters in my hands and have him shut down but good."

"Stalking! Jesus Christ Almighty man, you just said your two soldiers were actually stalking those two people out in the damn field, Captain. You're going to kill them two people without giving them a fair chance to surrender to us peacefully, Captain whatever the hell your damn name is. I'll not allow you soldiers to kill these two people just for the damn hell of it, or because you're pissed off someone killed some of your damn buddies, sir. I'm a fucking police officer who sworn an oath to protect and serve the civilians of this State, and I'm not going to allow your people to..." The officer's words were cut off when a high ranking Sheriff Deputy walked up behind the young man, and he rested his hand lightly on his shoulder and shook his head no, he then offered to the concerned officer. "Come on Eddie, this is a military situation going down here son, and we're ordered to take a back seat to their operation for the time being, son."

The Deputy Lieutenant cautiously led the young and angry deputy away from the special operation soldier who looked like he was ready to kill the officer, if he continued his complaint against his actions and that of his troops in the field.

Walker's actions did not sit very well with the rest of the mixed batch of police and State Trooper officers, gathered on the hotel property. The threat to kill the two subjects out in the field along with the threat just aimed against one of their own from the angry Marine Captain. There were nine police cars in the parking lot and Sergeant Ramirez noticed the terrible looks from the State Troopers and she complained at Walker. "Hey Bobby, do me a favor here and never try and think about ever becoming a Doctor."

"This is gonna be good, why is that Raz?" Walker asked her seriously as he stared at her for a long moment while he waited for her response.

"Because Bobby, your bedside manners leave a helluva lot to be desired, buster. You could've been a little more civil to that poor police officer a few second ago. You were really dumping on the young man, and all he was concerned with was for the two subjects."

"I'll watch my fucking manners when I don't have any of my soldiers in harm's way out in the damn field, hunting some armed fucking assholes who might have just killed a few of our people." Walker was seething as he continued to watch and tried to pick up his pair of snipers as they tried to lock onto the shooters hiding in the field.

"Gees Bobby, once this mess is over with, I'm going to fuck the shit out of you. Maybe that might put you in a little better mood." Sergeant Ramirez said as she tried a smile on Walker.

The Mutt butted in as always and he offered the female Sergeant with a smirk on his lips. "Hey girl, you're wasting your stinking smile on that one, little sister. He's not gonna be happy again until he gets all these stinking assholes no matter how much fucking you two do between the damn sheets with him, honey. But I'll tell you this much baby girl, if you wanna fuck the shit outta someone around here. Why don't you give me a little tumble between the stinking sheets for a change? At least I'll be smiling back at you while you're trying to kill me with your outstanding lovemaking abilities, Raz."

Ramirez smiled at the Mutt and then thanked him for his kind words, it made her feel a little better as she joined Walker trying to locate their two snipers stalking the shooters in the field.

"Hey baby, don't thank me, spank me." The Mutt replied with a larger smile as he tried to keep this conversation with Ramirez going longer. Mainly because he was bored to death with waiting for the two pointmen to find and then take out the two suspected shooters hiding from them.

"I don't know about you. You'll never change a bit will you, Mutt? You have a one tracked mind. Sex." Sergeant Ramirez complained at her friend and soldier.

"Hey Raz, what can I tell ya baby. I'm too wild to be mild. You can't tame what is meant to be wild and I'm so shallow you can't get you feet wet on me, sister." The Mutt retorted with a grin.

Their conversation was cut off by Walker, as he growled at his two friends and fellow soldiers. "Will you two shitbirds knock off the damn bullshit for a stinking minute for Christ sake? We got two fucking soldiers in harm's way working in the field hunting a pair of stinking armed god damn shooters. Pay a little attention to that damn situation for a fricking change, huh! We betta be ready to support them out there if they come under fire from these possible shooters."

"Hey Walker, are you really worried about those two shits searching for the damn shooters out there buddy? C'mon man, with those two stalking anyone's ass, they might as well hang it up right now. You know they'll get them two assholes out there real easy like, man."

The young Marine Captain Walker did not reply to the Mutt's last remark, as he picked up some slight movement a little further out in the field, and then he reported to his two stalkers over his handheld radio. "Ghost, I just picked up some slight weed movement about seventy five yards away from where you first entered the fucking field a few moments ago, man. It wasn't a definite pick up, but it's something you gotta pay attention to out there man."

The Ghost was so confident he was going to kill the two subjects, he replied in his handheld radio in a whisper. "Picked it up, I got one of the turds locked up in my fucking sight already, Walker. What are my orders against these two mutherfuckers out here, Walker?"

"If you got a positive MOE (Mark One Eyeball) on one of the fucking subjects, you're free to corpse the mutherfucker's ass. At your discretion Ghost, go postal on his stinking ass, man. You have clearance to kill your fricking target if you can get it done from where you're currently set up against the lousy scumbag, Ghost." Walker replied, also in a whisper in his handheld radio.

The Ghost did not respond to Walker's last orders as he fired his silenced weapon at the target he located. He watched his bullet actually hit one subject square in the middle of the forehead. He did not know if it was the male or female package at this point that he just killed, nor did he really care. The soldier fired a second round in the prone body just to make certain this one was out of the game of life and death. The Hunter was working ten yards off the Ghost's right side, and when the Ghost fired at the one target he picked up, it caused the other subject to move in response to the death of his fellow soldier a few feet away from where the other one was hiding. The instant the second target moved two silenced rounds hit the second shooter in the triangle of death in the chest area of the body. Then the Hunter gave the Ghost the thumbs up signal, and they both stood up and then causally walked over to the two downed bodies.

"Holy shit, what the hell are those two soldiers doing out there, dammit? Don't they know there are two people out there armed and dangerous?" One of the police officers cried out.

Captain Walker and the rest of his specially trained soldiers slowly walked out from behind their parked military vehicles, as the Captain lit another cigarette like he did not have a care or fear in the world. Then he walked out in the field towards his two pointmen already checking out the dead bodies of the two possible shooters they just killed. Then he replied to the concerned police officer who just warned him. "Hey pal, my stinking Vampires, (Snipers) know what the fuck they're doing out in the field at all times buster. If they're standing then they successfully neutralized the two fucking assholes they were sent out there afta, my friend."

CHAPTER TWENTY SIX

By the time the specialized soldiers along with the horde of police officers finally reached the two dead people. Both the Ghost and the Hunter had the bodies stripped, and held their personal belongings in their hands. Walker looked at the Ghost and he instantly began his report when his eyes locked on Walker's. "Captain, I have two passports for these two shitbirds here, sir. You know who they are? One of the two scumbags was with the stinking dude we called Bill at the titty bar up there in Washington the uther fucking day, sir. The passports say these two birds were damn Cuban shits. But one look at the asses and you can tell easy enuf that they're fucking A-rabs, sir. I can't believe I didn't pick up that fricking crap the uther day when we were talking to the assholes at the gin mill, Captain. We also found two loaded M-16's, with the same fucking type rounds that killed our people with these slugs, sir. They're the ones we used in I fucking raq.

"Captain Walker, we also found a loaded nine millimeter Colt C-13 pistol on each scumbag's bodies, sir. These are the same type hand guns that we flooded the Iraqi military with, when we decided to rearm their fucking dumb ass soldiers, sir. These two slugs moved in the bush against us like they were well trained soldiers, Captain. They kinda gave us a little bit of fucking sport out here before we finally located and got the dumb shits locked up in our sights, Captain. The male smuck had two thousand dollars American in cash on his lousy ass.

"The two also has some small change and twenty five extra rounds for their damn weapons on their person, sir. If you were to ask me Captain Walker Sir, these two pieces of shit are part of the four scumbags we're out here fucking looking for, and who hit some of our people a few days ago, sir." The Ghost reported to his Commanding Officer in an extremely angry tone. He was actually angry at himself because he did not detect the threat these four strangers were against his fellow soldiers back in Washington.

Captain Walker held his tongue, if the Ghost was branding these two terrorists as Arabs. Then why he did not mention it when they were drinking in the Bare Parts bar with the same people the other night.

"You were very lucky on this one Captain Walker. These two people could have been just a pair of hunting and they might have got lost in the woods and came out of the woods in this field, soldier. If they were just a pair of hunters and you ordered them killed, I would've arrested you for their murder on the spot, sir." Corporal McCollum growled while still trying to prove his point to the Commander of the dangerous soldiers, as he checked the bodies of the dead and then complained again. "Why the fuck did you have to strip them naked like this for, buddy? Couldn't you have left them some dignity in their death, especially the female subject, soldier?"

Walker looked at the faces of the two dead people and grew angry with himself. He instantly recognized the two, and they were with the man he knew as Bill and the other female from the bar. He met the two in the titty bar when he and his troopers were drinking with the two, and the others with them. He was fuming at himself because he knew he did not like something about the other two. Now he knew what it was, they were the killers of his people. He also knew once Colonel Leadbetter realized he was speaking to these two asshole a few days ago, he was going to rip him a new asshole for being sound asleep at the switch. His thoughts were interrupted when the Ghost bitched at one of the police officers bitching at him about the two dead people.

"Look stupid, if you think these two flaming assholes were just hunting out here and having some fucking fun in the damn woods, man. Then why the fuck were they in the bush armed with M- fucking 16 weapons and automatic pistols, buddy? You don't go fucking hunting for anything but god damn people with a five point five six brass clad, M-16 rounds, buster. You also don't go hunting with two fricking grand in cash stuffed in your stinking pocket either, man. And, if you're so stinking interested in why we stripped these two asses down like we did, that was to make certain neither of the two assholes had any fricking other weapons or possible booby traps or explosives hidden on their person. We don't want anyone else getting hurt by handling a fricking body that has a possible booby trap hidden on them, stupid. Enuf people died already because of these fucks, buddy." The Ghost growled at the officer as he glared at him.

"Hey Ghost, I see me a damn good set of booby traps on the dead bitch, man. Look at them damn cannons of hers. What a waste of a pair of stinking tits, man." The Mutt smirked, he was also angry because he was sharing drinks with these two people in the bar a few days back. His words netted him a hard punch in his back from Blind Date standing behind, as she bitched at him. "You're disgusting, you dirty old man you. I don't know why I am interested in you Mutt."

"Yeah baby and I'm gonna be a dirty old man until the day I fucking die, girl." He smiled.

"Mutt, if you don't knock the stinking bullshit off and get fucking serious on a damn mission for a change, asshole. I'm gonna stake you down to the ground, and let any woman you have defiled in your stinking life, take out their fucking revenge on your wasted body. Enuf screwing around and get fricking serious will ya man. This shit is damn important to us, buddy." Walker complained at his friend as he held him in his harsh glare for a moment, and then he turned to the other soldiers of the group and growled at them just as angrily.

"Okay people, I want these two lousy speed bumps (soldiers slang for dead bodies) dragged the frig outta these stinking weeds ten minutes ago, dammit. I wanna get a betta fucking look at the two assholes where we can see them a helluva lot betta than we can see them out here. Since you're being such a fricking funny man out here Mutt, you can give them a hand dragging these two assholes the hell outta here toot sweet, man. Secure their weapons and don't touch the damn things with your bare hands. I don't wanna fuck up any stinking fingerprints on the damn weapons, guys. I'll have a good number of plastic bags sent out to you people, and the ones who know how to handle evidence, will secure the fucking weapons inside the damn bags, along with any uther crap these two fucks had on their damn bodies.

"I also want everything the purps had on their persons to be carefully laid out on the ground in the parking lot of the damn hotel along with their stinking clothes. Maybe we can find out a little something more about these two stinking slugs from their clothes and any uther crap they mighta had on their lousy asses. Get a fucking move on it people. I wanna wrap this mess up as quickly as I can soldiers." Walker snapped at the Ghost, Hunter, Mutt and Sergeant Ramirez at the same time. The rest of his specialized soldiers from the group remained hanging around by the Humvees, in case there were anymore snipers hiding in the grass field.

Trooper Smith got Walker's attention, and offered. "Captain Walker, I have the people back there who can secure the weapons properly, and anything else you want secured at this crime scene, sir. These Troopers are well trained in crime scene and evidence preservation, Captain."

Captain Walker thought for a moment, and then he replied to the State Trooper. "That'd be great for my ass, Lieutenant. But first I want you people to remember, this fricking mess is still a fucking military investigation and operation, and it'll be handled by the soldiers of the United States, sir. Any and all evidence discovered on this damn crime site along with the stinking bodies, are to be handed over to me and my people for special processing, Lieutenant Smith."

"I understand that and my orders as well Captain Walker Sir. But I know your soldiers aren't as well trained in evidence gathering methods, and the protection of said evidence and properly securing the crime scene at the same time as my people are, sir. That's why I just offered a few of my people's expertise on this matter, sir. Captain Walker, I wish you'd understand that all here are on the same side, sir. There's no need to be so angry with any of us, Captain Sir. We're trying our best to help you apprehend these damn purps, sir. One thing I do suggest to you Captain Walker, I think you should cover the bodies over with blankets or something, sir.

"That's because there's going to be a helluva mess of damn news reporting helicopters flying overhead this situation in a few moments, as well as a horde of pain in the ass reporters showing up in the hotel parking lot at the same time, to see what was going down here, sir. I don't know about you sir, but I don't think we should allow these two dead people to be lying out in the open in the parking lot naked like they are, sir. It's not very good publicity for us and you military types you know sir. Sure as hell someone will complaining about their treatment sir."

Walker looked towards the sky, and he quickly picked up at least one helicopter, and it was rapidly closing in on their position as he watched it and then he grumbled at the concerned State Trooper. "Huh, I think the helicopter you just mentioned was coming to help spot the shooters out in the field is coming in now, Lieutenant. A day late and a dollar short as I stated sir. The stinking act would be over long before your damn chopper arrived on scene, sir."

"You're dead wrong on that one Captain Walker Sir. When you first told me this situation was going to be over before my helicopter arrived on scene, I immediately canceled the helo sir. The one you're picking up has to be the first news helicopter arriving on scene, sir."

Walker turned back to the good looking State Trooper, but he refused to admit he knew the two dead people, and he mumbled at him. "Yeah Lieutenant, I think you got a pretty good point there, sir. I believe I have something in my vehicles I could use to cover them damn pukes with, sir. I'll see to it when I get out of these damn weeds and back to my machines, sir." Walker shook his head and also ordering himself to calm down some.

"Captain Walker Sir, I have a blanket in my squad car, and I'm certain I can get another one from one of the other squad cars on the parking lot, sir. If not, I'm sure as hell we can get some blankets from the hotel, sir." The State Trooper Lieutenant offered with a smile on his lips to the Commanding Officer of the military personnel he was working with.

"Then you'll take care of that shit for my stinking ass, right Lieutenant Sir?" Walker asked the good looking officer as he tried to keep his eye on the rapidly approaching helicopter.

"Sure will Captain Walker and I'm damn pleased that you're starting to listen a little more to my suggestions sir." The State Trooper replied as he shot Walker a quick smile.

Walker did not reply to the State Trooper as he turned to the Ghost and growled at the soldier this time. "Hey Casper, when you get our guys to get these two lousy slugs the fuck outta these damn weeds, and dump their bodies on the stinking parking lot of this place. I don't want them left lying out in the open naked like this man. The State Trooper Lieutenant is gonna give you some stinking blankets cover over the damn speed bumps with the damn things. We have some nosey ass news reporters rapidly closing in on us real fucking fast from the stinking air, and I don't wanna hear any bullshit bout us not treating the stinking bodies of these lousy pukes with no respect, man. I also don't want any of you slugs admitting to anyone that we know or even knew either of these two flaming assholes before we killed the stinking pricks out here. You people read my ass about that last fricking order?"

The Ghost gave Walker a quick nod and then he roughly grabbed Lieutenant Elmasry's body by the leg, and he started to drag his body over the weeds towards the large parking lot. The Hunter moved in and he grabbed the other leg, and helped the Ghost drag the male body out of the field. Neither soldier showed any concern for the body of the dead shooter.

The Mutt was grinning from ear to ear as he roughly grabbed Sergeant Khalaifa's right leg, and then he started to drag her body over the weeds, broken branches and rocks sticking up here and there out of the ground. Her other leg got caught up in some weeds and placed the body of the dead female in a very disgusting position.

Sergeant Dorothy Ramirez watching what the Mutt was doing and she immediately rushed over to him, because she got terribly embarrassed over the way he was dragging the female's body out of the weeds. She took the other ankle and moved it so the dead woman's legs were closed as best as she could get them together. Then she snarled nastily at the Mutt as she walked by his side. "Hey dog man, when I get you back to the damn barracks. I'm going to beat the living crap out of your ass for what you have done to this poor woman's body, stupid. I can't believe you can be so damn insensitive to this woman's body after she was killed, man."

"Bitch, bitch, bitch. That's all you've been doing at me lately for Christ sake, Raz. You're starting to get too much like the Rambo Brass man over there in front of us, honey." The Mutt pointed towards Walker with his chin as he finished his complaint at Ramirez. "Man girl, you're taking all the stinking fun outta being a stinking soldier around here you know, girl. I wasn't allowed to take any stinking pictures of that naked Arab bitch we left alive back in the stinking Iraqi headquarters when we went after that fucking Colonel al-Adwani dude. Now, I can have a good look at this bitch Arab's body, without you jumping down my stinking throat and kicking me in the guts from the inside like you're doing, baby. You betta back offa on me some huh?"

"I don't care what you say stupid, it's about time you start treating women prisoners or their bodies with some respect buster, or I'm really going to get on your ass about it, Mutt. This isn't funny anymore you know, mister." Sergeant Ramirez snapped angrily at the Mutt, because she was really upset with him this time around.

The Mutt did not reply as the small group of soldiers came out of the weeds while dragging the two dead bodies behind them. Above them a news reporting helicopter got up to the hotel, and it was now hovering directly over the large hotel parking lot and a number of parked police cars and military vehicles, and their cameras were firing away at the action taking place below them. Two police officers came up to the soldiers and they immediately draped blankets over the two dead and naked bodies. The other soldiers had the belongings of the dead Iraqi terrorists, along with their clothes spread out neatly on the ground in front of their parked Humvees.

Walker was going through the wallet of the male lying at his feet, and he held the purse of the woman shooter looped in the fingers of his other hand. The weapons were laid out on the hood of his parked Humvee. Two ambulances pulled into the parking lot, and they parked their vehicles behind the line of police squad cars. The medics were waiting to pick up the bodies of the two dead terrorists once the soldiers and police were done with them.

The Captain was angry as hell, because he was not finding anything of worth on these two Iraqi shooters that stated they were Arabs, or where they might have truly came from, or who they might have been working with or for. He was killing off time, because he knew Colonel Bruce Leadbetter was on his way over to the crime scene, and he was going to take over command of the situation once he got there. That way, he and the rest of his troops would be free if and when the police located the vehicle observed leaving the parking lot, before the police or soldiers arrived at the hotel to get at the two snipers in the field.

He pitched the empty wallet of the male shooter on the ground along with the rest of the Arab's belongings, and then he started to go through the female's purse, once he got his fingers out of the two straps of the purse. He took the woman's wallet out and he quickly went through it, anything he did not want to hang on to, he just threw it to the ground. He did not find anything very interesting until he looked at the twelve picture pack the wallet held. He smiled as he saw the dead woman standing with who he recognized as General Hassan al-Zahar, and a second soldier obviously a Colonel in the Iraqi Army. He also immediately recognized the Iraqi Colonel as the man he knew as Bill from the strip joint up in Washington a few days ago. The guy he was drinking with at the stripper bar the other day, and he shook his head in anger. All three people in the picture were dressed in Iraqi military uniforms. The cash from the male terrorist was sitting on the hood of Walker's truck with a rock holding it in place.

He was wondering if this other man he knew as Bill from the bar in the picture, was this missing Colonel Hamoodi al-Qaysi he was warned about being the thought to be sniper from Colonel Leadbetter, earlier in the day. There were four other pictures of the female in the wallet, and she was standing with either General Hassan al-Zahar, or this other Iraqi Colonel.

He angrily ripped the pictures out of the wallet with a coating of fresh blood from the dead woman coating the outside of the battered and old wallet. The background in some of the pictures clearly showed the desert, along with a number of parked Iraqi military trucks in the pictures. He felt he just found all the proof he needed, to say these supposed Cubans were really the Iraqi fighters and terrorists who were killing some of his troopers for the past few days.

The fuming young Marine Captain stuffed the pictures in his pocket. What he intended to do if he had the time, he was going to fax the Police Commander up in Washington a copy of the pictures, and have him show them to his prisoner, and see if he would identify the other soldier for them. If this other dude was one in the same Bill and this Colonel al-Qaysi, he was going to take great pleasure with killing the man nice and slowly for deceiving him like he had done. Then talking with him before he killed his other two soldiers, something even the Iraqi soldiers could not do to his specialized troops. The Captain still could not believe he did not pick up the fact that this up until now, about the missing man he was still searching for.

The other police officers gathered in the parking lot of the hotel, quickly set up a number of roadblocks at all the entries to the hotel lot leading to this certain section of the large parking lot where they had the bodies of the shooters laid out. The police were trying to keep the growing horde of reporters and nosey civilians showing up in the lot in order to tape and see the action, off the hotel property. There were two news helicopters hovering overhead the area, and those reporters were the only ones getting any kind of decent pictures of what happened in the parking lot of the hotel between the police, soldiers and the dead people lying on the ground.

Walker and the rest of his elite troops were trying their best to keep their faces out of any pictures the reporters were taking of the police and soldiers moving around in the parking lot of the hotel, with weapons still held in their hands from a good distance away. The concerned Captain did not want any of his troops to have their pictures taken by the reporters, and having them flashed in every newspapers in the country, identifying them as soldiers.

This was so if his troopers were sent on another mission for the United States anywhere in the world, and if those soldiers on that mission under what was commonly referred to as a Black Work order, or no identification conditions. If any of the soldiers were somehow taken prisoner, the enemy would not be able to identify them as American soldiers through any file photos of the soldiers any reporters might have snapped of them in the past. The Captain also knew many enemy governments constantly monitored the newspapers and telecasts, and they usually pulled out pictures of anyone they found who interested them, and they filed them for future reference needs. The Marine Captain found himself cursing at the horde of reporters and civilians foolish enough to be caught up in his gaze, and there were plenty to go around for him to growl at.

He had enough of stacking pencils (killing time) and he walked over to his old sidekick, Lieutenant Frank Hall the Mutt, and he ordered the crazy soldier. "Hey Mutt, we gotta get our stinking people the fuck outta the damn limelight on the double quick man. These fricking pain in the damn ass reporters are snapping our faces with their damn cameras. Walk around and get the attention of the rest of our people, and then order them into the damn Grungies, man? Have some of the asses remove their shirts and hang them over the windows, so the snooping reporters can't get them on any damn film, buddy. Hey stupid, only have the damn men removed their shirts, wiseguy. Knowing you, you'd probably give the hens the stinking order to remove their damn shirts to cover the windows with, shithead."

"Man Walker, between you and Raz, you two guys are taking all the stinking fun outta being a fucking soldier around here you know. Now I can't even have the stinking chicks from our outfit show me some damn tits around here any longer, man." The Mutt complained as he sort of sidestepped while keeping an eye on the Captain as he headed off to carry out his orders.

"Never mind the fucking jokes, just get on with what I just ordered you to carry out, you walking sand bag. And get our people the hell outta the damn limelight as quick as possible as well, man." There was a slight commotion where many of the reporters were being bunched up, and he turned in that direction as he bitched at himself. "Now what with these damn slugs hanging around here, dammit?" the Captain complained as he showed the pictures he found in the wallet of the dead female terrorist to Sergeant Ramirez. She lowered her head and replied.

"Hey Walker, I recognized them right away man. I'm terribly sorry that I was trying to force you to be friends with these people we meet at the bar, Robert. What a damn fool I was, I should've followed your lead as always, lover. If you didn't like them then there had to be a damn good reason, and something was definitely wrong with them from the start of it, Robert. Can you ever forgive me for not trusting your judgment, Bobby?"

"Don't give it another thought baby. They kinda had me snookered as much as they had you and everyone else fucked over from our outfit." Walker smiled at his girlfriend as he stared at the mess of gathered reporters, as they were being forced out of someone's way. The concerned Captain smiled as he picked up Colonel Leadbetter coming right at him, and he was rudely pushing and shoving his way through the horde of reporters and civilians, snooping around to see what was going on at the hotel. One of the fools was stupid enough to run in front of the angry Colonel and drop down to his knee, and snapped a clear picture of the Colonel's face.

Now Walker was outright laughing as he watched the obviously fuming Marine Colonel yell something at the brazing reporter as he rapidly moved in on the stupid guy. His Commander angrily ripped the camera out of his hands and carried it passed the police lines. Once he was clear of the madding crowd being held off the hotel property by the police line, the Colonel opened the expensive camera and then ripped the film out of it, and he exposed it to the sun. Then he picked the camera high over his head and pitched it back at the complaining cameraman.

The expensive camera crashed to the ground at the feet of the upset reporter, and smashed into a number of pieces. Instantly, the reporter and cameraman started to complain to one of the police officers trying to hold them behind the barricades, as he pointed at the Colonel walking towards Walker. Again the Captain had to laugh as he watched the police nastily shove the reporter and upset cameraman away from the barricade they set up for this very reason.

Colonel Leadbetter stomped his way right up to Walker, and then barked at the young soldier. "What the fuck do you have going down over here for the love of God? Are these the lousy scumbags who were hitting on our people, Walker? They better be mister, or you're wasting my fucking time here, and you won't like the effects if you are, mister."

"Colonel Leadbetter Sir, I believe we have two of the lousy little pricks we were searching for down and out of it, by our machines over there sir. I also believe I have a picture of the missing fucking Colonel Hamoodi al-Qaysi, Colonel." He refrained from informing Colonel Leadbetter that they knew, and some of his soldiers even shared some drinks with the dead people a week ago at the titty bar around the massive military base.

"Out fucking standing mister! I knew if anyone could find these missing pricks, it was you and the rest of your pack of screaming squirrels, Walker. What about the vehicle that was observed leaving this fucking dump? Do you know if the people riding in the damn vehicle had anything to do with these other slugs we just capped here, Captain?" the still upset acting Colonel grumbled as he looked at the picture Walker handed him that he removed from the dead Iraqi's wallet.

"I asked the stinking cops the same question Colonel, and they reported they haven't been able to locate the missing vehicle as of yet, Colonel Leadbetter. But I'm willing to bet the ranch on it was this damn Iraqi Colonel we're on the alert about, riding inside the vehicle, sir. I think what happened here was these two shitbirds went out in the field to retrieve their weapons, so the four of them could go out and start doing their dirty work of killing our people again, sir. I also think someone musta witnessed these two asses with the weapons, and this Iraqi Colonel saw the civilians placing calls on their cell phones. He left these two uther pricks back here, and then he and another one of his stinking bastards made good their fucking escape from here, before we showed up on the scene and could get at and ice them, sir.

"Also Colonel Leadbetter, the stinking missing Iraqi Colonel shot out of the parking lot like the prick he is, to save his own stinking hide from us getting our damn hands on his ass, sir. I further bet he was shooting sparks outta his damn asshole he wanted out of the area so fast, Colonel. That's what I think happened here Colonel Leadbetter, if you were to ask me, sir."

"I asked you Captain and that was a good report from you, mister. However, I have another damn idea in mind though. Give me the rest of the pictures of the one you think might be this missing bastard Colonel we're now after, Captain. Sergeant Kirkpatrick, get your ass over here on the double quick. I have something I want you to do for me before I finish speaking with my Captain here." Colonel Leadbetter barked at his Staff Sergeant, and then he waited for the Sergeant to get to his side so he could tell him what he wanted.

The Captain handed Colonel Leadbetter the small stack of pictures of the man in question, and in return the Colonel handed them over to the Sergeant and ordered him. "Sergeant Kirkpatrick take these damn pictures up to the front desk of the hotel, and see if anyone can ID this prick."

Walker and the Colonel continued speaking, and when the Sergeant returned with a smile, he reported to his commanding officer. "Colonel Leadbetter, the guy at the front desk told me this person in the pictures was the guy who rented two rooms, sir. He also said he was the man who paid for everything for the other three people with him when he rented the rooms from the hotel, sir. He also knew the two killed by Captain Walker's troops, and he told me they were two of the three people with the guy in the picture, Colonel." The Sergeant smiled back at his Commander.

"Well Captain Walker, it looks like you're damn right about this sonofabitching prick in the picture, sir. That was good work on your part, mister. Captain, I guess there's one other order I have to issue to you and the rest of your war wacky pack of wild animals you're working with out here, sir. Go out there and get this bastard, but I now want this sonofabitch brought back in one fricking piece and still breathing or he can even be in puzzle form of a million fucking pieces and dead as they come for all I care, Walker. Either way, I want this lousy bastard as much as I want my next rate increase, sir." The angry Marine Colonel growled at his young Captain as he stared at him while waiting for him to go into action. His wait was not very long.

It only took a few more seconds for Walker to react to the Colonel's last orders. He turned on his heels and then he headed right for the three parked Humvees. He was already issuing orders to the rest of his troops as he climbed into the lead military jeep. But before the Captain could order his driver to pull out, Colonel Leadbetter walked up to his machine and began speaking with him again. The two military officers were soon joined by the interested State Trooper Lieutenant Smith, looking for any further orders from the Commander of the operation, before they shoved off on their continuing search for the few remaining missing terrorists.

COLONEL HAMOODI AL-QAYSI'S VEHILE HEADING FOR I-95 SOUTH

The extremely upset Iraqi Colonel Hamoodi al-Qaysi had to go down three extra exits for the main highway by means of a narrow two lane service road, before he was able to get back on Highway I-95, at a small exit not guarded by any police vehicles. Just as soon as he was on the highway, he remained heading south in the slow lane and drove the posted speed of the roadway. Before he got back on the highway, he noticed a police helicopter flying by him while he was heading southbound on the road. The Iraqi Military Officer knew instantly the police in the helicopter was obviously out looking for him. But he was driving behind the helicopter, and he did not feel the helicopter pilot would double back to check the road for a second time.

The cunning Iraqi Officer made certain he was surrounded by a few of the huge tractor trailers driving the road with him. One of the large machines was driving right behind him, and another one was driving directly in front of him, and there were two other huge rigs riding in the lane right next to him, actually boxing him in on the highway. It seemed like one of the trucks was trying to pass the other massive vehicles driving in the slower lane. Colonel al-Qaysi soon found himself completely surrounded by these three rigs, and he allowed himself a slight smile as he continued to follow the long line of massive trailer trucks running the road with him.

A young State Trooper riding on the road out searching for the missing Mercedes vehicle came up with an idea, and he picked up his radio and made a call. "To all truckers on CB Channel One, Nine, driving on I-95 north or southbound, this is Trooper Randolph, and I need your help people. Be it known to all rig drivers that we're out looking for a snow white, late model Mercedes Benz vehicle with heavily tinted windows. This is an emergency request; because it's believed the driver of this vehicle is the sniper who is killing the soldiers stationed in North Carolina. If any of you truckers spot this missing vehicle on the road, don't, and I repeat this, don't take any action against this vehicle yourselves. You're to call me back on this radio, and report this missing vehicle to me immediately. The driver and his passenger are believed to be heavily armed and extremely dangerous, truckers."

The State Trooper released the button to his radio and then he held his breath and waited for any response from any of the truckers out on the open road. He was certain this was the easiest way for him to try and locate the missing vehicle. He maintained his driving south on I-95, looking for the running vehicle.

"Hey Lame Duck, this is the Road Hog, and I have your back door for you, man. Look in your rear view mirror and tell me what you see trapped between our two rigs, fella." The driver of the trailing rig asked the rig in the lead of their so called convoy.

The driver of the Lame Duck truck looked in his rear view mirror as instructed, and instantly he picked up the snow white Mercedes, and the driver of the vehicle looked like he was trying to use his rig as a sort of shield to hide behind, while driving south on the road. Then the truck driver grumbled to the other driver in his radio. "Well, well, will you look at this shit we got ourselves here, good buddy? It looks to me like we got us a little white Nazi built car, and it seems to me that the damn driver's trying to use us as a blind for his ass, a shield against the Bears (State Police) out there searching for this dude, buddy. You stay behind my rig and glued to the guy's rear feathers in. Hey Spare Tire do you have your ears on good buddy?"

"Sure do Lame Duck and I heard what you and Road Hog were just talking about man." The driver of the third rig driving in the center lane replied to the Lame Duck driver.

"Hey Road Hog, I think we got us the guy that State Trooper's looking for, and he's trying to use us to hide behind. This is what I want you to do for me. I want you to pull your rig up right alongside mine and lock the sonofabitch in between the three of our rigs. I'm going to call this Bear on the road back, and let him know what we got us trapped over here. Let's see what he wants us to do about the dude, and if he wants us to squeeze this guy off the road."

"I copy and am moving up to close the side door on the guy, Lame Duck. I can't see in the car, those damn tinted windows, I hate the damn things. Them tinted windows stops me from seeing any of the seat covers (Women) riding in them cars, Lame Duck.

"You're doing perfect and I'm going to call the Bear back. This is the Lame Duck to the Statey who put out the call for help from us truckers riding on I-95. I believe we have the vehicle you're looking for all cornered in good and proper, sir. The driver of the damn vehicle is trying to use our rigs as a way to hide between while we're on the road, Trooper. We got the guy pretty well boxed in real nice and sweet for ya, sir." The driver of the rig reported to the police officer.

Trooper Randolph smiled as he replied to the driver. "Lame Duck, this is Trooper Randolph, sir. Look sir, I want you to keep the vehicle in question boxed in until I can catch up with your rigs, sir. But I don't want you guys to take any unnecessary chances with the damn driver though, sir. If he makes a move on you and it seems like he might endanger your rig or your life or the lives of any civilians on the road in any fashion, let him out of the trap immediately. We'll get him now we know where he is. What mile marker are you driving by at this time, Lame Duck?"

The driver of the Lame Duck tractor trailer remained silent until he spotted the next mile marker off the side of the road, and then he hit the exit before he found the mile marker, and when he saw it, he immediately reported back to the waiting State Trooper. "Hey Statey, this is the Lame Duck, sir. We just past Exit Forty Two on I-95 heading southbound, I have five other rigs with me, and a few more reporting they're closing in on my rig as we talk, sir. I have your little white Nazi car well locked in behind me and in front of another rig, and I have a third rig riding on the side of the wanted vehicle, sir. So we have him pretty much locked in the granny lane of the highway. We'll keep him locked up between our rigs until you people show up, and then you guys can do whatever the hell you gotta do with the damn driver, sir."

"I copy your last Lame Duck. Right now I'm just passing Exit Fifty Six heading your way at top speed, sir. I'm fourteen miles behind your rig. I just placed the call out, so maybe some other State Trooper who might be a little closer to you, will intercept your convoy sir. Thanks for the help Lame Duck. Someone will be back to you shortly, sir. Will remember the help, and we'll repay you somewhere along the way, sir. Good luck Lame Duck and stay safe. Over."

As the State Trooper was speaking to the Lame Duck rig driver, the State Police helicopter that passed that exit heading northbound a few moments ago, intercepted the call from the rig driver. When the Lame Duck gave his position out, the helicopter pilot instantly placed his airframe in a sharp turn to the right, and then he headed for Exit Forty Two at over one hundred and fifty five miles an hour. In no time flat, the State Trooper helicopter took up his new position one hundred and fifty feet flying directly over the five rigs, and the trapped Mercedes vehicle the rigs were complaining about driving between their rigs.

The moment the Lame Duck driver picked up the helicopter over his rig, the driver got in touch with the State Trooper he was speaking to a few seconds ago over his radio. "Hey Trooper Randolph, I have a Bear in the air, and he's flying right over my rig, good buddy. I thought you should know about this helicopter, sir. At least you know you have some help up here, sir."

"Thanks again for all the help Lame Duck, I just received a report from the helicopter pilot over your rig, sir. He was asking me to confirm with you if he was flying over your rig, sir. You just confirmed his concern, and I'll report same to the pilot. Thanks again for all your help Lame Duck. Stay tight, will advise you of what we want you to do next, if anything sir. Try and keep the vehicle boxed in for as long as possible. Until some cruisers catch up to you and they take over the operation to stop this vehicle, sir. They're responding as we speak Lame Duck. Out."

"Lieutenant John Smith, calling car, One, One, Five, Seven, come in please sir."

Lieutenant Smith was standing just outside his cruiser while speaking with Captain Walker when he heard his radio number called out on the CB radio, and then he offered to the military officer. "Hang in there for a minute Captain Walker Sir. I believe have a call coming in sir."

"Yeah sure, you do what you gotta do man. I got my own fricking problems I gotta handle here, sir." Walker replied as he talked with Colonel Leadbetter again.

"This is One, One, Five, Seven. Go with your traffic sir. Over." The young State Trooper Lieutenant replied in his radio.

"Lieutenant Smith, Trooper Randolph, sir. Be advised we might have just picked up the missing Mercedes vehicle in question, sir. The vehicle just passed Exit Forty Two on I-95, heading south in the slow lane of the highway, sir. We have the help of five trailers the driver's sort of have the wanted driver boxed in between their rigs, sir. The drivers will attempt to keep him locked in until your special unit of soldiers can catch up to them. Then the soldiers can take this operation over from that point forward, sir. Over sir."

"I got you and I'm leaving for Exit Forty Two as soon as I relay this information to the Military Commander of this operation, sir. Out. Hey Captain Walker."

Walker heard his name being called out and he looked at the trooper car. He picked up the young Lieutenant Smith waving him over to his vehicle. "Hold on a sec Colonel Leadbetter Sir, I gotta see what the hell this pain in the ass Trooper wants with my stinking ass, sir."

Walker headed for the car with the Colonel watching him. "Yeah, what's up Lieutenant?"

"We have a white Mercedes spotted and possibly trapped in at this time, sir. A number of truckers on the highway have the vehicle boxed in between their rigs, and the trucker's are stopping him from getting away on us, sir. They're about ten miles south of our present position, sir. We better get a move on it if you want to Command this damn thing, sir."

Walker smashed the trooper on his back, and then he took off in a dead run for his parked Humvee as the trooper started his car and pulled up before the three idling heavy military war machines. The lights flashing on his cruiser as the trooper waited for Walker and the rest of his troops to pull out, and then follow him to the highway. Colonel Leadbetter ran up to Walker as the Captain jumped inside the Humvee, and he asked him with concern. "What the hell's going down Walker? Since when do you ever leave my ass hanging out in the breeze like this, and leave this damn parking lot, Captain?" the Colonel stopped Walker from leaving the parking lot as he remembered his orders, and pulled him out of the Humvee moments before.

"Colonel Leadbetter Sir, a number of truckers spotted the possible vehicle we're looking for, and they're playing with the damn vehicle, it's reported at Exit Forty Two on I-95 sir."

"Out fucking standing Walker. Go and get the lousy sonofabitch so we can place a period at the end of this damn sentence. Remember Captain, we're looking for two fucking people, so the other one might be inside the damn vehicle along with this damn driver, sir."

"Roger that and thanks for reminding me of that fact, sir. It gives us a second target to get afta when we finally catch up with the damn vehicle, if it's the one we want that is sir."

McNip reversed the Humvee and straightened the machine out, and then his machine fell in line directly behind the State Trooper's lead vehicle. The other two Humvees quickly lined up right behind Walker's lead machine.

When the military vehicles were lined up properly behind the trooper's vehicle, the police officer put on his siren and started to move forward. The police working the parking lot of the hotel where the two snipers were killed, quickly removed the barricades and the civilians and news reporters on the other side of the barrier promptly got out of the way of the caravan of mixed military and police vehicles. As soon as the vehicles pulled out of the hotel parking lot, the two helicopters with a small horde of reporters stuffed inside them, left the area and followed the police car and three military trucks. The cameramen held the machines locked up in their view finders, and the civilians in all States of America were seeing the vehicles heading for Highway I-95 in living color. The cameras showed the three huge Humvees so close that the viewers were almost able to see some of the soldiers actually riding inside the machines.

The excited soldier branded the Mutt was looking out the side window of his Humvee, and he picked up the camera from the helicopter aiming right at him and he being himself. He stuck his hand out the window, and gave the helicopter and cameraman the bird. At the Fox News Studio, the young commentator was explaining to the public what they were witnessing, when he suddenly stumbled over his words when he noticed what the soldier was doing on the open feed, and he immediately apologized to all his viewers over the rude motion.

"I'm terribly sorry for the rude gesture you have just witness. You must remember that we're coming to you viva a live feed without the usual five second interval for editing purposes. So we were unable to edit this film before it was being shown to you viewers. Wait a second, I was just informed by our station that we're now going to that five second interval, so we can safely edit out any such further gestures, before they happen and are accidentally aired for our viewers. Once again, I must apologize to the viewers for anything offensive displays you might have just witnessed on your TVs. We're trying our very best to try and keep you well informed of everything that is happening in the Carolinas as they take shape for our viewers."

Walker noticed what the Mutt, (Lieutenant Frank Hall) did to the news helicopter, and he laughed over the display. He hated having the nosey reporters watching their every move, while they were on the road hunting down the sniper. He grabbed the radio and placed a call to Colonel Leadbetter, and then he began to bitch at his Commanding Officer in a hot tone of voice. "Nightstalker to Action Mountain. Come in sir. This is important Action Mountain. Over."

The Colonel heard his name being called out over the radio and he grabbed a mike from Sergeant Kirkpatrick and then replied to Captain Walker's call in. "This is Action Mountain, go ahead with your traffic Nightstalker. What the fuck's up so soon Captain? Where the hell are you, and what the hell are you up to, Captain Walker?"

"Colonel Leadbetter Sir, is there any way you can close off the stinking airspace over my sagging ass, sir? I don't want any of these damn news hounds seeing what the fuck might go down out here, sir. You know, in case we have to create some violence with this lousy little turd we're trying to run down and take into custody or other, sir."

"That good thinking on your part Captain Walker Sir, I'll place the airspace over the entire situation off limits for forty miles out in all directions to all civilian helicopters and aircraft. Until you tell me you got this missing bird." Colonel Leadbetter instantly broke off the communication with Walker, and then he enacted the Home Land Defense cause, and he immediately ordered all airspace over Highway I-95 in a forty mile area off limits to all civilian aircraft and news helicopters from Exit Forty Two out. Immediately, the two news helicopters were ordered out of the area, and they immediately complied as quickly for the new orders. The helicopters veered off the military machines and trooper vehicle.

When Walker was finished speaking with the Colonel, Sergeant Ramirez leaned forward in her seat and she smacked the Mutt on the back of his head, and then she glared at the soldier.

"Owe, what the hell did you do that fur Raz? That hurt like hell there, girl. I didn't do nuthin wrong to earn me a smack on the stinking noggin like that, sister." He rubbed his head.

"Don't give me any of that bullshit, mister! I saw what you did to that news helicopter reporter, and I didn't think it was very funny in the least, wiseguy."

"Hey Raz, why the hell don't you do me a fricking favor and do some cock chugging for a little while, until you end up with a mouth full of throat yogurt, huh? That hurt like hell girl." He snapped at her as he continued to rub the back of his head.

"Of you poor little baby you. I didn't know you got hurt so easily, buster. Usually it takes a round to make you cry like you're doing over a simple slap on the noggin, mister." Sergeant Dorothy Ramirez said as she smacked him in the back of the head again for good measure, and then she added to her angry words aimed at the Mutt. "And, you better also watch how you talk to me while you're at it mister, before you get me really upset with you, and I have to show you the error in your foolish ways of thinking and acting, buster." She gave the Mutt the look, informing him she was not fooling around with him on this one.

The Mutt did not like the harsh look coming from Sergeant Ramirez in the least, so he shut up and looked forward in the Humvee to get out from under her glare.

Blind Date put her hand in the air, and Sergeant Ramirez slapped hands with her, as they both laughed at her giving it to the dangerous soldier branded the Mutt. Even though the female French Sergeant had fallen in love with the Mutt, she never missed a chance to get on his case whenever he messed up around her.

CHAPTER TWENTY SEVEN

THE WHITE MERCEDES BENZ
HEADING SOUTH ON HIGHWAY I-95

The cunning but extremely angry Iraqi Colonel Hamoodi al-Qaysi picked up the police helicopter as it came around on them, and it started to hover right over his car while keeping pace with him. He understood they were discovered by the police, and instead of feeling he was hiding on the police by driving between the large tractor trailer rigs. He felt he was being trapped by the trailer trucks now. He glanced to his side at Major al-Shaya, and then growled at her nastily.

"Major, get the weapons from the rear seat of this cursed vehicle and chamber a round in each weapon for our use. The worthless police authorities have obviously discovered where we are, and I believe these god cursed lowly infidel trucks are working with the police, and they're trying to keep us trapped between their worthless machines, until the police assist the foul drivers in their attempt to stop us from escaping this foul land of lowly jackals. I believe all is lost to us, and we'll have the great honor to die for Allah just cause, and our country's sake. We'll give up our lives for Allah's just cause waged against all lowly infidels of the United States, woman."

Major al-Shaya reached behind her without question, and she pulled an M-16 over to the front seat with her. She immediately chambered a round in the weapon as she asked the Colonel with much concern in her voice. "Colonel al-Qaysi, what are you going to do now sir? We'll never escape the foul Americans alive, now they know where we are and where we're heading, sir."

"This worthless vehicle is much faster than these lumbering large cursed trucks, so at the right moment to take such an action against them. I'm going to drive off the side of the foul highway and use that narrow section of the road with the white strip painted on it, to pass this evil truck trying to block us from going faster than we're driving on this god cursed road. Major, you'll be ready with the weapon, and if the foolish driver tries anything against us when I make my move out to pass him. You'll shoot out his foul tires of the worthless truck out, and send him driving off the side of the highway, woman. I'll teach these lowly American infidels not all Iraqi soldiers are afraid of the worthless fools, and some of us are more than willing to fight them to our death, and to take as many of them with our honorable passing, woman.

"I'll prove to all these worthless infidels and jackals that some of us proud Iraqi soldiers are willing to die for our beliefs, and for Allah's sake and our homeland. Be ready with the foul weapon woman, we have a slight turn to the left rapidly coming up, and I'll use this curve as a sling shot move, in our attempt to get this foul vehicle past this evil truck trying to block us in. Then we'll go until I find the proper place for our death on this unending god cursed highway, be ready to react when I give you the foul word, Major. I'm going to start my move aimed against the worthless truck in a few seconds, Major al-Shaya."

Major al-Shaya opened the back window on the driver's side a few inches. Then she aimed the weapon out the window and prepared to shoot out the huge tires of the massive truck they would soon pass, if the driver tried to continue to block them in where they were trapped.

The driver of the truck trailing the Lame Duck noticed the rear window of the Mercedes open. Then he picked up the muzzle of a weapon slightly sticking out the window, and he reached for his radio and placed an emergency call to the lead driver of their six vehicle convoy. "Hey Lame Duck, it seems these two people know what we're trying to do to them, good buddy. I think they're going to try something on you in this next turn coming up. I just picked up a muzzle of a weapon sticking out of the rear window of the damn car a second ago, buddy. Do you want me to ram this car from the backside, and take them out of the damn game once and for all? I noticed a second person moving around inside the car also, good buddy. So there are definitely two people hiding inside the damn thing, my friend."

"Negative on that last Road Hog! We have to see what the hell the damn police want us to do with these people first. As much as I'd like to run over the damn car and be done with this damn thing, we don't own the trucks, and if we crash into them. We might cause a pile up that might kill a bunch of innocent people out here. Hang in Road Hog, I will..."

"Lame Duck, this is State Trooper Chopper Three, Five flying over your rig, sir. I heard what the other driver just told you, sir. I don't want you taking any chances with the driver of that vehicle, sir. If the suspects are prepared to shoot at your rig then I want you to break off your moving blockade of said vehicle, and allow said vehicle to pass your rig without any interference, sir. There's too much civilian traffic on the highway for you to try any heroics against our suspects, sir. It looks like the driver is setting up to pass your truck on this next turn coming up from the service lane side. If that's what the driver tries, you'll, and I repeat sir. You'll allow the vehicle to pass your rig, without you trying to continue to block him in any way, shape, or form, sir. You're now instructed to allow the damn vehicle to pass your truck, period sir.

"I only hope the passenger doesn't take it on his or herself to shoot at your truck as they pass by your rig either way, Lame Duck. If they do fire on your vehicle and you lose control of your rig, try and smash into the wanted vehicle and take it out, but only if they fire at your rig first, sir. At least one question was answered by your moves on the roadway, sir. We know for a fact now that there are two people inside the suspect vehicle, sir. Do you understand my orders as I have just issued them to you, Lame Duck driver? Over sir."

THE THREE MILITARY HUMVEES

Captain Robert Walker ordered McNip, Sergeant David Nirajima to continue following the speeding State Trooper cruiser as it flew passed the roadblock set up by the other police officers along the roadway. The excited Marine Captain watched as the Trooper's vehicle slid on the entrance ramp to I-95, and he quickly got control of the car. Then the Trooper ripped into the heavy flow of traffic. With his lights flashing and siren screaming, the Trooper got his vehicle moved into the speed lane, and the civilian traffic in this lane quickly got out of his way.

Captain Walker's lumbering Humvee, along with the other two heavy military vehicles had to struggle on order to get over into the speed lane, and then try and keep up with the faster moving trooper vehicle. All three Humvees had flashing lights blazing, but no siren. The three military Humvees worked their way through the heavy flow of traffic. All the time they were traveling, Walker was busy monitoring what was being said by the police in other pursuing squad cars. As well as he listened in on what the helicopter pilot was saying to the drivers of the tractor trailer trucks, and the police vehicles also involved in the pursuit of the wanted vehicle and terrorists trying to escape them on the highway.

Captain Walker looked behind him and grumbled at Sergeant Ramirez over his shoulder. "Dammit Raz, I hope to hell that we get there before any of these stinking police are able to stop the damn car we want on us. And, they get this lousy little prick the hell outta it alive and they secure his ass before we're able to get there and do him in as ordered. Before the stinking terrorists becomes a burden to the criminal system and our jail. The Colonel's gonna eat our asses for supper if that shit happens to ya, and we don't kill this dirty bastard first, dammit."

"Say Walker, you have to look at the bright side of this mess. As long as these people are stopped, who the hell cares how the police or we stop them. If the police are able to get the two suspected shooters out of their car, and they take them in custody alive, I think that'll be great for all concerned with this situation. The terrorists will no longer be a threat against us, Bobby. You understand I'm not very pleased with Colonel Leadbetter's orders of us taking these two people out, before anyone had a chance to question them properly, Robert. Maybe that way we can find out a little more about them and why they were doing this shit to us in the first place. Maybe being armed with that knowledge, we can stop another such attack from happening in the future, Bobby. I always felt we should try and take any terrorist captive, so we can properly interrogate them, and get what information they might have, before they die Bobby."

"How fucking romantic you truly are Raz. You're still trying to save the stinking world I see, girl. You know if any of these lousy turds are taken prisoner, the friggin bleeding hearts will stop us from interrogating them properly, so we can get any needed information from the little pricks. We can't even take them on a little swim on the stinking water board any longer, baby. Hell girl, it's more important to the fricking bleeding hearts to protect the lousy Arab criminals, than it is with protecting the innocent of the world against these damn nuts. These same stinking bleeding hearts will even try and stop us from asking them any stinking questions, before they can lawyer up and then we can never get any damn needed information from them.

"The way I see this mess coming out is, these damn A-rab bastards are looking to be erased from the face of the earth. There's no fucking pleasing them in any way, shape, or form. If we remove one tyrant from the fricking game, somehow we always end up looking like the bad guys in the damn act, Raz. Look at fucking Usama bin Laden for Christ sake, he's the perfect fricking example for my stinking bitch, baby.

"We supported the lousy bastard in the beginning on his rapid rise to power in the Arab world, and we even supplied the stinking fuck and his fricking groups of flaming assholes with a ton of damn weapons and cash. Once he got in the stinking position his ass was searching for, he immediately turned around and bit our stinking hand off, and then he spat in our stinking faces. We hafta learn that we can't trust any of these damn A-rabs or any other terrorist for that matter.

"There's no stinking honor or talking any damn sense with these people. They cry they're being prosecuted here in the States, because we Americans act like we hate the whole pack of dumb fucks. Look at what they're doing here and abroad on and against us and our interests. We have allowed them to come to the United States because they're running away from their ridged fricking governments, and people constantly killing each uther in the streets. Once they're here, the assholes begin to speak and training their hatred of us to their young and very gullible fools. And, we're the only people helping the lousy bastards outside of our usual allies.

"For Christ sake girl, none of the uther A-rab countries will complain, because A-rab terrorists are slaughtering uther A-rabs in their own damn lands. Just to force the stinking dumb ass bunch of people to follow their lead to Paradise, and their hatred of the West. Even Saudi Arabia, who states they're our fricking ally in the A-rab world, will demand the stop to the stinking deaths any Arab is suffering, because some pack of damn wingnuts want things to remain mired down in the stone ages. Even their great Holy Book, the Qur'an says any A-rab who kills, especially another A-rab, will never enter the Kingdom of Paradise.

"But yet these radical A-rab assholes will read the same words from their Holy Book, and they change them around to suite their own fricking needs and control over their fellow A-rabs. They will never make any peace with the damn Israeli's, no matter what the Jew State does to try and appease the A-rabs of the Middle East. It'll never be enough, the only thing these A-rabs want and understand, is complete annihilation of Israel, and that's bullshit and bad manners if you were to ask me baby. All the A-rabs see, and seem to want to see is war and fucking death.

"No baby, I can understand why so many people are beginning to hate the stinking A-rabs in the uther nations of the world. I wonder how the A-rabs feel, being hated by lands they were once a peaceful part of? The attack on the Twin Towers wasn't only an attack against us. Raz, there were people from all over the damn world killed in those two buildings. So in one swift attack, Usama bin Laden had successfully declared war on the world at large. Any nation that doesn't side with us in this ongoing war on terrorism, that is really a war on mostly A-rab lands, mind you. Are only opening themselves up to similar such attacks on their fricking soil in the future.

"Any uther nation involved in the war on terrorism has to take a stinking stand. They can't possibly stand in the middle of the road, because the only thing that'll be left lying in the middle of the road is stinking road kill. When we allow the damn terrorists to disrupt and change the elections of once free nations of the world. Then that nation is no longer a free and independent nation. Because that nation is now subjugated and bowing to the crazy demands of these lousy terrorists and stinking cowards, honey. That nation sold out their civilians, in hoping their move would stop any future terrorist attacks on their lands. Which we know damn well will never stop once the stinking terrorists get the upper hand in a nation they turned into a coward nation.

"Any stinking nations who gives into any terrorist demands, is just sending their country back to the stone ages, and they're also giving up the rights of their civilians to pursue a peaceful and free lifestyle in their own damn countries. Just because their weak ass stinking government officials couldn't tow the damn line and do what they had to do, in order to protect the people who put them in office, dammit. I'll tell you this much though Raz. I'll die with my lousy weapon locked in my hand protecting the civilians of this country, and I'll use every child we turned into soldiers to accomplish this feat. If only one American survives this lousy war on terrorism, and that one person is allowed to live under the freedoms our soldiers before us fought and died for. Then we've done what our laws demanded of their protectors of the civilians, and those soldiers haven't died in fricking vain, baby."

Walker's words were cut off when his Humvee was forced to jump in the speed service lane, in order to avoid a civilian vehicle that suddenly pulled between the leading Humvee and the Trooper cruiser, a few hundred yards ahead of the slower moving military vehicles. McNip roared with anger at the female driver as he carried out some quick and dangerous defensive maneuvers, to avoid plowing into the rearend of the civilian vehicle.

"Why you stinking bitch, you nearly killed all us for God's sake. If I had the time I'd put my head under the hood of this damn thing and rip out the damn governor, and then I'd run this machine right up your tight ass for ya." McNip floored the Humvee and got right up on her tail, and the driver must have noticed how close the large military vehicle was riding up on her, because she immediately put on her blinker and then moved out of the speed lane, and then she watched as the large military truck passed by her.

"Cut it out for fuck sake will ya man, and get a control of yourself and this damn machine for crap sake, McNip. We don't need you getting in a fricking accident when we might have the damn shooters in our stinking sights. We got more important things to worry about than some damn woman cutting us off and scaring your ass a little and..." Walker's words were again cut off when CoCo-G, who was driving the Humvee that was the last one in the caravan, called for Walker over the radio. CoCo-G got his tag name from one of the Japanese soldiers from the outfit. He said the Japanese language had no true word in it for the "N" word, but he dubbed the large black soldier CoCo-G. It was the nastiest word he could come up with for the black soldier, who didn't mind the word and even thought it was kind of cool to be branded CoCo-G.

Walker grabbed the radio and he barked in it. "What the fuck do you want from my friggin ass now, man? We almost just got killed in this damn thing, because McNip can't keep his fricking eyes on the damn road and avoid the uther stinking civilian traffic on the damn road."

"Hey man, you gotta calm down a little before you bust a stinking blood vessels or something, my friend. I just wanted to tell ya that we have a number of stinking police cars rapidly closing in on our stinking asses in a fast fricking hurry it up, man. I wanted to know what you wanted to do about them damn guys coming up on us, Captain." CoCo-G reported to his Commanding Officer, in case he was interested in what was going on behind his lead vehicle.

"What the fuck can we do about it CoCo? We can't jump in their damn vehicles with them fuckers, you asshole you. Keep your damn eye on them asses and see what the hell they're up to behind us, man. Keep me informed and if they want by us, let me know in a hurry man." Walker snarled at the driver of the other Humvee.

"Still the angry fucking dude I see, huh Captain? That's not what the fuck I meant by my question to you, rude dude. The stinking cop cars are coming at our asses like fire in our fricking lane man, and I wanted to know if you wanted to pull our vehicles out of this speed lane, and give them uther cars easy actions to pass us because they have betta speed than we do, man. Or do you wanna stay in this stinking lane, and force the stinking cop cars to dip into the center lane in order to pass by us, mister happy go lucky man? What's your damn pleasure, oh fearless leader of mine? It's your call to make here Captain, but I need some input from your ass, man." CoCo-G complained in his radio at the young and angry Captain.

"Keep it up buster and I'm gonna turn you inside out, so you can try and pass yourself off for a fricking white man, asshole. The stinking police cars can maneuver a helluva lot easier than we can in these slow ass moving machines. So we're gonna stay right where we are, and let them asses pass us on the inside lane, buster. Err... CoCo, I'll not bit your head off the next time we speak, man. That was a good question there, buddy." Walker added, feeling a little bad because he came down so heavy on the other soldier.

"What the fuck do you call that shit man? Was that supposed to be a stinking apology or what from your ass, man? If that was a fricking apology then keep the damn thing will ya Walker. I don't want you to hurt your fricking self like that again, man. You might end up needing a Tums to help calm down your stomach a little, because it hurt you so much to admit that you mighta been a little stinking wrong there, buddy." CoCo fired back at the new Marine Captain.

Walker smiled and shook his head over CoCo's rebuff of his apology, as he watched the five speeding State Trooper vehicles sped by him once their machines dipped back in the inside passenger's side of the Humvee. Two police officers in the speeding vehicles acknowledged Walker in the lumbering machine. As each cruiser passed the Trooper's cruiser escorting Walker and his people on the highway. The drivers blinked their lights in recognition of Lieutenant Smith. Then they left Walker's people in the dust as they increased their speed again.

COLONEL HAMOODI AL-QAYSI'S MERCEDES BENZ

The moment the Iraqi terrorist's vehicle entered the slight turn to the left, the Arab Colonel drove his vehicle wildly into the service lane of the right side of the highway, as he increased his speed at the same moment. Colonel al-Qaysi's car instantly sling shot past the heavy and much slower moving tractor trailer rig, desperately trying to keep the snow white Mercedes Benz blocked in between the three trailer trucks. The powerful Mercedes had little trouble passing the large truck, as the Colonel floored the powerful engine of the luxury machine, and the car kicked up the speed in no time flat. The high performance car went from sixty five, to eighty mph in mere seconds, as it quickly left the trailer trucks in the dust.

All the while the worried Iraqi Military Officer's vehicle roared past by the Lame Duck's rig, Major Serena al-Shaya had the barrel of her M-16 aiming out of the rear window of the vehicle. She had the weapon trained right on the rear set of tires of the cab of the big rig blocking them between the other few rigs on the highway.

When the terrorist's vehicle cleared the large rig, the female Major immediately pulled the weapon back inside the window, and then she closed it and struggled back into the front passenger's seat of the wildly speeding vehicle. The Iraqi Colonel held his speed up and the car quickly increased the distance he was opening up between his vehicle, and the trailing three rigs rapidly fading in the background. It was at this point he allowed himself a slight smile, and then he relaxed his hunched up shoulder muscles, the moment when he could no longer see any of the rigs in his rear view mirror. But his smile faded just as quickly as he looked ahead of his speeding vehicle, and he was stunned by what he was seeing coming up.

As Colonel al-Qaysi's car past Exit Thirty Eight on I-95, he noticed two State Trooper vehicles parked in the service lane of the highway. When the officers noticed his Mercedes speeding by them, the police cars flipped their lights on and then gave pursuit against him.

"I hate these worthless American fools and all they stand for in this hated world, Major al-Shaya. The loathsome creatures are like the troublesome locus, you cannot get rid of the lowly jackals no matter what you try against the evil things. How many of the foul police authorities does the

United States have anyhow, woman? They are as many as the head lice on a worthless Nomad's cursed filthy head." He roared at the female Major as the police cars started chasing after his vehicle. One cruiser immediately moved into the center lane, and the other police vehicle followed him in the speed lane, at a safe distance though.

As the Iraqi Colonel tried to get more speed out of his vehicle traveling at over one hundred and twenty miles an hour, he was constantly glancing in his rear view mirror. He noticed at least five more police cars suddenly catch up with the others driving behind him, and they had all the lanes of the highway completely blocked off from the civilian traffic trapped further behind them. The police cars were keeping a good distance between them and his speeding car though by traveling about ten car lengths or more behind his vehicle. He was feeling terribly trapped as he gave the car more gas, and tried to get more speed from the roaring machine.

What the angry Iraqi Military Officer and his female passenger did not realize was, ten miles ahead of his speeding vehicle, other police cars were closing off all entrances and exits to I-95, heading southbound. This was so the civilian traffic would be well out of the way for whatever happened on the highway with the terrorist's vehicle. Other police cars were moving the civilian traffic along before them, in an attempt to try and get the civilian traffic out of the way, before the terrorist's car caught up to them. Seven miles ahead of the police officers, the three lane highway dropped down to a narrower two lane highway, and at Exit Thirty One the police were going to stop the Colonel's car by employing road strips against the vehicle.

The road strips was a strip of rubberized material that had a large number of sharpened hollow tube type spikes secured to the strip which sprung up on command, and the tubes would easily punctured the tires of any vehicle the police wanted to stop relatively safely on the road. The police were able to immediately lower the spikes, once they disabled the fleeing car in question. This was so the pursuing police vehicles would not lose their tires to the same trap they just used to disable the fleeing suspect's car with.

The fuming Colonel al-Qaysi cursed aloud, because it seemed everywhere he looked, all he saw was more police cars lined up waiting for him to pass by them on the never ending highway. He never noticed the sudden lack of civilian traffic riding ahead of his machine on the highway. The upset Iraqi Military Officer even picked up a number of police vehicles parked in the middle of the two roads, and they had their lights on and the officers were kind of just staring at him as he passed by the parked squad cars on the side of the highway.

"Where in the good name of the Almighty Allah is all of these miserable, god cursed police cars coming from, woman? Is there that much evil crime committed in the foul land of Satan by these lowly jackals that they need so many worthless police officials to deal with their crime and criminals? Is there no end to the vast numbers of loathsome police cars that they have to stop us with, woman? Major al-Shaya, I want you to make certain there is a round chambered in my weapon, before I need the foul thing to defend myself with. If the worthless American fools want to stop us from leaving their miserable country so badly. Then we'll take as many of the worthless fools with us as we possibly can, woman." The fuming Iraqi Colonel snapped at the female Major sitting in the passenger's seat of the car.

Suddenly, three speeding Trooper cars appeared before the Colonel's vehicle, but what he did not see or understand was, he caught up to them, and they did not catch up to him. He slowed his vehicle down to seventy miles an hour, and he was forced to slow down even further. This was because the police cars were slowing him down with what the officers commonly referred to as a moving roadblock on the highway ahead of his fleeing vehicle. As his car was forced to slow down further, it allowed Walker's machines to close the gap between them much quicker.

The Middle East Colonel's vehicle was forced to slow down to fifty five mph, by the blocking Trooper cars driving in the three lanes before his vehicle. Another police cruiser was riding in each of the service lanes on the right and left side of the highway, and his vehicle was trapped between them all and forced to slow down even more, because of the wall of moving police cars driving ahead of him. Colonel Hamoodi al-Qaysi looked in his rearview mirror, and he noticed over ten other Trooper cars stacking up right behind his vehicle. Suddenly, he noticed the lack of civilian cars on the road, and he stared at the road ahead of the police cars.

Not seeing any civilian traffic driving on the highway wherever he looked, except for the north bound traffic, he decided to increase his speed to try and force the Trooper vehicles out of his way, or he was prepared to crash into some of them. He made a sudden charge at the police vehicles. His car was much heavier than the police vehicles, and it was more powerful as well. He easily caught up to the police vehicle riding directly in front of his machine, and he actually bumped into the police car as he tried to drive him off the highway. The slight bump from Colonel al-Qaysi's vehicle, caused the police car to swerve slightly in the lane, but the driver was able to maintain control of the cruiser before the car went off the road.

When Colonel al-Qaysi's car bumped the State Trooper's vehicle, orders came in to all officers involved in the pursuit of the believed to be terrorist vehicle. "To all moving roadblock vehicles, don't try and keep the subject vehicle hemmed in, if he tries something stupid like that again. I don't want any of you getting hurt by this guy. You're three miles away from the spike set up station, and we'll allow that to stop the bastards. Be aware, the road narrows again down to two lanes in a quarter of a mile of your present position. If the subject vehicle gets by the moving roadblock, those vehicles are to join the pursuing cars of said vehicle at a safe distance. We'll see what happens when the spike strips flatten his tires." The Trooper Commander riding in the helicopter ordered the rest of his State Troopers in the pursuit.

Colonel Hamoodi al-Qaysi grew angrier as he picked up the police vehicle regain control, and not crash his vehicle as he had planned for it. The fuming Iraqi Military Officer shook his head, and then he gassed his vehicle again, and in a matter of seconds he was bumper to bumper with the same police car again. When he closed the gap, the police officer gassed his car, and then he opened the way for the Colonel's vehicle to pass him by pulling off onto the left service road, and the Trooper then allowed the Colonel's car to pass him safely. The angry Trooper glared at the Iraqi Colonel as his car roared passed his vehicle.

Major Serena al-Shaya was scared to death over the wild way that her Commanding Officer was driving the speeding car, and she looked around herself. She was desperately trying to hang onto the dashboard with both her hands and her fingernails for dear life, as the car bounced and jumped all over the road because of the speed of the machine.

When the trooper car was out of his way, the Iraqi Colonel floored the car, and it shot past the police vehicle now driving on the service road. The wild Arab Military Officer pushed his vehicle even faster, until it was almost flying at a hundred and forty plus miles an hour on the open highway again. As the speeding vehicle entered South Carolina, the Colonel noticed a number of flashing red lights well ahead of his vehicle, and it seemed like the highway was again getting narrower on him. The two police cars momentarily driving alongside Colonel al-Qaysi's vehicle suddenly let up and they allowed him to pass them with ease.

The still fuming Iraqi Officer saw he had the road ahead of him all to himself now. So he maintained his speed until he realized the three lane highway was turned into a narrower two lane road. The surprised Colonel slowed his vehicle a little, until he was again riding in the speed lane. Then he opened his car again to the higher speed, and this speed was more comfortable.

Once Colonel al-Qaysi's car was on the two lane highway correctly, he concentrated his attention on the flashing lights he picked up about a mile ahead of his vehicle. The more the Arab Colonel drove, the more he noticed he was the only vehicle currently riding on the highway besides the horde of police vehicles. When he got close enough to see what the blinking lights were about, he noticed two more trooper vehicles parked off the side of the highway. The four officers were out of their vehicles, and he realized they had their weapons in their hands, and they were covering his car with them. He screamed at the female Major seated next to him.

"Major al-Shaya, the lowly jackals are going to shoot at us as we pass by their god cursed position. Get low and be ready to get out of this foul vehicle, and then shoot it out with the foul police authorities. Try to kill as many of the hated fools as you can, before allowing yourself to die by their worthless hands, woman. We'll show these hateful lowly American jackals the right way faithful Iraqi soldiers die when the time is near, and Allah is calling us home to be with him for all eternity, woman. We'll show the evil fools we're not afraid to die when we're right, Major al-Shaya." The still fuming Iraqi Colonel barked at his female soldier.

As the Iraqi Colonel's roaring Mercedes flew by the parked police vehicles, both he and the Major ducked down low in the front seat, and they waited for their vehicle to be riddled by a hail of bullets fired at them, from the police sitting off the side of the highway. But the bullets were never fired at them by the officers. Instead, the Iraqi Colonel felt a light, double bump under his car as he popped his head up to see where he was driving on the road. He looked behind him and saw the gaggle of police officers pulling something off the highway.

"I wonder what the devil that move was all about by these loathsome infidels, Major al-Shaya. The foolish police authorities had us right where they wanted us, and yet the worthless fools allowed us to drive by them without giving us any cursed trouble. The worthless desert fools they are, woman." As the Colonel complained to his second in command, he suddenly noticed he was starting to have a bit of trouble with keeping his car straight on the empty highway. The expensive luxury vehicle wanted to suddenly slide all over the road, and he was working harder than ever with the steering wheel, in his attempt to keep the car straight on the road.

The spike strips were used to puncture the front wheels of the car only. The police did not want to kill all four tires of the vehicle for fear of having the car slid off the road and crash.

Colonel Hamoodi al-Qaysi was forced to slow down to only sixty miles an hour, in order to maintain some safe control of his car, as he struggled desperately with keeping the vehicle driving true in the speed lane of the highway. The snow white Mercedes was bucking and sliding all over the road, and there were chunks of something bounced off the car's windshield, as he struggled to maintain control of his vehicle.

"Colonel al-Qaysi what is going on sir? What is suddenly wrong with the foul car? All of a sudden you are driving all over the road like you're losing control of the foul thing, sir." The Major cried as she tightened her grip on her weapon and the handle of the door of the vehicle.

"I have no idea what the devil is suddenly wrong with the foul German made worthless machine, woman. I can no longer go at the speed I want to drive this useless vehicle in, to keep us in front of the hated police authorities, Major. What is all this bouncing off our foul car windshield, Major al-Shaya? Put your worthless head outside the car window, and see if you can see what in damnation is wrong with this Germany piece of junk, woman. If I did not know any better, I'd swear to the Almighty Allah that I was driving this thing with flat tires, woman."

Major Serena al-Shaya did as she was ordered and she zipped her power window down, and then she poked her head out of the vehicle, and she look at the front end of the struggling vehicle. When she put her head out of the window, she was instantly struck in the forehead by a small piece of rubber, but she kept her head out the window until she saw the front tire on the passenger's side was flat. She could not believe the tire was flat, now she wondered how the police were able to flatten the tires without shooting it flat on them.

When the Major pulled her head back inside the car, she rubbed her face where she was struck by small shredded pieces of rubber peeled off the flattened tire. She checked her hand and noticed a small spot of blood on her finger. Then she reported to the worried Colonel still trying to keep the swaying car straight in the drive lane of the highway.

When she was able to catch her breath, Major al-Shaya reported to her Commanding Officer in an excited voice. "Colonel al-Qaysi, the front tire of the foul car on my side is flat. I don't know how the hated police authorities were able to shoot out the tire without my hearing a single shot being fired at us, when we passed the fools parked on the side of the highway just moments ago, sir. Somehow the god cursed lowly infidels were able to flatten the tire on us, Colonel. I don't believe one flat tire would make this fine car slid and shake like it is doing on us though Colonel. Something else must be plaguing this foul machine all of a sudden, sir." The concerned female Iraqi Major complained and she reported, and continued to rub the side of her forehead where the small chunk of tire struck her. Whatever struck her in the face was causing her some discomfort and pain. Again she checked her fingertips, but there was no more blood this time.

"You're correct with your worthless assumption of the situation, Major al-Shaya. One flat tire will not give me as much trouble as this miserable piece of junk is giving me, woman. The only thing I can see is the god cursed police authorities must have somehow been able to flatten the two front tires on this foul machine. That means we'll be forced to stop our car in the near future, or risk being involved in a crash on the foul highway. Major al-Shaya, I don't intend to end my life foolishly in a car crash on these cursed roads in the United States.

"Major al-Shaya, this is what I intend to do now that this foul made German machine is on the verge of failing us. I'll stop this good for nothing vehicle when I can no longer drive it safely, and then we'll make our last stand against these hated police authorities on this worthless highway. Our deaths will be well worth something in the pulse of the world, and we'll kill as many of the hated police jackals as we can, before we're finally killed in return by the loathsome fools. Remember these words my faithful sister of the desert sands of our ancestors, 'It's not murder to kill a lowly infidel, it's the true path to Paradise for us faithful followers of the sacred words of Allah." The upset Iraq Colonel fixed his jaw in an angry set, and then he stared straight ahead of his swaying car as he continued to struggle desperately trying to drive the damaged car.

The extremely upset female Iraqi Major did not reply to her Commanding Officer's last words, yet in her mind she was praying he would rethink his thoughts of trying to fight and kill the police, and he would think about giving up to them instead. She would much rather waste the rest of her life rotting away in an American jail, than by dying on the lowly streets of the United States, like the Colonel was preparing for. Or her being forced to return to her country only to suffer the terrible living conditions along with the other poor Arabs of their land, living under the constant threat offered by terrorist groups constantly ripping the Middle East apart. Or being forced to wait for another invasion of their sacred lands of Iraq by the United States and the rest of that country's Allies. Or from Russians or any other nation that wanted to place their worthless noses in Arab matters that only concerned the Arab peoples of the Middle East.

Colonel Hamoodi al-Qaysi dared a quick look in his rearview mirror, and he immediately noticed a police car was traveling two or three car lengths off the rearend of his powerful by struggling car. There was another police car riding in what he knew was called the slow lane to his right side of the highway, and two more police vehicles were about the same distance away from his struggling car. Silently, the angry Colonel cursed the two police vehicles, as he dared to give the terribly running car more gas, in an effort to try and open the gap between his vehicle, and the trailing police cars. But as soon as the powerful engine got the added gas, the struggling vehicle started sliding worse than before on the pavement of the road. If it was not for a number of quick actions carried out by the Arab Colonel, the vehicle would have surely went into a wild slid, and then crashed off the side of the road.

The trailing State Trooper squad cars noticed the sudden wild slid of the white car directly in front of them, and they immediately backed off their pressure on the terrorist's vehicle. But when the drivers of the police cars saw the Mercedes once again riding under some control, the officers instantly closed in again on the wanted vehicle. The Trooper driving in the speed lane requested permission to perform what the police officers commonly referred to as the pith maneuver against the fleeing terrorist vehicle. The pith maneuver was when a trailing police vehicle drove up to the side of the car they were following, and lightly tapped, or more shove the fleeing car on the driver's side fender, causing the wanted vehicle to spin out of control until it finally came to a stop either by crashing, or the driver giving up to the police officers. Then the police could easily block that disabled car with their vehicles, and get out of their machines and stop the driver from leaving the area. Thus ending further high speed pursuit of another vehicle the police were after.

The State Trooper Commander riding in the helicopter a hundred feet directly above the Iraqi Colonel's car, picked up the sudden slight slid, and he refused to give the requesting officer permission to carry out the dangerous pith maneuver on the still fleeing terrorist car. He felt all three cars were traveling at too high a rate of speed, and to try and carry out that dangerous maneuver against the driver of the damaged vehicle. It might send both cars in an uncontrollable slid and crash into each other, or off the road. The Commander had no intentions of placing one of his officers in that kind of danger at this time. He understood in a matter of moments, the Mercedes would be forced to stop, because of the terrible condition of the vehicle.

He was already picking up steam coming from the front end of the fleeing vehicle. Besides, the pith maneuver was usually employed on a much slow speed action to take, and at this time that move would possibly hurt some of his officers, and causing more trailing police cars to crash into one another, as they tried to dodge the possibly crashing cars directly in front of them. As much as he wanted to stop this terrorist car at this point, the wise Commander did not want any of his officers, or anyone else for that matter to get hurt in the process.

Suddenly, the Commander ordered the helicopter pilot to leave his present position, and then head further down the highway. He was looking for safe place to set up another spike strip setup. He decided to blow out the two rear tires of the damaged terrorist vehicle. He understood it was impossible to drive the car at any rate of speed with all four tires blown out on the vehicle. About a half a mile past the next exit, the highway went into a slight left hand curve, and the police helicopter past two parked Trooper cars already blocking the past exit to Highway I-95, and he read the number printed boldly on the roof of one of the trooper vehicles, and then he offered on his radio. "This is Chopper Command to State Trooper Cruiser Three, Four, One, Five involved in the roadblock on the entrance to I-95. Come in. Over." The Commander was please with this area for what he intended to do against the terrorist vehicle, and there were no civilian cars anywhere in sight on the highway in either direction at this time.

"This is Three, Four, One Five, Sergeant Rossberg here Commander. Send you traffic sir. Over." The driver of this squad car replied to his Commanding Officer.

"Sergeant Rossberg Sir, do you have a set of spike strips in your car?"

"Yes sir, I have a full setup with me sir." The Sergeant offered as he started his car.

"Good, this is what I want from you, Sergeant. I want you come down the highway to where I'm presently hovering, and then you're to set up the strips for action here, and we'll drive the terrorist vehicle right into the spike strip setup. I want to stop this god damn vehicle right here and now, dammit. This thing has gone on long enough for my likes, and I'm not going to wait any longer before this damn fool drives one of my Trooper's off the side of the damn highway, and hurt any of our people. Commander to lead pursuit car, I'm setting up another road strip here. You're to pursue this suspect car until it goes over the strips. Then I want you to perform the pith on the damn fool immediately after he goes over the spike strips, before he has a chance to increase speed on us again. We're going to stop this nut right here and now, if I have anything to do with it, Sergeant."

CHAPTER TWENTY EIGHT

The Trooper vehicle trailing Colonel Hamoodi al-Qaysi's crippled Mercedes, heard what the Commander was planning to carry out ahead of their vehicles, and he immediately tightened up on the fleeing suspect vehicle again. Then the Trooper concentrated his eyes on the car running before him. He glanced up and saw the helicopter about a quarter of a mile ahead of his vehicle at this time. Then his eyes went back to the Iraqi's crippled vehicle, as he watched every move the terrorist vehicle carried out in front of his vehicle.

Lieutenant John Smith's squad car finally caught up to the other Trooper vehicles riding behind the two cars tightly following the subject's vehicle. Captain Robert Walker's slower moving Humvees were lumbering almost a quarter of a mile behind the Lieutenant's squad car, and all four vehicles were traveling in the speed lane. The two trooper vehicles driving in front of the Lieutenant's car picked up his vehicle coming up on them rapidly, and they immediately got out of his way and soon his vehicle was the only one riding directly behind the Iraqi's Mercedes. Once Walker's Humvees past the other Trooper's vehicles, he had the second Humvee being driven by CoCo-G pull out before the other Trooper vehicles in the slower lane.

The Captain used his machine to block the other Trooper vehicles off him. So his people could be on the scene before any of the State Troopers could get there once they stopped the terrorist's vehicle, and the Troopers tried to stop what he was ordered to do with the terrorists. Complaints immediately filled the radios.

"What the hell are these damn soldiers doing riding in front of our vehicles like this, dammit? They're cutting us out of the damn pursuit of the subject's vehicle by their current actions being played out against us. Commander, we're requesting you make contact with the soldiers, and have them get their damn slower moving vehicles the hell out of our way so we can do our act, sir. If I knew the damn soldiers were going to cut us off like this. I would've never allowed them to get in front of my cruiser in the first place, Commander." One of the State Trooper Officer's barked angrily at the Commander in the helicopter over his radio unit.

The Commander in the helicopter knew his Trooper was correct with his bitch, but he also understood the soldiers were the ones in Command of this terrorist situation for the time being. So he grumbled in his radio but his gripe was more aimed at the Commander of the soldiers this time. "Captain Walker Sir, I want to inform you that we'll not stop you from doing what you have to do against the subjects in the suspect vehicle, sir. But I have to request you allow us to stop, and then get control over this situation before you and your soldiers react against the damn terrorists in the vehicle, sir. Until we stop this car and removed this vehicle from any further possible threat to the civilians on this highway sir, or to my Troopers, at the same time sir.

"Listen here sir, the damn suspected shooters are driving on my roads Captain Walker, and he's driving like a flaming asshole at that sir, and until I get him off my highway, he's not your problem sir. Once we have the suspect's car secured, we'll step aside and allow you and your troops to complete your mission as instructed by your Commander, sir. I must request you back off immediately and get out of my Trooper's way, Captain Walker Sir. Until we have complete control, and have secured this situation and subjects, Captain Walker. Then you'll be allowed to finish it off in any fashion you have in mind and were ordered to do, Captain."

The angry Captain glanced out the side window of the Humvee, and he picked up the Trooper vehicles stacking up behind his slower moving machines. He drew in his breath and then bitched at his driver. "Hey McNip, I think these lousy dudes are fucking right man, we betta let them stop this fricking car for our asses, man. Then we'll move in and deal with this damn pecker and his stinking bitch of a girlfriend. Pull back in the speed lane and then dip into the service lane to our left side, and then get the fuck outta the stinking Trooper's way for crap sake. We'll take that position until they stop this damn car for us, man.

"But McNip, I wanna remind you to keep up with the damn Trooper's vehicles, so we can go into action the moment these stinking guys stop this German made piece of shit that's falling apart right in front of us, man. Get back in the speed lane, and once there all three of our machines will move into the service lane. Four F, open the damn gap between your machine and mine, and allow CoCo to get back between us, man. Once he's riding in the speed lane, we'll all three move into the service lane of the damn highway and outta the stinking cop's way. People, check your weapons, if we receive any threat from these two fools in that damn car, we'll waste the bastards no questions asked, and no answers given people."

Walker watched out of the side window of his Humvee intensely, as the soldier branded Four F (Sergeant Frank Ferraro) back off his machine, until CoCo was able to get his machine back between the other two humvees. Once he was where he was ordered to be, the Captain's machine then slowly drifted into the left side service lane. The young Marine Officer did not breathe properly again until all three of his heavy war machines were driving flat out in the service lane. But even before he could let out his breath, the trailing Trooper vehicles pulled up, and they instantly closed the gap and past him like his three machines were standing still.

Captain Robert Walker stared as the flood of State Trooper vehicles roared past his slower moving military machine, and then he bitched angrily at his driver again. "Hey McNip, what the fuck's wrong with this damn thing anyway man? For Christ sake McNip, this damn thing's moving like we're carrying a crap load of fricking pianos inside it. Can't you get a little more stinking speed outta this damn thing?

This is really embarrassing man, we're being left in the stinking dust by the damn State Trooper cruisers, and I don't like it one bit, buddy. We're supposed to be the lead movers in this damn operation, and here we are, we're gonna come in afta all the stinking Trooper vehicles beat us to these miserable terrorists for crap sake."

"Captain Walker, I got the stinking peddle down to the fricking metal as it is, sir. If I could, I'd jump up and down on the shitting thing, push the damn gas pedal right through the stinking floorboards, if I thought it'd help with the damn thing any, Captain. Walker, I'd even jump outta the damn machine and get behind it and push the fucking vehicle faster if I could, sir. Bitch at the stinking government and not me, if you really wanna gripe at anyone about the stinking speed of these damn things, Captain. The stinking government's the one who put these lousy governors on the damn things, so we wouldn't go screwing around with the machines when they were in our possession sir. The brass hats don't want us to speed with the stinking things, Walker." McNip growled at the Captain as he kept his eyes glued to the road before him.

"Never mind that shit, keep your stinking sermon for after Church will ya buddy. Just try your best and keep up with the Troopers, dammit." He bitched at the driver as he stared out the window again. He could see the police helicopter, but he was too far behind the police cruisers to see what the troopers were doing with the target vehicle running ahead of them. All he could see was a mess of flashing red and blue lights, and the harsh glare coming from the headlights of the police cars, making it nearly impossible to see what the devil was going on ahead of him.

State Trooper Sergeant Rossberg broke his neck in his effort to try and get to where the Commander wanted him to setup the next road spike trap on the roadway. When he parked his car, he got out and ran to the trunk and threw it opened. He could see the duel headlights coming down the highway from his fellow officer's vehicles, and he knew they were almost on top of him. He pulled the strip set out of the trunk and then he ran to the middle of the highway and laid down the strip so it covered both lanes. The out of breath young State Trooper no sooner got back to the side of the road, than he was able to see the shower of sparks coming from the front end of the damaged Mercedes being driven by the wanted terrorist.

The Trooper pulled the line trigger, and the double row of super sharp hollow spikes snapped up to a standing position. It was none too soon, because as soon as the hollow spikes were locked in position, the crippled Mercedes came flying by his position. Instantly, the police officer heard the hiss coming from the two rear tires, as the suspect's vehicle shot by him. The Trooper then pulled the line again, and the spikes immediately went back to sleep hidden deep inside the heavy rubber forms, as the first of the cruisers sped by his position. The Trooper gave the other police officers the thumbs up signal, letting them know he successfully killed the rear tires of the wanted Mercedes.

The Troopers trailing the suspect vehicle increased their speed again, so they could catch up with the fleeing car, to see if this was enough to stop the Iraqi Colonel's car. The lead Trooper saw the Mercedes was sliding all over the road, but the driver still refused to pull over and stop. The way the vehicle was sliding all over the road, cause this Trooper to get on his radio and order the trailing Trooper vehicles to back off their pursuit because he did not want a pileup on the highway, if the suspect's car lost all control of his vehicle and crashed.

The Commander's helicopter was flying directly over the suspect car, and he was showering the fleeing car with his powerful floodlight, and when he saw the drive get control of the car after running over the spike strip, he cursed. Then he reached for the radio and placed a call to his troopers. "Okay lead car, it seems this damn asshole has no intention of stopping that damn thing, so I give you permission to do the pith maneuver, and send this asshole off the road. I want a period placed at the end of this sentence right now, dammit. This guy cost me enough down time and stress. Besides, its six ten p.m., and we have to take into consideration night setting in, and these two snakes sneaking out of the area using the darkness for cover. Stop them now!"

The lead Trooper vehicle instantly increased his speed, as the trailing cruiser slowed down, so he could get out of the way when his partner made his move against the subject's car. The rest of the following Trooper vehicles also slowed down, and this move was to give the lead car all the room he needed to do his act against the fleeing vehicle.

The lead Trooper cruiser given the okay to carry out the pith maneuver against the subject's vehicle rapidly closed the gap between the subject's vehicle and his vehicle, until his bumper was almost rubbing up against the bumper of the heavily damaged Mercedes. The Trooper's car then drifted into the service lane, and then the driver pulled the nose of his cruiser up until it was about a foot and a half past the bumper of the Colonel's damaged car.

At the right moment, the Trooper turned his wheel to the right, and the nose of his cruiser lightly bumped the rear panel of the Mercedes. The slight tap took the wheels, or what was left of them out from under the Mercedes, and the vehicle instantly went into a three spin twist. It took several second for the Mercedes to stop its harsh spin, and the machine ended up facing the wrong way on the highway, and the car instantly stalled out on the excited and angry Iraqi driver. The overheated motor of the Mercedes was covered in a heavy cloud of hot steam from the engine compartment, and this spin gave the disabled vehicle the excuse to stall out on the fuming Arab driver, and stay down and unable to be restarted.

The Trooper car that tapped the Iraqi's vehicle off the road, pulled to a stop across from the stalled vehicle some thirty five feet away from the disabled Mercedes with the known terrorists trapped inside it. The rest of the trailing Trooper cars pulled up and stopped directly across the road from the disabled vehicle, cutting off all civilian traffic heading southbound on the highway that was following the cruisers. The State Troopers and Sherriff Deputies jumped out of their vehicles, and they took up firing positions hiding behind their doors, or by the sides of their cars. The Troopers had their weapons out and aimed at the tinted windows of the stalled Mercedes.

Some of the Troopers were armed with M-16's for extra stopping power. Thirty three police officers were now hiding behind their parked cars, waited for either of the two trapped subjects to do something stupid, so they could react against them. Every Trooper wanted to end this thing as of this time, and hopefully without any loss of life.

Captain Walker's Humvees had to slam their breaks on because of how quickly the horde of Trooper vehicles stopped before them, and they took up defensive positions aimed at the two terrorists trapped inside the stalled vehicle. McNip, the driver of Walker's vehicle did not expect the police cars to stop right in the middle of the road and blocking the two lanes before him. Four F could not stop his Humvee in time, and his machine slid into the stopped Humvee being driven by CoCo-G, and his head went slamming into the steering wheel from the rear impact. CoCo stuck his head out the window and then he roared at the soldier branded Four F.

"Hey you stupid little prick you, what the fuck's wrong with your stinking ass anyhow for crap sake? You nearly killed my stinking ass up here dickhead. You wait until this mess is over wit you flaming asshole. I'm gonna show you how the fuck to drive that damn thing, by parking the stinking thing right on your stinking chest, motherfucker. Look at my ass, I'm fricking bleeding all over the damn place thank you very much, asshole." CoCo screamed at Four F as he wiped some of the blood from the small cut on his forehead with the back of his hand, and then he waved it at Four F so he could see his blood.

Buckethead dropped his mitt size hand on CoCo-G's shoulder, and he pulled his head back inside the window and growled angrily at him. "What the fuck are you yelling at that dumb prick for? The fricking ones we wanna deal with are sitting a few hundred yards ahead of our stinking asses, stupid. Here, let me get a look at your stinking noggin for ya. You're getting fricking blood all over the inside of this stinking machine on us man, and we're gonna get stuck cleaning the mess up when this fucking thing is over with, chump. Hmmmmm, you got yourself a nice little cut there black bird. Anybody in here got a stinking band-aid on them for this little cry baby here? I should stick it on his mouth instead of his damn noggin to shut him down some."

Caviar, the good looking young Russian female fighter announced to the American soldier. "Buckethead soldier you big fool, I have something I give you wrap around that black man head for him. It not real a bandage, but it do good until we get back to base, and he get look at by real you Doctor please." The pretty Russian female soldier handed Buckethead a white strip of cloth she removed from the emergency road kit to repair the machine with. It was not clean, but nevertheless Buckethead pulled CoCo's head closer to him and he looped the rag around his head twice, and then he ripped it in the center and made it so he could tie a knot in the light cloth, to hold it in place on his head.

"Hey stupid, that fucking thing ain't very clean you know buddy. Are you trying to poison my fricking ass or something on me, man? Can't you find something to cover my injury that's a little fucking cleaner than that is, so I ain't gotta worry about it becoming infected on me, buddy?" CoCo cried as he tried to pull his head away from the large soldier.

"What the fuck are you worried about asshole. If you were born to be hanged then what are you worried about bleeding to fucking death for, or getting a dirty bandage on it fur, stupid? This will do good enuf for you for the time being, just like the stinking Russian chick back there said it will, man. Until we get back to base and you can get worked on properly by the damn medics on the stinking base. If you don't like it then take the damn thing off your noggin and stick your stinking finger in the wound, just like that little kid did in the Dam, asshole. I don't give a flying fuck either way, just so long as you stop bleeding all over me and this damn machine, and crying like a little girl who got a stinking booboo on her finger, buster."

Captain Walker was on the radio the instant the two war machines made contact with each other. "Is everyone okay back there, dammit?" He asked, even though he was not really that interested in their condition, because he knew no one would be seriously injured in the little fender bender, as he added to his words. "This is what we're gonna do here people. We gotta get passed all these stinking police cars so we can get at this damn Iraqi Colonel and his fricking female friend inside the stinking stalled car. Then we'll settle up with his fricking ass good and proper, and get us some fucking payback for what he and his bitch done to some of our people. We're gonna pulled out onto the grass in the center divider of the highway, and then we're gonna drive by these stuffy ass cops giving me the stinking heebie jeebies by being so near them pukes.

"I really hate like hell being anywhere around all these fricking cops anyway man. Then we're gonna see what the hell's going on up there, and we're gonna act accordingly against these fricking terrorist shits we got trapped in front of our asses, guys. We're not gonna take any prisoners on this action if you people know what I mean by these stinking orders. Everyone's gonna follow me out of the damn Humvees and move into the grass area. Then we'll drive around these stinking cops nice and careful like. Don't hurt any of them stinking slugs, guys."

Buckethead reported back to his Commanding Officer in an excited tone of voice. "Hey Walker we got us a slight injury in this fricking little fender bender back here, man. CoCo got him a little cut on the stinking noggin, and he's bleeding like a stuffed pig all over the place."

"God dammit man, is he outta this damn thing, or is he still fucking operational, Bucket? I can't be lugging a fricking wounded soldier along with me, as we settle up with these damn pukes here man." Walker asked the large soldier with concern in his voice.

"He's still breathing okay fine enuf I guess, I ain't no fricking Doc you know Captain. All I know is he's crying like a little girl. But he's still good to go if he's needed in this damn mess, Walker." Buckethead reported again to his Commanding Officer.

"Jesus Christ Almighty, you people call yourselves damn soldiers? I have a good mind to trade the whole lot of you people in on one good looking Girl Scout, who can follow fricking orders and not get hurt in the process, dammit. Why the fuck are you bringing him up to my stinking attention for if he's not that bad hurt, asshole? What I meant by everyone being okay back there, was if someone was seriously hurt or not in the stinking fender bender. I don't wanna know about some little scratch on his stinking noggin, stupid. We're moving out, follow my lead troops."

The exhausted and extremely excited Iraqi Colonel Hamoodi al-Qaysi did everything in his power to try and get control of his wildly spinning car. He did not know what happened to the disabled vehicle, one minute he was driving pretty straight and okay on the highway, and the next thing he knew, everything was spinning wildly about him. When the disabled Mercedes finally slid off the side of the highway and stopped its spinning as it came to rest stuck on the soft grass, the motor instantly stalled out on him. His windshield was completely covered by a thick cloud of steam and oil spraying from the motor coming from the engine compartment, as Colonel al-Qaysi was trying desperately to restart the smoking motor steaming up, when an amplified voice called out to him from outside the damaged vehicle.

"You two people in the car, we know who you are Colonel Hamoodi al-Qaysi, this is State Trooper Sergeant William Schindler, sir. I'm the Commanding Officer for the State Troopers presently surrounding your vehicle, sir. Look Colonel we know why you and the rest of your people entered the United States, sir. Colonel al-Qaysi, no one has to die here today. All you have to do is throw all your weapons out the window of your car, and then you're instructed to come out of it with your hands in the air. Once you and your passenger are outside the vehicle, you both will walk ten paces with your backs towards me from your vehicle, and then you will lie down in the middle of the road. You will keep your hands well away from the sides of your body at all times, and then you will await further orders from me, sir. If you do as I'm ordering sir.

"Colonel al-Qaysi, I assure you that you'll not be injured by any of my Officers, sir. C'mon Colonel al-Qaysi and do the right thing here for all concerned, sir. Colonel al-Qaysi, as of yet your group has not killed anyone in the Unites States, sir. So your group has committed no serious crimes as of this time sir. All you have done wrong so far sir, was to sneak into the United States and you're only guilty of carrying illegal weapons and a number of minor road infractions I'm quite certain can be overlooked if you do the right thing here, sir.

"None of your people used the weapons in anger against anyone, sir. The crimes you have committed so far are no big thing, sir. A good lawyer might even be able to get you off the hook completely sir. So there's no sense of you and your friend dying for nothing here sir." The State Trooper Commander was trying his best to try and talk the two terrorists out of the vehicle peacefully, even to the point of lying through his eye teeth to the terrorists in the disabled vehicle.

The Mutt looked at Walker with a confusing stare, and then he bitched at the young Captain. "What the hell does that dopey little bastard mean by this flaming asshole didn't kill anyone, man? What the fuck is he trying to saying to these two pieces of stinking shit trapped in that damn messed up car, Walker? The two soldiers these scumbags killed were nothing to this stinking cop I guess, man? I got me a good mind to pop a fricking cap in that stinking Trooper's ass for dissing our people like that, Walker. This stinking guy's outright fucking nuts telling these two dumb ass slugs that they didn't kill..."

"Back off some dog man, the prick's just trying to bluff the little bastard outta the damn vehicle, that's all man. As far as I'm concerned, he's wasting his stinking breath on the lousy bastard that's as good as dead now, man. We have orders from Colonel Leadbetter to take the two friggin slugs out, and that's exactly what we're gonna do when we get the stinking chance to act against these two terrorists, man. Payback is a real fucking bitch and it's on the way my friend." Walker shot back at the Mutt.

The extremely angry Colonel al-Qaysi continued to try and start the stalled and still heavily steaming vehicle, but all the motor did was crank, and it refused to catch and fire into life again. While the Iraqi Colonel was desperately trying to restart the stalled motor, he continued to look out the front windshield. All he could pick up outside the vehicle was a horde of police officers hiding behind and, or standing by their parked cars while aiming their weapons directly at his car with hatred blazing in their hearts and eyes. There were so many police officers stacked up outside his vehicle that the confused Arab Colonel was unable to get a good number on just how many police officers there was stationed against him. The Iraqi Colonel turned to Major al-Shaya and noticed that she had the fear of God etched deeply in her wildly staring eyes. He then barked savagely as he glared nastily at her.

"Calm down before you do something rash Major al-Shaya, we have to keep our heads about us during this cursed situation we find ourselves trapped in, woman! Yes, it's true we're going to die on this cursed night, Major. So it's up to us how many of these god cursed lowly infidels we make share our honorable deaths with us, foolish woman. Major al-Shaya, check out our weapons, and make certain we have extra loaded clips for the foul things within easy reach while I try and restart this German made piece of junk. We should have remained in Washington and killed the worthless Federal Judge, and that lowly jackal waste of a Colonel who was taken prisoner by the god cursed American troops who had invaded our country, woman.

"If the great fool had followed his orders and died as he was instructed as a true follower of the Almighty Allah and His sacred word, and for his country's sake while battling the worthless American police authorities to his worthless death. We would not have been forced to come to this foul land and try and save, or kill the foul fool as we tried to do, woman. May the Almighty Allah take His revenge out on the worthless Colonel al-Adwani's foul head."

"Colonel al-Qaysi Sir, I have already checked out the weapons, and they are ready for use against the lowly infidels who have trapped us in this worthless vehicle, sir. I have two loaded extra clips for the M-16s, and an extra clip for our pistols as well, and I have placed them within easy reach of you, sir. Listen to the American police officers though sir. They're offering us life, and we're contemplating death as we Arabs always do, sir. Why do we not think about giving up to the hated American police as he orders us to do, sir? It's as he states to us my Colonel, we have killed no one in the United States and all we're guilty of, is carrying weapons into this hateful country, sir. I suggest we do as he ordered us, and we give up and..."

"Stupid foolish lowly woman of no account, you're so easy to fall for the evil lies of these lowly infidels spew from their worthless mouths. The jackal speaks only a half truth from his foul mouth to us, woman. Do you not remember that we have killed two foul American soldiers, and we have also wounded a third one of the cursed fools on our last attack against the hated infidels? The sons of a lowly camel in Washington are the ones who have killed no one. If this fool is offering anyone life from his lying mouth then he's speaking of the fools we have left in Washington to kill those two fools up there, woman. Major al-Shaya, remove these most troubling thoughts of giving up to these deceitful American jackals from your foolish head and looked after the foul weapons for us. I feel we'll have need of them soon, lowly woman.

"Look out the evil window of this poorly made German vehicle, and try and locate your targets you intend to end their worthless lives for, woman. If we're forced out of this German junk pile for any reason, we'll come out of this machine with our weapons blazing death at these evil infidels who have us so tightly surrounded. To die in the name of the Almighty Allah is all we live for, woman. The sacred eyes of Muhammad are watching us, and we owe it to His great pleasure to die honorably for His sacred words and truth. Major al-Shaya, get control of yourself, because I cannot restart this hateful thing that is completely worthless. So here is where we're going to die on this foul of nights for Allah's sake.

"Fate has given us the limelight to die most honorably for our beliefs in Allah, so that's what we're going to do on this night. Damn this foul German made car and the ones who have created it to the pits of hell for all eternity. It will not start no matter what I try against the foul and useless thing. Major al-Shaya, pass me a hated weapon so I might defend myself properly against this horde of jackals that have us trapped, until Allah allows me to come home to His waiting arms. What the devil is that foul noise I'm now hearing all of a sudden, Major? Are these hateful American jackals throwing even more police authorities at us now, woman? How many of these god hated police do they need to kill just two proud but extremely dangerous Iraqi fighters, and one of them being a woman fighter at that? Be most proud of yourself woman on this faithful day. If it takes this many American fools to kill the two of us then we have struck the fear of Allah into their worthless souls and minds, woman."

Captain Robert Walker's Humvees rumbled over the center meridian divider between the north and south bound lanes of Highway I-95, and then his machine drove up behind the Lieutenant's Trooper vehicle, while the other two military war machines remained parked in the grass off the main roadway. The Captain got out of the machine like he did not care if the subjects were armed or not, and he was bulletproof. He slowly walked over to Lieutenant Smith while lighting up a smoke again. He heard the other police officer yelling on the megaphone at the two terrorists in the vehicle, but he ignored him as he said to Lieutenant Smith. "Hey John what the hell's the game plan for you guys, sir? I'll give you a little time to make some stinking moves against these two assholes, sir. But when I feel the game's going on too long for our asses then I'm gonna move in and knock all the fucking cards offa the stinking table, sir."

"Captain Walker! We're trying our best to talk the two of them out of the damn car, sir. They know they can't possibly escape the trap we have set up against them, sir. I think we have a good chance of getting them the hell out of the vehicle alive, sir. Come on Captain Walker Sir, I know what you have in your mind, and I don't care if we get these two out of there alive or not, sir. But you have to give us a chance to try and end this thing without any further loss of life, and if they give us any problems. Then you can step in and do what your Colonel has ordered, sir."

Captain Walker's eyebrows arched slightly as he gave the young State Trooper Lieutenant an amused look and a half of a smirk.

"Yes Captain Walker Sir, if you remember right sir, I was standing right next to you when Colonel Leadbetter gave you the order to finish these two people off, and not to worry about taking either of them as prisoners, sir. No matter what your orders are from your Commander, sir. At least give us half a chance to try and work this damn thing out first, Captain. If we fail then you can do it in your military way as ordered, Captain."

"What the hell can I tell ya, Lieutenant? You got me dead to rights on this one, sir. Okay Lieutenant, play your little head games for a little while with the lousy sonofabitches in that damn vehicle, sir. But I'm telling ya this much Lieutenant, the first hostel actions carried out by either of these two fucking asses in that damn Mercedes, we'll immediately going hot against them whether you cops like it or not, sir. It's starting to get dark as it is Lieutenant, and I'm not gonna wait until they have an even chance of bugging the fuck outta here under the cover of darkness, sir. Then we'll hafta hunt the two assholes down again out in the stinking field. Right now Lieutenant, we have them right dead to right where we want them, and I'm not gonna allow this shit to get away from me again sir. Again Lieutenant Smith Sir, if anything goes sour on you guys, we'll move in immediately and take it outta your hands sir."

Colonel Hamoodi al-Qaysi gave up with trying to restart the stalled and overheated engine of his disabled vehicle. He felt he might have even flooded the motor with gas, so he knew he was going to be forced to wait before the car would restart for him. His mind was working overtime because he needed time, a diversion, something. He had to make a plan to try and escape the trap he was mired in, or he would surely die in the stalled vehicle.

He looked at the female Major Serena al-Shaya as he took hold of his weapon and brought it to the front seat, and then he barked savagely at her. "Major al-Shaya, we have to get out of this foul vehicle so we can make a proper stand against all these worthless lowly infidels who have us surrounded. We cannot possibly fight all these filthy jackals from the interior of this cursed and waste of a car. I'll keep you covered and you'll get out your door, woman. Once you're outside this worthless machine, you'll go right to the back of the evil vehicle. Then I'll come out while you keep me covered from there, and we'll attack our attackers.

"Once we're together again, we can either make a break for it and try and survive this trap, with each of us protecting the others back as we flee, and we try and make our way to the woods to the right side of this worthless heap of a cursed vehicle. Or we can fire at our selected targets, and kill as many of the god cursed police infidels as we can possibly kill, before we're finally allowed to start our journey to be with Allah forever in Paradise. Go at once foul woman, while I protect you from within this foul vehicle, Major al-Shaya."

Major al-Shaya hesitated for a brief moment, because she remembered how he left the two other members from their group out in the field by their hotel rooms, and she was scared to death he was going to try and do the same thing to her. All she could think of doing was just stare in a stunned manner at the angry looking Colonel, as if she was trying to read his mind.

"What is this I'm witnessing from you, evil woman from the sands of our vast desert? Am I going to have some trouble with you over this situation now, Major? If everyone did as I had ordered them to do, we wouldn't be trapped in the miserable situation we find ourselves mired in, woman. I have just ordered you to take your god cursed weapon and your foul body and get out of this worthless car, and then you're to take a position of protection behind this broken down worthless vehicle. Then you'll protect me as I come out to join forces with you, and that is what you'll do if you know what's good for you. That is, unless you want to die inside this worthless vehicle by my hand at this very moment, Major?" Colonel al-Qaysi snarled at her as he brought his weapon across his body, and then he aimed the barrel at her chest.

Again, Major al-Shaya hesitated and did not move an inch. She was scared to move a muscle. She was trembling and almost to tears. She did not want to die she wanted to live and have a family, and end her life of killing and living like a man.

"I see you chose to betray me on this cursed day as did the other fools we left behind in Washington, and at the time I need your faithful services the most, Major. This is fine with me evil woman, because I no longer have any further need of you or the constant trouble you keep offering to me. I'll give you five seconds to make peace with Allah, or you'll open that foul door of this loathsome vehicle, and then you will do as I have ordered you, woman. Or you'll simply die by my side by my hand, while I curse your soul and your ancestors forever." The fuming Iraqi Colonel moved the weapon into a better firing position in the confining front seat of the disabled vehicle, as he continued to glare angrily at the shaking female soldier.

Major al-Shaya could not take the Colonel's terrible look any longer, and she suddenly diverted her eyes away from the angry looking face of the seething Colonel al-Qaysi, and then she turned slightly and reached for the handle of the car door as if it was a mile away from her hand. She drew in her breath and then opened the side door of the damage vehicle. Instantly, the gathered State Troopers and other police officer outside surrounding the disabled vehicle, tensed up as they aimed their weapons at the door of the suspect's car opening slowly. Even Walker flinched slightly when he picked up the door moving on the car. Sergeant Ramirez ran up to Walker's side and she handed him his M-16 rifle. Then she took up a defensive position by the wheel of the parked Humvee, and she aimed her weapon at the suspect's car.

Once the door of the Mercedes was opened for enough for her to get out of the machine easily, Major al-Shaya took her weapon and then she hugged it close to her chest, and then she carefully and cautiously placed one foot outside the stalled car.

A State Trooper immediately growled in the megaphone as he warned the suspects hiding in the smoking car. "This is the State Police, you're surrounded at all ends, and you have no chance to escape your situation. You're ordered to throw any weapons you have out of the car. Then you will come out of the car with your hands raised above your heads. Then you'll walk ten paces away from the disabled vehicle, and then lie face down on the pavement and keep your hands away from the sides of your body at all times. You'll then wait until a police officer checks your person for any hidden weapons and the likes. Then you'll follow all orders given you by that arresting Trooper. Any failure on your part to follow any and all of my orders issued to you without hesitation mind you, might end with your death. Do you understand my orders as they are issued to you? I know you understand English so follow my orders as instructed.”

Major al-Shaya immediately froze in place she was scared to death by the Trooper's angry sounding voice and words, as he yelled at them. Now, she was not only being threatened with death from her own Colonel, but she was also being threatened by the police officer outside the vehicle. She did not know what to do next, and her body was trembling with fright and hesitation. She was shaking terribly as she hesitated again to move an inch.

“Worthless bitch born from the burning desert sand, and who has feasted upon sour mother's milk, you'll do as I have just ordered you to do. You'll pay no attention to what those god cursed worthless fools outside this vehicle are telling you to do. Get to the back of this cursed vehicle and take up a position of protection there, and then wait for me to catch up to you. I'll join you as soon as you're safely hiding behind this evil car, woman. Once we're together we'll consider their surrender terms from the hated police authorities. But only if the meaningless fools allow us to leave this foul land of Satan in peace.” Colonel Hamoodi al-Qaysi snarled at the shaking woman, as he moved his weapon again, and now he aimed it right at her face as he added to his threat against her. “You will step outside this foul thing, and you will do as I have ordered you, or you shall meet your fate right here inside this worthless German made vehicle, woman.”

The moment the car door opened, Captain Walker raised his hand in the air, and then he moved it to the left and pointed directly at the car. The instant he did this, both the Ghost and Hunter moved out and lied down on the grass and drew a bead on the stalled car and waited. The two pointmen and snipers of the Unit, picked up the female passenger sitting in the front seat, and they picked up she held a weapon in her hands. The Ghost got Walker's attention and then he held his hand up, raising two fingers and he spread them apart. This informed the Captain the one getting out of the car, was a female. Then he put his hand to the side and pointed his pointing finger and raised his thumb and made like he was firing a weapon.

Walker gave him a quick nod and the stop signal. This signal informed the Ghost he was not to take out this subject as soon as his eyes rested on her person.

The Ghost shrugged, not knowing why Walker did not want to take out the female target he had locked up and sighted in. He looked at the Hunter for a second, and he did the same by shrugging back at him, and then they both waited for further orders.

Walker was thinking if the Iraqi woman got out of the car with a weapon, he would allow the cops to do her in for them. That way he would not get the black eye for taking out a woman in this action going down on the side of the main highway.

Again, Major al-Shaya drew in her breath and then let it out in a rush, and she cautiously stepped out of the disabled car. Just as soon as her feet were planted on the asphalt of the road, she slid the rest of her body carefully out of the car. Then she made a mad dash for the rear of the stalled out car. She tried to run so fast she actually slid and fell against the bumper of the vehicle and hurt her knee. When she got her bearings, she leaned her back against the rear of the car, and she tried to get her breathing under some kind of control. She then took a quick look at the horde of police officers surrounding them, and saw her side car door was left opened. Then she turned and put the front of her body up against the trunk of the vehicle, and used it not only to hide behind, but also to lean against it to help stabilize her trembling body. The scared to death female terrorist was still trying to get her breathing under control, as she wiped sweat from running into her eyes with her right shoulder, as she tried to stabilized the weapon in her hands.

The troopers held their fire the moment they saw this suspect was a woman. They allowed her to get behind the car. The officers did not feel she was as big a threat as the male occupant of the vehicle. Besides, the police were still going under the assumption they were ordered to be backup support for this action being controlled by the elite group of soldiers. Since the soldiers did not do anything against this suspect woman when she got out of the Mercedes, they did not react against her either. Lieutenant Smith looked at Walker and he shrugged back at him.

Walker looked over his shoulder and made direct eye contact with the Ghost. The moment he looked at the Ghost, the Captain gave him a number of quick hand movements. He informed the Ghost to keep an eye on the woman subject, and if she made any threatening moves against the police or them, he was to take her out that quick in response to it.

Major al-Shaya finally got her breathing under control, and then she dared to give a quick look at the horde of police mounted against her and her Commander. All she picked up was police stationed everywhere she looked, and they were all aiming their weapons directly at her. She glanced to her right and noticed a number of obviously American soldiers kind of standing by their military machines and also staring at her. Her blood froze in her veins when her eyes locked onto those of Captain Robert Walker's, and he was giving her a chilling look of death stalking her. As she continued to stare at Walker, he gave her the signal to drop her weapon with his hands, and then walk over to him as quick as she could move towards him. Major al-Shaya nodded no at Walker at this point as she continued to defy his orders.

The Marine Captain replied with a simple shrug and a funny look, and then he drew his finger slowly across his neck as a further threat aimed against her. The Iraqi female Major swallowed hard, knowing what the soldier she knew as Captain Robert Walker, just told her what was going to happen to her if, she did not give up.

The female Iraqi soldier took her eyes off the American soldier, and she trained them on the horde of police officer still threatening her with weapons. She suddenly felt the car buck under her weight, and she leaned to the side and saw the Colonel closed the door she left opened on him. Now she knew why he forced her out of the car, he was going to do the same thing to her as he done to Lieutenant Malika Nabeel Elmasry and Sergeant Shurug Khalaifa a few hours before. But she was not going to allow him to get away with it on her. Her chest filled with rage as she thought of all she had done for this hateful Iraqi Colonel. She loved and respected him, and done things she never thought of doing for any other man in her life. Now this foul military officer owned her body, mind and soul, and here he was and he was going to leave her behind to be slaughtered by these loathsome American police officers and soldiers who wanted to kill her.

CHAPTER TWENTY NINE

The fuming Iraqi Colonel tried the stalled motor of the Mercedes Benz once more, but it still would not start for him, and then he noticed the heat gauge of the machine. It was plastered all the way to overheat, and he realized some rubber from his destroyed tires must have somehow damaged his radiator, or one of the hoses from the motor for the cooling system. He completely gave up trying to restart the motor, as he prepared for his death and his attack against the police officers surrounding the outside his stalled car.

In a sudden and swift move, Serena al-Shaya suddenly shoved her weight off the trunk of the disabled car. Then she stood straight and raised her weapon up to her shoulder, and she aimed it at the back windshield of the expensive car, as she roared at the Iraqi Colonel still trapped inside the disabled vehicle. "I shall not allow you to leave me out here to die in the middle of this cursed road like some kind of cursed animal, Colonel al-Qaysi. I'll not allow you to escape and leave me behind like you have just done to Lieutenant Elmasry and Sergeant....."

The instant the female Iraqi terrorist made the rash move with her weapon, by moving it up to a firing position on her body. Captain Walker raised his hand and pointed at the woman with the weapon in her hands with his finger. Just as quickly, the Ghost fired one round from his silenced M-16, and the female's head split opened and a spray a mist of red stained in the air, where the female once stood a heartbeat before. Major Serena al-Shaya's body slightly jumped in the air and was tossed backwards five feet before returning to earth in a heap of death crumbling behind the stalled vehicle. It seemed like a short lifetime before the body of the female Iraqi finally stopped moving, and it came to rest lying on the ground.

Captain Walker went in action right after the Ghost took out the female terrorist, mainly because he had enough of this nightmare. He turned and ran for his Humvee as he pointed at the huge war machines, and his troops piled into the heavy military machines. As he rushed for the machine, he gave the soldiers a bunch of rapid hand signals, so they knew what he wanted from them, before they moved against the surviving terrorist still trapped inside the disabled car. The three Humvees started up with a roar, and CoCo-G's Grungie moved out before Walker's, and he charged right at the stalled Mercedes. He pulled his Humvee right up behind the car, actually running over one of the dead Major's legs as she lay helpless on the ground, and he parked his Humvee tight up against and right behind the almost destroyed car.

Four F's Humvee pulled around Walker's machine, and he drove his machine to the front of the disabled Mercedes, completely blocking the car from being able to move forward an inch. The Captain's Humvee drove forward until his front bumper hit the side of the Mercedes, where the female Major got out of the vehicle, thus blocking the two doors on this side of the car. Once the three machines were up against the car, the soldiers piled out of the armor plated Humvees from the sides not facing the car, or out through the rear hatchback of the war machines. Then the elite soldiers lined up alongside their Humvees, and leaned over it and aimed their weapons at the windows of Mercedes. Walker got out by the driver's side door and left it opened, and then he looked through the window at the stalled car sitting off the side of the highway.

The young Marine Captain glared at the shadow he was able to detect moving around inside the car every once in a while. All the widows of the Mercedes were rolled up, making it almost impossible for the soldiers to see clearly into the vehicle, or seeing what the terrorist trapped inside it was doing against them. So they were stuck looking at the shadow they saw move in the car. The Captain pointed his weapon through the rolled down window of the Humvee, and he aimed it at the driver's seat of the car. He hated this Iraqi soldier for more than one reason. It was bad enough this Iraqi was killing some of his people, but to actually make friends with the soldiers he was trying to kill went against the grain on him.

He felt highly insulted by what this cunning Iraqi Officer done to him, and he was praying for any excuse whatsoever to shoot him dead for his crimes. He could see the Iraqi Colonel's form slightly through the dark tinted window of the once expensive car.

Sergeant Dorothy Ramirez along with the Mutt, Lieutenant Frank Hall, came up to the Captain from behind the military machine, with Ramirez asking him as she headed for him. "Well Bobby, now we have him thoroughly boxed in and he has only one way out of the car. What are we going to do with him now? It's a chinch this guy isn't going to come out of the car on his own accord. Do you have any idea how we're going to get him out of there?"

"I don't care if we have to drag his fricking ass the hell outta it through the damn key lock of the fucking door, sister. Right this moment I'm not gonna do nuthin that might cause this flaming asshole to react against us. We hafta see what the asshole is gonna do in there, before we react against his ass. We'll just sit by and wait him out for a while, and when I get tired of waiting for his damn ass to come outta there real peaceful like. That's when I'm gonna react and get him the fuck outta the stinking car one way or the uther. Just standby for the time being I guess." He happened to glance at the gathered police officers behind him, and noticed they relaxed their guard. State Trooper Lieutenant John Smith was standing in the open looking at him.

He nodded at the good looking State Trooper, and then he called out to CoCo-G in a booming voice. "Hey CoCo, did any of you fucking guys back there have the sense to check on the downed chick? Is she down for the count or what buddy, or do you guys need a stinking medic back there to help her out some, man?"

There was a long silence then CoCo reported back to his Commanding Officer. "Hey Captain, we had to drag her skinny little ass out from under the damn Humvee, sir. We musta ran her over when we pulled in the blocking spot on the rear of the damn vehicle, sir. Err... there's no need for any medic coming for her skinny ass, man. Halfa her once pretty head is missing Walker, and if that didn't kill her, went I pulled around this car sir. I hadta run her over to get my machine in the proper position to block this other bastard in."

"No prob with that shit CoCo, I really didn't wanna offer her any fucking help anyway, man. That's just one more stinking terrorist who'll never come back and bite us on the ass again. Okay sit tight for the time being I guess. I'm gonna get me a swallow of stinking water and then I'm gonna give it one shot at talking this asshole out of his metal coffin. One shot at it, and then we'll get him the fuck outta it in our own fricking way, guys." Walker said his words loud enough for the trapped Iraqi terrorist to hear his words from inside the stalled white car.

The concerned Iraqi Officer was smart enough to drop the front driver's seat down to where it was lying flat in the car. That way he was able to move around in the car a little easily, with much more room to move around in as well.

The Captain put up his weapon for the moment and then took a pull from the bottle of warm water Ramirez offered him. He looked behind the Humvee for a moment, and he noticed the Mutt and McNip were working on a long metal pole with some kind of a device attached to the other end of the pole by the two special operation soldiers. He walked over to the back of the parked war machine and snapped at the two soldiers. "What the fuck are you two shitbirds doing back here, and what the hell is that damn thing you guys are working on?"

The Mutt started speaking right off to his friend. "Hey Walker, we're setting up a nifty little smoke and tear gas popper on the uther end of this fricking detonation stick, man. If we really wanna drive that little prick the hell outta that damn luxury car he destroyed, man. Then we're gonna hafta use this here little thing to do it for us, man. All you hafta do is pop a small hole in the side window of the car. Then we can stick this damn thing in the car with him, and pop it off inside, and we'll choke the lousy sonofa fucking bitch outta the car nice and easy, man."

He watched as the Mutt wove the long thin string down the length of the stick, and put the end through a small hole at the other end of the stick, and then he offered. "Hey Walker, all we hafta do now, is just stick that uther end of the fucking stick into the damn car, and then we'll pull this here sting at the uther end and the stun grenade will go off inside the car for us as slick as snot, man. That lousy little A-rab prick in there ain't got a snowball's chance in hell of staying inside the fricking car after this thing goes off in there, Walker." The Mutt grinned proudly at his Commanding Officer as he stared in his eyes while seeking his approval of the weapon and what they were doing with the stun smoke grenade.

"That's fucking great man, where the hell didja guys get the damn thing from anyhow, Mutt? I can't believe you birds have come up with this idea all on your own, buddy." He said as he stared at the contraption he was rigging up.

"Walker, we got us all sorts of creepy looking shit stuffed in the back of our stinking machine for any kinda possible riot situation we might get involved in, man.

Although this ain't a fucking riot thing going off here, it's sorta like the same damn thing but different I guess, man. Instead of trying to stop a crazy ass mob from getting someplace they ain't supposed to be in. We got this fucking dude trapped in a place where we want him outta. Voila, we got this thing man."

"Good deal Mutt, I'm heading for the front of the truck. Ghost, when I give you the signal, I want you to pop a cap through the back windshield of the damn car. Try not to knock out the whole window and once you do it then the Mutt's gonna put his little toy in the car and drive this scumbag the hell outta the damn thing. Keep your eyes on my fucking ass, people."

He headed for the front of his machine again, and yelled out at the trapped Iraqi man hiding inside the stalled Mercedes Benz. "Hey Colonel al-Qaysi man. Bill! I know you can fucking hear me in there man, and I'm gonna give you one chance, and one chance only to come the hell outta that fricking car nice and peaceful like, man. If you ain't outta there before you run outta friggin time. Then I'm gonna blast you the fuck outta the damn thing nice and easy, mister. You have five fucking minutes to think it over buddy, and then I'm coming for ya stinking ass, man."

Inside the disabled snow white Mercedes Benz, Iraqi Colonel Hamoodi al-Qaysi tried to get a look at where Walker was yelling at him from outside his vehicle. Since he decided to die in the car, he wanted to take at least this one man out with him when he died. Even if Walker was the only man he killed on this night, before the soldiers or police killed him in return. Colonel al-Qaysi kept moving his head from side to side to try and see where Walker was standing outside his car. When the Iraqi Colonel finally picked him up, he noticed he was sort of hiding behind the opened door to the Humvee he drove up to his car in. The Arab Colonel did not know the Humvee was heavily armor plated, so he lifted his weapon to his shoulder and he aimed his weapon at right Walker's body mostly hidden by the heavy metal door of the Humvee through the side window of his stalled car.

The Captain was leaning against the front side door of the Humvee as he looked through the window at the Iraqi Colonel's trapped car. He was splitting his attention between watching the Arab Colonel's car and what the Mutt and McNip were still doing with the grenade on the end of a long pole. A muffled shot rang out, shattering the rear side window of the disabled Mercedes Benz, and it smashed into the heavy opened door of the Humvee. The hard impact of the round hitting the door of the Humvee sent Walker flying backwards and the round smashed the door close on the war machine at the same time. The Captain ended up sitting on his rearend on the ground by the back bumper of the Humvee. He also wacked the side of his head on the war machine, and he was bleeding slightly by his right ear.

Sergeant Ramirez saw what happened and she feared Walker might have been hit by the round fired from the Iraqi soldier. She rushed up to his side and checked his head.

The Mutt stopped what he was doing and looked at Walker as he mumbled. "What the fuck's wrong with your ass man? Don't ya know enough to keep your fucking head down when someone has a fricking weapon aimed in your direction, stupid? Man are you getting dumb."

McNip saw Walker was okay so he offered a slug of his own at him. "Hey Mutt, I bet Walker shit his stinking pants, man. I can't wait to look and see if he did man."

Walker glared angrily at McNip as he growled at him. "You wanna see some stinking shit buster, how 'bout I shit on your stinking puss for ya. You're damn lucky I'm so stinking tired right now man or I'd walk all up and down your skinny ass body for you, buster."

Walker rubbed the side of his head, and Ramirez yelled at him. "Don't touch it with your dirty hands like that will you please Bobby. You'll get it infected if you keep touching it like that mister. Oh God Robert, I thought he shot you through the damn car. If anything happened to you, I'd never forgive myself for it baby."

"No honey, he tried to shoot my ass but the damn door stopped the round from getting at my ass. But I'm gonna get him alright for that stupid ass move. Here comes the fricking wet ass hour, baby. You two fuckers got that damn thing rigged up yet?" Walker asked as he looked at the damaged door of the Humvee, and noticed the amount of damage the bullet had done to it. Now, he knew why his upper thigh was killing him so bad, because that was where the bullet struck the door against him. Next, he looked at the not so white Mercedes Benz any longer, and he saw the blown out window as he struggled back to his feet and let his breath out in a disgusted sigh, and then he glared at the stalled car.

"Hey Walker, it seems this lousy little fuck in there still wants to try and kill some of us pukes out here, man. I think it's time we go fucking hot and heavy on the stinking prick's ass for him, man. I'm getting kinda tired, and I wanna go back to the base and sleep some, man. I'm really beat up from the feet up, Walker." McNip complained as he walked over to Walker's side and then he picked up his weapon and handed it back to the upset Captain.

The Iraqi Colonel al-Qaysi cursed angrily from inside the disabled car, because he could not get a very clear shot at Walker's face from where and how he was sitting inside the car. But he was still able to tell he was standing behind the door of his military jeep. So he fired at the door, and when he saw Walker go flying backwards when the bullet struck the door of the jeep he smiled, thinking he either just killed him, or he wounded him. He even felt wounding the Marine Captain was enough to complete his revenge against the hated American soldier.

Walker looked at the shattered window of the Mercedes, and growled at the Mutt again. "Fuck that damn stick thing already man. The damn window's shot outta the stinking car. We can just pitch in a few stinking tear gas grenades in the damn thing and drive the lousy little Iraqi sonofabitch out of the fricking car from the uther side, man. We're going hot on the little fuck as of right now people. Everybody, when this stinking popinjay comes outta the car, take him out real quick and easy. No more fucking round with his ass, or someone else might get hurt by this damn little prick trapped in there. We gave him all the damn chances we're gonna give him.

"It's time he takes the long dirt nap, dammit. If he tries to stay inside the stinking car once the gas goes off in it, I'm gonna start up the fricking Humvee and push the damn car until it either crushes in on his lousy ass, or I turn it over on the little prick trapped in there. Let's get this damn thing over with this lousy dude who played us long enough round here as it is, people. It's time he goes off to his Paradise and gets the hell offa this damn earth, guys." Walker yelled out loud enough for his soldiers, the Iraqi Colonel, and the police to hear his angry words.

McNip went to the back of their Humvee and he fished around until he had four tear gas grenades in his hands. He kept two for himself and he handed the Mutt the other two. McNip designated the Mutt and himself as the grenade pitchers because that was how much he wanted to be part of the attack against this Iraqi murderer. He then showed Walker the grenades.

"Good fucking deal people, let's get this thing over with once and for all, dammit." Walker bitched at the two soldiers as he checked his weapon, because it fell to the ground when he was fired at by the Iraqi Colonel in the car. He pulled out his clip and ejected the round resting in the chamber of the weapon. Then he left the chamber opened and looked down the barrel to make certain no dirt got in it, and it could cause his weapon to blow up in his face, if he was forced to fire at the terrorist and the barrel was blocked. When he was positive the weapon was clear of dirt. He slapped his clip home, and chambered a round in the action of the weapon. When he was ready to work, he crouched down and took aim at the side of the stalled car. He nodded to the Mutt and McNip and they immediately pulled a pin a piece on two grenades, and then they tossed the burning grenades into the rear window of the disabled Mercedes Benz.

All Walker's troops went ready to fire the instant they saw him working on his weapon. They did not have to be told twice they were hot, because all the soldiers had to do was look at Walker's actions and they knew he was going in after the man who killed two of their own.

The elite specially trained soldiers watched as the Mercedes Benz quickly filled with thick eye burning smoke. The gas was pouring out of every opening in the once luxury but now all but destroyed car. The back seat of the vehicle started to burn from the extremely high temperature the burning grenades cause, as they went off and burned in the car.

The Iraqi Colonel's eyes were stinging terribly, and he was coughing his guts out, but he still tried to remain hiding inside the car until the last possible moment. At first he was trying to hold his breath and take quick little gulps of the bad air. But that move did nothing for the burning in his eyes, nose and mouth, whenever he drew in some of the arid smoke. Finally, when he had no other choice left in the matter, he opened the driver's side door that faced the wide grass field the side of the main road. He had no idea a number of police officers had worked their way in this area off the side of the highway, and they were waiting for him to try and reach the tree line some fifty feet away from the edge of the roadway and the Mercedes Benz vehicle.

The extremely upset Iraqi Officer again tried to remain hiding in the car, by taking in huge gulps of fresh air from the opened door. But with every breath he stole in the car, it was heavily mixed in with the burning tear gas, and causing his damaged lungs to burn more. Finally, the Colonel rolled out of the car while trying to use the body of the vehicle and boiling gas cloud as cover for him and his moves to try and escape the police officer's trap. Colonel al-Qaysi held his weapon in both his arms, but he was coughing so hard it was almost impossible for him to try and aim the weapon properly at the police officers, or soldiers surrounding him so tightly. Let alone trying to get a clear shot off that would possibly hit anyone outside the disabled car.

Once the Iraqi Colonel was out of the car, the Arab Officer leaned up against the side of the car while trying to get fresh air into his starving body. But nothing was helping him at this point. He rubbed his burning and tearing eyes with one hand that was the worst possible thing he could have possibly done, because it immediately irritated the effects of the gas on his eyes, while still holding onto the weapon with his free hand. He was desperately trying to see out of his burning and tearing eyes, but it was nearly impossible for him to do so. He was pulling in huge gulps of fresh air into his lungs, and trying to get his body back to normal.

Now the Iraqi Colonel knew he ran out of time, his main driving force was to try and kill some of the American soldiers or police officers, before he was killed by the ones he was trying to kill on the roadway. The Iraqi soldier's head was killing him and it was being pounded by a splitting headache caused by the huge amount of tear gas he breathed in inside the car. He felt his whole body was trying to shut down on him as he desperately struggled to breathe, and to also get his weapon under control at the same time.

The elite group of angry soldiers surrounding the Mercedes Benz and trapped Colonel al-Qaysi was waiting to see the first sign of their intended target moving around to get a clear shot at him. The soldiers were dying to be the one who capped the murderer of their fellow soldiers. Walker slowly moved forward until he was leaning his weapons across the hood of the Humvee, and he had it aimed right at the driver's side of the disabled car. He basically knew where the Iraqi Colonel was going to pop his head up, and it was only a matter of time before he did it. He wanted to be the first one to place lead in the Arab Colonel's forehead. He concentrated his aim at where he felt the wanted Colonel was going to appear when he tried to move.

Colonel Hamoodi al-Qaysi leaned heavy against the side of the car and he was still drawing in huge gulps of air into his burning lungs. His hands were shaking, and his body was trembling because of what the gas was doing to his body. He was terribly disorientated and his mind confused. The Iraqi soldier shook his head in an effort to try and clear his fogged over mind. When some of his vision came back to his eyes, he decided to act out.

Colonel Hamoodi al-Qaysi drew in a huge breath of air and held it and jumped to his feet and flipped his weapon over the roof of his car while roaring in anger, as he tried to get a good aim on one of the American soldiers he wanted to kill so desperately. As he roared his scream of hatred, it was suddenly cut off on him as he found himself staring into the flaming and wild looking eyes of Walker. The Iraqi Colonel stopped his roaring as he found himself staring at the angry looking American soldier. For some reason, his whole body froze up, and all the trapped Colonel could do at this point was to stare at the young and extremely angry American soldier he hated so much for invading his country almost a year ago and kidnapping his Colonel spy.

Walker could not understand why the Iraqi soldier did not take a shot at him, as he continued to stare at the foreign officer. He gave the Arab Colonel enough time to do it. But all his target did was locking their eyes together and staring at him.

Sergeant Ramirez was kneeling by the Roach's side while using the parked Humvee for their protection, she saw the stare down going on between the two soldiers, and she started to scream under her breath at her soldier. "Shoot him Walker. Take the god damn shot at the sonofabitch will ya for the love of God. Shoot him before he shoots you, Robert. What the hell are you waiting for, shoot him god dammit shoot him Bobby!" She knew she could not call out an alarm to Walker, for neither man fired on the other yet, even though they were standing only eight feet from each other. If she dared to call out the alarm to Walker, her call might cause the Iraqi Colonel to fire at him first. She was starting to sweat while watching the terrible stare down as it continued between the two angry men.

Walker stared so intensely at the wild looking trapped Iraqi soldier who he once knew as Bill, over the sights of his weapon, and he continued to wait. But when he felt he waited long enough to show the Iraqi Colonel he hated him with every fiber of his being, he finally pulled on the man. He fired the short three round burst off in less than a heartbeat, and then he continued to stare in the sights of his weapon as he saw two of the three bullets rip into the Iraqi Colonel's face. He could swear he actually saw the rounds in flight, and as they smashed into Colonel al-Qaysi's head. The third round hit the Iraqi Military Officer in the upper part of his neck as his body began to be pitched slightly backwards from the force of the other two rounds as they ripped into him square in the head.

Everything seemed to be happening in slow motion right before Walker's eyes. He watched in stunned amazement as the Iraqi Colonel's arm that held his weapon, when flying away from the right side of his body, and his left arm went up in the air and towards the back of his flying body. Colonel al-Qaysi's head snapped back violently as a light mist of blood stained the air where his head had been, and the first bullet hit his face and popped his left eye right out of the socket, as the round caved in his face. The second shot he fired at Colonel al-Qaysi, shattered his upper jaw and sent at least three of his teeth flying in the air along with some of his jaw bone.

The head of the Iraqi Military Officer's body was cruelly snapped backwards, forcing the rest of his body to follow the head in wild motion. The deadly weapon Colonel al-Qaysi was so desperately trying to hang on to, slowly left the falling Colonel's body, and it tumbled to the ground before the Colonel's back hit hard on the grass field, and his body came to rest lying in heap on the grass covered ground. The Iraqi Colonel's feet and legs were the last part of his body to come to rest from the three rounds assaulting his body

He landed hard on the back of his neck and shoulders with a sickening thug, and the fall knocking the remaining air out of his starved lungs, from the shock of the impact of his body landing on the hard grass ground. When his upper body finally hit the ground, his legs kept their forward movement going, almost causing the dead body to roll over the top of himself and onto his stomach and right side. But at the last moment and because his upper body weight, his legs stopped in the air, and fell back to the ground with his body ending up lying flat on his back. His eyes were staring the look of death as they slowly closed for the last time in his troubled life.

More weapons fire broke out as each of the elite soldiers part of the search for the terrorists who killed two of their own, took a three shot burst as they fired at the body of the enemy Iraqi Colonel. Each and every one of the specialized soldiers from Walker's Unit, wanted to put a piece of lead in the man who killed two of their own people. One after the other, the specialized soldiers stepped up to the Colonel's body, and fired at it until Walker raised his hand in the air in an effort to stop the soldiers from seeking their own sort of revenge against the dead Iraqi's body. The police saw what was going on and they did not react against it, because they knew the elite soldiers were taking their revenge on this killer's remains.

When the shooting ended, Walker came away from the side of his Humvee and then he slowly walked around the side of the disabled Mercedes Benz while lighting another cigarette. He was still limping slightly from the pain caused to him by the round the Arab Colonel fired at him, and it struck the door of the Humvee. The damage to the door injured his leg and he was really pissed off over the fact that Colonel al-Qaysi was able to harm his body before he took the killer out by ending his life for him.

Sergeant Ramirez ran up to Walker's side, and she punched him in the arm as she bitched at him angrily. "What the fuck do you call that shit you did back there, mister? Why the hell didn't you just kill the lousy bastard when you first aimed at his ass? You scared the living hell out of me by that dumb stunt of yours, Bobby. I couldn't believe you waited so long before you killed the bastard, Robert. What the hell were you waiting for before you took his ass out, Robert? I was going to do him before he fired on you. I thank God you fired at him before he fired at you, dumb ass. I still can't believe you waited so long before you took him out, Bobby."

"I fucking hesitated for that second because I wanted the lousy sonofabitch to see his death coming at his ass before I killed him. That was why I waited for the kill as long as I did." He growled as he limped around the civilian car and looked at the crumpled up body of Colonel Hamoodi al-Qaysi lying in a mess on the ground. His body was riddled with bullet holes from his soldiers seeking revenge against his body, and the dead man actually shit his pants in death.

State Trooper Lieutenant John Smith rushed from around the disabled car and looked at the downed body of the killer for a second, and then he said to Walker. "Man sir that was some shit you just pulled off back there sir. For a second Captain, I though the two of you were going to stare at each other until the cows came home, sir. Then I thought you were going to allow him to live until you pulled on the man. That was real cold blooded back there sir, and you have some fucking balls on your ass, Captain. Remind me never to get on the bad side of your ass for any reason sir. I have an ambulance moving up to get these two pieces of shit off my damn roadway, sir. Are any of your people hurt, Captain Walker Sir? You seem to be limping some sir do you need any medical attention for your injured leg sir? Are you hurt Captain Walker?"

He turned slightly and looked at the concerned trooper then replied. "No, I'm not hurt bad enuf to need any stinking medical attention, Lieutenant Smith Sir. Your words are kinda strange to my ass though sir, because I warned myself never to get on the bad side of you either, Lieutenant. I wouldn't wanna tangle with your ass in a hand to hand combat situation, sir. You're too fucking big to tangle with that way sir. No, none of my people are hurt in this action sir, and if they were, they'd refuse any civilian medical care. My soldiers would wait until they got back to our base before seeking any kinda medical attention I'm afraid, Lieutenant Smith."

"God dammit Walker!" the Captain heard roared at him from behind.

He turned and looked over the roof of the destroyed snow white Mercedes Benz and saw Colonel Bruce Leadbetter stomping his way towards him, along with the rest of his people and the other State Trooper Lieutenant. The fuming American Colonel had an ugly look on his angry face, and he was walking with a real purpose in each of his steps. He walked up to Walker, and snarled savagely at his face. "Well mister what the fuck do you call that god damn stunt you just pulled off back there mister? Since the fuck when do you allow some damn enemy scumbag to eye you down the barrel of a fricking weapon like he did to your ass, without you taking his fucking head off his shoulders, the first moment you get him locked up in your sights, mister?

"It looks like I'm going to have to get the whole lot of you people back on base, and once again turn you people into the born again killers you people are supposed to be, Captain Walker. Why the fuck did you people wait until that damn asshole got out of his car for, before you stopped his ass? Why the hell didn't you just fire in the damn car until you people knew the little prick was nothing more than a pile of dead shit and food for the fucking worms for Christ sake? Why the fuck did you people give this little bastard so many damn chances to live, dammit? Don't you people remember these two A-rab bastards took two of your own troops out, and you people were operating under my fucking orders of taking no prisoners on this fricking operation I sent your sagging asses out on?

"Don't you shitbirds know you were out here on a damn vengeance mission, and a vengeance mission is to kill with extreme impunity aimed against your fucking targets? This was a no prisoner operation, a search and splatter mission dammit! You people almost blew this one big time on me, and I'll be seeking some damn answers from the lot of you asses when I get you people back to base. Don't you people realize the level of fucking hell I can drop down on your dumb asses? Arrrr... fuck it, I see you got him Captain, good work mister. Everyone, I want you people to load up in them god damn Humvees. The restricted airspace over this mess has just been lifted on us, and I want all of you the hell out of the damn area ten minutes ago. I want every swinging dick and bouncing tits the hell out of here...."

"Hey Walker." A booming voice bellowed out at young Marine Captain.

Walker, kind of ignoring the angry Colonel's words aimed at him, turned his head and picked up the massive John Abbott, the soldier nicknamed No Neck, coming through the police line heading at him. He was grinning from ear to ear walking towards him not showing any signs of being wounded. The police officers got out of Neck's way, because most of them never saw a man so large and strong as this man appeared to be, and the officers did not want to get in his way. He was walking quickly through their ranks heading for the soldier in Command.

"Oh, by the way Captain Walker, I brought that sorry excuse for a fucking soldier with me, mister. He was in my office when the call came in you people stopped the Iraqi Colonel's car. I tried to order him out of my office so I could come out here and take Command of the situation. Did you ever try to give that asshole an order and expect him to carry it out properly, Captain?" The Colonel gave Walker a quick smirk as he watched Neck walking towards them.

"Yes Sir I sure did Sir, and I know what you're talking about Colonel Leadbetter Sir. He's too fucking big to argue with, and he's too damn strong to use weapons on his ass, sir. I'm glad to see him on his feet again though, Colonel Leadbetter." Walker was also grinning from ear to ear as Neck walked in the crowd of soldiers, and everyone gathered around the man. He was well like by all the soldiers from the specialized group, and now they had another reason to be pleased over. Not only did the soldiers get their revenge on the ones who killed some of their troops, but the wounded soldier was back in their ranks looking like he was never wounded.

Neck slammed a heavy hand down on Walker's exhausted shoulder, and the blow forced him to drop his shoulder a bit in response to the heavy hit, and to also absorb some pain it caused him. All the soldiers were trying to talk to Neck at the same time, but the reunion was broken up by the fuming Marine Colonel as he growled angrily at Walker and the other soldiers.

"C'mon you pack of Devil Rejects I hear some reporter helicopters are coming in on us at the moment. I don't want any of you slugs hanging around out here unnecessarily when the reporters get overhead, dammit. I happen to know there are at least five fucking news helicopters stacked up, and two of them have inferred capabilities on the damn aircraft. I want all you people the hell out of the area immediately, before they're overhead and working against us. Take this massive pile of dog shit with you, and get your troops the hell out of here double quick Walker.

"I guess I'll remain behind, and clean up this mess for your ass Captain. It's late, so there'll be no muster for tonight, sir. But I'll call muster tomorrow morning at Oh Eight Hundred fucking Hours sharp, to give you rejects from hell a sort of break. That'll give you people enough time to rest up from this fucking mess you just lived through. We have special training you asses have to accomplish before I can release you back on your damn leave time. And, you people can get back to whatever the fuck you people do to survive until the next time your government has and need of your outstanding services to your country, sir.

"Remember Walker, I can't release any of you shits until we accomplished the special training you people were ordered to report back to the base for in the first place sir. This mountain of shit doesn't cover that specialized training in the least, mister."

Colonel Leadbetter stopped barking at the young military officer, and then he waited for his group of specially trained troops to get in the idling Humvees, and the machines moved out and cut across the wide grass divide of the highway. Then the three war machines were heading north towards the military base at a high rate of speed. The first of the civilian cars were starting to show up in the northbound lane as the State Troopers lifted their roadblocks, and started to control the flow of civilian traffic as it drove by the scene of the deadly standoff.